Marching With Caesar®
Rebellion

By R.W. Peake

R.W. Peake

Also by R.W Peake

Marching with Caesar®- Birth of the 10th

Marching with Caesar-Conquest of Gaul

Marching with Caesar-Civil War

Marching with Caesar-Antony and Cleopatra, Parts I & II

Marching With Caesar-Rise of Augustus

Marching With Caesar-Last Campaign

Caesar Triumphant

Critical praise for the Marching with Caesar series:

Marching With Caesar-Antony and Cleopatra: Part I-Antony
"Peake has become a master of depicting Roman military life and action, and in this latest novel he proves adept at evoking the subtleties of his characters, often with an understated humour and surprising pathos. Very highly recommended."

Marching With Caesar-Civil War
"Fans of the author will be delighted that Peake's writing has gone from strength to strength in this, the second volume...Peake manages to portray Pullus and all his fellow soldiers with a marvelous feeling of reality quite apart from the star historical name... There's history here, and character, and action enough for three novels, and all of it can be enjoyed even if readers haven't seen the first volume yet. Very highly recommended."
~The Historical Novel Society

"The hinge of history pivoted on the career of Julius Caesar, as Rome's Republic became an Empire, but the muscle to swing that gateway came from soldiers like Titus Pullus. What an amazing story from a student now become the master of historical fiction at its best."
~Professor Frank Holt, University of Houston

R.W. Peake

Marching with Caesar Rebellion by R.W. Peake

Copyright © 2014 by R.W. Peake

For Julius Caesar and Titus Pullus
Veni, Vidi, Vici

R.W. Peake

Foreword

This book, *Marching with Caesar®-Rebellion*, marks a departure for me in more than one way.

Not only is it the first of this series that isn't written in the first person, it also is the first book after Titus Pullus' story. Probably not surprisingly, the combination of these two factors make me somewhat nervous.

It *was* surprisingly difficult for me to say goodbye to Titus Pullus, but when I embarked on this journey in telling his story, unlike Bernard Cornwell did with his brilliant (and one of my favorite) Sharpe series, I didn't leave any "wiggle room" to tell further adventures about the Roman who will always be my favorite character, no matter where this adventure takes me.

Another challenge in picking up the story, basically where it was left, was in the paucity of primary sources that talk about the beginning of the career of Tiberius and Drusus Claudius Nero; there are about two pages from Dio that discuss what marked the first campaign in which Tiberius was in overall command, the quelling of the rebellion in Rhaeti and Noricum. More specifically, there is one sentence devoted to his stratagem of crossing a lake to inflict a decisive defeat on the rebels. After poring over maps, I think the most likely location is the lake called Brigantinus (Lake Constance), where the city of Brigantium, or Bregenz is located. I suppose it could just as easily have been Genava (Geneva) and that lake, but I suspect that if that had been the case, Dio would have mentioned it and its relation to the famous wall erected by Gaius Julius Caesar at the southern end. However, I fully acknowledge that this is just a guess.

Also, for narrative purposes, I am being a bit vague on dates, particularly as it pertains to the end of Titus Pullus' career, and when the rebellion in Rhaetia and Noricum occurred, which was 15 BC. For that, I beg the indulgence of the reader.

One of the most interesting aspects of this period of Roman history, now that the reign of Augustus has been firmly established, is in the politicization of the Legions. When one reads accounts of this period, and the previous Republican period, carefully, what I found fascinating was in the behavior of what had previously been the stalwarts of the Roman army, the Centurions. In Caesar's account of the Gallic campaign, for example, for the most part the men who lost their nerve and acted in a fashion unbecoming to a man of the Legions

6

were usually Legates and Tribunes. It's not until the Imperial Period, where accounts of Centurions, or Camp Prefects, acting in a craven and cowardly manner, start to surface.

While some might consider it a leap, I don't believe it's a very far one to argue that this shift was due to Augustus' practice of putting men into positions of authority based not on their war record, but in their political reliability. Now that I know what I do about Augustus, it doesn't surprise me all that much; he was much more politician and administrator than warrior, and I can't help wondering how many of the military setbacks Rome suffered could have been avoided if he had assigned men to the Centurionate based on what kind of leaders they were, and not how loyal they were to him.

Ironically enough, even that practice didn't stop the habit of Legions selling themselves to the highest bidder, and I would argue that it probably made that very thing more likely. When you put soldiers who are more concerned with being on the right side into power than in doing their duty, bad things happen.

As always, I would be remiss if I didn't take the time to thank the fantastic team who has given me so much help in making the Marching with Caesar® series what it is. To my advance readers: Joe Corso, who has the keenest eye in spotting my many mistakes and always gives me great insight into what a reader might think; Stu MacPherson, one of the first and someone whose depth and breadth of knowledge, not just of the period in which I write, but in my fellow authors who love Rome as much as I do; and David St. Laurent, another brother Marine who stepped into the place of my dear, departed friend Robert (Curtis) Graham, MSgt. USMC (Ret), I thank each of you for your insight and comments.

To my long-suffering, ever-patient and eagle-eyed editor, Beth Lynne, and to Marina Shipova, who once more created a cover that tells the story before a reader opens the book, thank you seems so paltry to what you give me in support.

Finally, I want to thank all of the readers and I hope that you will follow me into this new chapter of Marching with Caesar®, and get to know the men and women who will carry the story forward, into the Empire.

Semper Fidelis,

R.W. Peake
March 9, 2014

R.W. Peake

Marching with Caesar: Rebellion

Prologue

The Centurion had been trained well, and he was experienced in his own right. At this point in Rome's history, it hadn't yet become common practice for Centurions to be in their posts because they purchased the position, and despite his youthful appearance, this Centurion had earned his way into the Centurionate. Nevertheless, this was the first time the Centurion had been in overall command, completely independent of higher authority, so he could be forgiven for his case of nerves on this occasion. He was a Pilus Prior, the Centurion of the First Century of a Cohort, which also meant that he was the commander of the Cohort. In this Centurion's case, it was the Fourth Cohort, which, as had been the practice of Roman armies going back as long as anyone could remember, was usually placed in the first rank of a Legion's battle line. Ever since the time of Gaius Julius Caesar, or as he was known now, Divus Julius, because of his status as a god, when a Legion arrayed for battle, they did so in the *acies triplex*, three ordered lines, consisting of four Cohorts in the front line, supported by three in the other two lines. Within the first line, the Fourth Cohort, under normal circumstances, found itself anchoring the left flank of, at the very least, the entire Legion, if not the entire army in the field.

Men selected to be a Pilus Prior of any of the first-line Cohorts were leaders of exceptional qualities and abilities, and this was especially true when the Cohort had become the basic unit of maneuver, sent out on independent operations such as this one. There had to be a first time for everything, the Centurion realized, but that didn't make it any less nerve-wracking, and this was certainly the case when it came to him. He had arisen this morning to find that his stomach rebelled at the very idea of food in it, and was just barely able to keep a cup of *posca,* the spiced wine that some favored as a way to start their day, in his stomach. Fortunately, he found that once he actually started the process of rousing the men of his Century, relying on the Centurions under his command to do the same, the familiarity of a daily routine helped to calm his nerves. Then, he had been so busy in making sure that every man of not just his Century, but the entire Cohort, had turned out carrying the necessary gear and was loaded down with the proper amount of rations for this operation that he didn't have time to be nervous.

Now the day was drawing to a close, and he was leading his Cohort towards the spot where the *exploratores*, those roving men who served as scouts, for both the enemy and for things like good sites for a camp, had told him was the right place for the Cohort to spend a night. Like any ambitious man, he had been excited and happy that he and the men of his Cohort had finally been chosen for an independent mission, even if he didn't care for the task itself. The province for which his Cohort and Legion were responsible for keeping under control was Pannonia, but maintaining the peace had proven to be quite a challenge. The man known as Augustus had supposedly tamed the wild tribesmen of this hilly, rugged country, but there was a running joke that made the rounds of the army stationed there that, if that was the case, Augustus had forgotten to inform the tribesmen of it. Although it couldn't be called open hostilities, from the viewpoint of the Centurion, and his men, it was a situation where the fighting had been punctuated by periods of peace and quiet. And as predictable as the changing of the seasons, another tribe had risen up, but this one was one of the strongest, the Daesitiates, although it was just one branch of them. That was why the Legate in command of what was known as the Army of Pannonia had decreed that it would take just a Cohort to march out and, in an operation he didn't believe would last more than a week, teach these barbarians another lesson.

The Pilus Prior had at his disposal an *ala* of cavalry, but they were composed of auxiliaries that he viewed as little better than the tribes against which they were marching, and they had vanished earlier in the day. This could mean anything, the Centurion understood; they could have found themselves struggling with the terrain, which was growing increasingly rugged. Or they could be dead already, and it was this thought that kept crowding into the Pilus Prior's brain as he marched at the head of his Cohort. Ranging perhaps a stadia ahead of him were two sections of men from his Century, each section charged with scanning both flanks for any possible threats. Ahead of them rode a half-dozen men from the *ala* who had been left behind, while another half-dozen were performing essentially the same job as the rearguard. Unfortunately, the task of guarding the flanks had been growing increasingly difficult with every mile they traveled and, according to what the Pilus Prior had been told, the forest terrain they had just entered lasted for about two miles. Once out of that, the site selected for the camp was a little more than a mile farther, and it took an effort of will for the Pilus Prior not to quicken his pace, knowing that at the end of this march was the work needed to make camp. Under normal circumstances, taking this track through the forest wasn't what the Pilus Prior would do, but this land was so rugged that the only alternative would have been to climb up the slopes of the hills that lined their direction of travel. It might have gotten them clear of the cover provided by the heavy undergrowth underneath the trees, but the jagged, rocky terrain would have slowed them down so much that they might as well have been standing still, and they never would have reached the selected site with enough daylight to make camp. Normally, building a camp in the dark didn't pose much of a challenge, provided the men didn't also have to worry about a volley of arrows or a sudden attack from the gloom. In short, the Pilus Prior had made what he considered to be the least bad choice of the poor ones available to him. Now he just had to hope that he hadn't made the wrong one.

Within a quarter mile of entering the forest, the slight depression of the track the Cohort was following was just barely visible, from a combination of the sun being blocked by the shoulder of a hill, but more from the thick, overhanging branches of the trees that crowded right up to the twin ruts of the track. The Pilus Prior had been informed that this track was going to be turned into a good Roman road at some point in the future, but it didn't help him at that moment. Between the gloom and the rough ground, he had to pay more attention to where his feet were stepping than continuing to scan for any threat. Behind him, he could hear the sudden jangling sound that told him one of the rankers had tripped, as the gear suspended by the pole each man carried jarred together. Sometimes, there was also a louder crash as the unfortunate lost his balance altogether and fell, which was always followed by a curse, although it was usually overpowered by a chorus of laughter as the victim's comrades enjoyed his misfortune. The Centurion didn't mind, as long as it didn't get out of hand, and he only had to turn about once to glare at the men of his Century for them to receive the message. Every so often, he would pause and step to the side of the marching column, looking down the neat rows of men, at this moment marching four abreast because of the narrowness of the track.

In between each Century was a gap of perhaps fifty paces, the delineation marked by the presence of the *signiferi* carrying their Century standards, the men like the Pilus Prior wearing the transverse crest of the Centurion next to them. Because of the rough ground, the standards bobbed up and down even more than normal, but even with this, the sight of so many men marching in unison, legs naturally moving in step with each other, even when they weren't required to keep in cadence during a route march like this, stirred the Pilus Prior every time he saw it. Despite the muted light, stray rays from the sun broke through the leafy foliage above them to bounce off a helmet here, or the point of a javelin there, creating a winking display that rippled along the length of the entire column.

Turning back from his latest inspection of his Cohort, the Pilus Prior noticed that the track ahead seemed to be sinking, but he quickly saw that it wasn't because it was sloping downward. Instead, over the years, the track had gradually sunk into the ground, but while it wasn't really any different than the part they had already traversed, it appeared that it followed a natural groove formed by the shoulders of two low hills meeting. On both sides of the track, the ground sloped upward, although it was still heavily overgrown, and as the Centurion drew closer, he saw that the slope on his right was steeper than the one on his left, although not by much. The track itself made a gentle curve to the left, blocking his view of what lay ahead, and it was this combination of things that gave the Pilus Prior a sense of unease and made him even more alert. At least, that was what he believed to be the case when thinking about it afterwards.

Once past the bend in the track, the Pilus Prior could see, barely, what looked like a circle of bright light, framed by green around the top half, and dark brown around the bottom half, and he knew he was seeing where the track left the forest. Somewhat to his dismay, however, the track still appeared to be sunken for at least as far as he could distinguish. He estimated that they still had more than a mile to go before they left the forest, and he was so absorbed in this that he almost missed it, although the truth was that he might have overlooked it even if he had been watching in the right direction. As it was, it was above his natural eye level, despite the fact that he was much taller than the average Roman. Yet, because of the slope, it was even higher, so that even when he did see it, the Centurion continued walking for a few paces as his mind registered not just what his eyes had seen, but what it meant. Nevertheless, it took another moment for him to act, and when he did so, it was actually to turn about and shout the command to halt the column. As was usual with a column consisting of six Centuries, the command had to be relayed, so there wasn't the same precision as if they were marching in the forum of camp. Starting with the Pilus Prior's Century, the column rippled to a halt, and even before the movement was completely finished, the Pilus Prior had his *cornicen* blow the notes that told the Centurions of the Cohort to come meet with the Pilus Prior. The five men came quickly trotting up to where he was still standing, seemingly absorbed in studying the foliage of a set of trees up the slope to the right of the column. His behavior seemed so odd that the Pilus Posterior, in command of the Second Century and the second in command of the Cohort commented on it.

"Did you decide to stop and count the leaves on the tree?" he joked, but in answer, the Pilus Prior pointed.

"See that?" he asked quietly, and, following his finger, the Pilus Posterior looked up in the same general direction his commander had been looking.

He, in fact, did see it, but before he could comment, the other Centurions arrived and were quickly informed of what the Pilus Posterior had noticed, so in a moment, they were all looking.

"Pluto's cock," muttered one.

"This is bad," said another.

"It is, but at least we saw it in time," the Pilus Prior commented.

What they were staring at, and what had caught the Centurion's eye, was what appeared to be a blazing white patch on not one, but three trees next to each other, each patch at roughly the same height up the trunk. On closer inspection, the Centurions could see that scattered on the ground around the trunks were piles of white chips, further sign that these trees had been chopped partway through, in obvious preparation for something. But for what?

Actually, the Pilus Prior, and the other Centurions, for that matter, knew exactly what purpose these trees served, but the Pilus Prior hadn't been looking at the leaves. What he had been doing, as he waited for his Centurions to reach his side, was to examine the wooded slope beyond the trees, searching for any further sign of danger. Like the others, he knew that these trees were going to be pushed across the track to block the Cohort; that wasn't in question. What he had to determine was whether or not this marked the beginning of the section of track that was the ambush site, or if these trees were to be dropped once the Cohort had moved past it. He thought hard as he tried to remember if this was the first sign he had seen, or if his eyes had actually caught sight of something similar earlier, but he had been too preoccupied for it to register as what it was, the sign of a trap.

Finally, he spoke up, his voice firm. "I think they were planning on trapping us farther ahead, and after we passed by, they were going to come down and finish these trees to block any retreat."

The Pilus Prior was relatively young to be in his position, and all but one of his Centurions was older than he was, yet while he hadn't been Pilus Prior all that long, almost all of them had learned to trust his judgment.

"And if this was the far end of the ambush, they wouldn't be waiting for us to figure it out," he finished. "They'd already be swooping down on us."

Not only did they trust him, what he said made sense; even so, they began to look about them nervously, their eyes relentlessly scanning both sides of the track.

"So, what do we do, Pilus Prior?"

It was a sensible question, but again, the Pilus Prior didn't hesitate.

"We didn't come all this way just to turn back because of some chopped trees," he said calmly. "Besides, we're supposed to teach these Daesitiates a lesson about the power of Rome, and I know they're sitting up there just ahead, watching us and wondering what's going on." He gave his Centurions a tight grin, which they returned. "So I suggest we don't keep them waiting any longer, do you?"

He got exactly what he expected in answer: a combination of growled acknowledgements, or smiles that held nothing but the promise of approaching mayhem. Quickly, he gave them the instructions of what he wanted, and since it wasn't anything unorthodox, it didn't take long before they were trotting back to their Centuries. Turning to his own men, the Pilus Prior rapped out his orders and, within a few moments, the column was ready to resume marching. And to face what awaited them.

The Daesitiates sub-chief that was given the task of setting the ambush was seething with frustration, and he longed for the moment when he could release his pent-up rage. Coupled with the anger was an acute sense that he had already failed in his task, and he resolved that someone would be punished for leaving some sort of sign that had obviously caught the eyes of the Romans. From his position a half-mile further down the track, he couldn't make out any level of detail, but he saw the column coming around the bend, then stop. That wasn't supposed to happen; it was well known that the Romans never lingered anywhere there was heavy undergrowth, because their style of fighting wasn't designed for it. That had been the reason for choosing this spot, but now it was apparent that his carefully designed plan wasn't going to bear the fruit he had hoped. Watching the Roman Centurions gather in a cluster, he could tell that they were looking up the slope, and it was in the general area where the trees had been partially cut. Yet he didn't get the sense that the Romans had spotted the men who were hidden there and were assigned the task of completing the felling of the trees. Yet, what other reason could there be? He felt the presence of his men around him; what he was most conscious of was the hard stare of his titular second in command, another sub-chief of a branch of the tribe who made it clear that he should have been given the overall command of this force. He was the head man of the village and the lands that occupied the valley adjacent to where the commander ruled, and as was usually the case, despite the fact they were from the same tribe, the two communities hated each other with the kind of passion that comes from close blood ties. The only thing they hated more was Romans, and this united them, for the moment. Still, the commander knew there would be a reckoning now that it was clear the Romans had sniffed out their trap. The question was, what to do? Despite his feelings for the other sub-chief, he knew the prudent thing would be to discuss what action they should take next, but his pride didn't allow for this kind of temperate behavior. Luckily, the Romans quickly resumed their progress down the track, and the sub-commander felt the tightening in his stomach and loosening of his bowels that always accompanied the knowledge that he was about to enter battle.

"Make ready," he called out, loud enough to be heard, but not shouting it at the top of his lungs.

Around him, he heard the rustling of the underbrush as men stood up, the clashing sound as the metal bits of gear hit against each other. Perhaps it was the noise that prompted his second to come storming up to him.

"Are you mad?" he hissed. "Surely you don't intend to go through with this now! Isn't it obvious that they know we're here?"

"Then all the more glory when we kill them to the last man." The commander said this loudly enough to be heard, and he was heartened when his boast was met by shouts of approval and agreement. The fact that the number of men shouting was only a small fraction of the force within earshot was something that he chose to ignore.

"That is a whole Cohort of Roman Legionaries coming, and they're expecting us to attack," the sub-commander insisted, trying desperately to avert what he knew would be a disaster.

Unfortunately for his cause, the commander wasn't willing to countenance the thought that his rival was actually thinking of the larger reason for which they were both fighting, and instead saw it as an attempt to undermine his authority and belittle him. That meant his response was calculated to be as insulting as it was possible to be and not bring the men belonging to each chief to blows immediately.

"I understand that this is dangerous," he replied with an icy calm that he didn't really feel, "and if you don't have the stomach for it, then I give you my permission to leave."

The other man reacted as if he had been slapped, the blood draining from his face, the shock and disbelief written plainly on his face. Despite the upcoming trial, which was just moments away, the men around the two were drawn to the pair, all eyes staring at them. And if some of them were coldly measuring not the sub-commander, but their leader, those eyes belonged mostly to the older, more veteran warriors, because they agreed with everything the sub-commander had said. Some of these men had faced the Romans before, when the Roman they now called Augustus had conducted his campaign here years earlier. They, better than anyone, including this hotheaded young sub-chief, understood the true might and power of the Roman Legions. When they had the advantage of surprise, and they could be contained within the killing ground with the felled trees, every one of them was committed to the idea of attacking. But now, their experience told them that this was a time to leave quietly, and wait for another day.

The sub-chief finally found his voice, although it came out as a hoarse whisper. "I won't be anywhere but in the middle of the fighting!"

Satisfied that he had scored a victory, the commander turned back to see how close the Romans were. Now that they had drawn close enough so that he could see the men in the ranks, while they still marched four across, they had spread out into what he supposed was their normal battle formation. More importantly, he could see that their shields had been unslung and the leather covers were off, so the red paint gleamed and the metal bosses shone dully in the subdued light. Suddenly, he felt his resolve slipping away when confronted by this naked sight of Roman power, and he could all too easily imagine the warriors of his tribe dashing themselves against the rocks that were represented by that wall of shields.

Even when something is expected, the actual moment action begins can be startling, and the Pilus Prior silently cursed himself for jumping at the sudden eruption of sound, in the form of roaring voices in full cry. The noise was quickly followed by movement, first by dozens of arrows slicing through the air, which he clearly heard as a whistling sound as more than one went rushing by, just a hand's breadth away. Whoever was in command of this ambush had not only failed in the larger sense, he had removed what small advantage he had by giving a shouted command, before the archers in his force had loosed their arrows. Granted, it was nothing more than a heartbeat's delay, but it gave most of the Romans in the column, who were already expecting contact, the chance to react by hunching behind their shields as they dropped the poles carrying their packs, resulting in most of the arrows lodging harmlessly in the wood of the shields. The Pilus Prior had used this lapse as well, by coming to a sudden stop, understanding that the archers loosing their missiles at him would have aimed at a spot where they thought he was about to be instead of where he was at. It worked, as the dirt track seemed to sprout arrows, still quivering as they spent their energy, just a pace away from where he was even then pivoting to his right in order to face the slope as a mass of howling warriors came bounding down to smash into the thin line of Legionaries. As he had ordered, the column split in two, with the man closest to each slope turning to face the threat, while the man who had been immediately next to him in the column braced him by grabbing onto the harness of his comrade and, in this manner, the men of the Cohort were facing the attack from both directions. It was thin, woefully thin, but the challenge of limited space worked both ways, since the men of the Daesitiates couldn't properly use the weight of their numbers because of the slope.

The men immediately behind the first line of warriors that were even then smashing into the shields of the Legionaries, trying to use the momentum gained from their dash downhill to knock the Romans off their feet, did have the advantage of higher ground, so they could thrust their spears down at their enemy, giving the defending Romans just one more thing to worry about as they ducked the spear points and parried the blows of their immediate attacker. What had been the relative quiet, marred only by the sound of treading feet and creaking of gear, was now obliterated by a riot of noise. The crashing sound of shields meeting shields provided the basis for this song of death and destruction, while the bright, clanging noise as sword blade met spear point, or another sword provided the melody, with the cries and curses of men being struck, either a mortal blow or even a minor wound punctuating the air in a discordant accompaniment.

The Pilus Prior had only the barest moment to appreciate his escape from being struck down by the initial volley of arrows as he quickly found himself assailed by a snarling barbarian warrior, his shield held high and sword pulled back above his shoulder, ready for the first opportunity to make a killing thrust. Like every Centurion, the Pilus Prior was without a shield, at least in the early phases of a battle, although they almost always took the first available one from a man out of the fight. However, this also meant that they spent most of their time training to fight without one, and the Pilus Prior's blade was already out in front of him, angled slightly across his body. For this initial round of combat, at least, his sword would have to serve as both offensive and defensive weapon, but in a move that surprised him so much that it almost ended matters right there, the barbarian facing him lashed out with his shield. It was so unusual for non-Romans to use their shields in anything but a strictly defensive manner that, when trying to piece it together later, the Pilus Prior had no recollection of how he avoided the smashing blow that would have, at the very least, knocked him flat. Yet he somehow did, although his desperate dodge put him in an awkward position that, while better than losing his feet, which was instant death, was not much better. In desperation, he lashed out with his sword in a wide, sweeping blow that violated the most common precept drilled into every Legionary that the point always beat the edge. He didn't know who was more surprised, he or the barbarian, because the edge of his blade caught his foe as he was following up his blow with the shield with a thrusting attack. This meant the barbarian's arm was extended, and he howled in pain as the edge of the Pilus Prior's sword sliced just above the handguard of his foe's own blade to carve a chunk out of the outside of the barbarian's forearm in a spray of blood and flesh that was as visually unsettling as it was painful. Still, the barbarian managed to hold onto his sword and, more importantly, brought his shield up in a move that knocked the Centurion's blade aside. This gave the barbarian the opening to make another thrust with his blade, yet the pain of his wound was so intense that instead he took a step backward to recover himself. Using the brief pause, the Pilus Prior risked a quick glance around him to check on the condition of his Century and to try to get a sense of how the battle was developing. He was heartened to see the two lines, thin as they might have been, facing outwards and unbroken, and that most of the prone bodies weren't wearing the uniform of Rome's Legionaries. That was all the attention he could pay, because he sensed a shift out of the corner of his eye as his opponent regained his composure and made to renew his attack. Before the barbarian could do so, however, the Centurion launched his own. Using a tactic that had proven to be devastatingly effective in the past, he appeared to have been paying attention elsewhere when he suddenly and without any preparatory move that might have alerted the barbarian, lunged in the barbarian's direction. His sword had been held in what the Legionaries called the first position, with the blade held low and parallel to the ground, and it was from this point that he began his assault. Seeing the threat, the barbarian dropped his shield to block the gutting blow, but even as he did so, the Centurion was altering the trajectory of his thrust. His first move had been a feint; a hard feint that meant that changing his angle of attack robbed the blade of a fair amount of force, but the throat is a soft target, not protected by armor. The point of his sword punched into the side of the barbarian's neck, cutting off the man's cry of anguish before it could begin, a spray of bright, arterial blood arcing through the air that briefly obscured the Centurion's vision of his now-slain enemy's face. The defeated man stood, tottering for a brief moment before collapsing in a heap, but his body hadn't even hit the ground as the Centurion was already moving, covering the dozen paces that had been between him and the greater safety of his Century. In doing so, he was able to dispatch two more warriors who had lost their awareness of his existence in their excitement of the battle and had moved to try to envelop what was the front of the column, turning their backs to him. Eliminating these two warriors was accomplished with a couple of quick but brutal strokes, then the Pilus Prior was standing, next to his *signifer*, where he belonged with his men. Only then did his mind have time to register the fact that the man he had just dispatched had been dressed in a fine green tunic, and was wearing the type of armor that marked him as not only wealthy, but a man of importance. However, it was only a passing observation and he quickly turned his attention to more pressing matters.

The barbarian warrior who was second in command had just seen himself get promoted, when his rival had been ended by a quick thrust to the throat at the hands of the Centurion in the front of the marching column. This was all that he needed; unlike his counterpart, he had understood the folly of what was taking place at that very moment, and his only concern at this point was to extract the warriors still remaining so they could be preserved to fight again.

"Sound the recall," he ordered to the man who carried the barbarian version of the *cornu*. To his credit, the man didn't hesitate and he blew his horn very quickly, in another sign that the warriors of the Daesitiates understood that their attack had been destined to fail, and they didn't need to hear the horn blow a second time before they obeyed. In fact, the men who needed to be reminded of their orders were the men of the Legion who, having repulsed this attack so easily, now wanted to pursue their advantage and chase these barbarians down. It took more than one blast of the *cornu* of every Century to remind the Legionaries that there would be no pursuit, but ultimately, they obeyed, and in a matter of a few moments, they were left alone, returning to their lines, still panting for breath.

After the sounds of battle, the only thing breaking the immediate silence was the low moaning of men, both Daesitiates and Roman who were lying on the ground, most of them holding their wounds. Quickly now, the shouts of Centurions filled the air, demanding that order be restored, in that most Roman of traits, trying to establish sense out of the most insensible of actions. Men were given the task of examining the bodies on the ground, both to find wounded comrades, and to find those barbarians who still lived to dispatch them with a quick slash across the throat. The Optios began moving through their Centuries, calling for those Legionaries that they didn't see immediately, most of them answering, while some remained silent, forcing the Optio to search through the bodies. Friends helped other friends bind up wounds, or in a few cases, squatted by a prone body, holding a hand and waiting either for help to come, or for the comrade to step into Charon's Boat, to take the long voyage across the river. In a very short period of time, order had been restored to the point where the Centurions left their Centuries to meet once again with their Pilus Prior, who stood calmly, wiping the blood from his sword.

"Not a bad day's work," the Hastatus Prior, commander of the Fifth Century, commented, despite the fact that he had a bloody neckerchief tied around his left forearm.

"No, not at all," the Pilus Prior agreed, his eyes narrowing at the sight of the makeshift bandage. "What happened to you?"

"I got careless," the other man replied casually, but his Pilus Prior wasn't moved by the other man's indifference.

"Make sure you have that seen to," he demanded. "We can't afford for it to get corrupted."

The other Centurion assured him that he would, then the other commanders had gathered. All of them congratulated their Pilus Prior. After all, it had been his sharp eyes that had given them the warning they needed. His reaction was to shrug off the praise, but inwardly, he was quite pleased. More than any of the others, he knew why he was in the position he was in, in both the larger and immediate sense.

"I had the best teachers," was his reply.

To that sentiment, there was nothing but agreement.

"Anyone who has Titus Pullus as an uncle, and had Sextus Scribonius as his Pilus Prior, better be good," joked the Pilus Posterior, and while there had been times this was a barbed jest, with the implication being that Gaius Porcinus had achieved the post of Pilus Prior because of his relationship to the great Titus Pullus, Porcinus knew at that moment, or chose to believe, that there was nothing but praise in this statement.

And he took it as he thought it was meant, with a simple nod in acknowledgement that, yes, he was indeed lucky and blessed to have been trained by the best.

"All right, give me a butcher's bill, and let's get the wounded patched up. I want to keep on the march so that we show up in their village not long after these bastards do," Porcinus announced, the idea of making camp now discarded.

Immediately, his Centurions fell to their tasks, as the Fourth Cohort of the 8th Legion, led by Quartus Pilus Prior Gaius Porcinus, made ready to resume their march and bring a taste of Roman iron to yet another recalcitrant tribe.

Chapter 1

Gaius Porcinus shifted in his chair, trying to ease the ache in his back. He had been seated at his desk for at least a full watch now, but it seemed that he had barely moved the wax tablets in front of him from one pile to the next. His system was simple; tablets on the right were those reports that he had to go through and verify, the stack on the left had been completed and tabulated. Sighing, he was forced to admit that it was nobody's fault but his own for putting it off so long, yet he was still getting accustomed to the workload that came from being the Quartus Pilus Prior, the Centurion in command of not just the First Century, but the entire Fourth Cohort. That, he recognized, wasn't exactly true; he had actually been in the post for more than three years, but he was breaking in a new Optio, now that his old one had been promoted into the Centurionate himself, although his Optio was new only in the sense that he was recently promoted to the post. In fact, he was well known to Porcinus and it had been Porcinus' decision to promote him from the ranks of the First Century. The man's name was Tiberius Numerius Ovidius and, as Porcinus was learning, despite the man's many qualities of leadership, the ability to write legibly wasn't one of them. If Porcinus was being honest, he suspected that this wasn't an accident, and in fact, he found it hard to blame Ovidius for preferring to be outside, on the training stakes with the men instead of cooped up indoors.

Sighing, the Pilus Prior, who was in his late thirties, but looked younger than his years, turned his attention back to the stack, knowing that wool-gathering wasn't going to get this chore done any sooner. He wasn't sure how long it was after he resumed work when there was a rap on the door to his quarters, the front room of which served as the Century and Cohort office. His desk was against the far wall from the door, while there was a doorway to his left that opened into his private quarters. That meant he was too far away from the door to open it himself, so he motioned to the slave who worked as the Century clerk to answer the knock.

The slave was Thracian by birth, and had been captured during a campaign that Porcinus had participated in as a Centurion of the 8th Legion, under the command of the Praetor of Macedonia, Marcus Primus. Since the Thracian's name was impossible to pronounce, he had been given the name Lysander, and Lysander rose to do Porcinus' bidding. Opening the door, he found another clerk, this one from the *praetorium*, delivering the week's batch of mail for the Century. Lysander took the sack containing the collection of scrolls, tablets, and the thin sheets of smoothly sanded wood that poorer Romans used to write on, and returned to his desk. This was part of Lysander's duties, so he untied the knot and dumped the contents on his own small desk, making enough of a racket that it caused Porcinus to jerk, ruining the letter he had been incising.

"Idiot," Gaius muttered, but Lysander knew his master well enough that he understood this was as far as Porcinus' berating would go. Instead, Porcinus, once he had corrected his mistake, looked over at Lysander, and simply said, "I'd forgotten today was mail day. Go ahead and stop working on the training schedule for the week and sort that mess out. I don't want to hear more complaints than we already do about how long it takes to get the men their mail."

"Yes, master," Lysander replied with a grin.

He knew even better than Porcinus did about the volume of complaints he would hear, but since many of those comments came with a cuff on the head or kick in the rear, he was more than happy to obey and get the chore done as quickly as possible. Working quickly, he read each name, cursing under his breath when whoever sent their missive forgot to include the Century number, forcing him to either remember or consult the official roster. Finishing even before Porcinus had reached for the last incomplete report, Lysander had divided the mail into six separate piles, one pile per Century. However, there was one piece left over, a scroll, sealed with wax, which Porcinus noticed when he lifted his head from the last report.

Pointing to it, he told Lysander sharply, "Don't leave that one out. Find out who it belongs to!"

Lysander shook his head as he picked up the scroll, and thrust it towards Porcinus.

"No, master. This one is addressed to you."

Porcinus frowned, forced to stand up and lean over his desk to take the scroll, and he examined the seal as he sat back down. A small smile played on his lips, although he said nothing. At least at first; then, conscious of Lysander's curious gaze and understanding that he would be pestered until he gave an answer, he gave an exasperated sigh.

"Fine. I know you're dying to know who it's from. It's from my uncle," Porcinus said, not elaborating any further, but Lysander understood to whom Porcinus was referring, since he only had one uncle.

In fact, Lysander, in some ways knew Porcinus' adopted father very well, even if it was in an indirect manner. It was because of Porcinus' uncle that Lysander was a slave, so unlike Porcinus, he didn't share his master's smile or sense of anticipation. However, he knew better than to let his feelings show, so he kept his expression in that carefully neutral state of any slave who wanted to avoid feeling the lash of their masters, verbally or physically, as Porcinus shook his head.

"He's probably writing to find out why I haven't come to visit him yet," he chuckled. "I think he writes at least once a month about that. Although," he said, frowning now that he had another moment to examine the scroll, "it's a little unusual."

When Porcinus said nothing else, Lysander, almost despite himself now that he had ascertained the identity of the correspondent, felt compelled to ask, "What's unusual, master?"

"Well," Porcinus pointed to the big red blotch that was the seal, "this is his seal, but this writing isn't his. He usually writes everything to me personally himself." Giving another small laugh, Porcinus laid down the scroll and finished, "I suppose he's getting lazy in his old age."

Turning back to his work, Porcinus decided that the letter could wait until he finished his work. It was in that spirit that he pointed mutely at the mail on Lysander's desk.

"It's not going to deliver itself."

Lysander simply nodded, then stood and began the process of preparing to deliver the mail to the Fourth Cohort.

By the time Porcinus was finally through, the late afternoon sun was slanting through the slits and un-shuttered window, casting a golden glow on the office and all its contents. He was thankful that, despite it being winter, the weather the last few days had been mild enough so that he didn't have to squint because of the poor light thrown by the lamps. Now that he was finished, he allowed himself the small luxury of standing up, stretching his aching back as he realized his ass had fallen asleep. Shaking first one leg, then the other, he walked into his private quarters to retrieve a small pitcher of wine and a cup before returning to the desk. With everything cleared away, all that remained on the desk was the scroll. After Lysander had finished his mail duties, Porcinus had sent him with the stacks of tablets to the *praetorium* and he had yet to return. Probably off somewhere looking for something to steal, Porcinus thought sourly, for he had learned that larceny was one of Lysander's vices. He had been beaten severely for it, but since in every other way he was exemplary, Porcinus had been lenient with him, so he could only hope that Lysander had learned his lesson. Pouring a cup of wine, he eyed the scroll, chiding himself for his reluctance to open it, so sure was he of its contents. What else could it be but another scolding about not bringing his family to visit? Just as he was reaching for it, there was a knock on the door again, and since Lysander was gone, Porcinus called for whoever it was to enter. The familiar figure of his Optio, Ovidius, filled the doorway before he marched to stand directly in front of Porcinus' desk and came to the position of *intente*.

"Optio Numerius Ovidius reporting that the men have completed their weapons drills and are now preparing the evening meal, Centurion."

Porcinus returned the salute, then asked, "How did it go?"

Ovidius, still unaccustomed to his new role, didn't feel comfortable enough at this point to break his position of *intente*, but he did look Porcinus in the eye as he gave a twisted smile.

"It went the same as always. The usual bunch whining about how we're doing too much stake work and not enough one on one."

"Is Fronto still waving his shield about every time he makes a first position thrust?"

Numerius laughed, but it wasn't a particularly nice one.

"No, I think I've settled that little problem. Fronto's bad habit is gone."

Porcinus raised an eyebrow.

"Do I want to know?"

"Probably not," Ovidius offered, and this time it was Porcinus' turn to laugh.

With the report done, he waved Numerius to a nearby chair, while he rose and went back to his private quarters, returning with another cup.

"Care to join me?" Porcinus asked.

"Have you ever known me to say no?" Ovidius scoffed, then accepted the cup that Porcinus had filled.

Sitting back down, Porcinus filled his own, and the two men chatted for a few moments about the daily training that never ceased in the Legions of Rome. Finally, Ovidius pointed to the scroll.

"Aren't you going to read that?"

Porcinus sighed, looking at the object on his desk, a frown on his face.

"I suppose so," he said finally. "It's just that I know what it's going to say."

Ovidius looked surprised and asked, "How can you know what it says before you open it?"

That was when Porcinus told him who the scroll was from.

"Ah," Ovidius said. "That's different." Giving Porcinus a grin, he added, "And you're right to be worried. I can't imagine he takes 'no' very well."

"It's not 'no'," Porcinus protested. "It's just 'not now.'"

"And how long have you been saying that?" his Optio said, laughing.

"Shut your mouth," Porcinus grumbled. Then, taking another breath, he said, "All right, then. I'll read it. Who knows," he grinned at Ovidius as he broke the seal, "maybe there was an uprising of Gauls or something exciting."

Ovidius laughed as Porcinus bent his head and started reading the scroll. The smile that had been on his face changed almost instantly as he recognized the hand in which this letter was written. Or more accurately, in whose hand it wasn't written. Silence filled the room as Ovidius sipped his wine, thinking of something clever to say, but he quickly saw that something was wrong. Leaning forward, he stared at his Pilus Prior intently as the other man read the letter. When Porcinus still said nothing, Ovidius cleared his throat, yet Porcinus gave no sign that he heard. Instead, his head tilted upward, in a sign that he was re-reading the letter from the beginning. Ovidius cleared his throat again, but when this still got no response, he finally had no choice.

"Porcinus? What is it? What's the letter say?"

Only then did Porcinus react, jerking his head as if he had been startled, and for the rest of his days, Ovidius would remember the look in his Centurion's eyes as he opened his mouth to speak.

"It...it's not from my uncle. It's from his scribe, Diocles. My uncle's dead." Porcinus gave a chuckle that held no humor." Although I suppose he's my father now, since that's what he was planning on doing, adopting me."

For a long moment, Ovidius could only stare, then he finally opened his mouth, but no words came out, because he was no less affected in his own way than Porcinus by this news. He knew that all men died, sooner or later, yet if there had been one man that Ovidius would have bet on as the one most likely to beat those odds, it would have been Gaius Porcinus' newly adoptive father, because Porcinus' father was no less known to Ovidius, even if it wasn't as intimately. In fact, it would have been safe to say that there wasn't a Legionary under the standard who hadn't at least heard of Porcinus' adoptive father. Finally, Ovidius found his voice, after a fashion, although what came out sounded to him like a strangled croaking.

"Titus Pullus is dead?"

As hard as the news of the death of the great Titus Pullus hit Gaius Porcinus, it was a shade when compared to the reaction of his children, particularly his oldest son, Titus, who had been named in honor of Titus Pullus. The youngster was nine years old, but although the man he thought of his grandfather had moved away three years before, rarely a day went by where young Titus didn't make some reference to his "Avus," although the subject of his Avus' horse, Ocelus, was usually involved. The boy and the giant gray stallion, who had been presented to Titus Pullus as a gift on his retirement from his post as Primus Pilus of the 10th Legion and assumption of the newly formalized office of Camp Prefect, appointed there by the man now known as Augustus, had formed a bond that was almost as strong as that between the horse and his master. Porcinus' oldest son, in fact, had been inconsolable, rushing off to only the gods knew where to sob out his grief, leaving Porcinus to comfort his wife and the other children. Iras, Porcinus' wife, was grief-stricken as well, but her husband understood that the emotions she was feeling were much more complex, and he didn't begrudge them. For the truth of the matter was that Iras had once been Titus Pullus' property, although it was the way into which she became part of his household that made the feelings that overwhelmed her so tangled. Pullus hadn't been Iras' first owner; she, in fact, had the honor, or misfortune, to be born into the service of the house of Ptolemy XII of Egypt, and like all his property, she had passed into the ownership of Cleopatra VII when Cleopatra's father, derisively nicknamed Ptolemy Chickpea by his Roman masters, had died. Complicating matters further, Iras was Cleopatra's half-sister, the product of a union between Ptolemy XII and one of his slaves.

The way Iras had come into the ownership of Titus Pullus merely added another layer that made her confusion of emotions at the news of his death understandable. Iras had been an instrument, wielded by Cleopatra, to seek the death of Titus Pullus, when he had been part of the force assembled at Ephesus, waiting for a fleet to be built to carry Cleopatra and her husband, the Roman Marcus Antonius, to their ultimate confrontation with the man who now was the undisputed single master of Rome. It had been Pullus' misfortune to be present when Cleopatra had uttered words that in essence revealed her plans to install her son with Julius Caesar, Caesarion, as sole ruler of Rome. And although she hadn't used the word "king," she didn't have to; after all, just the worry that Caesar's ambition was to crown himself king of Rome had seen his death. Afraid that Pullus would divulge her lapse of judgment, she had sent Iras as her weapon, with the mission of providing the household slaves already belonging to Pullus with poisoned provisions, under the guise of working for a merchant. This merchant had been well paid, but was given his own set of instructions; once Iras accomplished her goal of enamoring Pullus' slave, named Eumenis, and selling him the tainted food, the merchant was to dispose of the evidence, cutting Iras' throat. Unfortunately for Cleopatra, Deukalos the merchant was a man of huge appetites, and Iras was one of the most beautiful things he had ever laid eyes upon, so instead of doing as he had been paid, he took Iras into his bed. In fact, that was where she had been found, literally, when Pullus, with the aid of his friends Sextus Scribonius and Gnaeus Balbus, had unraveled the circumstances and learned the identity of the merchant, paying him a visit in the middle of the night. Accompanying Pullus that night had been his young nephew, still a Gregarius, the lowest rank of Legionary, and to say that he was smitten from the first moment was putting it kindly. In fact, it had been Porcinus who deduced that the young girl with the sheet pulled up to her eyes was Iras, and although Pullus' first plan had been to kill the girl, that plan had obviously changed. At first, it was because of the intercession of Pullus' woman, Miriam, who prevailed on Pullus to stay his hand, pointing out that Iras' very existence was perhaps the best revenge on Cleopatra. Over time, Iras had won first Miriam's, then finally, Pullus' trust, earning a spot in his household, and it wasn't long before she had won Porcinus' heart.

Now, she sat at the table in their quarters, and while her tears were genuine, like most women, especially wives and mothers, she had a practical side that even then was in operation. For as sorrowful as the news of Pullus' death was, it also put into motion a number of things that would have an enormous impact, not just on Iras personally, but more importantly, her family. Before he had retired as Camp Prefect, and left Siscia, where Porcinus and the 8th Legion were stationed as part of the Army of Pannonia, he had given Iras her document declaring her freedom, duly sworn and notarized. But it was his plans for her husband that had the largest impact, on her and her children, as well as Porcinus.

"I'm adopting you, and making you my heir," he had told them, shortly before he and his close friend and scribe, Diocles, departed for the villa he had purchased in Arelate. "So you'll never have to worry about money, at least."

That, naturally, made Iras very happy; the fact that the reason her now-former master had accrued so much wealth was to elevate himself, and more importantly to Iras, his heir to the equestrian class in the rolls of the citizens of Rome. But the most crucial thing that came from this elevation was the knowledge that Iras' children would be equestrians as well. Of the most immediate concern was the fact that neither of her sons would have to worry about finding themselves in the ranks of Rome's Legions, holding a sword and shield, as their father and benefactor had. This was a particular concern because Iras was no fool; she had seen how her oldest boy had loved her former master, and had, from almost as soon as he could talk, started telling anyone who would listen how he would be a man of the Legions, just like young Titus' father and his Avus. And from everything her husband Gaius had said, this was exactly what had led her husband to enlist in the Legions, because of the example set by the brother of his mother Valeria. Porcinus' enchantment had started when he was a little younger than Titus was now, when his uncle had visited, fresh from the conquest of Gaul where, like his general Gaius Julius Caesar, Titus Pullus had found his own measure of renown and fortune. The young Porcinus had been enthralled, and as his parents would learn, more to his mother's chagrin than his father's, the idea of life on a farm, emulating his father, had left him dead inside. In fact, although his uncle didn't realize it at the time, not only had he ignited a fire within his nephew that would only be quenched by enlisting in the Legions, he had provided the youngster with the vehicle by which he could achieve his dream, in the form of a small sum of money that he had entrusted to Porcinus' mother.

"This is for the boy," he had instructed his sister, "so when he's old enough, you give this to him to spend however he wants."

It helped that Pullus had given his sister what was, to her at least, a staggering sum of several thousand sesterces for her own use. However, Pullus' generosity had gone wrong as far as his sister was concerned, because Gaius used his money to find a man to help the young Porcinus swear into the 14th Legion by claiming to be the youth's father. To Pullus' credit, he had been unaware of this, and, in fact, had done what he could to prevent his only nephew from enlisting, although it was a halfhearted attempt. However, once he did learn of his nephew's enlistment, Pullus had used his influence, and money, as the Primus Pilus of the 10th Legion, to pluck the young *tirone*, the name for a trainee, from the 14th. The timing of this move could have been better; Pullus and the Legion were in the process of preparing for the invasion of Parthia, under the then-Triumvir Marcus Antonius, a campaign that not only failed in its objective, but would go down in Roman history as the most grueling and the costliest, with the exception of the expedition that had spawned this one. That first campaign had been three decades before, when Marcus Licinius Crassus and his entire army had met defeat at Carrhae, when only a handful of Romans had escaped with their lives. While that hadn't been the case with Antonius' campaign –he had been able to extract about half of his army from the vast expanses of frigid desert that constituted a large part of the Parthian kingdom – the ignominy suffered by Marcus Antonius was that the vast majority of his losses hadn't come from a Parthian arrow or cataphract's lance. It had been the land itself, and the brutal climate and conditions of privation that had claimed so many of Rome's finest Legionaries. This had been the first campaign for Gaius Porcinus, and while he never spoke of it, Iras knew that he bore the scars of all that he had seen and endured, because there were still nights where he would wake screaming in terror, shivering as if he had been submerged into an icy pool. These were the things that made Iras so thankful in the knowledge that her sons wouldn't have to endure these kinds of horrors, no matter if her husband never referred to them as such, or talked about them at all, for that matter. It was true that her youngest son, Sextus, hadn't expressed any interest or desire, but he had been too young for his huge uncle cum grandfather to have the same kind of impact.

Iras looked over at her husband, and even as her mind was working, she felt for him, seeing the look of sadness that had descended on his features, now that the shock had worn off. Better than anyone, Iras understood how her husband felt about Titus Pullus, and she ached for him now, wishing that there were words she could utter that would provide some balm for the fresh and gaping wound in his soul.

"It's just hard to believe," Porcinus broke the silence, his eyes fixed at some spot on the table, the wine cup in his hand still full. He turned to look at Iras, his eyes haunted. "I mean, I knew he would die, but somehow, I never thought that he actually would." Giving a self-conscious laugh, he lifted the cup to his lips, muttering, "I just thought that if anyone would cheat death, it would be him."

As he drained the cup, Iras studied him thoughtfully. No, she decided, it wasn't time yet.

Instead, she offered, "At least he died in his sleep. That's good."

Porcinus considered this for a moment, then shook his head.

"No," he replied quietly. "Somehow, I don't think he would have wanted to die that way."

"How then?" Iras asked, but Porcinus ignored the edge in her question, choosing to answer it as if she were asking because she wanted to know and not plumb his own thoughts about what kind of death he himself would seek.

"With a sword in his hand," Porcinus replied instantly, and his suspicions were confirmed when he saw Iras visibly flinch.

"And I suppose that's how you would want to die." Her tone was a combination of questioning and scornful; like most members of her gender, she didn't think much of men and their ideas of glory, honor, and duty.

Gaius Porcinus was every bit as dedicated to his Legion, Cohort, and Century as his adoptive father had been. Where he differed from Titus Pullus, however, was that he was also a devoted husband and father. So that, even through his grief, he knew he was swimming in dangerous waters, and understood that for the sanctity and peace of his home life that there was really only one answer he could give. However, it was partially because of his sorrow that, without making a conscious decision to do so, he chose to honor the man who had been the strongest influence in his life.

"Absolutely," he answered quietly. "I can't think of a better way for a Centurion of Rome to die, with a sword in his hand and enemy at his feet."

Iras glared at him, but he wasn't cowed, returning her gaze with a calm certainty that she had learned from long experience meant that he wouldn't be swayed. Consequently, Iras satisfied herself with a contemptuous snort that she knew with the same amount of conviction that he understood she didn't accept his statement. But this wasn't the time for a fight; in fact, the couple rarely argued, because that just wasn't in Porcinus' nature. Normally, his disposition was a closer match to that of his very first Centurion, the Secundus Pilus Prior and Titus Pullus' best friend Sextus Scribonius, a man who, as far as he knew anyway, was still alive and living in Alexandria.

It didn't take long for his thoughts to turn in that direction, and he commented to Iras, "I wonder if Scribonius knows. He's going to take it hard."

"I doubt he's heard yet, but he certainly will," Iras agreed.

He looks so sad, she thought, and she put her own small hand over his, which he took and squeezed gratefully. When their eyes met, she saw his were shining, rending her heart and telling her with no uncertainty that this wasn't the time to raise the practical considerations wrought by the death of Titus Pullus.

"He's just been such a huge part of my life." Porcinus was forced to choke back a sob, but he only did so with difficulty. "I just don't know what it will be like, knowing he's not there."

"I know." And in this, Iras was being completely honest.

Titus Pullus had been larger than life, in so many ways that it would have been impossible for her to describe. Physically speaking, it was certainly a true statement to say that Titus Pullus dominated every space he occupied. He had been born a large man, so huge that, according to his long-dead father, he had killed his mother in childbirth because of his size. This had been the pretext for his father's hatred towards Pullus, but in that hostility had been born a fire, which, when combined with the fact that he was taller and more muscular than almost everyone Iras or anyone else had ever met, made Titus Pullus a man destined for greatness. That greatness was tempered by the circumstances of his birth, but somehow, he innately understood that the only road that would take him to his ultimate destiny led him to the Legions. And it was in the Legions that the legend of Titus Pullus was born, as he not only survived a forty-two year career under the standard, but he achieved what was the highest rank available to a man of his birth, the post of Camp Prefect. This was an office that had appeared from time to time in the Roman military, but it had been made into a formal office, with a distinct set of duties, during the reforms wrought by the man who was the heir to Pullus' first general, Julius Caesar. Pullus' appointment to Camp Prefect had been a reward for his loyal service to Rome, but it wasn't without cost, one that Porcinus knew in his bones that he could never pay. As ambitious as Gaius Porcinus was, he had recognized at an early age that he wasn't possessed of whatever it was that fueled a man like Titus Pullus. And while he had some of his uncle's physical gifts, namely his height, his was a more slender build that, no matter how hard he worked, would never be as muscular as that of his adoptive father. But it was more than that, Porcinus knew, and if Pullus had been asked what his nephew was missing, he would have said that it was the gift of rage, a seething, dark, and lovely legacy given to him by his father's loathing, where there was an undercurrent of anger just waiting to be unleashed.

And now that his presence was gone, Porcinus thought, he realized that he did indeed feel adrift, as if whatever had moored him and given him his sense of stability and pride of place was suddenly missing. How could he compensate for that?

The personal trials of a Pilus Prior notwithstanding, the business of the Legions, and Rome, continued apace, so Porcinus found himself in his office the next day to begin business as usual. Unfortunately, he hadn't thought to tell Ovidius to keep the news of Pullus' death a secret, so it was only a matter of moments before the first man showed up, another Centurion from the 8th Legion, to offer his condolences. Porcinus took this in stride, understanding that every man who showed up was doing so because he himself had some sort of relationship with his deceased uncle. I have to start thinking of him as my father, Porcinus chided himself as the first man left his tiny office, only to be replaced by another well-wisher. It was understandable, Porcinus thought; Titus Pullus had been Camp Prefect for ten years, and had been the second in command of both major campaigns in which the Army of Pannonia participated. That made it natural for every one of these men to have some sort of connection to Pullus, and Porcinus had to admit that some of the anecdotes related to him by those paying their respects were quite funny. In fact, that seemed to be the overall gist of what men had to say about Pullus. Oh, they talked of his prowess in battle, or some of the acts they had witnessed, but by and large, these hard-bitten men talked about the amusing things that Pullus had done or said. Yet, as the day progressed, Porcinus noticed that these funny stories were almost always told in the context of how Pullus had managed to steady their nerves, or made them forget the dire peril that they were in at that moment. It was a profound lesson, the last in leadership that Titus Pullus gave to his adopted son, but it was one that would stick with him the rest of his life.

It wasn't until after midday that the current Camp Prefect stopped by. Despite the circumstances of his visit, Porcinus' face lit up in a smile as Aulus Honorius Macrinus knocked on his door. Not that he had to engage in such formality; Macrinus was the current Camp Prefect, and the successor to Pullus, who had made the recommendation for him to assume his post. More than that, Macrinus was the former Primus Pilus of Porcinus' own 8th Legion, and had been Porcinus' commander for his entire career, even if it was removed by several levels. While there had been a *quid pro quo*, in the form of Pullus' demand that his nephew and heir be promoted from where he had been the Pilus Posterior, commander of the Second Century, of the Seventh Cohort, in exchange for Pullus' support of Macrinus for Camp Prefect, Pullus would never have offered up his nephew if he didn't truly believe he was ready. Thankfully, for all parties, Porcinus had vindicated Pullus' judgment, and Macrinus held the younger man in high regard. Conversely, Porcinus thought of Macrinus in similar terms, so his pleasure at this call was unfeigned.

"I was sorry to hear about your uncle," Macrinus said after the initial pleasantries. "I didn't think anything could put him in Charon's Boat," he continued in an unconscious echo of Porcinus' own thoughts.

"I suppose he was just worn out," Porcinus replied as both men took seats. "After all, you saw him without his tunic. I've never seen anyone with so many scars."

"Nor have I," Macrinus agreed.

Macrinus regarded the other man thoughtfully. He had been more than a subordinate to Pullus; Macrinus was proud that he was one of the very few men that could call Titus Pullus a true friend. And it was as a true friend that Pullus had confided in Macrinus his plans and ambitions for his nephew. That, in fact, was one of the reasons Macrinus had come to visit.

"So what are your plans now?" Macrinus asked after the two had sipped their wine.

"Well, I'm going to take the Cohort out on a surprise forced march," Porcinus replied, hurrying to put his cup to his lips to hide his smile, knowing this wasn't what Macrinus was asking.

"That's amusing, Porcinus." Macrinus' tone was peeved. "But I think you know what I'm talking about."

"I do," Porcinus admitted, but his smile faded. "Honestly, I don't know. I haven't had much time to think about it."

"That's true," Macrinus granted, but while his tone was gentle, it was insistent. "But speaking as Camp Prefect, I'm going to need to know your intentions as soon as possible."

"I understand, sir."

Standing, Macrinus offered his hand, which Porcinus took, grasping the other man's forearms in the Roman manner.

"I'll let you know as soon as I can, sir."

"See that you do," Macrinus said genially. "And again, I'm sorry to hear about Pullus."

When the Prefect left, Porcinus had a few moments to himself before he was disturbed again, and he spent it deep in thought. What would he do?

Fortunately for Porcinus, despite Macrinus' words, he didn't have to make any decision immediately. It would take some time for the process of Titus Pullus' will to be retrieved from its location in the basement of the Temple of Vesta, where every Roman citizen, no matter how modest their status, kept their last will and testament. It was a peculiarly Roman trait; even if the only item to be bequeathed to a relative was a copper pot, it was likely that the owner of it had paid one of the lawyers hanging about the Forum every day to draft their will. Titus Pullus had quite a bit more than a copper pot to his name, so Porcinus was sure that it would take weeks, if not months before all the arrangements would be made to fulfill the provisions of his will. After that, he had no idea how long it would take for his own elevation to the equestrian status as Titus' heir to be ratified. Iras managed to wait for three days before she finally couldn't hold it in any longer and broached the subject that had been in the forefront of her mind since her husband had given her the news.

"Once your unc...father's will is opened," she made sure to correct herself, although she didn't really know why, "how long do you think it's going to be before you hear anything?"

Porcinus stifled his first impulse to snap at her for bringing such matters up so soon after Pullus' death, realizing that Iras had indeed managed to keep what he knew had been boiling inside her under control for three whole days. Instead, he gave her a weak smile, but could only shrug.

"I have no idea, my love. I've never been part of anything like this. I don't know if the will has to be taken back to Arelate, or if the lawyer who's handling the will in Rome just sends instructions back to Diocles about how to dispose of his estate. Or if he sends me a message at the same time. Then I imagine some sort of paperwork has to be done before my elevation is ratified."

Not surprisingly, this didn't satisfy Iras, but she also understood that her husband was right in that he had never had reason to have any experience with such matters. His father had died, that was true, but because of the generosity of Titus Pullus, the farm on which Gaius Porcinus was raised had instead gone to his youngest sibling and only brother, also named Titus. It had saddened Iras when word of Gaius' father's death had come, in a letter from Valeria, Gaius' mother and Titus Pullus' only surviving sister, but not for the reason one might think. It wasn't because Gaius was bereft at the news; in fact, it was the opposite. He had shown little emotion when he was informed. Iras knew it wasn't because the elder Porcinus had mistreated his son, but because her husband's affection and regard for a father figure had been transferred years before to Titus Pullus, probably all the way back to when Gaius was around young Titus' age and his uncle had shown up.

"So...what are we going to do?"

There, she had finally asked the question that kept her up nights, but now Porcinus just looked at her with an annoying placidity, the expression on his face telling her that he had given the matter little, if any, thought.

"About what?" he asked her, confirming her suspicions.

Iras was dangerously close to hurling the cup she was holding at his head, but it was then she caught the glimmer of his smile, and she recognized he was teasing her.

Scowling at him with mock indignation, she retorted, "You're lucky I can tell that you're teasing me, because I was about to bounce this cup off your head."

"*Pax*." He laughed, holding up his hands in surrender. Then, turning serious, he said, "I suppose that's something we need to think about. Macrinus came the day after I got the letter from Diocles and asked me, so you're actually not the first person to ask me." He considered for a moment, conscious that Iras' eyes were studying him intently. "If his will just transfers his status to me through adoption, I suppose it means that the money goes with it. But I don't know if his villa in Arelate is part of that or not. If it is," he shrugged again, "I imagine that it would make sense for us to live there."

Now that the words were spoken, Iras felt as if her breath was being snatched away at the scope of what they were discussing. Although both she and Gaius were well traveled; she had been part of Cleopatra's court, after all, and he had, of course, seen much of the world from within the ranks of the Legion, yet it had been many years since she in particular had traveled. Not until that moment, when Porcinus mentioned that relocating their family was a possibility, did she realize how much she had missed the excitement that comes from seeing new sights, and experiencing new tastes and smells. Yes, it was a hardship, and it could be dangerous, but to Iras, that just added spice to the stew of adventure, and she found herself fighting a smile at the thought of it.

"How long do you think it would take for us to get to Arelate?" Iras asked, her mind suddenly racing, filling with the enormity of what needed to be done.

"I think first we need to wait to hear from Rome, or Diocles," Porcinus cautioned his wife, standing up from his side of the table to place his hands on her shoulders, almost as if he were trying to keep her seated.

Which, in a sense, was exactly what he was doing, because he knew his wife very well. If this was allowed to get out of hand, he would come home from his daily duties to find his entire household packed up and ready to move.

"Until we hear, I'm still the Quartus Pilus Prior of the 8th Legion, and that's all that I am," were his final words, in a gentle but firm tone.

Iras understood his message, and accepted it. For the time being.

Winter in Pannonia could be bitter, but young Titus Porcinus always enjoyed himself, no matter what season it was. This winter was different, however, and Iras fretted that her oldest son would make himself sick. If, that is, he could make himself sick from sadness. Both she and Porcinus had assumed that Titus would behave with the resiliency that all youngsters showed when faced with tragedy, but it had been almost a month since the news of his Avus' death and Titus showed no sign of emerging from his melancholy. Finally, the boy could contain himself no longer, blurting out part of the cause for his ongoing grief and worry during the evening meal, and solving the mystery of his condition to his parents.

"Now that Avus is gone, who's going to look after Ocelus?" he cried, knowing that it wasn't manly, it wasn't Roman to shed tears in this way, but he couldn't seem to stop himself.

"You know that your Avus has Simeon," Porcinus told his son, not unkindly, but not wanting this display of tears to continue much longer. "He's been looking after Ocelus a long time now, and I'm sure he'll do a fine job now that Avus is gone."

"He can't take care of him like I could," Titus said with a ferocity and conviction that told Porcinus that his son was very worried that Simeon could indeed care for the stallion.

"I'm sure you're right," Porcinus agreed, his eyes meeting those of Iras, who was looking on with a bemused expression.

Like her husband, she had rarely seen her oldest boy display this side of his personality, and while she was amused, she was also a little fearful. Titus was a large boy; in fact, when her former master had been alive and still living in Siscia, Titus Pullus had told her that he was sure that he had been about the same size at young Titus' age. The boy's father was certainly taller than the normal Roman, by several inches, but young Titus, even at his age, was broad across the shoulders, giving a hint that he might actually emulate his adoptive grandfather in his size. Such thoughts gave Iras cause to shudder, but as quickly as it came, she reminded herself that Titus wouldn't have any reason to be put in a position where his size made him a target.

"What do you think is going to happen to him?" Titus asked his father, but much to his disappointment, his father refused to give him any hope.

"I suppose he'll live the rest of his days in Arelate, with Simeon to look after him," Porcinus said. Or, he didn't say, either Diocles or maybe I will sell him. Aloud, he told Titus, "But if I write and find out, will that snap you out of this...mood you're in?"

Surprisingly, Titus didn't answer this immediately, instead seemed to consider the question as if it was an actual proposition made to him by his father. Finally, he nodded, without much conviction, but still gave his mute agreement. Willing to take whatever victory he could get, Porcinus soon turned to other matters, talking to Iras about subjects in which Titus had absolutely no interest, and if he remained quiet through the rest of the meal, his sisters and brother more than made up for him. Although it was absolutely true that Titus was concerned about the fate of what had been one of his earliest companions going back to as long as he could remember, there was more to Titus' feeling of being unsettled. Even if he had been older than nine, he wouldn't have been able to verbalize the deep instinct that the death of his Avus had caused a fundamental shift, not just in Titus' life, but in that of his family. He knew, at least in general terms, that something called a will was going to have some sort of impact on them, but while his mother found it hard to contain her excitement, sending the message that whatever this will thing was, it meant good things, Titus' feelings on the matter were the exact opposite. Without knowing how, or why for that matter, he was sure that when the news of this will came to his family's doorstep, it wouldn't be bringing any happiness.

With his reform of the calendar, the man known as Divus Julius had finally ensured that the calendar was in step with the seasons, and it was just after the turn of the new year, in what would become known as the ninth year of the reign of Augustus, that the news for which Porcinus and Iras, with different degrees of patience, had been waiting finally arrived. At least, partial word, in the form of a cryptic message, not from Diocles but from what Porcinus learned was the lawyer in Rome charged with the handling of his adoptive father's affairs. Porcinus had received the message in his office, and even after reading it several times, he wasn't clear on its meaning. The only thing he was sure about was that the reaction of his wife wasn't going to be pleasant, because she would undoubtedly have the same questions that he did, and wasn't likely to be pleased with his lack of answers at the moment. Because of this prospect, perhaps he could have been excused for suddenly finding some particularly pressing matters that kept him from returning to his quarters at his normal time. Nevertheless, he recognized that further delay would be hazardous to the harmony of his house, so he trudged back home, carrying the scroll that was going to be the cause of the upset. On the walk, Porcinus reflected that perhaps the regulation against men of the Legions being married was, in fact, the wisest course to take. However, it was also the most ignored regulation, although if one were being technical, Porcinus wasn't married to Iras, at least legally. This was how most Legionaries were able to skirt the regulation; more importantly, it was what gave their commanders, at all levels, the pretext for ignoring the fact that when a Legion was in one area for any length of time, like the 8th was here in Siscia, there was a suspiciously high proportion of women and young children in the nearby town. And, depending on the campaign and the Legate in command, when a Legion did march, it carried a "tail" with it that was an army of its very own. It had been this way for as long as any man attached to the army could remember, and it was the unwise commander who tried to change this arrangement. Still, Porcinus entertained the brief thought about how uncomplicated his life might have been, then quickly dismissed it. While Gaius Porcinus loved the Legions, the truth was that he loved his family more, and it was perhaps this that was the biggest difference between him and Titus Pullus. It wasn't that Pullus had never had a family; in fact, he had loved two women in his life, and his first love, Gisela, had borne him two children, Vibius, named for Titus Pullus' longest, and, at that time, close companion Vibius Domitius, and Livia, named for the dead sister of Pullus and Porcinus' mother. This had been before Porcinus had become an adult and joined the Legions, so he hadn't seen the raging sorrow when his uncle's family had been wiped from the Earth in a plague that struck Brundisium, when Pullus was away fighting in Africa for Divus Julius, although he had met Gisela when she was still carrying Vibius. But Porcinus knew, and deeply loved, Pullus' second woman, and the one who Pullus had been given a special dispensation to marry legally on his elevation to Camp Prefect. Titus Pullus had met Miriam during his time in Damascus, when the 10th was marching for the dead Triumvir Marcus Antonius, and where Gisela had been coppery fire, carrying the voluptuous curves that spoke of her Gallic heritage, Miriam was slim and dusky, with dark features and a fine nose that bespoke her Syriac heritage. And as Porcinus thought, sadly, it had been her slim build that had doomed her and the too-large baby that was an echo of Titus Pullus' own birth, when his mother couldn't survive bringing her huge son into the world. It was not only the first event of Pullus' life, it was the seminal one that turned his own father Lucius against his only son, and drove the young Titus to seek a life away from the poisonous hatred of the man who sired him. Then, Pullus had watched the woman he loved, a woman who Porcinus was sure Pullus loved even more than he had loved Gisela, suffer the exact same fate. That, Porcinus thought sadly as he turned down the lane that led to his quarters in the town, had changed his uncle in a way from which he never recovered. He had become more like the Titus Pullus of his youth, at least in the sense that his only focus was the Legions, and advancing his career, a man with no softness in him, no finer feelings that would serve as an impediment to being the perfect man of the Legions. But at what cost? And in that answer lay the difference between Gaius Porcinus and Titus Pullus, because Porcinus had long before recognized that it was a price he was unwilling to pay.

"What does this mean, that there are 'issues with fulfilling the provisions of the will in its entirety'?" Iras scoffed, and even if the tone wasn't, the question itself was a reasonable one.

Unfortunately, it wasn't one that Gaius Porcinus could answer, at least to his wife's satisfaction. This meant that the rest of the evening was spent in what, to Porcinus at least, was an unprofitable manner, as Iras ran through every possible explanation to this riddle. It would have been one thing if she had pursued the answer on her own, but not surprisingly, she demanded that her husband participate. All that resulted was in two unsettled people retiring for the night, to toss fitfully through the watches of darkness, one of them because her mind wouldn't stop tearing at the knot of this mystery, the other because it is impossible to sleep when the person lying next to you never stops moving. It wasn't that Porcinus wasn't concerned; in fact, he was, but one of the more valuable lessons he had learned during his time in the Legions was the futility of worrying about matters over which one has no control. In fact, it had been during his first campaign, the ill-fated expedition against Parthia that he saw firsthand how corrosive and energy-sapping such behavior was, and until his dying day he would be convinced that more than one of his comrades who succumbed, not to a Parthian arrow or lance, did so because he was simply worn down from worrying about matters that they couldn't have done anything about. Porcinus wanted to know, perhaps not quite as badly as Iras, but it was worrisome nonetheless, yet he found he always felt better with a good night's sleep. That, he recognized, wasn't going to be happening, at least this night.

Looking back, Porcinus would never really be able to decide if it was a good or bad thing that neither he nor Iras had long to wait to discover exactly what that ambiguously worded phrase had meant. One thing that he did know was that the identity of the person who cleared up this mystery was a welcome sight, even if his task would prove to be so earth shattering. Only a full day had gone by, when Porcinus had once again returned back to his quarters, dreading the idea that he was essentially going to be forced to pick up what had been a singularly unsatisfying discussion for both him and Iras, that their talk was interrupted by a knock on the door. The timing couldn't have been better, at least as far as Porcinus was concerned, because the tenor of the conversation between him and Iras was growing increasingly heated, at least on one side.

"Are you expecting anyone?" he asked Iras, who shook her head.

She had her own ideas, however, as she retorted, "No doubt that it's your Optio or one of your men who you told to come rescue you from the clutches of your harpy of a wife!"

"If only I had thought of that," he sighed, but managed to duck the wooden spoon while moving to open the door.

Under normal circumstances, Porcinus would have determined the identity and purpose of the caller before opening his door; it was true the province was settled, but there had been attacks on Legionaries by the men who still refused to acknowledge the inevitable. However, he was sufficiently distracted that he forgot his normal precaution, and yanked open the door, which had a tendency to stick. The violence of the act startled the visitor, who uttered an undignified squawk as he leaped back a step, clearly expecting a reception in line with the abrupt nature of the opening of the door. Porcinus, framed in the doorway, didn't make a move of any kind, so the two men faced each other, frozen for a moment, both of them staring at each other. In Porcinus' case, it was a combination of shock and surprise, but not any fear, if only because of the diminutive stature of this unexpected visitor. Yet it was more than that, although it took Porcinus a moment to find his voice to identify this caller to Iras, who was even then demanding to know who had disturbed them. Finally, he managed a hoarse, gasping word, or name.

"Diocles?"

Naturally, he had aged, Porcinus noticed, after ushering his guest into his quarters, then stood there as he and Iras, as surprised as her husband, greeted each other, hugging for long moments. His black hair had been liberally sprinkled with strands of silver when Porcinus had last seen him, but now his head was almost completely an iron gray. The wrinkles, if not increasing in number, had definitely deepened, making longitudinal crevices framing his mouth, and accenting the corners of his eyes. Yet, his manner was still as vital as it had been when Porcinus had first met him, when he had still been a slave who belonged to Titus Pullus. Even then, the relationship between Pullus and this Greek, whom he had plucked from a pen containing the captured slaves and servants from Pompey's army at Pharsalus, when the then-Secundus Pilus Prior needed someone who could serve as a body slave, had transcended the master-slave dynamic. Diocles had earned something at least as valuable as his freedom; the trust of Titus Pullus, and his fidelity to his large master had been amply rewarded.

Now, standing there as Iras took his cloak, he looked careworn and tired, which was understandable since it was a long journey from Arelate to Siscia. Yet, it was more than that, Porcinus could see; he looked...worried. Having him take a seat, Porcinus sat with him as Diocles drank deeply from the cup of wine that Iras had poured, giving his wife a cautioning glare when he recognized that she was growing impatient. Finally, Diocles set the cup down, frowning down at it as he framed his thoughts.

"First, I want you both to know that I share your sorrow about Master Titus," he began, but he was cut off.

Somewhat to Porcinus' surprise, he watched as Iras placed a gentle hand on Diocles' arm, looking at him with a deep compassion.

"We're not the only ones suffering," she said softly. "I know how much you loved him yourself."

The words seemed to burst some sort of dam of grief inside the Greek, because without saying a word, he bowed his head and burst into tears. Within a matter of a few heartbeats, his body was wracked with sobs of the sort that came from such a deep well of sorrow that Porcinus felt the tears coming to his own eyes. Iras had risen from her chair and was now leaning over Diocles, who buried his head in her breast as he continued to pour out a grief that he had clearly kept bottled up inside as he performed his final duties to his master and friend. Finally, he regained enough of his composure that Iras relinquished her grasp, although her own face was wet with tears, making Porcinus feel a bit better about his own. A silence descended over the trio, punctuated by the sniffling of Diocles as he wiped his eyes.

"I don't know where that came from," he finally mumbled, then gave a self-conscious laugh.

"I do." Porcinus surprised himself. "This is probably the first chance you've had to grieve. I imagine there was a lot to do with..." He fumbled for words that wouldn't send his guest back into the abyss. "Well, with all that had to be done."

"Oh, there was a lot to do," Diocles agreed, a sad smile creasing his face as he stared into his cup. "Especially the funeral rites in Arelate. He was quite the well-known figure there."

"I can imagine he wouldn't have minded that." Porcinus said it without thinking, but it was the simple truth, and Diocles laughed in response, knowing that it was meant without any kind of rancor.

"No, he wouldn't," he agreed. "Although he didn't much care for the members of his own class who fawned all over him. And he really didn't like it when patricians came to visit him, because they always wanted something from him."

"That I can believe." Now Porcinus laughed, and Iras joined in.

Each of them had their own memories of Titus Pullus and his now-legendary clashes with the members of Rome's upper classes, which Diocles now used to introduce the purpose of his visit.

"Yes, well." Diocles cleared his throat, shifting uncomfortably in his chair. "Since there's no way to bring this up gently, I imagine I should just come out with why I'm here." He paused to take another gulp of his cup, wiping his mouth with the back of his hand before he continued, "Have you heard any word from Rome?"

Porcinus and Iras exchanged a glance, deepening Porcinus' unease even more.

"Yes," he answered. "Yesterday, in fact. But it was a...confusing message."

Diocles mouthed a silent curse as he closed his eyes.

"I had hoped I'd reach you before it got here. But I suppose it's better that it just arrived instead of you having to wait even longer to hear the news."

"What news?" Iras demanded, prompting an irritated glance from her husband.

"About your elevation into the equestrian class," Diocles replied quietly. "Rather," he corrected himself, "the fact that you're not being elevated into the equestrian class."

The couple sat in their chairs, neither of them able to speak for several moments.

"But...why?" Iras finally managed to ask, her voice thick with the shock and anger she was feeling.

Diocles considered carefully before answering, "I don't know for sure why. But," unconsciously, he shifted forward in his seat as his head dropped, his eyes suddenly looking about into every corner of the room, as if he was afraid of being overheard. "It comes from

Augustus himself. According to the dispatch I was given, and it was written in his own hand, he said that new information had come to light that impacted Titus' status as an equestrian. And because of that information, although Titus' name is allowed to remain on the rolls as an equestrian, Augustus wouldn't allow his heirs to maintain that status."

Now that the reason was known, all that remained was for the enormity of it to sink in for both Porcinus and Iras. Unfortunately, Diocles wasn't through.

"Also," he continued after taking a breath, "Augustus has decreed that because of this information, he is confiscating a portion of your unc...father's wealth. A significant portion, I'm afraid."

"How much?" Iras asked, although she felt a sick certainty that she had an idea.

"Three hundred thousand sesterces," Diocles replied, prompting a gasp even from Porcinus.

Iras, on the other hand, wasn't quite as circumspect, spitting out a string of curses that was no less vehement for the fact that she actually uttered them in her native tongue instead of Latin. Both men watched as she vented her rage, exchanging a wry glance, until Diocles finally held up a hand.

"The news isn't all bad. At least," he amended hastily, "on the money front. As well-informed as Augustus is, it seems that he seriously underestimated exactly how much Titus was worth, because, as you know, the qualification for elevation into the equestrian class, besides having a sponsor, is having a worth of 400,000 sesterces." He paused for a moment, happy at least that he could pass this piece of information to the younger couple. "Well, Titus had enough to be elevated into the Senate, if he had any interest. So technically, you still have enough, even after his confiscation, to become an equestrian." As soon as he uttered these last words, Diocles saw that he had made a mistake, seeing Iras' sudden look of hope, and he moved quickly to quash what he knew was a futile dream. "But that's meaningless, at least as far as becoming an equestrian. As you know, Titus was sponsored by Augustus himself, and he's removed his sponsorship. And," he finished meaningfully, "you would have to find someone who would be willing and powerful enough, to go against Augustus in the matter of sponsoring you for elevation. That, quite frankly, isn't going to happen."

Finished, Diocles lifted his recharged cup to his lips, and a silence settled over the three people, each lost in their own thoughts. Finally, it was Porcinus who broke the quiet.

"Well, at least we'll be the richest members of the Head Count in the history of Rome."

Diocles, his mouth full of wine, choked on the liquid before it finally came spewing out of his mouth as he began roaring with laughter, and was quickly joined by Porcinus. Only Iras didn't seem amused, but even she couldn't resist after a moment, although it wasn't as much because she saw the humor in the situation, as it was that she was swept up in the others' mirth. The laughter continued so long that it roused the children, who came streaming from their room, demanding to know what the cause of disturbance was.

"That's...interesting," was how Camp Prefect Macrinus put it, when Porcinus came the next day to announce that he, in fact, wouldn't be going anywhere. Although he didn't ask, Porcinus felt that his former Primus Pilus was entitled to know the circumstances, knowing that Pullus had considered him a close friend.

"That is one way to put it," Porcinus replied. "But I think you should know why."

Porcinus proceeded to explain the entire circumstances of this new development, leaving nothing out, including the fact that he was still a wealthy man, a very wealthy man. Macrinus absorbed this, his face giving nothing away, and he didn't speak until Porcinus was finished.

"I don't suppose this means that you don't need your pay, then, does it?"

Porcinus laughed, and even if it had a tinge of bitterness, the perverse humor of his situation wasn't lost on him.

"No, it doesn't," he told Macrinus. "If Augustus is going to ram his cock up my ass, I think I should at least be paid for it."

Now Macrinus laughed, nodding his head in approval.

"Good! I would have been more worried if you didn't view it like that." Turning serious, he asked Porcinus, "Have you informed Vettus of this?"

Porcinus shook his head, causing a frown to crease Macrinus' face, one that didn't need any more creases; the man already looked like a weathered pair of *caligae*. The man Macrinus was referring to was Sextus Vettus, the current Primus Pilus of the 8th Legion, and Porcinus' immediate superior. Bypassing him to go immediately to the Camp Prefect was a serious breach of protocol, and while Macrinus understood and appreciated why Porcinus had come to him first, he couldn't countenance this kind of behavior.

However, Porcinus, seeing and comprehending Macrinus' look, said hurriedly, "But only because he's taken the First out on a forced march. He's going to be gone for another couple of days."

"Ah, yes." Macrinus shut his mouth, a bit chagrined that he had forgotten. "Then I suppose I'm the appropriate person to tell." Before he spoke further, Macrinus gave the younger Pilus Prior a deep, thoughtful look. "I know this is a bitter blow, Porcinus. And I wish I could say that there wasn't an element of danger in your situation, particularly in the event that Augustus discovers that your uncle was much better off than he believed." Sighing, he stared off into space as he considered. "In fact, I think what would infuriate Augustus isn't if you tried to find a sponsor to elevate you, although I can't think of any man who would be foolish or desperate enough for money to do so. No, I think the fact that he didn't know Pullus had as much money as he did; that alone would be enough to make him take some sort of action." He gave Porcinus a level look, staring into his eyes. "I hope you know what that means."

"I do," Porcinus sighed. "Iras isn't going to be able to live in the villa she's dreaming about, either here or in Arelate. And she's not getting the extra slaves she wanted."

"I think that's probably the best approach," Macrinus agreed. "At least right now. In a few years?" He shrugged. "Who knows what could happen? He might forget. Or the gods may take him." The moment the words were uttered, a look that Porcinus might have thought was alarm, if he didn't know better, crossed Macrinus' face as he added hastily, "Not that any of us want that to happen."

Speak for yourself, Porcinus thought, but wisely kept to himself. Although, if the truth were known, he wasn't nearly as upset as he might have thought, and certainly not as much as Iras thought he should be. No, she was angry enough for both of them, but fortunately, her experience in the court of the Ptolemies had taught her a level of discretion when in public that meant he really didn't have that much to worry about when she went to the market and met the other Centurions' wives.

"So I have a lot of money that I can't spend," Porcinus summarized. "And I can't use it to help elevate my status. At least as long as Augustus lives."

When put so baldly, even Macrinus wondered why Porcinus wasn't angrier about it. It was true he didn't seem happy about it, but the Prefect would have expected a bit more fire, especially in private, with a man he trusted. At least, Macrinus mused, I hope he trusts me. Although, given the subject, and the times in which they lived, it was understandable. Ever since the rise of the man now known as Augustus, more commonly referred to as Princeps, it seemed that prudent men had learned to curb their tongues. If it was because in the past few years the more outspoken among them had exhibited a disturbing practice of suddenly disappearing from not just public but private life, then those who remained could probably be forgiven for not speaking out. With nothing else really to be said, Porcinus departed, leaving the Camp Prefect deep in thought. It was undoubtedly an injustice, but Macrinus forgave himself for thinking that at the very least, the 8th would still have one of its best Centurions. Yet, he was still troubled, not as much about the news itself, but the nagging question that wouldn't go away; why had Titus Pullus run afoul of Augustus, a man who he served faithfully and well?

That was actually the same question that troubled Gaius and Iras, even if it was for different reasons, but in this matter, the normally wise and well-informed Diocles couldn't provide much help.

"It's a question that's kept me up many nights since I received the message," he confessed to the couple.

It was his third night there, although it was the second time the three had the opportunity to talk, since Diocles had been asked to dinner by one of his long-time friends, reminding Porcinus that the Greek had lived here in Siscia for many years.

"And no matter how much I've thought about it, I can't think of one specific incident or reason that would put Titus in such disfavor with Augustus. Even with the Tribunal," Diocles continued.

What he was referring to had been the most challenging episode in a life filled with them, not just to Titus Pullus' career, but his life. The last campaign in which Titus Pullus participated, serving as second in command, was an invasion of Thrace by the then-Praetor of Macedonia, Marcus Primus. Primus, an example of the worst traits that were endemic in the patrician class rolled into one obese, pompous, and incompetent bundle, had claimed that his campaign was authorized by Augustus himself. It was an operation in which Porcinus had participated, his first as Centurion, as the Hastatus Posterior, or Centurion commanding the Sixth Century of the Seventh Cohort. As such campaigns went, it had been marred from the beginning by Primus' ineptitude and meddling, although when its true purpose had been revealed, it became clear that this was nothing more than Primus engaging in a treasure hunt. A treasure hunt on a vast scale, it must be said, composed of two Legions, the 8th and the 13th, and based on a nugget of information that Primus had overheard about the discovery of an especially rich vein of gold, in the mines owned by the Serdi tribe, outside of the city of Serdica. Although the campaign had seen some tough fighting, it ended in ignominy when Primus could no longer ignore the summons to return to Rome to face Augustus, who claimed that he never authorized any kind of campaign. What resulted was one of the most notorious trials in memory, culminating in the execution of Primus, yet what surprised those with knowledge of the situation was the Tribunal that was conducted after Primus' trial, where Titus Pullus was accused of knowingly aiding Marcus Primus in the waging of an illegal campaign against Thrace. It was not only patently false; Pullus' presence had been ordered by Primus who, as governor of Macedonia, held Proconsular imperium, making such a summons a matter of law. Furthermore, even when he brought the 8th and the 13th from Siscia, Pullus had been suspicious about the veracity of Primus' orders, and had demanded to see the orders issued by Augustus. Primus had produced them, but only after a delay of almost a full watch, and it was only later that Pullus learned Primus needed this extra time to transfer Augustus' seal onto a set of forged orders.

What was well known was that Pullus and Primus had been at odds from the very beginning of the campaign, as Pullus' instincts, honed over more than thirty years of service under the standard, told him that Primus was acting in a suspicious manner. None of that was enough to keep Pullus from being held before the Tribunal in Rome, but thanks to the energetic and imaginative defense provided by the Tribune Lucius Calpurnius Piso, and the appearance of his longtime friend and former Secundus Pilus Prior Sextus Scribonius, not even a Tribunal with instructions to the contrary could hold Pullus at fault. What Pullus had learned during that episode was that, contrary to his relationship with the man who raised him from the ranks, now referred to as Divus Julius, his relationship with Augustus wasn't nearly as close, or as cordial. In fact, from everything Pullus and Diocles were able to gather, the Tribunal had been conducted as a personal favor to Appius Claudius Pulcher, a close friend and supporter of Augustus, whose son had served with Titus Pullus in the army. Although Pullus and the son, after a rocky beginning, had developed at least a cordial working relationship, Pullus had been privy to misconduct on the part of the young Tribune. That had given the elder Claudius the pretext to view Pullus as a threat, but what Pullus had learned, directly from the son's mouth, was it was Pullus' impending elevation to the equestrian order that had incensed the older man. Claudius would have styled himself as an "old Roman," meaning that he viewed Pullus an upstart with pretensions above his class who had to be stopped. Yet, while that explained Claudius' motive, neither Pullus nor Diocles were ever able to determine why, at the very least, Augustus had allowed the Tribunal to move forward, even if he hadn't actively encouraged it.

"All I can think of is what happened at Actium," Diocles told the couple. "But even then, it was such a seemingly inconsequential moment that I find it hard to believe that even Augustus, who holds a grudge better and longer than anyone I've ever heard of, would still be angry. At least to the point where he would be this vindictive."

"I don't think we'll ever know," Porcinus sighed, but if he had resigned himself to this, Iras wasn't willing to let it go at that.

"There has to be more," she cried, the frustration causing her to bang a clenched fist on the table. "There has to be some sort of reason!"

"Not really," Diocles replied, and while his tone was mild, it didn't appease her in the slightest.

"Why are you so determined to find out why this happened?" Porcinus asked her. "All that's important is that it is. The why doesn't really matter."

"Yes it does," Iras retorted. "Because if we can find out the reason, then there's a chance we can at least fix it."

"I doubt that." Diocles laughed, probably the worst thing he could have done, but of the two men, he was the least cowed by Iras.

They had been fellow slaves, members of the Titus Pullus household, and they had a complex relationship. Diocles and Eumenis, the slave who died from the poison she had delivered under Cleopatra's orders, had been close friends, and while Diocles, probably better than anyone else could, understood how powerless a slave was, he still felt a reserve when dealing with her, knowing that she was the killer of his friend, even if she had acted under orders.

"Why do you doubt that?" she demanded. "Because we both know that Augustus doesn't do anything without having a reason. So we need to find out what that reason is."

Diocles didn't answer; she was right, he realized. Even if he didn't think they would ever discover it, she was correct that Augustus never did anything impulsively, unless it was perhaps gambling, at which he was notoriously bad. Otherwise, he was all cool calculation, every move and decision made with a deliberate eye and steady nerve.

Finally, he just shrugged. "Well, if you can find out, you're better than I am. Because I've thought of little else and haven't come up with a good reason."

With that glum announcement, the trio turned to other matters.

Not all the news was bad; it was while Diocles was there that he revealed two more pieces of information that would have a tremendous impact on Porcinus' family, particularly one member of it.

"Young Master Titus will be happy to know that his Avus mentioned him specifically in the will," he told the couple, lowering his voice to make sure that the sleeping children wouldn't be roused. "But he also specified two conditions."

"What are they?" Iras asked warily.

"The first is that you both have to agree to it," Diocles replied, looking at each of them.

"Uh-oh," Porcinus muttered under his breath, although with a wry tone.

"That's right: 'uh-oh.'" Iras scowled at her husband, but in the same playful manner, although Diocles could detect a note of nerves there as well.

"And the second?" Porcinus asked Diocles, but the Greek shook his head.

"Let's get the first out of the way before we go any further."

"We can't agree until we know what it is," Iras pointed out, ignoring the fact that Diocles was clearly about to continue.

"Yes, thank you so much for pointing that out," he said dryly. "It concerns Ocelus. Titus wanted young Master to have Ocelus, for the rest of the horse's days, however long the gods will it."

"What? That's out of the question," was Iras' first reaction. "That horse is massive! And I've seen him almost throw Pullus more times than I can count! No," she shook her head decisively, "impossible."

The truth was that neither man was particularly surprised at Iras' reaction; it was to be expected from a mother, and the two men exchanged an amused glance.

"I would just point out that Ocelus is in his dotage now, and from everything Simeon tells me, he's in excellent health, physically at least. But his days of jumping every fence, hedge, or ditch he comes across are behind him, I'm afraid. Besides," now Diocles' voice took on a shade of sadness, "he somehow understands that Titus is gone, I'm sure of it. Because he's been acting very melancholy, to the point that Simeon thinks that he will just...fade away. Unless," he made sure he was looking Iras in the eyes, "he has some reason to live longer. And we both know how much young Master loves Ocelus. For what it's worth, I think Ocelus loves him. At least," he amended, "as much as a beast can love."

Iras shifted uncomfortably in her chair, and she broke Diocles' gaze to stare down at the table a moment before muttering, "Well. That's different, I suppose."

"What's the other condition?" Porcinus asked quietly, now that he saw his wife had capitulated.

"That young Master come to Arelate himself to bring Ocelus back to his home," Diocles answered. "Not," he raised his hand in a placating gesture, "alone, of course. In fact, I would be happy to escort not just young Master, but all of you back to Arelate. After all, the villa is quite empty, except for us."

Diocles was secretly amused that the husband and wife wore similar expressions; jaws dropped, surprise clear for anyone to see. They exchanged a glance, and in that way that husbands and wives have, held an entire conversation in the space of time it took to look in each other's eyes.

"I do have some leave time coming," Porcinus broke the shocked silence.

Iras didn't say anything, instead letting out a brief, sharp squeal of delight that she tried to cut off by clamping her hand over her mouth. It was too late; the trio heard the distinctive rustling sound as the children, or at least the two oldest, roused themselves and came stumbling into the room, their eyes still slanted and swollen from sleep.

"What is it?" Titus demanded, suddenly alert and shooting a suspicious glance from his parents to Diocles.

He knew Diocles well, yet he and the Greek had a somewhat awkward relationship, but it was due more to the fact that Diocles didn't really know how to act with children than any dislike on the part of either of them.

Porcinus and Iras looked at each other, but Iras ceded to her husband the joy of making the announcement.

"Diocles just told us something that's very important." Porcinus' tone was grave, and he instantly regretted it because of the look of sudden fear in his son's eyes. "But it's good news," he hastily added, cursing himself for not thinking about how the boy would take such a portentous pronouncement.

"Well? What is it?" Titus demanded, the suspicion only partially dissipated, but the excitement of a surprise now the dominant emotion in his voice.

"Your Avus loved you very much. You know that, don't you?" Porcinus asked his son, and again cursed himself, because the mention of the man Titus had always thought of as his grandfather threatened a new round of tears. Porcinus was punished by a kick under the table form Iras, so he plunged on. "Of course you do. Well, he was worried about Ocelus, and who would take care of him. Simeon does a good enough job, but..." Porcinus' voice trailed off, and he gave a shrug.

Titus' expression had changed as rapidly as his father spoke, although he tried hard to rein in his hopes, which even so, were soaring.

"Your Avus wanted you to come to Arelate, and bring Ocelus back here to Siscia. This is his home, after all," Porcinus finished, but his last sentence was almost drowned out by Titus' shout of joy.

Not surprisingly, this roused the other two children, although the youngest, Miriam, was still a babe in arms. Suddenly, the house was filled with the babble of children's voices, and the lower tones of their parents as they tried to calm them down, to no avail.

"I wish I could, but we've just received orders," Sextus Vettus, the Primus Pilus of the 8th and Porcinus' immediate commander told his Quartus Pilus Prior. "There's some sort of mischief going on northwest of here, with the Rhaeti and Vindelici. Apparently, they've revolted, and we're on alert."

This didn't really surprise Porcinus; there are no real secrets in the army, and word had been rumbling with the men in the ranks for a few weeks that something was stirring with these people. The rankers had heard it from the townspeople, and Porcinus had long since learned that this informal network was more efficient, and accurate, than anything that emanated from Rome itself. Still, he was disappointed, but Porcinus knew better than to show it.

"Any idea if and when we move?" he asked Vettus.

The older man considered for a moment, weighing whether or not to answer, but he quickly decided that it would do no harm. He had known Porcinus ever since he had been brought into the 8th by the then-Prefect Titus Pullus, and while in the beginning Vettus had been sure that this youngster was being foisted on him by an over-involved uncle, Porcinus had quickly proven his initial impression wrong. Serving as his own Optio, Vettus had seen that there was iron in this young man's soul. Since then, Porcinus had never disappointed him, proving to be reliable, and while he was a bit soft for Vettus' taste, he was nevertheless an effective leader.

"If we do, probably not for at least a month, but not much longer than that," Vettus answered. Looking down at the tablet in front of him, he grunted. "It looks like Augustus' stepson Tiberius is going to be given the command, if it proves to be necessary." Knowing and trusting Porcinus, Vettus didn't mince his words. "Only the gods know if he's going to be worth an amphora of his own piss. Most of these nobles aren't."

Porcinus understood that Vettus was thinking back to the last major campaign in which the 8th participated, the ill-fated Primus expedition into Thrace. Since then, while there had been a number of punitive actions against the tribes in Pannonia, most of whom had proven to be quite resistant to the idea that they were now under the dominion of Rome, these operations had been of a short duration. Only twice had both of the Legions stationed in Siscia been sent out to quell local uprisings; otherwise, it had been Cohort-sized actions. In every one of these operations, the quality of the Tribunes assigned to the Legion had been widely varying, but they had been lucky in their Legate, Marcus Lucius Drusus Libo, who had just been announced as one of the two Consuls for the upcoming year. However, it had been more than eighteen months since the Legion had last marched into anything that could be called offensive operations, which meant that it was inevitable that the rust had to be knocked off the Legion. In some cases, that meant literally; despite preventive measures to keep their equipment in the best condition possible, torsion ropes would need replacement, the wooden bodies of the scorpions checked for cracks, along with an assortment of other tasks. While it wasn't likely that any of the javelins or swords stored in the long, low warehouses had actually rusted, both Centurions knew from experience that no matter how many conditioning marches they had conducted, the accumulated flab from the soft living of garrison life when compared to an actual campaign had to be burned off. Both men had experienced occasions when they were forced to march themselves, and their Centuries, into condition that would be considered battle-worthy for a Legion of Rome, and neither of them wanted to repeat that experience.

All of this summed up to one simple fact; Gaius Porcinus wasn't going with his family to Arelate. Iras took it as he had expected; not well, but he suspected there was still quite a bit of residual disappointment left over from the news about his and their children's status, so it was understandable. Titus, on the other hand, barely acknowledged the fact that his father wouldn't be going with them, which hurt Porcinus, although he hid it from the boy. His father understood the level of barely suppressed excitement that Titus was experiencing at the prospect of not only a trip, but returning with what would be the boy's first serious possession that would be his and his alone. Still, even if he wouldn't admit it, even to Iras, this sign of Titus' growing independence stung Porcinus, but he had the consolation of the other children, or at least the two who were old enough to understand that a separation was about to happen. Diocles would be escorting them back, yet while Porcinus knew the Greek would defend Porcinus' family with his life, the Centurion preferred to take steps that would make that unnecessary. One of the benefits of living in a military town was that there were men, hard men, available for work that profited from the experience they had earned under the standard. It was just a case of going into the town proper, and entering one of the many wineshops; Porcinus selected Mars' Delight, primarily because he knew the man who ran it, a former Centurion from his own Legion who had lost an arm during the Primus campaign. It didn't stop the man from operating a tightly run wineshop, although there was an edge of bitterness to him that meant on those rare occasions when Porcinus went out on the town with his fellow Centurions, he found being in the man's company a bit uncomfortable.

"*Salve*, Gaius Porcinus." The one-armed man wore the proprietor's false smile, but perhaps it was a shade warmer for his old comrade.

"*Salve*, Sextus Frugi," Porcinus replied, accustomed to the awkwardness of having to offer his left arm to clasp instead of the right.

"And what brings the Quartus Pilus Prior of the 8th Legion out? In the afternoon, even?" Frugi asked, but there wasn't anything in his question that gave Porcinus pause.

It was, after all, a sensible question, which Porcinus answered honestly.

"I'm looking for at least one good man, for a short period of work. Preferably two."

"Doing what?"

Porcinus proceeded to explain the trip his family was about to take. To his disappointment, Frugi didn't seem that enthused, and Porcinus was beginning to wonder if he had wasted his time.

Therefore, it was almost an afterthought when he added, "The main point is to allow my son to bring Ocelus back here to live."

Frugi visibly started.

"Ocelus?" he repeated. "Wasn't that your uncle's horse's name?"

Porcinus laughed. "That's the one."

Frugi's expression changed subtly, and he said, "Then that's a different matter altogether! If your family is going all that way, and it's to bring Ocelus back, then I can definitely help you!"

Porcinus had always been vaguely aware that the massive gray stallion of Pullus' was fairly well known, but he had always assumed that it was strictly because of his association with his adoptive father. He learned that day this was only partially true.

"It was back when we were taking Naissus the second time, after that fat bastard Primus was relieved and we were marching back to Siscia," Frugi explained when Porcinus asked why he was so familiar with a horse. "You remember that?"

Porcinus nodded; he indeed remembered it, because he had won his second *corona murales* as a Centurion of the Sixth Century of the Seventh Cohort. Frugi's mention of Naissus immediately summoned the memory of what had been in most ways a horrible day, one of blood, toil, and death, even if it was one in which he had distinguished himself and been rewarded for it.

"Well, our Cohort was the one that had the vanguard that day when our First Century was ambushed after they crossed the river. Remember?"

Porcinus, in fact, did recall this; the army was returning back to Siscia after what had been an extremely unprofitable campaign. Directly in the line of march stood the town of Naissus, which had already been assaulted five years earlier under Marcus Crassus. In all likelihood, the memory of that assault had been what spurred a force of perhaps three hundred warriors to ambush the Century leading the army, just after the Century had crossed the river. There had been no expectation of any kind of hostilities, so the surprise was total, and the advance Century had been savaged, not only suffering heavy casualties, but the loss of their standard.

"I saw your uncle's horse kill at least three of those Moesian *cunni* on his own, while your uncle was waving both his swords around like he was in the arena, except he was on the back of that horse! Ocelus kicked one's head in; it happened while we were crossing the river and your uncle and some of the Tribunes had galloped ahead of us. By the time we got to that side of the river, your uncle had gutted a half-dozen of the bastards, but then I saw Ocelus kick a man square in the chest and it sent him flying a good dozen paces! Then he reared and came down on another man and his head burst like a melon!" Frugi laughed at the memory, and Porcinus was smiling as well. "I'd never seen anything like it before. Well, you know the rest. We got them sorted out right quick."

Porcinus nodded his head, remembering the sounds of the *cornu* that had sounded down the column. His own Cohort hadn't been anywhere near the front, and the battle itself was short, if bloody. It was the aftermath, when Pullus announced that they would be punishing the city for harboring the men who had attacked them in such a cowardly fashion that impacted Porcinus more than this initial action. He was the first into the breach of the city wall, after it had been undermined, during a night assault, a rarity in itself. Then Porcinus thought of something.

"Wait, I thought you said Ocelus killed three men?"

Frugi's eyes widened and, for an instant, Porcinus thought he had caught Frugi out in embellishing an old soldier's story, which wasn't of any moment, but Frugi surprised him.

"He did! You remember that *cunnus* I mentioned he kicked in the chest? Well, as we came running up, I saw the bastard lying there, and I thought I'd end him, because I assumed the same thing you did, that at worst he had a few broken ribs. But when I got to him, his chest was caved in! It's true he was just wearing a leather cuirass, but still, I could have poured a tent section's whole pot of porridge into his chest!"

Porcinus expressed what he believed was the proper amount of admiration at Frugi's story, then politely steered the old soldier back to the purpose of his visit. By the time they were through, Porcinus was well pleased with the results, procuring the services of two men, both of whom he knew. One he knew quite well; Tiberius Libo had once been in Porcinus' Century, but when he lost his left hand and part of his arm when Porcinus' Cohort had been on detached duty and was attacked during one of the local uprisings that were such a prominent feature of being stationed in Pannonia, he had been cashiered. Fortunately, the kind of bodyguard work that Porcinus was offering didn't require the use of a shield, and Libo was one of the better men with a sword that Porcinus knew. More importantly, Libo had been one of the Legionaries that doted on young Titus when he was toddling around, and while Porcinus wasn't fooled, knowing that Libo was trying to curry favor with his Centurion, he could see that Libo was genuinely fond of the boy. That could only help if something happened on the way to Arelate. The other man Porcinus didn't know as well personally, but he was a veteran of the 13th who had opted to enjoy the fruits of retirement after one enlistment. Unfortunately, he was a much better fighter than gambler, and despite the tidy sum of money that he had earned through bonuses and loot, he not only found he needed employment, if the truth were known, he was bored. That was what brought Quintus Gallus into Porcinus' service, and while neither man worked cheaply, Diocles had brought what amounted as five years' worth of pay, sewn into the lining of his cloak, that was just a fraction of what remained of Pullus' fortune. It was still strange for Porcinus to think that he was a wealthy man, but at moments like this, he had to admit that it was a good feeling knowing that he could afford to provide this level of security for his family and peace of mind for himself, without it being a drain on his resources. With this detail taken care of, Porcinus returned to his duties, whistling a marching tune.

Porcinus' family departed for Arelate a week later, leaving in the pre-dawn darkness in a cart loaded with the younger children and all the necessary baggage for what would be a trip that took a month just to get there, at least that was the hope. Because it was still early in the year, a sea crossing, while quicker, was inherently more dangerous, which was something that neither Porcinus nor Iras was willing to risk with their family, a fact that neither of them communicated to the others and would serve to cause problems later. There would be a short passage by boat from Mediolanum to Placentia, but it would be by river, which wasn't a sufficient hazard that it needed to be avoided. Porcinus hugged and kissed the three smaller children, but when he came to Titus, who was sitting on the bench of the cart next to Diocles in the place of honor, relegating his mother to the back of the cart, he offered his hand. Even in the gloom, he could see the flush of pleasure creep over his son's face, although Titus matched his father's grave demeanor.

"I'm counting on you to protect your mother, brother, and sisters," Porcinus told Titus.

"I will, Ta...Father," Titus corrected himself, using the more formal title of the *paterfamilias*.

"And be careful with that gift I gave you last night." Porcinus added this in a whisper, wanting to make sure that Iras didn't overhear, not wanting to mar this event with what he knew would be an acrimonious argument. "In fact, I'd wait until you got to Arelate before you bring it out."

Titus, implicitly understanding this, and not wanting to rouse his mother's ire any more than his father did, shot a nervous glance over to where she was sitting on the wagon, and just gave a quick nod in response. Porcinus turned to Libo, who was sitting on his horse next to the wagon.

"Remember, Libo, Titus is in command," he said loudly, while throwing Libo a wink.

"I understand Centurion," Libo replied formally, but Porcinus could see he was fighting a grin. "Hopefully, he'll do a better job than the last Centurion I was under."

Porcinus couldn't suppress a chuckle at this, especially when he heard his wife snickering from the back of the wagon.

Turning to Diocles, who was going to be driving the wagon, at least at first, he said quietly, "Take care of them, my friend."

"With my life," the Greek replied, just as softly, and Porcinus knew Diocles was being completely sincere.

With that, the wagon carrying his family rumbled away, and Porcinus stood watching, waving back to his children as they departed on their great adventure. Once they were out of sight, he still stood, listening to the rumbling sound the wagon made as it bounced over the paving stones of the street, just before it turned onto the main road. When he could hear no more, only then did he turn to start his duties for the day, struggling with the feeling of sadness at seeing his family leave, and the relief at seeing his family leave. Gaius Porcinus would never know, because he would never utter it aloud, but like many professional men, there was a part of him that enjoyed the freedom to do his job, unhindered by the competing needs of family duties. All he knew, dimly, was that while a part of his mind would be worried until the moment his family returned safe and sound, he could lock that part away in a compartment, to be taken out only at times of his choosing, leaving the rest of himself free to attack the more immediate problem of getting his Cohort ready to march to war.

Chapter 2

It was during the beginning of the second week named for Mars, the war god, that the gates of the camp outside Siscia opened, and the vanguard of two Legions stepped out, heading north. It was early to be beginning a campaign, but this was to be a coordinated effort, with the two Legions from the Army of Pannonia working in concert with two Legions from Italia proper. First, however, the 8th and the 13th had to be met by their Legate, and contrary to what Vettus had been told, it wasn't Tiberius Claudius Nero waiting for them in Aquileia, which the Legions reached in five days. It was the other stepson of Augustus, Drusus Claudius Nero, who met them there, along with the complement of Tribunes, still six apiece for each Legion. Porcinus had learned from experience that it was in the hands of the gods as to which of the fine young men from Rome's greatest families would know which end of the sword to hold. The Legions had been led to this point by Prefect Macrinus, who, now that his duty was discharged, returned to Siscia to oversee the other Legions left behind in the province to keep an eye on the unruly inhabitants.

Another two days were spent in Aquileia; there was the inevitable shuffling among the Tribunes as their respective roles were defined by the young Legate, who, from what Porcinus had seen, looked to be barely out of his teens. This would have been cause for concern among the Centurions, but Drusus' headquarters staff made up in experience what the young man was lacking. His official second in command was a man in his late thirties, Publius Sulpicius Quirinus, although none of the first-grade Centurions knew him by anything more than reputation. Fortunately, that reputation was of a man who had experience, recently returned from Cantabria in the north of Hispania, and the campaign to subdue the last wild tribesmen who still refused to submit to Rome.

"We'll see who's really in charge the first week," was Vettus' judgment.

The day before their departure from Aquileia, there was a formation held, where the Legate formally introduced himself, and afterward, even the most skeptical man in the army had to admit that he had hit all the right notes. Self-deprecating, but at the same time exuding a confidence that Legionaries of every rank had come to expect from a noble Roman, Drusus also proved to be an excellent speaker, and most importantly, a good motivator. By the time he was through, the men were in full voice, roaring their promise to give their Legate cause to be proud, no matter what they faced. All in all, even Porcinus had to admit that it was an auspicious beginning to what was sounding increasingly like a tough campaign. It was at Aquileia that the strategy for the upcoming operation was announced, and Porcinus and the other Centurions learned that this was, in fact, the second phase of the campaign, one in which the young Drusus had already acquitted himself quite well. At least, that was the word put about, although the veterans of the 8th and 13th gave this talk little credence, knowing that it was equally likely to be the case of a few coins scattered among the scribes and slaves who always served as the information network for the men of the ranks. Only time and action would tell if the fulsome praise was deserved. What was known was that Drusus was coming from a series of actions against the Rhaeti, farther west of where they were headed now, and his brother Tiberius had taken over that initial effort. The strategy was ambitious, but thoroughly Roman; two forces coming from opposite directions, with plans to crush their enemies in between them. There was no subtlety, no artifice; just raw, naked power in the form of what would be a force of four Legions total, two apiece, along with the normal complement of auxiliaries and cavalry. The only discordant note was the weather; it was now the beginning of the last week of March, but even there on the coast, there was a raw bite to the wind that saw the men scrambling to find their fur-lined socks and don the *bracae* that had finally become approved for wear when the weather conditions permitted, although it was one of those prohibitions that in the past a wise commander ignored. Men had been wearing the *bracae* since almost the first year of Caesar's campaign in Gaul, certainly after the first winter in the colder northern climes, so when the army stepped out onto its march from Aquileia, those few men still alive who marched for Caesar would have recognized these men were prepared for spring in the mountains of Gaul.

The army marched north, reaching the foot of the mountains early on the second day, but despite the climb and the weather, they made good progress. Stopping at Julium Carnicum (Zuglio) the second day, the third proved to be extremely difficult, with a steep climb through a rugged pass that left the men gasping for breath. Because of the terrain, the young Legate made the decision to make camp early, in a narrow valley that was hemmed in on seemingly every side by towering mountains, where the snow extended down the slopes and into the valley proper. Fortunately, the snow wasn't deep, and there were already more bare patches of earth showing on either side of the roadway than was covered by snow.

About midday of the fourth day, after crossing the Dravus (Drava) River, the road on which they were traveling intersected with the major road running on an east-west axis, in between the towns of Aguntum (Lienz) and Teurnia (Tiburia). This road was wider and of much better quality than the northern route from Aquileia, and it ran in between the high peaks, although moving west meant that it was still uphill. Following the Dravus until it reached Aguntum, Drusus commanded that the army march straight through the small town, telling Porcinus that the Legate knew, if not from experience then because he had been told, the bad things that could happen when Legionaries were allowed to tarry anywhere near civilians and their property. Besides, Aguntum wasn't one of the towns that had shown any signs of rebellion, so the citizens were left unmolested, for the most part, although Porcinus knew from experience that there was at the least a bracelet filched, and more than one woman's bottom or breast got fondled, if a bit roughly. They made camp about ten miles west of Aguntum, although it was still early in the day, although the mystery of the early stop was quickly solved, after Vettus attended a meeting of senior officers in the tent of the *praetorium*, the headquarters of the army that was always located in the dead center of a Roman camp.

"Maybe he does know what he's about," Vettus' tone was grudging, "because he stopped us to give us our orders for tomorrow. It appears that Littamum (Innichen) is one of the outposts that was overrun. It's just ahead on this road, so he wants to be cautious in case there's a barbarian force still waiting there."

Porcinus thought this made sense, and he saw the others felt the same. He waited for more, and he was quickly rewarded.

"The 8th is going to be the lead Legion, but the First is going to be the vanguard."

So far, this wasn't unexpected; because of the fact that the First Cohort of every Legion was twice the size as all the other Cohorts, whenever there was some sort of initial contact expected, it had become customary for the First to lead the way. However, what Vettus said next wasn't as customary.

"But I want the Fourth immediately behind my Cohort," he continued, ignoring the whispers of surprise, and truthfully, disagreement.

Porcinus was no less surprised than the other Pili Priores, but he felt the flush of pleasure creeping up his neck, and was horrified at the thought that he would be seen blushing like a schoolboy who had just experienced his first kiss. He struggled to maintain his composure, and he had a hard time listening to the rest of what Vettus had to say. Fortunately for him, nothing that the Primus Pilus had to say concerned him. Dismissing his men, Vettus stood watching them file out, but he stopped Porcinus.

"I want to talk to you for a moment," the Primus Pilus said quietly.

Porcinus stood next to Vettus, waiting for the men to file out, trying to ignore the looks he was given by the Secundus Pilus Prior, a man named Lucius Volusenus, and the other Pilus Prior of the first line, Gnaeus Fronto. Once they had left, Vettus motioned to Porcinus to resume his seat on one of the stools in front of the Primus Pilus' desk, while he took his own.

"I wanted to talk to you about why I decided to have you following my Cohort on the march tomorrow," Vettus began.

"We all have to take our turn," Porcinus responded.

"That's true," Vettus granted. "But there's more to it than that. Ever since your actions against the Daesitiates, I've been watching closely, and I wanted to tell you something. But if you ever repeat it, I'll call you a liar to your face. Is that understood?"

Porcinus shifted uneasily; where was Vettus going with this? Nevertheless, he promised his Primus Pilus that no word of what he was about to say would escape Porcinus' lips.

Hesitating for a moment, as if gathering his thoughts or something else, Vettus finally said, "Your Cohort, and the way you run it, is the best in this Legion. Barring the First, of course." Vettus said this with a laugh so that Porcinus wasn't sure if he was being truthful, or just fulfilling his duty. Probably, Porcinus reflected, that's his goal. "But you've got a good head on your shoulder, and I think your choice of Ovidius was one of the shrewdest moves you could have made. Although he's not going to be much help at paperwork."

Vettus laughed at the face Porcinus made at this statement, mainly because he had learned how true it was.

"I don't suppose you could have warned me about the fact he can barely make his letters," Porcinus said, and while it was in a jesting tone, he was half-serious.

"But then you wouldn't have anything left to do," Vettus retorted. "I know you'd be bored."

"So you were just thinking of me when you recommended him," Porcinus said dryly, prompting another hoot of laughter from Vettus, who slapped the desk in delight.

"Exactly! I'm always thinking of my men first." Turning serious again, Vettus returned to the subject. "But I just wanted to tell you what an excellent job I think you're doing. And, of course, in the Legions, the way good work is recognized is by giving you more responsibility, and putting you in more danger."

Now Porcinus laughed, because it was a truth that he had often thought about. And yet, he was more ambitious than most men were, although he had long since recognized that his breast would never harbor the burning passion for advancement that had been his father's. How odd, he realized with a sudden start as Vettus stood, signaling the conversation was over; this was the first time he had thought of Pullus as his father, without reminding himself that it was through adoption. Iras had insisted that the moment would come when he would think in this way, but he hadn't been convinced. Clasping arms with Vettus, instead of rendering a salute, Vettus' parting words snapped him back to the moment.

"I don't know what to expect tomorrow, but my soldier's bones tell me that we might see a little excitement. So I'm ordering my boys to march with shields uncovered since there's no sign of bad weather. I'll leave it up to you what to do in that regard. Just be ready."

With that, Porcinus rendered a salute, which Vettus returned, then offered his hand again as well.

"Remember," he warned, "I never said any of this."

"Not a word," Porcinus agreed.

Despite the fact that he couldn't share it with anyone, Porcinus felt a glow of warmth against the chill of the night as he returned to his own tent. Words of encouragement, especially from a man like Vettus, made so much of the hardship and sacrifice worthwhile. Now, all he had to do was make sure he didn't let his Primus Pilus, or his own men, down.

Vettus' bones turned out to be right, although it wasn't right away; the outpost, little more than a way station where horses were kept for couriers, a ramshackle inn for travelers, and the barracks housing the twenty auxiliaries turned out to be deserted. At least, it was absent any live humans, although the vultures and other birds of carrion circling above the former inhabitants told the men of the approaching army a story that needed no translation. Marching through the station, once it was determined that there were no hostile tribesmen about, the men were subjected to the sight of corpses that seemed to be divided into two categories. Those few civilians, men, women, and at least two children that Porcinus saw, had been cut down where they were found, and for the most part their bodies were left undisturbed, although all half-dozen women were naked. It was the men who had obviously been the auxiliaries, or identified as Roman citizens, for whom special treatment was reserved, if special was the right word. Hung from their feet, all of the corpses had clearly been abused in some way, but there were a handful of them that, as hardened as Porcinus and his men were, turned their collective stomachs. These men had been flayed; the only question was whether it had been done while they were still alive, but Porcinus knew from experience that the huge dark stain underneath each body was a telltale that their hearts had still been beating, at the very least. All he could hope, and it was one shared by every

Legionary that marched by, was that these men, despite being auxiliaries, were senseless when this horrific act had been perpetrated.

Needing no urging, the army pressed on; Vettus had given Porcinus the basic lay of the land, so he knew that there was yet another point where contact with the enemy might happen. The next station was Sebatum (St. Lorenzen), and was about eighteen miles from Littamum, but while Drusus was disposed to stop short of the station, the word brought back by his scouts, who told the men of the vanguard the news by virtue of the way they were whipping their horses, changed his mind. He did order a brief halt, and Vettus, from his spot at the front, started trotting back to where the command group was located just behind Porcinus' Fourth. However, he was met by Drusus, along with Quirinus, so that as it happened, the impromptu meeting occurred right next to where Porcinus was standing, meaning he didn't have to try to find a way to eavesdrop.

"The scouts have reported that we've surprised the Rhaeti," Drusus told Vettus, then amended, "or at least one of their warbands. The Decurion estimates that there are perhaps two thousand men still remaining at the station, and unlike Littamum, they haven't killed everyone. Yet," he finished grimly.

Although the young Legate's tone was calm, even where Porcinus was standing several paces away, he could feel the undertone of tension underneath, and he supposed it was because of this last bit of news. Drusus paused, and Porcinus was standing at just the right angle to see the Legate shoot a sidelong glance at the older Quirinus, as if waiting for his second in command to add his thoughts. Or perhaps, Porcinus thought, to contradict Drusus, but Quirinus remained silent, creating an awkward pause.

"Yes, well." Drusus hurried to cover the gap. "So with that in mind, we're going to push on, but just with the 8th. I want your men to drop their packs; I'll have your slaves round them up and follow behind with the mules. I want to move as quickly as possible to catch these *cunni*, at least before they get away, if not before they slaughter our people there."

Porcinus saw Vettus suppress a smile at his young Legate's use of profanity, since it was clear that words used by rankers in every sentence was something that didn't usually pass his lips, although

Porcinus, for one, appreciated the effort the young noble was making to connect with his men. With the instructions given, Drusus and Quirinus trotted back to their spot, while Vettus paused for a moment next to Porcinus.

"Get one of your men to drop out and let every Century know what's happening," the Primus Pilus instructed Porcinus. "You heard the Legate. We don't want to waste any time." Before Porcinus turned to call to one of his men, a short, wiry Umbrian who was the best distance runner in his Cohort, Vettus grabbed his arm.

"Remember, we're going to be moving fast, so don't let too big a gap open up between your boys and mine. By rights, we should stop to at least catch our breath, but I have a feeling the Legate is going to get excited at the sight of these bastards and forget, so we're probably going to be shaking out into line, then heading straight for them." Vettus gestured to the narrow valley in which they were marching, and finished. "And if this is all the space we're going to have, we're only going to have enough room for your Cohort and mine, and that's if we go double line. So be ready to take the spot on the left."

Finished, Vettus trotted back to the front of the formation, while Porcinus sent his runner in the other direction. A moment later, there was a clattering sound that Porcinus hoped couldn't be heard all the way to Sebatum as the men dropped their *furcae*, the long sticks with a crossbar that they carried on their shoulders and from which their packs were slung. Since they had begun the march with their shields uncovered, Porcinus judged that it was safe to allow the men to keep them slung on their backs, although he mentally chided himself for not checking with Vettus. That thought was interrupted by the blown command to resume the march, and in a matter of a few heartbeats, the column was moving again. However, the normal chatter was notably absent as each man, understanding that a fight was a real possibility, retreated within themselves, doing whatever each did to prepare for what was coming. Men like Porcinus didn't have the luxury of introspection; there were too many details for a Centurion to worry about, and when one was Pilus Prior, those details were even more abundant. It was times like this that Porcinus would remind himself of whenever he felt the tug of ambition, because he didn't envy the load that his Primus Pilus was carrying as the 8th headed towards whatever awaited them just up the road.

As a result of his close relationship with his father, Porcinus had more of an idea than almost every other Centurion in the Legion, with perhaps the exception of the Primus Pilus Posterior, who was literally just a heartbeat away from bearing the same responsibility as the commander, the real burden of a Primus Pilus. It had become a tradition, when Pullus was still the Primus Pilus of the 10th, for Porcinus to share the evening meal the night before a likely battle with Pullus, Quintus Balbus, the Primus Pilus Posterior, and Sextus Scribonius, Pullus' best friend and the Secundus Pilus Prior, who was also Porcinus' direct superior back then. That gave him a unique insight into the things that occupied a Primus Pilus' mind the night before battle, but he could only imagine what was running through Vettus' mind at this moment. What he did know was that his ruminations did have one salutary effect; he was so intent on making sure he thought of everything he needed to remember that he had no time to be consumed with nerves. As the rhythmic tramping sound of a Legion on the march punctuated the air, which, even with the cold, raised a fine veil of dust, although it didn't seem to rise very far, Porcinus watched his men. While some were talking quietly, it was almost always to just the man next to them, the man with whom he would be standing, side by side to face whatever was coming. Porcinus knew from experience that none of the men would be able to remember what they had been talking about, after the fight, if it happened. Just the act of conversation was how some men girded themselves, indulging in a routine matter where the act itself was the important thing. In this manner, a man reassured himself, and those around him, that he wasn't overcome with fear, that his wits were about him and he was able to engage in talk, even if it was desultory.

Porcinus did take the time to pause from his spot at the head of the Century, first to exchange a quiet word with his Optio, Ovidius, then to wait for the rest of his Centurions. Immediately behind his own First Century came his Pilus Posterior, Publius Canidius, a swarthy man with wiry black hair that covered almost his entire body, which had earned him the nickname Urso. Where Porcinus was tall and lithe, Urso was the polar opposite, looking very much like one of the barrels that the army packed the salted pork into, with the only difference being he had arms and legs, the former sticking out at an angle from his body because of his massive chest. Like his namesake, he was almost as strong, although despite appearances to the contrary, Urso had a first-rate mind, and a devious streak to go along with it. Add to that the fact that Urso was an extremely ambitious man, and most importantly, had been sure the post of Pilus Prior of the Fourth Cohort was his, meant that out of all his Centurions, Porcinus trusted Urso the least. However, not at moments like this; of all the things Urso was, he was a good Centurion, and while Porcinus didn't like to admit it even to himself, was more than capable of running the Cohort. Therefore, it didn't surprise Porcinus to see Urso's Century march by looking determined, and more importantly, ready. Porcinus and Urso only exchanged a brief word, the Pilus Prior telling Urso that if it was possible, he would hold a meeting before they went into action, then the Second Century was gone. Normally, like every Cohort and Legion, the order of march was mixed up from day to day, mainly to keep men from the same Centuries in close proximity for day after day, where small grievances and disputes could fester. While Porcinus had never seen it happen, at least for that reason, he had heard from the older Centurions and even rankers whose Legate or Primus Pilus had been unwise, lazy, incompetent or a combination of the three, and had witnessed it.

Today was different, though, because of the anticipated contact that had been expected at Littamum, so that they were marching in Century order, meaning it was the Third that came next. Leading this Century was Aulus Munacius, a former veteran of the 10th who had chosen to retire rather than suffer the ignominy and humiliation inflicted on what to most of the Republic was the most celebrated and famous Legion, at the hand of Augustus himself. It was a topic that was never spoken of, at least in the ranks of the Legions currently marching, but it still rankled men like Munacius, and to a lesser extent, Porcinus. Augustus had held the fact that the 10th had served under Marcus Antonius against them, insisting that this had been a sign of disloyalty, ignoring the simple fact that the 10th had never been given a choice. After Philippi, while the two men who ruled Rome, three if you counted the non-entity Lepidus, divided up the entirety of the

Roman Republic and all its provinces between them, they had casually decided which Legions would march for each member of what was officially known as the Committee of Three for Ordering the State. It had never occurred to any man in the 10th, or any of the Legions for that matter, that a matter in which they had no say would be held against them later. When the second enlistment of the 10th ended, those men who had been part of the second *dilectus* sixteen years before, of which Munacius was one, were told that if they chose to re-enlist they would be combined with the 10th Legion that had marched under Augustus, or as he was known back then, Octavianus Julius Caesar. Like many of his comrades, Munacius had opted to retire, despite the fact that he was only in his mid-thirties at the time. Yet, here he was, fifteen years later, almost fifty, but tough as the leather of an old *caligae*, with a slight build that belied a strength that made him feared by his men. His story, when asked, was one that Porcinus had heard many times; he was a better Legionary than a farmer, so when the *dilectus*, the recruiting party that was enlisting for the 8th Legion just a couple of years after the disbandment of the 10th, Munacius had joined up as a leader of a tent section. He had been an Optio in the 10th, which was how Porcinus had known him, and it wasn't long before Munacius earned a promotion to that spot. When he had the chance, he had offered him a spot as the Centurion in command of the Third Century, and if Porcinus trusted Urso the least, it was the exact opposite with Munacius, although that didn't extend to the pair being close friends.

Next came the Princeps Posterior, Vibius Pacuvius, just a couple of inches shorter than Porcinus, making him among the tallest of all the ranks in the Cohort, but he was broader than Porcinus. Except where Porcinus was all muscle, Pacuvius had a soft look about him, but while it was true that he loved his food, and wine, he was as strong as his sheer bulk indicated. In stark contrast to his slightly portly build, his face was made hard looking, even savage, by the livid scar that started on his forehead above his right eye and moved downward across the bridge of his nose. Although he still had his left eye, it was a milky white in color, while the blade that had cut into him had done some sort of damage that made the eye constantly weep, which as Porcinus had learned, could be very distracting. It didn't mar his abilities. However, Pacuvius was also good friends with Urso, which Porcinus didn't hold against him, yet it did make him wary about the man. Like the preceding Centuries, his men were clearly ready, and Porcinus exchanged a word or two with some of the more veteran members, making sure to use their names as he called on them to be prepared. Porcinus was beginning to think twice about his decision to meet with every Centurion, because it meant that he would have to run, and quickly, to be back at the head of his Cohort, and he wasn't as young as he once had been.

Instead, he fell in step with Gnaeus Corvinus, the Hastatus Prior, essentially repeating everything he had told the other Centurions. Corvinus was a Spaniard, like Porcinus, and had grown up in the same province, Baetica, although at the opposite end from where Porcinus' farm was located. That was where the similarities between the two ended. Where Porcinus was as devoted to his family as a Centurion of Rome could be and still perform his duties, Corvinus had never had a relationship with a woman that wasn't measured in watches. Porcinus, following the example of his father and his Pilus Prior Scribonius, didn't drink much wine, although he knew that for appearances sake he had to be seen every so often in one of the wineshops in Siscia, standing his Centurions for a round of drinks. Corvinus spent as much time inebriated as possible, although it had never impinged on his ability to do his duty. Finally, while Porcinus was a stern but fair commander, Corvinus was known for the liberal use of the *vitus*, the vine stick that was the symbol of command carried by every Centurion. Despite this, his men loved him, because he came from the same gutter that they did, and for the most part shared the same pursuit of pleasure and debauchery. And as unalike as the two were, Porcinus counted Corvinus as his closest friend, not just in the Cohort, but the Legion. They both shared an irreverence for some aspects of life in the army, and they both loved their men in a way that neither of them could ever put into words, let alone share them with another.

Therefore, it was natural that Porcinus spent a bit more time with Corvinus before stopping to let the final Century reach him. Tiberius Verrens, the Hastatus Posterior, was the newest of the Centurions in the Fourth Cohort, having been in the post for only a year. And he was the youngest of Porcinus' Centurions, at thirty-one. He was also not

Porcinus' choice; in one of their most vigorous disagreements, Primus Pilus Vettus had insisted that Verrens be put into that slot when it became open. So far, however, Verrens had shown himself to be solid, but this would be his first major test as a Centurion of the first line. Like Porcinus, Verrens had been in the Seventh Cohort, and, at one time, had been Vettus' Optio, and while Porcinus understood and appreciated Vettus' loyalty to a subordinate, there were disquieting rumors about Verrens that were the reason Porcinus had been given pause to select him for the Sixth Century. Nevertheless, this wasn't the time to worry about it, Porcinus knew, so like he did with the others, he kept his talk with Verrens brief. Then, taking a deep breath, dreading the effort he was about to make, Porcinus began trotting back up the column to reach his Century.

Whoever was in command of the Rhaeti warband that had moved from Littamum to Sebatum was either inexperienced, or was grossly overconfident. That, at least, was the conclusion that Porcinus came to when he was informed that the Rhaeti seemed content to wait for the advancing Romans to come to them, on ground that favored the Roman way of fighting. Although the valley ran along an east-west axis, just before reaching the valley where Sebatum was located, the narrow valley carved by the river turned north and ran in that direction for a bit more than two miles, before turning back to the west. This was the opening into the valley and, by the standards of the countryside they were marching through, this valley was quite wide and almost flat, with only a couple of low hills in between the larger mountains that formed it. The station turned out to be more substantial than Littamum, and when he thought about it later, Porcinus thought that it was actually a nice spot that would probably grow into at least a small town. The station was located at the far end of the valley, which Porcinus had estimated was about three miles in width and four miles in length. Where the Rhaeti commander had made his error, for which he and his men would pay a dear price, was in not arraying his men at the point where the valley changed direction from north back to west. At this spot, the width of the valley was less than a mile, and the slope to the Romans' right was steep, while their left flank was anchored by the river. Within these confines, the disparity in numbers between the Rhaeti wouldn't have meant as much. Compounding his error, the commander also hadn't thought it prudent to post any kind of lookout on the hill that blocked the view to the east. That gave Drusus and the army the time to stop, hidden away from the Rhaeti, and conduct a quick conference, where it was decided that the width of the valley called for more of a front than two Cohorts. Porcinus was relieved and disappointed at the same time, but then Vettus told him that the Fourth Cohort was to stay next to the First, meaning that it was a certainty that they would face the Rhaeti.

The Romans appeared, at least from the Rhaeti leader's perspective, out of nowhere. One moment he and his men had been enjoying the fruits of their attack; this settlement had quite a few more women than the last one, and there had been three inns instead of one. Naturally, this meant more wine, and his men had fought hard, even if it was against only fifty auxiliaries. They hadn't even killed all of them; their commander, an auxiliary Centurion, had ordered his men to throw down their swords when there were a little more than twenty of them left. Obviously, they hadn't heard what the Rhaeti had done at Littamum, or the Centurion had lost his nerve. These men he was saving for later, to make an example of and to show Rome that it didn't own Rhaetia as they thought. As far as the rest of the civilians, perhaps two hundred total, he hadn't yet decided whether he would put them to the sword, if only because there was a fair number of them. Still, in the back of his mind was the idea that perhaps it was better to let them live, sending them south into Roman territory to spread the word that Rhaetia was free. Before he could ruminate further, however, a series of excited and alarmed shouts made him turn to see a group of his men, who had been busy looting one of the outlying buildings to the east, pointing and gesticulating back up the valley. Even as the leader began moving in their direction, one of his warriors came dashing towards him, except it took a moment for him to understand what his fellow tribesman was shouting. Once he did, he froze in his tracks.

"Romans! In the valley! They're already arrayed for battle!"

In yet another mistake in a day that was filled with them, the leader's mind went as motionless as his body, his mouth hanging open as he struggled to absorb this devastating news. How did they get here so quickly? They were already formed for battle? What should he do? Order his men to fight? Or was this a moment for discretion, to flee to fight another time? His warrior stood uncertainly, shifting from one foot to the other as he stared at his leader, waiting for something, anything, to come out of his mouth. The warrior would never be able to guess how long they stood together, him waiting for orders, the other with no idea what to do. But it was the leader's hesitation that basically made the decision for all of them, always the worst alternative for a commander. Once he snapped out of his fog, he saw that the Romans were barely a mile away, arranged in their damnably neat rows, marching in inexorable and oppressive unison. Even as he watched probable defeat and death approach, a part of his mind admired the discipline and precision that those Roman bastards represented, and he wished that his own men had even a modicum of it.

"Go alert the rest of the men," he finally croaked. "We stand and fight."

In yet another slight delay, the warrior stood staring in disbelief, then risked another glance over his shoulder, with the irrational fear that somehow since the last time he had looked in their direction, the entire Roman force had managed to sneak up on him.

Seeing the man's hesitation was the only thing that snapped the leader back to reality, and despite the lead ball that seemed to be burrowing deeper into his gut as he recognized that he was making a bad decision, his pride made him snap, "Go. Now! We're going to teach these Romans a lesson they won't forget."

Finally, the warrior left, thinking bitterly that there would indeed be a lesson given this day, but he was fairly sure who would be doing the teaching, and it wasn't the Rhaeti.

From his spot to the immediate left of the Third Century of the First Cohort, Porcinus watched the sudden flurry of movement as the barbarians finally recognized what was happening and reacted to it. Even from this distance of perhaps three-quarters of a mile, from the way men were dashing about, it was easy to tell that they had been surprised, and as they drew ever closer, Porcinus saw the telltale signs of an enemy very close to panic before the first javelin had flown their way.

"Look at 'em, boys," he called out loudly enough for at least his Century to hear. "They're already running about like scared rabbits!

This should be an easy day to get our swords wet! I don't know about yours, but mine is thirsty!"

As he expected, this was met with a roar of approval, but he was slightly surprised that the men of the First Cohort to his right, taking up twice the amount of space because they were twice the size, responded as well. By his nature, Porcinus didn't normally indulge in such bravado; while like most men of the Legions, there was almost an intoxication that took over in battle, before the actual fighting started, he didn't find himself feeling like a dog, straining at the leash, eager to bound forward to impose his will on another man. That had been one of his father's many gifts when it came to warfare, a raging fury where it seemed that Pullus had built up in his mind a whole chain of events that the enemy facing him had perpetrated against him, so that by the time the *cornu* sounded the charge, he hated his opponents with a passion that ran white-hot. Porcinus was more cerebral, in the mold of his former Pilus Prior Scribonius, although he had experienced moments in a fight when it seemed as if there was liquid fire running through his veins, and his sword sang a song of sweet and deadly music. Those occasions had always been reserved for the most desperate fighting in which he participated, but he didn't think today would be one of those days, although one never knew. Regardless of his own feelings, Porcinus had long since learned that most men responded to the kind of words he had just shouted, and if it gave his men an edge in battle that saw them walk off the field under their own power, he would engage in every trick that helped.

Somewhere in the First Cohort, a man began rapping his sword against his shield in a rhythm that matched the steps of the men, which was instantly picked up so that it became a thundering punctuation that had been the notice to the men standing across from whatever Legion that faced them that their death was at hand for decades, if not centuries. It was the sound of Rome's Legions about to engage in something that was, above all else, their business, the dealing of death and destruction, and while the pre-battle rituals of tribes like the Rhaeti made more noise, and were blood-curdling in their own way, this deceptively simple pattern of sound was all the more terrifying. It sent a signal of detachment, almost boredom, that this was all the Legions needed to prepare themselves for what all men knew, on both sides, was a fury of noise, sights, smells, and death, just moments away. Up and down the front ranks, Porcinus could hear other Centurions calling out to their own men, giving last-minute reminders to watch their spacing, to remember to brace the man in front of them, or they were shouting encouragement like Porcinus had done, so there was a rippling roar as each Century went through their own particular pre-battle ritual.

By this point in time, Porcinus could see that the Rhaeti were assembled in a ragged line, just on the eastern side of the last row of buildings. Unlike other times when Porcinus and his men had faced men they considered wild tribesmen, this group of men didn't seem interested in engaging in their own pre-battle ritual, which usually consisted of shouted curses, challenges, and promises of what each warrior would do to their enemy that normally included individual warriors rushing out from their line to issue a personal challenge. It was a challenge that was always ignored, at least in every battle that Porcinus had been a part of, although he had heard of times when a Roman had accepted. In those cases, it was almost always an officer, a Legate or a Tribune who was eager to make his reputation. Now, while Porcinus could hear a low, rolling rumble of noise that he knew was their shouting, it was so muted that it was more comical than anything. The line of the Legions continued to advance, until they were no more than a hundred paces away from the line of Rhaeti, then the *cornu* of the command group blew the notes that called a halt, instantly obeyed by the men, who came to a crashing stop. It was usually at this moment that an aggressive barbarian commander, hoping to surprise the Legionaries, would sound the order to begin their own wild charge, although it had never worked as far as Porcinus had seen. Instead, this bunch of Rhaeti stood in their ragged line, and now that they were close enough, Porcinus, and the rest of the men of the front rank, could see the look of fear, and more importantly, resignation on the part of men who understood that their future could be measured in just a matter of a watch, at most.

Nero Claudius Drusus, Legate in command of this army, guided his horse to a spot where he could be seen by the men of the front rank and Porcinus was forced to admit, despite his general ambivalence towards the nobility, young Drusus cut an impressive figure. More importantly, at least at that moment, he was believable as he curbed his stallion, a gray that reminded Porcinus of Ocelus, and trotted it in front of the cheering Legionaries. Holding his sword aloft, with the feathers from the crest of his helmet streaming behind him, just his presence was enough to rouse his men; despite all the troubles between the classes, the Legions of Rome were as proud of their patricians as the Rhaeti were of their chieftains, probably even more so. Because what was represented, in the form of a young man in his twenties, dressed in armor that would have cost a Gregarius more than five years' pay, was the continuity of Rome. More importantly, it was the promise of Rome, the eternal light in a world of darkness, and while not one man in the ranks could have articulated it, this ideal was so deeply embedded in each of them that it was a belief that was as much a part of them as the color of their hair or eyes. They were Rome, and for a brief moment, all the oppressive barriers of class, money, and title meant nothing, because this young noble, and the men who roared their approval at his display, were one. That was why Porcinus, even after all that he had seen his father endure at the hands of men like Drusus, found himself in full voice, along with the other men, shouting their pride. Once Drusus reached the end of the line, he wheeled his horse about, but this time at a gallop, then pulled up in a spray of dirt, in front of the First Cohort of the 8th, anchoring the far right. Porcinus had to lean slightly forward to peer down the ranks to where Drusus was, the young Legate holding his sword aloft as the blade, also of a quality that was beyond most of the men of the ranks, except perhaps the Centurions, caught the sunlight in blinding rays of light that Porcinus hoped was a good portent. The sword stayed in its upright position for what was perhaps a dozen heartbeats before suddenly sweeping down in a sharp cutting gesture. However, if the Rhaeti expected that signal to start their foes' march in their direction, they were mistaken, because it was just the signal to the nearby *cornu* player to play the notes that actually prompted the men in the ranks to step forward, each with his left foot. It was usual that, in larger-scale battles, the *cornu* player attached to each Primus Pilus would then relay his own order, because as far as the deep, bass sound carried, on a multi-Legion front, it still needed to be repeated. That wasn't the case here; although the 8th had been ordered to increase the front of their attack by two Cohorts, the 13th was in reserve, while the other Cohorts were arranged in the normal *acies triplex*. Porcinus nevertheless gave the shouted command to begin the march, as did the other Centurions, and with only a slight ripple, the leading Cohorts stepped out, heading towards the waiting Rhaeti. Who still stood there uncertainly, Porcinus observed, and while this was a blessing, it did make him curious, and a little cautious. Did the commander have something planned? Could he possibly be so incompetent, or so scared, that he was going to allow his men to stand there, waiting for the coming onslaught? Because, despite the fact that these Rhaeti had essentially no chance of defeating Drusus' men, there were things they could do not only to negate the Legion's overwhelming superiority, but to make the inevitable Roman victory costly. Yet, as they continued marching forward, the Romans saw the Rhaeti warriors not begin their own rush forward, in an attempt to close the distance so quickly that the Romans could only land one volley of javelins. Ideally, they would have dashed forward in an attempt to make their enemy go straight to the sword and drop the deadly javelins that were arguably the most devastating weapon in the Roman arsenal. That moment had passed, however, and Porcinus watched with astonishment as the Rhaeti still stood there, except now he was close enough to see the naked fear and uncertainty in the faces of his enemies. He also noticed how they kept looking about, as if searching for someone in authority to give a command and, despite himself, Porcinus felt a flicker of pity for these men, so badly led. It wasn't their fault they were about to be slaughtered, but just because he felt some sympathy for the men of the lower ranks, that didn't mean he would hesitate when it came time to kill them. When the *cornu* suddenly sounded the halt, it startled him, and he chastised himself for letting his mind wander now, of all the times. Just a moment later, there came the shouted command, this time coming from Vettus and one that was relayed down the front line Centuries. Immediately after he heard the Princeps Prior, commander of the Third Century of the First Cohort to his right shout the command, Porcinus repeated it.

"Ready javelins!"

He didn't need to look over his shoulder; the sound caused by the creak of leather and the disturbance of the air as eighty arms swept backward told him that his men were indeed ready. Points were aimed skyward; it always amused Porcinus when he talked to civilians who always expressed surprise when they had occasion actually to see men throwing the javelin, usually on the practice field outside camp, that the Legionaries appeared to be aiming for the sun, instead of for the posts that were their targets. What they didn't understand was that by throwing the javelins high in the air, there was some force that made them come plummeting to the ground at a much higher speed and velocity than even the strongest man could generate throwing in a flat trajectory. Granted, there were times when the enemy was moving quickly and closed to a point where that was the best way to take down their enemy, but this wasn't one of them. Since the Rhaeti hadn't moved, they were about to be subjected to the javelins at their most lethal.

"Release!"

Again, in a ripple that ran the length of the front line, the sky filled with the dark lines of the streaking missiles rising, rising, rising in the sky, and it always fascinated Porcinus how, when they reached their highest point, they seemed to hesitate before the weighted points, sought out by whatever god controlled these things, suddenly reversed themselves to begin hurtling downward. As usually happened, the eyes of both sides were fixed on the javelins, and even at this distance, Porcinus could clearly hear the low moan emanating from the ranks of the Rhaeti as all the men with shields held them above their heads, while their less fortunate comrades huddled as closely to a man with a shield as they could. Besides the moaning of the Rhaeti for what they were about to receive, the scene was strangely still, although that changed immediately as the iron heads began punching into their targets. Suddenly, the air was filled with a sound that was akin to hundreds of men striking wood with a mallet, but amid that, Porcinus and the rest of the men heard a more sodden, thudding sound that their experienced ears told them meant a javelin had managed to avoid being blocked by a shield and instead found a fleshy target. Following so quickly behind it that it was almost impossible to distinguish that there was a pause between the two came dozens of screams, of all pitches and registers, some pitched so highly that it felt like Porcinus' ears were being pierced by an awl, others more of a low moan of despair. There were a fair amount of curses as well; despite not speaking the language, none of the Legionaries needed the services of a translator.

"Ready javelins!"

The racket from the first volley hadn't even died down when the second command came, followed by the order to release, even more quickly than the first. This was intentional; by launching the second volley quickly, it deprived the enemy of the chance to regroup, and these javelins were still in the air when the *cornu* of the First Cohort sounded the command to resume the advance.

Perhaps the kindest thing to say was that the Rhaeti commander was still in a state of shock. Consequently, he was unable to utter anything of any value to his men, and, in fact, was in much the same state of helplessness as they were watching the Romans approach. Somehow, he managed to survive the first volley, despite placing himself in the front rank, as was only fitting for a commander of the Rhaeti. He weathered the second as well, except the screams of the men around him as they were struck down shattered any chance of him regaining his senses to do not just the prudent thing, but the only one that made any sense and order his men to flee the field. Men who were looking to him as the example saw someone seemingly at a complete loss, at least as a field commander. He did, however, draw his sword, longer than the Roman short, stabbing sword that the men of the Legions referred to as the Spanish sword, although it wasn't as long as those used by the Gallic tribes further west. The men around him who hadn't drawn their weapons, waiting for him to make a decision, followed suit, their lack of enthusiasm matching that of the leader's. Only one thing kept them pinned to their respective spots, preparing to do battle, even if it was half-heartedly, and that was the fear of shaming themselves in front of their fellow tribesmen by running away, overwhelming even the gut-wrenching dread represented in the line of Roman Legionaries facing them. The line that, with the volleys of javelins completed, had resumed their measured, steady progress, only for a moment before halting again. Those few men in the ranks of this warband who had either faced the Romans themselves, or heard from family members or fellow warriors that had, understood what was about to happen.

"For the sake of Voltumna," one of the veteran warriors, a tall, broad-chested man wearing a mail shirt that hung down to his knees, and armed with just a spear now that his shield was punctured, shouted to the supposed leader of the warband, "will you just have us stand here and be slaughtered? Give us the command to fight because it's too late to do anything else!"

That seemed to reach the leader who, shaking his head so vigorously that his carefully braided pigtails swung violently about his face as he emerged from the fog of shock that had surrounded him from the moment the Romans were spotted, came back to the moment facing him and his men. Even as he did so, he understood it was too late, but like his men, he couldn't bear the shame of running away, not now. Raising his own sword, he barely had time to shout out his command to begin a countercharge when there was a roar emanating from the lines of Romans as they broke from their steady, measured pace into the final dash to slam into the Rhaeti. The only solace the leader of the warband could take was by setting an example of leading the men he had commanded so poorly and be in the leading rank of Rhaeti to meet the onrushing Romans. Unfortunately for the Rhaeti, they were only able to generate the momentum gained from a dozen paces when the large, rectangular shields of the front rank of Legionaries smashed into them. Just as planned, the volleys of javelins that hadn't actually struck a warrior at the least had punctured a shield, and as the weight of the wooden part of the shaft dropped towards the ground, it bent the softer metal of the last foot of the javelin before the hardened tip. It was a refinement created by the great Gaius Marius, more than a century before, yet it was still devastatingly effective, meaning that those first warriors to meet the Legions did so, for the most part, with only their weapon and without their shield. Even without the extra mass of the shields, the collision of the two opposing lines, as it usually was, created a horrific, crashing noise that momentarily drowned out the full-throated cries from both sides. Leading with their shields, the men of the Legions held them with their elbows locked against their hipbone for the initial contact, something that all warriors across the known world who used the shield did as well. However, for a Legionary, that was only the first of a two-part movement when, after their shield met the first resistance, from wood or flesh, they would then punch their shield outward, straightening their arm, using the protruding metal boss of the shield that protected their grip as a potent weapon itself. Depending on where the boss landed on an opponent, it could do anything from staggering a man backward to crushing in a cheekbone and dropping the foe out of the fight.

Because of the success of the two volleys, very few Rhaeti in the front line had their shields, and up and down the line there was the sound of the solid, thudding impact as the Roman shields smashed the warrior across from them either backwards a step, or completely off their feet. Following so quickly behind the crash of the initial collision as to sound as if it happened simultaneously, there were short, shrill screams of mortal agony from men who hadn't managed to dodge their enemy's initial thrust, as the Spanish swords again showed their value in a fight like this. Bits of gear, splintered pieces of shields, helmets, even the odd body part flew a few inches above the heads of the fighting men in the eyeblink of time after the two lines met, along with a spurt of arterial spray from men whose lives were ended in that first moment. After the collision, and the initial thrust, the contrasting styles of the Rhaeti and Romans were clearly apparent to even a novice eye. While the Romans, still in fairly uniform lines so that each man's right, or unprotected, side was covered by their comrades' shield, worked with a methodical precision, the Rhaeti warriors seemed to be nothing but whirling motion and fury, those with spears thrusting repeatedly from any number of angles. The warriors with swords, usually of the upper nobility, favored an overhead attack that, if it landed, could render a man almost in two. Those that were deprived of their shields by the javelins had either drawn a dagger, or in some cases, a short sword similar to the Romans' Spanish blades, using them for both attack and defense, parrying the short, brutal thrusts that flickered out from behind the Roman shield wall. Sometimes it would come from between shields, like a brutal silver-grey serpent striking, whenever a Rhaeti offered the Legionary across from him an opportunity, but most commonly, the Roman Legionary favored the thrust that originated below his waist and came up from under his shield. Not only was it hard to defend, it tended to strike a man in an area that concerned him a great deal, and if landed, almost always resulted in the foe being out of the fight. Now, all the time the men of the Legions spent in the boring, repetitive work with the wooden stakes showed itself profitable as they thrust, cut, and hacked bloody gaps in the Rhaeti mass. Even if the Rhaeti were competently led, and allowed to work themselves up into their normal pre-battle frenzy, the end result wouldn't have been any different; it just would have cost the Romans more in lives. Arrayed in lines several men deep, with each Legionary holding the leather harness of the man ahead of him, the 8th performed like the machine that it was, so that by the time the man who was in the fourth rank moved his way up to be in the front line, facing the enemy, the bodies were already heaped up two and three deep. Those Rhaeti left who were still fighting needed just one final push to go from what they were at that moment, a disorganized, demoralized mass of warriors, into a panicked mob intent on nothing more than escape. That was when the real slaughter began, at least in larger battles than this one, but the Rhaeti had already lost half their number as it was.

The leader of the warband, the Rhaeti noble ultimately responsible for what was becoming a crushing defeat that would deprive the larger rebellion of much needed willing swords and spears, had at least shown great bravery, being one of the first to swing his long sword over his head as he met the onrushing Romans. Consequently, he was also one of the first to die, and since he hadn't bothered to designate a second in command, now those other members of the Rhaeti nobility, each of them commanding a small contingent from their own holdings, started worrying about themselves and their own men. Alternately calling out their own name, or in the case of the more powerful lords doing this while their standard-bearer waved their personal banner, these lords only served to add further confusion to the fighting. By attempting to extract themselves, yet not working together, all those Rhaeti nobles trying to withdraw instead doomed themselves and their men, when what was still a solid mass of fighting men fractured into their smaller bands, almost inviting their enemy to chop them up piecemeal. The more experienced Centurions, the Pili Priores, and the two Primi Pili, seeing this happening and understanding what it meant, didn't wait for the order from Drusus.

If this had been on the training ground, we'd be doing this over and over, Porcinus thought as, on the command from Vettus to his right, he led the leading three Centuries of his Cohort at an angle towards a band of Rhaeti who were even then backing away. The movement of the Legionaries of the Fourth Cohort was not performed with the smoothness Porcinus would have liked, but because of the bodies piled in their path, it couldn't be helped. Their target was one of the larger groups, perhaps three hundred in number, and Porcinus was leading three of his Centuries directly toward them, while Pacuvius, commander of his Fourth Century and the ranking Centurion of the second line, led the other three Centuries that were in reserve on a wider circuit around to cut off an avenue of escape. Overall, Porcinus was happy with the way his men had performed, and even happier that his butcher's bill at this point was only two wounded, one of them seriously injured from a spear thrust through the thigh. But he also knew that in many ways, the worst was to come, especially if Pacuvius was successful in blocking an avenue of escape, meaning that these men had no choice but to fight to the death. There were similar scenes taking place across the battlefield, so that if whoever was leading the band that Porcinus was confronting tried to move away from both Porcinus and Pacuvius, they would have to fight their way through other Cohorts. Just as a pack of wolves circles the crippled beast in the herd, the Cohorts of the 8th worked in a fashion that their four-legged counterparts would instinctively recognize. Porcinus himself had dispatched three Rhaeti, despite being limited offensively because no Centurion normally carried a shield in battle. They always did so if the opportunity arose, when one of their men had fallen and had no use for it, but since that hadn't happened, Porcinus had to rely on his skill using his blade in both an offensive and defensive manner. He was helped in his cause for two reasons; the first by virtue of being trained by Titus Pullus, who had rightfully been recognized as the best man with a sword in not just the 10th Legion, but in all the Legions, although Porcinus knew there were men who would champion another for that honor. The other reason was that, like his father, he carried his own sword, not one of the issue blades that Legionaries usually went through at a rate of one a season. This was a Gallic blade, made almost forty years before, for a young Titus

Pullus, and it had been a bequest to Porcinus that came along with the fortune, brought to him by Diocles. Of the two, at least at that moment, Porcinus appreciated the blade more; he vividly remembered the first time he had touched it as a young boy, when his uncle came to visit his farm, and he had eyed it covetously ever since. Barely breaking stride, Porcinus stooped to snatch up a torn piece of what looked like a Rhaeti cloak to wipe the blood from the sword, knowing that even as fine a weapon as this one would pit if the blood was left on the blade too long. Why this was so was one of those things that men talked about during the winter, each of them offering up some piece of arcane knowledge that supported their argument as to the cause for it.

Finished cleaning the blade, Porcinus started to sheathe it, then seeing that the band they were stalking had come to a halt, forming in what was a sloppy imitation of the Roman *orbis*, decided against it. The *orbis* was the formation of last resort, and Porcinus took it as a sign that whoever commanded these men had chosen to die fighting. Looking over to his left, he saw Pacuvius maneuvering the three Centuries he commanded so that they formed a rough semi-circle almost directly opposite from where Porcinus was marching his men. All around them, similar scenes were taking place; sometimes, it was just a Century that had brought to ground a small band, and the shouts and screams carried across the space in between each group as the short swords thrust and recovered, or rose and fell. The Rhaeti band Porcinus was heading for seemed content for the moment to stand and watch, but even from the distance they were, he could see them shifting about nervously, moving from foot to foot, with none of what Porcinus and other Romans considered foolishness by attempting to bolster their courage with shouted challenges and taunts. These men seemed resigned to what awaited them, and Porcinus supposed that it was understandable to an extent; it wasn't unknown that a defeated enemy was given a chance at living. He had seen it many times before, how desperately men would snatch at the chance of a life, even if it was going to be spent as a slave, rather than the unknown of death. As far as Porcinus knew, no orders about prisoners had been issued, and like all Legionaries, he was trained to obey the last order he had been given. And that order was to kill any who stood before him and his men, so when they were perhaps a hundred paces away, Porcinus had his *cornicen* sound the command to halt. Out of javelins, they would be going immediately to the sword, but he wanted to coordinate his movement with that of Pacuvius, and using a prearranged signal, he had his *signifer* raise his standard up and down three times. This was the signal to alert Pacuvius that an order was imminent, and after only a moment's pause, the *signifer* on the other side bobbed his standard three times in response.

"All right, boys," Porcinus shouted to his three Centuries. "Get ready to finish these bastards! We'll go on my signal!"

There was only a ragged cheer. However, Porcinus didn't expect anything more; it wasn't the most rousing pre-battle speech he had given, but this wasn't shaping up to be much of a fight. Staring over at where Pacuvius stood, Porcinus waited until he could clearly see him looking in his direction after presumably speaking to his own men. Once he saw his subordinate was paying attention, Porcinus snapped the order, and his *signifer* thrust the standard up into the air once, and was immediately answered by Pacuvius' own. Immediately following this, Porcinus' *cornicen* blew the notes launching the men of the Fourth Cohort at the waiting Rhaeti. Leading the way was Porcinus as he angled his own rush towards the enemy mass, aiming for what he assumed to be the leader of this group, a broadly built tribesman with streaks of gray in his pigtails that contrasted with the black of his long, flowing mustache. Standing next to him was a man akin to the *signifer*, holding a pole that carried a carved figure of a rearing stallion, but even without this telltale presence, Porcinus would have picked this warrior out as the leader. Over the years and across numerous battlefields, one leader learned to spot another, and while Porcinus' rush at the man seemed headlong and perhaps an attempt to grab glory, in the Pilus Prior's case, it was a matter of calculation. While his father would have sought out this man, in the beginning of his career to establish his reputation in the Legions, in his later years to maintain it, Porcinus' reason for doing so was based on a simple premise; cut off the head of the snake, the body dies. Although it wouldn't be completely accurate to say that grabbing his share of glory and renown wasn't part of his decision, most of it was based in the fact that Porcinus loved the men of his Century, and Cohort. Anything he could do that might help spare any of his Legionaries from being wounded or killed he would, including seeking out the warrior leading this bunch, knowing that he at the very least would be the best equipped of the enemy, if not the most skillful. And while Gaius Porcinus wasn't a swordsman on the same level as Titus Pullus, he was nevertheless very, very good, if only because he worked so hard at it. The leader of the Rhaeti warband had been turned slightly away from Porcinus as he shouted a warning to his men to brace themselves for the coming impact. However, some inner sense warned him that he had been singled out. Pivoting on one foot, he saw the Roman, wearing the transverse crest that he knew marked their Centurions, bearing down on him, his sword held just above his head, with the blade roughly parallel to the ground and arm pulled back, ready to strike.

The Rhaeti had just enough time for his mind to register the feral snarl of his opponent, the Roman's lips pulled back to show his teeth, his eyes just slits that gave the warrior no clue as to his foe's intentions or strategy. Without thinking, he raised his own sword, also parallel to the ground, but perpendicular to the point of the short, stabbing sword of the Roman, anticipating a parry whereby he would sweep his blade upward from its present position at chest level that would knock his enemy's thrust in a skyward direction. However, Porcinus' own move was a feint, and with a speed that bespoke of many full watches' worth of practice, he changed his angle of attack from one that came from above to one at waist level, the glittering point of his Gallic sword punching directly at the Rhaeti lord's midsection. It was one of Porcinus' favorite and most effective opening attacks, and it was normally a devastating move, yet Porcinus was not particularly surprised when his opponent managed to reverse his upward sweep in time instead to knock the Roman's blade downward. Porcinus knew from long experience that the men of the Legions weren't the only ones who practiced movements and maneuvers relentlessly, particularly men who had in essence climbed through the ranks of their own hierarchy to achieve the status this man clearly enjoyed. What did surprise Porcinus somewhat was the strength behind the parry, yet he was saved from not just the shame, but danger of having his own blade knocked from his grasp, since the downward force exerted by the Rhaeti's parry put enormous pressure on his thumb. The fact he maintained his grip wasn't because the lone digit of Porcinus' hand was exceptionally sturdy; although like every man trained by Titus Pullus, he performed exercises that made his hold stronger, it was due to the fact he practiced an unorthodox grip whereby he wrapped his fingers over the thumb instead of the thumb being on top of the fingers. This grip had been taught to Titus Pullus by Aulus Vinicius, his first Optio and the weapons instructor for Pullus' first Century, the First of the Second Cohort of the 10th Legion. Over the years, as Pullus rose through the ranks, he had required every man under his command to adopt what had come to be called the Vinician grip. Although it took getting accustomed to, the extra support meant that, as far as Porcinus had ever seen or heard about, no man trained in this manner ever had his sword knocked from his grasp. This time was no exception, although Porcinus' blade did bounce off the ground from the force of his enemy's parry. But in what seemed to be one continuous motion, using instead of fighting the momentum from the rebounding blade, Porcinus punched his sword forward, the point still aimed at the Rhaeti's midsection, this time coming from the opposite side. Again, Porcinus was frustrated, this attack foiled only by a desperate twist of the Rhaeti's torso that saw Porcinus' point slice forward and the edge of his blade slice along the links of the man's mail shirt. The only advantage Porcinus gained was that his flurry of attacks came so quickly that the Rhaeti had no time for his own offense. Both men understood this was a moment of incredible danger; as focused as they were on each other, it meant they were vulnerable to attacks from the men around them. Yet, as Porcinus instinctively knew, this was where he, and every Roman Legionary, had a tremendous advantage, because he trusted the man to his left in a way that none of their foes could with their own comrades. Simply put, all of Rome's enemies thought of themselves as warriors, while the Legions thought of themselves as a single entity, a machine where every part relied on the other. This gave Porcinus a level of freedom that his opponent simply couldn't afford, and the Roman was ruthless in exploiting this fact. All around them were the shouts and screams of men fighting to the death, yet while Porcinus' attention never wavered from his foe, the Rhaeti lord couldn't stop his eyes from flickering to the side when the edge of his vision picked up a sudden rush of movement. This was all the opening Porcinus needed, and again with a speed that was impressive, he made another lunge, low and hard. Despite the fact that the Rhaeti's distraction was for the barest instant, it was enough, and his eyes bugged out in disbelief and an agony that Porcinus could only guess at as the Gallic blade cut through the links of mail to bury itself several inches into the Rhaeti's gut. Grimacing, both from the effort and because of what he knew would follow, Porcinus twisted not the blade, but his entire body from the waist, putting his full weight behind the move that disemboweled his now-vanquished foe. That was when the Rhaeti's low-pitched groan suddenly escalated into a scream of such agony that, no matter how many times he heard it, and caused it, made the hair on Porcinus' neck stand up straight. Like with the unorthodox grip, using the force of his whole body instead of twisting his arm in the manner in which most Legionaries were taught, this was a refinement taught to him by Pullus, because it was devastatingly effective in more than one way. By using his whole body, Porcinus ensured that the razor-sharp edge of the Gallic blade sliced through not only his enemy's stomach muscles and intestines, but the links of chain mail, something that couldn't be accomplished with twisting the wrist unless one possessed the strength of a Pullus. It was not just effective, it was dramatic, and that was also Porcinus' goal since, by the time he completed his movement and withdrew his sword, the Rhaeti's inner organs, no longer constrained by the taut muscles and the security of the mail vest, came bursting forth in a sight and with a smell that anyone who saw it would never forget. Dropping to his knees, his face gone suddenly as pale as the white of a politician's toga, the Rhaeti's scream subsided to a low moan as his eyes rolled back in his head, sparing himself the sight of watching his own intestines dropping in an obscene heap, coiled and gleaming, in front of him as his legs failed. Somehow, Porcinus didn't know how or why, the Rhaeti stayed tottering on his knees for a moment, prolonging a spectacle that had arrested the attention of every man around him, both Rhaeti and Roman, before finally falling forward, mercifully covering the pile of intestines and gore.

Just as Porcinus had hoped, the dramatic disemboweling of their leader created an instant and dramatic effect as the men immediately surrounding their lord threw down their weapons and, in an unconscious mimicking of their slain leader, dropped to their knees.

Those Rhaeti slightly removed from the scene only became aware of what had happened through the actions of their comrades closer to it, causing a rippling effect as the warriors followed suit in dropping their weapons and falling to their knees, hands out in supplication. And as was usual, the killing didn't stop immediately; men whose fear and bloodlust had been aroused were not only unwilling, they were unable to suddenly stop their swords from rising and falling, so that perhaps a dozen men of the remaining Rhaeti were chopped down even as they screamed for mercy. Since Porcinus hadn't lost his *vitus*, he used it to bash men liberally about the arms and shoulders, his other Centurions following suit, until the killing stopped. Finally, what was left was one group of men, all of them still on their knees and moaning in fear or despair at what awaited them, surrounded by another bunch, panting and still wild-eyed with the fury of the moment. Ovidius, moving from his spot at the back of the Century, obeyed Porcinus' snapped order, stepping forward and taking the wooden standard from the Rhaeti bearer, who refused to meet Ovidius' eyes as his hands fell limply away from the status symbol of his slain lord. Thrusting it aloft so that the men of the entire Cohort could see it, Ovidius' action elicited a spontaneous cheer, yet even as they did so, Porcinus was looking about, realizing that he might have made a mistake. All over the valley, similar struggles were taking place, except it was clear that the Fourth Cohort had subdued their foes first. What worried Porcinus was that, in being the first, while other Rhaeti bands were trying to surrender, none of the Centurions commanding the Legionaries facing them seemed inclined to accept it, and no blasts from Drusus' personal *cornicen* had sounded that would warrant a cessation. It wasn't a huge worry for Porcinus, but he was acutely aware that there were other members of the Centurionate who viewed him as unnecessarily soft, and while he normally didn't pay much attention, neither did he want to give these critics fodder. In his attempt to keep his men from being put at more risk, perhaps he had been hasty, and while he would not only order it, but participate, he didn't relish the idea of slaughtering men who had surrendered. More importantly, he knew his men didn't care for the idea either.

The sun had traveled to less than a hand's width above the western mountains before most of the resistance from the scattered bands of Rhaeti warriors on the valley floor were subdued. Porcinus was slightly relieved to see that he wasn't the only Centurion who had stopped the slaughter, although he and those men were definitely in a minority. Very quickly in the aftermath of this band's surrender, Porcinus had gotten the surviving Rhaeti disarmed, while those warriors suffering from anything but the most minor wound were dispatched with a quick slice across the throat. While this was going on, Porcinus took the time to look about more carefully, his experienced eye traveling the width of the valley to get a sense of the situation. All in all, it was a by-now familiar scene; Legionaries owning the field and moving about the wreckage, human and otherwise, with a practiced efficiency, busily searching bodies and grabbing the trinkets and coin that made all the marching, digging and fear created by fights like this worthwhile. There was a more substantial pile of bodies spread along a line running on a roughly north-south axis, marking where the Rhaeti had originally chosen to stand and fight. Moving in a roughly westward direction from there were other heaps of bodies, while in a couple of spots bands of Rhaeti that were either possessed of a stronger collective will, or more likely, better led, were still fighting. And at the far, western end of the valley, just on the other side of the still-smoking ruins of the station that had been Sebatum, Porcinus could just make out a swirl of movement that looked like perhaps a Cohort moving rapidly away from the rest of the army. Although it was impossible to make out much detail, Porcinus guessed that at least one band of Rhaeti had managed to fight their way to a point where they could turn and flee, and now what looked like a Cohort was in pursuit. Moving his attention nearer to his location, he began the process of trying to decide what needed to be done next. It was after he determined that there was no Legion eagle on which to move his Cohort back into their proper position that he realized it was his own First Cohort that had gone off in pursuit of the enemy. Although this was unusual; most of the time, one of the higher number Cohorts that hadn't been engaged normally conducted pursuits like this, Porcinus just assumed that Vettus had either been ordered by Drusus to chase after the Rhaeti, or had found himself in a position where his Cohort was the logical choice. Of the two, Porcinus was more inclined to think that it was the former, thinking that it was the kind of thing an inexperienced Legate would do, either forgetting or never realizing how important the presence of the First Cohort was to re-establishing order and a semblance of a proper formation.

"What do you want us to do with this bunch?" Urso's question pulled Porcinus from his thoughts, turning to see his Pilus Posterior jerking his thumb over his shoulder to where the prisoners were now sitting, miserable and seemingly resigned to their fate.

That appearance, Porcinus knew, was deceiving. If Drusus ordered these men be executed, as it appeared to be the case judging from what was taking place everywhere else, it was extremely doubtful they would remain passive.

"Keep an eye on them." Porcinus stared for a moment, trying to estimate how many remained, made difficult now that they were huddled together, each man seeking the simple solace of close contact with a comrade. "Your Century should be enough."

"My Century?" Urso groused. "Why mine? Why not Verrens'?"

While it was true that it was traditionally the last Century of a Cohort that was stuck with some of the more mundane, and usually unpleasant tasks, it certainly wasn't in the regulations.

In fact, Porcinus would have been inclined to agree, but something in Urso's tone irked him, prompting him to respond, "Because I said your Century will do it, that's why."

Gaius Porcinus wasn't a Centurion the men called a "yeller," which was self-explanatory; neither was he a "striper." He used his *vitus* judiciously, like moments before when he had stopped his men from killing essentially unarmed and helpless men, nor was he a Centurion that ordered floggings if he could avoid it. However, Urso knew his Pilus Prior well, and understood the tone in his superior's voice and what it meant. Stiffening to the position of *intente,* he rendered a salute that was meant to be seen by the Legionaries nearby, once more acknowledging not only Porcinus' rank, but his authority. As he left to shout at his men to spread out around the prisoners, Porcinus moved in the general direction of the mounted command group, thinking that he would find the Secundus Pilus Prior who, since the First Cohort was gone, would be the ranking Centurion in the

Legion. It took some time, but he finally spotted Volusenus standing with a small group of other Centurions, and as Porcinus trotted over, he could see that most of the Pili Priores were already there.

"Glad you could join us." Volusenus was, under the best of circumstances, a normally surly man, but he clearly didn't relish the idea of being in command of the entire Legion, even if it was temporary. Without waiting for any response, Volusenus looked about, asking, "Who's still missing?"

Quickly determining that it was the Pili Priores of the Seventh and Ninth Cohort, by process of elimination as each of the Centurions present pointed out where their Cohorts were located in the wide valley, they saw that Seventh had apparently been co-opted either Drusus by or the sub-Legate Vinicius, and appeared to be involved in some sort of work in the smoking ruins of Sebatum. Meanwhile, the Ninth wasn't immediately visible, but after some intense searching, what the gathered Centurions assumed was their missing Cohort was spotted climbing up a slope on the northern side of the valley, having previously been hidden by the bulk of a smaller hill. From where they were standing, the Ninth was visible just as a series of roughly rectangular shapes, three of them leading another three, which they knew were the Centuries aligned in their normal configuration. Perhaps two stadia ahead of the Ninth was another dark mass, although this one was irregularly shaped, and Porcinus judged that this group contained perhaps slightly more than a Century, around a hundred men. Whoever was leading the Rhaeti seemed to have the idea that he and his men would climb up the steep slope of a mountain that, while it didn't have the craggy peaks of most of the mountains in this part of the world, was nonetheless extremely steep. For a moment, all the Centurions were absorbed, watching as the Pilus Prior of the Ninth drove his men, who they all knew had to be near exhaustion, in his dogged pursuit of this band of stragglers.

"I hope he knows what he's doing." Volusenus finally voiced the thought that Porcinus was sure was running through all of their minds.

He didn't know the Ninth's Pilus Prior, Quintus Maxentius, all that well, but Porcinus felt sure that he wasn't doing anything that he hadn't been ordered to do. The only thing that troubled Porcinus was who had given the command, because if it was Drusus, that was a bad sign.

When Gaius Porcinus had a chance to reflect later, he was struck
by the thought that such an inconsequential action as the one that took
place at Sebatum, one that would never have even been entered into
the Legion diary as anything more than a skirmish if it wasn't for the
presence of young Drusus, could have such a lasting and far-reaching
impact. It certainly hadn't seemed that way as he and the other Pili
Priores, minus the missing Cohorts, finally got their men formed up in
something resembling a proper formation, even if it was missing three
Cohorts. Then the men of the Seventh were finally released from the
onerous task of pulling down the scorched walls and clearing the
smoking debris of the buildings that had already been consumed by
flames, pulling several charred corpses from the ashes. When they
came marching back to where the rest of the 8th was standing, there
was the usual round of jeers and good-natured bantering, silenced only
when some Centurions lashed out with the *vitus* to remind the
Legionaries that this wasn't winter camp. Porcinus had received the
reports from his Centurions of their casualties, and he was happy that
none of his men had been killed outright. One Legionary of the Fourth
Cohort had suffered a serious wound to his side, and it was unlikely
that he would live long, but Porcinus had seen stranger things happen
than a man that the *medici* and the physicians had given up as dead
refusing to submit to a ride in Charon's Boat. He also knew that it was
in the hands of the gods, and he made a mental note to slip a coin
surreptitiously to the wounded Legionary's close comrade to pay the
camp priests for a sacrifice. I'll do it as soon as we make camp,
Porcinus thought, if the man is still alive, seeing and understanding
that matters were still too confused at that moment. Drusus' second-
in-command, Vinicius, had come trotting over to Pilus Prior
Volusenus to inform him that the young Legate had yet to decide if
the army was going to push on a few more miles, or if they would
make camp at a site that was perhaps a mile back towards the eastern
end of the valley that was flat enough to accommodate the entire army.
Even from where Porcinus was standing, he could see just by his
posture that Vinicius was having a difficult time suppressing his
impatience and irritation with the young Roman nobleman who, from
everything Porcinus had observed, had decided to take the fact that he

was given command of this part of the army, despite his youth, seriously. As fine a figure as the boy cut on a horse, and as bravely as he might have behaved, he was still a novice at the art of warfare and campaigning. It was this inexperience that, belatedly, Porcinus understood was the cause for what was about to happen. In reality, the catastrophe had already occurred, but it was only when Porcinus heard a shout and turned to see one of his own Centurions pointing to the far western end of the valley, and he saw a smudge of dust that was the presage of the bad news. Still too far away to make out anything more than a dark mass that seemed to roll slowly along the ground just below the cloud, Porcinus turned to his men and gave the order for them to sit down, still in formation, to wait this new development. At that moment, neither Porcinus nor any of his fellow Centurions, for that matter, were worried, all of them assuming that the First Cohort was returning after finally running down its band of Rhaeti and putting them to the sword. All of the prisoners, those that Porcinus had taken and the other stragglers rounded up by the other Cohorts, were now being guarded by a Century other than Urso's, one from the Eighth Cohort, a task more in keeping with one from the third line. Unfortunately, by the time that happened, Urso and his men had lost out on the chance for stripping the dead in their part of the battlefield, which Porcinus estimated was perhaps three stadia in width in its entirety, at least where the Rhaeti had made their first stand. Because they had scattered, there were clumps of bodies spread across the valley floor for perhaps a mile around where he was standing. The surviving civilians were being addressed by Drusus, and Porcinus watched, amused, as the Legate curbed his stallion, because Porcinus could see that on the side away from the small cluster of disheveled citizens, Drusus was digging his heel into the side of the horse in order to make it act precisely in the manner it was. Shaking his head, Porcinus sighed, thinking that this was something a young man would do; create a situation that gave him the opportunity to show himself in the best possible light. He just hoped that this trait didn't extend into the way he conducted the campaign, but he had a feeling that it was a forlorn one.

Tearing his gaze away, Porcinus looked back at the returning First, and when he thought about it later, this was when he felt the first stirring of unease. It was nothing specific that he could identify; perhaps it was in the slightly darker mass at the front of what he could now make out as the rows of Centuries of the First. Whatever it was, it was enough to rivet his attention to the First as it approached, and he was only dimly aware that he wasn't alone. The heads of almost every man in the 8th were now facing to the west, and what Porcinus did notice was that the steady buzzing of men talking, sharing their experiences and stories that were inevitable after a battle, or arguments that they picked up where they left off before the fight started, all of this had stopped. At the very edge of his vision, he noticed that Urso was drifting closer, and he was quickly joined by the other Centurions; Pacuvius, Canidius, Corvinus, and Verrens. They stood in a little group, as silent as their men, each of them coming to grips with what the sight of the First meant, since the First Century was leading the way and now close enough to make out the details, explaining the slight mystery of what Porcinus had thought of as a darker mass at the head of the formation than would be normal. He felt his mouth open, and it suddenly seemed as if the world was threatening to fall away from under his feet, so dramatically that he took a staggering step back, stopped only when Urso grabbed his arm. Blood that had drained from Porcinus' face came rushing back at this lapse, yet when he glanced over at Urso, opening his mouth to explain this sign of weakness, he saw that his swarthy Pilus Posterior was no less affected, and, in reality, wasn't even looking at him. Instead, like every man there, his gaze was fixed on a sight that was seen fairly rarely on a battlefield owned by Rome's Legions.

Leading the First Century, and the whole First Cohort, were the Centurions of the Cohort, but only five of them were walking under their own power. Two pairs of them, side by side were each holding aloft a corner of what Porcinus and the others could see was a Legionary shield, carried with the concave side up so that it could hold, almost cradle, the body being borne by the Centurions. Like most things with the Roman army, there was nothing spontaneous about this procession, nor in the use of the shield. While Centurions falling during battle was a common enough occurrence, when it was the Primus Pilus, the event called for a solemn ritual whereby his body was borne from the field in the manner that Porcinus and the rest of the 8th Legion was watching. Even as he reeled in shock, Porcinus' mind registered how Vettus' legs dangled limply over the edge of the shield, both of them swaying in morbid time to the movement of the Centurions bearing his body. His helmet was still on, hiding his head and face from immediate view, but when they were still thirty paces away, Porcinus could clearly see that the shield was only partially successful at trapping the blood that had pooled around Vettus, so that it dripped in a slow but steady stream from the leading edge of the shield.

"What...How...?"

Porcinus heard the words, but didn't know who said them; in fact, it had been him, yet such was his shock that he wasn't aware that he had uttered a word. By this point, the Centurions bearing Vettus had come abreast of where Porcinus and his Centurions were standing, and with no command being given, they all stiffened to *intente*, rendering salutes to their now-fallen Primus Pilus. Only then did Porcinus regain enough of his equilibrium to notice that every man bearing Vettus either had tears streaming from his eyes, or looked very close to joining his comrades in sharing their grief. Since Porcinus' attention was focused on the sight in front of him, he heard the approach of what he assumed was Drusus before he saw it, the drumming hoof beats telling him that he was coming at a gallop, and he wasn't alone. The noise became so loud that it wrenched Porcinus' head to the right so that he watched as the young Roman nobleman drew on the reins of his stallion, bringing it to a skidding halt. Immediately behind him was Vinicius, and the other members of Drusus' staff, but Porcinus only had eyes for Drusus, so he saw the look of shock and dismay on the younger man's face as he looked down from his saddle at the corpse of Sextus Vettus.

"Sir, it is my sad duty to report, as the Primus Pilus Posterior, of the death of our Primus Pilus, Sextus Vettus. He fell on the field, and up until his last moment was leading his Cohort and Legion in a manner befitting Rome's Legions."

The Centurion, a man named Quintus Frontinus, was forced to pause, head bowed as he fought to regain his composure. All other sound had ceased, except for a low moan that to Porcinus' ears could have been the wind, or coming from the prisoners awaiting their fate; or it could have been from the men of the 8th. Wherever it came from Porcinus didn't really care, but he did note that this was the quietest he'd ever heard a battlefield.

Frontinus had regained enough composure to continue. "As far as your orders, we pursued the last band of Rhaeti out of this valley, and we eliminated the last resistance. While our overall casualties are low, as you can see, it was quite costly."

Porcinus thought he sensed a rebuke in Frontinus' words, in tone if not in what he actually had said, and, shooting a quick glance over at Urso, who was nearest to him, he saw that he wasn't alone. Clearly, it wasn't lost on young Drusus either, because his fair features suddenly turned a bright red, and Porcinus inwardly winced, certain that Frontinus' words, no matter how deserved they were, would not go unpunished. However, he was in for quite a surprise.

"You are right, Primus Pilus Posterior Frontinus," the young Roman replied quietly. "It is much too costly when we lose a man like Sextus Vettus, no matter how many of these rebels we kill." Straightening in the saddle so that he sat taller, and raising his voice at the same time, Drusus called out, "No matter how much of a victory this is, we have suffered a loss that I'm afraid can't be easily repaired. And I know you men of the 8th feel this grief the most keenly, but know that I, too, mourn the death of a great Centurion, a great Roman, and a great man, particularly since I am the cause of it."

He paused then, letting the words settle over the slumped shoulders of the men of the 8th Legion. Porcinus became aware that now the sound of low-pitched, quiet sobbing could be heard, clearly coming from every one of his Centuries, and he was sure that it was the same in every other Cohort. For so many of these men, Vettus was the only Primus Pilus under whom they had served, yet for men like Porcinus, the tie to the Primus Pilus ran even more deeply. Drusus, apparently deciding enough silence had gone by, resumed speaking.

"I have decided that we will make camp here. However, I excuse the 8th from their duties in order to give them time to prepare for the funeral rites that are in a manner and style befitting their Primus Pilus."

Without another word, at least that were audible to anyone other than Vinicius and his staff, Drusus wheeled his horse about and went galloping away, leaving the men of the 8th to grieve.

"I started out as his Optio," Porcinus said quietly, staring down into the cup that was holding unwatered wine. "He was the Pilus Prior of the Seventh at the time, and I had transferred in from the 10th."

The Centurions of the First Cohort and the Pili Priores were now gathered together in the tent of the Primus Pilus, the only tent large enough to hold all of them. The camp had since been erected, and the men of the Legions were performing the tasks of a Legion of Rome after battle, including this meeting.

"Yes, that's when your uncle made sure you were taken care of, wasn't it?"

This came from Volusenus, and Porcinus felt the flush rising up his neck, aware of some of the looks he was being given by the rest of the small group of Centurions.

However, he had become accustomed to such small, cutting remarks, and replied calmly, "That's right. After the 10th Equestris was merged with the Veneria, after Actium. And after Parthia," he finished quietly, and he was pleased to see that his last remark had hit home.

Although he had only been a Gregarius, actually barely more than a *tirone*, a Legionary still in the first phase of his training, Gaius Porcinus' participation in what was acknowledged throughout the army to be the harshest, most grueling campaign, not just in recent history, but in the annals of the Roman army, no matter what side a man found himself on in the great struggle between the Triumvir of the East Marcus Antonius and the Roman now known and referred to as only Augustus, marked him as a hard man in his own right. Just surviving what became a death march through the vast wastelands of Parthia and Armenia was an achievement in itself, but Porcinus had also won the most coveted and honored individual award, the Civic Crown. He won the award during the last of the seventeen engagements that the army of Marcus Antonius fought with the Parthians, led by Monaeses, a Parthian prince who had duped the Triumvir into believing he had been bought and paid for with Antonius' gold. The 10th, acting as a rearguard, was protecting the army as it crossed the final river that marked the spot where the Parthians would stop their relentless stalking and pursuit. Understanding that this was their last chance, the Parthians had thrown not only their waves of horse archers, but the dreaded cataphracts into the assault. In the ensuing fight, Porcinus' Pilus Prior Scribonius was struck down and lying helplessly, waiting for the next Parthian lance to end his life, when the young Legionary leapt between his Centurion and the Parthian who was trying to end Scribonius. It had been one of those blindingly quick, unthinking actions, but it had resulted in Porcinus having the right to wear the simple award, a crown made of woven grass, on festival days and on parade in full uniform. At this moment, sitting in the large tent of the Primus Pilus, it served an even better purpose, stilling the acid tongue of men like Volusenus, and Porcinus was pleased to see that more than one Pilus Prior tried to hide a smile at his gentle but firm rebuke.

Understanding that he had lost the honors in the exchange, Volusenus chose to remain silent by taking a deep swallow from his own cup.

Taking that as a tacit submission and seeing that the others were still looking in his direction, Porcinus continued, "As I was saying, I started out as his Optio, and next to my father," Porcinus couldn't resist adding this subtle jab at Volusenus, "and my first Pilus Prior Scribonius, he taught me more about the Legions than anyone else."

"I remember that," the Pilus Prior of the Third, Gnaeus Fronto spoke up. "I was his Hastatus Posterior then, and when I saw you show up, I was sure that you wouldn't last more than a month as his Optio."

Fronto chuckled at the memory, and while that might have been taken as an offense, Porcinus knew that it wasn't meant that way, so despite the circumstances, he found himself sharing Fronto's amusement.

"Too soft," Porcinus supplied the unspoken criticism, knowing how often it had been uttered, by many, including Vettus. At first, anyway.

"Too soft," Fronto agreed, then lifted his cup in Porcinus' direction. "But you had a good teacher to drive that out of you. Vettus was a hard man. A fair man, but a hard one."

"That he was." This came from Frontinus, his eyes still puffy from the grief that he was feeling, although it was something none of the assembled Centurions would make any comment about. "As hard as the sword he was carrying. And," he finished with a quiet chuckle of his own, "his tongue was about as sharp as well."

This brought the first real laughter from the assembled men, each of them dipping into his own well of memories as individually they recalled a moment that fit Frontinus' description. None of them had thought their respective moment was amusing at the time, and if forced to tell the truth, they would admit that many of them were carried from the site of the tongue-lashing by a pair of wobbly legs. Porcinus, with his unique perspective, wouldn't have placed Vettus in the same class as his father in terms of not only sheer volume, but intimidation, although much of Pullus' ability was due to his immense and muscular size, since he liked to tower over the recipient, with barely the width of a hand between him and his victim. However, no man rose to the rank of Primus Pilus without having the ability to cow other men, particularly other Centurions, all of them hard men in their own way.

"So, how do we go about this? And are we going to use money from the burial fund for the entire Legion, or just the First Cohort?"

Volusenus' question could have been considered rude because it jerked the attention and focus of the Centurions from their moment of honoring Sextus Vettus, privately and in their own way. Yet, neither could it be argued that this was what they were there for, all the Pili Priores and the Centurions of the First Cohort, gathered in the Primus Pilus' tent in the dusk after a battle that none of them would ever forget. Reluctantly, the Centurions turned their attention back to their purpose, and the next third of a watch was spent discussing the manner and style in which they would send their Primus Pilus to the afterlife. Finally, it was decided that each Cohort would add funds to that of the First, not only to pay for a tomb and inscription of the appropriate size and ornateness fitting for Vettus, but to pay for the most expensive sacrifice available, one of the sacred white bulls from the small herd that traveled with the army. Normally, they were reserved for holy days, or extraordinarily propitious events, and not surprisingly, at least to most of the Centurions, this was the most contentious issue. The only thing that wasn't unexpected, at least to Porcinus, was the reason behind the group of Centurions who argued against it. Expense wasn't actually what they took issue with; it was the idea of proportion, and as arguments went, it was one that was familiar, not just to Porcinus, but to every man. This was because it was a topic that, especially in the aftermath of battle, was always the subject of debate and, in essence, it was a simple question. What honored a man more; a larger sacrifice, or a more elaborate headstone? Sacrifices to the gods were all well and good, some of the Centurions argued, but they were temporary symbols of the regard in which a man like Vettus was held. Whereas the grander the tombstone, the greater the honor being done to the deceased. While on the surface this was true, Porcinus was experienced enough; some would use the word "cynical," to understand that at least part of the reason these men who felt this way argued so strongly was that, as was the custom, there would be an inscription included where all could see who had provided the memorial. In this way, their own names would be immortalized in stone, and would serve as what some might call an ostentatious display of their regard for and loyalty to the deceased. Only a Roman could make something political out of a headstone, Porcinus thought with equal parts amusement and mild disgust. Fortunately, at least as far as Porcinus was concerned, those who wished to pay for the bull held sway, the losers of the debate surrendering the point with varying degrees of grace.

Once the details for Vettus' funeral rites were settled, it was ostensibly time for the Centurions to disperse and make their own preparations to honor their Primus Pilus. Yet, nobody moved, but Porcinus was not only unsurprised, he was mentally counting the heartbeats before one of his counterpart's nerve finally broke, and they uttered what was really on everyone's mind, at least as far as most of them were concerned.

He didn't get past ten before Maxentius, who looked not only as if he was grieving, but on the edge of exhaustion after pushing his men up the steep slopes after their quarry, blurted out, "So who's going to be named Primus Pilus, do you think? I mean, permanently." His eyes darted an apology over to Frontinus who, according to the regulations, was now the acting Primus Pilus.

While Porcinus was on the younger side of the Centurions, he had still been in the army long enough that he had been able to watch what he knew was one of the most disturbing elements of the reforms wrought by Augustus, at least as far as his father and the Centurions of his generation were concerned. Before the reforms, promotions were more a matter of custom than regulation, but despite there being nothing written down, to Romans, what had been practiced by their ancestors in these matters carried more weight than some words scribbled on parchment or wax tablet. And the tradition had been that Frontinus would not only step into the shoes of his former Primus Pilus temporarily, it was almost always ratified and made permanent. But then, the great civil wars had come, and while only a couple of the men there had been in the ranks for the first civil war, pitting Divus Julius against Pompey, none of them had been in the Centurionate. However, all of them had been at least in the ranks for the second civil war that lasted for more than a decade, and they had witnessed how potent a political weapon the Legions had become. It had been about the only thing that then-Octavian and Antonius had agreed upon; whoever controlled the loyalty of the Legions controlled the greater prize of Rome. And while most of the men in the ranks who carried the most influence among their comrades marched for the contender for the title of First Man in whom they believed the most, or at least believed would win, there were Centurions who saw an opportunity for personal gain. These were the men who sold their respective Legions to the highest bidder, and while it was true that, at some point in the titanic struggle between Augustus and Antonius, almost every Primus Pilus and Legion had either chosen or been forced by circumstance to switch sides, most of the time it was for considerations other than money. But Porcinus supposed that it only took one Primus Pilus who was, as his father liked to say, crooked as a warped *vitus*, to make Augustus suspicious of all Primi Pili and their motives. That attitude was what had led to the disbandment and merging of the 10th, when Augustus had accused the men of Caesar's greatest Legion of disloyalty for "choosing" Antonius over his own cause. Because of his relationship with the Primus Pilus of that Legion, Porcinus had seen firsthand how angry and hurt it had made his father, who argued, unsuccessfully, that in the aftermath of Philippi, when the two victors had split the army into two parts, neither he nor any of the men, of any Legion, had been asked which side they preferred. No, Pullus argued, almost to the point where it cost him his career, they had followed orders, and ended up on the other side of Our Sea, marching into Parthia. Even then, at the decisive battle of Actium, when the 10th had been designated as one of the Legions that would accompany the fleeing couple of Antonius and Cleopatra, the 10th had refused to board ship, and had marched for Augustus ever since. Titus Pullus had never really forgiven Augustus for what he viewed as this unwarranted punishment, but as Porcinus had since discovered, neither had Augustus forgiven Pullus. Which was why Porcinus was still sitting in the tent of the Primus Pilus and not with his family, enjoying his father's villa in Arelate. At least, that was the conclusion that Porcinus, with Diocles' help, had reached.

But now, Augustus had taken very careful and painstaking steps to reduce the chances of any surprises wrought by a greedy Primus Pilus. At least, that was the assumption, because what had been a tradition in the Roman army was no longer observed. Promotions to the rank of Primus Pilus of a Legion were determined by one man, and one man only, and that was the Princeps, the first among "equals," which was a term that a man only laughed at when he was alone and out of earshot of anyone else that might betray him. Now Maxentius had prodded the boil of the problem with the needle by raising the question that Porcinus suspected was foremost in every man's mind. Frontinus, shifting uncomfortably on his stool, just looked down at the floor, mumbling something that nobody could hear, but Porcinus assumed was some sort of words to the effect that Augustus' will would be done. Which was true enough, and there was a part of Porcinus that held out hope that it would be Frontinus who would receive the confirmation that his temporary assumption of the post would be permanent, because he was as suitable a candidate as anyone that Porcinus could think of. First and foremost, he was respected; although Porcinus didn't like to admit it, there had been some truth in the charge that, in the beginning anyway, he was too soft. That was due to the fact that Porcinus, like many young and inexperienced leaders, confused being liked with being respected. It was a lesson he learned quickly, but it was with some chagrin whenever he thought back to some of the early mistakes he made as Vettus' Optio, when the hard-bitten men of the First Century had seen him for what he truly was, a green-as-grass Optio who barely knew which end of the *vitus* to hold, and taken advantage of him, without any mercy. Frontinus was a striper, but not excessively so, and he was as tough as old boot leather. Because he commanded a Century of the First Cohort, he had twice the men of a normal Century, yet managed to keep his men in line, despite the fact that his Optio was considered one of the weakest, not just in his Cohort, but in the Legion. Porcinus had little to do with the man, but from his observation, it seemed that he suffered from the same malady that had afflicted Porcinus when he first assumed the role of second-in-command of the Century. He was earnest, and hard-working, and...soft. That, Porcinus mused, might be a mark against Frontinus, because he hadn't corrected the situation, despite the fact that the Optio had been in his post for more than six months. That was long enough to correct the issue, either by strengthening the spine of the Optio or replacing him. Although that seemed on the surface to be a detail that would hardly be likely to reach the ears of Augustus, Porcinus knew otherwise. Again, through his relationship with Pullus, he had learned that, as the saying went, when a sparrow fell in the Forum, Augustus knew about it before it had actually hit the ground. A detail like a weak Optio was exactly the kind of thing Augustus would know about, and was likely to use as a disqualification of Frontinus. Because, although he wouldn't say it aloud, Porcinus suspected that it was unlikely that the new Primus Pilus of the 8th Legion was even in the tent at this moment.

No matter who dies in the armies of Rome, the Legions continue their work, and this death was no exception. Normally, with casualties so light, the army wouldn't have bothered to pause a day like they did after a larger battle where they suffered heavier losses. But because of Vettus, they spent the next day in place, and the funeral rites that sent Vettus, along with the half-dozen other unfortunates who had fallen to the afterlife, were carried out perfectly. The white bull, drugged to just the right amount so that it was docile, but could be led to the altar for sacrifice, gave itself to the gods with what the priests said was a willing spirit. Smoke from the seven pyres rose into the air, the sacred words intoned, and the ashes allowed to cool before being scooped up and placed in their urns. Vettus' remains went into a temporary urn, since the one that would be his permanent repository had yet to be created, then reverently deposited in a spot on the wagon belonging to the First Cohort. Meanwhile, the mounted scouts continued their aggressive patrolling, moving westward, deeper into Rhaetia, bringing back reports of armed bands whose tracks had been found, although they all seemed to be retreating back to the northwest, into Rhaetia itself. In reality, this meant that their rebellion was over, at least as far as any active attempt to seize more territory in their name. Despite this, none of the men, at least of Centurion rank, were under any illusion that this battle would be punishment enough, so when the orders were given to break camp, and to continue marching westward, nobody was surprised. Only slightly more of a surprise was that no word had come from the *praetorium* concerning the status of Frontinus and his role as Primus Pilus. Another of the long-standing traditions in the Roman army was that all leadership positions be filled before they resumed the march, after a battle. But this was a slightly different matter than deciding who would lead the Sixth Century of one of the Cohorts of the third line, so little mention was made of it.

As far as Frontinus went, he performed the duties of the Primus Pilus, and relied on his Optio to run the Second Century. Unfortunately, especially for the men of the Second Century, the Optio's performance proved that the opinion held about him by most of the Pili Priores was justified, it very quickly becoming clear that keeping the men of the Second under control was beyond his capacities. As any experienced Centurion, or Optio, for that matter, could attest, whenever there was a sudden vacuum of leadership in the hierarchy of something like a Roman Legion Century, there would be men who sought to take advantage of that absence. The names of some of these men would be well known, not just to the Centurion and Optio in command of the Century, but their respective Pili Priores. These were the troublemakers, the malcontents, the shirkers and malingerers, of which every Century, Cohort, and Legion had a portion, some more than others. The one small saving grace was that, since these were men of the First Cohort, the relative scale of their particular perfidies was lesser than what might be found with the men of, for example, the

Tenth Cohort. What negated that one small advantage was that these men were more competent in every way, and that included their ability to take advantage of a weak Optio. In the first three or four days on the march after Sebatum, the transgressions were minor; lagging a bit when summoned back on the march after a rest break, a hesitation when the Optio told one of these men to do something. But since the Optio was either unwilling or unable to take sterner measures, it wasn't long before these men decided to push the boundaries of acceptable behavior even farther. Normally, this was something that only faintly interested Porcinus; he had men like that in his own Cohort, and he understood the effort it took to keep these men under control.

But as he pointed out to the other Pili Priores one evening in camp, when they had gathered in Fronto's tent, "Unless Frontinus gets a handle on his old Century, his chances of being confirmed as the permanent Primus Pilus will be seriously damaged."

It was either in Fronto's, or Porcinus' own tent that had become the informal meeting spot for the Pili Priores of the 8th, as it seemed every day brought new rumors or fresh speculation based on what a clerk attached to one of their Centuries had overheard when dropping off his daily report at the *praetorium*. Porcinus supposed that going strictly by hierarchy, it should be Volusenus' tent where they met, but he was such a disagreeable sort, and was famously stingy with his hospitality that it had devolved onto Fronto and Porcinus. Fairly soon, it just worked out that the meetings alternated between the two men's tents, which neither of them minded, if for different reasons. For Fronto, it meant that his resources wouldn't be stretched by hosting the gathering every single night, because Centurions were nothing if not thirsty creatures. Not only did he have a wife and family to support, over the years and thanks to the largesse of all the bonuses and bounties paid to the men of the Legions, his wife had developed very expensive tastes. That meant anything he could do to reduce expenses was welcome. For Porcinus, it was based more in his ambivalence towards this political side to the Centurionate. Not only was he not normally inclined towards meddling with such things, he had observed enough of the sometimes horribly dangerous path that his father had to tread, in order to fulfill his ambition to become an equestrian. It certainly wasn't the expense; he was still coming to terms with the idea that he was an extremely wealthy man, and if he had known Fronto's situation and worries about money, he would have instantly offered to absorb the costs for every night's refreshment.

"I told Frontinus that," Marcus Sabinus, the Quintus Pilus Prior spoke up. "But he said he was too busy with everything else to worry about whatever mess Paetinas is making."

Servius Paetinas was the hapless Optio, and while Porcinus knew that Sabinus and Frontinus were friends, having come up through the ranks; he seemed to remember that it was in the 20th, one of Caesar's Legions, Porcinus didn't get any sense that Sabinus had gotten through to his friend. His belief was confirmed with what Sabinus said next.

"I wasted my breath," Sabinus continued. "Honestly, he's so absorbed in just trying to keep up with all the various duties that he barely had time to listen to what I had to say."

With that somewhat gloomy assessment, the tent was quiet for a moment as each man thought about what they had learned this night. When nobody seemed inclined to share with the others, Porcinus cleared his throat, his signal that not only was he about to resume speaking, but he wanted to change the topic.

"Has anyone heard more about Drusus and what happened the other day?"

Although this subject was as potentially explosive as Frontinus' prospects of being named permanent Primus Pilus, it was no less important. In fact, it could be argued that this was even more crucial, because it impacted more than just the 8th Legion. And in the intervening time between the battle and this, the fifth night after it, the full extent of the catastrophe that had befallen the 8thhad become clear. This news came from a variety of sources; most of the time, it would be from a clerk who was friends with one of the slaves that was attached to every tent section, but there were also snippets of conversations that were overheard by the Centurions themselves whenever their daily duties took them to the *praetorium* after camp was made. The best information, however, came from the other Centurions of the First Cohort itself, particularly Frontinus and the Primus Princeps Prior, Gnaeus Bassus. They were nearby when Drusus had, in what Porcinus could only believe was a bout of insecurity, countermanded Vettus' order for the Tenth Cohort, which was already standing at a spot nearer to the western end of the valley, to conduct the pursuit of the band of Rhaeti that to that point had managed to elude all attempts to pin them down and bring them to battle.

"Primus Pilus, I gave you the order," Drusus had supposedly said, and depending on whom one talked to, he had either shouted it, or at the very least, spoke in a stern manner to Vettus who, surprising none of his Centurions, responded calmly.

That, apparently, at least from what Porcinus could gather, had further agitated the young Legate, and he told Vettus that it was the First Cohort specifically and no other that he expected to pursue the fleeing remnant. And, showing the same flair for the dramatic, it was what Drusus said as Vettus saluted and turned to lead his Cohort that would turn out to not only be prophetic, but would haunt the young nobleman for the gods only knew how long.

"I expect you to completely crush these scum, Primus Pilus," Drusus had called, and from all accounts, he made sure that he was heard by the entire Cohort. "Do not leave one man alive. I expect complete victory. If you don't achieve it, then don't bother returning."

It was the kind of thing Porcinus and the others had heard before, from haughty young Tribunes mostly, but Tribunes could be laughed off, and for the most part were ignored. A Legate, however, was another matter, especially one who was widely considered to be at least in contention for the title of Princeps when Augustus crossed the river in Charon's Boat, although none of the Centurions could ever recall hearing a Legate say anything as harsh and unforgiving as what Drusus had told Vettus. That, Porcinus reflected, was because by the time a Roman reached the status of Legate, he had been on campaign, usually several of them. This wasn't the case with Drusus, and it was just one more troubling sign as far as Porcinus and most of his compatriots were concerned. Hence the interest in the young nobleman's mental state here on this fifth night.

"Have you seen the boy?" Volusenus scoffed. "Now he's moping about, acting as if he's Atlas and got the world on his shoulders. I heard from Caleus," Volusenus referred to his personal slave, "who talked to some slave friend of his attached to the boy's household that he's not eating or sleeping." The Secundus Pilus Prior shook his head, and spat onto the dirt floor of the tent. "It's disgusting that he carries on this way."

"I actually think that's a good sign," Porcinus interjected mildly, unsurprisingly earning a scornful look from Volusenus. Neither fazed nor intimidated, he continued, "It shows he knows he made a mistake. That counts for something, at least in my book."

"Bah." Volusenus was equally unmoved. "So he made a mistake. We all have, and we all have made mistakes that have gotten men hurt. But you don't see us carrying on like a woman, wringing our hands and whining about it."

Porcinus wasn't the only Centurion who took notice of the callous disregard Volusenus seemed to be showing for the circumstances behind Drusus' behavior, and he saw Fronto stare at Volusenus with barely disguised hostility. He wasn't alone; in a moment, even Volusenus couldn't ignore the hostile gazes of at least a half-dozen of his counterparts, causing his face to flush and turn his already swarthy features even darker. Only then did he seem to realize how his words could have been taken, and he shifted nervously on his stool.

"I...I didn't mean anything disrespectful to the memory of the Primus Pilus," he said hastily. "I was just talking."

"Yes, you were 'just talking,'" agreed Publius Philo, the Sextus Pilus Prior, but his tone wasn't friendly. "It seems you do a lot of that, just...talking."

Volusenus' eyes narrowed at the insult and, for a moment, it looked as if he intended to make an issue of Philo's words.

Then, Fronto intervened by saying simply, "I agree with Porcinus. I think it's a good sign that the boy Legate is actually shaken up because of what he did. Although," he felt compelled to add, "It's not like what happened with Vettus was something that anyone could have foreseen."

That, also, was true, Porcinus knew. And of the larger tragedy of Vettus dying, this smaller one was in some ways worse, because Vettus hadn't been dispatched by a Rhaeti warrior he was facing on the battlefield, with his sword in hand. That at least would have been fitting. Instead, it was an act that every Centurion had seen happen across hundreds of battles and skirmishes, a case where the gods turned their face away from a man. Vettus, despite the harsh manner in which he had been addressed, was carrying out his orders to the letter that Drusus had demanded. But the First Cohort was operating at a disadvantage; they had been forced to run across the valley floor to close the distance to the fleeing Rhaeti band, meaning that not only were they winded, their cohesion wasn't what it should have been. The secret to the success of the Legions was their discipline, but part of that discipline was represented by how tightly they held to the space between each man, and the width between each rank. Not surprisingly, running over rough ground, especially for a long distance, shattered the cohesion of even the most disciplined and well-trained units. Vettus, probably still smarting from the stinging rebuke from Drusus, was leading from the front, as a good Primus Pilus does. However, in his desire to carry out Drusus' orders, he had ranged too far ahead of the front ranks of his Century, so that when the probably scared and undoubtedly desperate Rhaeti had flung his javelin, it was a case of a number of factors coming together that ended with this result. Obviously, Vettus couldn't add his own perspective, but from what was pieced together, he had just come to a stop and was in the process of turning to point to the spot where he wanted his Century to line up. Apparently, he had turned his back to the enemy, still more than thirty paces away, which was normally something an experienced man would never do if he was isolated. But it wasn't until Vettus turned around to see he had outrun his men to a point where he didn't have immediate support that he realized his mistake. The only conclusion that made any sense was that either the man who flung the javelin that killed him released immediately after Vettus turned his back or, somehow, Vettus didn't pick up the movement out of the nearly five hundred Rhaeti. Because Vettus had gained some twenty paces on his men, when his *aquilifer* tried to shout a warning, he was too out of breath and too far away to do more than cry out in anguish and frustration when the point of the javelin, arcing down through the air, struck Vettus in the hollow just above his left collarbone, punching through the mail to pierce his heart, whereupon he took a staggering step back towards his Cohort before dropping in a heap, already dead by the time his body hit the ground. Every Centurion present in the tent had either seen, or at least heard from someone who had witnessed such random events happen during a battle, but none of them had ever seen or heard about it happening to the highest-ranking Centurion in the Legion. Now, those men Vettus had relied on the most in leading the 8th were left trying to cope with what was a devastating loss, made worse by the uncertainty the future held for their Legion. If any of them were to articulate their fears, none of them would have mentioned the campaign itself as a cause for worry; they had all been on multiple campaigns. And this one, at least to this point, was shaping up to be little more than a matter of killing a few tribesmen to remind the others that they were ruled by Rome. Whether it stayed this way remained to be seen, but their larger concern was the unknown posed by their Legate, and whether or not he, in fact, did learn from his mistakes.

The army's pursuit of the Rhaeti continued, and for those uninitiated in tribal rebellions of this type, it was a frustrating business. Fortunately, Porcinus and the men of the 8th had a good deal of experience fighting what at times seemed to be a phantom enemy, as small bands of warriors would suddenly coalesce to strike at a minor Roman settlement, inflicting as much damage as they could in a limited amount of time. The damage was usually in the form of burned buildings, sometimes still smoldering as the advance guard of Drusus' force would arrive. Fairly quickly, it became apparent that the goal of the Rhaeti was more than just the destruction of property. It was around the third or fourth settlement that the Romans understood there was a method to what the Rhaeti were doing, in the form of the mutilated corpses of every male Roman, all of whose genitals had been hacked away. And for men experienced enough to understand the signs, it was apparent that this was done while the unfortunates were still alive. Yet it was more than that; women weren't immune to this treatment, although it was confined to women who had been carrying children. Even for those hardened to such things, the sight of fetuses ripped from their mother's wombs not only turned stomachs, it created a cold fury, especially in men like Porcinus, who could too easily imagine that it was Iras lying there, with one of his children being ripped from her belly. The message the Rhaeti were sending couldn't have been clearer: We will drive the Romans out of our lands and remove them from existence. At least, that was how it was presented to the men of the Legions by their Centurions, but every man wearing the transverse crest knew that they already had a receptive audience for their message. Still, as Porcinus and his compatriots knew, the anger of the rankers helped to dull the frustration, and the complaining that would normally have resulted from trudging through what was becoming increasingly challenging terrain, in pursuit of phantoms.

"It's like trying to tie a knot in a wisp of smoke," was how Ovidius put it one night as he sat in Porcinus' tent, going over the events of the day.

Or, more accurately, the non-events, Porcinus thought dismally, because he was no less frustrated than any of the men, at least as far as closing with the enemy and crushing them in battle was concerned. That feeling was compounded by the fact that it was his Cohort that had been in the vanguard that day, meaning that he and his Century had followed the column of smoke still streaming into the sky and been the first to come upon what, even by this point, was an exceptionally gruesome scene. Whoever had commanded this band hadn't been content just to slaughter the inhabitants of what had been a clearly prosperous settlement. It also hadn't been purely Roman; there were already two distinct towns, one belonging to the Focunates, the tribe in whose territory the settlement lay, which was located on the north side of the Aenus (Inn) River, and the Roman, arrayed on the southern bank. Seeing the scene, Porcinus instantly understood that it was no accident that it was only the structures on the southern side that lay in smoking ruin, while the collection of small but sturdily built huts, with their tightly woven roofs of thatch, were completely intact and, from what he could see, unmolested. It was also no surprise that their occupants, the Focunates, who from what could be gathered by scouts and spies, hadn't been part of this rebellion, were nowhere to be seen. Well, Porcinus thought grimly as he and his men entered the settlement, they're in it now, because Rome isn't going to make a distinction, not anymore.

Even as he understood it was a futile endeavor, Porcinus ordered his men to spread out through the three rows of streets, looking for survivors amid the rubble of the buildings. While he watched, he was struck by the odd juxtaposition of the neat lines made by the good Roman streets, and the smoking hulks of the shops, trading posts, and homes that had been enclosed by them. The contrast was made even greater by the sight of the Focunates settlement across the river, which seemed to have no sense of order to it at all, looking very much like the occupants of each structure had simply looked about and decided that this was a good spot to build upon. His thoughts were interrupted by a shout from Corvinus, whose Century he had sent to the center of the small town where, like in every Roman town, the forum was located. Even before Porcinus had drawn near enough to see his friend's expression, he knew that something even worse than what he was already seeing was coming. Reaching Corvinus, there was no mistaking the pallor underneath the Centurion's normally swarthy features, made even more noticeable by lips pressed so tightly together that his mouth appeared to be nothing more than a thin gash sliced into the bottom of his face by a very sharp knife. In fact, Porcinus thought, if I didn't know better, I would think he's trying to keep from throwing up.

"You need to see this," Corvinus told him quietly, but there was a catch to his voice that unsettled Porcinus even more than his friend's expression. "But you need to prepare yourself."

"Why? It can't be anything I haven't seen before," Porcinus replied, but Corvinus only shook his head in response.

As he followed Corvinus, his friend's bulk blocked his view for a precious few more heartbeats. Later, Porcinus wasn't sure whether that had been a blessing or a curse. For a moment, he stared uncomprehendingly at the knot of men, huddled roughly in the middle of the forum. This place, he would only learn later that its name was Veldidena (Innsbruck), had yet to be consecrated and officially entered as a Roman town, which meant that there was no obligatory statue of Augustus. Instead, it appeared that the locals had settled for a statue of what Porcinus assumed was Jupiter Optimus Maximus; it was impossible to tell because the statue had been toppled and smashed to pieces. But that wasn't what the men were looking at, and for the rest of his days, Gaius Porcinus would find himself wishing that he had just turned around and walked away, before his mind comprehended the awful sight that his eyes were seeing. A crude frame had been erected, perhaps twenty feet long. In construction and style, it was similar to the kind of frame farmers erected when it was time for slaughter, and as apt a comparison as it may have been, Porcinus immediately regretted making it, even if it was only to himself. Suspended from the frame were eight bodies, all strung up with their feet pointing skyward, their arms now dangling limply just above the ground. Underneath each of them was a huge pool of blood, barely congealed and telling the Legionaries that what had taken place had occurred within perhaps the last watch. Unfortunately, that was the least gruesome of the details seared into Porcinus' brain, along with every other man who saw it. The fact that every victim was a woman was apparent, not from the usual telltales of their sex, but because just below each of them dangled the unborn fetus of the child she had been carrying. Despite himself, Porcinus noticed that each tiny corpse was in varying levels of development; two of them could have been babes in arms, while the others ranged from very small, but perfectly formed, to one that had to have been at least six months away from birth. While he had seen this type of butchery before, what made this even more gruesome were the signs that the warriors had taken the extra step with the better-developed fetuses by mutilating them, leaving no question about the message they were sending.

"By the gods...." Porcinus was barely aware that the croaking, strangled voice was his own as he stared in horror at the sight before him.

"I don't think the gods were watching over this place," Corvinus said bitterly, standing next to Porcinus. "I've never seen anything like this before."

"Neither have I and I hope I never have to again!" Porcinus shook his head violently, in a vain attempt to banish the image that was now seared into his memory.

"They were alive when those...*cunni* savages did this, Gaius." Corvinus' mouth twisted into a bitter grimace, and he finally spat the bile that had been pushing its way into his mouth from his stomach.

"I can see that," Porcinus replied quietly. Closing his eyes for a moment, he uttered a brief prayer then continued. "Let's cut them down and at least give them the funeral they deserve."

"Are you sure you want to do that?"

Porcinus turned at this new voice to see that Urso had arrived on the scene. Frowning, Porcinus was about to remind Urso that he had given the Second Century instructions to move to the western end of the settlement, but refrained. Just because you don't trust him doesn't mean he doesn't have something valuable to say, Porcinus remonstrated with himself.

Instead, he asked, "Why do you say that, Urso?"

"Because I think this is something Drusus and that bunch should see," Urso replied, and while he was addressing his superior, his eyes never left the sight that had drawn their attention, for which Porcinus couldn't blame him.

Considering for a moment, Porcinus nodded and said simply, "You're right. He should see this. Thank you, Urso."

For a brief moment, Urso looked startled, as if he had been expecting a reprimand, and it gave Porcinus a small sense of satisfaction, as he thought, No, that's what you would do. But I'm not you. Which is why I'm the Pilus Prior and you're not.

"Er...you're welcome, sir." And while Urso clearly meant it as a statement, it came out sounding like more of a question, causing Corvinus' mouth to quirk in an unconscious smirk.

Ignoring the underlying current, Porcinus turned his attention to more immediate matters.

"Did your boys find anything? Alive, I mean?"

Urso shook his head, and in this Porcinus was sure that his regretful expression wasn't feigned.

"Just bodies."

Despite expecting this, Porcinus still felt a sense of disappointment. During this exchange, the men of both Porcinus' Century and that of Urso's had joined with Corvinus' men, each of them in their own way strongly affected by what they saw. It was one of the few times in Porcinus' experience that the sight of a Legionary retching and vomiting up the contents of his breakfast wasn't the immediate cause of merciless teasing and taunting by his comrades. Each of them seemed to understand that they were seeing something that would haunt their dreams for the rest of their collective lives. Recognizing how it would look to have his men milling about in the forum, no matter what the cause when the command group arrived, Porcinus gave the appropriate orders to get men back to what needed to be done, as little as it may have been. Nothing really left to do but clean up the mess, he thought bitterly.

Urso's suggestion had proven to be a smart one, because not only did Drusus and his officers see the carnage in the forum of Veldidena, the young commander ordered that the entire army march past the bodies, in order to see for themselves the barbarity of this enemy. Porcinus wasn't sure if the young nobleman had thought this through for himself, if it had been suggested to him by a more experienced man like Quirinus, or it was just a happy accident, but the result was the same; the complaining about the futility of trying to catch these Rhaeti, which had been steadily growing, became much less pronounced. That didn't mean the men still weren't frustrated, as Ovidius was opining that very night in Porcinus' tent, but Porcinus was fairly sure that seeing the results of the Rhaeti butchery would quell the men's normal proclivity to grumble.

"We're marching drag tomorrow, so remind the men to have their neckerchiefs loose enough that they can pull them up if it gets dusty," Porcinus told Ovidius, who nodded his agreement.

"So, do you think we're ever going to catch any of these bastards? I mean, again?" Ovidius asked Porcinus, who only answered with a shrug.

"Well, I think between what happened when we caught that one band at Sebatum, and what they're doing to the settlers, they're going to keep running and hope we give up."

Even as he said it, Porcinus knew it was a ludicrous statement, and he was affirmed in that view by Ovidius, who dismissed the idea with a snorting laugh.

"As if that would happen," his Optio retorted.

Porcinus couldn't suppress a laugh himself, and just shrugged.

"Well, it was a thought."

"Any news about the other thing?"

The moment the question came, Porcinus understood that this had been the real purpose behind Ovidius' visit to his tent that night. He also knew that it wasn't just a case of Ovidius being nosy; he was being pestered by the rankers, who were just as interested as the

Centurions of the 8th Legion as to who would be named as their permanent Primus Pilus.

"No," Porcinus sighed. "Nothing yet, other than Volusenus is doing his best to run the Legion and show Drusus he's the best choice."

"Drusus?" Ovidius regarded Porcinus with a cocked eyebrow, his skepticism unmistakable. "What does Drusus have to do with this? He's too young to make a decision like that. I'm sure Quirinus is going to be the one who Augustus is going to listen to, not Drusus."

"I wouldn't be so sure about that," Porcinus replied, but without any real conviction.

In fact, if he had been pressed, he couldn't have given any solid arguments supporting his reasoning; it was a feeling, nothing more, that young Drusus was figuring prominently in the Princeps' plans for Rome and her future.

After moving north from Sebatum, following the Rhaeti to Veldidena, the trail went cold, resulting in several frustrating days spent in a camp erected a short distance to the west of Veldidena, along the Aenus River. Despite appearances, however, Rome and her armies weren't sitting idly, waiting for something to happen. While Drusus had his cavalry *ala* scouring the rugged country to the north and west, word arrived by courier that Drusus' brother, Tiberius, in command of the other two Legions, was now approaching from the north, through Cisalpine Gaul. Finally, it appeared that the Rhaeti would run out of room to maneuver, and would be brought to ground. On the fourth day in camp, Lysander came hurrying back from the *praetorium* with news that a courier had arrived while the Thracian was delivering the daily report.

"I had already delivered the report, but I decided that you'd want to know what the courier was about," Lysander told Porcinus, the slave still slightly out of breath from his run.

"That was good thinking, Lysander," Porcinus agreed, secretly amused at the Thracian's not-so-subtle attempt to win some sort of favor from his master.

Regardless of the motive, Porcinus was indeed grateful. It was yet another lesson he had learned from his father, the wealth of information that could be gathered from those in the lowest places in the Roman army pecking order.

Clearly pleased by the praise, Lysander continued, "The courier was from one of the *ala*. They've picked up sign of the band we were trailing. They've joined up with another band, and Decurion Camillus estimates that the two groups total more than two thousand warriors."

Lysander stopped, and Porcinus assumed he was catching his breath, but after a moment, the slave still remained silent.

"Is that all, Lysander? Did the courier not give any idea where they were headed?" Porcinus' tone was gentle, but Lysander's face still flushed.

"Oh, er...yes, master. I'm sorry," he replied. "But, yes, it appears that they're now heading northwest. Apparently, the reason we lost their trail is because they followed the Aenus up into the mountains..."

"Yes, I know that." Porcinus' patience was beginning to wear thin. "That's why we've been sitting here, because we lost their trail."

"Yes, master. Sorry." Lysander's face, which had returned to its normal coloring, darkened again. "But the reason we lost the trail is because there's a very narrow pass that leads over those mountains into the country on the other side. According to what I heard the courier say, the trail is literally in the shadow of those peaks we can see off to the west and is very hard to find. He said that Camillus suspected this to be the case, but personally, I just think they got lucky and stumbled on it. You know how those cavalrymen like to exaggerate..."

"Lysander." Porcinus' tone was quiet, but his slave knew his Pilus Prior well enough to know that this was when he was close to losing his temper which, while rare, wasn't something that Lysander was willing to endure.

"Yes, master. A thousand apologies. But the point is that this trail is passable only to cavalry, or lightly armed men on foot. There's no way that the army and all its wagons can negotiate it."

"So we're going to have to find another way around," Porcinus finished, but Lysander shook his head.

"No, we did have to, but Camillus has already found a way. It will add a day to the pursuit, but now that he's found the Rhaeti, he promised our Legate that he wouldn't lose sight of them again. The courier knows the alternate route."

Even as Lysander was finishing, there was a blast from the *bucina*, the horn used to relay commands within a camp. The series of notes that sounded now summoned all the senior Centurions to the *praetorium*.

As Porcinus rose and grabbed his *vitus*, which no self-respecting Centurion ever left his tent without, he told Lysander, "Go alert the Centurions to get the men ready to break camp. I have a feeling our young commander isn't going to want to wait until morning to get going."

Before he exited the tent, Porcinus stopped and looked over his shoulder.

"And, Lysander, thank you for warning me. The Fourth is going to be the first Cohort ready because of you. I won't forget that."

He didn't wait for an answer, but Lysander's smile was enough.

Just as Porcinus had predicted, Drusus had called all the Pili Priores to give the order to break camp, immediately and without the usual work of filling in the ditches and burning the towers that was standard procedure.

"We're already going to lose a day by taking the long way around. I don't want to delay any more than we must," was how he explained it to the Centurions.

This made perfect sense, and Porcinus was one of those whose head nodded in agreement and approval. There was little more to be said, and the Centurions were dismissed to their duties. Despite himself, Porcinus couldn't help feeling a little smug in the knowledge that Ovidius had already begun the process of rousing his Century, and the other Centurions the rest of the Fourth Cohort. That feeling was only intensified when the Fourth Cohort was the first to be formed up, their tents already struck and their stakes recovered, with everything packed on the Cohort mules. Normally discouraging such displays, for a number of reasons, this time, he indulged his men by allowing them to make good-natured taunts and jeers at their comrades in the other Cohorts, who took it with varying degrees of grace. Not surprising Porcinus in the least, the one man who seemed to take the fact that his own Cohort wasn't leading the way badly was the Secundus Pilus Prior, Volusenus, who glowered at Porcinus, making no attempt to hide his anger. Which, also unsurprising to Porcinus, he took out on his own Legionaries, bashing any of them within reach with his *vitus* as they scrambled to take their place in the formation. As was usual, the Cohort designated to lead the march – this day, it was going to be the Fifth Cohort of the 13th – was lined up and ready to march out what had been the front gate. Because of this, the 8th, being the second Legion in the order of march, was forming up in the area of the forum, where the men occupied themselves waiting for the order to begin by watching the *praetorium* being taken down, the sections of which were too big to go on mules and instead packed in wagons. The *praetorium* of a Roman army camp was always the first thing erected and the last thing struck, without exception, and Porcinus idly wondered why this was so. Like so much of life in the army, the origins of this custom was lost to men of Porcinus' era, going so far back that there was nobody alive who could possibly remember how it had come about. It was the same thing with the ditches, walls, towers, and stakes used for the parapet that were created and thrown up every day on the march, again almost without exception. In fact, Porcinus tried to pass the time waiting for the *bucina* to sound trying to think of the times on campaign where the Legions hadn't created a camp, and the only time he could recall was in Parthia. Just the thought of that campaign, his first and still the most brutal and trying of his career, made him shiver as he thought of it. Fortunately, the call to begin the march sounded, yanking him from a place that was painful to think about. While the Parthian campaign was famous throughout the army, and any man who could say he had been part of it was given a measure of respect over and above what they might have earned on their own, for Porcinus it had been his initiation into a world that he had dreamed about ever since his adoptive father had first shown up on his family farm, arriving from the conquest of Gaul, which was all people talked about in those days. Except, like with so many things, what the young Gaius had imagined, and the harsh, brutal, and bloody reality were so different that it was hard to reconcile the two ideals in his mind. Still, it had marked the beginning of what was a promising and fruitful career in the Legions, one that he wouldn't have traded for anything.

Because of the relatively late start, Drusus and his army didn't cover their normal twenty-five miles, but did manage to cover almost fifteen before stopping to make camp. Where two branches of the source of the Aenus met, instead of continuing to the west, following one of them up into the mountains like the Rhaeti had done, Drusus' army turned north, following a track that led up to a pass that, while narrow, was still wide enough for the army to traverse. It was just on the other side of that pass where the army made camp. Continuing the next day, they headed on a northwesterly course before, using a narrow valley found by their scouts, they turned to the west again. Even as they marched, mounted couriers came galloping by Porcinus and his Cohort, either heading for where the command group was located near the front of the column, or in the opposite direction, carrying messages and instructions to the detachments presumably out scouring the area for the Rhaeti. Very quickly, on the second full day of marching, word filtered down to Porcinus, through Lysander, that the enemy had been spotted, and that they appeared to be heading in the direction of a large lake.

"According to what I heard, this lake is almost entirely surrounded by mountains, except for a spot where the Rhenus leaves it at the southern end of the lake," Lysander explained during a rest stop. "The Decurion's report said that it appears that the band we're following is meeting up with at least one more band."

As it happened, Porcinus had called an impromptu meeting of his Centurions and Optios, gathering them out of earshot of the men of the Cohort, who nevertheless tried very hard to listen in, without appearing to be doing that very thing. This was such a common occurrence that it didn't rate comment, but Porcinus had learned early on to hold these meetings even farther away than what might be considered a safe distance. Lysander's news unsurprisingly unleashed speculation on the part of Porcinus' Centurions about the meaning of this new piece of information. It was Corvinus who supplied the most likely reason.

"I bet they're going to make a stand, using the lake at their back to keep from being surprised. And if what Lysander heard is correct, they'll use that open ground, with the river on one flank and these mountains that are supposed to be there on the other."

Even as this was immediately accepted by the others, Porcinus noted with quiet amusement Urso's displeased expression, which he tried to hide with little success. He wanted to be the one to say that, Porcinus thought, so that the others would look at him the way they're looking at Corvinus.

"Well, more fools them is all I can say," scoffed Aulus Petrosidius, Urso's Optio and, from everything Porcinus had observed, a man cut from the same cloth as his direct superior. "It doesn't matter what kind of ground they pick, we'll crush them!"

Although Porcinus agreed with the assessment, he didn't care for the careless tone Petrosidius adopted, also understanding that the Optio was saying this as much to impress Urso with his eagerness to get stuck in as any other motive. The problem was that his words were at odds with his actions; from everything that Porcinus had seen and heard, Petrosidius wasn't the most avid when it came time for the actual fighting, always hanging near the rear of his Century, and quick to volunteer for messenger duty. Not that this wasn't technically what an Optio's duties were, but during his years under the standard, Porcinus had witnessed that there were men who adhered to the letter of the regulations with more zeal than others. Petrosidius was one of those men, and it was because of this trait that, of all the Optios in his Century, he was last on Porcinus' mental list as being worthy of advancement.

"That's certainly true, Petrosidius," Porcinus interjected, stopping the Optio, who was clearly warming to the subject of wading in the blood and guts of their enemy. "But we want to crush them and have as many of us as possible live to see another sunrise, neh?"

Petrosidius flushed, but whatever sharp retort he might have uttered was tempered by the knowledge that this was his Pilus Prior, and as soft as he may have been, according to Urso, at least, he was still his commanding officer.

"You're absolutely right, Pilus Prior." Urso came to his Optio's rescue, not wanting Petrosidius to say something stupid. "Whatever costs us the least in lives is the best way to go about it." Turning back to the matter being discussed, he addressed Lysander. "Did you hear anything more about this force Tiberius is supposed to be bringing? Any idea how close they are?"

Lysander shook his head.

"No, master. I haven't heard anything about that."

Whatever questions or discussion this answer would have engendered was cut short by the *bucina* call, signaling the end of the break.

"All right, you lazy bastards! On your feet!"

Some of his Centurions might have thought Porcinus was soft, but the tone and volume that issued from him, along with the swipes of the *vitus* aimed at a couple of men who were a bit too leisurely for his taste, would have earned the hearty approval of his adoptive father.

As they followed a very narrow valley, a fair amount of what passed for level ground was taken up by a raging torrent, slowing the army's progress. The country through which they were passing had a rugged beauty, with the towering peaks on either side of their line of march still covered in snow, despite the fact it was now early summer. If it hadn't been for the difficulty of traversing such terrain, with the men reduced to a narrow front along a track that was barely wide enough for one wagon to pass through, Porcinus would have marveled at the beauty of it. It also reminded him of the worst part of the Parthian campaign, struggling across the shoulder of the huge Mount Ararat, where he had almost died when his then-close comrade, a veteran named Vulso, had slipped and fractured his skull. It had been in the midst of a howling blizzard and, over the years, Porcinus had often wondered if a similar event had happened later in his career, after he had been seasoned and endured the hardships that came with marching more than a single season, if he would have done the same thing. Such speculation was pointless, he knew; still, he couldn't stop himself from letting his mind go in that direction. In Parthia, he hadn't hesitated, leaving the formation to dash down the icy slope that had caused Vulso to slip and fracture his skull, but in his haste to rescue his friend, put both of them in danger. The result was that for a period of time that even now Porcinus couldn't determine the length of, he had clung desperately to a bare rock with one hand, while clutching Vulso with the other. Because of the raging wind, none of the men trudging by heard his shouts for help. At least, that was what they all had claimed, something that Porcinus had long suspected wasn't necessarily the case, although he didn't begrudge anyone for worrying about their own survival at that moment. Still, by the time he summoned the strength to drag himself and Vulso back up the slope to the narrow trail, the once-vast army of Marcus Antonius had marched by, leaving the pair behind. Vulso hadn't regained consciousness, forcing Porcinus to sling his tentmate over his shoulder and stagger along the track, with the extremely faint hope of surviving the conditions long enough to get back to the relative safety of the camp the army would make at the end of the day. Not surprisingly, at least to himself, Porcinus' strength had finally given out, and he had collapsed, but not before hollowing out a space in the snow that provided a modicum of shelter. Very quickly, he and Vulso were covered by snow, where Porcinus lapsed into a state of semi-consciousness, only roused by the sound of approaching horses, and he somehow found the strength to stand erect, scaring both animals and riders, but enabling rescue of both him and Vulso. Although he had received no official decoration for his act; in fact, he was forced to endure one of the worst tongue-lashings of his career from his Primus Pilus, who administered it not as a Centurion but a badly frightened uncle, Porcinus' act had won him a reputation among his comrades for extreme bravery and willingness to risk his life for a friend. Unfortunately, his efforts had been in vain; Vulso never regained consciousness and died a few days later. These were the kinds of thoughts that occupied Porcinus as he occasionally glanced up at the massive peaks above him and his men, slowly drawing to what they all hoped would be the decisive encounter with the Rhaeti.

The track they followed to the west finally emptied out into a wider valley, at a point almost a full day's march south of the shore of the large lake. By the time Drusus and the army reached this point, all doubt about where the Rhaeti were heading, and their intentions, was removed. The band of warriors they had been following had linked up, not with one or two other bands, but four different groups, bringing their numbers up to more than ten thousand warriors, according to the scouts. As confident as the men of Drusus' army were, these numbers were daunting, particularly when it was learned that whoever was commanding this combined army had picked his ground very well indeed.

"There's another river that runs into the Rhenus at an angle that creates a barrier," Quirinus, acting in Drusus' stead for this briefing, announced to the senior Centurions the night they reached the wider valley. "So that in between the Rhenus, this river, the lake, and the mountains, they've got a very strong position. We can't flank them because of the Rhenus and the mountains, and they're entrenching on the other side of that river, which we'll have to cross to get to assault their position. It's not deep, and it's got a rocky bottom, but it's more than a hundred paces wide, according to the scouts, so it will slow the men down some."

The second in command of the army paused for a moment to let the Centurions digest this and, as he expected, none of them showed any happiness at the prospect of leading their men against a defended position with these kinds of aids. It wouldn't stop them; every one of them knew that and none held any doubt about success. But unless the Romans could offset these advantages in some way, it was likely to be a very bloody business, and Quirinus smiled thinly at the sight of the men looking at him, half-hopefully and half-resigned to the idea that no such help was forthcoming.

"However," he finally said, drawing out the word as if savoring the sudden change of expression and posture that swept through his audience. "They're not the only ones with a trick or two up their sleeves. In fact, that's where our commander is at this moment, working out the details of a little surprise we're going to be springing on these savages."

A current of pleased surprise rippled through the Centurions, but as Quirinus anticipated, their collective expressions became expectant as they waited for him to divulge what was in the works. Despite their obvious question, Quirinus responded with a shake of his head.

"Unfortunately, I can't divulge what that surprise is. To anyone," he added forcefully, casting a glance at the two Primi Pili, both of whom gave every appearance of being disposed to argue this point. For his part, Frontinus was willing to take this admonishment at face value, acutely aware that his status was temporary and very much in doubt. His counterpart, Sextus Traianus, however, wasn't as willing to be put off in this manner, and opened his mouth to argue.

Seeing this, Quirinus' expression hardened, unwilling to countenance this sign of disobedience, snapping, "That is final, Traianus. No exceptions. Until our commander deems it appropriate, the nature of this…wrinkle we're working on will remain confidential. Is that understood?"

Although Traianus seemed intent on continuing to dispute this, he saw Quirinus' expression and, wisely, shut his mouth before anything came out, responding only with a curt nod. By regulation and custom, this was a sign of disrespect at the very least, but Quirinus had been leading men for quite some time, and was wise enough to know when ignoring such signs of disobedience was the best course, and this was one of those. Satisfied he had made his point clear, he dismissed the Centurions, telling them as they departed that they could be expecting orders to move towards the enemy the next morning.

"I don't know what the plan is, but I hope it's a good one, because there's a lot of those bastards waiting for us," Pacuvius said when Porcinus informed his Centurions during his briefing later that evening, held in his tent.

"If you wanted to live forever, you shouldn't have joined the Legions." Corvinus' words were mocking, but his tone was sufficiently playful, and just as Porcinus had hoped when he instructed him, the laughter in the tent was hearty and dispelled the mood created by the news of what awaited them.

Once the mirth had dissipated, Porcinus turned their attention back to the matter at hand.

"Whatever Drusus has in mind, what we do know is that we're going to be in action soon," he continued. "So I want an inspection of the men's javelins. Make sure the wooden pins are in good shape and don't need to be replaced. Also, check their shields to make sure the dampness hasn't warped the wood. We don't need anyone's shield falling apart on its own because someone was too lazy to wipe the moisture off it in the mornings like he's supposed to."

Pausing, he waited for questions, but when none were forthcoming, he dismissed the others, calling on Corvinus to stay behind. This wasn't unusual, so none of the others looked askance at their counterpart, with the exception of Urso, whose mind simply couldn't grasp that his Pilus Prior didn't have some deeper motive than spending time with another Centurion simply for the sake of friendship. Shooting a suspicious glance at Corvinus, he left without saying anything, Porcinus watching him exit the tent with a rueful shake of his head.

Corvinus wasn't blind to Urso's suspicions either, saying, "Is it just me, or did it just warm up a bit?"

Porcinus laughed, then waved to his friend to follow him into the second chamber of the tent, which was cut roughly in half by a partition. This part served as Porcinus' separate quarters, and as a Centurion and a Pilus Prior, it was larger than the one Corvinus occupied. Porcinus' quarters were a reflection of the man; tidy, but with a number of small touches that gave a keen observer some insight into its occupant's character. Sitting on his personal desk was a small portrait of Iras, which Corvinus thought was exceptionally well done. Nevertheless, it still didn't really capture Porcinus' wife's true beauty, something that Corvinus, with his reputation, was wise enough to refrain from commenting about. His Pilus Prior wasn't the suspicious, or from what he had seen, the jealous sort, but considering how Corvinus had never tried to hide his appetite for conquests of women, single or otherwise, the Hastatus Prior thought it best he keep his opinion to himself. Sitting down in the other chair, he accepted Porcinus' offer of wine, despite knowing that it would be heavily watered. If he had been in his tent, alone, the refreshment would be more potent, but he accepted his superior's abstemiousness with as much grace as he could. They sipped from their respective cups in companionable silence, before Corvinus decided to open the conversation.

"So, I know what the official word is, but unofficially; any idea what our great general Drusus has in mind for his master stroke?"

As usual, while Porcinus secretly enjoyed, and shared, Corvinus' irreverence, it still made him uncomfortable. Bitter experience, albeit secondhand through Pullus, had taught him that those that were socially superior to men like him and Corvinus tended to look rather dimly at the slightest hint of mockery or ridicule, even if it was in jest.

Still, he felt sufficiently safe within his tent to offer Corvinus a smile, although that was about all he could give his friend.

"No," Porcinus admitted, somewhat ashamed since he normally had a better idea of matters in the *praetorium*, thanks to Lysander, primarily. "I don't have a clue."

"Any guesses, then?"

Porcinus considered for a moment, then said with a shrug, "The only thing I feel fairly certain about is that it has to do with his brother, Tiberius. But exactly what, I really can't say. Just having him reinforce us before we face these bastards would be a help, but from the way Quirinus was talking, I think there has to be something more involved than just that."

"Maybe they've learned how to fly over these fucking mountains." Corvinus chuckled. "And they're going to drop on the Rhaeti out of the sky."

Porcinus laughed at the thought, but as it would turn out, Corvinus had come closer than either of them realized.

Despite being prepared for what they would encounter, the sight that greeted the army of Drusus was still sobering. For reasons that, again, nobody in the *praetorium* who knew would divulge, the young nobleman hadn't seemed very eager to close the remaining distance to the Rhaeti. In fact, the next day, they had marched barely half of the fifteen miles when Drusus ordered the halt, prompting a dull uproar of speculation. Men immediately began wagering on not only what it meant, but when they would do battle, since it appeared that their young general was losing his nerve. Quirinus was singularly unhelpful, tersely informing the Centurions that, while the moment of battle was approaching, it had still not arrived. This time, Traianus was joined by Frontinus in an attempt to pry more information from the second in command, but Quirinus refused to budge, finally losing his temper and ordering them from his sight. Therefore, the sighting of the Rhaeti host was delayed for a day, which, in Porcinus' opinion, exacerbated the consternation and unease that the men seemed to experience once they did come close enough to the lake and the Rhaeti position. Making matters worse was the fact that the Rhaeti commander was using the Romans' seemingly leisurely approach to his advantage by improving their position. Not normally known for their skill, or enthusiasm for that matter, for erecting static defenses, whoever was commanding this group of Rhaeti didn't seem to be cut from the same cloth as his fellow tribesmen. The natural advantages of the position he selected were formidable enough, but on the other side of the river from the Romans, he had somehow prevailed upon his warriors to dig a ditch that ran parallel to the riverbank. He had chosen to set up his defenses at a point where there was barely a mile between where the smaller river turned from its generally east-west orientation, to the north to feed into the lake. The distance from the riverbank closest to the lake and the ditch varied, from perhaps fifty paces to at least a furlong, but that was about the only weakness Porcinus could see in the position. Although the ditch itself wasn't huge; the surveying party, consisting of Drusus and the command group, the *praefecti fabrorum*, the Primi Pili and, of course, an armed escort, had reported that it was nowhere near the width and depth of that created for a Legion camp under normal condition, let alone that of Caesarian proportions. Still, it would slow down an assault, which was its primary intent. Drusus ordered their own camp to be built a little more than a mile away, so that as soon as they had the chance, the Centurions from both Legions trooped out the Porta Praetoria to go conduct their own survey. As was normal, Porcinus went first with Frontinus and the other Pili Priores, then later in the day brought his own Centurions out for an inspection. It was a solemn bunch that stared at the wall, created from the dirt of the spoil from the ditch, which was lined with Rhaeti warriors, essentially doing the same thing that they were, trying to get a sense of what their enemy had in store for them.

"This is going to be a right bastard of a job," Verrens muttered as Porcinus, his Centurions, and Optios slowly walked perhaps half the distance of the Rhaeti position.

Privately, Porcinus agreed with Verrens, and in fact, his Hastatus Posterior was just unconsciously echoing his Primus Pilus, since Frontinus had said almost exactly the same thing earlier. While it was true that a mile and a half, which was what the engineers had announced as the total distance of the ditch and wall, counting the part that curved almost all the way to the shore of the lake, was a lot of ground that had to be covered, even with ten thousand men, the reality was that there appeared to be three, or perhaps four points along the line where an assault was feasible. And the Rhaeti chief had already shown he knew what he was about, so Porcinus, like everyone else on the Roman side, assumed that the enemy understood that as well. It was also true that the Romans had one distinct advantage, aside from the Legions themselves, when it came to assaulting a fixed set of defenses, and that was their artillery. Although it was next to impossible to knock down a dirt wall, since the dirt of the wall just absorbed the rocks used as ammunition, while a stone or even wooden wall would crack or break under bombardment, the ballistae and scorpions would at least serve to force the Rhaeti to keep their heads down. This would help negate the problem of being under missile fire for at least part of the approach, although as Porcinus well knew, they would have to cease-fire once the Centuries got ready to throw up the ladders in order to avoid killing their own men. That was the idea, anyway, but like every other Centurion, Porcinus possessed enough experience to know that sometimes the enemy didn't cooperate, and there was always some intrepid slinger, archer, or javelineer who was willing to run the risk of being skewered by a scorpion bolt. All in all, Porcinus thought glumly, Verrens had summed it up perfectly. This was going to be a right bastard of a job.

That evening, a briefing was held in the forum of all Centurions and Optios. The forum was needed because, while the *praetorium* was a large tent, it couldn't accommodate 240 men. However, the forum was also problematic because it was out in the open, meaning that for as long as there had been a forum in a Roman army camp, Legionaries had contrived numerous ways to make sure they were within earshot. That meant that whenever possible, these meetings were actually held outside the camp, usually near one of the side gates, either the Porta Dextra or Porta Sinister. Because of the proximity of the enemy, this wasn't possible, so instead, Drusus ordered the provosts to cordon off the area, several paces beyond the edge of the forum, in an attempt to discourage eavesdroppers. This, Porcinus understood, was a futile gesture, something he knew from experience since, more times than he could count, he had been designated by his tentmates to be the ranker to sneak into a nearby tent to listen to what the Centurions and officers were discussing. Knowing what lay in their future was almost an obsession with men, of all ranks, which was understandable, particularly at moments like this. And while Drusus was indeed young, he was either very shrewd, or he had been given very good advice, although that only became apparent sometime after the fact. That evening, he gave no hint of dissembling, or withholding any information as he outlined the plan for the next day. Because, as he announced immediately once everyone was gathered, there would be no more delays; the Legions would be assaulting these walls the next day. When he thought about it later, Porcinus concluded that it was the youth of their general that emboldened what took place immediately after that announcement when, if he was being fair, Porcinus acknowledged was only the verbalization of the exact same thing that was running through all of their collective minds.

"What about your brother and the two Legions with them? Aren't we going to wait for them?"

There was a sudden silence as men who had been whispering to each other just a heartbeat before suddenly stopped, both because they also wanted to know and from shock that Traianus should commit such a breach of etiquette and discipline. Although he was as surprised, and uncomfortable, as he assumed his compatriots to be, Porcinus also noted that Traianus didn't seem the least bit worried, or apologetic. In fact, Porcinus realized, he looks as if he either already knows the answer, or has already been forgiven in advance. For his part, Drusus didn't seem to be taken aback, or uncomfortable, deepening Porcinus' belief that this had been arranged between the two of them. But why? he wondered, even as he listened intently for what the general had to say.

"The forces under my brother's command are very close by," Drusus said calmly, although he had dropped the volume of his voice a bit. "In fact, they will be arriving at any time now. They may be here in time to support the assault, but I can assure you all of one thing." Drusus paused, and despite himself, Porcinus felt his body leaning forward, just like the men around him. "You and your men won't have to worry about sharing in the spoils of victory, because no matter when they show up, I know that the army I am leading is more than up for this challenge, so the reward will be yours and yours alone!"

The resulting cheer was spontaneous, and loud, which was precisely the effect for which Drusus was looking. Even Porcinus, who could sense the artifice of the moment, added his voice to the chorus of shouts, but unlike his comrades, his cheering had nothing to do with the idea of not having to share in the profits that would accrue from the coming battle. Money was the least of his concerns.

Drusus continued the briefing, informing the Centurions in general terms the plan for the assault, while telling them that their written orders, with the detailed instructions, would be issued before nightfall. The briefing concluded with another round of cheering for the young general, and this time, Drusus did look surprised, and pleased. Porcinus walked back to his Cohort area, his Centurions and Optios with him, running down the list of items that had to be attended to before the next day. The Legion armorers would be opening up their shop to sharpen blades for those men who didn't attend to this chore themselves. Porcinus knew that his father had always done this himself, not trusting anyone with his treasured Gallic blade, and it was a habit that Porcinus decided to continue. With some surprise, and a sudden twinge in his heart, he realized that this would be the first time he would be performing what had become Pullus' ritual, carefully working the blade with a stone, using a few drops of oil. When he thought about how he had longed for that sword, Porcinus became sad, not really thinking through what that would mean. All he had known, from the moment he first laid eyes on it when Pullus had visited his farm, then through the years he had marched with his newly adoptive father, was that he wanted that blade. The fact that it was almost as legendary as the man who had first carried it was only part of his reason; the larger force behind his desire was that, in some small way, he would emulate and honor the man he admired and respected more than any other. But, now that he had it, he finally understood in a real and visceral way, the import of what it meant to carry this sword into battle. Not only was it the final, concrete sign that Titus Pullus no longer lived, it carried with it a huge burden to live up to, that of a man who always led from the front and never tasted defeat. This, he realized as he walked into his tent to retrieve the Gallic blade, was what it meant to be the heir of Titus Pullus.

Even before the sun had risen the next morning, the camp containing the Legions of Drusus was swarming with activity, and not all of it was devoted to the coming trial. Porcinus' day started with Frontinus informing him that his Cohort would be among the first Cohorts to assault the Rhaeti position, along with the First, and in even more of a surprise, the Sixth. Although it wasn't a regulation engraved on a bronze tablet like the other laws of Rome, it had been the custom for at least a century, once Gaius Marius had reorganized the Legions from their Velites, Hastati, Principes, and Triarii four-line organization into the Cohort and Century Legion, that the lowest number Cohorts were always the first into battle. When arrayed in the *acies triplex*, which Porcinus knew was his father's old general Caesar's favorite method of deployment, the First always anchored the right end of the first line. And while sometimes the order of the adjacent Legions were switched, so that it might be the Fourth next to the First, as had happened in the last battle, it was much rarer for the higher numbered Cohorts to be in the front line. Despite the fact this was going to be an assault and not a set-piece battle, the principle was still the same; it would normally have been the Second Cohort, along with the Third, instead of the Fourth and Sixth. At least, that was what the Secundus Pilus Prior was arguing with Frontinus, as Porcinus watched, slightly bemused, but also extremely interested in hearing why Frontinus had decided as he did. In this, he was to be disappointed, however, because the acting Primus Pilus refused to give Volusenus any reason, other than to say that his decision was final, and that the Secundus Pilus Prior needed to get his own Cohort ready, since they would be part of the second wave and would undoubtedly see action. Once he determined that there was nothing more forthcoming from Frontinus, who dismissed him with a wave, Porcinus headed back towards his Cohort area, only to be caught up by Volusenus, who had stalked after him.

"So how much did you offer him?" Volusenus made no attempt to hide his anger, or his scorn, staring at Porcinus in the gloom with unconcealed fury.

It took Porcinus a moment for the words to register, and his jaw dropped in astonishment.

"What? You don't think I offered him a bribe just to be the first over the wall, do you?"

Volusenus gave a mocking laugh.

"That's exactly what I'm saying, and don't bother denying it! Why else would it be your Cohort and not mine?"

Gaius Porcinus shared a number of traits with Titus Pullus, but a volcanic temper wasn't one of them. Normally, he was very slow to anger, but there were few things guaranteed to raise his ire more quickly than the kind of thing that Volusenus was charging him with now. As always, he was acutely aware that men like Volusenus still viewed his rise up the ranks as being a direct result of favoritism and the patronage of his adoptive father. He also understood that there was nothing he could do that would convince Volusenus and those of a like mind that he, in fact, belonged where he was, that while having Titus Pullus as his mentor certainly helped in some ways, in others it was just as much of a burden as it was an aid to his advancement. Like now, he thought bitterly, and despite the fact he knew his attention should be elsewhere, that there were more important matters to attend to than the pique of the Secundus Pilus Prior, he felt the slow, coiling burn of anger building deep in his gut.

"Maybe it's because my Cohort is better than yours, in every way," he said this quietly, but with an intensity that was unmistakable. "My men are better trained, they're tougher, and they're better led. That's why he picked us and not your bunch."

If Porcinus had slapped Volusenus across the face, it was unlikely he could have looked more shocked. But that was instantly replaced by rage, and Volusenus reached out to grab Porcinus by the left bicep, squeezing hard. As strong as his hands were, however, through his anger there was a bolt of uncertainty when there was no give in the other man's muscle, at all. It was as hard as iron and, for the first time, Volusenus realized that, while Porcinus didn't have the same musculature as his uncle, who Volusenus had served under as well, the younger man was tightly muscled, without an ounce of soft flesh. For his part, Porcinus didn't react strongly, making no attempt to pull his arm out of Volusenus' grasp.

"Let go of my arm. Now," was all he said, again quietly, but there was…something in his voice and, when Volusenus looked into Porcinus' face, that same thing was reflected in his eyes.

It was anger, but it was a cold, calculating type of anger, not the hot rage that Volusenus had been feeling, at least up until this moment. Suddenly, Volusenus glanced down to see that Porcinus' free hand was no longer empty, but was now holding that Gallic sword of his uncle. However, that wasn't what acted like a bucket of water drawn from one of the icy streams that bounded down from the snow-covered mountains being dumped over his head, dousing not only Volusenus' anger, but his nerve. No, it was what Porcinus was doing as they both remained, almost motionless, staring at each other with Volusenus still clutching Porcinus' arm that triggered in Volusenus a memory. A very painful, humiliating memory, in fact, when as a young, newly promoted Optio, he had done something very foolish. Lucius Volusenus was good with a sword; every one of his comrades said so, the best man in his Century. This had been when Titus Pullus was the Camp Prefect of the Army of Pannonia, and nearing the end of his storied career. But even then, despite having no need to do so, Pullus spent at least a third of a watch, every day, working the stakes with a *rudis*, the wooden training sword, just as if he was still a *tirone*. As Volusenus had watched him work one day, the older man stripped to the waist, displaying a body that, despite the toll of the years and countless battles, was still impressive to behold. Volusenus had decided that while the old man handled a sword fairly well, he himself was still the better man. And, it must be said, with a great deal of encouragement, in the form of taunts and teasing from his comrades, he had taken up a long-standing challenge to face the Camp Prefect in a mock duel. This challenge had been in place since before Volusenus even joined the Legions, when Pullus was still the Primus Pilus of the 10th Legion and, in fact, it dated all the way back to when he was a young Gregarius and had been chosen as his Century weapons instructor by his Pilus Prior, the great Gaius Crastinus. It was one of the first things that newly arrived Legionaries were told when they joined the Army of Pannonia, that at any time they felt up to it, they could challenge the Camp Prefect to see who was the better man. The fact that Volusenus had never personally seen anyone take up this challenge was certainly in the back of his mind, but between his own confidence and the pressure being put on him by his friends, the moment he uttered the idea aloud, there was really no graceful way he could back out.

The beating Volusenus received at the hands of a man thirty years his senior was still a memory that caused the Secundus Pilus Prior to cringe when he thought about it. And in the pre-dawn morning of this day, more than a dozen years later, the sight of Gaius Porcinus, motionless except for just the tip of his downward-pointed sword, which was moving in small but easy circles, brought that memory flooding back. Suddenly, Volusenus felt his body break out into a cold sweat, and he was acutely aware of a single, frigid drop trickling down between his shoulder blades, causing them to clench together involuntarily. In the space of a couple of heartbeats, no more, the pain of that day, both the physical pain from the cuts, bruises, and broken nose, and the emotional torment of being thoroughly humiliated in front of his closest friends, swept every vestige of anger from Volusenus' mind and heart. His hand jerked away from Porcinus' arm and his mouth opened, but no sound came out. Porcinus continued to stand there, motionless, except for the sword, which kept moving, and without any words being said, both men understood that something had passed between them that would stay there for the rest of their lives. And from that point forward, Volusenus would never view Porcinus in the same way, as a man who was there only by the favor of a superior. Suddenly, and still without saying a word, Volusenus spun abruptly about, and walked unsteadily away towards his own Cohort area, leaving Porcinus to stare after him. He didn't move immediately; he decided that it was a good idea to let his heart and breathing go back to normal before he faced his men with the news that they were about to earn their pay. Only when he was back to what passed for his normal, calm state did he sheath his sword, mainly so he didn't have to see his own hand shaking as he did so.

It was only when the time for dawn came and it didn't get any lighter that the men of the Legions realized their endeavor this day had been blessed by the gods. At least, that was what the camp priests were proclaiming about the thick fog that almost completely obscured everything but the closest objects. As his Cohort made their preparations, Porcinus observed that while the torches that lit the section of the camp wall nearest to him were barely visible, those farther down, or the ones that were permanently lit outside the *praetorium* were completely hidden by the thick veil of misty, wet fog. Whether or not the gods had a hand in this Porcinus somehow doubted, but what was certainly true was that this helped the Roman cause immensely. At least, he amended, it will help, once we start the assault. At that moment, however, as men made their final preparations and the *bucina* sounded the call for assembly to march out of the camp, the fog made matters decidedly more difficult.

"Hurry up, ladies! You know I expect you to be in formation before the second blast of that damn horn, not the third! I don't give a fuck if you can barely see! Each of you should be able to find their spot blindfolded by now!"

Porcinus could clearly hear his Optio, and he could tell the general direction the sound was coming from, but between the quickly moving bodies and the gloom, he couldn't determine his exact location. By the gods, I can barely see the back rank of my own Century, he thought with some dismay. Still, he could see enough to know that his Century was all there, in formation and ready to start the day's work. Under normal circumstances, he could have simply looked to his left from his spot at the head of his Century to see the rest of the Cohort arrayed behind him, but on this morning, that was impossible. Consequently, he made his way down the Cohort street, and while he wasn't surprised to see that the rest of his Centurions and their Centuries were also formed up and ready, he was nonetheless pleased. Exchanging a quiet greeting with each of them, he quickly moved back to the head of his Cohort, and gave the order to march. They would pass through the forum, on the way to and out the Porta Praetoria, heading into battle, and as always, Porcinus found the thick, crunching tromp of hobnailed soles comforting. It meant that he wasn't going to be facing these Rhaeti alone, and as long as his boys were with him, he had no doubt that they would not only survive, they would prevail. Although he didn't think about it much, Porcinus was dimly aware that this was what it meant to be a professional soldier, marching in the Legions of

Rome, the quiet confidence that comes from knowing that one is the best. And they were; of that fact, neither Porcinus nor any man in his Cohort or the Legion held any doubt about. Today, they would prove it once more.

As they maneuvered into position, the fog turned out to be quite a challenge, and if the matter at hand hadn't been so serious, Porcinus would have found it somewhat amusing to see the normally well-drilled, well-oiled machine that were the Legions acting more like the mob of warriors they were about to face. Men were running into each other because Centurions found themselves marching their Centuries right into another Century, both of them trying to occupy the same space. To Drusus' credit, he quickly understood that the normal method of aligning each Century and Cohort by sight wasn't going to work, so he ordered the Tribunes, most of whom were actually older than he was, to guide each Century into their spot. Nevertheless, it took more than a third of a watch to perform what should take barely a third of that time, and that was just for the 8th. Not that it mattered that much; originally, Drusus' plan had called for the sun to rise on a Roman army already arrayed for battle, each Cohort of the assault element lined up across from the spot in the Rhaeti defenses to which they were assigned. But even after the sun had risen above the shoulder of the mountains to the east, it was barely visible as a pale, ghostly orb in the sky, casting a light so paltry that Porcinus was sure that he had seen nights with a full moon almost as bright. The difference was that the fog, reflecting the sun's rays, turned the entire world around them into a gray, indistinct mass, where the only recognizable shapes were the men of his Century, and parts of the Centuries on either side of his. Punctuating this strange sight were the normal sounds of a Legion about to go into battle; the *cornu* of each Cohort was sounding his call, while Centurions continued shouting orders, as the horses of the command group and Tribunes neighed and snorted, passing on the vibrating nerves transmitted to them by their tense and nervous riders. All in all, Porcinus thought this was already the strangest battle he had ever been a part of, and it hadn't even started yet! He was standing in his spot, with the Second Century of the First Cohort to his right. Whereas normally each Cohort aligned in a three-

Century front, with a Century behind each one, the orders for this day had specified a narrower but deeper formation front of two Centuries side by side. However, unlike the First Cohort, where Frontinus arrayed the Second next to his First, Porcinus had opted for a different formation. The second Century in the front line, to his immediate left, wasn't the Second, but the Fifth, led by Corvinus. As he had expected when he gave the order, Urso hadn't liked this at all, but in a rare show of temper, Porcinus had cut him off short before he could splutter more than a couple of words in protest. It was only a few moments later that Porcinus admitted to himself that his confrontation with Volusenus was still running through his veins, and his blood had been up, so that he felt slightly ashamed at his show of temper. Now, as he and his men stood and waited for the sound of the *cornu* that would signal the next phase of the plan, the beginning of the artillery barrage, he found his mind going back to his argument with the Secundus Pilus Prior. Behind him, his men were talking quietly to each other, and there were even a few laughs, which Porcinus knew was a good sign. Although, he thought, they aren't laughing nearly as much as they had been the last time they faced these *cunni*. But that was to be expected, since this was an entirely different proposition than routing and chasing a disorganized, poorly led and highly outnumbered mob. Using his ears more than his eyes, Porcinus strained to try to determine exactly where matters stood with the deployment of the rest of the army. From what he could determine, it sounded like the 8th was finished, but now the Tribunes were busy guiding in the 13th. Judging that there was still some time to go, Porcinus walked over to where Corvinus was standing. His friend was essentially doing the same thing Porcinus had been, but had actually untied his helmet and lifted one earpiece as he cocked his head, intent on trying to hear anything useful.

"You look like an idiot doing that," Porcinus commented, prompting a mock scowl from Corvinus.

"You're just jealous because you didn't think of it first," Corvinus retorted.

Porcinus laughed, but his heart really wasn't into the normal banter that they both normally enjoyed so much, particularly before a trying moment like this. Sensing this, Corvinus gave him a quizzical look, one eyebrow cocked as he waited for Porcinus to say what was on his mind. Porcinus, on the other hand, was struggling to come up with the proper way to broach a subject that, by rights, he shouldn't be bringing up with a Centurion of a lower grade. Under normal circumstances, Porcinus strongly discouraged the kind of gossip about other Centurions that some of his compatriots seemed to thrive on, and didn't normally indulge in it himself. This, he told himself, isn't a normal circumstance.

With that in mind, he finally blurted out, "I think I've finally figured out why Volusenus hates me so much."

If Corvinus was surprised at Porcinus' words, his face didn't show it. He didn't respond immediately, however, just looked at his Pilus Prior, waiting for him to continue. At last, Porcinus did, describing the scene that had taken place earlier that morning between him and Volusenus, including what had led up to it.

"He thinks you bribed Frontinus?" Corvinus asked doubtfully. "That's what he said?"

"Exactly that," Porcinus confirmed. "But I think I finally know what the real source of the problem is."

"I always thought it was just because he's a bitter *mentula*. And he thinks you're soft," Corvinus added helpfully, causing Porcinus to laugh again, even though he didn't particularly want to.

"That's part of it, but that's not the cause. In fact, I don't think it has as much to do with me as it does my father."

For a moment, Corvinus didn't appear to understand and, in fact, he was trying to determine how it was possible for Volusenus to have any knowledge of Porcinus' father. All Corvinus knew of him was that he had been a farmer in Baetica. Then he remembered, and his face cleared.

"Ah. You mean Titus Pullus."

"Yes. I should have said 'my adoptive father,' but yes, that's who I'm talking about."

Corvinus frowned, still not seeing any connection.

"But what does Pullus have to do with Volusenus hating you? You mean, because he thinks you're in the Centurionate because of Pullus greasing the wheels?"

Something in the way Corvinus said this caused Porcinus to turn and study his friend's face intently, his own expression suddenly growing impassive.

Porcinus didn't speak for a moment, then asked quietly, "Is that what you think, Gnaeus?"

Corvinus looked startled, and if it wasn't genuine, he was doing a good job of acting like it, Porcinus thought, the other man shaking his head.

"By the gods, no," Corvinus exclaimed. "I've known you a long time, and I've seen you in action, so no, I know that you're where you belong on merit, not because of favor." Porcinus' expression softened, but Corvinus felt compelled to add, "But you know that there are men who think that. You do realize that, don't you?"

Porcinus nodded.

"Yes," he admitted, a bit grudgingly. "I know, and I know that Volusenus is one of those, but I think it goes deeper than that with my father. Frankly, it was something I had forgotten, but today, when he grabbed my arm…"

"He did what?" Corvinus asked sharply, his face registering shock. "He physically put his hands on you?"

Again, Porcinus answered with a nod. Corvinus let out a low whistle. What Volusenus had done in laying a hand on another Centurion was forbidden not just by regulation, but by a deeply held and long-standing custom. It was almost unthinkable for a Centurion to do something of this nature, for the simple reason that if it was allowed to happen, without any kind of punishment, it wouldn't be long before the senior leadership of the Legion would be settling disputes by brawling, or worse. A Centurion's person was considered sacrosanct, even by other Centurions of all ranks, and Volusenus' action in grabbing Porcinus' arm told Corvinus more about the depth of the Secundus Pilus Prior's enmity towards Corvinus' superior than anything Porcinus had said.

"What did you do?"

"I…I'm not sure," Porcinus admitted, for the first time looking a bit unsettled himself. "All I really remember was him grabbing me. Then, the next thing I knew, he had let go."

"Probably because he realized what he had done," Corvinus suggested.

Now Porcinus' face took on what to Corvinus seemed to be an almost sheepish expression, as if he were a child caught trying to filch a candied fig.

"I don't think so," Porcinus replied, pausing for a moment before finishing with, "I think it had to do more with the fact that I must have drawn my sword."

"You drew your sword?" A moment before, Corvinus would have sworn that he couldn't have been more surprised and shocked than he had been, at least until this moment now.

"I think so," Porcinus said with a shrug. "The truth is, I don't remember drawing it. I remember him grabbing me, then it was just…there, in my hand."

"Well, I can see why he let you go," Corvinus said with a muted chuckle.

It wasn't really funny, but in all the years he had known Porcinus, he had never seen him act in a manner that suggested he would do something like this and, frankly, Corvinus didn't know how else to react.

"It was more than the fact that I drew my sword," Porcinus said quietly. "I was doing something with the sword that's become a habit, I suppose. It's something I picked up from watching my fa…Pullus," he corrected.

Corvinus frowned as he thought for a moment, before replying, "I bet I know what it is. It's those circles you make, isn't it? That's what you were doing and that's what Volusenus saw."

"Exactly!" Porcinus was happy that he didn't have to explain, that Corvinus had finally known what he was talking about. "When Volusenus looked down and saw me doing that, he turned white. It was like he'd seen a *numen*," Porcinus was referring to the disembodied spirits that all Romans knew haunted particular places, like forests. "And I realize now that he had. Or at least," he amended, "what he saw brought back a memory that was very powerful."

The dawning of realization crossed Corvinus' features as his eyes lit up.

"By the gods, Gaius! If you're talking about what I think you're talking about, then that's exactly what happened. I'd forgotten all about that myself."

"Like I said, so did I. But Volusenus clearly hasn't."

"Nor would he," Corvinus agreed. "I didn't see it personally, but I certainly heard about it. And I saw him afterward. His nose looked like a plum!"

"I didn't see it either," Porcinus said, "but the gods know I fought my father enough times to see him make those damned circles. And it was always when he was toying with me, about to teach me a real lesson about who the best man with a sword was. It got to the point where, when I saw him starting to draw those circles with his sword, I wanted to just throw mine down and call for mercy."

Porcinus finished this with a laugh, but it was one tinged with memories both sweet and painful as he remembered the harsh lessons dealt him by Titus Pullus. What had happened to Volusenus wasn't unusual; over the years, many men had tried to best Pullus, but none had succeeded, and with every victory, Pullus' reputation had grown. Which was exactly what Titus Pullus wanted to happen; as much as Porcinus loved and respected his father, he also was honest enough to acknowledge that humility simply wasn't part of Pullus' makeup. It was as if, even in the last days of his career, Pullus was trying to prove himself to others, somehow convincing himself that other Legionaries doubted him and his ability with a sword. But what was out of the ordinary was the severity of the beating Volusenus had taken at the hands, or *rudis*, of the Camp Prefect. What Volusenus hadn't known, and Porcinus did, was that he had caught Prefect Pullus at a particularly bad time, not very long after the death of Pullus' wife Miriam in childbirth, and immediately after the campaign conducted by Marcus Crassus' grandson by the same name. During that campaign, Pullus had lost the little finger of his left hand, bitten off in a savage fight with a gladiator named Prixus who had been one of Crassus' bodyguards. But it was also that Volusenus, undoubtedly goaded by his friends, had been loudly proclaiming that, in essence, a new champion had arrived, and that once Volusenus was through, men wouldn't be talking about Titus Pullus as the best man with a sword in the Legions any longer. Of all the things a man could say, Porcinus knew from experience and observation that this would bring out a side of Titus Pullus that was terrible, yet awesome to behold. What Porcinus knew, however, that nobody else, with perhaps the exception of Pullus' best friend and longest companion, Sextus Scribonius, was aware of, was how badly and deeply scarred Pullus was, and it had nothing to do with the marks crisscrossing his body. When Miriam died, something in Titus Pullus had died as well; the softer, kinder side of the man had withered away, to be replaced by the iron that had filled the rest of his soul. It was out of this pain that the beating of Volusenus emanated, and created a memory that the Secundus Pilus Prior would never forget, no matter how hard he tried. And, in his confrontation with Porcinus, the humiliation and hurt from that episode had come roaring back to him, shaking him to his very core. However, it also marked a turning point in how Volusenus viewed Porcinus, something that would only become apparent later.

Finally, the expected signal from Drusus' personal *cornicen* came, sounding the notes that gave the men who were manning the artillery pieces the order to begin their barrage. The sound also served to break the moment between Porcinus and his friend, with the Pilus Prior returning to his own Century, but only after offering his hand and wishing Corvinus luck. This was in itself, something of a ritual, and soldiers by nature are a superstitious bunch, making it unthinkable for either man to skip this small and private moment. In fact, Porcinus had already done the same with his other Centurions, for the same reason, but while he normally did so in order, the reason Corvinus was last went all the way back to the very first time Gaius Porcinus led his Cohort in battle, some three years before. For reasons neither man remembered, Corvinus was elsewhere when his new Pilus Prior came to offer his wishes, making Corvinus the last man instead of the penultimate as Porcinus had intended. Yet, since the battle that day - from what Porcinus recalled, it was an action against the Daesitiates - he had been loath to change back to what would be considered the normal order. What Porcinus did remember was that Corvinus had made some comment that was both witty and helped to dispel the almost paralyzing case of nerves that Porcinus had been suffering from up until that moment. Had that been the start of their seemingly unlikely friendship, Porcinus wondered. Shaking his head, as if to banish the line of thought his mind had chosen to pursue at this moment, he was experienced enough to know that this wasn't uncommon. At least as far as he was concerned, his mind tended to stray off in odd directions at the most unlikely moment, like this one, as he and his men waited for the command to advance. Although he never asked anyone else about it, what Porcinus was experiencing was, in fact, very common among his comrades, even if the subject matter varied from one man to another. For some, it was recalling some escapade of carousing in the past; for others, it was reminding themselves to take care of what was in reality a mundane and unimportant piece of business, like buying a new lamp because the one they had was leaking oil. Whatever it was, the minds of men about to go into battle did what they could to protect themselves by avoiding dwelling on all the horrible things that could possibly happen, using memories or odd pieces of unresolved business as fodder for the imagination instead. Which was why, when the deep, bass notes of the *cornu* finally did come rolling through the fog, Porcinus physically jerked in surprise. Chagrined at this display of nerves, he risked a quick glance over his shoulder, but thankfully, between the fog and the fact that his men were occupied with their own thoughts, none of them had noticed. Suppressing a chuckle at his behavior, for what was likely the hundredth time, Porcinus reached down and pulled his sword partway out of the sheath, checking to make sure that when the time came, it wouldn't stick. Then, once the third and final call came, he filled his lungs to bellow, along with the other Centurions of the front line, the command to step forward. With a slight ripple that was unavoidable when a large number of men began moving, no matter how well trained and disciplined they may have been, the assaulting Cohorts began moving in the direction of the Rhaeti position. The assault had begun.

It was no more than a hundred heartbeats later that Porcinus was struck by a thought that was both worrying and, at the same time, absurdly amusing. I wonder if we're even headed in the right direction, he mused, although he continued in the same direction without faltering. Glancing over to his right, he was reassured that the First Cohort was still there and visible, but his relief was short-lived as, even as he watched, the left-hand Century started to disappear into the mist. He realized with a growing horror that the First was marching at a slightly different angle! The original plan had called for the two Cohorts to stay side by side, focusing on what would be a relatively narrow spot of the Rhaeti position. It had been selected both for the wall's distance from the rapidly running river, which Porcinus could hear flowing across his front, although he still couldn't see it, but also because the engineers had determined that there was a dip in the wall, effectively lowering it. From their vantage point when they were conducting their survey, they were able to determine that this wasn't due to an indentation in the ground; more likely, it was the Rhaeti charged with constructing this portion of the wall being lax with his warriors, allowing them to do more leaning than shoveling. It was well known by the Legions that the warriors of barbarian tribes like the Rhaeti despised manual labor, thinking it beneath them, so it was entirely plausible that the area where Porcinus and Frontinus' Cohorts were heading had a shallower ditch to go along with the lower wall. Nevertheless, Porcinus had stressed to his Centurions the strong likelihood that this was an illusion, or that the engineers had simply made a miscalculation. This was why the men of the Fourth Cohort were carrying more hurdles, the tied bundle of branches that would be thrown down into the ditch, as well as more wicker baskets filled with dirt that would be dumped onto the branches, than the engineers had estimated would be required. The hurdles and baskets had been evenly divided among the four trailing Centuries, which would be passed up through the ranks to the First and the Fifth, whose men would perform the actual act of filling in the ditch. In addition, there were two sections from each of the lead Centuries, who were tasked with carrying the ladders that would be used to scale the walls, and although the engineers had maintained that it wasn't necessary, Frontinus had insisted that the ladders be constructed taller than they needed to be. In short, everything possible had been thought of, and was another example of why the Legions of Rome were so feared.

Now, all the carefully laid plans seemed to be threatened because, with every step, the First Cohort was drawing farther away from the Fourth. This was worrying enough, but what compounded Porcinus' fear was his doubt about who was in error at this moment. He felt sure that he was maintaining the proper heading, but he also recognized he could be the one who had somehow changed the angle of his approach. When he had first realized what was happening, he had opened his mouth to shout a warning to alert Frontinus that something was amiss, but had stopped himself. With the fog so thick, the Romans had been handed one huge advantage, and that was in their ability to approach as closely as possible before the Rhaeti could pinpoint their exact position. He was under no illusion that the Rhaeti would be caught completely by surprise; he was sure, that at this moment, there were warriors lining the walls, straining their eyes in this direction, trying to determine exactly where the approaching lines were. They had undoubtedly heard the *cornu* calls and, in all likelihood, the front lines of the advancing Romans had approached to a point where the Rhaeti could hear the sounds of the advance. But shouting would pinpoint at least Porcinus' position more accurately than the general noise made by the sound of hobnails striking rock and the creak and rattle of leather and metal rubbing together. Consequently, Porcinus shut his mouth, clenching his fists in frustration, unsure what to do, although he continued to march, while his men continued to follow. Deciding that he had no choice but to carry on, at least until he reached the river, Porcinus forged ahead, the sound of water rushing over rock drawing ever closer. Finally, he picked out a change in the grayness, in the form of what looked like a dark line, and within a matter of a few more steps, Porcinus saw the width of the line extend to the point he could see the river. It wasn't until he was no more than twenty paces away that he could make out enough detail to give him an idea of what the crossing would be like, and he let out a soft curse. Despite the fact that he was half-expecting something of this nature, he was still disappointed to see that the crossing was going to be more challenging than they had been told. The river was swiftly running; that they could see beforehand from the scouting, but viewing from a distance, then being just a few steps away were two different matters. As planned, Porcinus called a quick halt by thrusting a clenched fist into the air, and behind him, he could hear his men come to a crashing stop, the odd pebble sent skittering across the rocky ground by caligae sounding very loud to Porcinus' ears. This was the very kind of sound that experienced warriors would know was unnatural, being very different from the background noise of the rushing river, and Porcinus' breath caught in his throat as he waited to hear some warning shout from the Rhaeti position. Straining to listen, trying to block out the sound of the rushing torrent, Porcinus could hear a buzzing sound that he knew from experience were men talking, telling him that the Rhaeti were truly out there, somewhere. After a moment, he allowed himself a sigh of relief; there had been no sudden shouts that would indicate alarm, telling him that so far, at least, the Rhaeti hadn't been alerted. Of course, he realized, this was about to change, because there was no way to muffle the sounds of hundreds of men splashing across this river. The best hope for the Cohort at this point, Porcinus realized, lay in the fact that crossing this river wouldn't take long, because the men would be at their most vulnerable once they waded into the water. However, his eye told him that this hope was, in all likelihood, a forlorn one, and he chided himself for hesitating. Regardless of how difficult it would be, this river had to be crossed; the problem of where the First Cohort was could wait until they got across. Even as this thought crossed his mind, he heard the unmistakable sound of men splashing into the river, upstream from him somewhere.

Looking over his shoulder, he called out just loudly enough to be heard, "Follow me. It's time to get wet."

Then he stepped into the river, gasping from the shock of the cold water as it went rushing around first his feet, then quickly rising up to mid-calf. He could feel the rocks under his feet shifting, confirming his worst fears that the footing wasn't composed of the smoothly rounded and flat stones that the engineers had insisted composed the river bottom. Their reasoning was sound enough; unlike the Rhenus, which was flowing in the opposite direction, this small river emptied into the large lake. By the time a river neared its end, the action of the water usually had smoothed out the stones that composed the riverbed. But this river was different, and although in that moment, Porcinus didn't put much thought into why, it had occurred to him that, because the mountains from which this river sprang were so near, it made it less likely that the bottom would be smooth. This was being confirmed as, within his first few steps, his foot slipped on an uneven and slippery rock, almost losing his balance and falling to the side. Although he caught himself, the swift current compounded the problem, but his troubles were just beginning. By the time he had gone twenty paces, the water was already just below his crotch, and he wasn't more than a third of the way across. Behind him, he heard the first rank of his men come splashing into the water, and he mentally began counting, even as he continued wading. He didn't get past ten before that sound he was dreading happened, as an alarmed shout reached his ears from somewhere to his front. Within the span of a dozen heartbeats, the Rhaeti on the walls were in full cry, and now that his men knew there was no need for silence, they began shouting their own challenges. Punctuating this was the sound of a heavy splash, followed by a shouted curse as one of his men lost his footing in the river. Porcinus was now halfway across, and he was dismayed that the water was now up to his waist, which, because of his height, meant that most of his men would be submerged up to their lower chests. The depth also made it even more difficult to keep his footing because of the current, so he supposed it was inevitable that, despite his care, he lost his balance when the rock under his left foot suddenly dislodged from its position. Instantly, he was submerged, fighting the panic that threatened to overwhelm him as he felt his body tugged downstream. Within the span of a heartbeat, his speed picked up tremendously, so that when his side struck a larger rock, while it stopped his momentum, it also robbed him of his breath. The water itself, which had been perfectly clear, was now murky from the movement of both his men and the men of the First Cohort upstream, making it impossible for Porcinus to get his bearings. Bouncing off the rock, he felt his body spin around, and the force of the blow caused him to involuntarily open his mouth in a gasp of pain, which was the worst thing he could have done, his mouth and lungs suddenly filled with icy water. I'm going to drown; this was the thought that came blaring into his consciousness, although the voice in his head was devoid of emotion, simply stating what had become an obvious fact. I'll never see Titus and Sextus grow up, I'll never hold Iras again, or kiss my daughters when they get married. And not because I had a sword thrust into my guts, but because I lost my balance and drowned in this river.

When he had a chance to reflect on the moment later, Porcinus concluded that those thoughts and images of never seeing his family again had provided whatever it was he needed to decide not to die. That, and the fact that Corvinus had appeared out of nowhere to grab his harness and yank him to the surface, he thought ruefully, although he was extraordinarily thankful that his friend was paying attention. There had been no chance at that time to properly thank Corvinus, who half-dragged, half-carried his Pilus Prior the rest of the way to the far side of the river, before dropping Porcinus to the ground and collapsing on his own. What Porcinus did remember was rolling over and retching violently, sure that half the river came spewing out of his mouth and nose. Taking several ragged gulps of air, Porcinus thought that he had never smelled or tasted anything so sweet. Unfortunately, the part of his mind that was detached from the ordeal and focused on his job forced him to stop enjoying the moment, and he climbed unsteadily erect, water still streaming from his tunic and armor. Corvinus had also regained his feet, but when Porcinus turned to his friend, intent on thanking him for the rescue, the sight that greeted him yanked another gasp from him. In one of those strange moments that occur in moments of great danger, Corvinus, who was facing Porcinus, had much the same reaction.

"You're bleeding!"

Both men had uttered the same words, at the same time, and they stared at each other in shock. How was it possible they had both been injured in the same spot, Porcinus wondered? Then Corvinus suddenly bellowed with laughter, confusing his Pilus Prior even more as he gaped at Corvinus, who was pointing at Porcinus' face.

"We're not bleeding," Corvinus gasped between laughs. "It's that fucking cheap dye we use for our crests. It's run out and down our faces!"

Porcinus touched his face, and when he drew his hand away, he saw that his fingers were covered in red. It took only an instant of inspection for him to see that this wasn't really the color of blood, but a slightly brighter red. One of the innumerable details that Augustus had changed about the army was the regulation that Centurions' crests had to be dyed red, changing it from the traditional black or white of the past. It was one of those things that, when one thought about it, made sense, since the horsetail crests of the men were still black, making it easier for a commander to pick out his Centurions. Of course, it didn't take long for one of the wags in the ranks to point out something that was equally as obvious, that it made the Centurions better targets, not only for the enemy, but for rankers with a grudge. Whatever the reason, the dye supplied to the Centurions for such purposes had immediately been cursed by the members of the Centurionate for its lack of fastness and tendency to fade quickly. Or, Porcinus thought ruefully as he took a corner of his wet tunic to wipe the dye from his face, while Corvinus did the same, to run when it got wet. While the two were thus occupied, their Centuries had managed for the most part to wade across, but although they had managed to do so without any man being swept away, when Ovidius, the last of Porcinus' Century to cross, came to find his Pilus Prior, it was to report that several men had lost their javelins and two men had lost their shields. While this was bad news, it was also not unexpected; when faced with a choice of using both hands to maintain balance, or be swept away, it wasn't uncommon for men to choose losing javelins. Losing a shield was more uncommon, but Porcinus knew that there was nothing gained by worrying about it now. By this point, he could see that both his and Corvinus' Centuries were across and fully formed up, their shields now uncovered and ready for use. Walking across the rocky riverbank, he and Corvinus resumed their spots, and Porcinus shouted the order to continue the advance towards the Rhaeti.

The first arrow came streaking out of the fog to skip and clatter harmlessly across the rocky ground, but it was quickly followed by another, then another. At first, the missiles landed well wide of the Cohort, hitting several dozen paces to the right of the First Century. That's where the First Cohort should be, was the thought that flashed through Porcinus' mind. At least he thought so, although he was forced to acknowledge that it was just as likely that he was the one to veer off course as Frontinus. They had been within earshot of each other as they crossed the river, but now, despite straining to hear, he could no longer even pick out the odd noise that might tell him they were still fairly nearby. It was as if the First Cohort had simply been swallowed up whole by the fog; for all Porcinus knew, that was the case all along the front. What if we're the only ones still about to assault the wall? This was a worrying thought, but he forced it from his mind, concentrating on peering into the gray veil ahead, hoping to catch a glimpse of the ditch at the very least, anything that might tell him exactly where he and his men were. Then, after perhaps a dozen more paces, something emerged from the fog off to his left that caught his eye. It was perhaps twenty feet beyond the last file of the Fifth Century, but when Porcinus determined what it was, he felt a flood of relief. It was nothing much, just the remains of what they had guessed was the foundation of a stone wall that was perpendicular to the line of the Rhaeti ditch. But there was no doubt about its identity, and more importantly, its location, because it was the only landmark of its type anywhere near the spot where Porcinus' Cohort was supposed to cross the ditch and assault the wall. At least we're in the right place, he thought, but whatever comfort that brought was immediately banished as the barrage of missiles that came hissing out of the mist started to shift, coming ever closer to the men of Corvinus' Century.

Before Porcinus could give the order himself, he heard Corvinus' voice ring out the command, "Shields up! And if any of you *cunni* get hit by these blind bastards, you're on a charge!"

There was some laughter at this, although it was muted by the shields that the men had raised above their heads. And, as Porcinus feared, a moment later came the first shout of pain as one of the arrows found a gap between shields, and what little humor remained was gone for the foreseeable future. Porcinus resumed his position at the front, thankful that at least they were past the rocky riverbank where the footing was better. There was still no sign of the ditch, and perhaps Porcinus could forgive himself for temporarily forgetting the distance from the river to the ditch, considering all that had transpired to this point. He didn't stop moving forward, understanding that now that the Rhaeti were aware of their general position, every moment spent in front of the walls increased the peril for his men, and the overall success of the assault. Unfortunately, it had become clear that Drusus had suspended the artillery bombardment soon after the order to advance, which meant that there was nothing to deter the Rhaeti archers from massing along the wall and raining arrows down on the heads of Porcinus and his men. Despite this fact, Porcinus didn't fault Drusus' decision, because as bad as it might get when they were finally spotted by the Rhaeti, having scorpion bolts and ballistae rocks slamming into the unprotected rear of his Cohort would be even worse. Walking steadily forward, Porcinus felt extremely vulnerable, both because of the difficulty seeing an arrow streaking in his direction because of the fog, which under the best of visibility was something of a challenge, but at that moment, the only protection he had was his *vitus* in his left hand. It was common practice for Centurions to pick up shields, except that would only happen when one of his Legionaries no longer needed it, usually because the man was dead or had been wounded and dragged to the rear to safety. And because two of his men were missing their shields already, he would have to wait even longer than normal. Even as this thought passed through his mind, in the very last space of time in which to react, his eye caught the blurring line of an arrow and, without any thought, he leaned his body slightly to the right, hearing the hissing sound of the missile pass by his left ear by no more distance than the span of a hand. His heart, which was already beating more rapidly than normal, but keeping a steady rhythm, suddenly leaped in his chest in a delayed reaction to his narrow escape. It was yet another lesson he had learned from Titus Pullus, that the best and really only way for a Centurion, in the most exposed position of the Century, to avoid being skewered was to not think about the fact that men were sending arrows in his direction.

"In situations like that, thinking will not only get you in trouble, it'll get you killed," Pullus had explained. "The best and only way to keep from being hit is to trust your body to know what to do. Just relax, and you'll be fine."

It was advice based on the experience of years spent as a Centurion, first of a Cohort, then of an entire Legion. Compounding matters, Pullus made a tempting target by virtue of his very size, because even now, after many years under the standard, Gaius Porcinus had never seen a Legionary the size of his father. In fact, he was just an inch shorter, meaning that he was the tallest man of not only the Centurionate, but almost of the entire Legion. However, while

Pullus had seemed to be almost as broad across the shoulders as he was tall, Porcinus was lithe in build, with a frame that never seemed to pack on extra pounds, no matter how hard he had tried early on to emulate his mentor. Porcinus still had an enormous appetite, but he had long since stopped the exercises that someone, he no longer remembered who, had prescribed for him to build bulk and muscle. And right at this moment, he was thankful that he was more narrowly built than Pullus, particularly after that last close call. More arrows went streaking past him, although none came as close as the one a moment before, but behind him, he could hear that some of the missiles were at the very least finding shields. The sound was much like a mallet striking a block of wood, yet when compared to the alternative, the wetter, sucking sound as the barbed tip struck flesh, it meant this was music to Porcinus' ears. Still, he knew that it couldn't last forever, and it was just as he finally saw the ditch looming across his front through the fog that he heard the second, dreaded sound. This time, there wasn't a shout or cry of pain, but a low groan, followed by clattering thud as a man, one of his boys, collapsed to the ground. From bitter experience, Porcinus knew that, at the very least, whoever had been hit was seriously wounded, most likely mortally.

"Give his shield to one of the men who needs it," he yelled over his shoulder, even as he offered a silent prayer for the fallen man.

The ditch was now clearly visible, meaning that the danger was about to become much greater, as the men of the assaulting Cohort came to a halt. Speed was now of the essence, and Porcinus moved from his spot in front of the Century to a position from where he could supervise the next phase of the attack. The first step was the men of the trailing Centuries, all of whom had successfully negotiated the river, with the exception of Verrens' Century, who had lost a man swept downriver, passing the bundles of hurdles forward to the men of the First and Fifth, who threw them down into the ditch. It was at this point, when Porcinus had done a brief inspection of the ditch that he had seen the engineers had been in error, because the ditch was just as deep and just as wide as it was further along the Rhaeti fortifications. In fact, this came as no surprise to Porcinus, and he silently gave a brief prayer of thanks to the gods that he had planned accordingly. Of course, as it was turning out, nothing connected with this operation was going as intended, because when Porcinus went to give the order, he was informed by Urso, Munacius, and Pacuvius that at least one man from each Century had lost the bundles they were carrying. In the case of Munacius' Century, it was worse; five of his Legionaries had either been forced or opted to lose their burdens, which were presumably now swept downstream and were probably floating in the lake. Of the men who were carrying the wicker baskets, it was even worse, which in all honesty didn't surprise Porcinus that much, since the dirt was heavier, and was more likely to drag a man under. Regardless of the reason, it meant that he would have to husband his resources to the point that there was only going to be one solid path across the ditch instead of the planned two. Within a matter of moments, the hurdles were thrown down, and the baskets of dirt emptied onto them, but it wasn't without cost. Despite the best attempts of comrades to cover the men charged with this task, it was probably inevitable that some of them would be struck and, in the space of a dozen heartbeats, Porcinus was forced to watch three of his men get hit by Rhaeti missiles, one of them being hit by three arrows, the one striking him in the throat a mortal wound. Even so, he managed to fall forward, into the ditch, in his last act to help his comrades. Porcinus' own throat tightened at the sight, recognizing the dead Legionary, his name Marcus Figulus, one of his most veteran men. Figulus was a Gregarius who hadn't even earned the status of an *immune*, one of those men with a special skill that earned them extra pay, but as far as Porcinus was concerned, he was part of the solid core of veterans that formed the beating heart of his Century. It was a loss that he could ill afford, and the fact that it happened before the ladders had actually touched the wall was something that Porcinus hoped wasn't an omen. Arrows were now flying thick and fast, their hissing passage almost matching the sounds of the river and shouts of his men as they finished filling in the ditch. Seeing that it was done, Porcinus moved quickly; now was the time to draw his sword and to make sure he was the first one across the ditch. Before he did so, however, he stooped to pick up Figulus' shield, which the man had dropped to the side of the formation before beginning what turned out to be his final task in the Legions. The distance to the wall from the ditch at this point was no more than twenty paces, but still the fog was so thick that, while it was visible, Porcinus couldn't make out any level of detail. The Rhaeti lining the wall were simply dark objects protruding above the darker line of the wall, yet he couldn't tell which ones were archers, making it difficult for him to anticipate when one of them would be loosing his missile. Keeping the shield in front of him while trying to peek around first one side, then another, then underneath, Porcinus was doing his best to keep the Rhaeti from targeting him as he advanced; the fact that if he couldn't pick out individuals among the enemy meant they were in the same straits never occurred to him. Despite the lack of visibility, one or more Rhaeti archer managed to strike Porcinus' shield, so that before he had gone a dozen steps from the ditch, there were four arrows embedded in his shield. He didn't dare risking a look behind him, but between the blurred lines made by other arrows, and the distinctive sound, he knew his men were in much the same shape he was. Understanding that every arrow striking his shield weakened it to the blows of spears and swords that would be coming shortly, Porcinus quickened his pace from the fast walk to a trot. Now that he had committed himself and his men, the sooner they got to the wall, the more quickly they would be sheltered from the missile fire, because once they were at the base of it, any archer would have to risk leaning over and exposing himself to a javelin in the face. It was one of the ironies of combat, but it was also a truth in this case; the closer he and the Cohort got, the safer they would be. Although he dashed the last dozen paces, it wasn't fast enough to keep another arrow from striking his shield, and this time the range was so short that the impact almost knocked the shield from his grasp. Barely managing to keep his grip, he nevertheless made it to the base of the wall, where he crouched, his shield over his head, watching as his men closed the remaining distance.

Both the First Century and the Fifth Century, which had resumed its position adjacent to the First after crossing the ditch, were in the famed *testudo* formation, which by necessity moved more slowly than if they were in open formation. Except, by this point, both Centuries looked more like giant hedgehogs, so many feathered shafts were protruding from the shields of almost every man in both formations. The racket produced by what had become a hail of arrows was almost deafening, but Porcinus managed to fill his lungs and bellow the command to pass the ladders, carried by men in the middle of the formations, to the front. What happened next was the product of the endless training that most Legionaries bitterly complained about during the long winter months, but at moments like this, the benefit was unmistakable. With the men of the outer files still holding their shields above their heads, the Legionaries in the center two files detached from the formation, with the men of both lines carrying a ladder. A total of four ladders would be thrown against the wall; ideally, it would have been twice as many in this section of the wall, but Porcinus had put the thought of the missing First Cohort out of his mind as something that he could do nothing about. It would be up to his Cohort, at least in this area.

Now, speed was of the essence, so the men carrying the ladders moved as quickly as it was possible for four men, each holding a section of the heavy wooden ladder, to go. Four ladders went up against the dirt wall of the Rhaeti stronghold at the same time, and Porcinus, Corvinus, Ovidius, and Corvinus' Optio, Tiberius Sulpicius, were the first to mount. As they did, the men standing immediately behind them were hurling their javelins up at any target that presented itself. The clattering racket of the barrage of arrows had stopped, replaced now by shouts, curses, and screams on both sides of the wall. Just as Porcinus had feared, the Rhaeti archers weren't the only missile troops; now that they had closed the distance, even with the fog there was nowhere to hide, with only shields for protection from the enemy javelins that were being hurled down now. Although not the same as the Romans' weapons, with the added weight and softer metal shaft, they were nonetheless formidable in their own right, and Porcinus heard first one, then another thudding into a fleshy target. Even with his own predicament, holding a shield in one hand and clutching the rungs of the ladder with the other, while trying to anticipate a javelin being hurled in his direction, he winced at the sound of at least two more men out of action. The best he could hope for was that they were only wounded, and not seriously. Putting that out of his mind, he paused for a moment, his head now just three rungs from the top, waiting for the next volley of javelins from his own men.

Hearing the section leader left in charge of the supporting Legionaries shout the command, "Prepare javelins!" Porcinus tensed, waiting for the next shouted order. In the instant before the section leader gave the next command of "Release!" one of the Rhaeti popped up from behind the parapet that Porcinus had seen was composed of a motley collection of shields, logs, and even some rocks, to hurl his own missile directly at Porcinus. He didn't see the man do so directly; he was just aware of a sudden movement out of the corner of his eye, and just as he had been trained by his father, without thinking, he flattened his body against the ladder an eyeblink before the javelin thrown by the Rhaeti went slicing down behind him. Before he could shift back to his ready position, the javelins of his men hurtled upward, two of them slamming into the body of the unlucky javelineer, throwing him backward out of sight. Porcinus knew this was his only chance, despite not being prepared as he had been an instant ago, meaning it was a clumsier ascent up the final three rungs than he would have liked. Even as his right hand released its grip on the final rung, he thrust upwards with his legs as his now-free hand reached for his sword.

Clearing the ladder to land on the dirt parapet, in the fraction of a heartbeat of time he had to take in the situation facing him, he saw a bearded, heavyset Rhaeti to his left, his face still registering surprise that Porcinus assumed was due to his sudden appearance next to the warrior, but before Porcinus could lash out, using the boss of his shield, the man toppled backward without as much as a push from the Pilus Prior. His mind barely registered the sight of a javelin protruding from the man's chest before he tumbled down off the wall to land with a heavy, lifeless thud on the ground. With that man dispatched, the nearest Rhaeti to his left was at least a half-dozen paces away, enabling Porcinus to whirl his head around to the right, just in time to see a snarling face, spittle flying from lips peeled back in a savage grin. As startling as the expression might have been, Porcinus was more concerned with the heavy, leaf-bladed spear that this new attacker had pulled back so that his arm was behind his ear, preparing to plunge the spear into Porcinus' side. Once more, the watches of training paid dividends as, without conscious thought, Porcinus swept the blade of the Gallic blade upward, just as the Rhaeti brought his arm forward with massive force and a speed that Porcinus' eye could barely track. In the instant before the point of the Rhaeti's spear punched through the mail armor protecting Porcinus' chest, his own blade, the one that he had spent so much time and care honing, met the wooden shaft perhaps two feet below the deadly spearhead, slicing through the oak shift as if it was a twig. Porcinus didn't notice the sight of the now-detached spearhead spinning crazily over his shoulder, so intent was he on recovering and bringing his sword back into position to strike. And strike he did, with a hard, punching thrust that snaked past the round, wooden shield that the other man was holding with his left hand, the finely pointed blade plunging through the boiled and hardened leather cuirass as if it wasn't there, a foot of the blade burying itself in the chest of the Rhaeti. Porcinus' opponent let out a strangled, gurgling scream as blood showed in his open mouth. Twisting the blade, both to free it and inflict more damage, Porcinus withdrew his blade and, with his right foot, kicked the man, who managed to remain upright for another heartbeat, sending him flying backward, directly into the path of three more warriors who were rushing to the threat posed by this tall Roman. The leading Rhaeti tried to dodge the now-dead man, but instead was knocked down by the impact from the bulk of the corpse hitting him. This in turn caused the other two men to pause as they tried to maneuver around the tangled mess of flesh, giving Porcinus the chance to turn his momentary attention back to his left. He was protected on that side by his shield, which he was still holding up tight against his shoulder, but he had turned just in time to see the warrior, who had been paces away, had closed the distance and was preparing to launch his own attack. The weapon this man held was a sword, a longer one favored by the Gallic and barbarian tribes in this region, but just like the previous attacker he was poised to strike, the sword pulled over his head and ready to slash downward onto Porcinus' head. However, even as Porcinus braced himself, raising his shield to meet the expected blow, a helmeted head popped into the corner of his vision, followed instantly by a silver-gray blur that shot out to strike this attacker in the side. Because he was wielding the sword with both hands, and the attack was so swift and unexpected, the Rhaeti had no chance to defend himself. Like the previous victim, this man issued a scream, then collapsed at Porcinus' feet, twitching for a moment before going still. Surprised, but understandably pleased, Porcinus watched as his benefactor finished his own ascent of the ladder, joining his Pilus Prior. The man was Spurius Natalis, a veteran on his second enlistment, and he grinned at Porcinus, who grinned back.

"Let's sort this out," Porcinus told Natalis, who sketched a salute.

Without having to be told, the veteran turned to Porcinus' left, allowing Porcinus to return his attention to the men who had just then disentangled themselves. He understood that time was impossible to judge at moments like this; his best estimate was that he had been on the parapet for the span of no more than fifty heartbeats. Risking a quick glance over the parapet, he saw that the ladder he had used was completely filled with men, one man's head immediately underneath the heels of a comrade. Within another few heartbeats, presumably he and Natalis would have help, and it would be sorely needed, because Porcinus could see a mass of movement along the parapet in both directions as the defenders in the area were alerted to this incursion by their enemies. Compounding matters, Porcinus could just make out a disturbance through the fog on the ground in the general direction of the lake, and while he couldn't make out details, he was sure it meant that more Rhaeti were heading in his direction from inside the fortifications. It was impossible to tell numbers, but he understood speed was absolutely of the essence; the more men of his Cohort he could get up onto the wall, the better all of their chances of success. And to do that, these enemy on the wall had to be killed. Turning so that he was squarely in the path of those warriors who had been delayed by the body of his first kill, Porcinus dropped his hips while drawing his sword back into what the Romans called the first position, the blade held at waist level and parallel to the ground, poised to strike a gutting blow. His shield was in front of him in a perfectly vertical position; in the brief pause, he had knocked the arrow shafts from his shield with a quick swipe of the sword, but he was under no illusions that it hadn't been weakened. Only the next few moments would tell if it was fatally so. The parapet was wide enough for two men abreast, which the trio of warriors were quick to take advantage of, a pair aligning side by side, with the third warrior just behind the first two. As worrying as the numbers were to Porcinus, his bigger concern was how they had chosen who would be in front, and to an inexperienced observer, they would have been surprised to know that it wasn't the first two men that worried Porcinus the most, but the warrior immediately behind them. This concern was based in the fact that the leading men were armed with the long swords, along with shields, one a round shield, the other the larger kite-shaped variety also favored by warriors in this region. However, the trailing man had another weapon, the same kind of spear as the first warrior that Porcinus had dispatched, and the Pilus Prior knew he was the bigger threat, as odd as it may have seemed. He had seen it before; a Legionary would be engaged with one or two men, his shield protecting him from one attacker, and his sword the other. Except that left him vulnerable to a third attacker, and when that attacker had the superior reach provided by the war spear, he was in mortal peril. Instinctively, Porcinus knew that most men in his position would say that his best, and really only tactic was to act defensively, until one of his men could come to help. With that in mind, he did the opposite thing from what would have been the prudent course and conduct a defensive fight. Instead, Porcinus abruptly took a lunging step forward. By doing so, he threw off his attackers, with the one on his shield side preparing to bring his sword down in an overhand blow while the man directly across from his sword had his arm drawn back in a mirror image of Porcinus' own position. Their intent was clear; force Porcinus to raise his shield to keep from having his brains splattered on the dirt wall, allowing the second man to gut him. Or, if Porcinus chose to block the lower thrust, the only protection his head would have was his helmet, and he knew very well that it would do little good against a blow with as much power behind it as this Rhaeti was about to unleash. But by taking a step towards, not away from his attackers, both enemy warriors quickly had to adjust their aiming point, which they could have done fairly easily if that was all Porcinus had done. Most importantly, Porcinus' move had clearly been unexpected, surprising both men and causing them to hesitate for the fraction of a heartbeat Porcinus needed. Even as his body was moving, so was his shield, Porcinus punching it forward as well, aiming at the man to his left, who had been preparing the overhead attack. He had no illusions that he would land a solid blow, and as he had anticipated, the Rhaeti moved his own, round shield to meet the iron boss that protruded from the center of Porcinus' curved rectangular one. As attacks with a shield went, it wasn't much, but it was just enough to cause this man to pause in his own offensive maneuver and moved him back a half step, giving Porcinus the instant he was hoping for, and he didn't waste the opportunity. In the space of time it had taken for the Rhaeti trio to close with Porcinus, his experienced eye had taken at least a partial measure of his foes, and he had seen that of the three, the weakest link in the chain was the man to his right, holding his sword low. Calling him a man was not entirely accurate; this was little more than a boy, barely old enough to shave, wide-eyed with the combination of fear, hatred, and wild excitement that Porcinus knew was the most likely expression of every man in his first battle. His stance was too closed, making it easier to unbalance him, and the way he held his sword told Porcinus that he still needed more practice. Unfortunately for him, the gods had decreed that he wouldn't get that opportunity, or so Porcinus hoped. Feinting a thrust from the first position, but again in the same movement and with the smoothness of practice, Porcinus' hand and arm suddenly changed direction. The Rhaeti youth was completely fooled, dropping his kite-shaped sword even lower to block what looked to him as an attempt by this Roman scum to geld him. In the timespan remaining to him, his brain barely had time to register that somehow the point of the Roman's sword suddenly shifted position, quickly reappearing to his left, just above his lowered shield. His eyes actually never left Porcinus' face, which set in the grim, determined expression that he had been wearing since ascending the ladder, the face of a hardened professional, so his eyes didn't track the point of the Roman's Gallic blade slicing into the soft spot on the left side of his neck behind his trachea. And, just as quickly, the blade was gone, like a striking serpent, which in many ways it was, leaving a standing corpse. Porcinus didn't wait for the young warrior to collapse, using the sudden relaxation of the Rhaeti's body as the youth still stood, slack-jawed and seemingly oblivious to the bright shower of arterial blood spraying from his neck, shoving his victim into the man with the spear, still just behind the pair of attackers. Happening as quickly as it did, Porcinus was able to catch the spear-wielding warrior before he could make a thrust with his own weapon, and now the man had to deal with a limp body hurled against him, in a repeat of the tactic Porcinus had employed to delay the trio the first time. Then, lights of a million colors exploded in Porcinus' head, while it felt as if his knees had suddenly lost their ability to hold him erect, and he realized with a dull horror that the first attacker had recovered more quickly than he had anticipated. He was barely aware of the heavy blow to his left shoulder that had occurred immediately after the shock to his head, staggering back as he desperately tried to keep his legs underneath him. The boy he had killed was now lying in the dirt, a pool of blood growing, and the Rhaeti with the spear had stepped over the body to join the first warrior who had landed the blow to Porcinus' head. Everything within Porcinus' vision was different than it had been just a heartbeat before; it seemed to him that somehow the dirt wall that he was standing on and that seemed so solid had suddenly become tilted, putting him in danger of sliding off. Although he knew it was deadly important to keep his focus on his two foes, he was almost overwhelmed with a sudden lethargy, and the detached part of his mind took note of the smile on the face of the man wielding the sword, which held nothing but evil. It was the look of the other man that arrested his attention, who even then was once more pulling his arm back, spear held at shoulder level in preparation to plunge it into Porcinus. It was an expression that seemed out of place to Porcinus, more suitable for after the battle, when men mourned their dead, a look that his objective mind recognized was one of grief, sending a spark of realization in what Porcinus was sure was the last moment of his life. The boy he had just killed had meant something to this man, and with an odd calm, Porcinus thought that it was fitting that it would be the Rhaeti with the spear taking his vengeance. Yet, even as one part of his consciousness accepted his coming demise, some other part, acting in concert with his body, rejected that notion, and it was with a stab of surprise that Porcinus felt his left arm moving his shield up in time to block the enemy's thrust, as if it had a mind of its own. Although he felt the jolting shock run up his arm from the force of the blow, there was a disembodied, disconnected quality to what was happening that made it seem as if he was outside of his body, watching himself playing the part of a gladiator in the arena, facing two opponents. Again, there was a flash of silvery gray to Porcinus' left front, as the surviving Rhaeti swordsman unleashed his second attack. This time, it was the horizontal stroke favored by barbarian warriors, with the simple aim of decapitating their enemy. Because the point of the second warrior's spear was still buried in Porcinus' shield, and was even then being viciously yanked as the warrior tried to both retrieve his spear and to pull the shield from Porcinus' hand, there was no defense left, nothing that Porcinus could do, and he knew it. The sword was halfway through its swing, perhaps two hands' width away from Porcinus' left shoulder when, in the small space between Rhaeti sword and Roman body, there was another darting flash of movement, this one going in a perpendicular direction to that of the Rhaeti's blade. There was a brief shower of sparks, but it was the clanging sound of metal against metal that made Porcinus flinch. Then there was the bulk of a body, and even at the edge of his vision, Porcinus could tell that the helmet and armor was Roman.

"Good thing I got here when I did."

Porcinus knew he should recognize the voice, but it was as if the fog that enveloped everything outside of his body had somehow managed to find its way inside his mind, making even the simple task of identifying his savior impossible. Besides which, he wasn't out of danger, and he was alert enough to understand that. Finally, on the fourth yank, the Rhaeti's spear came free, and as if by agreement, all the combatants paused for a moment. Only then did Porcinus risk a glance to his left to see that he had been saved by Aulus Galens, another of his veterans, who gave him a tight grin. Porcinus knew he should say something, but realized he couldn't string together words that would make any sense, so he settled for a brief nod before turning back to face the other two men. His legs felt a little steadier, but he was aware that he had taken a serious blow to his head and he was still lightheaded and reeling a bit. He would have liked to take the time to at least reach up and feel for any damage, but his foe with the spear, driven by grief, was unwilling to wait, and with a shouted challenge, he lunged forward again. Once more, the arm moved, and the shield met the point of the spear, but above the normal, deep thudding sound came a higher pitched cracking noise, a clear signal that Porcinus' shield was fatally weakened. This development had one salutary effect; more than anything else he could have done, that sound served to drive at least some of the fog from his mind. With his head clearing, Porcinus understood that, although the odds were evened, he wasn't out of danger yet, because, in all likelihood, the next attack from his enemy's spear would split his shield in two. This gave him the impetus to resume the offensive, ignoring his instincts that told him he still needed time to recover his senses. As his opponent approached, weaving the spear in an elliptical pattern, while holding his shield out in front of him, Porcinus closed the distance as well, exposing the disadvantage of the spear as a weapon. Anyone wielding it needed a bit more room than warriors armed with swords, even the longer Gallic blades. Consequently, the Rhaeti was faced with the choice of taking another step back, but when he did, his rear foot hit the body of the dead youth, who still looked up at Porcinus with the shocked expression the Roman had seen on many faces, over many battlefields. Understanding what it meant, the warrior immediately lunged forward again, and this time the two men crashed together, shield to shield, Porcinus feeling the shock of the collision travel through his body, down through his legs. At the instant they met, Porcinus' worst fears were realized as his shield issued a resounding, splintering noise, sounding much like when breaking a board, and he could see daylight streaming through the gap running from top to bottom just to the left of where his hand clutched the handle that was protected by the boss in the center of the shield. The shield didn't fall into pieces; for the moment, it was held together by the metal strip that ran around the edge of the shield, but his opponent, hearing the sound as well, summoned more of his strength to put even greater pressure on the shield. More out of desperation than any sense of tactics, Porcinus, who had been meeting the shoving pressure of the Rhaeti with his own strength, suddenly relented, not just moving his rear leg backward, but relaxing his entire body and leaning backward as well. It was the kind of move that no warrior with any experience would succumb to, and Porcinus would wonder later if his foe had just been so out of his mind with grief that he had lost his head. Whatever the reason was didn't matter; what did was that it worked. The warrior stumbled headlong in Porcinus' direction. Porcinus was now standing with almost all of his weight on his right, rearmost leg, and the look on the Rhaeti's face told Porcinus that he knew his fate was sealed. Porcinus didn't hesitate, thinking it oddly fitting that both this man and the youth should die the same way, with a thrust to the neck. The Rhaaeti collapsed at his feet, and although Porcinus probably felt the warm spray of his enemy's blood splashing on his lower legs, the Pilus Prior wouldn't take notice of that until much later, when he would try to remember how it happened as he cleaned it off.

Porcinus' attention had immediately shifted to what was now the lone remaining warrior, but he turned just in time to see Galens, countering the Rhaeti's attempt to take Galens' head from his shoulders, launch a training-ground perfect thrust from the first position, burying his blade half its length into the Rhaeti's abdomen. This Rhaeti was wearing mail, but it hadn't stopped the Roman blade, and the man's mouth opened as he emitted a guttural moan that was more eloquent in expressing his agony than any words he could have uttered. Seeing the effective end of the fight, Porcinus had no need, nor had he the desire to watch Galens finish in the manner he had been trained, twisting the blade, then ripping it out, bringing a gout of blood and offal with it. Only now did Porcinus take a moment, stepping away from what had become a small pile of bodies on the wall, both to check himself for damage and to take stock of the overall situation.

Between the fog in the sky and what he thought of as the fog in his head, it was impossible for Porcinus to judge how much time had passed, but what he could see was that he and Natalis were no longer alone. Perhaps half his Century had reached the rampart, and there was a brief moment when the progress of the rest of the men ascending the ladders was stopped as those on the rampart milled about. Such was Porcinus' mental state that he began looking around, angry at this sign of disorganization, wondering where someone in charge was to straighten out the mess of confusion.

"Pilus Prior!"

While it was the first one he heard, Ovidius had shouted at his Centurion no less than three times, and was now shoving his way past the men standing on the wall, concerned at the sight of Porcinus standing motionless, seemingly with nothing on his mind but to stare vacantly up at the pale, barely visible white orb that was the sun. Finally, Porcinus jerked his head around, and despite himself, Ovidius stopped in his tracks, now very concerned at what he saw. There was a creased dent in his Centurion's helmet that ran front to back, just below the edge of Porcinus' transverse crest, the sight of which under other circumstances would have caused Ovidius to chuckle, so bedraggled and faded from the dunking in the river that it flopped forward. But what Ovidius was seeing was no cause for laughter, if only because of the look in Porcinus' eyes.

"Sir! You've taken a bastard of a blow to the head." Ovidius said this as quietly as he could under the circumstances. Reaching his Pilus Prior's side, Ovidius paused to snap over his shoulder at a knot of four men, "Don't just stand there like fucking imbeciles! Spread out and make room for the rest of the boys! And you," he pointed to one of the men, who happened to be Natalis, "move down the wall and find Corvinus. He's the only other Centurion up here so far. Ask him to come attend to the Pilus Prior. Now!"

Without waiting to see if he was obeyed, knowing that he would be, Ovidius turned back to Porcinus, who was looking at Ovidius with what seemed to be mild amusement.

"At least someone's in charge," Porcinus muttered, and it was his tone as much as what he said that caused Ovidius to laugh.

"You are," Ovidius reminded Porcinus.

Looking at the Optio in some surprise, it took a moment for the words to register. Now that the crisis of his personal battle was over, Porcinus felt the clarity of thought he had experienced seem to slip away, and he began to shake his head in an attempt to clear it. The stabbing pain it caused stopped him in mid-shake, although the pain itself did seem to help dispel some of the cobwebs. Ovidius, seeing the gesture, mistook Porcinus' intent.

"Right now," he said carefully, "you are in command, sir. But...."

His voice trailed off. Porcinus looked at Ovidius, squinting and peering at his Optio as if seeing him for the first time.

"But if my brains are scrambled, I shouldn't be," he finished for Ovidius.

If he saw his Optio's shoulders sag in clear relief, he gave no sign. Despite knowing what it would mean, Porcinus forced himself to shake his head back and forth, yet as unpleasant as it was, the pain lancing through his head did more to bring him back to the present than anything he had done before. When he returned his gaze to Ovidius, his eyes were bloodshot, but the look in them was clear; at least, Ovidius thought, clearer than a moment before.

"I'm all right now," Porcinus said, inspecting the rampart over Ovidius' shoulder.

His eyes narrowed as he spotted Corvinus, weaving his way through the men of Porcinus' Century, and he shot a glance at Ovidius, who shrugged.

"I wasn't sure..." he began.

"You did the right thing," Porcinus cut him off. "But I'm fine now. Take," he paused for what seemed an exceptionally long time, and Ovidius thought for a moment that his Pilus Prior's wits had left him again, but Porcinus finished, "the even numbered sections, and get them facing that direction, down on the ground." He pointed in the general vicinity of the lake. "It's hard to tell, but it looks like these bastards are trying to get something organized to head this way."

When Ovidius followed Porcinus' finger to where it was pointing, he saw that it indeed appeared to be the case that something was happening deeper inside the Rhaeti position. Because of the fog, it was impossible to make out any details, but Ovidius could see that what appeared to be a darker gray mass that hadn't been there just moments before, and was growing wider even as he watched. That could mean only one thing; more Rhaeti were running to form a line of warriors, preparing to face the men of the Fourth Cohort. What wasn't clear was what whoever was commanding this bunch intended, whether he would lead them to the wall to try and retake it, or if he had resigned himself to losing the wall and was going to wait. Oddly enough, Ovidius actually felt better seeing that dark line of men, because Porcinus had seen it as well, and understood what it meant immediately. This was why he was sending his Optio and half the Century down off the wall to form a line, in anticipation of what the Rhaeti over there might do, a sure sign to Ovidius that his superior was thinking clearly.

Oblivious to his Optio's thoughts, Porcinus continued, "I'm going to take the rest of the men and head that way." He pointed to the right, off in the general direction of where the First Cohort should have been.

As both men were gazing in that direction, they saw movement similar in nature, and obscurity, to what was going on to their front. But while the gathering line in the direction of the lake could only mean the presence of the enemy, it wasn't the case to the right. It could be Rhaeti who were disturbing the gray curtain in that direction, yet it could also be the First Cohort. For whatever it was worth, Porcinus didn't think it was Frontinus and his men; while the fog muffled the noise to an astonishing degree, he was relatively sure that he would have heard some sound that identified whoever was over there as Roman. By this point, Corvinus had reached the two men, and despite everything that was going on, he rendered his Pilus Prior the proper salute. Only then did he step closer, the concern on his face clear to see, embarrassing Porcinus. Corvinus let out a low whistle as he inspected the deep dent on Porcinus' helmet.

"How are your brains not on the ground?" he asked, and while he made sure his tone was light, there was real wonder behind the question.

Porcinus shrugged because he honestly didn't know, although he offered the only thing that had come to him as an explanation.

"Right before he hit me, I shield-punched him. I didn't think I made a solid hit, but it must have thrown him off-balance more than I thought."

"Well, you are stronger than you look." Corvinus laughed, then he turned serious. "But thank the gods you are, or you wouldn't be talking to us."

Using that as an excuse to turn the conversation back to the business at hand, Porcinus asked for a report.

"My Century is on the wall, and we've extended about 100 paces that way." Corvinus indicated back over his shoulder. "We've killed about a dozen of the enemy, but right before I left, we could see that a bunch of them farther down were working up the nerve to head back this direction."

"And if that's so, why are you standing here?" Porcinus asked crossly.

In answer, Corvinus shot a glance at Ovidius, who, for the first time, looked uneasy.

"I, well, I thought your brains were scrambled," the Optio said.

That, Porcinus thought ruefully, was an accurate assessment of his condition, at least a few moments before. Instead of continuing on this topic, Porcinus dismissed Ovidius to gather the sections of men and descend off the wall. As the Optio moved away, back in the direction of the Fifth Century there came a shout of warning, followed instantly by the distinctive sound of metal, wood, and flesh colliding together.

"You better get back to your men," Porcinus ordered, and Corvinus didn't hesitate, pushing his way through newly arrived Legionaries that Porcinus recognized were men of the Second Century.

It didn't take more than a heartbeat longer to spy Urso, the stocky man snarling orders at his Century. At the moment, Porcinus didn't particularly want to have an exchange with Urso, not when his wits weren't at their sharpest, but he knew it couldn't be avoided. Before calling the Pilus Posterior to him, Porcinus quickly arranged the men of the odd-numbered sections of his Century, of which Galens was one, into a compact group, sending them off to his right.

"I want you to extend our position out 100 paces that way," he instructed the Sergeant of the first section, "but don't go any farther. Wait for me!"

By the time he was finished, Urso was standing next to him.

"Well, that took longer than expected." The Pilus Posterior's voice was cheery.

Too cheery, Porcinus thought sourly; he's happy that it took us longer than normal.

"The fog doesn't help much." The time it took to say it was the only time Porcinus was willing to devote to this topic. "What's your status?"

"My Century," Urso took a quick glance over his shoulder, just in time to see one more man ascend the ladder to join the mass of men standing there already. Turning back, Urso finished, "is all formed up and ready to move. At your orders, of course."

How does the man manage to make everything sound like he's doing me a favor, Porcinus wondered bitterly, but again, wasn't willing to dwell on matters that couldn't be worried about at this moment.

"Good, very good," Porcinus said briskly. Indicating the ground off the wall where Ovidius was finishing forming his men, he ordered, "Join Ovidius. Tie into his left flank and extend the line that way." Porcinus pointed in the direction where the sounds of a small but vicious fight could be heard, where Corvinus and his men were up on the wall. "Get in a position where your men can put some javelins into whoever those *cunni* Corvinus and his boys are dealing with."

"Ah, the Fifth Century needs our help." Urso said this jovially enough, but there was no mistaking the barb in the comment. "Well, me and my boys are more than happy to lend a hand."

"Then why are you still standing here talking?" Porcinus snapped, instantly regretting losing his composure, even if his words had the desired effect.

Urso's face flushed, but his salute was perfect as he replied, "As you command, Pilus Prior."

Without another word, Urso stalked back into the fog.

Once Porcinus rejoined the half of his Century that was still on the wall, he saw that, although the shapes he had seen farther down the wall were clearly Rhaeti, whoever was in charge of them had decided that even a half-Century's worth of Roman soldiers was something that it was best to avoid, presumably leaving the wall to join the mass of Rhaeti forming up. Despite this development, Porcinus wasn't willing to count on the fact that matters would stay this way, so once the Third Century was on the wall, he had that full Century replace him and his men. However, neither was he willing to have the Third stay put either, because there still had been no sign of the First Cohort.

"I want you to move, slowly, down the wall. Put at least a section out in front of you just to the point you can't see them anymore in this *cac*," he instructed Munacius. "Try to find the First, and when you do, send a runner back to let me know. I need to find out what Frontinus wants us to do."

With that done, Porcinus took his men down off the wall to rejoin the rest of his Century, and fairly quickly, the First and Second were joined by the Fourth and Sixth. Debating with himself for a moment, Porcinus decided to leave Corvinus up on the wall, for the same reason he had Munacius to the right; with this fog, it wouldn't have been very hard for a bunch of Rhaeti to come creeping up from that direction to fall on his flank. This by far was the strangest, most confused operation in which Porcinus had ever participated, let alone held a leadership position. The only thing he was sure of was the location of his own Cohort; in fact, it could have been as if he and the Fourth were conducting this assault all by themselves. It was a world of shadows, the fog, to this point, not showing any sign of letting up, which to Porcinus was the strangest part of a strange day. However, as he would later learn, because of the fog, both external and in his mind from the blow, his perception of time had been seriously altered. By this point, barely a sixth part of a watch had elapsed since he and his Cohort had crossed the shallow river. The amount of time that had elapsed from the moment his feet touched the wall, to the moment Ovidius had reached his side numbered in the hundreds of heartbeats, no more. The only value this information would have held for Porcinus was by informing him that the assault was still in the early stages, and had not dragged on through much of the day as he originally thought. Not helping his mental state was the nagging worry that came from the isolation and lack of information, and he brutally shoved the thought that the assault had failed everywhere else and his men had been abandoned back into the recesses of his consciousness. He could only worry about what he could control; this was yet another valuable lesson he had learned, mostly through observation of both his father and his first Centurion, Pullus' best friend, Sextus Scribonius. Pushing that idea into the front of his mind, he turned his attention to the mass of Rhaeti warriors that had begun their advance. Although they were still just an indistinct shape, Porcinus could see enough to understand that unless he did something quickly, the ends of the enemy line would overlap his own, on both ends of his formation. The ideal solution would have been to call his two Centuries from their spots on the wall, but he quickly discarded that plan. Swiftly determining not just the best course, but the only one available to him, he snapped out a series of orders. Reacting without any hesitation and with a smoothness that only came from intense practice, the rearmost four ranks of his Century began sidestepping to their right, moving quickly until they had detached themselves from the rear of his Century. Then, with a few steps forward, the detachment moved so that it was directly adjacent to their comrades of the front four ranks, while the Century on the left flank, the Sixth, performed the same maneuver. It was at moments like this that it was easier for a Centurion to see his losses, as men shifted up a file whenever a man ahead of them fell. This made the rear rank always the most ragged, and Porcinus was dismayed to see that, in fact, there were only three men in the rear of the ranks that had just moved into their new position. Seven men? His Century had already lost seven men? Recognizing this line of thought as another thing over which he had no control, he forced his mind back to the more practical issues. Helping him in this cause was, for the first time that day, the blaring of a horn, except that it wasn't a Roman one, and the sound, even muffled as it was, clearly came from the direction of where the Rhaeti were preparing themselves for whatever they were planning. Obviously, the signal to begin the advance, the last note hadn't died out when a great shout followed behind it, rolling across to where Porcinus and his men were waiting. Immediately, the dark mass started moving, advancing out of the gray mist, and despite the threat, there was something oddly comforting in the sight. This was the kind of fight that Romans understood and at which they excelled.

"All right, boys! Prepare javelins!"

Porcinus didn't have to turn around, knowing by the sound of creaking leather and the sudden, harsh intake of breath from the lungs of his men that every one of them had their arms pulled back, stretching as far as they could go, the points aimed skyward, waiting for the next command. They were forced to wait, however, as Porcinus refrained from giving the order, wanting the Rhaeti to advance even closer. Even now, they were closer than he would normally have allowed an enemy to approach, but there were two factors working in his favor; the first was the most obvious, and that was the limited visibility created by the heavy fog. It made judging distance difficult, but as hard as it was for Porcinus, he knew it was the same for his counterpart, whoever it was, ranging along the back of the moving mass of Rhaeti. This difficulty was the second factor that caused Porcinus to wait longer than normal because it had slowed the Rhaeti advance. Normally, by this point, a barbarian enemy would just be beginning their headlong charge at their enemy, yet not only were they still advancing at a slow walk, they hadn't stopped for their usual ritual of working themselves up into a frenzy.

"Release!"

Finally, men whose muscles had begun quivering from the tension swept their arms forward, while at the same time twisting their torsos to swing the entire right side of their bodies violently in the same direction as the missiles they were launching, giving every ounce of energy and momentum into their throws. As often happened, Porcinus heard a low, moaning sound rolling through the swirling gray, the sound of men who had either experienced, or had heard of the devastation that was plummeting their way. And the fog worked in Porcinus' favor even further, making it almost impossible for the enemy warriors to look skyward and pick out the javelin that was even then slicing downward that posed the most threat to them. The moan changed into a series of shouts and screams as the hardened iron points either slipped past an upraised Rhaeti shield, or punched through one with enough force to strike a fleshy target. With the howls of pain and anger rolling across the space between the two forces, to Porcinus' experienced ear it sounded like the enemy had been especially hard hit by this volley, more than normally would be expected at this range. Also, he understood that many in the Century had already thrown a javelin when assaulting the wall, meaning that a second volley might only launch twenty javelins.

Deciding on the spot, Porcinus shouted, "Drop the javelins, boys! These *cunni* are ready for the slaughter now! Let's not keep them waiting!"

If the men of Porcinus' Cohort had been less seasoned, he wouldn't have skipped that order of launching their next and final javelins, but without looking back, he began sprinting toward the Rhaeti, confident his men were behind him. Before he had gone a few paces, his faith was justified by the answering roar of his men, just a couple paces back. Dropping their javelins and drawing their swords while on the run, every one of Porcinus' men raised his voice, uttering his own war cry or, in some cases, just an incoherent howl of rage and hatred, whatever worked to stiffen their resolve and send them hurtling headlong into their enemy. Porcinus' ears hadn't deceived him; once within a dozen paces, in the handful of heartbeats of time he had once

the details of the enemy line became clear enough to make out, he saw
that the Rhaeti were still in utter disarray, with the bodies of the men
skewered by the volley serving to impede those of the front rank
remaining upright and uninjured. Those who didn't have that problem
and had blocked the missiles with their shields were impaired by the
soft metal shafts bending on impact, the butt end of the javelins now
pointing toward the ground and rendering the shield useless. That was
all the time Porcinus had, as, in full stride, he picked a man who was
frantically trying to extract the point of the javelin from the kite shield
that had protected him. It was almost impossible to do what the Rhaeti
was trying to do, because of the hardened triangular head of the
javelin, and it was absolutely impossible to do it quickly. Only at the
very last instant did Porcinus see the man's eyes raise from the shield,
widening just a fraction before the Roman, putting his shield, his
second, hard up against his left shoulder, with his hand pulled in tight
to his waist, slammed into him. The next thing that came into Porcinus'
vision were the bottoms of a pair of the type of boot Gallic tribes
favored, as the warrior flew backward into the Rhaeti to his right, who
in turn staggered and lost his footing. Barely breaking stride, and while
not taking his eyes off the Rhaeti in front of him who were still upright,
he gave a hard thrust down, the point of his blade unerringly punching
into his fallen victim's throat, even as the man was just beginning to
try to climb back to his feet. Because of his position at the far right of
the thin line of Romans, and with his order to extend his flanks, it was
actually Porcinus, his *signifer* to his left, and the next two men of what
had been the Fifth Section but were now in the front line that
overlapped the Rhaeti. Without giving any orders, the other three men
smoothly followed Porcinus' lead as he made a slight turn to the left,
squaring himself so that he was now the one facing the left flank of
the Rhaeti formation. Making this adjustment without any hesitation,
and still at almost at full speed, Porcinus, Felix the *signifer*, and the
Gregarii Mela and Bovinus were able to hit their counterparts of the
four ranks of the Rhaeti before any of them were able to turn squarely
to face the new threat. One moment they had been in the second, third,
and fourth lines of men, waiting their turn to have at the hated Romans,
and now they found their collective wish for the chance to draw blood
coming true earlier than they had expected. Not surprisingly, in the

short period of time these men had left, none of them found this sudden opportunity to their liking. Within a matter of another few heartbeats, the four Romans had slain or badly wounded their opponents and had begun to push into the left side of the Rhaeti formation. The deaths of their friends gave those warriors deeper in the formation the chance they needed to understand and position themselves to meet this unexpected thrust, although none of the now-dead men felt particularly happy that their sacrifice had made it possible. And while Porcinus, as the Pilus Prior, didn't have the support of a row of men behind him to grab his harness, the other three did, their comrades moving quickly around into their proper positions. Shouts of alarm and surprise sounded from the Rhaeti, the reaction to this sudden development rippling across their massed bodies, delayed a bit because of the fog. Men who were perhaps a dozen deep in the Rhaeti formation, more a tightly packed mob than a formation with proper intervals between each man, were at the outer limit of visibility because of the thick fog. A result of this handicap was that the word of what was happening had to be passed back through the formation to the Rhaeti warlord in command of this line of defense, since their use of horns was limited to very simple and basic commands, like giving the order to attack, halt, or retreat. Information like the appearance of an enemy force on the flank was just something they had never thought important, and they were paying for it now.

Porcinus quickly saw that, while his move around the edge of the Rhaeti had been instinctive, it was the best decision he had made so far that day. Even before the rest of the three files of Romans had taken their place behind Felix, Mela and Bovinus, Porcinus and those men had cut their way deeply into the formation. When he was recalling events later, he realized that if there had been a quicker thinking Rhaeti standing in the mass of the milling barbarians who actually understood the opportunity being presented to him, he would have jumped immediately into the space behind Porcinus and the others that was only occupied by the Rhaeti dead and wounded at that moment. Fortunately, his own men had reacted so quickly that the span of perhaps ten heartbeats where this might have been possible hadn't been enough. Where the main Roman line and this new smaller line met was a death trap for any Rhaeti foolhardy enough to try and drive a wedge into that angle. If he attacked the Roman now anchoring the main line of Romans, he was completely exposed to his left to Bovinus who, despite the name given to him when he was a *tiro* for his placid nature and habit of chewing on blades of grass, was anything but cow-like in battle. Conversely, if the Rhaeti had chosen to face Bovinus, he would have the same dilemma, and worse from the sixth Roman of the front rank who wouldn't even have to dodge a blade to stab him in the back. This was proven to be true very early on, and it prompted the Rhaeti to, instead of pressing against the Roman line, contract backward a step. They had finally managed to change the orientation of their formation to mirror that of the Romans, so that Porcinus and his men on the flank were now squarely facing the Rhaeti across from them. The file of men who ordinarily lined up behind Felix, even if it was normally farther back, but were now on the outer edge of the flanking part of the Roman formation, had turned to face to their immediate right, with shields up and ready for any attempt by the Rhaeti to, in effect, do what Porcinus had done, and get around them to turn the flank. Porcinus alone was the most exposed Roman, although that was nothing new to him, and he had changed his facing slightly so that he was able to keep an eye on both his rank of four men, and the file behind Felix now protecting the right. It was somewhat awkward, but when one of the Rhaeti, who had pulled back a few paces, decided that this presented an advantage, he was disabused of that notion by way of a strong thrust to the gut that left him lying on the ground in a pool of blood, gasping his last breaths as he tried to hold his intestines in with one hand. Still, Porcinus knew that the larger situation was precarious; the only way to keep the Rhaeti from enveloping this small part of his Century was to keep them occupied by cutting more deeply into the formation.

"Come on; let's not stand about," Porcinus shouted. "Let's get this done!"

Giving a blast of his bone whistle, blown in a distinct pattern, it was immediately taken up off to his left front, where the Fourth Century started and his ended, immediately followed by a shout from the men of the rank immediately across from the Rhaeti, signaling their acknowledgement. With a unity and smoothness that wasn't quite parade-ground perfect, but was close, the front rank leaped forward to engage their enemies, and the noise level shot up accordingly. Porcinus wasted no time in taking satisfaction in how his men were performing their maneuvers, jumping across the space the barbarians had given him, lashing out with the borrowed shield. His opponent was a short, wiry man, very agile and lightly armored, who, even with the crush of men around him, was able to take a hopping step backward so that the Roman's shield hit nothing but air, sending a jarring bolt of pain up Porcinus' arm. Frustrated, Porcinus nonetheless kept sight of where Felix was on one side, and the nearest Gregarius to his right rear, a recent replacement named Flaminius, knowing that if he pressed his foe too closely he would separate from his men and isolate himself. Fortunately, the Rhaeti seemed to accept what he clearly took as a challenge from this Roman Centurion, because almost as quickly as he had taken a step backward, he again made a hopping move towards the Pilus Prior. While doing so, he whipped his sword out from behind his shield, a large round one with a spike protruding from the boss, in the horizontal, arcing blow the Gauls favored. Where this attack was different was that it wasn't aimed at his neck; in fact, it was the opposite. Porcinus reacted, but he was caught by surprise, both by the speed and the target of the assault, so that when he dropped his shield to cover up the spot above his greaves and below his knee, he only partially deflected the blow. A searing pain came from where the edge of the Rhaeti's sword sliced into the side of his upper calf, just before it was deflected from its path. Porcinus heard a sudden hissing sound, like a serpent, and was only dimly aware that it was coming from his own lips, which were tightly pressed together. The damage had been done to his left leg, and he was reluctant to put pressure on it although he did so, but despite the pain, he didn't think it was more than superficial. Nevertheless, the Rhaeti's intent had been clear; he was going to cripple the Roman before going in for the kill, and this realization fueled Porcinus' resolve to exact vengeance. It was a dirty way to fight, at least to Romans and the Pilus Prior was now determined to make this scum pay. The Rhaeti, his hair a dirty blonde in both coloring and hygiene, had his hair in plaits, while his beard was arranged the same way, except for the small bones tied in them. They're supposed to be the finger bones of the enemies he's killed,

Porcinus thought, proclaiming his status as a great warrior. That detached part of his mind was able to take in such details even when he was thusly engaged in a deadly contest. But over the years, what Porcinus had learned was that it was just as likely to be the larger bones of small animals; much conversation on this topic had gone on around the Legion fires over the years, and it had become accepted wisdom, supposedly because those animals suspected of supplying those "knuckle" bones had been dissected and compared, that it was the thigh bones of ground squirrels that supplied this supposed symbol of great prowess. Porcinus didn't have any way of knowing at this moment whether it was true, but by believing that it was, he stoked the fire of his determination to kill this man. Launching a sudden attack of his own, this time when the Rhaeti did his hopping step backward, Porcinus was ready for it, thinking with grim satisfaction that no truly great warrior would ever perform the same maneuver twice in a row. That was reserved for those men who liked sitting by the fire, drinking their disgusting ale and boasting about the men they had slain, instead of staying out in the elements, training. Like us, Porcinus told himself as he mimicked the hopping step to keep the distance closed between the two. The Rhaeti's eyes grew wide as he felt the solid press of flesh and wood behind him, hemming him in as Porcinus grimly shot his shield arm out, or at least pretended to, making his enemy commit to blocking with his own shield. By bringing his shield across his body, even though it was only partially, it created enough of a gap between the left edge of the shield and his arm that there was a little triangle of space. Even as he had thrust his shield out, Porcinus' right arm was already moving, counting on the Rhaeti to fall for his feint, and the point of his sword punched right through the mail coat and padded leather lining. If his blade hadn't already been covered with blood, Porcinus would have seen more than eight inches of the tip of his sword covered in it, and almost immediately after withdrawing the blade, small frothy bubbles appeared, oozing out from the rent in the mail coat. Blood came gushing from the man's mouth as he took a staggering step, looking at Porcinus almost accusingly, blaming the Roman for his death. Which was appropriate; that was the last Porcinus gave any attention to his now-vanquished foe, already seeking another target, and relieved that his leg hadn't given out from underneath him. Around Porcinus, his men were doing much the same as he was; engaging the Rhaeti across from them, and using their skills and teamwork, vanquishing their foe, either by killing them or inflicting an incapacitating wound. The latter barbarians, if they weren't grabbed by one of their comrades and dragged to the rear, or were unable to move themselves, were only alive as long as it took for the Romans to occupy this newly vacated ground. Aside from bracing the man in front of him, the role of the Legionary second in line was to dispatch any enemy who was bypassed by his comrade in front, but who was still breathing. A sudden, brutal downward thrust, a blur of silvery gray, and those Rhaeti who weren't killed immediately quickly joined their comrades who were. Step by bloody step, foot by deadly foot, Porcinus' Cohort continued their work, grimly but with the detached professionalism that was the hallmark of the Legions. By this point in battle, all the extraneous shouting and cursing was missing, as men on both sides saved their collective breaths for the fight. The only shouts now were either orders from a Centurion or Optio, or what came from striking a telling blow, either in triumph or pain, punctuated by the hollow thud when a blade hit a wooden shield, or the sharper clang of metal on metal. Although it was normal for this phase of battle, in Porcinus' experience it was even more subdued than normal, the fog seemingly absorbing the sound in some way, making the normal din of battle muffled, as if there was an enormous wet cloth draping the combatants.

The Pilus Prior had lost track of the number of Rhaeti he had dispatched, but his arm was beginning to ache from the exertion, so he took the opportunity of a brief pause to take a step backward, within sword's reach and protection by the outside file. Glancing over to his left, he could just barely make out the white stripe sewn into the shoulder of his Optio's armor, frowning a bit at the sight of Ovidius, who wasn't in his assigned spot to the left rear of the Century, but was, in fact, in front. This was something he had talked to Ovidius about before; his Optio's excitement and eagerness for battle often meant that he pushed his way to the front, but that wasn't the primary duty of an Optio. By putting himself in front, Ovidius was unable to perform his primary job, which was to make sure that the Gregarii of the Century didn't take a step backward, and that any man who fell was immediately replaced in his spot by shifting the appropriate file up. The former wasn't something that Porcinus worried about; his men were veterans, and the chances of them suddenly turning about and fleeing was minimal, especially in this fight, but the First Century was taking casualties, which meant that Ovidius should be making sure men moved into the right spot. Understanding that this wasn't the moment to do anything about it, Porcinus turned his attention back to the mass of Rhaeti warriors, and while he was heartened to see that his men had pushed the barbarians back several dozen paces, leaving a sizable number of dead in their wake, what concerned him was what he sensed more than saw. Peering through the murk, he could just barely discern movement at the rear of the Rhaeti formation, which was almost invisible. Relying on his instinct rather than what his eyes were telling him, the rangy Pilus Prior, aided by his height, determined that even as his men were whittling them down, more Rhaeti were coming from the gods only knew where, adding their numbers to the mass of barbarian warriors already fighting. For the first time, Porcinus felt the glimmering of doubt; if they were replacing every warrior his Legionaries killed, it became nothing more than brutal mathematics.

Even as Porcinus stood there, regaining his breath and recovering from his exertions, he saw two of his men fall. One of them immediately began crawling back through the ranks of his comrades, aided by men deeper in the formation who grabbed him by the harness and helped drag him to the rear. The other man was clearly more seriously wounded, because immediately after falling his only action was to pull his shield over his body, curling into a ball to bring as much of his body as possible under the protective cover. He thought it was a Sergeant of the third section, a man from Hispania like himself by the name of Aulus Severius, but he couldn't be sure in the brief moment he had to observe the action. From his experience, Porcinus understood that this man, whoever it was, was very seriously wounded, perhaps mortally. Either way, he wasn't returning to this fight. What this meant was immediately clear to Porcinus; if matters continued as they were going, with more Rhaeti joining this fight, he was going to run out of men.

When he was thinking about it later, alone in his tent, Gaius Porcinus was still unable to separate all that occurred in what he calculated was no more than a sixth part of a watch after he made his grim observation. After their initial advance, the four Centuries of his Cohort that had been part of the fight with the body of Rhaeti who had formed down on the ground once the wall was lost to them had been brought to a grinding halt as more Rhaeti joined the mass of barbarians fighting them. One moment, Porcinus and his men had been steadily pushing the barbarians back, then suddenly, they were stopped in their tracks as the barbarians halted their own backward movement. Porcinus still wasn't sure if it was because their numbers had been bolstered by warriors drawn by the sounds of fighting, although he suspected that was the case. All Porcinus could be sure about was the fact that he and his men had been stopped from pushing their foes into the lake, and his premonition of running out of men seemed certain to come true. His first inkling that there was a change was from a sudden eruption of noise coming from an unexpected quarter, back in the direction of the lake, to the Rhaeti rear. It started with what, to his ears, sounded like cries of alarm, despite the fact he couldn't understand the words, followed a moment later by a noise that sounded exactly like what was assailing his ears and was caused by his men and the Rhaeti who were still fighting furiously. Except this time, the sound was coming from the rear of the enemy, rising very quickly in pitch and fervor to match the fighting to his immediate front. With extreme rapidity – Porcinus' later estimate was the span of no more than two or three dozen heartbeats – what had been the noise of a furious fight degenerated into the sounds of a complete panic and rout. Just a moment later, Porcinus saw a surging movement headed in his direction, caused by men whose only thought was to flee. So out of their mind with fear were they that they ran headlong into the backs of men who were still stoutly resisting the onslaught of Porcinus' men, and the result was a slaughter that was both complete, and inevitable. It was the most confused battle in which Porcinus had ever participated, from the moment the *cornu* had sounded the advance, but as hectic and disorganized as it had been, he couldn't argue about the outcome. It was the source of their possible salvation that had all the men talking, of every rank.

"Of all the things I was expecting, it wasn't that," was how Porcinus put it to Corvinus, the night of the battle, as they sat in the Pilus Prior's tent.

Corvinus didn't reply immediately, but nodded his agreement as he sipped from his cup. He was sporting a bandage around his upper arm, courtesy of a thrust from a Rhaeti spear that he had only partially blocked. His superior was essentially unmarked, except for the normal bumps and bruises that were an inevitable byproduct of life as a Centurion of Rome, along with a gash just above his greave that hadn't even required being stitched up. He did have to draw a new helmet from stores, Porcinus reminded himself, rubbing the knot on his head gingerly. And there were links on the shoulder of his mail coat that would need to be replaced. Porcinus was thankful that, even now, the throbbing in his head had begun to diminish.

Setting the cup down, Corvinus finally replied, "You have to admit, it was a stroke of genius."

While Porcinus was certainly impressed with what turned out to be a planned stratagem on the part of the young commander of the army, he wasn't willing to go that far.

"I don't know about 'genius,'" he said, shaking his head as he thought of what his father would have said if he had heard someone utter such words about anyone other than Divus Julius, who Pullus maintained was the greatest general, and Roman, who ever lived, presumably up until his last breath. "But I admit it was…inspired," he said, finally found a word he thought it was appropriate.

"The men still think that it was a trick of the gods that the fog was so thick," Corvinus said, prompting another shake of Porcinus' head.

"They're going to believe what they want, no matter what the truth is." Porcinus' tone was rueful as he stared into his cup. "But you heard Quirinus; Drusus was told by locals that there's almost always a thick fog coming off the lake in the mornings."

"True," Corvinus conceded, "but that doesn't explain why it lasted past noon today."

Porcinus just shrugged; if he were being honest, that thought had occurred to him as well, yet he still wasn't willing to ascribe this seemingly unusual phenomenon to an act of the gods. Maybe my father's opinion of the gods rubbed off more than I thought, Porcinus mused to himself, but aloud, he said, "Be that as it may, that fog turned out to be a blessing, no matter where it came from."

"That it did," Corvinus agreed, accepting another cup of wine when Porcinus proffered the jug, reaching across the desk. There was a momentary silence as the cup was refilled, then Corvinus settled back into his chair before continuing. "What I'd like to know is how in Hades Tiberius and his men managed to row all the way across the lake and find the right spot to land. That," he raised his cup in a salute, "is more a sign of the gods' favor than the fog, if you ask me."

This was something that Porcinus found hard to argue, so he didn't try. Honestly, it was a surprise, albeit a happy one, and a puzzle how Drusus' older brother had managed to navigate from the far northern end of what had been described as a ten-mile-long lake with a fleet of flat-bottomed transports carrying the two Legions that composed his part of the army, and landed exactly where they were most needed. It had been Tiberius and his men who were the cause of the sudden disruption and commotion at the rear of the Rhaeti formation, as five Cohorts from one of Tiberius' Legions had followed the noise of the fighting in Porcinus' area to slam into the rear of the warriors with whom Porcinus and his Cohort were engaged. The rest of Tiberius' force had spread out from the lakeshore, and from everything Porcinus had heard, used the same tactic to march to the various spots where Tiberius' brother's Legions were fighting. From the gossip coming from the *praetorium*, through Lysander, the only flaw had been in the timing of Tiberius' landing; the original plan had called for his men to actually land first, as soon as it was light enough for the men who were rowing the transports to see the lake's southern shore. How they were supposed to accomplish that with the fog, which again, according to Lysander, was a key factor in the plan, Porcinus didn't know. But that didn't really matter; what did was that it worked, and now that it was dark, those Cohorts that hadn't participated in the assault were still hard at work. And although what they were doing wasn't as nerve-wracking or dangerous as the assault, it wasn't without its own challenges, and even with the casualties his Cohort had taken, Porcinus was happy that his men had earned a rest and, most importantly, the chance to miss what was currently taking place. As he and Corvinus sat there, although they didn't comment on it, they both could hear the sounds that always came in the aftermath of a Roman victory, especially when it was at the end of a rebellion like this. Shouts of despair, answered by the cries and calls of other voices, these almost always higher-pitched, followed by short, sharp words in the form of commands by those Legionaries designated for the task of separating and shackling prisoners; this was the noise that the leather of Porcinus' tent couldn't block. It was brutal, but it was efficient; in short, it was the army of Rome going about a part of its business that wasn't talked about around the fires, yet was almost as much a part of what the men did as fighting Rome's enemies. Jointly, Tiberius and Drusus had given the orders that every Rhaeti man of fighting age, whether there was any evidence that they had been part of the battle that day or not, was to be put in chains and sold into slavery. The fate of the women and children had yet to be decided, but it was still necessary to separate the male combatants from the rest of the Rhaeti, which was taking place just outside the confines of the Roman camp. Because of the location of the Fourth Cohort, next to the camp wall, the sounds of families being torn apart were clear for both men to hear, but of the two, only Porcinus was affected in any way. He supposed that was because of his own family; it was all too easy for him to imagine that it was Iras, Titus, Sextus, and the girls being herded into the enclosed area that was set aside to hold them. This was something he had never uttered aloud, and never would to any of his comrades, no matter how much he trusted them. It was just something a Legionary of Rome didn't talk about, the fickle nature of Fortuna, and the capriciousness of the gods, particularly on this topic.

"Have you heard what's next?"

Corvinus' question brought Porcinus back to the present, but the only answer he could offer the other man was a shake of his head.

"No. I imagine it's going to take a few days to sort this mess out." He waved a hand in the general direction of where the Rhaeti were being segregated. "After that? I have no idea."

"Hopefully, we'll just pull guard duty," Corvinus mused. "Gods know we need the time to let the boys heal up."

"The ones that are going to," Porcinus said grimly, thinking of his trip to the hospital tent less than a third of a watch before.

It was his last official duty of the day, one that came after every battle, and of all the onerous tasks that Centurions had to perform, Porcinus hated this one above all. Seeing his men with their wounds of varying degrees, almost all of them doing their best to let their Pilus Prior know that they would be ready to fight again soon, was hard enough. But it was the trip to a section of the tent that was separated by a leather partition, called Charon's Boat, that was undoubtedly the worst. This was where the men the *medici* had deemed to be beyond hope, but who had yet to succumb to their wounds, were kept, a place that stank of fear and death. It was kept deliberately darkened, with only a single lamp near the opening, with a lone *medicus* there to do what he could to ease their suffering. Usually, that comfort was accomplished with a spoonful, or more, of poppy syrup, but Porcinus knew that the *medicus* assigned there also had another tool, a razor-sharp dagger, to be used when a man's torment became too much. It was a place where there was a constant, low-pitched moaning coming from a number of the inhabitants, most of whom were either semi- or completely unconscious. Not all of them, however; Porcinus was always acutely aware of the stares coming from those who the gods hadn't seen fit to allow to lapse into a stupor, who were forced to endure what had to be an unspeakable agony, compounded with the knowledge that the number of breaths allotted to them was dwindling every moment. The first time Porcinus had been forced to visit Charon's Boat, he hadn't been sure what to expect, but he prepared himself for at least an accusing glare from one of his men who, if he was being honest, Porcinus was at least indirectly responsible for putting there. What had shaken him to his very core was how his entrance was met from those men still conscious, with looks of what could only be described as hope, as if Porcinus was coming with some magic potion that would miraculously heal their wounds and make them whole again. Their pleading, no matter that it was silent, was a burden on him that was almost impossible to bear, and it was at moments like this that he cursed whatever it was in him that had spurred him to be more than just a Gregarius in the ranks. The night of the battle by the lake, Porcinus was bitterly aware that this would be the reception greeting him, but he steeled himself to enter. All things considered, he was lucky; he only had two men in the Boat, and one of them from the Fourth Century, a youngster who had only been with the Legion for about six months, had died even as Porcinus kneeled by his cot and held his hand, feeling it grow cold almost immediately. As the man gave his last, rattling gasp that Porcinus had heard so many times before, he was struck by the bitter irony of the fact that this man had been a replacement himself, and now he would need to be replaced.

When Porcinus had joined, originally by the *dilectus* held for the 14th Legion that was raised by the then-Triumvir Marcus Antonius, losses in the ranks weren't replaced, at least not with any regularity. In fact, there had been no regulations covering this event; like most things in the Roman world, because it had been done this way since the beginning of the Republic, it was still that way early in Porcinus' career. This meant that over the course of a sixteen-year enlistment, Legions would be whittled down, little by little, from the toll of fighting, marching, disease, and just ordinary exposure to what was an incredibly harsh existence. From what Porcinus had been told by his father, it was Divus Julius who had first instituted the practice of drafting men into a Legion that had suffered losses, but what Porcinus knew as a fact was that Augustus had codified this from practice to regulation. Now the Fourth Cohort was replacing replacements, he thought bitterly, even as he moved to the bedside of the second man. Feeling thankful and guilty at the same time that the man was unconscious, Porcinus only lingered long enough to say a prayer, then hand the *medicus* a coin. He told himself it wasn't from the stench caused by the man's punctured bowels, barely contained by a wrapping of gauze that was kept moist.

"If he wakes up, and he's suffering, you know what to do," the Pilus Prior told the other man quietly, who didn't reply, but gave a somber nod.

Returning back to the relative cheer of the larger tent, Porcinus stopped to talk to each of his men, making what he thought were the same, tired jokes about how they had managed to avoid normal duties. As often as he had made these jests, Porcinus recognized that although he had uttered them many times before, most of the wounded hadn't heard them, unless this wasn't their first time in the tent. Thankfully, there were only three of these men, and Porcinus thought up something different for each of them, a quick story of some past transgression, but with a comic twist, or complimented them for some off-duty exploit, usually involving some form of debauchery that, up until that moment, they were sure he hadn't known about. As soon as he was able, Porcinus hurried away from the tent, his stomach churning as it always did from the sights and sounds. What Porcinus didn't realize, nor would he have believed if he had been told, was how the men of the Fourth Cohort valued and appreciated these small signs by their Pilus Prior. Because the sad truth was that not every Centurion did what Porcinus did, and those who did rarely spent as much time or exerted as much effort as he did trying to lift their spirits. It was a characteristic of many fighting men, this reluctance to spend any time in the company of those who were wounded. In fact, many such men seemed to have a superstitious fear that the bad luck that had befallen their wounded comrades was somehow contagious, and whatever *numen* would strike twice and claim two victims, the original and the unfortunate man who had some sort of interaction with him.

"I wouldn't change places with Frontinus right now for all the money under Augustus' mattress."

Once again, Porcinus was yanked from his thoughts, but he was actually thankful, knowing as he did the morose place such ruminations as Charon's Boat would take him. Besides, the performance of the First Cohort was a topic of both immediate interest and long-term implications.

Smiling thinly, Porcinus replied, "I don't know; Augustus probably has a lot of money under his mattress. A lot."

What Porcinus didn't say, had never said, and had no plans to divulge to anyone, even to Corvinus, who he trusted more than almost any man he knew, was that Porcinus himself was a fabulously wealthy man. Even if he couldn't spend it.

"I don't care how much it is," Corvinus responded adamantly, emphasizing his point with a shake of his head. "After what happened today, I don't think any amount of money would be worth what's going to happen to him."

Although Porcinus wasn't willing to go quite that far, he did agree with Corvinus' overall point, and said as much.

"It was almost impossible to see in the fog," the Pilus Prior continued, half-heartedly. "So it's easy to understand how it happened."

Corvinus supplied his answer, in sentiment at least, with a derisive snort.

"That didn't stop us," he pointed out. "We were in the same fog as Frontinus and his bunch."

That was as indisputable as the presence of the fog, and Porcinus heaved a sigh. The fact was that he liked Frontinus well enough, but in the intervening time since the death of Vettus, the Pilus Posterior hadn't given any sign that he was up for the job as Primus Pilus. Porcinus could only imagine how difficult it was to be thrust in that role, yet the truth, however harsh, was that every Primus Pilus Posterior in every Legion of Rome knew that what happened to Vettus was not just a possibility, it was a likelihood, and that for as long as there had been the advent of the organization of the Legions into Cohorts, it had been a tradition for the Pilus Posterior to be promoted to the Primus Pilus. This was no longer automatically the case, although as far as Porcinus knew, the Centurion supposedly selected by the clerks who operated out of a wing of Augustus' villa at least came from the same Legion. Of course, Porcinus and every man marching under the standard knew the story of hard-working clerks poring over service records to make their selection was a fiction; one man, and one man only selected the Primus Pilus of each Legion. As Porcinus thought about it, he recalled he had heard mutterings about the last two or three times a Primi Pili was replaced. Two had been under circumstances similar to those of Vettus, having been killed in battle, but the third had been the talk of the army for weeks afterward. While the Pilus Prior never put much stock in this kind of gossip, there was one common thread in every version Porcinus heard, and that was the third Primus Pilus, supposedly of the 22nd Legion, had been implicated in a plot against the Princeps. This certainly wasn't the case with Frontinus.

"Besides," Corvinus pressed, "it wasn't just getting lost. It was how long it took them to get into action. From everything I've heard, none of the First Cohort even got their swords wet."

"I heard that too," Porcinus granted, although that was as far as he was willing to go in criticizing Frontinus.

Seeing that his Pilus Prior wasn't going to add anything more, Corvinus recognized when to stop with this line of conversation, and taking that as his cue to leave, the Centurion drained his cup, then left Porcinus to his thoughts. Corvinus was right, Porcinus mused as he watched his friend push the flap separating Porcinus' private quarters from the Cohort office aside and exit. It was bad enough that Frontinus had lost his bearings in the fog, although Porcinus still wasn't sure that the same thing wouldn't have happened if their spots had been reversed. The First of the 8th had been the element farthest to the right of the assault, with nothing but the slope of the mountains that anchored the left side of the Rhaeti stronghold to their own right. However, the spot they were given to assault was a stretch of wall starting a bit more than a half-mile from where the dirt wall merged with an extremely rocky precipice that protected the Rhaeti from any flanking maneuver. Somehow, shortly after the command sounded to begin the assault, Frontinus had changed his angle of march, which originated directly across the expanse of open ground from the chosen spot. Without any way to get his bearings, Frontinus had somehow turned at an oblique angle from his original path, heading, as it turned out, directly toward the slope instead of the wall. From what Porcinus had gathered, Frontinus had gotten so turned around, he marched his Cohort parallel to the wall instead of perpendicular to it. Porcinus had also heard angry muttering that at least two other Centurions of the First, the acting Pilus Posterior, and the Princeps Prior, commander of the Third Century, had run from their spot to warn Frontinus of their suspicions that the Cohort was heading in the wrong direction. But Frontinus had refused to listen; Porcinus suspected that his intransigence was due as much to the identity of the two Centurions as what they were saying. They had been the pair who were the loudest and most insistent in their opinion that Frontinus wasn't up to the task of being the permanent Primus Pilus. Well, he thought, they were right, although the gods only know if that was why they tried to get Frontinus turned around. Whatever the cause, the First only stopped when the ground in front of them began tilting upward, and Frontinus was forced to confront the fact that he had indeed led his men astray.

If that had been all that happened, it would have been bad enough, but then Frontinus compounded his error, and this was what Porcinus had the hardest time understanding, or forgiving. Instead of just acknowledging that he had made a mistake, Frontinus had then, at the very least, misled, if not outright lied to the other Centurions, telling them that just before the assault, he had been given new orders by Drusus. Supposedly, these new orders called for the First to ascend the slope a couple hundred paces before turning to move across the slope, in the direction of the lake. Once at a point where they were behind the wall, they were to descend the slope and attack the Rhaeti from behind. Even without fog, this would have been a dangerous plan; they had all seen that the lower slopes of the mountains were bare of any real cover, so there would be no hiding this attempt. With the fog, while their movement was covered, it also made already treacherous footing decidedly dangerous, and they hadn't gone more than a hundred paces before several men lost their balance and went tumbling down the slope. Several had been injured, and two men were killed even before the assault had properly begun. Still, Frontinus refused the entreaties of his Centurions to descend the slope, insisting that he was following orders. Piecing it all together later, once the men who had taken part in the assault were back in camp, at about the same time Porcinus and the Fourth reached the wall, Frontinus was just beginning his ascent of the slope. By the time the Fourth had taken the wall in their area, and Porcinus sent Urso along the parapet seeking to link up with Frontinus, the First Cohort was struggling across the slope, at least heading towards the lake. The truth was that Urso had never found the First, but as much as Porcinus didn't trust his second in command, or like him, he couldn't fault the action that Urso had taken. Coming down off the wall, he had slowly marched his Century back in the general direction of where the rest of the Cohort was then fighting the enemy formation that had gathered a short distance from the wall. Urso and his men ran into resistance, but it was poorly organized and led, and they inflicted a number of casualties without suffering many themselves. Meanwhile, Frontinus and his men struggled across the slope, until they came to where the wall met the precipice. This was when Frontinus discovered there was a steep ravine, where a small rivulet had cut a deep groove in the side of the mountain that had been hidden from the eyes of the engineers. Not especially wide, it was nevertheless an obstacle that had to be traversed in order for Frontinus' supposed plan of descending behind the wall to work. Seeing that as a sign, even if not from the gods, Frontinus' Centurions, all five, had urged him to give the order to descend the slope and throw their ladders against the wall, and start the assault. Still he refused, instead ordering that the ladders his men were carrying for the assault be lashed together to be used as makeshift bridges across the chasm. The results of this haphazard attempt were nothing short of disastrous, as a half-dozen Legionaries from the First Cohort fell to their deaths while trying to cross the shaky contraptions. As bad as this was, matters were destined to get worse for the hapless Frontinus, who discovered, to his horror, that the sheer face of the precipice extended around the curve of the slope, preventing them from descending. And for Porcinus, the fact that Frontinus, even then, refused to turn back, was perhaps the greatest of his errors, yet he insisted on continuing to push on. It wasn't until Frontinus and his men were close enough to the lake that they could hear the lapping of the waves hitting the shore that the angle of the slope lessened to a degree that allowed them to descend. While it was true they were now well behind whatever Rhaeti line there might have been, they also had arrived too late to be of any use whatsoever. By the time the First Cohort was arranged in a single line of Centuries and were prepared to sweep parallel to the shore, Tiberius' Legions had landed, and the fighting was essentially over. And while Porcinus hadn't come out and openly agreed with his friend, his opinion was much the same as that of Corvinus; Frontinus' career was over.

Chapter 3

It took almost a month for Gaius Porcinus' family to travel to
Arelate, and for young Titus Porcinianus Pullus, a name that he still
was trying to settle into, it had been the most exciting, but agonizing
period of time in his young life. As excited as he was to make this
journey, it was only a shade compared to his anticipation at being
reunited with the big gray horse that had belonged to his adoptive
grandfather. Seemingly with every mile that passed, as he and his
family, accompanied by the two bodyguards, Gallus and Libo,
plodded along, first to Emona (Ljubljana), then to Tergeste (Trieste),
the boy's excitement grew. So too, did his pestering of his mother,
who he was sure was determined to move as slowly as it was possible
to go. His little brother Sextus, just a shade more than five years old,
looked up to his older brother and could be counted on to adopt Titus'
attitude and actions, in every detail. Naturally, this didn't make Iras'
life any easier, who was still nursing the fourth child of Porcinus'
family, the second daughter. Valeria, who was seven, was as attached
to Titus as her little brother was, a fact that Titus found to be unsettling
in the extreme. As far as Titus was concerned, he was practically a
man; the fact that even if his chronological age didn't attest to this, his
size caused people constantly to misjudge his age, only served to
support this belief. While he didn't know it, he was almost identical in
size at ten as his granduncle had been at the same age. Titus' father
was much taller than the average Roman, but in one of those quirks of
nature, young Titus was much brawnier than his father, who was slim
and wiry in build. It had always been this way, and young Titus vividly
remembered the times the man he thought of as his grandfather had
taken him aside after he had used his size to his advantage with one of
his friends. Even now, several years later, Titus' ears burned at the
memory of how ashamed he had felt as his grandfather quietly talked
to him about what it meant to be blessed by the gods to have his size.
That hadn't been the way Titus Pullus had put it to him; by the time

the younger Titus was old enough to understand, his grandfather had severed all ties with all gods, Roman and otherwise. It was something that the young boy had only heard snatches of whispered conversations between his parents, but like all children, what Titus knew and what his mother and father thought he knew were vastly different. Titus had never met Miriam; his only knowledge of her came from his mother, who spoke of her with obvious love and regard. Only once had he brought Miriam up with his grandfather, but while the elder Titus' answer was gentle, the boy had instantly understood that just the mention of Miriam brought his grandfather a great deal of pain. It wouldn't be until many years later, when the younger Titus was an adult, that he would learn the full story. All he knew during the time he was chafing to get to Arelate was that Miriam had been important to his Avus, and for reasons he didn't understand, something to do with Miriam had caused his Avus to sever ties to the gods. So, without invoking the gods, what his grandfather had told him was that just because he had been born to be larger than other boys, that didn't give young Titus the right to use that size to intimidate or terrorize other children. His Avus didn't yell; Pullus had never raised his voice to his grandson, his quiet tone and gentle admonishment was in many ways worse, because what young Titus had felt in that moment wasn't embarrassment, or even anger. What he had felt was shame, and it was a feeling that even now, a few years later, still stuck with the boy. Since that talk, young Titus had been careful not to literally throw his weight around, and, in fact, had backed down on more than one occasion when he had been sure he was right. However, despite his size, Titus was still a boy, and experienced all the vicissitudes that childhood brings. And although the first couple of days on the road were exciting, very quickly, the novelty of the journey and the new sights wore off for him, particularly as every mile traveled brought him closer to what, even then, he was thinking of as his horse.

The only break in the jolting monotony of riding in the wagon driven by Libo, who somehow had been appointed as the permanent driver, which he handled with skill despite the missing hand, was when Gallus spent time helping him hone his riding skills. While Libo spent his day in the wagon, he still had his own mount, tied to the back, plodding along at the same pace as the mules in the traces up ahead.

Titus was curious about this, but when Gallus succinctly explained that it was in the event that the party ran into some sort of trouble, the boy felt a jolt of equal parts fear and excitement. This had been on the second day of the journey and, since that point, Titus spent a good part of the time daydreaming of what it would be like to be set upon by bandits.

On the night after reaching Emona, where they spent the night at an inn, Titus and his mother had quarreled when he had decided that it was time to unveil the secret gift his father had given him the night before they had departed. That gift, which his father had told him was an early birthday present, since Titus would turn ten while they were on the journey to Arelate, was the most precious thing in Titus' possession, at least until he and Ocelus were reunited. It was a perfectly crafted Roman sword, of the type that men still referred to as the Spanish sword. Titus' sword was the same in every detail except its proportions; it was about three-quarters of the size, and while he had no appreciation of such things, the boy was dimly aware that it must have cost his father dearly to have it crafted for him. But unlike the toy swords his friends carried, almost all of them made of wood, although some of the boys whose fathers were Centurions like his had ones made of metal, this one actually had an edge.

"When we're together again, I'll teach you how to put a really good edge on it," Porcinus had told Titus. "But it's still very sharp as it is, so you be careful with it!" His father had become very serious then, using the same tone of voice that Titus only heard on those occasions when he had sneaked into the camp to spy on his father as he did his job. It was what Titus thought of as his father's Centurion voice. "Titus, this is a tool, just like a hammer, or a chisel, or an axe. But this tool's primary purpose is to kill another man. You must always keep that in mind whenever you handle it, because a sword doesn't have a conscience; it can bite its master just as easily as it can bite its master's enemy. Do you understand?"

Titus, his manner matching the solemnity and gravity of his father's, assured Porcinus that he did, swearing that he would always treat it with respect.

"Good." Porcinus nodded. Then, he added, "And this is something your mother doesn't need to know about it. It's just between us men, right?"

Although his father had given him a grin and a wink as he said this, Titus knew perfectly well his father was serious, and that Porcinus' admonishment was at least partly based in a healthy dose of fear of his wife, and her temper. This was something that Titus not only understood, but shared with his *paterfamilias*. In many ways, his mother, despite the fact that he was now as tall as she, was more fearsome than his father, so it wasn't hard for him to agree that it was, in fact, a very good idea not to bother his mother with such trifling details as a sword.

However, that had been before the talk of bandits, after a few days on the road where Titus' imagination was given free rein. Although they were traveling on a good Roman road, and there was a fair bit of traffic going both ways, including small detachments of mostly auxiliary troops marching to and from various outposts, Titus became convinced that every bend and every section of road surrounded by forest was a perfect spot for an ambush. It was well known in Siscia that the native tribes that occupied the area were always seething with unrest, still chafing under Roman rule, despite the obvious improvements to their overall living conditions. Now these barbarians were lurking, just waiting for the chance to fall upon a vulnerable traveler, and Titus was sure that his party made a tempting target. The fact that there were three grown men; Diocles, who was riding his own horse Thunder, a roan gelding whose name was far more fearsome than the horse itself, Gallus, who always ranged ahead, looking out for the same thing that Titus did, and Libo driving the wagon, didn't mean anything to Titus. In his imagination, they would be beset at any moment by a huge band of bloodthirsty barbarians. And while he didn't need any help in his fantasy, the night they spent in Emona, the first night under a roof of the trip to that point, only fueled his conviction. Choosing an inn that, although it wasn't of the quality where one would find a traveling patrician, was nonetheless of a clientele and cost far above what a drover, wagon driver, or average trader could afford, the party took two rooms, one for the family and one for Diocles and the bodyguards. Regardless of the quality of the other guests, the type of gossip and conversation was much the same in every inn, and the topic was almost exclusively about the rebellion that was occurring up north with the Rhaeti. Although separated by a good distance, the men and few women gathered in the common room that served as both dining room and tavern made it sound as if these rebellious, bloodthirsty warriors were just outside the outskirts of Emona. There was much talk of how dangerous it was traveling at this point in time, and Titus was too young to understand that the people who made such statements did so to add spice to the mundane reality of their particular journey. From his limited experience, grownups were the authority, and everything they said was taken without any skepticism or questioning of motive. To Titus, that meant the danger he had spent the previous days imagining was, in fact, very real. That night, he tossed and turned, disturbing Sextus and Valeria, both of them mumbling in protest at their own disturbed slumber, wrestling with the dilemma posed by his promise to his father. Finally, he dropped off to sleep, but only after coming to a decision.

That decision prompted what would be one of the first two crises of the trip, when Titus, after demanding some privacy that kept his party waiting outside the inn, finally emerged from inside. Although it took a moment for her to discover the cause, what Iras noticed immediately was the different way that Titus carried himself. Whereas before he had tended to slump, conscious of how he towered above his friends, this morning shortly after dawn saw him walking with his shoulders thrown back and, if anything, was clearly trying to appear taller than he actually was. In that moment, Iras caught her first glimpse of her firstborn not as the child he was at that moment, but the man he would become, and the effect on her was an emotion she hadn't ever experienced. Equal parts pride, fear, and a sense of loss at this first sign of the inevitability of adulthood washed through her, and her vision suddenly clouded as her son strode to the wagon, becoming a shimmering image that suddenly reminded her of her native country of Egypt and the mirages that were a feature of that barren land. Unknown to Titus, who was only aware that, just as he had hoped, all eyes of his family and the others were on him, he won a reprieve of a few precious heartbeats of time before his mother wiped her eyes with the hem of her cloak. This moment didn't last long; before he reached what Titus thought of as the safety of the wagon, where he could settle in among the pieces of luggage near the back of the wagon that he had claimed as his spot, his mother spied the cause of this dramatic entrance.

"Stop. Right. There."

Titus, like every child experienced with the tones used by parental figures and the meaning of each, knew his mother's words, sounding as if they had been bitten off, meant instant obedience was the only safe choice. So he did as she commanded, freezing almost in mid-stride, which would have left him with a foot hovering above the ground. However, he did plant both feet on the ground, and while he didn't remember doing so, both Gallus and Libo would hide grins at the sight of the boy bringing himself to the perfect position of *intente*, in an unconscious mimicry of his father and every man of the Legions.

"What is that?"

If Titus had had a moment to think, he would have determined that pretending ignorance was probably the worst tactic he could have used, but he was still a child, and like all children, their favored method of dealing with consequences was to delay them by any means.

Consequently, his reply, "What is what?" was such a bad choice that Diocles, already sitting on Thunder, winced, while Gallus suddenly had a coughing fit that sounded suspiciously like a laugh.

Titus' siblings weren't so circumspect; both Sextus and Valeria suddenly bursting out in giggles at their elder sibling's expression as much as his words.

"Don't you dare pretend you don't know what I'm talking about," Iras hissed, and Titus instantly knew that this was going to be a seriously uncomfortable moment.

Nevertheless, he drew himself even more erect than he had been, and in his best attempt at sounding like the grownup man he so desperately wanted to be, he replied, "This is my sword. Tata gave it to me before we left. He had it made for me, and it's actually a real sword. Look." He drew the short blade, liking the hissing sound it made as it left the specially made scabbard. Swept away was any attempt to be adult about this, his enthusiasm and excitement about this fabulous possession just too overwhelming. "Isn't it beautiful, Mama? Truly?"

If Titus had hoped that his mother would be awed by what even Diocles could see from his spot on Thunder was beautiful workmanship, it was in vain. His mother was completely unmoved by the dull sheen that even then picked up the light from the torches at the entrance to the inn. All she saw was a weapon, a dangerous object in the hands of a boy who she was convinced was much too young to have anything like that in his possession. It would have given Titus little comfort to know that her anger at that moment was more with her husband than with her son; while she couldn't share his excitement, she did understand why a young boy would have such feelings. Unfortunately for Titus, his father wasn't there to share in her wrath.

"I don't care how beautiful you think it is. You're taking that…thing off and you're going to give it to me for the rest of the trip. When we get to Arelate, we'll talk about it. But until then, you're not to touch it again. Do you understand me?" Holding out her hand, she finished, "Now, give it to me."

"No."

From where Diocles sat, able to see both Iras and Titus, it was impossible for him to tell who seemed to be the most surprised, the boy or the mother. In fact, Titus was the more shocked of the two; this was the first time in his life that he had so openly defied his mother, and in some dim recess of his mind, he recognized this as an important moment. This was his first open act of independence, and in the length of time it took him to utter the small but powerful word, his resolve hardened into something as strong and unyielding as the black stones that paved the road on which they were traveling. Iras, on the other hand, was stunned into speechlessness, which Porcinus, if he had been there, would have wryly congratulated his son for achieving, since it was extremely rare that his wife was ever at a loss for words.

Finally, Iras managed a strangled whisper. "What did you say?"

"No," Titus replied, but he didn't say it defiantly, just as a simple statement of intent.

Whatever had caused Iras' momentary uncertainty vanished, and as resolute as Titus was, he felt his knees shake at the expression that now took over her face. I've never seen her this angry, he thought, but somehow, that only made him more determined to prevail. He had no way of knowing, but this was a trait with which Porcinus and Diocles, even more so, were very familiar.

It was a single-minded, almost mulish stubbornness and a refusal to submit that had been a hallmark and defining trait of young Titus' adoptive grandfather and, watching the scene before him, Diocles felt as if a giant but invisible hand had suddenly seized his heart, squeezing it hard. Oh, Master Titus, if only you could see your namesake right now, he thought, what would you say? Would you counsel the boy to listen to his mother? Or would you be proud that he's refusing to submit, something that you would have done at his age?

Oblivious to the Greek's thoughts, Iras suddenly found herself on the ground, leaping off the wagon seat with a lithe grace that hadn't been diminished by the years or childbirth. The baby, in a basket on the seat, who had been asleep, was apparently disturbed by the sudden movement and slight rocking of the wagon caused by her mother's dismounting, and began to cry. Libo, seated on the other side of the basket, was torn between what looked to be an interesting moment and trying to soothe the baby. Meanwhile, Iras, now on the ground, crossed the distance between the wagon and her son, who hadn't moved from his original spot a half-dozen paces away from the wagon, roughly equidistant between it and the inn.

Watching his mother approach, Titus fought an almost overwhelming urge to flee, knowing that by giving in to it, he would not only shame himself, he would draw the laughter and mockery of the small crowd of travelers who had been drawn to this small drama being played out. Do not run, he told himself, and although he had no way of knowing it, while this was the first time he would be guided by this inner voice, it was far from the last. Regardless of his inner turmoil, by the time he made the decision to stand his ground, the choice was gone because his mother was standing in front of him, her breathing harsh, blasting against his face as she placed herself almost nose to nose with Titus. Both mother and son had a moment where their thoughts were completely in unison as they both realized with a sudden surprise that they hadn't been this close in some time, and that Iras was now shorter than her son. Not by much, but he was still only ten. Unfortunately for Iras' cause, this boosted Titus' confidence, bolstered by having the high ground, in a manner of speaking.

"I'm not going to tell you again, Titus," Iras said softly, but with an odd detachment, he saw how her nostrils were flared and her eyes dilated, both of them signs that she was on the edge of doing something drastic. "Give me the sword."

"No, Mama," he said again, but before he could stop himself, he hurried on with a pleading tone. "You heard the talk last night. It's dangerous right now because of the rebellion. We're going to need every sword…"

"That's what Gallus and Libo are here for," his mother cut him off.

"I know, but it can only help to have me armed as well. You do see that, don't you?"

"What I see is that you're too young to have a dangerous weapon. What your father was thinking…"

Now it was Titus' turn to cut his mother off in mid-sentence.

"What he was thinking was that I'm ready to have this." He gestured to the sword, understanding that drawing it again wasn't a good idea.

"Well, he was wrong," Iras snapped. "And I'll talk to your father about it later."

"He's the *paterfamilias,* Mama," Titus tried to reason with her, thinking that perhaps a legal argument would help his case. "What he decides is law. You know that."

The look that Iras gave her son was one he would have cause to remember over the course of his life; a half-scornful, half-amused expression that would become one with which he was all too familiar, always coming from the women that would be in his life.

"You're just a boy," Iras retorted. "You don't know anything about things like that."

As soon as she said it, Iras recognized that she had made a horrible mistake, probably the worst thing she could have uttered under the circumstances. Before she even finished, she saw her son's expression change, his lower jaw suddenly jutting forward in a look she knew all too well. Oh no, she thought, why did you have to say that, Iras?

"I'm more than halfway to being a man." Despite his best effort, Titus couldn't hide the hurt from his voice. "And I'm already as big as some men, Mama. I'm bigger than you." Horrified, he felt the tears welling up in his eyes, and only he would ever know the willpower it took to keep them from filling his eyes. "So I'm not giving you the sword."

He didn't see it, but he certainly felt the shock of pain as her hand snaked out to slap him, hard, across the face. It was like a sudden fire erupted across the whole left side of his face, and he let out a gasp of pain, but it was his mother's eyes that suddenly filled with tears. Without thinking, he reached up to touch the side of his face, yet somehow, the tears that threatened to burst forth a moment ago had suddenly dried up. It was with equal parts surprise and unease that Titus recognized why; as much as his face and his feelings hurt, more than anything, he was angry. And it was a kind of anger towards his mother that he had never experienced before, not the kind of anger a child has when they think they're being treated harshly or unfairly by a parent. It was an anger that Iras saw in her son's eyes and, despite her own rage, gave her pause. A sudden feeling of almost overwhelming sadness came over her as she recognized that not only had she lost this battle over a sword, she had lost a part of her son as well. When she looked back later, nothing ever seemed the same between mother and son after that.

The next crisis actually came later that day, after a tense two watches of a silence that enveloped everyone. Titus spent the entire time riding Libo's horse, but instead of passing the time next to Diocles or Gallus, he chose to ride by himself a short distance away from the wagon. However, when the party reached the point where the road split, and without any discussion Diocles, who had joined Gallus ahead of the wagon, turned in the direction that would take them to Tergeste, Iras ordered a halt.

"Why are we going that direction?" she asked Diocles, although she knew the answer.

Diocles sighed; he had been warned by Porcinus the probability of this happening.

"We're going to Tergeste to catch a ship," he told Iras. "It will be faster than taking the overland route through Aquileia."

"By ship?" Iras shook her head. "No. Absolutely not. I won't take my family by sea. We're going overland."

"Iras, it's going to take longer if we go overland," Diocles replied patiently.

"I don't care," Iras shot back. "I'm not in any hurry. Are you?"

Since the wagon had come to a halt, Titus had drawn closer, but to this point, he remained silent. He was about to open his mouth when Gallus beat him to it.

"Mistress Iras," the bodyguard was always respectful, something Iras appreciated, "I'm with you about not wanting to go by sea."

Iras looked over at Diocles triumphantly, but it was short-lived.

"But, while I don't want to, I also think it will be safer to go by sea than to continue overland," Gallus said quietly.

Staring at him in disbelief, Iras exclaimed, "Not you too? Surely you're not scared by all the talk at the inn last night! I expect it from Titus; he's just...young." She caught herself from using the dreaded "boy" that had caused the original problem. "But that rebellion is more than a hundred miles north of here!"

Gallus' face flushed, but his tone remained calm.

"No, I'm not worried about the Rhaeti," he replied. "At least, not right now. But we're going to be passing through countryside that's even rougher than this, and the fact is that there are bandits along the Via Postumia."

"He's right, Iras," Diocles put in. "It's just safer in the long run if we take the ship. And the voyage is short, barely more than a day. We've been on a lot longer voyages than that."

"Only if a storm doesn't come up," Iras said stubbornly, but Titus could see that she was weakening.

Nothing more was said for several moments, but when the silence was broken, it was by Titus.

"If you want to take the overland route, Mama, then I agree."

Iras looked over at Titus in surprise, then she quickly recognized his words for what they were: a peace offering. In a flash of insight, she also understood what at least part of his motive was and, her anger still outweighing any desire to make peace with her son, that made up her mind.

"Fine," she sighed. "We'll go by ship."

Don't think I don't know you, Titus, Iras thought with grim amusement. You wanted to go to the overland route because you think there might be trouble. She again looked over at her son, and favored him with a smile that communicated that knowledge.

Despite Iras' fears, the voyage went smoothly, the weather cooperating and allowing the crossing to take the expected amount of time. Landing at Ariminum (Rimini), the party resumed their journey, this time in relative safety as they traversed the Via Flaminia to the northwest. After the novelty of the sea voyage, as short as it was, barely two full days from the time they left the port at Tergeste to when they tied up at the dock in Ariminum, the monotony of daily travel resumed its hold on Titus. Traveling through the peaceful countryside of Aemilia, as active as Titus' imagination was, he was hard-pressed to see danger anywhere as he and his family rolled past miles of ordered farmland and large estates. More out of boredom, the boy began spending time with Diocles, who he had known his entire life, but only as his grandfather's servant. The fact that the Greek wasn't in the Legions had caused Titus to dismiss him as someone worth talking to, a fact that Diocles viewed with quiet amusement. Very quickly, Titus learned that while Diocles hadn't wielded a sword, he had been involved in almost every exploit of his adoptive grandfather from the first civil war onward, and had seen things and been witness to events that were spoken of with great awe and even greater respect. Their first day spent together, Titus learned that Diocles had been at Pharsalus; while the boy only had a very rudimentary knowledge of this battle that shook Rome down to its foundations, he did know that adults like his father considered it to be a very important event. Somewhat to Titus' surprise, however, what he found he enjoyed the most was the Greek's stories about his grandfather that didn't have to do with battle. Young Titus Porcinianus Pullus had no way of knowing that this trip would turn out to be one of the most formative periods of his young life, over and above the tangible effects of what was an unusual amount of travel for a boy his age.

For Iras, it was a mixed blessing; while the stories distracted Titus from his preoccupation with the idea that they were under threat of attack at any moment, she feared that her former fellow slave and friend was planting ideas and thoughts in the boy's head that would be incredibly difficult to root out and destroy. She had known from the moment her firstborn came that her former master would cast a giant shadow over the boy's life, but she had pinned her hopes for the future of her family on the very thing that she knew would be so alluring to her boy: the prowess and achievements of Titus Pullus.

When Iras had been sent by Cleopatra VII, who was actually her half-sister, the result of a quick union between their father Ptolemy and one of the palace slaves, to assassinate not just Titus Pullus, the Primus Pilus of the 10th Legion, but his *de facto* wife, Miriam, she had accepted that this was her fate, to be used as a weapon of revenge by her queen. She ultimately failed in her mission; the only casualty was Pullus' slave Eumenis, who had tasted the grain that Iras had poisoned when she worked for Deukalos, who had been convinced by the stack of gold coins offered to him to take Iras on and allow her to perform her mission. Deukalos was given strict instructions by the emissary sent by Cleopatra, that once she performed her job, Iras was to be disposed of and never seen again. But Deukalos was a weak man, in every sense of the word. Enormously fat, his appetite ran to matters of the flesh as well, and when he saw Iras, who was a true beauty that even now caused men to stop and stare, his resolve had failed. Instead, he had sent his wife to visit relatives while he took Iras to his bed, which was where she had been found by an understandably angry Titus Pullus. He hadn't been alone; in fact, even as she thought about it these years later she felt a flush as she thought of how it was Pullus' nephew who had first determined her identity, and actually had seen her naked for the first time when he yanked the sheet that she was hiding under off the bed. While Porcinus had been shot by Eros at that moment, if she were being honest, Iras' first thoughts about the young Roman hadn't been tinged with love, or lust. No, her first concern was practical, and that was in winning another few moments of life, stopping the vengeance that Pullus thought was his due because of not just the death of one of his slaves, but by virtue of the fact that Iras' ultimate target was him and Miriam. To this day, Iras still wasn't sure how it had happened, but while she wasn't a normally religious person, she had always felt that it was somehow ordained by the gods that she would be spared. The vehicle of her salvation had come with what she had overheard between her mistress Cleopatra and one of her counselors, where the queen had ordered that in the event that Iras was unsuccessful, the job be finished by a group of hired mercenaries. Fortunately for Iras, they had believed her, and after dispatching the merchant in his home, she was thrown in a sack and carried along with Pullus and his party of men, consisting of two of his Centurions and best friends, Scribonius and Balbus, and Gregarii who the giant Roman trusted with his life.

Over the years, Iras had often thought of the irony created by the fact that the burden of carrying her, bound and gagged, had fallen to the man who would become her husband and the love of her life. Their run through the streets of Ephesus (Selçuk), from the merchant quarter where Deukalos lived, to the temporary quarters of the Primus Pilus and his wife had been one of exquisite discomfort and fear for Iras, bouncing around inside the dark sack. When they arrived at Pullus' quarters, the attack by the group of mercenaries had already begun, but the men Pullus left behind, guarding against this very possibility, had stopped the attackers from breaking in and slaughtering Pullus' woman. Falling on the mercenaries from the rear, Iras' only clues about the short, sharp fight came from what she could hear before she was abruptly hauled somewhere else. She was unceremoniously dumped out of the sack onto the floor of what turned out to be Pullus' apartment, marking the first time she ever laid eyes on a woman who would become the most important figure in her life, even more than her mother. In the very beginning of their relationship, Iras had viewed Miriam as simply a means to an end, the best tool she possessed at her disposal to live another day, because Miriam's husband made it very clear he had every intention of killing her. While Pullus was occupied elsewhere outside the apartment, Iras had pleaded with Miriam, still a stranger, to spare her life. And it had worked; when Pullus returned, grimly determined to exact vengeance while sending a message to Cleopatra, his woman had bravely stood between the giant Roman and Iras. Reasoning with him that, ultimately, it would alarm and shake Cleopatra more to see that Iras lived, Miriam had persuaded Pullus to stay his hand. From that shaky beginning, a relationship formed between Iras and the woman she rightly viewed as her savior, and if her transferal of loyalty to her new mistress was dictated by a sense of honor, over time, the bonds of affection for this quiet, calm, and good woman had cemented their relationship. Iras was integrated into Pullus' household, becoming Miriam's attendant, and she had never wavered in her service and loyalty towards her mistress. It wasn't until months had passed, and Pullus had relented from his early practice of chaining her every night, never forgetting the circumstances under which she had entered the collective lives attached to the Pullus name, that her relationship with Gaius Porcinus had begun. Oh, she had known from the very beginning, in the barely lit bedroom of a now-dead merchant's house, when the young Gregarius had yanked the sheet off of her, that he had wanted her. That was something Iras had long grown accustomed to, the covetous and appreciative looks from men, but never before had she been slightly interested in returning those gazes with what could be considered encouragement. And, being truthful, much like the beginning of her relationship with Miriam and Pullus, there was a healthy streak of self-interest when she let Porcinus know that she was as interested as he was in pursuing matters. That, she thought ruefully as she sat on the wagon seat watching her son and Diocles deep in conversation, had been before. Before she had learned what kind of man Gaius Porcinus truly was, before she found herself falling in love with him. She had mistakenly assumed that the nephew was merely a younger version of his uncle, in temperament if not in size, yet fairly quickly, she learned that there was much more to Porcinus than she originally thought. He was as ambitious as his by then-famous uncle, but with a softer side to him that Iras only occasionally glimpsed in Pullus. It wasn't that surprising that the rolling monotonous rhythm of the wagon took her thoughts to a place of real sadness and loss, and Iras was honest enough to admit that there had been more to Titus Pullus as well, and that much of what had shaped the large Roman was born from tragedy. She hadn't been part of his household when he lost his first wife and his two children to a plague, while he was off in Africa fighting at Thapsus under the man they called Divus Julius now, but Diocles had been there and seen the aftermath firsthand. The Greek hadn't spoken of it often, but when he did, it had always been with sense of heartfelt loss and sympathy for his master. However, she was there when Miriam had died during childbirth, and was a witness to the final transformation of Titus Pullus, as the last remaining soft spots in his soul were blasted away by heartbreak. He became, according to men like Sextus Scribonius who had known him since he was sixteen and a Gregarius in the newly formed 10th Legion, the man of his early years, ruthlessly ambitious and only truly comfortable when he was in battle, doing what he did best: killing his enemies. While she and Gaius didn't speak about it much, it had saddened her a great deal to watch what she considered the best part of Titus Pullus the man wither away and die, just as the mistress she had come to love did trying to give him a son. But even in the midst of death, both physical and spiritual, love had grown between Iras and Gaius and, while she was still relatively young, she was mature enough to reflect on the path the gods had chosen for her life, and realize with quiet satisfaction that she had absolutely no regrets. Still, it was hard for her to quell a pang of unease as she watched her son learn what it meant to be the son of Gaius Porcinus, and the adopted grandson of Titus Pullus. The incident with the sword was enough to worry about; now she had to fret about the exploits of a legend and the impact it would have on her son.

Just a day less than a month after they departed, the family of Gaius Porcinus rolled into Arelate. Unknown to any of them, the *paterfamilias* had just faced the Rhaeti on the lake, and was now marching with an army of four Legions, now that Drusus and Tiberius had reunited, heading for Noricum. In Arelate, young Titus was almost beside himself with excitement, barely able to contain his fidgeting in the back of the wagon as his brother and sister hung over the side, peering at all the new sights and sounds. Unlike Siscia, Arelate was very Roman in its layout and in the style of building, and while there were traces of this in Siscia, Arelate had been founded from the ground up as a veterans' colony and was not built on a native settlement. This meant that the forum was in the middle of the town, where the streets were laid out in a manner that any Roman Legionary would instantly recognize, while the brick *praetorium* was located along one edge of the forum. Augustus had recently commissioned a number of new projects, including an arena and theater, neither of which had reached Siscia at this point, at least in a permanent form.

Normally, Titus would have found everything that was going on around the wagon as it rattled along the paving stones as interesting as his siblings did. At this moment, however, the boy only had thoughts for a large, gray horse that he had convinced himself knew he was coming, and would be eagerly waiting for him in his stall. Diocles had trotted Thunder ahead of the wagon to alert Agis, now the second most senior member of Pullus' household, that Porcinus' family was arriving. Libo had a bit of trouble maneuvering the wagon through the stone archway in a wall that, to Titus, was almost as tall as the one surrounding the fort at Siscia. That wall, made of dressed stones and not the more common brick, surrounded what appeared to be almost an entire block just a few streets away from the forum. As inexperienced as he was in such matters, Titus could easily see that the people who lived in this part of the town were the wealthy ones and, for the first time, he had an inkling that his grandfather hadn't just been important in the Roman army, but had been one of those rich people that all his friends talked about becoming. Once inside the walls, Titus stood erect in the back of the wagon, craning his neck to take in his surroundings.

"How many times have I told you not to stand up while the wagon's moving?" Iras snapped, but before he could either utter a retort or comply, the wagon creaked to a halt.

Without waiting, Titus leaped over the side, landing on the ground and immediately running up to Agis, demanding, "Where's Ocelus? Where's his stable? Where's Simeon? I need to talk to him about Ocelus!"

Poor Agis, already hampered by being somewhat slow of mind, was further encumbered with a stutter. Fortunately, this only showed itself in moments of stress; unfortunately for Agis, the sight and sound of a very excited ten-year-old boy, an overgrown one at that, was something he considered very stressful.

"M-m-master T-t-t-titus?"

In his excitement, Titus had forgotten about Agis' stutter; it had been several years since he had last seen the slave, after all. Just as he was about to open his mouth and shout at the hapless man, now in his middle age, balding and with a slight paunch, he had a vision of his grandfather, and their talks. Would Avus yell at Agis for stuttering right now, Titus wondered.

Knowing the answer immediately, the boy took a deep breath, and asked in a softer tone of voice, "I'm sorry for yelling, Agis. Can you tell me where Ocelus is stabled? I want to see him."

Despite being soothed by the youngster's words, Agis still didn't trust himself to speak. Instead, he simply pointed to a building at the far corner of the compound. Without a word, Titus spun about and headed for it at a sprint, leaving a confused Agis standing there, unsure what had just taken place. During that exchange, Diocles had helped Iras, who was holding the baby, down from the wagon. Walking with her to Agis, Diocles grinned at his erstwhile friend and compatriot.

"I'll bet you can't guess what young Master Titus is here for, can you?"

Agis laughed at this, feeling more at ease now as he greeted Iras warmly. For a moment, the trio stood there, regarding each other and, if they had been so disposed to share their thoughts, they would have discovered how similar they were to each other. Each of them had been a member of Titus Pullus' household; all three had been slaves. Now, each of them had their freedom, and Iras was married to a Centurion, a fabulously wealthy one at that, and had a family. For Diocles and Agis, however, matters were more complex. Whereas they had their freedom, the ability, and the means, thanks to the generous bequest from their former master, to go and do as they pleased with the rest of their lives, neither man had shown any inclination to do so. It was something that Iras had been curious about, and had brought up with Diocles on the journey, but the answer he gave her had somehow seemed, at the very least, incomplete. The Greek had mumbled something about making sure that all the bequests and instructions of Pullus' will were carried out to the appropriate degree, but when Iras pressed him about his plans after that, he had been vague. Deliberately so, if Iras was any judge. It was something that she was determined to get to the bottom of before they left Arelate to return to Siscia. By this point, the other two children had been helped down by Libo, who held Valeria by the hand as he led them to their mother. Introductions were made; Valeria had been a toddler when she had last seen Agis, and Sextus a babe in arms. Agis turned and called out; immediately, a girl and an older woman who Iras deduced was the girl's mother emerged from the villa.

"This is Glenora." Diocles indicated the older woman, whose iron-gray hair was pulled back tightly against her skull, while her hands were red and chapped, something that caused Iras a momentary pang of guilt.

It had been quite some time since she had done the kind of work around their house that caused hands to look like Glenora's. Oblivious to Iras' discomfort, Diocles called the other female, and as she approached, Iras saw that she was older than Iras had first assumed, perhaps in her early twenties.

"This is Birgit," Diocles announced, and in a flash of what her husband would have called feminine intuition, Iras understood that, whatever this Birgit's role was in the household, she played a much bigger one in Diocles' life.

As the two women greeted each other, Iras and Diocles' eyes met, and her suspicions were confirmed by the rapid flush that swept over the Greek's features. Why, you're old enough to be her father, Iras thought with some amusement as she introduced her children to the other two women. Gallus and Libo had unloaded the wagon by this point, and Agis beckoned to them, moving towards the wing of the villa where they would share a room. Before they entered, while the whole group was outside, a shout caught their attention. It came from the stable, and Iras, her mother's instinct immediately engaged, turned and thrust the baby, who had managed to stay asleep, into the unready arms of Diocles, who was the closest to her. While he took the little girl immediately, if Iras had been in a better frame of mind, she would have burst into laughter at the look on the Greek's face, who held the sleeping child in his arms as if he was afraid the infant would turn into some sort of deadly serpent. By this point, Iras was already several paces away, heading for the stable when the door to the building flew open, flung wide as if it was kicked. Iras' mind barely had time to register this before a gray blur burst into view, the sight accompanied by a drumming, thundering sound that came up from the ground into Iras' body. Before she could do anything more than gape in astonishment and fear, a large gray horse, with no saddle, but with a boy on its back clutching a handful of rein and mane, went thundering past her, shooting through the still-opened gateway and into the street. Within a half-dozen heartbeats, Ocelus and Titus had disappeared from view, although their progress could be tracked by the shouts of alarmed citizens in the streets. Closing her eyes, the image that was burned into her mind was the last thing her eyes had managed to capture, the sight of her son wearing the broadest smile she had ever seen him wear. She was only vaguely aware of being joined, but when she turned expecting to see Diocles, she was surprised to see that not only was the Greek there, but there was another man beside him, panting heavily. It took her a moment to recognize the face of Simeon, who, up until a few moments before, had been Ocelus' caretaker. He had come sprinting after his charge and the boy, but even in his old age, Ocelus was the fastest horse he had ever seen, and Simeon came from Armenia, where horses were their life, and had seen many, many horses.

"I'm sorry, mistress," Simeon said, his Latin still carrying the heavy influence of his native tongue.

He had come into Pullus' ownership as part of the spoils of the campaign in Armenia conducted by Marcus Antonius, back when the 10th Legion was under the command of the Triumvir of the East, and Pullus had proven to be a fair master. But unlike Diocles and Agis, Pullus hadn't manumitted Simeon, meaning that he technically belonged to Porcinus, which meant Iras, and she wheeled on him, ready to take her anger out on him.

Before she could speak, Simeon hurried on. "I tried to stop him. I swear it by all the gods, I did! But he tricked me! He promised he wouldn't ride him yet, that he just wanted to put a bridle on him to walk him out! He waited until I turned my back, then he hopped on Ocelus, and before I could do anything, he was gone!"

Iras' anger instantly deflated. Between the fact that she still was very sensitive to the lot of a slave, having been born into servitude herself, and the understanding that what Simeon said was, in all likelihood, the truth, her only reaction was to shake her head.

Oblivious to the obvious relief of Simeon, she muttered, "That boy is going to be the death of me."

Titus knew that he was going to be punished for what he had done, but in all honesty, he felt that whatever his mother meted out would be worth it. His reunion with Ocelus had been everything he dreamed of and more. Flinging the door to the stable open, he had startled Simeon, but Ocelus was standing in his stall, ears pricked forward and looking in what Titus was sure was an expectant way at the door. Titus was right, as far as that went; Ocelus had picked up the boy's scent in the short period of time it took Titus to run to the stable. Sliding to a halt, Titus' view of Ocelus started shimmering as he felt a torrent of emotion burst forth, coming up through his chest and his throat so strongly that he physically felt like he was going to choke with it. He had known he would be excited, and happy to see what was now his very own horse, but he hadn't expected this sudden feeling of sadness and loss that threatened to overwhelm him as the import of why Ocelus was his hit him. Simeon was frozen in the position he had been in when the door burst open, with a pitchfork in his hand, about to toss the sweet hay it held into Ocelus' stall. Squinting for a moment, Simeon relaxed when he realized that it was the boy, his master's grandson or something. Simeon had never been sure exactly what the familial connection was.

"Master Titus?"

Titus didn't trust himself to speak, so he only nodded, but as he did, he walked slowly to Ocelus, who had lowered his head over the half-door of the stall. Truthfully, Titus didn't have anything to say to Simeon; the boy had instinctively seen the Armenian horseman as a rival for the big gray's affection, and of all the things the boy worried about, it was the idea that Ocelus had forgotten him, and he belonged wholly to Simeon. As he was about to discover, his fears were unfounded, because when he was close enough to reach out and touch the old stallion, Ocelus, nostrils fully dilated as he breathed in the scent of the boy, reached out with his mouth, and grabbed at Titus' tunic. Instantly, Titus' anxiety disappeared, and he gave a laugh of such pure delight that Simeon couldn't help but smile himself.

The Armenian had known about his master's bequest of the horse to the boy, and he had been informed by Agis that the boy and his family were on the way. But he had held out a hope, a slim one he knew, that somehow, someway, the boy would either never show up, or Simeon would at least be allowed to continue caring for Ocelus. When one is a slave, it doesn't pay to wish for more than the barest of essentials; a kind master, enough food, a safe and warm place to sleep. Wishing for more than that was unwise, Simeon knew, but he had been around horses his whole life.

Oblivious to Simeon's turmoil, Titus and Ocelus got reacquainted, and it delighted Titus immensely that it was Ocelus who made the first move. It was a little thing, that tugging at his tunic, but that tug represented what had been a daily ritual that went back as far as Titus could remember. He had vague, fragmented memories of being carried, either by his father or more commonly his grandfather, as the younger Titus clutched the apple he insisted that only he give to Ocelus. Once Titus began walking, he would still be accompanied, but under his own power, he would go to see Ocelus to give him his apple. One day, Titus couldn't remember exactly when, he had tried to trick Ocelus, approaching the horse with empty hands, telling Ocelus with all the sincerity he could muster that he had forgotten to bring the apple that day. The gray wasn't fooled, however; his sense of smell was so much keener than Titus' that the boy never had a chance of tricking the horse. Immediately, Ocelus had thrust his warm, velvety nose into the folds of Titus' tunic, snuffling and sniffing until he found where the boy had secreted it. And although Ocelus had torn Titus' tunic in his attempt to get to the apple, much to Iras' consternation, not once, not ever, had the giant horse bitten the boy. Now, in the stable at Arelate, Ocelus had picked up the game as if it had last happened just the day before, and Titus was sure that there would never be a moment in his life, no matter how long it was and how much he accomplished, where he would be happier than right then.

"He remembers you," Simeon's voice broke the moment, and despite himself, Titus scowled at the man.

"Of course he does," Titus retorted with more assurance than he had felt just a moment before. "I knew he would."

"They never forget anyone," Simeon said simply.

Then he turned to resume his task, and Titus recognized that, at the very least, he owed Simeon a debt of gratitude for taking what he could see was good care of the gray. Not that Titus wouldn't have happily performed all the mundane and sometimes unpleasant tasks associated with the care of an animal of Ocelus' size, but he hadn't been here.

"Simeon." Titus' tone was tentative. "I just wanted to say…thank you. Thank you," he repeated with more confidence now that he had uttered the phrase, "for taking good care of Ocelus."

Simeon's dark face beamed at the compliment, and he gave the boy a deep bow that, if Titus was older, he might have taken as a mocking one.

"It was my greatest pleasure, Master Titus. Ocelus and I are old friends. Aren't we?" He put down the pitchfork to reach up and give the horse a pat on the neck, prompting a soft nicker in response. Or, at least, Titus thought, as much of a sound as a horse can make with a mouth full of apple.

"Has he been exercised today?" Titus tried very hard to make his tone casual, just one horseman conversing with another, but even to his own ears, he could hear how false it was.

Realizing that, he gave Simeon a grin, and of all the things he could have done to soften the Armenian's defenses, that was it. Instantly transported back in time to when he was Titus' age, in Armenia, he could vividly recall the intense longing in his own ten-year-old heart when he asked, no, he begged his father to be allowed to take his father's prized stallion out for a ride.

"Why, no, Master Titus, he hasn't had his exercise today." Simeon grinned back, and at least for the moment, Titus' antipathy towards the Armenian was obscured by their common love of horses. "I think he could use a bit of exercise. Just to stretch his legs, yes?"

Without waiting for an answer, Simeon took a bridle hanging from a nail pounded into one of the vertical support beams. Ocelus caught the movement and suddenly tossed his head, his own excitement rising at the thought of being allowed to do what he had been born to do. Obediently dropping his head, Ocelus waited patiently as Simeon brought the bridle up and over his ears before cinching it in place. Taking the bit with no more than his usual reluctance, Ocelus began pawing at the dirt floor of his stall, signaling his eagerness to get started. Simeon had turned to get the saddle, but Titus could wait no longer. Opening the gate, the horse came out almost bouncing with suppressed energy. Impulsively, Titus grabbed a handful of mane, and using a slat of the stall as a boost, threw himself upward and straddled the back of the big stallion.

"Master Titus! You shouldn't ride him without a saddle! It's been a long time since anyone has ridden him bareback!"

Titus laughed and shook his head.

"I'm sorry, Simeon, but I'm not getting off. I've waited too long for this."

Only another horseman could understand, but while Simeon did, he had a more practical objection, and it was one that at least temporarily dampened Titus' mood.

"What will your mother say when she sees you go riding by without a saddle? She might have me whipped!"

Although this last was an exaggeration, as it had been years since any of Titus Pullus' slaves had felt the lash, it did cause Titus to pause.

Thinking for a moment, his face brightened. That was when he gave Simeon the concocted story, what the Armenian would tell his mother just moments later. Then, with a kick to his ribs, Titus launched Ocelus at the partly closed stable door, who opened it by simply lowering his head and using it as a battering ram. Titus' shout of joy was still ringing in Simeon's ears after boy and horse had disappeared.

When he would think back on it later, the next ten weeks that Titus and his family spent in Arelate held some of the happiest moments of his life, and some of the most momentous. The first full day wasn't the best one for Titus, because as punishment, he was barred from all contact with Ocelus. While Titus didn't like it, he also understood; he had been gone a full watch on his ride with Ocelus, who had behaved and performed as if all the years and associated wear and tear had never happened. The bond between boy and horse that had begun forming even before Titus could remember was cemented on that ride. That made the next day even more painful, but it passed, even if it was too slow for Titus. After that, boy and horse quickly developed a routine, and whenever Titus was missing from the villa, he could be found in the stable caring for his newest and most treasured possession. Iras had expected her son to be eager to perform most of the chores that were involved with the upkeep of a large animal, but when she saw him willingly mucking out not just Ocelus' stall, but the entire stable, it gave her pause. To Iras, this was the first sign that he was becoming a responsible man, and much like Titus had experienced at his first meeting with Ocelus, albeit not as strongly, she again felt the tug of competing emotions, a sense of pride in her son, and the ache that comes from understanding that time never stood still.

Fortunately for Titus, Iras' attention on her son was distracted, not just by the other children, as Sextus and Valeria had been left by their older brother to their own devices. And Pullus' villa was very large, with many rooms, nooks, and crannies that deserved to be explored by the two younger children. That alone would have been enough, but Iras had other matters occupying her attention. Starting the first night, when the family sat down to a meal prepared by Glenora, discussions had begun between her and Diocles, the talk focused on the practical matters involved with not just the villa, but Pullus' entire fortune.

"One reason that we've escaped notice from Augustus so far as far as the part of Master Titus' fortune that he hasn't taken already is because most of it is in property, not cash," Diocles explained.

This made sense to Iras, and she said as much.

Diocles continued. "Master Titus allowed me to invest his money as I saw fit. You know he never really cared about money, other than as a means to an end. And," Diocles' mouth twisted as if he were tasting something bitter, "Augustus made sure that he paid for that end."

Diocles' anger at what Augustus had done was fully shared by Iras, who had her own reasons for the sentiment she now expressed by uttering an oath, in her native language, as she spat between two fingers. Despite the fact that they were alone, in Pullus' villa, Diocles nevertheless visibly flinched.

"I hope you know better than to do that where anyone other than me can see it," was how he put his concern to Iras. "Especially around here. We came through the forum, remember. Didn't you see that statue of him in the center?"

"I saw it, and I'm not stupid," Iras assured the Greek. "Remember, I grew up with the Ptolemies."

Mollified, Diocles continued, noticing as he did that young Titus was trying very hard to appear as if he wasn't listening, engaging in desultory conversation with Valeria next to him. The boy is trying to become a man, all at once, he thought, although he gave no outward indication that he was aware of what Titus was doing.

"The only restriction Master Titus put on me was that none of his money went into farms." He gave Iras a smile, and she noticed for the first time that the Greek had lost a lower tooth. Had it been recent, she wondered. Diocles paused for a moment as he sipped from his cup. "So most of the estate is now invested in a couple of mining ventures, a shipping company, that sort of thing. All of them are doing very well. The income just from the interest is a few thousand sesterces a month."

The way Diocles so casually mentioned a sum that was beyond Titus' imaginings had a tremendous impact on the boy, but he could see his mother was no less impressed. She had let out an audible gasp at the news, and she sat back in her chair, her meal completely forgotten.

"And we can't touch any of it," she finally spoke, her voice laced with bitterness.

"No," Diocles granted. "At least, no, you can't touch most of it, not in a lump sum anyway. I've figured out a way to divert some of the money in a way that I don't think will attract any attention. I think you'll be safe if we don't take more than a thousand sesterces a month from the sum."

While this didn't satisfy Iras completely, she was forced to acknowledge that just that amount would be more than her husband's yearly pay several times over. Still, it wasn't enough, but for Iras, it was about more than just the money. Born a slave, she had been subject to the whims of the small proportion of the wealthy of both her native Egyptian and adopted Roman society for her entire life. In her view, while her former master Titus was the one who had achieved what was an impressive rise in the rigid hierarchy of Rome, he had actually been fortunate enough to die ignorant of the malevolent gift that the man called Augustus would bestow on his heirs. It was her husband, and, most importantly, her children who were bearing the real brunt of Augustus' vindictiveness. And although it was nothing she would ever utter aloud, especially around Diocles or her husband, a part of her anger was directed at Pullus himself, who in life had always seemed determined to antagonize his social superiors at every opportunity. It had almost cost him everything; she still could easily recall, the memory even now causing her to shudder, the dread inspired by that period of time when Pullus had been recalled from Siscia to go to Rome to stand trial. Every day, she worried that a knock on the door would bring the news that Pullus' luck, almost as celebrated among the men of the Legions as that of his first general, Divus Julius, had run out. That knock had never come; at least, not right away. It was only after he died that his family and heirs learned of the poisonous gift bestowed on them by the man who controlled Rome. If only he had just kept his mouth shut more often, Iras thought as she sat at the table, listening to Diocles.

Focusing on Diocles' last words, Iras interrupted, "You think you can do this? You're not sure?" She shook her head emphatically. "Augustus has eyes everywhere. That's too big a risk to take."

"I didn't say it wasn't without risk," Diocles retorted with asperity, clearly nettled by what he saw as Iras' lack of faith in him. "But not even Augustus can track a hundred sesterces here and a hundred there. Besides," he added, "he thinks he's won already, and I'm sure he's got other, more pressing concerns by this point."

That, Iras had to concede, was all true, but she still couldn't resist a bitter jab.

"He thinks he's won? That's because he did win!" She pointed at Titus and the other children. "They won't be equestrians! They won't have all of this!" She waved a hand to indicate the villa. "They'll have to make their own way in the world!"

"Is that really such a bad thing?" Diocles asked quietly. "Iras, you've seen what happens to the generations who haven't had to work for anything. Look at Rome. Look at the patricians and the old plebeian families and how they've done nothing noteworthy despite all the advantages they've been given. By Hades, look at some of the rich equestrians, the merchants who give their children everything, and how they do nothing but drink, gamble, and carouse and cause all sorts of trouble! Is that what you really want for Titus? For Sextus? Or Valeria? Or...Miriam?"

His voice caught as his throat threatened to close over the last name, that given to the babe who even then was cradled in Iras' arms. Diocles, if for different reasons, had loved Miriam as much as Iras did, and it was another tie that bound two together who otherwise would have had little to do with each other. Although, in most ways, Diocles understood the dilemma facing Iras when she was sent to murder his master, Eumenis had been Diocles' closest friend, the second slave that Titus Pullus had brought into his household. It had been extremely difficult for Diocles to forgive Iras, and even now, there was a barrier between the two, a reserve that Iras sensed, and understood. Nevertheless, they had much more in common with each other, and over the years had often worked in concert behind the scenes to affect an outcome between their respective masters. If there wasn't much affection between them, there was respect, and Iras took what Diocles said seriously.

Sighing, she replied, "No, that's not what I want. For any of them. But it's just so…unfair that Augustus can do something so petty and underhanded to a man who served him so well."

"That, I completely agree with," Diocles said. "But you of all people should know that fairness, justice, whatever you want to call it, isn't part of the world we live in." Chuckling, he finished, "No matter how much philosophers talk about it."

Turning to other matters, the two adults at the table continued their discussion. Meanwhile, Titus had heard and absorbed everything they had said. The fact that it was the first time that his mother, Diocles, or anyone had actually discussed the circumstances behind what had happened to Titus' Avus so openly in front of Titus meant that it had an impact that would have tremendous implications.

When Titus wasn't riding or caring for Ocelus, he explored Arelate, always finding something new and interesting, usually in the side streets and alleys. Initially, Iras wouldn't allow him to go out without an escort, and for some reason, it was always Gallus who volunteered for the duty. But very quickly, Titus and Gallus came to an understanding that the fact that Gallus spent all of his time sitting in a tavern drinking wine as Titus wandered around alone wasn't something Titus' mother needed to know. Consequently, Titus and Gallus would leave the villa, walk to the far end of the forum and around the corner, where Gallus would stop at his spot, while Titus continued his exploration. Although, at first, Titus was a bit nervous in unfamiliar territory, he grew in confidence each day, gradually increasing the distance each trip. By the end of the first week in Arelate, he had traveled down to the river harbor, where the wharfs were located, a bustling, noisy place that he found particularly exciting. Although he couldn't articulate why he did so, he always made sure that he remained in a hidden spot as he made his observations, watching the gangs of slaves assigned to the loading and unloading of the ships, while their overseers walked about, whips at the ready. Other slaves, identified by the bronze placard worn around their necks with the name of their owner inscribed on it, were hurrying in all directions, some carrying crates or pushing small carts, others carrying tablets that Titus assumed were messages of some sort. There were several wharfs jutting out into the river, which was very wide; in fact, it was the widest river Titus had ever seen, which made the two bridges across all the more impressive. He had heard someone say that it was the Rhodanus (Rhone), but that was all he knew about it. It was still a remarkable sight, even if it did smell so much that he had to cover his nose with his tunic when he got close, at least until he became accustomed to the stench. Each wooden dock was long enough to accommodate at least two wide ships on each side, and whenever Titus came to the river, he rarely saw any berths empty. Across an open area that had been built up from the riverbank and was made of wooden planks, there was a line of stone buildings, and around the entrance into each building, there were usually at least a couple of men talking. Titus never got close enough to make out what these men talked about, although sometimes, they looked like they were having a very friendly conversation or even sharing a funny story; other times, they did a lot of shouting, waving of arms, and pointing fingers at each other. One day, he had sought out and asked Diocles about what he had seen, thinking that the Greek would know, so he was disappointed when the answer was one word, "Business."

"But what kind of business?" Titus asked, but Diocles only shrugged.

"All kinds," the Greek replied, his eyes never leaving the scroll he was examining.

Seeing that he wasn't going to get any more than this, Titus left his Avus' study, where he knew he could always find Diocles. The boy liked going into his grandfather's study, mainly because he was sure that he could still smell his presence, a combination of leather from the harness that still hung from the stand that was just like the one his father used to hang his own on, the rich odor of the hundreds of tightly wrapped rolls of vellum that Titus knew was something called a library, but more than anything, Titus was sure he could still smell him. Even if he had uttered this aloud and had been asked, he wouldn't have been able to explain it, and a tiny piece of his mind chided himself that it was his imagination. How could the scent of anyone still linger, months after they were dead and gone? As far as the scrolls went, when Diocles had told him that one day these books would be Titus', he had scoffed at the idea. To his surprise, Diocles hadn't been upset about this lack of interest, and, in fact, had laughed.

"Don't worry," he assured Titus. "Your Avus felt the same way when we first met, and he was a lot older than you. That will change."

Titus didn't see how that was possible; while he had learned his letters, and he could write his name, further literacy was something that had been put off by his parents as something to be done later. And why would anyone want to read when they could be outside, doing something much more interesting? Still, just like his conversations with Diocles on the trip, this exchange planted a seed in the boy's mind that would gradually take root and grow into a full-fledged idea.

As interesting as the wharf was, once Titus made his other discovery, the allure of the waterfront quickly fell by the way. Once he had wandered around the western part of Arelate up to the river; he hadn't worked up the courage to cross on one of the two wooden bridges to do any exploring on the other side, he turned his attention to the area to the northeast of the forum. His Avus' villa was located at what he had been told was the southwest corner of the forum, just a block away from the southern boundary. Normally, this would have meant just walking straight across the forum, but there was too much construction going on, so he had to skirt around by heading east on the main road, called the Via Aurelia, before turning north. Gallus' spot was a short distance from the southeast corner, so the day Titus went in that direction, it worked out perfectly.

Once past the forum, the boy took the first street north, coming upon the newly constructed theater a block later. Despite his general lack of interest in anything to do with theaters, he found his feet slowing as he looked up, slightly awestruck by the sight of the soaring columns, still white and gleaming in the morning sun. The pediment had intricately carved figures, and while he knew that what he was looking at was something from the myths his father and others had told him, he wasn't sure which one it was. What was unmistakable was the statue of Augustus, who had paid for this building and to whom it, and from what Titus could see just about every other public building here, was dedicated. Stopping, he stood staring at the statue, recalling the conversation he had listened in on at the dinner table the first night, and he felt a cold, hard lump forming in his stomach. It was a strange and unsettling feeling, one that Titus had never experienced before, and his confused mind tried to sort out and identify the rush of emotions. He could easily tell he was angry, but at what? A statue? A cold lump of stone? As he stood there, still staring hard at the statue, his brow furrowed and with a hard scowl on his face, it slowly came to him and, in that moment, Titus took another, tentative, step towards manhood. He recognized that what he was angry at was what the statue represented, that while he didn't hate the marble, he hated the man who it depicted. For young Titus, it was simple; he had learned that it was because of this man that his mother was upset, and Diocles was upset, and although he didn't show it, his father was upset. The man represented by this statue had committed an unjust act against not just his Avus, which was enough of a horrible crime in itself, but against his family. Suddenly, the thought of baby Miriam came unbidden into Titus' mind and, for a moment, he thought that the lump in his stomach was somehow real and was about to burst. She was a baby! Granted, she was a nuisance; she made a lot of noise, and her *cac* stunk up the whole room, but his mother had assured Titus, Sextus, and Valeria that they had done the same thing, and he had no reason to doubt this was true. But what had she done to this man that her future would be such that it worried his mother to the point Titus was awakened by her crying the night she and Diocles talked? What crime had she committed? Or Valeria or Sextus? What had he, Titus Porcinianus Pullus, done, other than be named for a man who everyone Titus knew told him was a great man, perhaps one of the greatest Legionaries in all of Rome's history? He still hadn't moved, but there was a shift inside him, as the anger turned into...something else. Something that he had even more trouble identifying than the original emotion that had rushed through him. It was a hard, bitter resolve that somehow, in some way he, young Titus, still just a boy, would find a way to right this wrong done to his family. And part of that, Titus knew, meant that it was his duty to exact vengeance on Augustus. If he had been even a few years older, this was something that he would have quelled within himself immediately, shoving it back down into his gut, where it would remain undiscovered and unheard. But he was still a boy of ten, and to a boy that age, all things are possible; the only obstacle in the way was his number of years, but that would change and in a few more years, he would be a man. And when he was a man, for Titus, it was a simple proposition.

"One day, I'm going to kill you."

"You're going to kill who, boy? Who are you talking about?"

If it was possible for a boy of ten to drop dead of fright, Titus was sure that it would have happened to him at that moment. He whirled around, his heart suddenly hammering so hard that he could hear it in his ears, beating so loudly and so fast that he was afraid the man staring down at him would hear it as well. Did I say that aloud? he wondered. He must have, but he certainly didn't remember doing so.

"Who are you talking about, boy? I'm not going to ask you again."

Titus opened his mouth to answer, but nothing came out. The man's features were completely obscured because he was standing with the sun to his back, causing Titus to squint up at him, but he still only saw the man's outline. That meant he didn't have any warning when a hardened hand lashed out to slap him across the face.

BAM!

Stars of every color burst in front of Titus' eyes, and he took a staggering step backward, but he didn't lose his footing. Although he didn't know it, his assailant was secretly impressed by that; he had hit the boy hard, and he was sure that other twelve- or thirteen year-old boys would have been on their backs, crying their eyes out. Titus' eyes were certainly filling from the pain, but somehow he managed to avoid crying out or letting the tears spill down his cheeks.

Instead, he managed, "I…I…I wasn't t-talking about anyone. I was just…talking."

The man laughed, but it wasn't a pleasant one.

"So you're just talking to yourself? Are you addled in the brain, boy? Is that it?"

By this time, Titus had managed to shift his position just a bit so that the man blocked more of the sun, giving the boy the opportunity to see his assailant more clearly. What met his eyes wasn't encouraging; the man looked much like Gallus and Libo, an older, hard-bitten man whose eyes watched him coldly. There was a scar, white with age, running down the side of his face from just below his left eye to the corner of his mouth, which pulled one edge into an expression that looked as if he was leering with just one side of his face, but there was nothing friendly or humorous in his countenance.

"No." Titus decided that answering the man's question about his mental state was the best way to avoid a subject he didn't want to go into. "I'm not…addled."

WHAM!

This time Titus did fall backward, and for a moment, he was suddenly sure he had lost the vision in his left eye. Despite the pain and what would quickly turn out to be temporary blindness, the boy scrambled to his feet, more out of instinct than anything else. It was a good thing that he did so, because the man had aimed a hard kick with his foot at the spot where Titus had been just a moment before. Staggering, Titus held one hand to his left eye, although he kept the right one fixed on the man, who again gave him a smile of pure malice. It was only then, now that he had some distance between the man and himself that he noticed the tunic and belt. His heart sank; was this man an off-duty Legionary? But while he couldn't immediately identify it, he sensed that there was something different, that while similar in style, what he was looking at wasn't a Legionary. That was when Titus saw that instead of a sword, the man had a cudgel, held by a leather thong strapped to his belt.

"I think you were talking about murdering the Divine Augustus," the man spoke.

"No, I wasn't!" Titus' reply was instant and uttered with as much conviction as he could muster, even if it was a lie.

"Oh?" the man sneered. "You just happened to be staring at his statue and talking about killing someone else?"

"Yes!" Titus cried. "I just happened to be staring at the statue and I was thinking about someone else when I said it."

"Who?"

Titus' mind raced, but he was almost as surprised at the words that came from him as the man to whom he was speaking.

"Simeon," he replied.

"And who is this Simeon? And what's he done that you're going to kill him? Is he a playmate of yours and he stole one of your toys?

Although the mocking tone lacerated Titus' already bruised pride, he understood that he was being baited.

"No, he's a full-grown man. Like you. Bigger than you," Titus added, happy to see the smirk on the man's face fade a bit.

Something came over the man's face, and he shifted slightly as he tilted his head, as if looking at Titus with new eyes.

"Ah," he said softly. "It's like that, is it? He's made you his bum boy?"

The part of Titus' face that hadn't already been reddened from the two blows suddenly flushed with a heat that made him feel as if he had been out in the sun all day.

"No! It's nothing like that!" he insisted. "He's…he's our groom. And he wants to keep my horse even though my Avus gave it to me!"

The man didn't say anything, clearly waiting for Titus to continue, so he did, telling essentially the truth to this man he had come to believe was some sort of city guard. At least, it was the truth as Titus had believed it when he had first arrived in Arelate, but it was close enough that when he told the guard the story, it had the ring of sincerity to it. When he was finished, the guard scratched his chin, squinting at the boy thoughtfully.

Finally, he asked, "What's your name, boy?"

The change that came over the man the instant Titus gave his full, newly adopted name was instantaneous, and it caused Titus to chastise himself for not saying it sooner. Already his eye was swelling closed, and in the back of his mind, he knew he would have to come up with quite an explanation for it when he went back to the villa.

"You're the grandson of Titus Pullus?" the man asked doubtfully, as he suddenly didn't seem to be so sure of himself as he had been a moment before.

"Yes," Titus answered, his voice throbbing with pride. "My father is Gaius Porcinianus Pullus. He's the Quartus Pilus Prior of the 8th Legion."

The man closed his eyes for a moment as he swallowed hard.

"Well," he finally said, "you should have said something earlier."

Titus stared at him in astonishment, but as he was about to open his mouth and argue, he caught himself. Thinking quickly, he realized that he was going to have enough to explain without prolonging an argument about how this guard had come upon him, and what he had been saying. For reasons he couldn't articulate, he understood that he would be in just as much trouble from Iras, and Diocles for his indiscretion, as he was from this guard.

"Yes, sir," he mumbled. "I'm sorry, sir."

Clearly surprised, the guard stood there for a moment, unsure what to do. Like Titus, he had no wish for this little incident to become known by those above him. It was true Titus Pullus had been dead for several months, but the man was a legend, especially here in Arelate. And legends, dead or not, had friends. If it became known that he had cuffed Pullus' grandson, while he didn't think much bad would happen to him, it was enough of a question that he had no intention of finding out.

"Well, young Pullus." The guard now did favor Titus with a grin, but while Titus wasn't disposed to make an issue of this incident, neither was he willing to forgive, and he glared at the man, who ignored the look. "I need to be on about my business, and I'm sure you do as well."

Still not completely mollified, Titus nevertheless turned to go, but by this point, he had forgotten he wanted to explore the northern part of the town. Besides, he was no longer in the mood, so he began heading for the forum. Seeing the boy heading in that direction, the guard had a sudden disquieting thought; what if the little bastard was going off to find one of the officers of the *vigiles*? Or even worse, went straight to one of the Urban Praetors?

"Oy! Boy! Master Pullus!"

Titus turned slowly, his expression wary, but he didn't say anything.

"Do you like the arena?"

Unsurprisingly, this got Titus' attention and interest. Still unwilling to speak, he answered with a nod.

"Would you like to take a peek at some of the gladiators training? The *ludus* is just up the street." He jerked a thumb back in the direction that Titus had originally intended to go. "And I know the *lanista*. He owes me a favor, so I can get you inside the grounds while they're training."

Strictly speaking, this was a lie; if anything, it was the other way around, and the guard owed the trainer, but the guard was determined to get in this pup's good graces, and if he had to owe the trainer more, so be it.

Suddenly, Titus forgot all about his eye.

That day, Titus found a new pastime, one that almost rivaled spending time with Ocelus, and for the remainder of the time he spent in Arelate, whenever he wasn't with Ocelus, he could be found at the *ludus*, watching the gladiators train. The fact that this happened more than once, that the *lanista* allowed him to watch, and not just from some hiding spot, but up in a small box of seats that overlooked the training arena, came about as a result of what Titus was certain was the best news he had ever heard. When he had returned to the villa after his run-in with guard and after his first glimpse of the *ludus*, once he had endured the thorough questioning from Iras about the cause of what was well on its way to becoming a black eye, he had sought out Diocles. Naturally, he had lied to his mother about the cause of the damage, insisting that he had simply not been paying attention to where he was going and walked directly into a low-hanging beam of some sort. Iras had been completely unconvinced, but quickly determined that she would never learn the real story behind her son's first black eye. Finding Diocles in the study as usual, Titus began the conversation by casually mentioning that he had wandered by the *ludus*. The reaction he got was totally unexpected, as Diocles looked up sharply from the ledger he was writing in, piercing Titus with a gaze the boy was sure he had never seen before on the Greek's face.

"And what were you doing over there?" Diocles' tone told Titus instantly that he was in dangerous waters. "That part of town is no place for you, Titus. Very…unsavory people inhabit that area."

Titus shrugged, suddenly becoming intensely interested in a loosely rolled scroll that was lying on a waist-high cupboard crammed full of them, fingering it idly with his eyes fastened to it.

"I was just curious," he said. "I've never seen where the gladiators train before."

Diocles said nothing for a moment, just continued staring at the boy, and Titus had the sense that he was deciding something. Finally, without saying anything, the Greek got up from what he still thought of as his desk, tucked in a corner of the spacious study, and walked to the door. At first, Titus thought that Diocles was leaving the room; instead, he shut the door, taking care not to slam it, but easing it closed before throwing the bolt.

Seeing Titus' face as he turned around, Diocles grinned at the boy as he said, "Your mother has very, very sensitive hearing."

Immediately seduced by the idea of some sort of conspiracy aimed at keeping his mother in the dark, it brought an answering grin to Titus' face, and he waited as Diocles returned to the desk and took his seat again. Immediately, all signs of levity left his face and demeanor.

"What I'm about to tell you is a secret, Titus," he began, which naturally arrested the boy's undivided attention. "In fact, it was the only secret I kept from your Avus, and for that, I do feel some regret. But he trusted me to invest his money." Diocles' voice trailed off as he stared at something Titus couldn't see, and as impatient as Titus was for his grandfather's secretary and friend to continue, he sensed that this was something that had to come out on its own, without any prompting.

Diocles went on, "And when I looked at all the various ventures that were the safest bets, and had the best potential for the long term, I saw there was one type of business that was better than anything else I looked at." Now he glanced at Titus, gauging the boy's reaction, and was cautiously pleased to see the dawning of understanding on his face.

Before he could continue, Titus interrupted, speaking slowly, "So…you're saying that you invested in the *ludus*?"

Diocles hesitated before answering, "No, I did more than invest."

Titus stared at him, comprehension slowly coming to him, and he couldn't stop a small gasp of astonishment.

"You mean, we own a *ludus*? We own gladiators?"

When put this way, even if it was true, it caused Diocles to wince, a reaction that Titus didn't understand in the least.

"Why do you look like that? This is the best!" Titus exclaimed, forgetting in his excitement to keep his voice down, causing Diocles to dart a glance at the door as he held his hands out in a placating gesture to the boy, silently begging him to lower his voice.

Titus understood instantly, and whispered, "Sorry. But, still…." A broad grin split his face, and Diocles imagined this was much the same look as when Titus was reunited with Ocelus. "We own a *ludus*!"

"Your parents own a *ludus*," Diocles admonished sternly. "And it's much, much more complicated than that."

Titus understood and acknowledged the first part of the Greek's statement, but he was prompted to ask, "Why is it complicated?"

Diocles sighed, silently castigating himself for indulging the boy and thereby opening up a topic that he wasn't sure Titus was ready to hear. Don't underestimate the boy, he thought as he looked at Titus carefully, evaluating the oversized youth, trying to determine if his internal age matched his size.

Finally, he made his decision and said quietly, "Titus, I'm going to trust you, and I'm not going to treat you like you're still a child. I'm going to talk to you man to man. Understand?"

Titus' face was solemn, and while he said nothing, he nodded his head.

"I know you were listening in on the conversation your mother and I had a few nights ago, even though you were pretending you weren't."

Diocles got his answer by the rush of blood that came to Titus' face, confirming what he had only suspected to be the case.

"So you know that because of Augustus, your family has to be very careful. You understand this, right?"

Now Titus answered, his words rushing out in a torrent of emotion that he had bottled up.

"Yes, I know what he did to us! And I'm going to exact vengeance one day! I swear on the black stone!"

If Titus had thought Diocles would be pleased by this show of loyalty to his Avus and family, he was proven wrong. Before he could react, the small Greek had leaped from his chair, moved from behind his desk, and crossed the few paces to where Titus was standing. Grabbing Titus' left arm in a grip that made the boy wince, Diocles' face came just inches away from the boy, and Titus had never seen that expression on the man's face before.

"Don't you ever say anything like that again, boy! Ever! Do you understand me?"

As he spoke, Diocles emphasized his words by shaking Titus, and while he was alarmed, the boy was also impressed; he hadn't known this Greek who stood just a couple inches taller than he already was possessed this kind of strength. But it also served to emphasize how seriously Diocles had taken what he said, and Titus' immediate next thought was the memory of the guard who had given him the black eye for uttering essentially the same thing.

"Y-yes, Diocles! I understand!"

If he had thought that would assuage Diocles, he was wrong, who shook his head and continued squeezing Titus' arm.

"That's not good enough! You said you would swear on Jupiter's black stone that you would have revenge on Augustus. Well." Now he relinquished his hold on Titus' arm, but it was only to walk to the large chair with a table next to it that Titus had been told was where his Avus spent most of his time, reading. The table was cluttered, and it took Diocles a moment to retrieve what he was looking for, but when he returned to Titus' side, he was holding something in his hand. Thrusting it in front of Titus, Diocles said, "I want you to put your hand on this and swear to me that you will never, ever utter those words, or anything like them, aloud again."

Titus looked down at Diocles' upturned hand, and it took a moment for his eyes to focus on the object he held in his palm. It was a round, metal disk with a hole drilled in it near the edge, through which there was a leather string. As Titus stared down at it, his vision suddenly clouded when his eyes took in the small words etched on the disk. Those words were more accurately described as a name, and it was a name that Titus instantly recognized, because it was almost identical to his own new name, even if in simpler form.

"This is your Avus' identity disk that's given to every man when he retires from the Legions," Diocles quietly confirmed Titus' guess. "I wasn't supposed to give it to you until you donned the *toga virilis*, or," he added something that Titus found disquieting, "in the event I don't live that long, your parents were to give it to you. Your Avus wanted you to have it so that you would remember him, and how much he loved you."

Titus' composure had begun to crack when he laid eyes on the disk, but Diocles' words shattered it completely, and he felt a huge, wracking sob coming up from within him. Before it came out, Diocles grabbed his arm again, squeezing it so hard that it served to arrest his grief, even if it was momentarily.

"No. You can't cry right now, Titus," Diocles told him firmly. "Not until you put your hand on this disk, like a true Roman man, and swear to me that you will never, ever say anything about Augustus that can be used against you or your family, ever again."

Titus put his hand over the disk, feeling the warmth from Diocles' own hand, and he would never know where the strength and resolve came from, but his voice was strong and his eyes clear as he said, "I swear it, on the memory of my Avus, and for my family. I will never give Augustus cause for suspicion."

For the remainder of his life, young Titus Porcinianus Pullus had cause to remember that day, and every time he did, he silently thanked Diocles for performing one more act of loyalty to his family.

There was a happier outcome to that talk with Diocles, and that was in the form of a small scroll, written by Diocles, and hidden by Titus in a hole he found in the brick wall that made up part of Ocelus' stable, that he gave to the *lanista* on the second visit there. The *lanista's* name was Maximius Vulso, a man a bit younger than Diocles, but older than Titus' father, with a shaved head and a large black patch covering one eye. Even with the patch, Titus could see pink, puckered skin that extended down Vulso's cheek. More impressive was how tightly muscled the man was; his tunic was stretched tightly across his chest, while his biceps bulged so much that, to Titus, it looked as if the muscles were about to burst through the man's skin. Running down his left arm was another long, pink scar, and he was missing a fair number of teeth for a man his age. Yet, somehow, Titus wasn't afraid of him, even when Vulso, after reading the little scroll, stared at the boy with his good eye, clearly appraising him in much the same way he would with a new slave brought to the *lanista*.

"So you're Pullus' grandson, neh?"

Titus nodded, but didn't say anything.

"Speak up, boy!" Vulso growled. "Don't act like one of those bum boys that hang around down by the theater!"

Despite the man's fearsome tone, Titus found himself grinning at the man, who was clearly surprised at the boy's lack of fear.

"Heh. Maybe you are Pullus' grandson after all," he muttered, handing Titus the scroll.

Then, he winked at Titus, marking the beginning of a most unlikely friendship.

"Well, according to that chicken scratch I'm to let you wander around," Vulso said, then spat on the ground. "But that's not happening, boy. I don't need one of my men lopping your head off just because you got in the way. So, whenever you're here, you're either by my side, or you're sitting up there." He pointed up to the box seats, covered with an awning. "But don't expect me to have one of the girls wait on you." Vulso gave Titus another wink. "At least not for a couple more years."

That was how Titus found himself spending part of his day at the *ludus*, usually after taking Ocelus out for a ride, rubbing him down, and attending to the other chores required for keeping his horse happy and healthy. None of this went unnoticed by his mother, but no matter how much she pestered and questioned her oldest son, she never learned his true destination. This didn't come to Titus without a cost; very grudgingly, he began to allow Sextus and Valeria at least to witness his daily ritual with Ocelus, making them stand to one side and watch as the horse nosed about for his apple. That was how it started, at least; within a few days, Titus gave in to the constant begging by both of his siblings to be allowed to feed the horse their very own apple. Not surprisingly, Ocelus was clearly in favor of this concession, but it only took one time for Titus to discover, much to his chagrin and disgust, that three apples a day was too rich a diet for his horse. He did exact some revenge by forcing Sextus and Valeria to participate in cleaning up the mess, but this didn't stop them from clamoring to be allowed to feed Ocelus. Very grudgingly, at least at first, Titus allowed his siblings to participate, each of them allowed to hand Ocelus his apple, alternating between the three of them. And while at first, Titus was very put out, he began to enjoy watching his brother and sister and the joy they got from being allowed to participate in what they knew was something very important to him. This he would never admit to anyone, especially to them, but it made him feel like...a big brother. There was another price Titus had to pay in order to spend his time at the *ludus*, and that was a hefty bribe to Gallus. Naturally, Titus didn't have money, nor was that what Gallus was interested in; he was an avid fan of gladiatorial games, so the price of his complicity in the conspiracy to keep Iras in the dark was accompanying Titus to the *ludus*. Although Titus was somewhat apprehensive, Gallus and Vulso hit it off immediately, both of them recognizing a kindred spirit in the other. Titus was mature enough to understand that Gallus' enthusiasm for the blood sport, and his obvious appreciation of some of the finer points helped Vulso's acceptance of this sudden addition to the spectators. Very quickly, Titus came to value Gallus' presence, as he would point out some nuance or provide some clue as to why one of the sweating men down in the training arena performed a certain maneuver. Therefore, nobody involved was surprised when Titus worked up the courage to initiate a conversation with Vulso, who hid his amusement and treated the youngster with a gravity that Titus was too young to know was mostly feigned.

"Can you show me how to fight?"

The truth was that Titus had rehearsed in his mind a much lengthier, more compelling request, but when actually in the moment, all those carefully rehearsed arguments were nowhere to be found in his mind.

"Show you how to fight? For what?" Vulso laughed. "You're rich. Don't you know that, boy?"

Titus opened his mouth to explain how this was not the case, but stopped himself, Diocles' demand fresh in his mind.

Instead, he just said, "I don't care about that. I want to learn how to fight. To protect myself." Suddenly inspired, he added, "In case someone tries to rob me!"

Vulso stifled a smile, deciding not to point out that a boy as rich as Titus Pullus had been, no matter what his origins, would be able to hire men like Vulso and Gallus to protect him.

"All right," he relented. "I'll show you a few tricks of the trade. But," he glowered at Titus, "if I do, you have to agree to do what I tell you, when I tell you to do it, without any questions. Understood?"

Titus actually hesitated a moment, wondering about the deeper implications of his oath, a sign that even in the short period of time since he had left Siscia, he was beginning to mature. But the lure of what was being offered was too strong for anything more than a momentary pause.

"I swear," he said to Vulso.

While he was satisfied, Vulso still had a surprise for Titus.

"Good," the *lanista* grunted. "Then you can begin by doing this."

Dropping to the ground in a prone position, Vulso began to push himself up and down, performing several repetitions while Titus stood and watched. Once he was finished, Vulso stood and indicated that Titus should perform the same action. The boy did, but if he had known what he was about to experience, he might have instantly regretted his decision.

Understandably, it was Iras who noticed her son moving gingerly about the villa a few days after his second trip to the *ludus*.

"Why are you limping?" Iras demanded of her son.

Titus froze; he had been heading to the stable with his brother and sister with him; it was Valeria's turn to feed Ocelus his apple.

"I...I tripped yesterday," was the best that he could come up with, and he saw his mother's eyes narrow, the sure sign that she wasn't fooled.

But then, salvation came from what was, to Titus anyway, an unlikely source.

"I saw him, Mama," Valeria spoke up. "He tripped over his own feet when he was trying to show off." She gave a girlish giggle at the imagined sight. "It was really very funny!"

It was Titus' expression; crestfallen, embarrassed at the thought that his little sister was witness to his clumsiness, that convinced Iras the cause for her son's limp was as her daughter had described it, and her response was to roll her eyes.

"Well, you just need to be more careful," she admonished, something with which Titus wholeheartedly agreed, assuring his mother that he would indeed be more careful.

As the trio of children made their way to the stable, Titus didn't say anything to his sister, but favored her with a wink and pat on the head that she would remember for some time to come. If Titus were being honest with himself, he would have been secretly relieved that his mother discovered the truth, because he had never been this sore in his short life. The first exercise that Vulso had demonstrated had only been the first of many, and the *lanista* hadn't relented at all just because of Titus' age. Although he didn't know it, young Titus had started a training regimen, preparing for combat, at an even earlier age than his Avus, who had wheedled and begged a veteran of Sertorius' rebellion in Hispania to provide a twelve year-old Titus Pullus and his best friend at the time, Vibius Domitius, a similar type of instruction. While the two styles of fighting were different; Legionaries were part of a tightly knit team and trained in a manner that reflected the knowledge that there were men on either side providing support, while with a gladiator, he was almost always the sole combatant, performing for a crowd, the underlying fundamentals were the same. And the basis for both was a solid platform of overall fitness, although Titus wasn't in the right frame of mind to appreciate this. Still, he performed the exercises prescribed for him by Vulso, while Gallus served as observer and morale booster, encouraging the boy as he struggled through the regimen. And while he was loath to admit it, it wasn't long before Titus noticed a difference in himself; he was slower to tire, and tasks like mucking out the stables that had taxed him before left him feeling as if he hadn't done them at all. That made it easier for him accept the fact that he had, to this point, been unable to show Vulso what was still his second-most treasured possession, the sword given to him by his father. Finally, perhaps a dozen days after he had begun the program given to him by Vulso, he managed to smuggle the sword out of the villa, hidden under his cloak. This day, Titus was determined to force Vulso to allow him to begin training with his sword, prepared to argue and use his status as the grandson of the owner of the *ludus* to allow him to do more than the infernal exercises. When he and Gallus arrived at the *ludus*, and Vulso pointed to what had become the boy's accustomed spot for doing his exercises, for the first time Titus didn't obediently move. When Vulso, so accustomed to obedience that it took him a moment to understand what was happening, finally stopped to stare at Titus, the boy still didn't move.

"I want to start training with this." Titus' voice shook, but he stood defiantly, still not moving.

He had produced his sword, and for a moment Vulso stood rooted himself, then burst into laughter at the sight, pointing at Titus' small weapon.

"Boy," he was laughing so hard that his words came out in wheezing gasps, "where did you get that thing? You couldn't kill a dog with that, let alone a man!"

Titus was infuriated by Vulso's dismissal of his sword.

"My father had this made for me!" His voice throbbed with the fury and passion that coursed through his body. "It's not a toy sword! It has an edge just like yours!"

While Vulso's first instinct was to continue laughing, he saw the boy's face, and something in him relented. Instead, he took the time actually to look at the blade that Titus had drawn from his scabbard, and realized with some surprise that it wasn't the toy sword he expected.

"Let me see that," he demanded, and with only a slight hesitation, Titus presented it to Vulso.

Examining it closely, despite his initial skepticism, Vulso was impressed.

"That," he admitted, a bit grudgingly, "isn't a bad sword. Even if it is a bit small," he added.

Handing it back to Titus, he gave the boy a grunt whose meaning only became clear when, without saying anything else, Vulso turned and beckoned Titus to follow him. Leading the boy out into the training ground, he strode to the far corner of the yard, where there was a series of wooden stakes. Titus immediately recognized them; there were several rows of similar stakes just outside the walls of the camp where his father worked in Siscia. He couldn't count the number of times he had watched men of the Legions, from the rawest *tirones* to men like his father working the stakes. So he wasn't surprised that Vulso expected to start here, nor when Vulso picked up one of the wooden swords that were placed on a rack attached to the outer wall of the building. In one motion, Vulso whirled about, tossing the sword to the boy, who just managed to catch it without fumbling too badly.

Vulso grinned. "Let's see whether you know what you're doing, boy." Pointing to a stake, he said, "Show me your forms."

When Titus squared himself on a post, he instantly recognized the value of the exercises that Vulso had put him through. Before leaving Siscia, it would have been a struggle for him to keep the tip of the *rudis*, the wooden sword used for training the Legions and gladiators that was also lined with strips of lead to make it even heavier, level and parallel to the ground. He had been able to do it, but his arm shook with the effort; now, he was amazed and pleased to see the tip not wavering at all. Going into a crouch, Titus pulled his arm back while turning his hips so that his right foot was behind his left a short distance, enabling him to use the extra power generated by his lower body when he twisted as part of his thrust. He held the position, knowing that Vulso would want to critique it, and the *lanista* did exactly that, walking up to the boy, hiding his smile at the sight of the scowl on Titus' face as the boy tried to exude a fierce confidence. Circling the youth, Vulso stared down at Titus, grunting in a manner that didn't inform Titus one way or another about his thoughts, but his only action was to kick Titus' right foot a bit wider apart from his left. Apparently satisfied, he turned to walk back to a spot where he could observe, then something caught his eye. Staring down at the boy, his gaze was focused on Titus' right hand, which was clutching the sword.

Pointing, Vulso asked, "What by Cerberus' balls is that? Who taught you to hold a sword like that?"

Titus had expected this reaction, but his hand continued grasping the *rudis* the same way as he answered, "This is how my father holds his sword." He gave a shrug. "It's how all of his men hold their swords too."

Vulso was about to open his mouth and tell the boy he didn't care if Hercules had held a sword that way, it wasn't the way he or the gladiators he trained held it, but his eye was caught by a motion from Gallus, who was standing nearby.

Walking over to Gallus, Vulso turned his back to Titus and moved close to hear Gallus whisper, "The boy's telling you the truth, and furthermore, his father isn't the one who started training that way. You know who did?"

Vulso shook his head.

"Titus Pullus," Gallus said quietly. "Or at least, he's the one who made the men of his Century fight that way. Then his Cohort when he became Pilus Prior, then the 10th Legion when he became Primus Pilus."

"Who taught him?" Vulso asked, more out of curiosity than any real desire to know.

Gallus shrugged and replied, "I don't know. I seem to recall hearing that he was in Gaius Crastinus' Century when the 10th was raised."

"Well, that's not how I train my men." Vulso spat on the ground, then scratched his chin, clearly thinking about it. Finally, he shrugged and said, "But I don't really care if he wants to hold his sword that way as long as he can do his forms."

As it turned out, Titus couldn't, for the simple reason that his father had never taken the time to teach him all the things that came with the unorthodox grip. Although he had told the smith who crafted Titus' sword to equip it with a slightly smaller handle, thereby allowing Titus to wrap his fingers around and on top of his thumb, rather than the other way around, he hadn't explained to Titus that it would be awkward at first, even for a novice who had no experience with gripping a sword in the conventional manner. In fact, the reason Titus failed to impress Vulso when he demonstrated the thrusts and cuts the *lanista* demanded was because his hand and wrist lacked the strength to move laterally outward from his body, which was the one weakness of the grip. Titus Pullus had dubbed it the Vinician grip, because it had been his first Optio, Aulus Vinicius, who had trained every man of the First Century, Second Cohort of the 10th Legion, commanded by then-Pilus Prior Gaius Crastinus. Crastinus would go on to become the Primus Pilus of the 10th, falling at Pharsalus during the defeat of Pompeius Magnus, but earning everlasting glory and fame in doing so. However, at the *ludus*, Vulso wasn't sufficiently impressed to allow Titus to continue holding his sword the way his father did. For the time he was in Arelate, and until his father finally did take the time to train him, young Titus gripped his sword the way almost every other man in the Legions and arena did.

Iras glared at her oldest son, seated at the table in the dining area of the villa in Arelate, but Titus kept his head bowed, refusing to look at his mother.

"First it was a black eye, now it's this?" She pointed first at the huge, purplish bruise that ran from above Titus' left elbow, all the way up and disappearing under his tunic, before her finger traveled to point accusingly at the boy's head.

If it had just been that, Titus mused, he probably wouldn't be sitting there at the table, but as hard as the bruise was to explain, the large gash on his scalp that had required an even dozen sutures, provided by the slave at the *ludus* who served much the same function as a camp physician assigned to a Legion did, was even more so. It was due to this obvious sign of injury that forced Titus to confess to his mother what he had been up to when he was a way from the villa and not with Ocelus. He felt slightly ridiculous with the huge white bandage wrapped around his head, although his bigger complaint was the splitting headache he was suffering. Having his mother yelling at him wasn't helping it either, but he knew that there was no avoiding it, so he absorbed her words in silence. He didn't even want to imagine her reaction when the bandage came off and she saw that part of his head had been shaved to keep the wound clean. His mother's ire wasn't reserved just for her son; seated next to him, with much the same hangdog expression, was Gallus.

"And you." She turned to point at the bodyguard. "I trusted you with my boy, and this is what happens? Him," she gestured to Titus, "I understand that he's going to do something stupid. He's just a boy…"

"I am not just a boy," Titus interrupted, but this time Iras was too far gone in her anger to worry about soothing his feelings.

"Yes, you are," she snapped right back. "And this proves it! What were you thinking? That you were going to learn how to be a...a...gladiator?"

Iras at her most scornful was a dish that neither her husband nor her children cared for at all, and Gallus was finding it just as bitter.

"The boy wasn't training to be a gladiator, mistress," Gallus put in. "He was only doing the same things that the boys in the Legions do. It's true Vulso is a *lanista*, but he was in the Legions as well, and..."

"I don't care if he was a Primus Pilus," Iras cut him off. "He had no business letting a boy," she shot a glance at Titus, daring him to object at the word, "do something as dangerous as fighting against a slave trained to kill in the arena!"

When put that way, Gallus found it hard to argue, so he didn't try. The truth was that the opponent that Titus had faced could only charitably be classified as what Iras was describing. One of the relatively recent wrinkles added to gladiatorial games had been in exotic and unusual pairings. It was becoming the case that the audiences attending the games no longer appreciated the contests because of the skill involved between the pair, or pairs, battling on the sand. Along with the blood, the crowd clamored for variety, something unusual that they could then talk about as they left the arena to go soak themselves in wine and relive what they had just seen. A few months before Titus and his family arrived in Arelate, Vulso had taken delivery of one of those oddities that the *lanista* believed would titillate the crowd. Although the new arrival was fully grown, he was an inch or two shorter than Titus, but with the normal size head and torso of a fully grown man. The dwarf had been given the name Spartacus, a mocking tribute to the gladiator slave that had terrorized Rome a century before. The circumstances that saw Titus and Spartacus standing in a circle made of the other trainees and attendant slaves was completely on Titus' shoulders. The boy did understand this truth, although it didn't help much at this moment, with his mother howling like Cerberus. He had been pestering Vulso for days that he was ready to face a real opponent instead of the stupid stakes, and while he wasn't sure, Titus suspected that Vulso had finally relented just because he didn't want to listen to him anymore. Earlier that afternoon, Titus had gotten his wish, yet while he wouldn't admit it to anyone but himself, the dwarf Spartacus had soundly thrashed him. Much to his chagrin, and pain, Titus nevertheless learned a valuable lesson, that thrusting and slashing at a wooden stake had absolutely nothing in common with facing a living, breathing opponent. This was even more true when that opponent was seething with anger and humiliation at being matched with a child, no matter how overgrown that child was. As Titus sat there while his mother focused her anger on Gallus, he took consolation in the fact that he had managed to score his own damaging blows on Spartacus, but even he was forced to admit that he had lost the fight, long before the *rudis* cracked against his helmet, turning his world black. Fortunately, he hadn't been unconscious long, so his next memory was of a ring of faces peering down at him, the expressions on each ranging from real concern to the kind of smirk that Titus had seen from his friend Marcus on the one occasion Marcus had managed to best him at wrestling. In fact, Titus' thoughts after his defeat by Marcus and that moment lying on the sand of the training arena were remarkably similar; he would find a way to get even. Avenging his loss to Marcus had been easy; this time would be more problematic because of what came out of his mother's mouth.

"You're not to go anywhere near that place again," she commanded.

Titus' instant thought was how easy that would be to disobey, although looking over at Gallus, he recognized that the bodyguard was no longer an ally he could count on. However, his mother wasn't through.

"That's why you're confined to the villa for the rest of the time we're here." Seeing Titus' face go white, she did add, grudgingly, "You can still take Ocelus for your daily ride. But," she pointed that cursed finger at him again, "you're going with Libo, not Gallus." She looked disdainfully at the bodyguard, who was finding something extraordinarily interesting on the floor at his feet. "We've seen how much he can be trusted to keep you out of trouble."

Most children, particularly given the circumstances that found him wearing a bulky white turban about his head like those wild tribes from Africa were supposed to, with a raging headache, would have recognized that their opportunity for doing as they willed was over. All parents had a tone of voice that informed their offspring that they had officially reached the end of the tether that their respective parent allowed to give their children freedom, and Titus had recognized that tone immediately. But Titus Porcinianus Pullus wasn't like other children, either in size or temperament, and while he had no way of knowing for sure, he instinctively knew that somehow his Avus would understand that he had no intention of obeying his mother, and would approve.

"Libo," Titus pointed excitedly at something just off the trail, "what is that?"

The bodyguard, who Titus had come to learn wasn't as much surly as he was just taciturn by nature, followed Titus' finger, peering off into the vegetation that lined the Via Aurelia.

"I don't see anything," Libo muttered, cursing the fact that this boy's vision was so sharp.

"It looks like a box of some sort. Don't you see it?" Titus insisted. "It's right there, at the base of that tree."

If this had been the first time, Libo wouldn't have been willing to indulge the boy, but Titus had proven to have extraordinarily sharp vision, and much to Libo's chagrin, had proven to be right every other time he spied something. And if the truth were to be known, Libo found these rides otherwise excruciatingly boring, so he didn't mind what had become something of a game he played with the boy, who he was extremely fond of, in his own way. Titus would point something out, and Libo would try and find whatever it was, while Titus provided hints until he determined what it was. If Libo was disposed to think about it, he would have found it somewhat amusing, in a sad sort of way, that his life had been reduced to finding excitement in a mundane game. Although Libo felt an attachment to Titus, going back to the days when he had marched in the ranks of Titus' father's first Century in the Seventh Cohort and had been one of the rankers who escorted the toddling Titus to give Ocelus his apple, he didn't have children of his own. And, as anyone with children knew, they could try the patience of even the most devoted parents, and Libo was no parent. At least these rides with Titus were better than the endless chatter of the younger children when he drove the wagon to Arelate. Now he stared in the direction that Titus had pointed, squinting as he tried to see whatever it was that Titus had spotted.

Finally, he grunted in frustration, and said, "There's nothing there. Your eyes are playing tricks on you."

Titus laughed, but he continued to point.

"You're just getting too old to see anything. It's right there, just like that big nose on your face!"

"My nose isn't that big," Libo protested automatically, then caught himself.

You're arguing with a child about your nose, he thought with equal parts disgust and amusement. This is what your life has been reduced to? Seeing that Titus wasn't going to be swayed, Libo heaved a sigh.

"Fine. I'll prove that there's nothing there."

Moving his horse a bit closer, Libo slid off the horse and began striding to the tree. He would tear those shrubs around the base out by the roots just to prove to the boy that he wasn't always right. Libo was almost to the tree when he heard a surprisingly loud, sharp SMACK, followed by a sudden whinny of shock and pain. Whirling about, he was too late to stop it, but in time to watch his horse bolting up the Via Aurelia, heading away from Arelate, leaving a small cloud of dirt clods and dust in its wake.

"Sorry, Libo!" Titus shouted this even as he was kicking Ocelus in the ribs, causing the old horse to respond instantly with a huge, bounding leap, in the opposite direction of Libo's horse. Calling over his shoulder, Titus shouted, "I promise I'll tell Mama that I tricked you!"

Libo was too astonished to be angry, although that would certainly come over the third of a watch it took him to find his horse.

Titus had planned his escape well, even as he knew that the consequences would be dire. But as far as the boy was concerned, he had unfinished business that couldn't wait, especially since his mother had announced that it was time to return to Siscia. They were scheduled to leave in just two days' time, making this the last opportunity for Titus to exact his revenge. The fact that his sutures had only been removed a few days before, while the bruising was now a faded yellow, meant nothing to the boy. He was grimly determined to even the score with the dwarf Spartacus, and this would be his last and only chance to do so. Although he was set on this course, it wasn't without considerable apprehension. He had prepared himself the best that he could, given the circumstances, but he knew that sneaking out of the room he shared with his siblings every night to go out into the courtyard to work on his forms wasn't the best kind of training. His Avus had installed a set of stakes when he moved into the villa, in what turned out to be an ill-advised attempt to have Diocles, Agis, and Simeon join him in the exercises that he performed daily, without exception. In fact, when young Titus first set eyes on the stakes, Diocles had informed him that his Avus had done the exercises on the very last day of his life. But while Titus performed his own exercises next to the stakes, he made sure that he didn't strike the stake, afraid that the noise would rouse unwanted attention. It was the best he could do under the circumstances; as he rode Ocelus at a fast trot back to Arelate, he hoped it would be enough.

Vulso was tempted not to let the boy into the *ludus* when he showed up on his big gray horse, but there was something in the boy's eyes, a sort of fire that hinted at the chance for something interesting happening. Signaling to the guard, the grillwork iron gate was yanked open, and the boy urged his horse through the archway. Entering into the yard, a sudden change came over the gray horse, his nostrils dilating and taking in the vast array of scent, but while Titus had no way of knowing, it was the sounds of men engaged in combat, even if it was just in training, that triggered Ocelus' reaction. Without any warning, the horse suddenly reared in the air, front hooves rising high and lashing out. Titus felt himself falling backward, the reins jerked from his hand, although he just managed to catch a handful of mane before he slid off the back. Ocelus came back down, snorting, with his ears pricked forward, making a series of little hops as he was assailed by the sudden memories of when he had been younger, and the man was on his back. They had been a team then, striking down the enemies of the man, and Ocelus was just as much of a warrior as the man, with several kills to his credit. If there had been a smell of blood, thick and coppery in the air, it was very unlikely that Titus could have controlled the big horse at all. As it was, once he resumed his grip on the reins, it took several heartbeats before he had Ocelus under control.

"Looks like your horse is ready for a fight," Vulso remarked, careful to give the gray a wide berth.

Titus didn't answer for a moment, still trying to get Ocelus completely under control, and when he patted the horse's neck in an effort to calm his mount, Titus could feel the quivering muscle under his hand. Vulso is right, Titus thought; Ocelus is ready for battle. Well, so am I.

Once Ocelus settled down, only then did Titus slide from the horse's back, walking over to Vulso on knees that he desperately hoped weren't shaking visibly. Stopping in front of Vulso, he was only slightly reassured by the fact that he didn't have to tilt his head up very far to look the *lanista* in his one good eye.

"I'm here to fight Spartacus again." He was proud of himself because his voice wasn't unsteady at all.

If he had expected Vulso to be surprised, the *lanista* didn't show it. Nor was he particularly welcoming to the idea.

"You had your chance, boy," he said dismissively. "Why should I let you get whipped again?"

Titus had come prepared. From where it was hidden inside his tunic, he produced a leather bag, which he held up and, in imitation of what he had seen men do when making wagers with each other, shook the bag so Vulso could hear the metallic clink.

"Because I'll give you this. If I win, I get it back; if I lose, you get to keep it."

The eyebrow above Vulso's patch was the one that arched as he eyed the bag with the other.

"And how much is in there, boy?"

"Fifty sesterces," Titus said proudly, because to a boy of ten, and, in fact, to a vast number of adults in Roman society, it was a huge sum.

He wasn't prepared for Vulso's reaction; he began roaring with laughter, and it was a harsh, mocking kind of laugh that lacerated the boy's pride.

"Fifty sesterces," Vulso managed to gasp as he wiped his good eye. "Boy, I piss that away on one night's dice."

"It's all that I have," Titus mumbled, mortified as he felt a sudden rush of tears threaten to embarrass him even more than he already was. Swallowing hard, pushing the emotion down, he looked at Vulso and asked stubbornly, "Well? Are you going to let me fight him or not?"

"Not for fifty sesterces," Vulso sneered. "You'll have to do better than that."

A feeling of desperation came rushing up, bringing back with it the tears that he had swallowed. Not only was it important that Vulso agree, Titus was acutely aware that the time he had to effect his plan was limited. Even now, Libo might have found his horse and be riding for Arelate, and Titus knew that it would take no time whatsoever for his mother to figure out where Titus had gone.

"What do you want, then?" he blurted out, but even as he did, he feared he knew the answer.

Even so, he thought his heart would burst out of his chest when, in answer, Vulso simply pointed over Titus' shoulder. Right at Ocelus.

"If you want to fight Spartacus, you have to put your horse up," Vulso replied.

The truth was that Vulso had no real desire to take Titus' horse. He actually liked the boy a great deal, but he also didn't need the headache that he knew would accompany giving in to Titus' request. He had already experienced one taste of Iras, who had come with Diocles to let the *lanista* know exactly what she thought of a man who would let a boy spar with a grown man. Vulso had made the initial mistake of pointing out Spartacus' size, but immediately regretted it, understanding that the best and only defense was just to ride out the storm. She was, after all, the owner of the *ludus* for all intents and purposes, so whether she was a mouthy woman or not was beside the point. Now, with Titus standing before him, he was making a very shrewd guess that this big gray stallion, advanced age or not, meant more to Titus than just a means of transportation. All in all, his judgment was sound, but he underestimated the resolve of the boy.

Titus swallowed hard, but he didn't hesitate, answering, "All right. My horse Ocelus is yours if I lose." He paused for a moment, then added, "But if I win? You have to protect me from Mama."

Vulso laughed, but offered his arm, which Titus took.

"I'll go let Spartacus know he's about to win me a horse."

As Vulso strode away, the enormity of what he had just done struck Titus, and his knees, which he had forgotten about, started shaking again.

Unsurprisingly, the prospect of the rematch between the dwarf and the boy stopped all the other activity in the training yard, something that Vulso normally wouldn't have allowed. However, his men had been working hard, and he decided they had earned at least a slight diversion. They formed the perimeter of the rough circle, a living boundary that would serve as the crowd at the same time. And every one of those men, with very few exceptions, were looking forward to one of their own, no matter if he was a dwarf or not, give this rich young sprout a second beating. That was because, to these men, Titus' heritage and circumstances didn't matter. All they knew was that he was somehow connected to the faceless owners of this *ludus*, which in turn meant these hard-bitten men belonged to them as well. How Titus Pullus had earned the kind of money it took to own a *ludus*, even if it was unknowingly, that it had been by way of his strong right arm and sword, didn't matter to any of these men. What they were aware of was that this boy's privilege and rank stank in their nostrils, making what was about to happen something they were more than happy to witness. The fact that it was the first time Titus ever experienced any of this; the hostility of the trainees at the *ludus* had been completely unexpected, created a huge impression on the boy, something that he would have cause to remember for the rest of his days. In his mind, he was one of them; the son of a Legionary, a man who earned his living with his sword, and the realization that they didn't reciprocate this view was another pivotal moment in his young life, reminding him that there was often a large gap between what he perceived and what others did. Gripping the *rudis* and hefting the small, round shield that to Titus was barely bigger than the plate he used to eat his meals on, he was all too aware of the hostility surrounding him, seeming to wash over him in waves as the onlookers jeered and taunted him. Standing there, waiting for the dwarf to appear, Titus had never felt so alone in his whole life, and the unfairness of the hostility on display threatened to overwhelm him. Why did they hate him so? What had he done to any of them to warrant this kind of enmity? They should have been cheering him, his bravery! He was just a boy, after all, and he had come here to face what was a grown man, no matter if the gods had seen fit to encase him in the body of a child. Titus knew from bitter experience that Spartacus was much, much stronger than a child his size, yet here he was, ready to face him again. As he stood there, fighting back the combination of nerves and tears, understanding what was at stake in the horse he loved more than anything in his life, the fear and hurt started to turn into…something else. And in this moment, completely unaware of it, the boy Titus Porcinianus Pullus experienced the transfer of that wonderful but dark gift, something that had first been bestowed to his Avus many, many years before, on a barren hill in Hispania. On that occasion, during Titus Pullus' first campaign, his First Century of the Second Cohort, 10th Legion, along with the Second, had been ambushed and surrounded by the rebelling tribesmen. The situation was dire, yet in that moment, the young Titus Pullus, still just a Gregarius and barely more than a *tirone*, had experienced something that he, and others who witnessed it, attributed as a gift from the gods. It began as a fit of anger that quickly grew into something more, a divine sort of rage that gave Pullus the strength of two men his size, while not robbing him of his awareness. By the time the battle was over, Pullus was standing alone, amidst a pile of bloody corpses, and the beginning of the legend of Titus Pullus had been born. It was that gift, that sense of fury that was fueled by the hostility of the men surrounding him that flowed into young Titus at that moment, and he received it as a completely unexpected feeling of an almost molten wrath, which caught him completely by surprise, and frankly, frightened him. A spate of sweat suddenly burst forth, almost instantly soaking his tunic and running so heavily that it threatened his vision. He quickly wiped his brow with the sleeve of his tunic, as the anger in him continued to build, turning into a focused point of rage, hatred, and determination. They were jeering him? They were booing him? That was bad enough, but as he exchanged hard stares with each of the men directly across from him on the far side of the circle, he imagined that these men were just counting the moments before they got the chance to ride his horse. His Ocelus, his beautiful horse; the thought of these grubby, dirty men pawing at his stallion, and even worse, how confused and frightened Ocelus would be at this sudden change from everything he knew, was the final piece that pushed him fully into the spot where his Avus had been those years ago. The sudden appearance of Spartacus, who had pushed his way between the watching trainees, gave Titus the proper place to focus his killing hatred. But it was the sneer on the dwarf's face, the expression of disdain that sent the clearest sign of contempt and served to launch Titus, much in the same way a bolt from a scorpion is released with the yank of the lanyard.

Despite his best attempts, Titus was never clearly able to recall the sequence of events that culminated with him standing, panting and bloody, over the prone body of the dwarf that had been known as Spartacus. His first real recollection was the total silence, except for the harsh sound of his own breath in his ears, and it was another moment before his eyes had focused sufficiently on the external world around him to take notice of the faces of the men standing a few paces away. They looked stunned, and the first thought that came to Titus was that their faces wore the expression of the pig he had once seen slaughtered, immediately after one of the slaves had struck it with the mallet right between the eyes. His next sensation was of a slight cramp in his right hand, and he looked dully down at it to see that the *rudis* was still clutched in it. It was a *rudis* just like any of the ones on the rack, yet it looked different to him somehow, and it took a moment for him to realize that the one he was clutching was covered in blood. Blood and...was that hair? And what were those pinkish-gray bits that seemed to cling to one edge? The rush of bile was completely unexpected, forcing its way from between his clenched teeth, and he was just able to lean over to spill the contents of his stomach out onto the sand without getting any on himself. Even as he was retching, he expected to hear the mocking laughter from the assembled men, except the silence was still total, although that wasn't destined to last. Just as he felt confident that the last bit of what had been his breakfast was now safely out of his stomach and stood back up straight, his vision was filled with the contorted face of Vulso. And Titus could instantly see that he was angrier than Titus had ever seen him in the short time of their association.

"You little...*cunnus*! You killed my dwarf! You killed Spartacus!"

"I...I did?" Titus was no less surprised at this news than Vulso had been just a few heartbeats before when he watched it happen.

"Oh, don't play cute with me, boy," the *lanista* snorted. "You saw he was down! You saw him lift his hand and you know what that means! But you kept on until you beat his brains out!"

Titus had been sure that he had vomited the last of whatever was left in his stomach, but he had been wrong. His reply was to suddenly turn aside and retch one more time, and oddly enough, this did more to assuage Vulso's anger than anything Titus could have said.

"You didn't know, did you?" he asked softly, more to himself than to the boy, although Titus still managed to shake his head.

Once the spasms that racked him subsided again, Titus stood erect again, his eyes red and streaming, and it was only partially from the strain of vomiting.

"No, Vulso, I don't remember." His voice sounded strange to Titus, hoarse and somehow different. Trying to think, he could only add, "The best I can remember is bits and pieces. But I don't remember him going down, and I don't remember anything about what happened...after." Titus looked into Vulso's eye, his expression clearly beseeching the *lanista*. "Please, Vulso, I swear by all the gods, I don't remember!"

Although Vulso was still angry, almost despite himself, he felt his heart soften towards the boy. While it was certainly true that obtaining the dwarf had cost Vulso dearly, not to mention the time and effort that had gone into training him, the reality was that it wasn't Vulso's money. In fact, he thought, the boy had just cost his family a pretty penny, and it was with this idea in mind that prompted him to forgive the boy with a grunt and clap on the boy's shoulders, which sagged with relief. The others weren't so disposed however, and Titus heard a ripple of angry whispers and muttered curses all around him, yet if Vulso was disturbed or intimidated by this, he certainly didn't show it.

"Shut your mouths!" he roared, turning about so that he could glare at as many men as possible. "This is none of your business! It's between me and the bo...between me and Titus!" Returning his gaze back to the boy, he spoke softly enough so that only Titus could hear. "Besides, you've got enough trouble as it is."

Titus gave him a questioning gaze; Vulso's only response was to indicate with his head something behind Titus. Even as he turned about, the boy had a premonition of what he would see, but despite preparing himself, the sight of his mother, Diocles, Gallus, and a very angry Libo might have been enough to cause a new round of retching. Fortunately for Titus, there was nothing left to come up.

Whirling back around to face Vulso, Titus whispered, "Remember our deal! You agreed that if I won, you'd protect me from Mama! You'd tell her something that would keep her from being mad at me!"

Vulso gave a harsh, barking laugh.

"That was before you killed my dwarf," he countered. "Besides, did you really think there would be anything I could say that would keep her from being angry with you? You disobeyed her, didn't you?" Vulso's tone changed as his gaze flickered between Titus and his waiting mother, who had pushed her way through the small crowd and even now was standing, arms crossed and with an expression that Vulso was sure didn't bode well for the boy. "There are consequences in life, Titus," he continued, not unkindly. "Consider this the consequences for what you just did, that I won't lift a finger to help you with your mother. Besides," he said just before he turned away, "I have a feeling that you'll be paying for this a long time, long after your mother flays you and has forgotten about it. You never will."

Iras would never be able to decide whether it was better that she arrived at the *ludus* when she did, or if it was some sort of punishment by the gods. Not particularly religious, she nevertheless couldn't help the feeling that being forced to watch her firstborn son perform the kind of act that she knew, albeit indirectly, that her husband and men like him took part in quite often was a sentence by the gods, and a harsh one at that. She had been prepared to come charging in, completely unafraid and unmindful of the type of men she was shoving aside as she pushed her way through the ring of spectators. But she arrived too late; or, as she was forced to admit to herself later, she had arrived just in time to get another glimpse of the man her son would become. All of the words she prepared had clogged in her throat, which shut closed almost as soon as her eyes had picked out her boy. It was just as he knocked Spartacus to one knee, and while the dwarf still had his shield and was holding it up above him as he vainly tried to regain his feet, she had watched as her boy, her precious baby, had rained down blow after blow, battering the small round shield. Even from where she was standing more than two dozen paces away, she heard a sharp crack an instant before the shield split in two, but Titus didn't relent at all. Instead, he immediately shifted his attack to the dwarf himself, knocking aside Spartacus' attempt to block the wooden blade with his own as if it wasn't there. And when Iras thought about that moment, as she often did, she also had to admit to herself that she felt a moment of a savage satisfaction, watching Titus strike the first scoring blow directly on the dwarf's helmet. That little vermin, after all, was the one who had given her boy what would become a prominent scar, so he was getting no more than he deserved. And she was completely aware of why this was happening in the first place, understood that more than Titus' scalp had been lacerated, that his pride and image of himself had taken a beating as well, qualities that her son had more of than most boys his age. But she was totally unprepared for what came next. Clearly stunned, Spartacus had held up his hand in the signal of surrender, and with his other removed his helmet because it had been knocked askew and was obscuring the dwarf's vision. Titus clearly didn't see, or even worse to Iras, didn't care that he had done it; he had conquered his opponent because he hadn't stopped. To Iras' untutored eye, the only reason she could see as a possible source of Titus' confusion was when the dwarf, still holding his own *rudis*, had tried to clamber to his feet and, in doing so, gave Titus the impression that he wanted to continue the fight. Whatever the truth was, what followed would be seared into Iras' memory, as it was in that of Diocles, who had managed to reach her side. Spartacus had tried to defend himself; to Diocles, that was his mistake, because it sent the obvious signal to Titus that he had yet to capitulate. The first blow Spartacus somehow managed to deflect, but that was the last one, and in just another moment, it was over. Neither Iras nor Diocles, nor, for that matter, any of the onlookers were able to count the number of blows, or tracked which was the one that cracked open Spartacus' skull and spilled his brains out onto the sand.

Despite the training and harsh reality of their lives, gladiators and novices alike had been shocked into silence and immobility. There was just a blur of motion, then Titus was standing over the body of the dwarf, who still twitched, his limbs jerking spasmodically. Then there was the exchange with Vulso, which Iras could only partially hear, although for a moment she had tensed, ready to launch herself at the *lanista* if it looked like he was about to strike Titus. But he hadn't, and that was when Titus had turned around and walked, no, he had marched to face his mother. As he approached, Iras was struck by an irrational wave of fear, her eyes drawn to the *rudis* still in his hand, wondering why he still clutched it, all manner of horrible images leaping before her mind's eye, no matter how hard she tried to shove them back. But then, she looked into her son's face, now close enough to see the expression in his eyes, and any thought of her son as a possible threat vanished. He looked, she decided, like what he really was, despite his size, a little boy. A boy who had just been scared out of sleep by a bad dream and was coming to his mother to be comforted, so it was pure instinct that pushed her forward, intent on rushing to meet her son, to be there. Fortunately for both of them, Iras caught herself, stopping her motion before she had gone more than a couple paces. Instead, she stood erect, her head tilted up and her expression impassive, like one of the statues of Livia Drusilla that were popping up everywhere. A Roman matron, waiting for her son to greet her in the proper manner; at least that's what she told herself she was doing. After all, she was still angry, and it wouldn't do to start fussing over Titus until that matter was resolved once they were away from prying eyes. Nevertheless, as Titus closed the remaining distance, he saw her eyeing him up and down, looking at what he assumed were the bloody spots on his body and tunic, trying to determine if it was his own. Just before he stopped in front of her, he remembered to drop the *rudis*, and the thudding sound it made as it hit the sand was the loudest noise to that moment, as everyone still stood, motionless and silent. The boy was as acutely aware as his mother that all eyes were on the pair, with perhaps the only exception being Diocles, who stood directly to his mother's right.

Diocles was only looking at Titus, although the boy was too absorbed to take notice of the expression on the Greek's face, a curious mixture of sadness, relief, and pride. Titus had no way of knowing this, but while Diocles hadn't been part of his Avus' life when Titus Pullus experienced his first...fit, or whatever it could be called, he was there for what turned out to be the last one. It had been outside Serdica, when the Legions under Marcus Primus were assaulting a fortress that guarded the southern approach to the city. Granted, it had been at a distance, but even from his vantage point, Diocles saw enough of what his then-master had done, and had naturally heard about it in the immediate aftermath of the battle. Now in Arelate, he was seeing evidence of this divine madness somehow being passed on to his master's namesake, and that recognition had a profound effect on the Greek.

"I know you're going to punish me," Titus broke the silence. "But this was something I had to do."

All the words, all the angry recriminations and haranguing that Iras had been preparing to unleash on her son evaporated in that instant. It wasn't just what Titus said, or even the expression on his face as he stood before his mother, looking her in the eye, calmly. What stilled Iras' tongue was the recognition that, as well as she thought she knew her son, there was a part of him that she had never glimpsed until just a few moments before. There was a seething, volcanic fury there, and it was buried so deeply within him that, when she witnessed it for the first time, she was caught completely by surprise. As unprepared as she had been to witness her son's violence, she was even less ready for the incredibly powerful wave of sadness that washed over her, and for a moment, Iras was sure her composure would crumble in perfect harmony with her breaking heart. What demon put this anger, this rage inside you, my son? Yet somehow, despite the almost overwhelming urge to do so, she refrained from reaching out to Titus, who still stood there, silent. Finally, she opened her mouth, and even she wasn't sure what was going to come out.

"Let's go back to the villa," she said quietly. "We need to pack to go back home."

Without waiting for an answer, she turned about while Gallus and Libo cleared a path through the men, who grudgingly gave way. Titus was acutely aware of the hard stares of the other gladiators and trainees, but none of them laid a hand on him as he followed behind his mother. Once clear, Titus walked over to where Ocelus was standing, held by a slave who, just as he was trained, dropped to his knees to allow the boy to step up. Titus was thankful; he suddenly felt close to collapse and he knew there was no way he could have leapt onto Ocelus' back without help. The gray had settled down, but Titus could feel the barely contained excitement of the horse, and he worried that there would be a repeat of his behavior. Fortunately, Ocelus was docile enough as he trotted out of the *ludus*, pulling up beside the others. Suddenly, the boy leaned down and extended a hand to his mother.

"Mama, let me help you up. You've never ridden Ocelus with me!"

Iras hesitated for a moment; unlike her son, she didn't love horses. However, she also knew that this was about more than riding a horse, so she took his hand as he pulled her up behind him. They both pretended they didn't see Gallus reaching out to give her a surreptitious boost. Putting her arms around her boy, Iras and Titus trotted away from the others.

Chapter 4

As scheduled, Gaius Porcinus' family left Arelate shortly after dawn two days later. Naturally, Titus rode Ocelus, but Libo was liberated from the duty of driving the wagon; riding next to Iras was Simeon. That, Iras thought as she sat next to the Armenian, was a surprise, but nothing compared to the shock of the other two extra travelers accompanying them back to Siscia. Thinking about it made her glance back in the wagon, a smile on her lips at the sight of Birgit, sitting cross-legged across from Sextus and Valeria, and cradling young Miriam, who, as was her habit, whenever the wagon started moving, was sleeping soundly. Birgit was telling the two children a story from her own childhood; she was from Gaul, up near the Rhenus somewhere. Not surprisingly, Iras' gaze turned outward from the wagon, over to the other surprise where Diocles was once more riding next to Titus. Between their respective horses, and the size of their owners, it was the young boy who was actually a full head taller than the Greek next to him, but that didn't seem to matter to either of them. She had only been informed the night before that Diocles intended to accompany them back to Siscia, although she felt a certain satisfaction as she recalled the conversation. He hadn't been expecting that, she thought triumphantly, glancing back at Birgit once more.

She was supervising the packing of the last bit of baggage when Diocles had approached her. For several moments, neither of them said a word, standing side-by-side and occupied with their own thoughts. It was Diocles who broke the silence.

"I've decided," he began after clearing his throat, which Iras had learned long before was the precursor to the introduction of a topic that the Greek either thought important or possibly contentious, "that I'm coming back to Siscia with you."

Iras hadn't been expecting that, and she looked at him in open-mouthed surprise. She had been preparing herself for a somewhat emotional parting, because as much as she and Diocles differed, they had so much more in common.

"But why?" she asked, not trying to hide her astonishment. "You belong here!"

"No, I belong with Titus," Diocles said calmly, preparing himself for the reaction that came from what he knew Iras would see as criticism.

"Why?" she flared. "We're doing just fine without you."

"I'm not saying that you aren't." Diocles tried hard to avoid sounding defensive. "But I've noticed that the boy can barely read."

In answer, Iras just closed her eyes and shook her head.

Finally, she replied tiredly, "I know. It's something that Gaius and I have talked about, but we were afraid to hire a tutor just for him, because of..." Her voice trailed off.

"Because you didn't want to attract the attention of Augustus that you were giving your boy an education that's more like what the son of an equestrian would receive rather than the son of a Legionary, even if he is a Centurion. Is that it?"

Iras nodded, relieved that she had no need to say it aloud.

"Well, that's why I'm coming back with you," Diocles said gently. "What would be more natural than a slave who's become a freedman continuing to serve the family that freed him?"

In that, Iras understood Diocles was absolutely correct. It had been the case for centuries, by this point, that many slaves, particularly those like Diocles who had held high positions in a Roman's household, once they were given their freedom, chose of their own free will to stay employed in the service of their original masters. That was inarguable, although that wasn't Iras' only objection.

"What about you and Birgit?" she had asked Diocles, whose expression instantly became guarded.

"What do you mean?" He was looking everywhere but into Iras' eyes, and she wasn't disposed to humor him.

"You know exactly what I mean," she snapped. "I've seen the way you look at her. You're in love with the girl."

Diocles' already dark features became even more so as his face flushed.

"So what if I am?" he asked stubbornly. "What does that matter? Besides," his face betrayed his misery then, "she doesn't know that." Diocles stared hard at Iras. "And I don't want her hearing it from you!"

"You men are such fools," Iras scoffed. "Of course she knows how you feel! And she feels the same way! Anyone with eyes can see that."

The look Diocles gave Iras was so fraught with hope and fear that any temptation she might have felt to torment the Greek evaporated. She recognized that expression; it was the one she had seen on Gaius' face, and she assumed that it was on hers as well, the night Titus Pullus had discovered the two of them together for the first time. By the time the Primus Pilus discovered the affair, the two had been seeing each other secretly for months, and were hopelessly in love. Iras' mistress Miriam had known and remained silent, and it was her influence that night that stayed Pullus from demanding that Gaius sever all ties with the then-slave. And, being honest, she wouldn't have blamed Pullus; Gaius was a free Roman citizen, and Iras was a slave. Although Iras knew that Miriam still harbored hopes of bearing Pullus a son, the giant Roman had already made it clear by this point that Gaius would be his heir. And all that was threatened by Gaius' love for Iras.

This memory was in Iras' mind as she looked at Diocles, and was what prompted her to say in a more kindly tone, "Diocles, I promise you. Birgit feels the same way about you as you do about her. Does that change anything?"

Diocles hesitated as he thought about it before reluctantly saying, "I imagine it would. If Birgit feels as you say she does, then yes. I would probably stay here."

Iras considered this for perhaps a half-dozen heartbeats before speaking again.

"That's why she'll come with us."

Naturally, it hadn't been quite that simple. Glenora had wailed at the thought of her daughter going somewhere she had never heard of, but she also was aware of Birgit's feelings for Diocles. So it had been a tearful farewell earlier that day, although very quickly, Birgit's tears had dried as she was swept up in the excitement of a journey, and of a new life. Now, as Diocles and Titus rode alongside one another, it was hard for Diocles to keep his attention on what Titus was saying, his thoughts still whirling from all that had transpired since the previous day. While he and Birgit hadn't had more than one hurried conversation, it had been one of the happiest talks of his life, because she had shyly informed Diocles that, yes, what Iras said was true, she felt the same way that he did. It hadn't been long after this moment, snatched between the various chores as the entire household bustled to make ready for departure, that Diocles was struck by another thought and it was this one that he was wrestling with as he rode with Titus. If she had felt the same way, how long had it been so? How much time had he wasted, had they wasted? Diocles was in his late fifties, and although he was in excellent health, since the passing of his friend and former master, he had become acutely aware of the passing of time, and the fleeting nature of human life.

"So did Avus ever have something happen to him like what happened to me?"

It took Diocles a moment to make the shift from his internal musing to focus on Titus' question, but even then, he didn't make the connection to what Titus referring to, prompting him to ask, "Like what happened to you? What do you mean?"

Titus looked over at him, giving Diocles a level stare without saying anything, giving Diocles the answer.

"Ah," the Greek said softly. "That." He paused for a moment, trying to decide the best way to answer the boy. Finally, he decided there was only one approach to take. "Yes," he answered, "Your Avus did indeed have that same kind of thing happen to him. I wasn't there for the first time it happened. Or times," he corrected himself, not seeing Titus suddenly sit up straighter, "But I certainly heard about it from people like Scribonius. You remember him, don't you?"

"Of course I do," Titus said, somewhat indignant at the inference that he might have been too young to recall his Avus' best friend. "He's the first one who taught me my letters. I remember him very well."

"Ah, yes. I'd forgotten about that," Diocles said lightly. "Sorry, Titus. It's part of getting old." He frowned for a moment, trying to gather his thoughts. "Anyway, I heard about the first time from Scribonius and Vellusius."

While Titus knew who Publius Vellusius was, he only had a vague recollection of the man; by the time Titus was a toddler, Vellusius was just about to retire from the post of bodyguard for the Camp Prefect, a job that had been invented out of thin air by Titus Pullus as a way to allow one of his oldest friends and a member of his original tent section to stay connected with the army. What Titus remembered was of a man with very few teeth, but whose completely gray hair always stuck up, making him look like some sort of odd bird.

"It was in Hispania, as I recall," Diocles continued on, "in your Avus' first year with the 10th. That was when he won his first set of *phalarae*, you know."

Titus did indeed know, although he had learned this from his father and not his Avus. The set of three gleaming disks, which in those days were emblazoned with a bull, was the original symbol of the 10th Legion, and were in a chest that Diocles had brought to Siscia with him, containing all of Pullus' decorations. Titus had longed to touch and hold them, but Porcinus had forbidden it, not wanting them to get smeared with childish fingerprints.

"But while that was the first time, it wasn't the last. From what I know, it happened at least twice more before I came into his service. All I can tell you is that I was there the last time it happened to him. Or," he corrected himself, "for him. Because it definitely saved his life."

As Titus listened, Diocles explained what he had seen that day outside Serdica. When Diocles finished, Titus didn't say anything for quite some time, the two plodding along a short distance from the wagon in total silence.

"So," Titus finally spoke, "what caused it? And why did it happen?"

Diocles thought for a moment, then shrugged.

"That I don't know for sure. What I can say is that the men who saw it happen all attributed it as some sort of...fit, but one that came from the gods. As to why? The only thing that each time had in common with the other was that your Avus and the men around him were in mortal danger. And then...whatever it was that possessed your Avus took over, and they were no longer in danger."

Diocles looked over at Titus, trying to determine how the boy was digesting this, but Titus' face was expressionless.

Finally, Titus asked, "So he didn't have any control over it either?"

"No," Diocles replied. "As far as I know, he didn't know when it was going to happen. It just…did."

Titus considered this for a few more moments, staring off in the distance.

Finally, he turned back to stare straight ahead as he said, "Do you think I have what my Avus had? That I was having a…fit?"

Now it was Diocles' turn to be silent as he thought about his answer, knowing that he had to be careful in his response to the boy.

"I don't know," he said finally. "But from what I saw, it would appear to be so. Yes," he finished thoughtfully, nodding his head, "I think that very well may be the case, that whatever it was that your Avus had, you do as well."

"Well, it's a curse." There was no mistaking the bitterness in Titus' voice.

"No." Diocles' tone was sharper than he intended, and he took a breath before continuing in a calmer manner. "I can see how you'd feel that way. But it kept your Avus and the men around him alive! And it only came to him in moments of great danger. It wasn't as if he was just walking down the street and suddenly drew his sword and started chopping people's heads off." Despite the grim subject, as Diocles had hoped, the image he was depicting caused the boy to grin. Seeing that he had the boy's full attention, the Greek continued making his case. "Now it's true that it's a terrible, terrible gift. And I know that your Avus felt the same way about it that you do. I think that's the most important thing, to be aware that it comes with a price. Titus," he turned so that he could make eye contact with the boy, "I can't tell you the number of nights that your Avus woke up drenched in sweat, crying out because of the dreams that haunted him. And while he'd never talk about them, I know that at least some of them had to do with those times he had his fits. That's the price that comes with it, Titus. But your Avus died, in bed, in his sleep, and I can tell you he was at peace when he did. And the only reason he was able to live to the age he did, and die the way he did, was because of that gift from the gods. But it's not without cost. I won't lie to you about that."

Titus didn't say anything, instead responding to Diocles' words with a slow nod, before turning away to resume staring off into the distance.

It wasn't until much later that he said anything, and Diocles had become absorbed again in his own thoughts, so he missed Titus muttering, "If I have to have these fits, I should be able to control them."

Much as had happened on the trip to Arelate, very quickly the monotony of what seemed to be endless days plodding along encased the travelers. Moving east, they retraced their journey on the Via Aurelia, traveling along the coast. Most of that time Titus spent with Diocles, who had decided to start his tutoring of the boy as soon as possible. Naturally, it was impossible for Titus to work on anything requiring writing, so Diocles confined his lessons to topics that could be orally transmitted. It came as no surprise to Iras, or Diocles, for that matter, that Titus' favorite subject was history, particularly that part of history in which his Avus had participated. Very quickly, Diocles determined that if he did as Titus wanted, they wouldn't talk about anything else but the conquest of Gaul and the civil wars. Therefore, Diocles made a rule that the mornings were devoted to the topics that he wanted to cover; early Roman history, of course, but also Greek history, which was Titus' least favorite, and mythology, in which he was moderately interested. Only after they stopped for their midday break and Diocles then questioned the boy on what he had learned earlier in the day would the Greek relent and begin talking about Titus Pullus, the Republic, and Caesar.

Iras, either sitting next to Simeon, or when she would trade places with Birgit so she could nurse Miriam and spend time with Sextus and Valeria, watched the pair as they rode alongside the wagon, with mixed emotions. She was happy that Diocles had provided a way to help improve her son's education, but she couldn't help worrying about the boy's almost obsessive interest in Titus Pullus. It wasn't that she didn't want the young Titus to know about his great-uncle and adoptive grandfather, yet she did fret that her son would have the same spell cast over him by Pullus' exploits that her husband had experienced. She had heard more times than she could count how Titus

Pullus' visit to Gaius' farm to see his sister Valeria and her son, young Gaius, had been the pivotal moment of Porcinus' life and, as she watched Diocles and Titus together, she could almost feel the giant Roman's shadow falling across the boy.

The weather held for the first week, but just a day from Genua, a huge storm came rolling in from the sea. Even with a paved road, their progress was slowed by sheets of rain, driven almost horizontal by the wind. The thunder and lightning that accompanied the rain made the younger children whimper with fear, and despite their best efforts to stop it, water streamed through the cracks in the seaward side of the wagon to form puddles in the bed. It didn't take long for Gallus, who had been appointed the *de facto* leader of the trip, to decide to find shelter, which they did at a farm where they were given space in the barn, only after Iras grudgingly dropped some coins into the hands of the farmer, who eyed the group with the kind of suspicion that locals always seem to have for anyone from outside their world. The weather didn't break for two days, costing Iras even more money, and the enforced closeness of the barn – the farmer's wife had taken one look at Iras and Birgit and, knowing her husband as she did, had forbidden them to enter the ramshackle house – wore on the entire party's nerves. Not that there was an appreciable difference between the barn and the house, Iras had muttered to Birgit. Fortunately, the weather was fine after that, or at least good enough to keep traveling. Reaching Genua on the tenth day of the journey, they turned north, and they were all happy to leave the coast. It was at Placentia, two weeks into the return journey that they heard the first word of what had occurred to the north, at place they were calling Brigantium.

"It was a bloody fight. At least, that's what I heard," was how Iras and her children were informed, but it was only Titus who had instantly known that what the two men next to them in the inn were talking about concerned his father and his Legion.

"Let's go outside," Titus told his brother and sister, who protested at being pulled from their meal of bread and cheese, but Titus wouldn't be swayed.

Grabbing what they could, the pair of younger children allowed themselves to be led by the hand out of the inn, as Iras mouthed a silent thank you to Titus, who merely shrugged in reply. Diocles, Birgit, and the two bodyguards were sitting with them at the same table, but by unspoken consent, it was Gallus who turned to the man who was speaking.

"*Salve*, friend." Gallus' tone was genial, but the man, who appeared by his dress to be some sort of merchant, eyed Gallus, taking in his soldier's boots and belt, along with the sword, and seemed hesitant to engage in conversation.

Ignoring the look, Gallus asked him, "We couldn't help but overhear you talking about that fight up in Rhaetia."

"So?" The man was clearly suspicious, and he kept glancing from Gallus to Libo, not seeming to see the women or Diocles at all. "I was just talking. There's no crime in that, is there?"

Gallus put up a placating hand.

"*Pax*, friend," he said soothingly. "I mean no harm. And no, it's no crime to talk about such things."

"Then why do you want to know?" The merchant's tone turned belligerent; only then did Iras and the rest of her party notice how red-rimmed his eyes were.

His companion was apparently not as inebriated, because he looked decidedly nervous. Gallus was doing his best to be patient, but Iras knew the man well enough to hear the strain in his voice as he tried to reason with the merchant.

"We're just curious. We've been down in Arelate, and this is the first we've heard about any of this. We just wanted…"

"I don't give a brass *obol* what you want," the man snarled, and he tried to lurch to his feet.

Fortunately, his legs weren't ready to support his weight, so he collapsed back on the bench, and Iras heaved a silent sigh of relief. Gallus was clearly angry, but before he could say or do anything that would make the situation more difficult, Iras spoke up.

"I'm sorry." She adopted the manner that she had learned in the palace in Alexandria, that of a meek, slightly scared woman. "He's just asking for my benefit. You see, my husband is a Centurion in the 8th Legion, and he was probably in this battle that you're talking about. Those are his children that just went outside." Suddenly inspired, she lifted Miriam up above the table, where she had been gurgling and cooing as her mother tried to eat her own meal. "This is his youngest daughter. That's the only reason Gallus here is asking."

It was a good idea, and it would have worked if the man hadn't been so drunk. Instead, her words brought a leer to his face as he looked from her to Gallus, then to Libo. Diocles, seated next to Birgit, instinctively pulled her closer to him and away from Gallus, who she was seated next to at the table.

"This is not good," he muttered so that only she could hear.

"So, you say that your...husband is in the Legions?" the merchant asked Iras, but she knew from his tone that he wasn't going to wait for an answer. "But here you are with him," he jerked a thumb towards Gallus. "So my question is, how does this husband of yours know that brat is his?" He pointed to Libo. "Or his, for that matter? No respectable woman would be out traveling with this sort. Besides, Legionaries aren't allowed to be married. Everyone knows that!"

The merchant didn't see the blow that knocked him from his spot on the bench. Iras did; so did Gallus, Libo, Diocles, and Birgit, because none of them were the ones who landed it. Titus had put his brother and sister in the wagon, and was returning, determined to hear about the battle his father had probably been in, and was just in time to hear the merchant's last words. He hadn't stopped to think; he had just launched himself at the drunken man who insulted his mother. They both landed on the floor, between the benches, with Titus on top, and the boy began pummeling the man, who was too stunned to do more than cover his head with his arms. Gallus took his time pulling Titus off the man, while the other patrons of the inn roared with laughter at the sight of a boy attacking a grown man. It took considerable effort on Gallus' part to stop Titus, and it was with no little surprise that the bodyguard realized that this boy, even at ten years old, was almost as strong as a full-grown man. Finally, Gallus wrested Titus away as the merchant, his face red from the combination of drink, embarrassment, and the result of several of Titus' blows, struggled to a sitting position. Handing Titus to Libo, who now had his one hand full with the struggling boy, Gallus leaned down to the man, offering his hand to help him up. The look of surprise on the merchant's face was so comical that Iras had to suppress a giggle, despite the fact she was still angry at the slur.

"You're lucky it was just the boy," Gallus said, "and that's his mother you insulted."

For a moment, it appeared as if the man was going to slap Gallus' hand away, but then his companion spoke up.

"That's more than you deserve, Mela. You insulted the lady. By rights, you'd be looking at your liver right now."

Grumbling under his breath, the merchant nevertheless took the offered hand and sat heavily on the bench. The other travelers, sensing that the entertainment was at an end, slowly returned their attention to their own business. With that matter settled, at least for the moment, the merchant was at least willing to talk.

There are some things that are better off unknown; at least, that was the conclusion Iras came to after hearing about the battle on the lake against the Rhaeti. The merchant had described it as a great victory, but also claimed that the casualties among the Legions were heavy, particularly so with the troops under the command of the young Drusus. At the same time, the name of Tiberius was being spoken of as a great general, and the ultimate architect of the masterstroke of attacking the enemy in the rear by rowing across the lake. All Iras knew was that her husband was involved; the merchant had been certain that the 8th was one of the attacking Legions. The only consolation came from the fact that this distracted Iras a great deal from the monotony of the trip, as the family continued their journey, through Placentia and on to Mutina. It was at Mutina that the party heard that the Legions had moved up into Noricum, where other tribes were rebelling. More troubling than that was the first muttering about unrest back in Pannonia. Despite this news, it didn't change the route on which Iras had insisted; no amount of arguing or persuading could convince her to put her family on a boat again. What Gallus couldn't understand was why Diocles, who had been able to convince Iras the first time, chose to remain silent this time. Unknown to Gallus, neither Iras nor Diocles were the real cause of this change of heart; Birgit was terrified of the idea of a sea voyage of any length. And Iras, who hadn't been excited about the idea of another sea passage herself, had been receptive to her fears. Her motives weren't entirely based on fear; she also wanted to give Titus as much uninterrupted time with Diocles as she could. Once they returned to Siscia, as Diocles and Iras had discussed it, they had decided that the Greek would begin tutoring the other children as well. Going further, they agreed that the best way to dispel any talk of young Titus being groomed for ideas above his station was to offer Diocles' services to the children of other Centurions as well. With that in mind, Iras wanted Titus to have the undivided attention from Diocles for as long as she could get away with, although it was not only the other children who were upset with the idea that their big brother wouldn't spend at least part of the day with them in the wagon, or ride behind it on Ocelus. Now that both Birgit and Diocles had declared their feelings for the other, they seemed determined to make up for the time they had lost mooning over each other in Arelate. On this, Iras had held firm; they were stopping early enough in the day that the pair could enjoy their nights, although she noted with quiet amusement how often Diocles started the day looking haggard, as if he hadn't gotten any sleep, while Birgit was positively beaming with happiness. Titus had noticed this as well, although his attitude was more of bemusement than anything else; he understood the sexual act well enough, given how often he heard his parents panting and moaning, but he just couldn't quite grasp why adults seemed to be such fools about it. He had heard often enough men referring to it as an itch that needed to be scratched, which puzzled him even more, thinking of the analogy literally. When he scratched an itch, it obviously felt pleasant and brought relief, but he didn't do it any longer than it took to stop the itch. And he didn't keep scratching after it stopped itching! When he brought this up to Gallus, understanding that Diocles was hardly in the right frame of mind to discuss such matters, the bodyguard had laughed and given him the same answer adults always seemed to give.

"Don't worry. One day, you'll understand."

He seriously doubted that.

One other pleasant byproduct of taking the overland route was that it gave the travelers the chance to see more of the country than they would have taking the same way back. At least, it started pleasantly enough, except the farther east they moved, the more disturbing the signs became that there was something going on. It started with small things, most often expressed in the demeanor and greetings that came from other travelers, but it didn't take long for all of them to notice that the traffic heading west was getting heavier by the day. It was when they were still two days away from Emona, the last town they would pass through before reaching Siscia and home that the nature of the traffic changed as well. Before they had gone five miles of that day's journey, Iras counted no less than a dozen carts and wagons, each of them heavily loaded and accompanied by what to any observer looked like families. However, none of the westbound travelers said anything, or even acknowledged the calls of Gallus, or Libo, about why there were so many people on the Via Postumia. Finally, Gallus and Libo together forced a wagon to stop by blocking the road next to their own wagon, at a spot where the wagon driver simply couldn't swing wide onto the dirt next to the paved road because it was too muddy. The driver, clearly alarmed, leaped from his seat, waving what to Titus looked like nothing more than a stave or perhaps a pick handle, but he was quickly joined by two teenage boys who had clambered down from the back of the wagon, each of them armed with their own pieces of wood.

Gallus held both his hands out, as Libo did the same, calling out, "*Pax*, friend! We mean you no harm! We're just trying to find out why everyone seems in such a hurry heading the opposite direction that we are."

The man, clearly unconvinced, scowled suspiciously at the pair, then his eyes darted over to where Titus and Diocles were sitting on their horses, just behind their own wagon. It appeared that he was weighing his best options when Sextus and Valeria chose that moment to pop their heads out from their wagon to have a better view of what was a break in the monotony. Seeing the children, the man visibly relaxed, although his demeanor didn't change.

"You mean you don't know?" His tone was still suspicious.

"No," Gallus assured him. "We're coming from Arelate, returning to our home in Siscia...."

He got not further as the man gave a snorting laugh that held no humor.

"No chance of that," he said, shaking his head to emphasize the point. "If you're smart, you'll go no farther than Emona."

"But why?" Titus was the one who asked this question, ignoring the envious stares of the two youths who were trying to determine how someone their age could afford a horse like that, even as old as it was.

"Why?" the man echoed, then gave that humorless laugh again. "I'll tell you why, boy. The entire province of Pannonia has risen up in revolt, that's why! Those barbarian scum are killing every Roman they find! None of us are safe!"

This declaration prompted Iras to stand up from where she had been playing with the children and, at the sight of her, the man finally relaxed.

It didn't change his near-hysteria, however, as he turned to Iras. "Mistress, you need to listen to me! You're not safe, nor are your children! You'd do well to turn around right now and follow us out of this cursed place!"

"But our home is in Siscia," Iras replied calmly. "We've been away a long time and just want to go home."

The man shook his head impatiently, insisting, "You'll never make it to Siscia! I told you, the entire province is in rebellion! The Legions are nowhere near because they've been sent over to Rhaetia and Noricum! Siscia is defenseless!"

"That's not true," Gallus interjected firmly. "There are three Cohorts of auxiliary troops that are always left there."

"If you want to put your lives in the hands of a bunch of barely trained rabble that aren't even citizens, that's your business. But you shouldn't be putting the lady and her children in danger because of your misplaced faith!"

Like all men of the Legions, even those no longer under the standard, neither Gallus nor Libo viewed the auxiliaries as the equal of Legionaries, yet they also knew that they were much more than "barely trained rabble." Nevertheless, Gallus instantly saw that there was no reasoning with this man, who seemed very close to losing his mind from fear. Instead, he turned to Iras, the question clear in his gaze.

Without hesitation, she spoke up loudly enough for everyone to hear. "I thank you for your concern, sir. But we're going to Siscia. I have the utmost faith in the men of the auxiliaries, and I also know that if matters are as you say, the Legions are even now marching here."

Staring at her disbelievingly, the man's mouth hung open for a moment before he made one last attempt.

"Lady, I beg you. If you insist on heading east, I can't stop you, but I implore, no, I beg you for the sake of your children not to go farther than Emona."

Rather than argue further, Iras simply said, "We will stop in Emona."

With nothing further to be said, the bodyguards moved aside and allowed the other wagon to pass.

Because of the rattling din of the wheels rolling over the paving stones, the man didn't hear her finish, "For the night. Then we go on to Siscia."

Iras had much cause to regret those words. When they reached Emona, the fear of the citizens was at a fever pitch, brought on by news of a series of raids on some small settlements and farms to the north. It was impossible for Gallus to determine what was fact and what was the fevered imaginings of terrified townspeople, but he determined that, at the very least, something serious was taking place. That night, at the same inn they had stopped at on the way, which was almost deserted, Iras, Diocles, and the bodyguards discussed matters. Insisting on attending was Titus, taking the charge given to him by his father of protecting the family extremely seriously, even if it had been given in jest. It was a sign of Iras' worry that she not only didn't forbid his attendance, when he showed up wearing his sword, she only made a half-hearted attempt to have him put it back in the wagon. The talk was tense, as the two bodyguards tried to convince Iras that just because the man they had met a couple days before on the road was almost out of his mind with fear, it didn't mean his advice wasn't sound. But as Porcinus could have told them, and as they had learned over the course of this trip, Iras could be incredibly stubborn. In fact, when she and Porcinus argued about who had given what trait to their children, the charge that Titus' bullheadedness came from her was one she found impossible to refute. That characteristic was fully engaged during what quickly became a heated discussion.

Finally, Diocles threw up his hands, exclaiming, "Pluto's cock, woman! Must you always win?"

The fact that the Greek had used an epithet that had been his former master's favorite, coupled with Iras' knowledge how rarely Diocles used such language, actually did more to shake her resolve than any of the other, reasoned arguments she had heard from the trio of men. Yet ultimately, although there was much truth in what Diocles said, Iras had made up her mind that the safety of her family was best guaranteed by reaching Siscia. Her reasoning wasn't entirely based on emotion; the fact was that Emona wasn't a fortified town, nor did it have more than a Century of auxiliaries. The citizens were pinning their hopes on the fact that Emona was at the far west end of Pannonia, while the depredations that were taking place were occurring to the northeast, almost directly north of Siscia. Not without some logic, the citizens of Emona were convinced that because of Siscia's location and importance, it would bear the brunt of whatever the rebelling tribes had in mind. However, it was equally true, and was a major factor in Iras' reasoning, that Siscia was much better prepared and defended than Emona. Most compelling to her was the thought that this would be where Gaius would come, along with the rest of the men of the Legions. And just like had happened on the trip to Arelate, it was Titus who tipped the scales, although this time it was in the opposite direction.

"Whatever you decide, Mama," he told her quietly, ignoring the mutters and groans from the three men.

The last time Titus said this, he had his own reasons, and Iras had recognized it as an attempt to manipulate her. This time, however, she viewed his words as a lifeline, her only ally in what was turning out to be at the least a contentious exchange. And she grabbed it, not thinking nor particularly caring whether or not her son's motives were pure.

"Thank you, Titus." She smiled at her son. Drawing courage from his support, she turned back to the others and said, "We're going on to Siscia."

As is normally the case with such things, and as the rebels intended it, when the attack happened, it happened quickly, and they picked their spot well. It was the third day out of Emona, with Siscia just a bit less than two days away. At a spot where the road ran along the Sava to the left, and there was a heavily wooded hill to the right, a force of more than a dozen warriors, members of the Latobici tribe, to whom this part of Pannonia belonged, came bursting from their hiding place. In conception, it was a perfect plan; in execution, the leader of the band was too eager, so that Libo, who was riding ahead of the wagon as a scout, had a crucial moment that gave him the instant of warning he needed.

"Ambush!" he shouted, drawing his sword and performing the only maneuver that ever had a chance against a surprise attack.

Lowering his blade out in front of him, he savagely kicked his horse in the ribs, aiming the beast directly at the nearest barbarian warriors, just coming out of their hiding spot. Gallus, riding next to the wagon, turned to shout a command at Simeon, but the Armenian had reacted instantly as well, jerking one rein to begin turning the wagon about.

"Head back to that farmhouse!" Gallus shouted, and Simeon, who had essentially made the same decision at the same time, merely gave a grim nod as he brought the whip he carried on the seat next to him down on the back of the twin pair of mules.

There was a sudden, vicious lurch that knocked Iras from her feet, just as she stood to get a better look at the cause of the disturbance, and the children let out a frightened cry at the sight of their mother losing her feet. Miriam, who had been nestled in Birgit's arms, sound asleep, was awakened and began adding her own lusty cries to the noise, contributing to the chaos. It was this combination of events that alerted Titus and Diocles, riding a few dozen paces behind the wagon, but it was the older Greek who reacted first.

Taking in the sight of the wagon that was just beginning to turn back in their direction, he leaned over to look past it in time to see Libo strike down one of the leading warriors before he was surrounded by at least a half-dozen Latobici, all mounted as well.

"We have to get up there to keep those *cunni* away from the wagon," Diocles commanded the boy, who didn't hesitate, drawing his sword, small though it was.

Diocles drew his own blade, one that he had begun carrying for the previous several days, and together, they moved at the gallop past the wagon.

Iras had regained her feet, and her eyes widened in horror at the sight of her son heading in the opposite direction of the wagon, screaming at him, "Titus! No! Don't you dare! Come back here!"

Titus, his face set in a determined scowl, shouted back, "I have to help keep them off the wagon, Mama!"

Ocelus, his stride now opened, never faltered as they went thundering past, the old stallion already opening a gap on Diocles' Thunder and closing the distance to Gallus, who had hurried to join the other bodyguard. Iras continued shouting at her son, almost obscured by the dust raised by Ocelus' and Thunder's hooves, and she was sure that this was the last sight she was going to have of her son, still alive and breathing.

The farmhouse that Simeon was heading for was abandoned, but hadn't been burned by this warband, although it had been thoroughly looted. The leader of the raiding party had forbidden his warriors to torch the buildings, not wanting the column of smoke to alert anyone traveling the road. That wasn't his only reason; they were operating close to Siscia, and the Latobici knew from firsthand experience how quickly the Roman military moved. He wanted to scoop up as many solitary wagons and travelers as he could before being forced to melt away back into the hills. He and his men were unprepared for this kind of response, however, as his men swarmed around the first Roman, who had done the exact opposite thing the leader had expected. Nevertheless, he wasn't worried, yet even as some of his men surrounded that first Roman, he saw another galloping up, his sword also drawn. Shouting to alert the pair of his warriors closest to him, he headed directly for Gallus, bringing the spear he carried up and level, aimed directly at the onrushing Roman. He saw two more riders behind the man he was aiming at, and, for a moment, he considered that the prudent course might be to withdraw, but when they got closer, he saw that one was a boy, the other a slightly built man with dark features and almost completely gray hair. Dismissing them as a threat, he discarded the idea of a retreat, returning his attention to his rapidly closing adversary, who had veered his own mount in his direction to meet the challenge.

"You know what to do," the leader shouted to the other two warriors just before he and Gallus met.

They, in fact, did, each one splitting on either side of the Roman, wheeling about to turn perpendicular to Gallus, both of them waiting to see how Gallus met the attack of their leader. What Gallus did, much like Libo's act, was completely unexpected. Instead of continuing to head straight for the leader, he suddenly veered to his right, changing his aim from the Latobici leader to the warrior to his left, who had just come to an almost complete stop. Robbed of his mobility, this warrior, armed with a sword, desperately brought it sweeping up in a last-ditch attempt to block Gallus' thrust as the Roman went galloping by, but he was an instant too late. Gallus' arm jerked from the impact; he was an infantryman by training and had never fought from horseback, so although he braced himself, between the force of the thrust and the motion of his horse, he felt his blade yanked from his grasp, leaving it lodged deep in the ribs of the Latobici warrior. The man gave a wheezing gasp, reeling in the saddle as a froth of blood suddenly appeared on his lips before toppling from the back of his horse to land with a dull, lifeless thud onto the dirt near the road. Gallus had scored a kill, except he was now unarmed.

The Latobici leader, momentarily thwarted by Gallus' maneuver, had flashed by the pair, unable to bring his spear up and over the head of his own horse to bear on the Roman. Viciously yanking the reins of his horse, whose head was jerked by the motion, he wheeled about, lips pulled back in an evil grin as Gallus desperately tried to turn his own mount, intent on returning to the corpse of the first man and retrieving his weapon. The leader's horse leapt forward, and it became a desperate race back to where the body lay, the slain man's horse trotting off a few paces before deciding to graze. It quickly became apparent that the leader would cut Gallus off, but again, the Roman didn't do what would have been the understandable thing and veer away in an attempt to open the distance. Instead, he turned his horse so that it was heading in the general direction of the leader, but at such an angle that, to the Latobici, it appeared that the Roman had lost his head from fear. There was no safety in the direction the Roman was headed; on the other side of the road was the river, which was too wide and deep to cross. All the leader had to do was nudge his own mount with his knee to adjust his own trajectory to intersect the man. Once he dispatched this Roman, there was only the original man to worry about, and although whatever was happening was behind him, he was sure that his men had already dispatched that one. Then it was just that boy and the old man before they could run down the wagon.

He never saw the blow that killed him, so he didn't know that it was actually the boy he had dismissed who struck it. One moment, his entire being was focused on the fleeing Roman, who suddenly pulled up as if realizing his flight was futile, then there was a searing, unspeakably intense pain in his back, starting just below the ribcage but lancing deep into the very center of his being. There was the feeling of some sort of foreign object entering his body, then it was gone almost before he realized it was there, leaving nothing but an agony. For some reason, the grip on his spear suddenly relaxed, and he felt it bouncing off his thigh as it fell to the ground, just before he felt himself toppling off to the side. The impact with the dirt was tremendous, although he barely felt it over the agonizing pain in his back. His last conscious thought was a feeling of surprise at the sight of a large, gray horse that went thundering by, and the boy holding a bloody sword. Where did he get that? the leader wondered. It was so small.

Titus reached Gallus, and together they rode over to the first Latobici corpse, where they were joined by Diocles, the pair of them watching as Gallus slid off his mount and ran over to the body, wrenching his blade from it. Meanwhile, the third warrior, seeing the fate of his leader and other comrade, had decided that he would be better off rejoining the part of the raiding party that was in pursuit of the wagon.

Quickly remounting, Gallus muttered, "Thanks, boy. I thought I was done for."

Titus was sufficiently distracted not to bristle at being called a boy, as Diocles pointed east down the road.

"Libo's in trouble!"

Gallus began heading in that direction, but he was stopped by Diocles.

"We can't," the Greek said quietly.

Gallus looked at him as if Diocles had lost his mind, but the older man was steadfast, pointing in the opposite direction. Even then, the half-dozen mounted men in pursuit of the wagon had closed the distance to within perhaps two hundred paces.

"We have to protect the wagon," he insisted, and Gallus instantly saw that he was right.

Cursing bitterly, Gallus turned his horse.

"But we can't just leave him," Titus protested. "I'll go help!"

"No!" Diocles shouted, the fear sharp in his voice. "You can't, Titus! There are too many of them!"

Reluctantly, Titus looked again, and with a sinking heart, he saw that Diocles was right. Gallus was already headed after the wagon, and Diocles was clearly anxious to follow. Still, Titus looked at Libo, and he saw that the bodyguard was bleeding from a wound to his torso and one leg. Yet he continued to fight furiously, and Titus saw what he had to do.

"I'm going for help," he turned to Diocles, his voice eerily calm. "I'm going to ride to Siscia. It's our only chance."

Diocles' mouth opened to argue, then shut it. The boy was right, he realized.

Instead, he gave a quick nod, saying only, "May the gods go with you, Titus."

"Tell my mother," Titus said, then turned and jabbed Ocelus in the ribs.

Even as dire as the situation was, Diocles couldn't suppress a shudder at the thought of being the one to tell Iras that her son was risking his life.

What Titus had seen was what gave him the idea. Libo's tactic of attacking the attackers had taken him off the road in the direction of the lower slope of the hill, just short of the line of trees. That left the road itself open, a clear path leading to Siscia, yet despite his youth he knew that time was of the essence.

"Okay, boy, I need you to be strong for me," he whispered to Ocelus, who replied by flattening his ears, then, before Titus even touched the horse's flanks, the gray stallion leapt into motion.

Within no more than three heartbeats, the giant horse was at a full gallop, his hooves thudding along the paving stones of the Via Postumia, the wind roaring in Titus' ears. Despite the gravity and danger of the overall situation, Titus felt a grin plastered on his face, his lips pulled back in a combination of joy and from the force of the wind rushing past. Almost before his mind could register, the distance to where Libo was just then reeling in the saddle was halved, while the warriors surrounding the Roman were clearly intent on landing the final blow that would unseat him. That meant none of them were paying any attention to the lone rider heading their way at a full gallop.

Titus almost made it undetected, but it was a matter of just a few heartbeats' difference between a clean escape and what happened, when Libo, wounded in at least a half-dozen spots, finally was too slow in parrying a thrust and took a spear in the throat. He fell from the saddle, dead before he hit the ground, enabling the two warriors nearest to the road to turn their attention away. Simultaneously they spotted the large gray stallion pounding toward them, and although they both reacted instantly, they underestimated the speed of Ocelus. They intended to intersect their quarry, but they completely missed, reaching the road well behind the fleeing boy. Shouting to their companions, the pair began their pursuit, and they were quickly joined by two more men, while the remainder of the Latobici turned back to the west to join the warriors who were pursuing the wagon. Ocelus was running full out, his neck extended flat, ears back, and mane whipping in the wind. Titus could feel the strands lashing his face, and would have several small welts on his cheeks later. At that moment, however, he was intent on escaping; he had seen everything as it happened, and even then, his heart was heavy at the thought of Libo's death. The image of the thrust that killed Libo came to his mind, but he risked closing his eyes for just a moment, forcing the picture away. Titus had become a decent horseman, yet he was still afraid risking a backwards glance, so he only turned his head towards his shadow, trying to catch a glimpse of any pursuers by looking for their own right behind him. Seeing nothing, he finally risked a quick peek over his shoulder, and was relieved to see that his pursuers were several dozen lengths behind him. Ocelus was still running smoothly, but Titus was worried; his horse was old, although he hadn't really exhibited much signs of aging since he and Titus had been reunited.

"Keep it up, boy," Titus shouted to the horse. "When we lose them, I've got an extra apple for you!"

Ocelus' ears, flattened against his skull, only twitched in response, the horse continuing his smooth, ground-eating gait. While Titus wasn't that experienced, he knew at some point soon he was going to have to slow down his horse, but then so would his pursuers. What he was counting on was the fact that their horses were already more winded when they started their pursuit than Ocelus; his hope was that this would make the difference in his escaping. As Ocelus continued along the road, Titus desperately tried to remember the country to the east and what opportunities it provided for him to lose his pursuers. From what he remembered, the ground was mostly open, the road following the Savus all the way to Siscia. Then, he recalled that, perhaps twelve miles ahead, there was a heavily forested ridge on the northern side of the road. It was a bit unusual; the ground around it was flat and open, but Titus remembered that Gallus had told him that the ridge was riddled with caves, which might give him and Ocelus the chance to hide and lose his pursuers, should they continue to chase him. His hope was that they would give up, and do it soon, especially because while the ridge was his best chance at losing them if they continued the chase, it was on the other side of the Savus. He had swum with Ocelus before, but never under these kinds of circumstances, and while he wasn't sure, he thought he had spotted one of his pursuers carrying a bow. First, however, he had to get there, so he risked another glance behind him, and was heartened to see that the gap remained the same. However, they were still back there and showing no signs of giving up.

The wagon just barely made it to the farmhouse, the mules giving their last bit of energy to do so. Simeon wasted no time, leaping from the wagon before it came to a complete stop.

"Mistress," he shouted. "Get your children in the house! I will do what I can to hold them off!"

Even as Iras did as Simeon commanded, jumping down from the back of the wagon, then turning to grab Valeria's hand and roughly pull her out of the wagon, Simeon went sprinting past her, back in the direction of the riders, who were less than fifty paces behind them. Meanwhile, Sextus, clearly frightened, jumped out by himself, and last was Birgit, clutching Miriam, but leaping down with an agility that was surprising, although it was fueled by fear. Iras barely had a moment to wonder what Simeon had planned, but as she hurried her children to the door of the squat, stone farmhouse, she saw something in one of his hands, while the other drew back to his cheek. Only then did she remember that among the many things that Simeon had told her over the course of their return to Siscia was his prowess with a bow. She had the odd, fleeting memory of him telling her how he had been one of Armenia's corps of dreaded horse archers, trained in the same manner as the Parthians, if not as renowned, before he had been wounded, captured, and made a slave. Before she even shut the door, she saw Simeon release an arrow, draw another from a quiver he had slung across his back, nock, and let a second one fly. What she couldn't see were the results, but she heard a blood-curdling scream that she barely recognized as coming from one of the rebel's horses. Slamming the door shut, she was about to throw the locking bar down, then thought better of it. She didn't know where Gallus, Diocles, or Titus were at that moment, but she was sure that they would be trying to reach the farmhouse as well. The children were whimpering with fear, yet surprisingly, Birgit seemed to be the calmest, holding Miriam, who was squirming mightily while the Gallic girl murmured to the two older children words in her native tongue that she had begun using with the children even before they left Arelate. At first, it had irritated Iras that the girl was using words that she didn't know, but it was something she had planned to bring up and never gotten around to. Now it didn't seem to be so important, and it was having a good effect on Sextus and Valeria, who were even then calming down. Outside, Iras caught a series of shouts and what she assumed were curses, including what was clearly a cry of pain that she could tell didn't come from Simeon. There was the sound of hooves and she heard at least two sets that began sounding as if they were coming from the opposite side of the house from the wagon.

Suddenly alarmed, she told Birgit, "Watch this door! If anyone other than Simeon or the others come in, scream."

Without waiting for Birgit's reply, she scurried as fast as her *stola* and traveling cloak allowed to the far side of the farmhouse. It wasn't a huge house, but it had four rooms, and she could tell by the smell of the room she moved into from the main one that this was used as a stable, most likely for the more valuable of the departed farmer's animals. Normally, she would have been careful where she stepped, but she had no time to do so, because she spotted that there was another door, this one large enough for animals. It was closed, yet before she reached it, a blast of light destroyed the darkness as the door was violently flung open. Startled, she let out a terrified shriek, trying to slide to a stop but slipping in a pile of manure and falling, hard, on her rear.

"Iras! It's us!" Diocles shouted, holding a hand out to her as he pulled Thunder's reins to lead his animal into the building.

Gasping in a combination of relief and pain, Iras struggled to her feet. Right behind Diocles was Gallus, who the Greek made room for by leading Thunder into the far corner, where he dropped the reins.

Approaching Iras, Diocles' nose wrinkled and he said, "You smell like you stepped in *cac*."

It was an odd thing to say, at an odd time, and the incongruity of the moment caused Iras to laugh, despite her state of mind. That was when she noticed something.

"Where's Titus?"

Diocles hesitated for an instant, and Iras, mistaking the reason, uttered a muffled, choking sob and collapsed in a dead faint.

"What did you do that for?" Gallus demanded as Diocles dropped to his knees.

"I didn't do anything," the Greek protested as he gently slapped Iras' face.

When he didn't get any response, he reluctantly increased the force of his attempts. Finally, her eyes fluttered open, slowly coming into focus. Looking up and seeing Diocles, she gasped and tried to sit upright.

"Titus!" She said the name as both a question and a lament, needing to hear, but fearing the answer.

"He's fine," Diocles answered quickly.

Her face flooded with relief, but it was short-lived.

"Then where is he?" she demanded again.

There was no putting it off, and Diocles decided it was best to plunge in.

"He's gone for help. To Siscia."

For a moment, her face registered no comprehension, then she sat bolt upright. Disdaining Diocles' offer of help up, she climbed to her feet.

"Are you mad?" She was furious now, completely oblivious to what was happening around her and her condition of just a moment before forgotten.

Gallus, meanwhile, hadn't bothered to stay put, but moved quickly back into the main room.

"It was his idea, Iras," Diocles said, then added quietly, "And it was a good one. The only one, really."

"But what about Libo? Surely he would have been better suited," Iras protested.

Diocles hesitated, then replied, "I don't know for sure, but I think Libo is dead. The last time I looked back, I couldn't see him at all, which probably means he's off his horse. And if he was unhorsed..." His voice trailed off, but his meaning was clear.

"But why Titus?" she wailed. "He's just a boy!"

"Because he's an extraordinary boy." Diocles was trying to remain patient, aware that his attention was needed elsewhere. "And he's got Ocelus."

Iras was almost overwhelmed by a confusing array of emotions at Diocles' words: pride, fear, anxiety, and a feeling of helplessness that threatened to paralyze her. But there was a rational part of her mind that acknowledged everything Diocles was saying was true, and that Titus was the best, and perhaps their only hope.

"If anything happens to him..."

Diocles put a hand on her shoulder and assured her quietly, "He'll be fine, Iras. He'll get through and bring help. I know it."

"I hope so," Iras managed.

Absently, she reached up to pat Diocles' hand, then moved back into the main room. Just as she entered, she saw Gallus leaping to the door to yank it open.

Simeon came stumbling in, his quiver empty, but still with his bow, gasping, "They're right behind me!"

Gallus and Simeon put their shoulders into the door to slam it shut, but even so, had to struggle to close it as a single, brawny arm shot through the gap, clawing at the air. The sight of that elicited a scream from the children and Birgit, who clutched Miriam and shrank back into the far corner of the room. Gallus managed to draw his *pugio*, and with his left hand, he jabbed it downward, stabbing the forearm of whoever was still trying to keep the door from being closed. A howling yell emanated from the other side, but the arm was withdrawn, leaving a bloody smear on the wall next to the doorway. The door slammed shut, and Diocles quickly dropped the locking bar into place. They had won a few moments, but that was all. Quickly taking stock, Gallus saw that although the walls were made of stone, making it impossible to fire, the roof was wood. He knew it wouldn't take long for the raiders to arrive at the idea themselves, and their only chance was to keep them from climbing the roof. Like most farmhouses, this one had a loft spanning half of the room adjoining the main one. If it was used in the same way as most such structures, the farmer's children slept up there. Telling Simeon to keep watch, which he could only partially do through a crack in the shuttered window, Gallus beckoned Diocles to follow him. Climbing the ladder, both men had to crouch as Gallus inspected the planks that formed the roof, testing them until he found what he was looking for. Taking his sword, he used it to pry the plank he had selected by placing the tip in the crack between it and the support beam that it had been nailed to, wincing at the noise as the board screeched in protest. He did the same for the next two planks, so that there would be a space wide enough for a man the size of Diocles.

Turning to the Greek, he said, "If you hear anything, and I mean anything, up there, you're going to have to go out on the roof and stop them."

Diocles' face turned pale; nevertheless, he nodded his grim understanding, drawing the sword he had been given a few days earlier by Libo. Gallus dropped down, and ran to where Simeon was standing.

"They're looting the wagon," the Armenian said quietly, still peering through the crack.

"How many do you see?" Gallus asked.

"Five," Simeon replied, then turned to Gallus. "Did you manage to count how many there are?"

Gallus shook his head, but said, "I can't be sure, but I know there were at least a dozen."

Simeon thought for a moment. "I know that I killed at least one."

"As did I," Gallus responded, "and the boy killed another."

Iras looked up from comforting the children, wide-eyed.

"Titus did?" she gasped. "He killed a man?"

Gallus nodded, but he was thinking furiously about other matters.

Turning to Simeon, he asked the Armenian, "Can you handle a sword as well as you use a bow?"

The Armenian grinned.

"Not as well, but I know which end to hold."

Gallus laughed, except it was cut short by the realization that there wasn't an extra sword in the house. The only way his plan would work is if Simeon used Diocles' weapon. And if any Latobici chose the same moment to climb the roof to set it alight, Diocles would have no way to stop it. Deciding quickly that it was worth the risk, Gallus ran into the other room, and told Diocles that he needed his sword. Although the Greek was confused, he complied, handing it hilt first to Gallus.

"I'll bring it right back, but it might be a little bloody," Gallus called over his shoulder as he returned to the main room.

Handing it to Simeon, he quickly explained what he was planning. It was to the Armenian's credit that he didn't hesitate once he learned what it was.

Titus had slowed Ocelus to a canter, then finally to a trot, but only did so when he saw his pursuers slow their own mounts. He, or rather Ocelus, had managed to increase the gap back to his pursuers, who were perhaps a quarter mile behind him. And looming ahead of him was the lone ridge that he had remembered, off to his left front, the heavily forested slopes beckoning to him. The only problem was the silvery ribbon that was the Savus, glinting in the sunlight, in between Titus and the possible safety of the ridge. Glancing at the sun, Titus estimated he had no more than a full watch of daylight left, but he would reach the ridge before dark. This was disappointing; his hope had been that he would be able to use the cover of darkness to cross the river, because he had had enough opportunity to see that one of the Latobici was armed with a bow. In fact, the warrior had attempted a long distance shot twice, although both had fallen well short of their target. Now he had a decision to make, whether to attempt to cross the river and risk being struck by arrows as his pursuers stood on the riverbank, or to forego the possibility of losing them by not even trying to reach the ridge. Nagging at him was the worry about Ocelus; he had been unable to stop to rest his horse, who, for the first time, was showing signs of fatigue. He had been run into a good sweat, making his coat a darker gray than normal, and his head was bobbing a bit with each step. Nevertheless, Titus was sure that his pursuers' mounts were in at least as bad condition, and he had every confidence in his horse, no matter how old Ocelus was.

"I haven't forgotten my promise," the boy told the horse, more to break the silence than for any other reason. "You're going to get an extra apple. But no more than that," he added ruefully, remembering the aftermath of his short-lived experiment, when he had allowed both Sextus and Valeria to give Ocelus their own apples.

It was the worry about Ocelus that forced Titus' decision. He had to find a place to elude his pursuers to allow his horse to rest, for at least a watch. Despite his youth, Titus understood that this was a horrible risk to his family; every watch he delayed in reaching Siscia meant his mother and siblings were still in danger. Yet, he reasoned with himself, if Ocelus finally did founder, his family, in all likelihood, would die along with him, because he held no illusions that the Latobici would show him any mercy. He didn't know that the man he had killed was the nominal leader of this raiding party; what he did know was that he had slain one of their number, and that marked him as a combatant and not a boy. Under other circumstances, Titus would have taken great pride in that distinction, yet for the first, and what would turn out to be the only time in his life, he wished that they would view and treat him as just the ten-year-old boy he was, no matter what size he might have been. Following that thought was an even more unwelcome one; what if his efforts were in vain? What if it was already too late? As quickly as the idea came, he shoved it away with a shudder, refusing to let his mind go into that dark corner of his consciousness and open that door again. This may have been what prompted his next action. Suddenly pressing hard into Ocelus' right flank with his knee while drawing the reins in the opposite direction, Titus gave his horse a hard kick in the ribs.

"Let's go, boy!" he shouted, as much to startle Ocelus as anything. "Let's go swimming!"

As he had hoped, the combination of his cry and the physical commands he was given caused Ocelus to respond instinctively with a leap to his left. Where he got the reserves, Titus would never know, but the gray stallion went to the full gallop, heading directly for the river. Titus looked over, and his heart leapt with joy at the sight of the four barbarians engaged in some sort of discussion and not paying attention at that moment. He knew that it wouldn't last; even as he was turning his attention back to the front, he saw a quick jerk of one of the Latobici's heads, attracted no doubt by his own movement. Between the distance and the wind already roaring in his ears, he couldn't hear the cries of alarm, but the four warriors immediately put their own mounts into motion, heading at an angle for the riverbank. Nevertheless, Ocelus, without any hesitation, went plunging into the river, his powerful legs churning up a fantastic spray of water and mud. In no more than the space of three or four heartbeats, Titus could feel his horse's legs lose contact with the river bottom, as he became buoyant as well. Clutching tightly to the saddle, Titus turned to see that his pursuers had yet to reach the riverbank, but they were closing the distance rapidly, and he wasn't quite halfway across. Ocelus was still swimming strongly, but Titus could hear how labored his breathing was becoming, his lungs working like the powerful bellows that they were, his nostrils fully dilated. Although he had very little experience in judging such matters, Titus thought that he would have to get at least fifty paces beyond the riverbank to be out of bowshot. And that was only if the bowman stayed fully on his side of the river and didn't enter the water. Glancing back again, Titus' heart sank as he saw that the pursuing tribesmen had reached the bank, and while three of them went plunging into the water, one of them had drawn up and hopped off his horse. As Titus watched in helpless horror, he saw the man draw his bow back, and point it slightly skyward, judging the trajectory of the arrow he was about to loose. There was an instant's pause, then Titus saw a dark blurry object streak into the air, arcing up then down, moving so quickly that the boy's eye could barely track it. And there was nothing he could do to avoid it, but fortunately the archer's aim was wide, Titus hearing a hissing sound an eyeblink before the arrow created a splash as it entered the water, off to his right.

"Come on, boy, we're almost there!" Titus urged Ocelus, trying to keep the fear out of his voice, brought on as much by the sight of his horse's head, his nostrils less than an inch above the water, as he was by the near miss.

Even as he said this, there was another hiss, except this time it was to his left, and it was much, much closer, the entry of the arrow splashing Titus in the face. They were so close to the other side, he thought, although Ocelus' hooves still hadn't touched bottom. Just as this passed through his mind, Titus felt as if somehow one of the Latobici had managed to sneak up behind him and punch him in the shoulder, hard. It didn't hurt, at least at first, but in very quick succession, the pain came in the form of a piercing agony right at the junction of his left arm and torso, just above the armpit, followed by the realization that he had been struck by an arrow. It was a reflex action for him to release his grip on Ocelus with his right hand to reach around to feel for the arrow protruding from his back. But although he instantly realized he had made a mistake relinquishing his grasp of Ocelus, it was too late, as just then the horse's hooves touched bottom and the stallion made a surging leap forward. Titus slid right off the back of his horse, and almost instantly went under the surface of the water. This, in fact, was a good thing, because in the space he had occupied just a heartbeat before, another arrow came slashing down. In all likelihood, it would have been a mortal blow; instead, it splashed into the river harmlessly in the gap between the boy and his horse, who was now chest-deep in the water. Meanwhile, Titus was fighting against the panic that came from being hurt, and underwater. He knew how to swim under normal circumstances, but these were not normal circumstances; the pain in his shoulder had begun in earnest, making any movement of his left arm excruciating. In the confusion of the moment and in his near-hysteria, he lost track of where the surface was, causing him to thrash his one arm and both legs. He was close to drowning as he fought his body's almost overwhelming urge to draw in a breath, which, as far gone with fear as he was, he understood would spell his doom. Maybe that wouldn't be so bad; the thought flashed through his mind, and it was so powerful that it caused him to stop struggling, his body going limp as he began to accept this finality. He was only vaguely aware of a sudden disturbance just above him, then he felt as if his right arm was clamped in a vise as he was violently jerked upward. Just as his head broke the surface, his body finally prevailed, and he opened his mouth to take in what he was sure would be a lungful of water. Instead, his reward was what he thought was the purest, sweetest air he had ever inhaled; it wouldn't be until much later that he would learn his father had experienced something very similar not long before. His right arm was still gripped by something powerful, and his left arm was too painful to lift, but what he was feeling at that moment was a whisper compared to the agony that was about to hit him. Just as the last of the river water streamed from his eyes, out of the corner of his vision he saw a large, gray snout, with big yellow teeth firmly clamped to his arm, dragging him backward onto the riverbank. Before he could appreciate what Ocelus was doing for him, he was almost overwhelmed with agony as the shaft of the arrow protruding from his back came into contact with the ground, shoving the head of the missile deeper into his body. For a horrifying moment, he was sure he would faint, yet there was some part of his mind that refused to submit, the imperative of the need to flee still too powerful.

"Let go, Ocelus," Titus groaned through clenched teeth. "I'm out of the river now."

While not completely true; his feet were still in the water, Ocelus relented, but what relief Titus might have felt from the sudden release of the grip of his arm was overwhelmed by the throbbing agony of his other shoulder. For the remainder of his days, Titus Porcinianus Pullus would never know where he got the strength, not only to stand up, but to climb up on Ocelus' back, using just one arm to lever himself back into the saddle. Just as he settled onto his horse's back, another dark blur went streaking by a few inches away from his head, and it caused Ocelus to jerk his own up. Without waiting for the command, the gray horse spun on his rear haunches, and began at a canter to head towards the ridge, the boy slumped over in the saddle, the three pursuers still in mid-river behind them.

It was impossible for Titus to determine how long he'd been unconscious, or if, in fact, he had been at all. He remembered fragments and pieces of the next watch, but no whole memories remained. It was more impressions; Ocelus laboring underneath him as he began ascending the slope, entering the relative security of the trees, yet still managing to move quietly, something his Avus could have attested to about the big horse. He was vaguely aware that the sun, now a hand's width above the horizon, was to his left as Ocelus began climbing. But he had no memory that would tell him how, the next time he was aware of it, the sun was to his right, and it was barely two fingers above the horizon. It took him a moment to determine that he had somehow reversed his direction, doubling back on his own trail, but higher up the hill than his original path, so that he was heading back in the general direction of the river, and the road. Had he done that, or had Ocelus done it on his own? He could feel his horse shuddering underneath him, and even through the pain, his heart started hammering as he realized that Ocelus was near collapse. He had to find a place to hide, so he forced himself to concentrate, desperately searching for one of the caves that Gallus had said riddled this ridge. Barring that, some small cleft or fold in the hillside would have to do, anywhere that would be hard to spot. Of course, if these warriors were good trackers, it might not matter, he thought grimly, but he refused to dwell on that, focusing instead on what he could do. When he found what he was looking for, it was completely by accident, and, in fact, he almost missed seeing the gap in what looked like just part of a section of sheer rock face. It was the sight of a small tree jutting out at an odd angle, different from the symmetrical arrangement of all the other trees that were growing straight and tall from the hillside, that caught his eye. Even then, it was just one of those things that the eye catches without the mind registering it as anything but something a little odd, and that was almost the case with Titus. He could have been forgiven; he was as close to collapse as his horse, his left side was useless, and he had never been this tired or in as much pain. Yet, somehow, his mind snagged onto the sight of that odd little tree, much as a man being swept downstream will grab at a root or branch. Nudging Ocelus in the direction of the tree, Titus approached from directly downhill from the rock face, where the small tree seemed to jut out from behind the rock, but with only the upper portion of the tree showing. Through the fog of pain, fear, and fatigue, his curiosity was aroused, so he guided Ocelus up the slope. Only when he was perhaps a half-dozen paces away could he see that what looked like sheer rock was actually a giant slab of the same type of rock that made up the ridge, but set out a distance from the rest of the rock face. What Titus didn't know was that it was that tree that had caused this to happen, or more accurately, one of the tree's ancestors, when a tiny seedling had managed to wedge itself in a fissure that, over thousands of years, slowly widened. By the time Titus found it, the gap between the lone slab and the rest of the rock face was just wide enough to accommodate the trunk of the tree, with a bit of room to spare. As Titus was about to discover, it was just wide enough for a boy and his horse to squeeze past. And it was from another accident of nature that gave the pair someplace to go, in the form of one of those caves that Gallus had talked about. This one had been created by the presence of a small but steady flow of water, supplied by a spring that originated at the very back of the small cave. And much like the tree had, over the thousands of years, the trickle of water had formed a depression in the rock floor, creating a small pool. It wasn't perfect, however; Titus saw that he would have to dismount, and that while he and Ocelus would fit completely in the small cave, his horse wouldn't have the ability to turn around. When it came time to leave, he would have to back Ocelus out, and although he had done this before, it was always in a stable or stall, never in a small cave in the wilderness. Titus was too far gone in his misery to give that more than a passing thought, however, and as carefully as he could, using the nearby tree branches to help, he grabbed one with his right arm and swung himself out of the saddle. When he dropped to the ground, he couldn't suppress a groan of pain at the jar of the impact, and he had to stand for a moment, leaning his head against his horse's flank to allow his head to stop spinning. After a moment, he felt strong enough to take Ocelus by his bridle and lead him into the cave. Immediately, the horse, already smelling the water, headed for it, dropping his muzzle deep into the pool to suck in the liquid. As he did so, Titus staggered into the cave behind Ocelus. The sun was almost down, and he knew that he couldn't risk a fire, even if he had brought his firebox with him, so it was with a good deal of reluctance that he finally looked down to his shoulder, knowing that he had to do something while it was still light. He had been aware of a change in the nature and location of the pain and, as he forced his mind to focus, he realized that the change had come when Ocelus had dragged him from the river. His tunic was still damp from the immersion, but as he craned his neck to peer over his shoulder at his back, he could tell that the blood around the wound had dried there, although there was a warm, sticky feeling in his armpit. Gritting his teeth, he lifted his left arm; despite his preparation, he couldn't stifle a muffled sound that was part sob, part moan, and it was loud enough that it disturbed Ocelus, who jerked his head up from drinking to turn and look inquiringly at his boy, water dripping from his muzzle.

"It's…all right," Titus muttered. "I'll be fine."

Ocelus continued to look at Titus, as if trying to determine whether the boy was telling him the truth. Then, he turned his attention back to the water, thrusting his muzzle back down, leaving Titus to attend to himself.

For some reason, this bothered Titus, who glared at the horse and said hoarsely, "Well, thank you for not paying attention! It's nice to see all you care about is drinking your fill. I hope you get a stomachache!"

As quickly as it had come, his fit of pique faded. No, he didn't want Ocelus to get sick; he still needed the giant horse, and for more than just his ability to carry him to Siscia. It was because of Ocelus that he wasn't already captured, and hadn't just given up. Returning his examination to his armpit, he saw the cause of the sudden discomfort, and he also somehow realized that despite the added pain, what he was looking at was actually a good thing. The arrow had hit Titus in the upper back, but his young bones, particularly his shoulder blade, had been strong enough to deflect the missile. Rather than punching through the bone, it had turned, the point scraping along the shoulder blade and lodging up against it. Then, when Ocelus had dragged him and the end of the shaft had come into hard contact with the ground, the force had driven the point deeper, but because of the angle, it had continued along his shoulder blade and punctured the skin of Titus' armpit. He could see the point of the arrow, bloody and dull, sticking out no more than the width of a finger, poking its head out enough that, if he wanted, he could grasp the head of the arrow with the thumb and forefinger of his right hand. Not that he wanted to do anything with it, yet despite his youth, Titus was a child of the Legions. And over the course of his young life, he had heard much talk from men, usually around the stoves of their section huts, where he had the run of his father's Cohort area as he performed odd jobs and did errands for the rankers, just like every other Legionary child. While much of this talk was about whores, and carousing, almost an equal amount was focused on the more practical aspects of the Legionary's life. And dealing with wounds was one of those realities of their lot, so it was natural that they would discuss the best way to deal with such things among themselves. This knowledge had been absorbed by the boy who, like all children, were akin to the sponges at the bottom of the sea who obtained their sustenance from the water around them by sucking it in, taking what was needed and discarding the rest. That was how Titus knew what he must do; the question was, would he have the courage to do it?

The plan devised by Gallus and performed by him and Simeon had worked perfectly. Bursting from the farmhouse, they had attacked the five rebel warriors at a moment when they had all been absorbed in the find of one of them, the small chest of coins that was concealed in a larger trunk filled with clothes. It was a small fortune by anyone's standard, so the rebels were understandably distracted when Gallus leaped into the wagon, followed closely by Simeon. Although their styles were vastly different, the two men worked well together, and in very little time, they thrust, hacked, and chopped down the Latobici rebels. The attack was so sudden, so severe, and so thorough that the remaining half-dozen rebels, who were stationed out on the road, keeping lookout per the orders of the newly promoted commander had no time to react. At least, they had no time to stop the slaughter of their friends, but even worse, they gave Simeon the chance to replenish his stock of arrows. Standing in the bed of the wagon, the Armenian held his bow with an arrow nocked at the ready, but the Latobici had experienced enough loss from this small party. The new commander gave the order to withdraw; normally, this would have been the first challenge to the new leader's authority, because there had been friends and kinsmen lost to this puny party of Romans. However, the knowledge that there was a larger party nearby was sufficient to quell any possible unrest among the remaining tribesmen. Consequently, they were content to withdraw out of bow range, while sending two of their number to the far side of the farmhouse to keep watch and one man to find the larger band and let them know that there was loot to be had and losses to be avenged. Fortunately for Iras and her family, Gallus understood that the danger hadn't passed, so when she put forth the idea that they try to force their way through what was admittedly a small force, he was firm in his refusal.

"This isn't over," he told her quietly, only after he pulled her into the stable with the horses, away from the children. "They've gone for help, and if we get caught out in the open again, there's no way to guarantee that we'll be lucky again."

Iras considered this, but only briefly, knowing that the bodyguard was right.

"Very well," she sighed. "We'll stay put."

Nodding his acceptance of her agreement, Gallus went to tell Diocles and Simeon and make dispositions. Now that they had access to the wagon again, Gallus and the other men transferred the contents into the farmhouse. Iras tried to ignore the fact that more than one box or crate had the blood of the rebels on it, but Birgit was unable to suppress a gasp at the sight. This naturally attracted the attention of the children, yet somewhat to Iras' dismay, they seemed more interested than repulsed. The mules had been killed where they stood in their traces, although Gallus had acknowledged to Iras that if forced, they could hitch the horses to the wagon, but moving from this spot was only a last resort, and only if they were forced out. Now that the threat of missile fire was gone at least temporarily, Gallus had Simeon open the shutters on the two large windows that faced the road and the surrounding countryside. At the same time, he sent Diocles to the opposite side of the building, where he opened the large door so that he had a similar vantage point to the Armenian. There were still blind spots, of which Gallus was all too aware, but his instinct told him that the remaining tribesmen would be content to wait for reinforcements. He also understood that they weren't expecting to wait long, because he assumed that they knew that one of their number had escaped and had gone to get help. If he were the leader of whatever raiding party was nearby, he would be acutely aware that Siscia was barely more than a day's hard march away. His position was defensible, but only for a short period of time; it was all up to Titus now.

Decurion Decimus Silva looked over his shoulder at the men riding behind him. His first thought was that he at least felt confident his men looked like he did; tired, hungry, and just worn down from days in the saddle, despite the fact that this day had just started. Silva was the Decurion of one of the two *ala* of cavalry attached to the Army of Pannonia, but this one, the most veteran one, was on the trail of Latobici rebels, whose lands were in the westernmost corner of Pannonia. It hadn't surprised him that these barbarians had rebelled; they were the closest to Rhaetia and Noricum, and he had learned from bitter experience that the flames of uprising were quick to spread, and it was almost always a matter of proximity. And although the rebellion had been crushed in those two provinces, it hadn't taken long for word to reach Pannonia. Equally unsurprising was the fact that the absence of the two Legions permanently stationed in Siscia had been taken as a sign from their gods that the time was right to throw off the Roman yoke. The Latobici were the first, but Silva, a veteran of more than a decade spent in Pannonia, knew they wouldn't be the only tribe to test Rome's strength. To that end, the entire army of four Legions, now under the command of Tiberius, because of his seniority to his younger brother, had just recently returned to Siscia. They weren't going to be there long, only spending enough time to refit, replenish their larders, and make repairs to artillery and other equipment. Tiberius had decreed that no more than a week be spent in Siscia, which meant that the Legions, even with the tasks assigned to them, would have a chance to rest. That wasn't the lot of the cavalry, and while Silva had experienced this reality more than once in his career, that made it no less bitter a draught to swallow now. Most of all, he was worried about the horses; the men could fend for themselves, but without their animals, they were no better than infantry. The very thought of that made Silva shudder, remembering the times he had watched his ground-bound counterparts hard at work with shovels and picks, digging the ditch and building the wall of that day's camp. Not for him; he much preferred a life in the saddle. Nevertheless, there were drawbacks, and this was one of those times, because he and his men had been given all of one night's rest in Siscia before being sent out to scout the province. Now they were following the Sava to the west, with the nearest landmark, a large, lone ridge that thrust up from the surrounding countryside on the northern side of the river, barely more than two miles away. That was the side Silva and his men were on, although he had a section of six men on the other side, paralleling his line of march. To that point, they had seen signs of activity in the form of clusters of hoof tracks, and every remote farm they came across was deserted, although Silva had known this was the case from the talk in Siscia. The town was crammed with families who had chosen to flee rather than try and fight for their homes and farms, something that Silva originally had neither sympathized with nor understood. But after a decade of service in this region, where there had been easily a half-dozen uprisings of varying levels of seriousness, he held a better appreciation for the fact that property was fine, but one's life was more important. He had long since lost count of the times he and his men had come across the smoking ruin of a farm, or small settlement of a dozen families, where the settlers had chosen to fight. And for the most part, they had paid a heavy price for that defiance. Now, riding along the Sava, his one hope was that they would be able to stop this rebellion with the Latobici before the infection spread. First, however, they would have to find them, and Silva was growing increasingly frustrated at the elusiveness of their quarry. As was normal, Silva was riding near the front of his command, although he had another section of a half-dozen men spread out in front, riding as outriders and scouts.

This was to avoid being surprised, of course, but also to give Silva that instant of time he might need in the event that one of his scouts was the one who surprised the enemy. The six men were paired up, so that one could race back to the main body to let the commander know whatever new developments had arisen while the other maintained an eye on whatever it was they spotted. It was the man from the pair Silva had deployed to his right front who came galloping back, and even before the rider reached him, Silva knew that something potentially important had been seen, or had happened. Not willing to wait, he put his own mount into a canter, heading to meet the scout, the two intersecting a short distance away from the main column.

"Decurion, Postumus and I found a boy! He's mounted on a beautiful horse, but he's been hurt! He's babbling about his family, and how they were ambushed."

Silva looked past the man, but he couldn't see anything except the forested flank of the lower slope of the ridge, now a little more than a mile away.

"Where is he?"

"He came out of a cave! He scared the *cac* out of ol' Postumus." The trooper grinned, showing a smile missing several teeth. Clearly enjoying the memory of his friend so discomfited, the trooper, Metellus was his name, seemed to forget his real purpose. "I mean, he just came out of nowhere! I thought Postumus would fall off his horse, and you know...."

"Metellus," Silva interrupted. "Enough of Postumus. Where are they now?"

Metellus started, a guilty expression crossing his seamed features. "Yes, sir. Sorry. They're up about halfway up the slope, on the side facing the river. At least, that's where they were."

"Well, let's go meet them." Silva turned and called for the rest of the *ala* to follow him.

As he did so, Metellus lingered for a moment, rather than ride back to his partner, which would have been the proper thing to do. Silva was about to snap an order that he do that very thing, except he knew Metellus and that, despite his proclivity to wander in his reports at times, he was a good man who wouldn't be hesitating if there wasn't a reason.

"What is it?" Silva asked the man quietly.

A frown creased the other man's features, and he shook his head in clear frustration.

"I don't know, sir. I mean, I don't know how to explain it."

"Well, try. Come on man, something's eating at you. What is it?"

"It's just that I know I've seen that boy before. And if he is who I think he is..." Metellus shrugged, but when he didn't say anything more, Silva's patience finally snapped.

"We don't have the time for this." Silva was clearly angry.

"Yes, sir. Sorry, sir. But I think that the boy is Porcinus' oldest boy. Titus, isn't it?"

While there were a number of men with the same name, there was only one that Silva, or Metellus for that matter, knew anything about, and of the two, Silva was much more familiar with the family Porcinus. In fact, he had been a guest at their table on more than one occasion.

"Pluto's cock," the Decurion swore.

Then, raising his hand and circling it in the air in the signal for a rapid advance, without waiting to see if his men followed, he kicked his horse into a gallop, heading for the ridge.

Titus had spent a miserable night; cold, afraid, and in a great deal of pain. But he wasn't alone, and he was sure that the only reason he survived the night without giving in to despair was the presence of his giant friend and savior. The horse generated a fair amount of warmth, and if Titus had felt up to it, he would have done more to make the cave impervious to the lonely wind that whistled into the gap between the standing rock and the ridge, before swirling around in the cave itself. He didn't even have a cloak; it had been in the wagon since the day was warm, and he supposed that when all things were considered, he was lucky it was still summer, even if it didn't feel like it. He was only vaguely aware that his underlying condition contributed to his chill, and even now, in the early dawn as the outline of Ocelus grew more defined, Titus wasn't sure where he had gotten the strength to do what he had. Still, he knew it was the right thing to do; even though his shoulder still throbbed, it wasn't with the same intensity as before. That was because he had removed the arrow from his shoulder, and had done it the only way available to him, by pushing the head of the arrow the rest of the way out from under his armpit. His first attempt had been by grasping the small part of the arrow protruding from the skin, but it was simply too slippery, and too painful. Although he had no idea how much time had elapsed, it was fully dark when he realized that he would be unable to do it by himself. He was in nearly total darkness; all he could see was the bare outline of Ocelus, who was dozing in that way that horses do, his breathing deep and steady. Titus had managed to remember that he had secreted Ocelus' apple away inside his tunic, but it had understandably been crushed. Still, he fed Ocelus most of the pulpy remains while he saved some for himself. He had also drank his fill of the water, once the small pool had replenished itself after his horse drained it several times. Once he had regained his senses from his first attempt, he had moved cautiously about, feeling carefully until his right hand found the wall of the cave. Maneuvering so his back was close to the wall, he leaned forward as he made the final adjustments to his position. Then, taking a deep breath, he sat slowly upright, moving an inch at a time until he felt the feathered end of the arrow touch the wall. As much as he thought he had prepared himself, he still couldn't stop letting out a cry of pain, but worse than that to him was his eyes filling with tears. He was sure his father wouldn't cry like a baby, or his Avus either, but no matter how much he tried, he couldn't stop his lower lip from trembling, which he recognized from his childhood as a sign that he was about to act like his little sister Miriam when she was hungry or tired. Then, through the tears, came the anger, the same kind of anger that had overwhelmed him when he exacted his vengeance on Spartacus. But while it scared him somewhat, it proved to be oddly comforting and, more importantly, it gave him the resolve he needed. Sitting up straight, he leaned back against the arrow, shoving the point through the skin, whereupon he fainted, falling sideways onto the floor of the cave. When he regained his senses, he didn't think that much more time had passed, but he also knew that he wasn't finished with what needed to be done. Unfortunately, he was mistaken in the belief that the hardest part was over. His initial idea had been to use his sword to cut the shaft now that he could feel the arrow jutting out several inches from under his left armpit. However, although he could bring the sword up and across his body, even touching the blade to the shaft was too painful to bear; the effort of moving the blade back and forth to saw through the hardwood was unthinkable. Titus sat, slumped over, for several moments as he tried to think what to do, finally arriving at the only solution available to him. He knew that the shafts of arrows were made from the hardest wood available, but he was a very strong boy. Besides, he realized that he had no other choice. One more time, he braced himself as he reached over with his right hand, grasping the shaft right behind the point. Silently counting to five, he violently rotated his hand, using his forearm and wrist muscles. Stars burst in front of his eyes as, for a third time, he passed out. But even as he fell, a part of his mind registered that he had heard a distinct, snapping sound, and it was the sweetest music he had ever heard.

Withdrawing the shaft after he came back to consciousness was the easiest part of all, although it was still extraordinarily painful. Most worrying was that the bleeding had started again. Fortunately, it stopped fairly quickly, and with the immediate crisis over, Titus was left with his thoughts. It was very difficult, but he forced himself to think through what he needed to do. Originally, he had thought to spend a watch or, at most, two letting Ocelus rest, but that had been before he had gotten hurt. Now he was worried about trying to travel at night, afraid that he would somehow lose his way, or even worse, stumble into the Latobici, who he assumed were still searching for him. Not long after he found the cave, he had heard voices shouting in a strange tongue, down the slope from his hiding spot. He fought the urge to panic then and, for a moment, he was afraid that Ocelus, picking up the scent of at least one other horse, would betray his position. Fortunately for both of them, the moment passed, and he hadn't heard anything since. Now that dawn was here, he knew he needed to press on; in fact, at least two parts of a watch had passed before the sun first peeked over the hill, but Titus had been unable to summon the energy to leave this spot. Finally, it was Ocelus who began expressing his frustration at being forced to stand in one position by stomping his hooves, snorting, and whipping his tail back and forth.

"All right," the boy mumbled, pulling himself to his feet. "We'll go."

Titus had never been this tired, this hungry, and in this much pain in his life, as short as it may have been, but he knew that he had to push on now; there was no more excuse for delay. Taking Ocelus' bridle, he coaxed the horse backward and, to his quiet relief, Ocelus obeyed. Once out, but while still in the space between the standing rock and the cave, Titus tied one rein to the trunk of the twisted tree.

"Stay here," he commanded his horse. "I need to go look and see if those *cunni* are still around."

Despite the fact that it was just him and his horse, Titus still darted a guilty glance over his shoulder in a reflexive action, although it made him feel better to utter a word that adults used, but was forbidden for him to use by his mother. Walking carefully, he moved through the trees on the slope until he reached a spot where he could see down to where the river and road ran across his front. It was a fairly small area that he could see, and he honestly didn't know what he was looking for, but after a moment of observation, he decided it was safe. Returning to Ocelus, he used the tree once more to help him into the saddle, then nudged the horse forward. Moving slowly at first, Titus guided Ocelus along the slope, while the boy craned his neck in every direction, looking nervously about for any sign of the men who were trying to kill him. He had pointed Ocelus in a generally northern direction, with an idea to come down the slope so that the ridge was behind him, and he was parallel to the river. He had no desire to cross the river again, and if all went well, the next time he would do so was at the bridge outside Siscia. Despite his best effort, he couldn't keep his mind from dwelling on the one topic that frightened him more than anything he could imagine, and that was what was happening to his family. Added to that was a growing sense of guilt at his delaying the resumption of this ride for help; what if that third of a watch or two was the difference between help arriving in time? How would he live with himself? How would he explain to his father that he had failed in this simple, but so very important mission? It was Ocelus who jerked him from his thoughts, when the horse suddenly stopped, his head coming up and ears pricking forward.

Titus thought his heart would leap out of his chest as he stared in the direction Ocelus was looking, whispering to his horse as if Ocelus could answer, "What is it? What do you see?"

Naturally, Ocelus didn't answer, except with a gentle puff of breath, blown through his huge nostrils, and if Titus had been more experienced with horses in general, he would have recognized the sign that Ocelus had picked up the scent of one of his own. Titus continued staring down the slope, sure that he was following his horse's line of sight, but he couldn't see anything. Finally, he urged the horse forward, but they had only gone a few paces when this time both horse and boy stopped, in perfect concert. It was voices! Titus reached down for his sword, although he had no intention of fighting; this would be another chase. He just wanted to be ready, so he slowly drew the sword a short way out of its scabbard before putting it back, making sure it was loose in the event he was forced to draw it.

"That's when I told her, 'If you think I'm going to pay for a fuck that bad, you don't know Gaius Postumus!'"

It was the combination of the name and the fact the man was speaking Latin that prompted Titus to forget all ideas of fighting or fleeing. Kicking Ocelus, he went into a trot as he shouted, "Eyo! Eyo! I'm Titus Porcinus! My father is Gaius Porcinus! I need help!"

Chapter 5

The period of time between his son being brought into Siscia, under escort by six of Decimus Silva's troopers, and the reunion with the rest of his family, was the most agonizing and frustrating of Gaius Porcinus' life. Even after it had all been resolved and his family restored to him, shaken but unharmed, the memory of those three days would still cause Porcinus to jerk awake at night, his heart beating as rapidly as if he was about to enter battle. However, as terrifying as the thought was, he couldn't even have imagined if this horrifying event had happened just two days later, because he and the 8th would have been gone. The men had been busy, as were their Centurions, their new overall commander Tiberius pushing the Legions under his command hard to replenish their supplies and refit so that they could march again. Even in the short period they were in Siscia, couriers seemed to arrive with every watch, bringing news of tribes all across Pannonia who had decided that it was an opportune moment to rise against Rome. Porcinus, like his counterparts, hadn't been all that surprised; they were veterans of this province, and this was actually a fairly frequent occurrence. This time, however, was slightly unusual because it appeared to be more than just one or two tribes. Still, neither Porcinus nor his men were particularly worried; they had seen enough of Tiberius in action by this point to have a good deal of confidence in their Legate. After the battle on the lake, when Tiberius had assumed overall command of the now-combined armies, with Drusus' cooperation, if not his approval, he had wasted no time. Marching his army rapidly eastward up into Noricum, in a series of short, sharp actions, the Legions had essentially handed the same fate to those rebels that had befallen the Rhaeti, although for unknown reasons, Tiberius hadn't ordered all the rebels into slavery as he had the Rhaeti. Nevertheless, in less than a month, both provinces were pacified, only to have Pannonia flare up. Returning to Siscia, they had been there four days when Porcinus, in his office incising yet another interminable report into a wax tablet, was interrupted by Lysander. He had been irritated at the way the slave flung open his door, but one look at Lysander's face told him that something was, at the very least, amiss. However, he was totally unprepared for what came out of the Thracian's mouth.

"Centurion, you need to report to the *praetorium* immediately."

It was Lysander's face more than the words that initiated a surge of fear in Porcinus, but he didn't hesitate.

Moving from behind his desk, he demanded, "What is it? Why do you look like that?"

Lysander hesitated for a moment, but seeing Porcinus' own expression, hurriedly replied, "It's your son. He's here. He was brought in by some of Silva's men."

Porcinus froze while his mind raced as he tried to make sense of what Lysander was saying.

"Titus?" he asked. "You're saying that Titus is here?"

Lysander nodded, but seemed at a loss to explain further. Cursing, Porcinus pushed past the slave. Under normal circumstances, he would have been careful not to be seen running in the direction of the *praetorium*, knowing the kind of panic this caused with the rankers; this time, he didn't care. The guards outside had either been told to expect him or, seeing his face, had no desire to try to stop him, and he pushed past them and into the building without being challenged. Entering the main room, where minor clerks had small desks and the Tribune named officer of the day had his own area, where he served as both commander of the guard and watchdog for the Legate, it took a moment for Porcinus' eyes to adjust. Then his attention was drawn to a small group of men, huddled together, except that as Porcinus headed in that direction, he saw they were actually surrounding something. Nearing within a few paces, he saw that the something was someone, and that someone was his son, Titus. But it was a Titus he had never seen before; drawn, haggard, and most disturbingly, with a large dark patch on his tunic that Porcinus recognized all too easily. For a moment, he was sure his knees would give way, but he forced himself at least to appear calm as he walked to the group. Then Titus saw him, his entire being becoming animated as he pushed past the men to run to his father. Completely forgotten by the both of them was any sense of decorum or sense of how a Centurion of Rome, or the son of one, should behave. In that moment, it was a scared but relieved little boy greeting the one man who could make everything better, his father.

Porcinus almost fell backward as Titus, momentarily forgetting the awful pain in his shoulder, barreled into him. On the fast ride to Siscia, one of the troopers assigned by Silva to accompany him who was experienced in such things, bandaged Titus' shoulder. The bandage was little hindrance now as the boy threw his arms around his father, although the sudden movement elicited a yelp of pain from him.

Alarmed, while Porcinus returned the embrace, he asked, "Titus! What's the matter?"

Looking down at his son's arm, he gasped at the sight of the bandage, which had a small spot of red on it.

"Pluto's cock," he said without thinking. "You're hurt!"

"Mama's going to be angry you used that language." Titus' voice was muffled by Porcinus' tunic, the boy having buried his head in his father' chest, breathing in the scent of leather, olive oil, and sweat that he had always associated with his father.

Despite the situation, Porcinus couldn't help laughing, although it was quickly cut off by the mention of Iras.

"She'll forgive me," he replied quickly. Then, with considerable effort, both because Titus was clinging to him so tightly and from his concern that he would hurt his son, Porcinus gently pried Titus loose so he could look the boy in the eye. "Titus, where is your mama? Where are your brother and sisters?"

Titus had sworn an oath to himself that he wouldn't cry, especially here in the *praetorium*, in front of the hard men his father worked with, but the mention of his mother and siblings was too much, and to his horror, he felt his eyes filling with tears. Despite his distress, he managed to give Porcinus what was in essence his very first report to a superior, even if it was his father. When he was finished, Gaius looked to one of the troopers who had brought Titus in, a man he knew by sight, but not by name.

Understanding the unasked question, the trooper hurried to assure Porcinus.

"Decurion Silva's already on his way to your family, sir. In fact, he might be there by now."

While this was indeed good news, unsurprisingly, it did little to assuage Porcinus' worry. He took Titus by the hand, something he wouldn't have normally done, yet it was a sign of their mutual distress that Porcinus did so, and Titus allowed himself to be led from the *praetorium*. However, when it became clear that Porcinus was leading him to the building adjoining the headquarters, where the hospital and *medici* were located, Titus balked.

"I need to take care of Ocelus," he told his father.

Although Porcinus understood and appreciated his son's concern about the gray stallion, he assured Titus that Ocelus would be taken care of, but Titus refused to budge from his spot, pulling his hand from his father's.

"I'm not going in there until I take care of Ocelus," he said quietly.

Porcinus was prepared to lift his son, big as he might be, and carry him to be seen to, but Titus' words stopped him.

"He saved my life, Tata. I wouldn't be here if he hadn't saved me."

"I know. He's a great horse." Porcinus was trying to be patient, understanding at least how important it was to Titus. "But he'll be fine."

Still, Titus remained rooted to the spot, shaking his head in a certain way that Porcinus had seen too many times. However, all the previous times had been about candied plums, or when he was supposed to be in bed.

"No, Tata," Titus repeated. "You don't understand. Ocelus saved my life, and I have to take care of him. You've always taught me that you have to see to your men before anything else. Well." Titus took a deep breath, looking up into his father's eyes for the first time to make sure Porcinus could see how serious he was. "Ocelus is my responsibility. He's a comrade just like Corvinus is to you, and he's tired, and he's hungry. I need to see to him before they look at me."

Porcinus fought the hard, sudden lump that formed in his throat, and as beside himself with worry as he was, he had never been prouder of his son than he was at that moment.

"All right," he finally spoke, his voice husky. "Let's go take care of Ocelus."

If that had been the only battle Porcinus had to fight in those nerve-wracking days, it would have been enough. Unfortunately, he had already been through what would be the first of many clashes with his superior; at least, his newly appointed, permanent superior, in the form of Primus Pilus Quintus Barbatus.

Barbatus had been waiting for them at Siscia. This was something of a surprise, if only because, after the debacle that was the First Cohort's performance at the lake, all the Pili Priores had expected that Frontinus would be immediately relieved of his duties. But that hadn't happened; in fact, nothing official had come from the *praetorium* about the poor performance of the largest and strongest Cohort of the Legion. The first several days of the march to Noricum were tense; as the army made camp every night, the Pili Priores of the 8th, minus Frontinus, who did his best to pretend nothing was happening, gathered together, again in Porcinus' tent, as they speculated on what they viewed as an inevitability. However, when it didn't happen, at least not in the timeframe they expected, the speculation grew more rampant and wilder by the day, at least in Porcinus' opinion.

It turned out to be Volusenus, the most disagreeable of the Pili Priores who, despite being banished from these impromptu gatherings, had come up with the prediction that was the closest to the most accurate.

"It's going to be someone Augustus picks. And trusts," he had said sourly, this during a rest stop on the way back to Siscia. "Chances are, he's going to be waiting for us in Siscia."

That, as it turned out, was exactly what happened, although at least in Porcinus' case, he didn't hear about it right away. In fact, he learned of it through Corvinus, who came barging into his office their first night back. That he didn't observe the normal proprieties was something that Porcinus was about to admonish him for, but one look at his friend's face told him that there was something important going on.

"Have you heard?" Corvinus asked without any preamble, and without asking leave, he dropped into the chair on the opposite side of the desk.

"Come in," Porcinus said mildly, eyeing the jug in Corvinus' hand.

It didn't surprise him that Corvinus had wasted no time in finding something to drink; this first night back was the only time the men had been given to do with as they saw fit before they were to begin the process of making ready to go out again. And Legionaries wouldn't have been worthy of that name if most of them didn't immediately set off in search of their particular favorite when it came to some type of debauchery. That Corvinus was sitting here, even with wine, and not off with his men checking to see if there had been an arrival of new whores, told Porcinus whatever it was Corvinus had to impart was important.

"No, I haven't heard anything other than Lysander complaining about all this piling up." Porcinus pointed at a pile of tablets disgustedly.

"We have a new Primus Pilus," Corvinus said, which, not surprisingly, caught Porcinus' full attention.

"We do? As in an officially appointed one?" Porcinus asked cautiously.

Corvinus nodded as he swallowed his mouthful of wine before passing the jug to Porcinus, which the Pilus Prior waved off.

"Trust me," Corvinus said quietly. "You're going to want that."

Taking the jug, Porcinus stared at Corvinus, but his friend refused to say anything until Porcinus had actually gone through the process of taking a swallow of wine.

"There," Porcinus said peevishly. "Now, out with it."

"Our new Primus Pilus is Quintus Barbatus." Corvinus' voice was still quiet, but if he expected an immediate reaction from Porcinus, he was to be disappointed.

Porcinus frowned, but made no immediate comment. The name was familiar, yet he couldn't place it immediately, which caused him to shake his head in frustration.

"I take it I should know who it is by the way you're acting," he commented.

In answer, Corvinus stood and said, "I'll give you a hint."

He didn't say anything more; instead, he made a show of first tapping the hilt of his sword, then drumming his fingers on it. It was the latter action that jarred Porcinus' memory, but still, he wasn't completely sure.

"Wait," he gasped. "You mean…that Barbatus? The one who went into the Senate building?"

Corvinus nodded grimly, but asked, "Is there any other?"

"I'm sure there are," Porcinus shot back, nettled at his friend's tone, then chuckled as he added ruefully, "Although I can't think of any others."

Now that he knew, Porcinus sat back in his chair to consider this, but not before he grabbed the jug back from Corvinus, ignoring the man's smug look.

Thinking for a moment, he asked, "But I don't remember what Legion he was with before this. Was he at least a Pilus Prior? If not, he had to be in the First Cohort somewhere."

Corvinus again shook his head, telling Porcinus, "Neither."

Porcinus was growing frustrated; he knew that his friend was at least partially toying with him, but he also was aware that he didn't keep as close track of the movements of other Centurions as his friend did, and probably as he should have.

"So are you going to keep me guessing?" he snapped.

"He was in the Praetorian Guard," Corvinus told him then, seeing his friend didn't make an immediate association with this name, referred to them in the old manner. "The Brundisium Cohorts."

Hearing the old name, the original one given to them by the then-Triumvir Marcus Antonius, so called because that was where the original Cohorts had been raised, jarred Porcinus' memory. He drew in a sharp breath as he made the association, and all that it implied, particularly when connected with the name Quintus Barbatus. Barbatus was a legend in the army; not, Porcinus thought, in the same league or for the same reason as his adoptive father. No, Quintus Barbatus' reputation had very little connection with prowess in battle, or the kind of leadership that was so valuable on the battlefield. Although, Porcinus allowed grudgingly, doing what he had done did take a certain amount of courage. As Porcinus recalled it, Barbatus had been a Centurion, but in either the Ninth or Tenth Cohort, in one of the Legions that the man then known as Gaius Octavianus Caesar had raised, using what was rumored to be the war chest of his late adoptive father, Julius Caesar, for the funds. He did this to contest what he said was his rightful inheritance, which was controlled by Marcus Antonius. This was relatively early in the second civil war, when, after the Battle of Mutina saw Antonius' defeat, the young Roman, who, even then, insisted on being called Caesar had chosen, instead of pursuing the fleeing Antonius, to march on Rome instead. Ostensibly doing so in the name of his men, it was, in all reality, nothing but a power grab, and it was Quintus Barbatus who had volunteered to represent the young Caesar's interests in the Senate. Ignoring centuries of custom and tradition, he had appeared in the Curia, fully dressed in his uniform, and most importantly, fully armed. When an outraged Cicero had demanded by what right the young upstart, as he was viewed then, claimed the right to all that he demanded, Barbatus' reply had been non-verbal, at least at first. What had been spread about the campfires of the Legions was that he performed the action that Corvinus had mimicked for Porcinus as his hint about the identity of the man. It hadn't surprised any man under the standard that the old men of the Senate were thoroughly cowed, and quickly agreed to Octavian's demands. As far as Porcinus could recall, Barbatus had dropped from sight; apparently, however, he had stayed close to his master. And if it was true that he was fresh from a Praetorian posting, which Porcinus had no reason to doubt, that meant Barbatus had spent most of his time in Rome. That in itself was meaningful; as relatively stable as Rome had been the previous several years, Porcinus knew how much of that stability was superficial. He only had to recall the ordeal of his father during Pullus' tribunal as part of the Marcus Primus affair. In one important way, Primus and Pullus had something in common; they had been made scapegoats, although in Primus' case, his problems were compounded by his gross incompetence and greed. Whereas with Pullus, he was meant to be a symbol to other men of his station about the danger of aspiring to improve themselves, and how dimly a small but extremely powerful segment of the Roman elite viewed that very idea. Pullus had escaped, at the time seemingly unscathed, while Primus was executed, although it had become clear that Primus' greatest crime was one of association, particularly with a man named Lucius Murena, who had served as Primus' defense at his trial. The reason Murena ran afoul of the man, who at that time was referred to as the Princeps, first among equals, which even then was a thinly disguised fiction after Actium, was because he had been implicated along with a man named Fannius Caepio in a plot to assassinate Augustus. Whether or not this was indeed the case, Porcinus had no way of knowing, but Porcinus was on the campaign to Thrace under Marcus Primus, and, in fact, had been his first campaign in the Centurionate, meaning he had witnessed what an enormous fool the man had been more closely than if he was still in the ranks. Enormous in every way imaginable, Porcinus chucked to himself as he thought back to those days. Primus had been enormously fat, and had to have the muscled cuirass that Legates wore specially made. Even now, a few years later, Porcinus had never since seen a muscled cuirass made with a potbelly big enough to cook a tent section's porridge in.

Finally, unable to recall anything useful about Barbatus, he shook his head in frustration, telling Corvinus, "Well, we're going to find out soon enough what kind of Primus Pilus he is."

"That we are," Corvinus agreed.

It wasn't very long after that when Lysander came to tell him the new Primus Pilus was calling an assembly of all Centurions at the beginning of the next watch.

"He said that there's no need for full uniform, that this is an informal meeting," Lysander informed him.

When it was time, Porcinus stood and picked up his *vitus*.

"Let's go find out what our lives are going to be like."

The first meeting of the Centurions of the 8th Legion and their new Primus Pilus was remarkable only in how unremarkable it was, at least in the beginning and considering what Barbatus had to say. Initially, he hit the right notes; he was proud to lead a Legion that even now was referred to as one of the Spanish Legions, despite the fact that relatively few men were actually from Hispania, and none were left from the first *dilectus*, held by the late Gnaeus Pompeius. He touched on some of the Legion's most famous exploits, starting with the Gallic campaign. Most of his talk was spent on what he expected of the Legion, which were the usual things a Primus Pilus would; tight discipline above all, attention to detail, instant obedience to orders, all the normal expectations that Porcinus and the others were sure they were already providing. It wasn't completely a waste of time, however, at least as far as Porcinus and few of the more observant among the Centurions were concerned. What was instructive to them wasn't what Barbatus said, it was his appearance. Even now, the prevailing style of haircut in the Legions, at least here in Pannonia, was still closely shorn, a look that Titus Pullus would have recognized and approved of. This was especially true with the Centurions, a holdover from the days when Camp Prefect Pullus had bellowed at those he viewed as being too shaggy that hair might be the pride of a woman, it was the shame of a warrior. Pullus always wore his hair closely shorn, a remnant of his early days as a *tirone* when his head had proven to be too large to fit into a helmet with the felt liner in it. Naturally, his adopted son had followed the example set by his father, yet so had the other Centurions, not just of the 8th, but the 13th and the other Legions as well. The only exceptions were the constantly rotating set of fine young men from Rome, who had adopted the type of hairstyle that was favored by Augustus since he was a young boy, with hair well past the ears. Pullus always took great delight in reminding everyone that the Princeps' reason for this had been to hide a rather unfortunate set of ears, which Pullus claimed looked like the handles on an amphora of wine the way they stuck out. Yet now, it appeared that this hirsute style had made it into the ranks, at least into the ranks of the Praetorian Guard, because Barbatus' hair, iron gray as it was, was almost to his shoulders. However, it was slicked back so that the hair lay flat against his skull, giving the appearance of a closely shorn head. Was that…pomade in his hair, Porcinus wondered? If that were all, it would have been enough to get the men talking, with the Centurions leading the way. But he also wore more jewelry, in the form of rings, than any man of the Legions that Porcinus had ever seen, at least of the ranks. There were a few Tribunes who wore such finery, although very quickly, they discovered that not only was it something the men quietly sneered at, wearing rings in the field, on campaign in particular, was impractical. Most striking of all, at least to Porcinus, was in the singular lack of scars the man sported. As he surreptitiously examined Barbatus while the man droned on in a voice that had a nasal, whiny quality to it that was quickly wearing on his nerves, Porcinus couldn't spot anything that might be thought of as a battle scar. He hadn't worn his full uniform; as Porcinus had been informed, this was a more informal first meeting than a full inspection, and the man's skin had that pink glow that was a sign of significant time spent in the baths. Although his tunic was the regulation soldier's tunic, dyed red, it was easy to see that the cloth and the dye was of a much higher quality than was seen in the Legions. It was as Porcinus was examining Barbatus' tunic that the Primus Pilus closed his remarks, and in doing so, gave the Centurions their first warning that there would be changes.

"As I said, I'm proud to be here," Barbatus said, but then there was a slight change in his demeanor as he seemed to make a point to look each man in the eye as he continued, "but I come from the Praetorian Guard, and our standards, especially in appearance, are much higher. And consider this fair warning; I will be expecting my Legion to meet the standards to which I've become accustomed, not the other way around." Pausing a moment to let this sink in, he finished with, "That is why I'll be holding a full inspection of the Legion, at the beginning of third watch tomorrow."

There was a moment of stunned silence, then it was quickly broken by an uproar of noise as a large number of Centurions voiced their protest. Porcinus wasn't one of them, mainly because he thought enough of his comrades were making it clear that what Barbatus was demanding was not only unreasonable, it was contrary to what Tiberius had ordered.

"*Tacete!*"

This didn't come from Barbatus, but from the man who had just been demoted back to his Second Century, much to his obvious relief, Frontinus. And while he may not have been considered fit to be Primus Pilus, he still was respected enough that the men quieted down quickly. Meanwhile, Barbatus stood, his face impassive, yet having made no attempt to establish order. Instead, he looked at Frontinus, who seemed to realize that since he had been the one calling for order, he was expected to speak for the group.

"Sir," Frontinus began, but Barbatus cut him short.

"Primus Pilus, Pilus Posterior," Barbatus said this quietly, but there was something in his voice that Porcinus could see others had noticed as well.

Frontinus reddened, but his voice was steady. "Er, yes. My apologies. As I was going to say, Primus Pilus, the problem with what you're ordering is that it would keep the men from performing the duties that the Legate has commanded in order for us to be ready to resume campaign at the end of the week."

Barbatus' reaction was to appear puzzled, and it made Porcinus wonder if he had been so anxious to meet the Centurions that he hadn't gotten a full briefing from Tiberius. That belief was quickly dispelled.

"I'm not sure why you're telling me something I already know, Pilus Posterior," Barbatus replied, again with a calm demeanor. "I know exactly when we're supposed to march, and we will be ready. But that doesn't have anything to do with my inspection. That's separate from what the men already have to do."

If Frontinus looked perplexed, he was only mirroring the feelings of almost all of the other Centurions. One exception was Porcinus, who was experiencing a sinking feeling in his stomach as he thought, I know where this is going. Unbidden, he was reminded of Marcus Primus again, and the disastrous and farcical attempt he had made to impose his authority by demanding a full inspection, under almost identical circumstances. Porcinus' only hope was that Barbatus knew more about how to conduct an inspection than Primus had.

"But, Primus Pilus, how are the men supposed to do both? At least, without staying up all night?"

For the first time, Barbatus showed some emotion, the glimmer of a smile, and his tone was almost cheerful as he replied, "Why, I doubt they can do both without staying up all night, Pilus Posterior." Raising his voice for the first time, he added iron to his tone as he finished, "As I said, gentlemen, I expect this Legion to meet my standards, not the other way around. This Legion will be the match of any Cohort of the Praetorian Guard. At least in looks, if not in ability."

And with that insult serving as the last word, Quintus Barbatus had introduced himself to his new Legion.

That was three days before Titus had come into the camp, which meant that Porcinus was already worn down. Matters hadn't improved between Barbatus and the Legion, and they had gotten much worse between Porcinus and Barbatus. It was after the inspection when the new Primus Pilus conducted individual meetings with his Pili Priores, in their order. That wasn't unusual; in fact, it was expected. But while Porcinus wasn't sure what to expect specifically regarding himself, it certainly hadn't been the reception he received from Barbatus. When he reported, he had behaved in the prescribed manner, squaring himself in front of the Primus Pilus' desk, then rendering an impeccable salute as he informed Barbatus that he was reporting as ordered. That had been the last normal moment of their meeting. It started when the Primus Pilus didn't acknowledge the salute, choosing instead to sit back and examine Porcinus, still standing rigidly with his fist against his chest, waiting for the acknowledgment in the form of an identical movement, before finishing the salute by extending the arm outward. Porcinus was forced to stand there for a period of time that he couldn't calculate before Barbatus had returned the salute in a perfunctory manner.

"Sit down," he said curtly.

Naturally, Porcinus did, holding his helmet on his left knee in the proper manner, making sure to keep his back erect and not touching the back of the chair. It was a good thing he did so, although when he thought about it later, he wondered if that had helped at all. Barbatus continued his inspection of his Quartus Pilus Prior, making it clear by his expression that he wasn't impressed with what he saw. In and of itself, this didn't disturb Porcinus; he had learned to accept that, unlike his father, he didn't quite look the part of a Centurion. Even now, approaching forty years old, he still had a fresh-faced look about him that Iras, and friends like Corvinus, teased him about. The addition of a few scars had helped, but he had long since given up trying to build up the same kind of musculature that had made Pullus so recognizable. All he had was the height, yet, if anyone, he most resembled Scribonius. Nevertheless, his record was exemplary in the area that mattered; he had won a Civic Crown, and a Corona Muralis, although none of that seemed to matter to Barbatus.

Finally, Barbatus spoke again, and Porcinus imagined that the room had suddenly become frigidly cold.

"Gaius Porcinus." Barbatus spat the name as if it was some sort of indictment, puzzling Porcinus even more. The mystery was cleared up with Barbatus' next breath. "The nephew…" he made an exaggerated mock bow, which was slightly ridiculous since he was seated, "…I apologize, the adopted son of the great Titus Pullus." Barbatus' lips curled back in a sneer. "A traitor to Rome."

Gaius Porcinus didn't have the volcanic temper of Titus Pullus; in fact, his father had often worried that Porcinus was missing what he considered an essential ingredient to making the perfect Legionary, that sense of fury that fueled a man and kept him fighting through the most extreme times of danger. Furthermore, Porcinus understood that Barbatus was baiting him, and that giving in to the rage he did feel would be playing into this man's hands, so it was with a titanic effort that he quelled the sudden itch in his sword hand, as if the appendage was begging to have a blade in it so he could find out what this man was made of, literally. Consequently, he said nothing, yet when he thought about it later, he wryly wondered if somehow his father's *numen* hadn't suddenly decided to inhabit his body, because when his only reply was to stare at Barbatus levelly, communicating everything that needed to be said through his eyes, it was the Primus Pilus who broke the gaze.

Suddenly appearing to be interested in the scroll in front of him, Barbatus dropped his head, pretending to scan the document. Seeing the man discomfited so gave Porcinus a small sense of victory, except that he still wanted so much more.

"Yes, well," Barbatus broke the silence, which had stretched out for more than a dozen heartbeats. "I've looked at your record. It's…acceptable," he sniffed. Then, he looked back up, seemingly recovering his nerve to finish. "But in my opinion, it's hardly worthy of someone who is a Pilus Prior in a front-line Cohort." Barbatus smiled at Porcinus, but it was a leering, knowing one, and he winked. "I bet that cost your…father a pretty penny, to buy your post."

Without thinking, Porcinus replied, "I wouldn't know about that, Primus Pilus. I myself don't have any experience in buying a posting. Perhaps you could enlighten me on how it's done." He gave the other man a cheerful grin. "In the event that I want to buy my way up, you understand." Even as he continued, a part of him shouted at himself to stop now, but he couldn't resist adding, "How much does the post of Primus Pilus cost, for example?"

Barbatus' smooth and freshly oiled features darkened, and Porcinus saw that his lower jaw was trembling.

"How dare you?" he hissed, all sense of decorum or aura of command that Porcinus had come to expect in a Primus Pilus gone, and his lips pulled back in a snarl of fury. Well, he's at least missing a couple of teeth, Porcinus thought. "Are you insinuating that's how I was promoted to this post? That I bought it?" Still seated, he leaned forward threateningly, and his voice dropped to a near whisper. "I would be very, very careful if I were you, Pilus Prior Porcinus."

Although it took an effort, Porcinus returned the man's glare with a look of wide-eyed innocence, falling back on that fresh face to appear as if he was shocked that Barbatus had so misconstrued what he had said.

"Why no, not at all, Primus Pilus! And I apologize if that's how it sounded! I know that Augustus would only appoint the most capable man to such an important position! It's just that you are clearly knowledgeable about such matters, and I'm truly curious about this topic since I've never seen it happen. Or heard of it," he finished, and while his expression remained the same, his message was clear that, Primus Pilus or not, this was a topic Barbatus had best not pursue any farther.

The Primus Pilus glared at Porcinus for a moment, clearly trying to determine the real intent behind the words.

Finally, he grunted and sat back, saying only, "Fine. As long as we understand each other." He regarded Porcinus for a moment longer. "I will say that it appears that the warning I was given about you appears to be fully justified. I was told that whether he was your real father or not, you had adopted many of Pullus' bad habits."

Now Porcinus' surprise was unfeigned as he asked, "Warned? By who? Who in Rome could possibly know about me?"

For the first time, Barbatus smiled, but it wasn't pleasant in any aspect. It was the smile of a man who's sure that he will land a final blow, and it will be a crippling one. And, in many ways, he was correct.

"Why, Augustus, of course," he replied cheerfully. "He knows all about you. And he warned me specifically that you might have been infected by your *uncle's*," he put special emphasis on the word to let Porcinus know that he for one didn't accept the idea of Pullus adopting Porcinus, "aspirations to climb above the station set for him by the gods."

As angry as Porcinus was, he was also puzzled by something, which prompted him to prolong what was a disastrous conversation by asking, "But it was Augustus who sponsored my father. And I happen to know that because of the proscriptions, he's made the path to being elevated to the next class easier."

"That's true," Barbatus conceded. "And for those who are truly qualified, and possess the right character, the Princeps is vigorously working to ensure those men are elevated. Your uncle, as it turned out, wasn't truly fit to be an equestrian, which is why Augustus corrected his mistake."

"Only after my father died," Porcinus pointed out, equally unwilling to concede the role of Titus Pullus to him as Barbatus.

"That," Barbatus' tone was more grudging now, "is also true, but that's because Augustus is a truly merciful man, and frankly, he's a bit soft-hearted. Particularly when it comes to men who marched with his father."

Again, Porcinus knew better, but he couldn't resist.

"I wasn't aware that Gaius Octavian the elder ever marched with the Legions," he said gently. Then, before Barbatus could answer, he continued, "Ah. I forgot. You were referring to Augustus' adoptive father. Not his real one." His brow furrowed as he pretended to think about it. "What was Augustus' relationship to Divus Julius again?" Snapping his fingers, he smiled. "Ah, yes. It was his uncle. His great uncle, in fact, wasn't it?"

Barbatus' jaw had started trembling again, but he seemed to sense that any further exchange would just be worse, and he needed to cut his losses.

"That's true," he said curtly. "But hardly the same case as with your…situation." Trying to regain the upper hand before dismissing this upstart, he added, "As I said, Augustus learned of your uncle's true nature, but he is a merciful man. However," he glowered at Porcinus, "he also doesn't make the same mistake twice. And I am letting you know that I'll be watching you to make sure that you don't get any silly ideas."

"Ah." Porcinus returned Barbatus' gaze levelly. "So you're saying Augustus made a mistake. That's....interesting."

As angry as Barbatus was, he couldn't help feeling a stab of alarm at Porcinus' words, and as the Pilus Prior had seen so often in connection with the man who ran Rome, his eyes suddenly darted to look to the corners of the room.

"You're dismissed, Pilus Prior," he said stiffly.

No matter how things between them had transpired, Barbatus could find no fault with the correct manner in which Porcinus stood, rendered another salute, which the Primus Pilus returned with a haste that was in direct opposition to their greeting, and marched out the room. Feeling the stabbing glare of Barbatus boring into his back, Porcinus was awash with conflicting emotions, but the overriding one was one of a rueful chagrin. Congratulations, Gaius, he thought, you won that battle. But you probably lost the war.

Despite the small drama being played out, the work of the Legions continued as men of all ranks hustled about in the controlled chaos that was an army preparing to move. Like his father, this was something at which Porcinus always marveled, how what seemed to the eye to be complete confusion and random, disconnected movements was actually a carefully orchestrated operation, one that would see a fully equipped army, ready to march at the appointed time. His normal appreciation of all that was taking place was tempered by his worry, but to anyone who knew him, they wouldn't have been surprised that it wasn't the sudden downturn of his career prospects. Instead, almost his entire focus was on the safe return of his family, and being there to comfort his oldest son. Like all children, Titus' wound seemed to start healing overnight, but it wasn't his physical welfare that concerned Porcinus. The boy spent one night in the hospital building, and it had been extremely hard for Porcinus to resist the urge to spend the night at Titus' bedside. Fortunately for both of them, he had memories of his own embarrassment when Titus' namesake had fussed over him when he was wounded. Besides, the boy was already well known among the men of the Legions stationed in Siscia; the fact that he now bore his own wound, and the circumstances that had earned him this mark of valor made him a minor celebrity, so the less seriously wounded men crowded around his bed. Porcinus' last sight of his son that first night was of a beaming Titus, answering the questions of clearly impressed Legionaries. Even the camp physician, a Greek named Philandros, was captivated by the story of Titus' ride.

"Your boy is a rare one, Centurion," the Greek had told Porcinus. "Not many ten-year-olds, even his size, could have done what he did."

"Yes, I know." Porcinus, standing at the door of the hospital, looked back fondly at the small crowd gathered around the bed. "But he had help."

"Yes, the horse. Ocelus, isn't it?"

Porcinus nodded, unprepared for the sudden surge of emotion at the mention of the big, gray horse, who, at that moment, was enjoying an extra helping of oats and barley.

"I remember hearing stories about your uncle and that horse when I first arrived here," Philandros went on, oblivious to the glimmer in Porcinus' eyes until he turned to glance at the Centurion. Seeing the emotion, the physician turned quickly away, not wanting to embarrass either of them, but asked anyway, "Are any of them true?"

Porcinus managed a laugh past the lump in his throat.

"It depends on which one it is," he answered, still looking at Titus. "But from what I've heard, yes, most of them are true."

"Remarkable!" Philandros exclaimed. Then, "Well, if you will excuse me, Centurion, I must shoo the admirers from young Achilles. He needs to rest."

Without waiting for a reply, he left Porcinus, who lingered for only a moment more before returning to his quarters, but not before paying a quiet visit to the stable to give his own quiet thanks to a horse, carrying an apple with him.

The day before the army was scheduled to leave, there was still no sign of Iras and his family, and it forced Porcinus to do something that he had desperately hoped he wouldn't have to do. Approaching the office of the Primus Pilus, he tried to ignore the knocking of his heart against his ribs, but he was forced to pause for a moment to gather himself before entering the building. As he expected, the two clerks assigned to a Primus Pilus for the clerical work were at their respective desks. The senior one, Porcinus thought he was a Macedonian named Perdiccas, the other named Crito, looked up at the sight of the Pilus Prior, his lips compressing. Like happened so often, Perdiccas had assumed the attitude and viewpoint of the Centurion to which he was attached, and the fact that there was no higher rank than Primus Pilus meant that Perdiccas was quite often a pain to deal with, looking down his nose at free Romans because they were of a lower rank than his master. One mark in Frontinus' favor, at least as far as Porcinus and most of the other Centurions were concerned, was that he hadn't tolerated this type of behavior in Perdiccas, yet it was clear that the lesson had been lost.

"Yes, Centurion Porcinus? What can I do for you?"

The smile Perdiccas offered was more a grimace of distaste as he made it clear he didn't appreciate being interrupted. Porcinus was forced to resist the urge to use the *vitus* in his hand, as Frontinus had, to remind this slave of his place.

"I need to speak to the Primus Pilus," Porcinus answered shortly.

"And what is it concerning?"

This was too much for Porcinus under any circumstances, but while it would have irritated him before, his frame of mind was such that before he could catch himself, he had taken a step forward to lean over the desk and glare down at the Macedonian.

"None of your fucking business, slave," Porcinus snarled, and while a part of him was somewhat ashamed at his behavior, more than anything, he was pleased to see all the superiority and bluster vanish as Perdiccas cowered.

"I'm sorry, master," Perdiccas whined. "It's just the Primus Pilus has been very specific in his instructions to us about being disturbed. As you can imagine, he's very busy."

That, Porcinus was forced to acknowledge, was, in all likelihood, the truth, and he chastised himself for lashing out at a man who was powerless to resist anything that either he or Barbatus chose to do to him. It had been yet another lesson passed onto him by his father, that there was no honor or strength in bullying the helpless.

Taking a deep breath, Porcinus said, "Very well. I understand that you're just doing your job. Will you please go request that the Primus Pilus take a moment to see me? It's really quite urgent."

Perdiccas inclined his head, the haughty manner instantly returning, as if he were bestowing a favor, yet he did as Porcinus asked, moving to the door leading to the Primus Pilus' quarters. Knocking on the door, Perdiccas' voice was pitched too low for Porcinus to make out what he said, and he heard Barbartos' response only as a muffled noise, but he did manage to catch his own name. He tried to keep his breathing steady, and he was half-expecting to be denied, or at the very least, be made to wait. Consequently, he was very surprised when the Macedonian turned and beckoned to him.

"The Primus Pilus will see you now."

Porcinus, thrown off-balance by this quick agreement, hesitated for a moment, then hurried across the outer office to where Perdiccas was waiting, hand on the latch. The thought flashed through his mind that this was most probably what Barbatus intended, putting him on his back foot, as they liked to say in the Legions, so Porcinus took one more deep breath before nodding to Perdiccas. He was barely conscious of the smirk on the Macedonian's face at this sign of nerves when he moved past the slave to march, once more, into Barbatus' private office. As he crossed the few paces to stand in front of the desk, Porcinus' nose wrinkled involuntarily. What was that smell? he wondered. It had a fruity, cloying scent, but it was oddly familiar. In the space of time it took for him to reach where Barbatus was again seated, he placed the memory, helped by the sight of some items sitting on a small table off to his left. The items were a bronze, highly polished disk, a small jar and what Porcinus assumed was a hairbrush made of boar bristles exactly like the one that his wife used every night. He remembered the first time he had been confronted with this odor had been, in fact, during an inspection, the one performed by Marcus Primus that was such a disaster. When it became Porcinus' time for the man who was the Proconsular governor of Macedonia, endowed with the imperium that awarded him the title of Legate to stand before him, he had almost been knocked flat by the smell coming from the fat little man. And while the odor he was assaulted with in Barbatus' office was essentially the same, during the inspection, it had competed with whatever perfume Primus had apparently bathed in. At least, Porcinus thought as he completed his salute to Barbatus, he's not wearing perfume. The surprises continued when Barbatus returned the salute immediately instead of playing the little game with which he had tormented Porcinus at their first private meeting. In fact, if Porcinus was any judge, the Primus Pilus appeared impatient, which was understandable. If, that is, he's not in a hurry to go back to brushing his hair. This thought threatened to mar Porcinus' composure, and he roughly jerked his attention back to the purpose for which he had come.

"Well?" Barbatus asked, the moment the official exchange was done. "What is it? I'm very busy. In fact," he apparently couldn't resist at least one jab, "I'm surprised you have the time to spare to come see me."

"Yes, sir, I'm sorry to bother you." Porcinus refused to acknowledge the barb. "But this is very important. I wouldn't have disturbed you otherwise."

Barbatus raised an eyebrow.

"Oh? What is it? One of your men lose a javelin? Or there are some chickpeas missing from your Cohort's barrels?"

Now Porcinus was forced to resort to yet another trick he had been taught by Pullus, biting hard on the inside of his cheek. The sudden stab of pain distracted him enough to stop the retort that had come to his mind before it escaped his lips.

"No, sir," he hesitated for a moment before plunging on. "It's about my family. I..."

Barbatus' expression changed, but only a little, and Porcinus assumed he was trying to appear to be sympathetic.

"Ah, yes. Your family. Bad business, that. Most unfortunate, but I'm sure you're proud of your boy. What's his name?" He gave a humorless chuckle, telling Porcinus he had known the answer before asking the question. "Ah, yes. Titus, just like his...what would he be? His great uncle?"

"Yes, just like Augustus and Divus Julius." The words came out before he could stop them, so he hurried on, seeing the sudden flush again, "But yes, sir, and thank you, sir. It means a great deal to know that you're so concerned."

You're not the only one who can smear honey on a turd, he thought, while Barbatus struggled to come up with something appropriate.

Hurrying on, Porcinus said, "It's just that Decurion Silva hasn't returned from escorting my family back yet. I know he's expected any day. And," he took a breath, "I request permission that I be allowed to stay here until I'm sure my family is safe. Then I'll catch up with the Legion, wherever it is."

He had barely gotten it out when Barbatus snapped, "Denied."

For a moment, Porcinus wasn't sure that the man had said anything, and if he had, it wasn't that word. Seeing Barbatus staring at him, that thought was quickly dispelled; there was no mistaking the malevolent triumph in the man's eye. He's paying me back for the last time we met, Porcinus thought dully. Knowing that it was futile, he nevertheless made the attempt to change the man's mind.

"Sir, I am asking…no," he closed his eyes for a moment, then continued, "I'm begging you to allow me to stay behind. I swear on the black stone that the moment they come into camp and I see them with my own eyes and that they're safe, I'll flog my horse to death to catch up with you. That could be by tomorrow night!"

"And it might not," Barbatus pointed out evenly, which, as much as Porcinus hated to admit, was no more than the truth, no matter the intent behind the words.

"No," Porcinus granted, "it might not. But, Primus Pilus, it's my family."

"Which, by regulation, you're not allowed to have," Barbatus retorted. If he was attempting to look like he at least regretted matters, he was doing a horrible job of it. "I'm sure you know the saying, Pilus Prior."

"I do." Porcinus didn't bother hiding his bitterness. "'If the Legions wanted you to have a wife and family, they'd be in the *quaestorium* and the quartermaster would have issued them to you when you were a *probatio*.'"

"Exactly." Barbatus nodded, as if pleased that Porcinus was acknowledging the fact. "It's why I never took a woman myself. A Legionary, of any rank, can't afford to have such entanglements."

That was when something fell into place in Porcinus' mind, seemingly disparate pieces of information and observation suddenly coming together so well that he had the irrational fear that Barbatus could hear them clicking together like a puzzle. Of course, no such thing happened, but this sudden revelation had nothing to do with the moment at hand.

"Please, sir," Porcinus tried one last time, and it was only through a huge effort of will that he didn't shame himself by dropping to his knees in front of the man's desk, dully recognizing that while it would be what Barbatus wanted to see, it still wouldn't make any difference.

"As I said, permission is denied." Barbatus signaled that the interview was over by suddenly picking up a scroll and pretending to examine it with great interest.

Despite his distress, Porcinus retained the presence of mind to render the proper salute before stepping back the correct distance, then turning about. He was almost to the door when Barbatus called out.

"Porcinus, it would be most…unfortunate if you were to decide to disobey your orders and not be there leading your Cohort in the morning when we march out of here. The consequences would be…severe."

Knowing that it would have made Barbatus extremely happy if he were to do that, Porcinus could only exact a small revenge by assuring the man, "Don't worry, Primus Pilus. I understand your orders, and will obey."

This was the customary method a subordinate acknowledged his orders, and Porcinus couldn't count the number of times he uttered those words in his career, but never before had they tasted so bitter.

It was often said about Titus Pullus that his luck was second only to that of his first general, Gaius Julius Caesar. Yet, in a smaller way, Gaius Porcinus had been as favored, even if it was not quite as dramatically as his father. And in another manifestation of that luck, shortly before dark of the day before the army was to depart, once more Lysander came running to find his Pilus Prior. This time,

Porcinus was talking to Urso, in the Pilus Posterior's own small office, when the Thracian slave appeared, panting like a dog on a hot summer day.

"What's gotten into him?" Urso asked sourly, irritated at the disturbance.

He had been letting Porcinus know how he, Urso, had solved a number of problems that had cropped up that, according to his insinuation, his superior was too distracted to address. Porcinus hadn't missed the subtle jab, but the truth was that Urso was right; his mind had been elsewhere, and no matter the man's motives, Urso, truly had provided a valuable service to the Fourth Cohort. He was in the process of telling Urso that very thing, which compounded the Pilus Posterior's annoyance at the disturbance since it interfered with Porcinus finishing. Like many men who have a streak of insecurity in their makeup, Urso needed praise for its own sake; the fact that, in his mind, it sent the signal to his nominal superior that he was the better man was just a bonus.

"What is it?" Porcinus cut off his praise of Urso, turning to Lysander, not daring to hope what it was about.

It took just a moment for Lysander to regain enough of his breath, but it was an interminable wait before Porcinus heard him say, "Pilus Prior Porcinus! I happened to be by the gate just now. I was just delivering the messages you ordered me to send, and…"

"Lysander." Porcinus' voice was gentle, as he was almost eerily calm. "I don't care what you were doing. What is it?"

Lysander flushed, but the words tumbled out. "It's your family! I just saw Silva and his men escorting a number of wagons in, and I saw that your wife was in one of them!"

Lysander and Urso were abruptly by themselves, staring at the back of their superior, who was sprinting in the direction of the main gate of the camp as if Cerberus was hot on his heels.

"Thank the gods," Lysander said as he watched Porcinus disappear from sight. "I'd been making sacrifices every day that they'd come back."

The truth was more complicated than that; while Lysander had indeed been sent to deliver messages, he had taken the opportunity to loiter by the gate, waiting for a chance to give his Pilus Prior some good news for a change. Lysander thought a great deal of the Pilus Prior, a fact of which Porcinus was completely unaware, because the Thracian hid it well under a guise of indifference.

For a brief moment, the gulf between free man and slave was forgotten as Urso slapped the Thracian on the shoulder.

"So was I," he said, then turned and walked back into his office, leaving a surprised Lysander to stare after him.

The Thracian would have been even more surprised if he had known that Urso was telling the truth.

The reunion, although brief, was everything Porcinus could have hoped for, and more. Completely disregarding the stares of other Legionaries of all ranks, he greeted each member of his family with a fierce hug and kisses, especially for the females, although Sextus couldn't escape without receiving one as well. Fortunately, he was still at an age where he didn't mind his father showing that kind of affection.

Before he was allowed to do any of it, however, he supplied Iras with the answer to her first question.

"Where's Titus?"

"He's here." Porcinus had thought quickly enough to have stepped close to his wife, so he was there to catch her when her knees buckled.

"Silva told me he'd been hurt! How bad is it? Where is he now? When can I see him?"

Laughing, the only way Porcinus could stop the torrent was by covering his wife's mouth with his own, and for a moment, the rest of the world was forgotten as the couple reveled in the comfort of the other. As all married couples know, before there was a family, before the children, there had been just the pair of them, a man and a woman who loved each other. And both of them were sure that they never loved the other more than at that moment, no matter if it was in front of dozens of leering Legionaries.

"He better be at home in bed," Porcinus told her. "Although I won't be a bit surprised if he's not."

Iras looked alarmed.

"Where would he be? He's been hurt! From what Silva said, it was serious!"

"It wasn't just a scratch," Porcinus allowed, immediately regretting his choice of words as Iras tore herself away from his grasp, glaring at him.

"So if that's so, why is he up?"

"I don't know that he is," Porcinus protested, and a part of him had to admit that he and his wife were giving the witnesses to this exchange a fair amount of fodder for the inevitable story time around section hut stoves that night. "I just said he might be."

"And where could he possibly be?" she demanded.

"Well, if he's not where he's supposed to be, the only other place he would be is with Ocelus."

Only then did Iras' expression soften, and she relaxed somewhat.

"Oh." She looked a bit embarrassed. "Well, that's understandable. From what Silva told me, Titus claims that it was Ocelus who saved him."

"That's what I heard too, from Titus," Porcinus agreed. "Although he hasn't given me any details yet."

"He can tell us about it tonight at dinner." Iras, as always, turned to the practical matters at hand.

Porcinus put a gentle but restraining hand on her shoulder.

"He might, but he might not. He might not be ready to talk about it yet."

Iras nodded, her expression suddenly becoming one that Porcinus couldn't readily identify. She cast a glance over her shoulder, happy to see that Birgit and Simeon had the children a short distance away, while Diocles and Silva were engaged in some sort of discussion.

"Did you know Titus killed a man?" Then she remembered, and corrected herself. "Actually, he killed two men."

Porcinus felt his jaw drop; in fact, Titus had said nothing about such things. The only piece of information that the boy had given him was about Libo, who Titus had seen fall, the boy barely able to mention it without bursting into tears again. His father hadn't pressed him then; he understood very well how such things like this came out, in fits and starts, and only when the teller of the tale was ready.

"Did you...see it?" Porcinus asked, cautiously, almost as worried about his wife witnessing that as his son performing the act.

Iras nodded slowly, her eyes suddenly becoming unfocused.

"I saw one of them," she said softly, then looked up at her husband with haunted eyes. "Gaius, it was horrible. I've never seen him like that before, and it was…" She stopped and simply closed her eyes.

"I know it's a terrible thing, but he was doing it to protect you and the family," he said gently.

Iras' head jerked up, her eyes suddenly open and searching his face as she realized he had misunderstood that she wasn't talking about the Latobici. She opened her mouth to correct his assumption, then closed it. No, she realized, that's for later.

"Well, we still have a lot to do," she said instead, her tone bright, and if it was forced, she was pleased to see that Porcinus didn't seem to notice.

In fact, Porcinus had detected the strain in her voice, and it was the experience of a long and loving partnership that he somehow knew that there was something Iras wasn't telling him at that moment. His first reaction was to think, well, there's time for that. Then, he remembered with a sinking heart that this wasn't true; he had just tonight, and the orders had been issued, not by Barbatus, but by Tiberius himself, that the men of all ranks were confined to the camp this night before departure. This was standard, and had been so for as long as anyone could remember. But, like all things Roman, this also was dependent on how much a man was willing to pay to the right person to be granted a pass.

Thinking quickly, Porcinus leaned down and whispered in Iras' ear, "Did you bring some of Titus' hard cash with you from Arelate?"

Surprised by the question, Iras leaned away, searching her husband's face.

"Yes," she whispered slowly. "But why?"

"I'll explain later, but tell me where it is in the wagon. I need to get some of it."

"How much?" she asked sharply, suddenly suspicious.

Inwardly, her husband groaned; of all the times for Iras' natural parsimony to come up, this wasn't the time.

Still, he kept his patience, and assured her, "I'll explain later, but it will be worth it. Trust me."

And ultimately, Iras did trust her husband implicitly. Quietly, she told him which crate contained the small chest of coins.

The amount of the bribe had caused Porcinus to wince; it was still difficult for him to think of himself as a wealthy man, so a hundred sesterces to the provost to write a pass that allowed him to leave the camp still made him wince. However, before he was in his quarters in the town more than a few moments, he realized it had been worthy every sestertius. As he had predicted, Titus hadn't been in bed; he was down in the small stable built underneath the two floors that comprised the Porcinus family's apartment. He was still pale, and his arm was in a sling, but when Sextus and Valeria, squealing with delight, came running to greet him, the smile on his face made it hard for his mother to believe he'd ever been hurt. Laughing, he couldn't avoid wincing when the two came crashing into him, jarring his arm.

"Careful," Iras called out. "Your brother's hurt."

"I'm fine, Mama," he called to her, and she could see that he truly was.

She stood for a moment, just soaking in the sight of her children as she held the baby, and although not a religious woman, she offered up a prayer to Isis, Ptah, and the other gods of her childhood, something she did very seldom. Miriam was in her arms, her other children were safe and reunited, and she would remember that moment for many years to come.

It wasn't all good; Porcinus hadn't been home for more than a hundred heartbeats before he told Iras that this reunion and celebration of the family Porcinus would be confined to just that night. Luckily for Porcinus, this didn't come as a surprise to Iras; Silva had been the one to inform her when they were still on the way to Siscia. He and his *ala*, minus Titus' escort, had arrived in the night of the same day that Titus was found. Despite the happy outcome, Iras still didn't want to think about the fear that had seized her heart when Gallus alerted them to the sound of approaching horsemen. Then, although they made a straight line back to Siscia, the Decurion had insisted on sending patrols out to spots where he knew there might be settlers, and they escorted another three frightened groups of them back to the main column. Fortunately, the warband of the Latobici, while large enough to wipe out Iras and her family, was no match for an *ala* of veteran Roman cavalry, and they had been reduced to being spotted twice on nearby ridges, watching the column make its way to safety, frustrated and impotent to strike. When Porcinus told Iras that he was leaving the next day, it was hard to hide his relief when she took it as she had, an unwelcome but accepted fact. It made the atmosphere that last night as joyful and easy as he supposed it was possible to be. As his family sat at the table, with the usual noise and what seemed to be chaos, he studied the scene before him, and it was hard not to shake his head in a combination of wonder and bemusement. It had been immediately after he had told Iras about his departure when in turn she had explained how his household had suddenly grown. The truth was that he hadn't been completely surprised when he spotted the gray head of Diocles and, in fact, he was happy when Iras told him why he had returned to Siscia.

"We should have thought of that," was his only comment.

The addition of Birgit was slightly more surprising, if only because of the cause.

"That old dog." Porcinus had laughed, earning a sharp jab from his wife, who gave him a scowl that was marred by the smile that threatened it.

"Everyone deserves love," she had said simply.

"And if anyone does, it's Diocles," Porcinus agreed. "He spent most of his life devoted to Titus. It's time he enjoys himself." An impish urge overtook him, and he grinned down at his wife. "And he picked a lovely way to do it!"

"Thank you for telling me that," Iras said sweetly. "Now I know I need to watch you like a hawk!"

"And I need to sleep with one eye open," he muttered, but burst into laughter at her nod in response.

Simeon was the biggest surprise, especially after Iras told Porcinus of the way his relationship with Titus had started.

"But Titus saw that Simeon loves Ocelus as much as he did." She looked at the dark Armenian, seated at the far end of the table, trying to look like he wasn't uncomfortable.

The boy and man had instantly picked up their relationship where it had left off, as Titus relayed to the Armenian Ocelus' exploits on his dash to get help. Two people who loved horses, Porcinus mused, as he watched the pair, their heads almost touching as Titus related his adventure. In fact, it was Titus who not only insisted that the Armenian be allowed to eat with the family, but that he sit next to Titus. Normally, Iras would have refused on general principles that slaves had no place at the table, but this wasn't a normal occasion, and still fresh in her mind was the memory of Simeon, bow in hand, giving her and her family time to scramble to safety. If for nothing other than that, Simeon would always have a place in the Porcinus household. There was only one more thing that Iras had yet to relate to her husband, but she made the decision that this was a subject best left until after dinner and when they were alone. For the moment, she was content to let Porcinus enjoy his last night with his family, before he marched off to war.

It was later that night, after husband and wife had consummated their reunion, when Iras finally told Porcinus the entire story of their trip to Arelate, particularly as it pertained to Titus and the dwarf Spartacus. Porcinus was sitting up, back against the wall as he stared off into space, trying to make sense of what he had just been told by Iras.

"What was that *lanista*, what was his name? Vulso? What by Juno's *cunnus* was he thinking?"

Surprisingly, Iras was the more pragmatic and understanding of the two.

"You know how Titus is," she told her husband. "I'm sure that he was just like we are; he got worn down by Titus' insistence to face someone live. And," she pointed out, "would you rather have had him face a full-grown man?"

"No," Porcinus conceded, but he was unconvinced, not to mention that he was made uneasy by the idea that, on this topic anyway, there appeared to be a reversal of roles. Usually, he was the one to try and point out a reason why Titus should be forgiven some transgression, or allowed some privilege. "But that doesn't mean I wanted him fighting a dwarf. I've seen them fight before." Porcinus was, or at least up until this moment, an avid follower of the blood sport, and kept up with the fortunes of a number of gladiators. "They're short, that's true, but they're strong!"

"All I can tell you is what I saw that day," Iras said quietly, and Porcinus could be forgiven that he didn't see the shudder that came with that statement. "That dwarf may have been strong, but he didn't stand a chance against Titus."

Despite himself, Porcinus felt a glimmer of pride, and he cast a sidelong glance at Iras and asked, "He was that good, neh?"

He expected an outburst, but instead, she just heaved a sigh and shook her head.

"I don't know if he was good, or if he was just...mad. I tell you, Gaius, I've never, ever seen anything like that."

"I have," her husband said quietly, but his gaze was somewhere far away, so he didn't notice Iras give him a sharp glance.

She had heard that same tone of voice, but it had been from Diocles, when they had discussed the episode at the *ludus*, and he talked about Titus Pullus.

"So," she couldn't help asking, although she was still hesitant, afraid to hear the answer, "was it with your father? Did you see Pullus do that?"

Porcinus didn't answer, verbally at least. He gave a slow nod, his gaze never wavering from the opposite wall. There was a silence for several moments, but he was acutely aware that she was still staring at him, and he sighed, understanding that she needed to hear.

"It was in Parthia," he began.

Over the next few moments, he described events that he had never spoken of before, at least to her or in her presence, and despite herself, she listened in rapt fascination. She had seen Titus Pullus in action; more accurately, she had seen the aftermath of what he had done, on the night she had been taken at Deukalos' villa. But she had never witnessed it firsthand, nor had her husband ever gone into detail about anything concerning his adoptive father. Only once, back when Sextus Scribonius and Gaius Porcinus had spent a night at the table talking, in that horrible time after Quintus Balbus, Pullus and Scribonius' best friend, had been killed and Pullus, blaming himself, had begun drinking heavily, had she heard anything remotely like what her husband talked about this night. For once, Porcinus spared no detail, telling Iras everything. Once he was done, Iras sat, absorbing it and trying to decide how honest she should be with her husband.

Finally recognizing that she had never hidden anything from him concerning their children, she turned to him and said, "That sounds almost exactly like what happened to our son. It was horrible, but..." Her voice suddenly trailed off, unwilling to continue.

Porcinus finished for her, "But it was awesome and, in a terrible way, beautiful to behold." He looked over at her, giving her a strange, level look. "Isn't that right? There was something horribly beautiful about it?"

Iras shuddered, but then, she nodded.

"Yes," she said softly, even as she hated herself for admitting such a thing about her son, her beautiful, first-born son. "Yes, it was. It was if he was..."

"Born for it," they said in unison.

They sat, both of them absorbed in their own thoughts, staring off into space, side by side, but both alone.

Porcinus slipped from the house in the pre-dawn, kissing his youngest children as they slept, then on an impulse, he roused his oldest son.

"Come with me," he whispered.

Despite being groggy, Titus could tell that this was important, and he didn't make his normal protest about being roused. He was a boy who liked his sleep, but he understood this was different. Leading his boy to the table in the main room, Porcinus indicated that Titus should take a seat, which he did, watching quietly as his father lit a lamp that he placed on the table between them. Sitting down, he regarded his son for a moment, thinking with more than a little sadness how much older Titus seemed since he had left for Arelate. He tried to tell himself that it was the light, but he knew better. Gathering his thoughts, he finally broke the silence, keeping his voice low.

"I have to leave in a little while," he began, but Titus spoke up.

"I know," the boy said simply. "I heard you telling Mama."

Porcinus couldn't stop a smile as he shook his head. Of course you did, you little sneak.

"So you know that I'm going back on campaign?"

This time, Titus only nodded, looking down at the table.

"Before I left, I wanted to talk to you."

"About what?"

There was something guarded, wary in the boy's tone as he looked up and studied his father's face.

Sighing, Porcinus realized he only had one choice, and he said, "I want to talk about what happened in Arelate."

At first, Titus gave no reaction, still watching his father, before he asked suspiciously, "What about Arelate? We were there a long time."

Biting his lip, Porcinus fought the urge to speak sharply to the boy, knowing that it would do more harm than good.

"I think you know what I'm talking about," he replied gently.

Neither spoke for the next several heartbeats, but it was Titus who broke first, his shoulders suddenly slumping and, in that moment, Gaius once more saw the boy.

"You mean," Titus whispered, "about Spartacus?"

At first, Porcinus was confused; Iras hadn't mentioned the dwarf's name, so it took a moment for him to make the connection.

"Was that his name?"

Titus nodded, his eyes suddenly looking everywhere but at his father, and Porcinus could see them shining in the lamplight.

"Titus, let me ask you a question. Did you set out to kill this…man?"

Porcinus found it hard to form the word, thinking, by the gods, he's just a boy! Only then, did Titus look up, shaking his head emphatically as his eyes searched his father's face.

"No, Tata! I swear it on the black stone! It was just that…he beat me the first time." Titus closed his eyes, swallowing hard, then continued. "And yes, I wanted to beat him. But I didn't want to kill him!"

"I know you didn't, Titus." Porcinus reached out and put a hand on his boy's shoulder, careful to grasp his right shoulder and not the injured one. "But in battle, sometimes, some men, something happens to them…" He stopped, struggling to find the right words.

"What, Tata? What happens to them? Are they…" Porcinus saw Titus swallow hard, as if the word was blocking his throat, "…cursed? Is that what it is, Tata? That I've been cursed by the gods?"

Porcinus was suddenly scared that his own composure would break as he tried to force the words out in a rush, assuring his son,

"No, Titus! No!" He shook his head emphatically, and forgetting himself, squeezed his son's shoulder as he shook the boy. "In fact, it's the opposite."

"How is it the opposite?" Titus struggled with the big word, triggering the thought in the back of his mind that Diocles hadn't returned a moment too soon.

Instead of answering directly, Porcinus asked his son, "You remember how much everyone looked up to your Avus, don't you?"

Titus nodded vigorously, the memories of Arelate still fresh.

"Oh, yes," he replied. "Hardly a day went by when one of his men didn't come by and talk about what a great Legionary he was! They talked all about the things he'd done!"

And most of them weren't there, Porcinus thought with a grim amusement, but decided this wasn't the time to bring that up.

"Well, when your mother told me what you'd done to…Spartacus, you know what it reminded me of?"

Titus shook his head; he was still too sleepy to recall that there was some relation between his Avus and him that Porcinus was driving at, just as Diocles had mentioned to him on the trip back.

"It reminded me of your Avus, when we were in Parthia," Porcinus said. "I saw your Avus do something very, very much like what you did, when we were in a great deal of danger. When I asked him about it later, do you know what he told me?"

Titus shook his head again, but there was a dawning expression of hope on his face that made Porcinus' heart ache, understanding how desperately his son needed this.

"He told me that it was a gift from the gods, Mars and Bellona, to be specific. And it was a gift that only came to him at moments of great danger, and he was suddenly blessed with the strength and speed of two men. Is that how you felt?"

"Well," Titus' tone was doubtful, "I don't know about two men. But while I didn't remember any of it right after, over the next few days, I remember bits and pieces." He considered for a moment, then gave a thoughtful nod. "But yes, I think that might be something like what happened to me. The one thing I remember more than anything was how slowly he seemed to be moving, like, like…" He struggled for a moment as he tried to come up with an appropriate example.

Then he brightened. "It was like he was in honey, but the way honey is on a cold day. And I wasn't." As quickly as it had come, the spark vanished as his shoulders slumped, "But, I should have stopped, Tata. I should have stopped beating him. But, I…I just couldn't."

That was when the tears finally burst forth, and Titus leaned forward, into his father, who put his other arm around his boy, holding him closely and murmuring the kind of things he did when he was holding his newborn son for the first time, experiencing a complete, yet terrifying love that he had never encountered before. Finally, Titus was spent, and Gaius' tunic was soaked, but he didn't mind. In fact, unknown to anyone but himself, as soon as he returned to his quarters in camp, he changed his tunic to a fresh one, but put this one down at the very, very bottom of the pack that would go on his mule, and he would forbid Lysander from washing it. When Titus sat up, he had returned to his state of being a boy who wants to be considered a man, and Porcinus felt compelled to offer him some sort of encouragement while at the same time impress on his son the gravity of what they were talking about.

"Titus," he began, sounding awkward to his own ears, although Titus didn't seem to notice, "you've been blessed like your Avus was. If you continue growing as you are, you'll be his size." Suddenly inspired, he joked, "And your mother and I will be broke." He was rewarded with a grin. "But," he became serious again, "this other…gift, because that is what it is, Titus, it's a gift from Mars, it comes with a price. It's not like the toy gifts you get on your name day, or on Saturnalia." Thinking for an appropriate analogy, he settled on one that he thought would make sense to Titus. "It's like Avus' gift of Ocelus to you. Because Ocelus isn't a toy, or a candied plum. He's a living, breathing creature, and with that comes responsibility. Do you understand?"

Titus nodded solemnly, assuring his father, "I do, Tata. And I take care of Ocelus!"

"I know you do," Porcinus agreed. "Your mother has told me how well you've taken care of him since you were in Arelate. And I'm very proud of you for that. Well, this other gift, this ability that you have in moments of great danger, that comes with a responsibility as well. Do you know what that is, Titus?"

Porcinus was expecting a shrug, or a mumbled response that Titus didn't know, so he was extremely surprised when instead, his son nodded.

Looking his father in the eye, he said quietly, "I can't abuse it. I can't just use it when I'm mad at Sextus or Valeria. Because I could hurt them very, very badly." His lower lip began to tremble at the very thought, and he hurried to finish. "Because I would never forgive myself if I hurt my family, Tata."

It was hard for Porcinus to contain his relief, but he wanted to make sure he drove home the whole point he was trying to get across.

"That's very good, Titus," Porcinus assured the boy. "I'm really proud of you for understanding that. But," he held up a finger, and his voice hardened just that fraction that told Titus his father was deadly serious, "that needs to extend to more than just your family. You're probably going to be bigger or stronger, as it is. So if you were to abuse this gift of the gods with anyone other than an enemy, and I mean a real enemy and not just when you're mad at your friends like Quintus Pacuvius or Gnaeus Figulus," Porcinus named Titus' two closest boyhood friends, "then you're going to draw the wrath of the gods down on your own head. You must know when the time is right, and only then should you open your heart and let that gift flow through you."

Titus considered this, which Porcinus took as a good sign, that he didn't immediately give his father his promise. But he could see Titus was still troubled.

Finally, he blurted it out. "How will I know when it's going to come? How can I call it if I really need it? Did Avus tell you how he did it?"

Porcinus hesitated, but he understood he couldn't lie to his son, not about this. This wasn't about something inconsequential, like whether or not he was getting something he had asked for.

"No, Titus," he said at last, shaking his head sadly. "As far as I know, and from what Avus told me, he never knew when it was going to come. Just that it was going to come, and when it did, it was always when he needed it most, never before. Or after," he added.

Porcinus stood then, and he had never been more reluctant to leave his family than he was that night. However, he also knew that it was highly likely that Barbatus was going to be checking his quarters to see if he was there. As long as he returned soon, he could simply tell Barbatus that he had either been wandering around his Cohort, or was with another Pilus Prior. He had said his goodbyes to everyone else, but as he did when they left for Arelate, Porcinus offered his son his right arm, thinking the boy would appreciate another sign that his father viewed him as a man. But when Titus stood up and threw himself into his father, wrapping one arm tightly about Porcinus' torso, Porcinus was more than happy to return the hug and savored this moment when his son still acted like a little boy.

Chapter 6

The Army of Pannonia, four Legions strong, marched out of Siscia; the fact that it was just after dawn didn't dissuade the crowd that lined the road leading out of the Porta Praetoria to see the men off. As was normal and had been the case for centuries, Tiberius and Drusus, riding side by side at the head of the column of men, pretended they didn't hear the shouts of "Tata" and "husband," also ignoring the sight of young children suddenly darting out of the crowd to run alongside a part of the column. Whether or not it happened to be next to the man who fathered them was not of any interest to Tiberius, Drusus, Quirinus, or any of the high-ranking Romans who, if they had taken an interest, would have been forced to do something about it, since it was expressly forbidden by regulations for any rankers to have families. Centurions were allowed to marry, but only with a special dispensation, although this was also generally ignored. From the time that the Roman army on campaign first gained the "tail" that constituted those women and their children who insisted on coming along, there was one requirement and one only; that the tail neither impede nor require any assistance from the Roman war machine.

What had been discovered fairly early on was that there was a symbiotic relationship between the camp followers and an army on the march. The women of the Legions provided many valuable services, over and above of a carnal nature, and, in fact, eased the strain of supplying such a large, well-equipped force by supplementing certain items. Tunics were mended instead of replaced; spare bits of gear were bought from those merchants who also accompanied the army, relieving the *quaestorium* from handing these out to the men. To an outside and uninformed observer, it may have appeared strange for a Legionary to go outside the supply system and pay a premium for an item of equipment, but there was a cost associated with an officially issued piece of gear over and above the number of coins. For small pieces, it was usually a swat or two with the *vitus*, but for other, larger pieces, along with a deduction in pay came an official punishment, and that could be as harsh as execution. Therefore, it made perfect sense that men in such straits would find themselves outside their marching camp, wandering in the area of ramshackle shelters and wagons that was the home of the camp followers. The family of Gaius Porcinus wasn't one of those families who traveled with the army; in fact, it was very rare to see the woman of a Centurion traveling with the camp followers. The same was true with the children, except for one select group, those sons of Centurions who were perhaps in their teens, but still not of majority, and for the most part had declared their intent to follow in their fathers' footsteps. In those cases, it was literal, as these boys tagged along, often serving as their fathers' body servant and, as such, they relieved the army of the cost of a slave's upkeep on a campaign. To be sure, there weren't many of these boys, perhaps fifty in total, spread among the four Legions. But to Porcinus' consternation, one of Titus' friends, Quintus Pacuvius, was one of those boys; the fact that he was the son of Vibius Pacuvius, Porcinus' own Princeps Posterior, in charge of the Fourth Century, meant that Titus was convinced he should be allowed to accompany his father as well. Fortunately for Porcinus, the fact that his son was still recovering from his wound gave him the clinching argument that the real reason wouldn't have, which was that Porcinus' opinion that his son was too young. Although Titus had pouted when he brought it up at the dinner table the night before, before Iras could say a word, his father pointed out that his sutures hadn't been removed.

Unfortunately, that didn't stop Iras from adding, "Besides, you're too young! You're only ten! Quintus is thirteen!"

Porcinus stifled his groan, yet somewhat to his surprise, rather than lash out and argue in his usual manner, the boy gave his mother a long, thoughtful look, as if trying to decide how forthcoming he should be.

Finally, all he said was, "I'm not only the same size as Quintus, I've already seen battle, Mama." Porcinus would always wonder who had been the most shaken by his words, the mother or the son, because Titus had immediately dropped his eyes to his plate and mumbled, "But Tata's right. My arm still isn't healed." Then he heaved a sigh that, to Porcinus, almost sounded like he was relieved to have this as a reason for staying behind.

It was true that the boy was silent for quite some time after that, before he and Simeon had begun talking of Ocelus, but that was as far as it had gone. However, Titus still had one surprise in store for his father when he appeared that morning on Ocelus, who he had walked a short distance away from the gate where the greatest part of the families were concentrated. That hadn't been the surprise, however; sitting in front of him was Valeria, while behind him, his arms around his older brother's waist, was Sextus. The two younger children looked every bit as excited as one might expect, both because of the occasion of the army leaving, yet more for the thrill of not only being allowed to ride their brother's horse, but the fact that it was his idea.

"You'll have the best seats in the house." Titus had grinned as he told them.

Naturally, they needed no persuasion, and while Iras was a bit bemused at her oldest boy's generosity in sharing something he had jealously guarded at the beginning, it still gladdened her heart. Now she stood next to the big gray horse, cradling Miriam, who was peering out at the spectacle of an army on the march from her swaddle with a great deal of interest. Next to Iras were Diocles and Birgit, and despite having some time to become accustomed to the idea, when Porcinus saw the pair, he had to stifle a grin at the sight of the pair holding hands. Under normal circumstances, the Legates turned a blind eye to men, usually Centurions by virtue of the fact that they walked alongside a marching column, stopping for a moment to say last goodbyes before hurrying to catch up with their Century. Porcinus had already warned his family the night before that, now with a new Primus Pilus, and even more because of who it was, this would be one time that Porcinus did no such thing, not wanting to give Barbatus the slightest excuse to make an issue of it. Consequently, when he drew level with his family, who was waiting for him, it was with some regret that he only gave them a wave, blowing a surreptitious kiss to his wife, although the nearest rankers saw it and made their normal good-natured comments and catcalls.

"Shut your mouths," Porcinus said to them, but it was equally equable, more because it was expected than anything else.

But he was a bit surprised when Titus turned Ocelus and began walking the horse alongside the column. When Porcinus gave him a warning glare, his son was completely unrepentant.

"You said you wouldn't be stopping. You didn't say anything about us walking with you for a bit," he said cheerfully.

Despite a slight worry that Barbatus would take exception even to this, Porcinus couldn't stop a laugh.

"Maybe you should be a lawyer," he told Titus ruefully, his comment his tacit acceptance of this development.

Titus and his siblings kept pace with their father for about a half-mile, stopping just before they reached the last signs of the outer reaches of Siscia.

"Take care of them," Porcinus repeated his instructions of the night before, indicating Sextus and Valeria.

"I will," Titus assured him, and there was something different in the way he said it.

It was almost as if, Porcinus mused, he was already a man. With a last wave, Porcinus, along with the Fourth Cohort, went marching off to the north in search of rebellion.

They didn't have to march far; barely more than two days' march to the north, the Varciani tribe, in fact, had risen up just a matter of days before Tiberius' army had arrived in Siscia, although it had taken them longer to get organized than the Romans. That meant their depredation and raids on the Roman settlers and small settlements had been minimal, and Tiberius was determined to keep it that way. It was a normal topic of conversation, particularly while the army was on the march, the relative merit of the Legate in overall command, yet this campaign was different. What talk there was about how Tiberius and Drusus handled the Legions and themselves was usually in short snatches of muttered conversation between the Centurions. It didn't take Porcinus long to see how, contrary to past campaigns, the Centurions of the 8th Legion kept their conversations restricted to one or two close friends, and almost always within their own Cohort. Gone were the meetings in one of the Pili Priores' tents that had been an almost nightly occurrence in the aftermath of Vettus' death. And while Porcinus assumed that their new Primus Pilus had something to do with it, not until he and Corvinus discussed it at length one night, albeit in whispers, did he get a better idea why.

"Everyone's scared," Corvinus told Porcinus. "Especially after something Barbatus said just a couple days after he took command, that Augustus had picked him because he was sure of his loyalty and that the Princeps has some doubts about the 8th."

This was the first Porcinus had heard this, and he said as much, commenting, "Where was I? Why didn't I hear about this?"

Corvinus gave him a long, level look that told Porcinus the answer, which the Pilus Prior supplied, "Because I had other things on my mind, like where my family was."

Corvinus only nodded in answer, and they sat for a moment in a companionable silence.

Finally, Porcinus broke it by asking, "And what do you think? Is that true? That Barbatus is here to spy on us?"

Corvinus considered for a long moment before answering slowly, "No, I don't think so. At least, I don't think that's the only reason. I mean," he hurried on, "I think that might be part of why he's here. But I don't think spying on us is his primary assignment..."

His voice trailed off, unwilling to say anything more, despite Porcinus being sure that what they were saying was pitched so low that their words couldn't be understood outside the tent. Slightly irritated at his friend for making him work it out, Porcinus thought about it, slowly realizing that Corvinus' emphasis on one word was important. As he turned it over in his mind, he felt his eyes widen as he looked at Corvinus.

"You mean," he whispered, "Barbatus is spying on Tiberius?"

Corvinus didn't reply, just kept looking at Porcinus before giving a small nod, which was quickly followed by a shrug.

"That's what I've heard, anyway. Although I have a feeling that Drusus is under watch too."

Porcinus sat back on his stool, grabbing a cup to take a drink of watered wine as he thought about what he had just heard. Although it made some sense, Porcinus still was unsure, and his lack of certainty was down to what to him was the obvious flaw.

"But if Barbatus is watching them, and us, he's going to be too busy to go to the latrine, let alone do his job."

Corvinus favored Porcinus with a slight grin as he tapped the side of his nose.

"There are some advantages to crawling in the gutter," he told his Pilus Prior. "And one of those is you hear things that others don't, because they're at home tucking their children in and listening to their women nag them about the gods know what." He just dodged the cup that Porcinus threw at him, laughing for a moment before turning serious again. "Did you know that the First Cohort got plumped up?"

"Plumping up" was the term Centurions used when men lost in the ranks were replaced, and it was a common occurrence before a campaign. However, Porcinus hadn't thought it would or could have happened in the short week back in Siscia.

"How did that happen so fast? Where did they come from?" Porcinus asked. "They didn't come from us."

"Because they came with Barbatus," Corvinus answered.

Porcinus thought that was unusual. When the First Cohort plumped itself up, those men always came from the higher numbered Cohorts of the same Legion, while the other nine Cohorts received men from the various recruiting parties that were out scouring the Republic for men who qualified, usually whether they actually did or not. This was what Porcinus was referring to, because as a front line Cohort, the Fourth was always one of those that the largest Cohort in the Legion drew on first, and that hadn't happened in their week at Siscia. In fact, Porcinus had been somewhat expecting it because of the losses the First had suffered against the Rhaeti, but had put the inactivity down to the lack of time. Now he was hearing that the First had indeed replaced their losses.

"Where did he get them from?" Porcinus asked.

Corvinus told him, "They came from the same place Barbatus came from. The Praetorian Guard. In fact," Corvinus took a sip before adding his last piece of information, "what I heard was that the men come from his Cohort."

Porcinus considered this, and as he digested it and decided what it meant, he exchanged a look with Corvinus that told him his friend was thinking along the same lines.

"So Barbatus brought his own spies with him."

This disturbing revelation about the eyes among them aside, there was the more urgent question of the Varciani. Silva's *ala*, now reunited with the army and back in their role as scouts, had located the main body of the rebels, a bit more than sixty miles north of Siscia. The rebels had managed to burn out a small settlement that had formed around a natural springs, which once belonged to the Jasi tribe and supposedly had medicinal qualities. However, when they caught sight of Silva and his men, they had, perhaps surprisingly, headed south a short distance, back in the general direction of the main body of Tiberius' army. Regardless of appearances to the contrary, there was a good reason for the leader of this Varciani warband doing so; if he had led his men north of the Dravus River, or even worse, eastward toward the Ister, or as it was becoming more known as, the Danuvius, it would lead them into wide open country that, while it had patches of heavy forest, was the perfect kind of terrain for the Legions of Rome to deploy in their favored formation. Compounding matters further was the presence of a huge lake, Pelso was what the locals called it, located in that direction as well, meaning that sooner or later, the Varciani would have found themselves trapped in a triangular wedge of land with the Danuvius to the east, the lake to the north, and the Legions to the south. Nevertheless, what Porcinus and the other veterans of Pannonia understood was that, while the rebels were closing the distance to their enemy instead of gaining some breathing room, they were heading into territory that veterans of the region knew from bitter experience was a nightmare to control. In area, it was very small; a strip of land about thirty miles running east to west and no more than ten miles north to south. And considering that the Varciani band numbered some seven thousand men, to those unfamiliar with the area, it was hard to believe that there was any way to hide a force of that size. Unfortunately, Porcinus and the others knew better. Heavily forested, mostly with birch, poplar, and other trees that at this time of year were in full foliage, there were very few flat, open areas where an army of the size of Tiberius' could deploy. This was especially true because, at least if the Varciani leaders behaved as they had before, the warriors would break into smaller bands to melt into the hundreds of small pocket valleys, draws, and hidden glens that riddled the area. Adding to the difficulty was what the Legionaries had discovered the first time they chased a rebelling tribe into the area, that a fair number of the low spots between the low but steeply sloped hills were marshy, with thick, sucking mud that left the men filthy, tired, and frustrated. What had always been most puzzling to the Romans was that the ability of natives to hide hadn't been confined to just their infantry, but their cavalry as well, which took a great deal more space. Yet, whenever a tribe's warriors, infantry, and cavalry entered into this territory, they all just…vanished.

"We're going to be here for a month, just like last time," muttered Munacius of the Third Century. "And the men are going to be pissing and moaning the whole time."

"Good thing it's only the rankers doing it," Porcinus commented, hiding a smile by taking a drink from his cup.

The other Centurions snickered at their Pilus Prior's subtle jab at the Princeps Prior, who reddened slightly before chuckling himself.

"Fair enough," he said with as much grace as he could muster, but he understood that there was a serious message behind the Pilus Prior's words. "And I'll make sure that my boys don't do more than the usual complaining."

Porcinus inclined his head in silent thanks, as the others murmured similar assurances. Because as they had all learned, their Pilus Prior was in some professional peril; whether it had come from Corvinus, Porcinus didn't know, but it had become very clear that his Centurions were aware of the enmity Barbatus held toward their leader. As Porcinus also discovered, again in the form of quiet, snatched conversations, not only had the Centurions of his own Cohort become aware, but the other Pili Priores, who he had sought out one at a time, had also learned of the identity of the newly added men of the First Cohort. Never in his entire career had Porcinus seen the kind of atmosphere settle over the Centurions of the 8th Legion that permeated it now, and he wondered if the 13th, the 15th and the Legion that was normally stationed on the Rhenus, the 22nd, were experiencing similar issues. Nobody knows who they can trust, he thought with some dismay on the day they reached the southern edge of the rough country. He knew he trusted Corvinus implicitly; Munacius and Verrens almost as much. Pacuvius was a close friend of Urso's, but in and of itself that wasn't an indictment of his loyalty, although Porcinus also didn't discount that it was meaningful. As far as Urso was concerned, Porcinus already guarded what he said and how he conducted himself with his Cohort's second in command. Still, it was just one more thing to worry about, as if the coming ordeal wasn't enough.

Very quickly, the men of the Legions found themselves in what, for most of them, was familiar and hated territory, both physical and otherwise. Ironically enough, under normal circumstances, Porcinus normally enjoyed these kinds of operations, at least as much as one can enjoy a kind of operation where what seemed to be a normal, routine day was suddenly made more challenging by either plunging into calf-deep mud, struggling up a steep slope covered in heavy underbrush, or worst of all, a sudden, screaming attack by rebelling tribesmen. What Porcinus liked was that the terrain was tailor-made for operations by smaller units than Legions, as detachments of Cohorts were given an area to search. Not only did he enjoy the challenge and independence, the fact that he was away from the prying, hostile eyes of Barbatus and his spies in the First Cohort made it even better. Almost as quickly as the rankers, Tiberius recognized the nature of the challenges facing his army, so that once more, he split his forces, although this time he was even more drastic in his dispositions than with the Rhaeti, splitting his force into four, consisting of one Legion each, with a detachment of cavalry and auxiliaries of missile troops with each. He basically positioned his forces so they were roughly aligned with the four points of the compass, completely surrounding the area of rough country. What was not lost on Porcinus or any of the other Centurions was that the 8th stayed under the direct command of Tiberius.

"I wonder how much that cost Barbatus?" was the way Corvinus introduced the topic the night that the new dispositions were made.

"You really think he bribed Tiberius to keep us with him?" Porcinus asked, more genuinely curious than doubtful.

Corvinus shrugged, but said, "I wouldn't bet against it. If he's been assigned to keep an eye on the youngster, then this is a good way to do it. Besides, if he did, he's probably not using his money. Or he's going to be reimbursed by Augustus as an expense."

This made Porcinus laugh, thinking with a mixture of amusement and bitterness how matters like spying on a superior could be considered to be so routine that it would be subject to normal rules of business, where an employee could expect to be reimbursed by their employer for expenses incurred. With that thought lingering in his head, Porcinus bid his friend good night before he made his last inspection of his Cohort area, walking the streets and listening to the low buzz of conversation coming from the tents now that the command to retire had sounded. The next day, Tiberius was taking the men into a particularly rugged section of ground, and from past experience, and in his soldier's bones, Porcinus felt sure that there would be some sort of contact with the rebels the next day. Up to that point, there had been frustrating glimpses of men hurrying up and over the next hill, and tracks of both mounted men and infantry, but it had been a case where the Romans had been just a bit too late. This latest tactic by Tiberius, Porcinus thought, was a good one, and was going to bear fruit. Ideally, the pressure from all sides would compress the rebels into one spot where all four Legions could come to bear. However, there was one possible flaw in Tiberius' strategy, and while it wasn't a huge one, it did stick in the back of Porcinus' mind as a nagging worry. Although it was extremely faint, the leader of the rebels had one chance of extracting his men from the trap they had put themselves in, and that was to concentrate his forces then head for one Legion to fight their way out. Even with the terrain in their favor, the Varciani couldn't hope to defeat even a single Legion, but they could conceivably force their way through the Legion lines to flee. And depending on how much damage whatever Legion they happened to face inflicted, Porcinus and the army might find themselves either in pursuit, or returning to Siscia.

"We'll find out one way or another tomorrow," Porcinus muttered to himself as he lay down on his cot, falling asleep immediately as he always did on the march.

Sometime during the night, the weather changed, Porcinus and most of the men awakened by the clap of thunder, followed quickly by the sound of a hard rain against the canvas of their tents. That the rain was now hitting canvas instead of leather was yet another change wrought by Augustus, since canvas was cheaper to produce and, unlike leather, didn't tend to split apart suddenly once it became saturated to such a point where it couldn't support the weight of the trapped water. While Porcinus and the other veterans appreciated this, along with the fact that canvas was lighter in weight, there was one drawback to it when compared to the leather, and it made itself apparent that night. When it rained hard, the drops striking canvas were simply louder than they had been under leather, meaning that men who might have slept through the storm were invariably awakened, and if they were like Porcinus, found it almost impossible to fall back asleep. Fortunately, the rain had slackened by the time the *bucina* sounded the call to start the day, yet it also meant that very quickly the Legion streets became a churned quagmire of mud. And with a sky the color of lead sling bullets, it didn't appear that it would be letting up, at least for the foreseeable future. It was shaping up to be a miserable day, even without the prospect of any action. The only blessing was that Tiberius had commanded that the camp not be taken down, and the Tenth Cohort was assigned the duty of manning the walls while the rest of the 8th went hunting. After a quick breakfast, Porcinus and the other Pili Priores assembled at the *praetorium* for their commander's briefing. Naturally, Tiberius was there, but his brother, Quirinus, and Marcus Vinicius, the other three men of Legate rank, were absent, each of them in command of another Legion. The only other men present besides the Pili Priores were the Tribunes nominally attached to the Legion, men who Porcinus rarely bothered learning their names. The days where a Tribune actually commanded a Legion in anything but name had passed long before, and, in fact, was barely practiced during his father's time as well.

"We're going to split up into forces of three Cohorts each," Tiberius announced as soon as it had quieted down.

He pointed down at the model of the area that his *praefecti fabrorum* had created, based on what little information existing maps had provided, their own observations, and from some of the men who were familiar with the area. It was not built to perfect scale, perhaps, Porcinus noted, or at least, he hoped that the hills didn't tower so steeply above the narrow ravines that Tiberius was pointing at. Despite his youth, Tiberius always seemed to have a perpetual scowl on his face, the corners of his mouth turned down in a manner that, if Porcinus was being honest, quite reminded him of his oldest son when he didn't get his way. Still, there was also a brisk air of assurance about the young man, and Porcinus had to admit that he had already proven himself as a general.

"The force that I will lead, consisting of the First, Second, and Third Cohorts, will head north up this narrow defile that's about a mile from camp. The second force, consisting of the Fourth, Fifth…"

Before he got any farther, he was interrupted by the clearing of someone's throat, in a manner that made it clear it wasn't because the owner had a tickle.

Clearly irritated, when Tiberius looked up to see who it was, there was an almost imperceptible change in his manner, so slight that Porcinus, standing near the rear of the group because of his height, was willing to admit he might have imagined it.

"Yes, Barbatus?"

"Sir." Barbatus made no outward sign that he was aware of Tiberius' irritation, or at least, if he saw it, he was ignoring it, which Porcinus thought was telling in itself. "I'd like to make a suggestion, if I might."

Tiberius didn't verbally reply, but gave his permission for Barbatus to continue with a perfunctory nod.

"I'd like to request that the order of Cohorts be changed, at least for the one under your command."

While this wasn't unheard of and, in fact, under some generals, it happened fairly frequently, Porcinus was extremely surprised that a new Primus Pilus, handling his Legion in his first campaign, would make such a bold suggestion as to shake up the identity of the Cohorts most likely to see battle. As he glanced around, the tall Roman could see that he was far from alone. The other eight Centurions looked, if not troubled, then at least puzzled.

Either oblivious to the consternation, or ignoring it, Tiberius instead merely asked, "Who did you have in mind accompanying me?"

"The First, naturally," Barbatus replied, "and the Second. But instead of the Third, I'd like the Fourth instead."

More than one man sucked in a breath, yet none were more shocked than Fronto, the Tertius Pilus Prior, and Porcinus himself. Even Tiberius seemed aware that this was not only unusual, but could be taken as a slap in the face by Fronto, so he didn't answer immediately. Porcinus was close enough to see the young general's eyes dart from Barbatus to Fronto, as if willing the Primus Pilus to make some sort of further comment that might explain away what could be taken as a serious insult. Barbatus seemed oblivious to Tiberius' silent importuning, holding his helmet under his arm, and calmly returning the general's gaze.

Finally, Tiberius was forced to ask, "Is there a reason why, Barbatus?"

Every Centurion knew that Tiberius was handing his Primus Pilus a chance to make at least some sort of explanation that would remove the sting from his request, but again Barbatus didn't hesitate.

"None that I would care to go into with you at this moment, sir. Later, I'm more than happy to do so. But right now, it would take too long to go into."

Now there was no hiding the shock on everyone's face, and there was an audible gasp around the room. The only men who didn't appear discomfited were the Tribunes, all of whom were watching this drama play out with the avidity Porcinus normally saw at the arena.

The silence that followed started out as uncomfortable, but in the span of however many heartbeats it lasted, it became excruciating. Finally, Tiberius gave another, single, abrupt nod.

"Very well." His tone was curt. "We don't have any more time to waste on this kind of thing. So," he took a deep breath before continuing, "The First, Second, and Fourth Cohorts will be with me…."

Frankly, Porcinus didn't really hear much more of what was said; he had heard the part that was important to him and his men, and the rest of the time Tiberius spoke, his mind was whirling with the import of this new development.

"We move in a sixth part of a watch," Tiberius concluded.

Then, without another word, he faced about and stalked off, heading to his private quarters.

Nobody moved for a moment, then Barbatus barked, "You heard the man!"

Filing out, Porcinus took care to hang back and put as much distance between himself and the Primus Pilus, who had yet to don his helmet. He probably doesn't want to muss his hair until the last moment, Porcinus thought sourly. Then he felt a hard, unfriendly jab from behind. Spinning about, he faced a furious Fronto.

"What by Pluto's cock was that?" Fronto hissed, making no attempt to hide his anger.

Porcinus put his hands in the air, trying to placate the other Pilus Prior.

"I have no idea, Fronto! I swear it! I'm as mystified as you are, believe me!"

Fronto didn't answer immediately and just stared hard into Porcinus' eyes. Then, his body relaxed and he shook his head.

"I believe you," he muttered. "Juno's *cunnus*, I knew you didn't have anything to do with it before I asked you. I just wish I knew what that bastard is up to."

"That makes two of us," Porcinus replied fervently.

Then there was nothing more to be said as each man headed to rouse his Cohort for the day's work.

"The bastard has something planned," was Corvinus' immediate assessment, the first words spoken after Porcinus informed his Centurions of their change in assignment.

The other Centurions, although they weren't as vocal, were clearly as disturbed as Corvinus was and, while that made Porcinus feel better, the fact that Urso seemed equally upset puzzled and troubled him. He had expected his second in command to be positively beaming at this development, but he looked anything but happy. Porcinus couldn't devote any more time to this topic, as he had the Cohort *cornicen*, a veteran named Sextus Nigidius sound the command for the Cohort to assemble at the intersection of the Cohort street and the Via Praetoria. The men were assembled and ready in a matter of moments, whereupon Porcinus gave the command to march to the forum to meet Tiberius and the other Cohorts. It was a small victory, but he was nonetheless pleased to see that his Cohort was the first to arrive. However, it was made even better when, after the arrival of Volusenus

R.W. Peake

and his men, the First Cohort came marching up last. The crowning blow was that Tiberius was mounted and waiting as well, and there was no mistaking the even darker glower he gave Barbatus.

"So pleased you could make it, Primus Pilus," the general said sourly, looking down at the Primus Pilus, who at least had the good grace to appear embarrassed. "But I can see your judgment about the Fourth is to be commended! They were here first and I can tell they're frothing at the mouth to get stuck into the enemy!"

As could be expected, this brought a roar of approval from Porcinus' men, and Porcinus was no less pleased himself, and he made no effort to hide his grin as Barbatus strode past, glaring at him. Once the First made its way to the front of the column, the command was sounded, and the Cohorts under Tiberius went looking for trouble. And Gaius Porcinus somehow knew that, at the very least, he and his men were going to find it; if it were just from the enemy, he would be satisfied.

When the column reached the point where a small tributary stream came down out of the hilly country; Porcinus wasn't sure where it led, but he assumed it ended up in the Savus, which was directly south behind them, the command was given by Tiberius to change from marching column to one that prepared the Legion for battle. They would still move in column, but unlike the narrow front of four or six men abreast designed for rapid marching on roads, it was doubled in size, going to either an eight-man or ten-man front, with more space between files. With the First Cohort, it was somewhat more difficult because it was double the size, although it normally was a simple case of sixteen men across. That wasn't possible here, because the defile was too narrow, so they were aligned like the other Cohorts, making their formation longer. Shields were uncovered, and it appeared that all was ready. Although the Fourth was part of this group, they were still placed at the end of the column, meaning they had to wait for a period before they could begin moving. Once they finally started, they hadn't gone more than fifty paces, however, before there was another halt.

"What now?" Porcinus muttered, although they resumed the march quickly enough.

Almost immediately upon entering the defile, the mood of the men changed, as the idle chatter and banter stopped and men began peering up the slopes. Operating under their standard procedure, Porcinus sent a section from his Century to scramble partway up the slope to the left, as did the other odd-number Centuries, while the even-numbered sent a section to the opposite side. This was an important duty, even though it was one that was universally loathed by the men because, as brush-choked and rough as the terrain along the bottom of the defile might have been, it was still better than forcing one's way across a heavily forested slope. Particularly important was keeping pace with the rest of their comrades who were marching down below, which meant it was a duty that was always rotated to keep men fresh, and depending on how rough the going was, the sections might be switched during more than just the midday break. They had moved perhaps a mile up the defile when the *cornu* from the front of the column sounded the call for the Pili Priores to come to the front, and Porcinus trotted forward, catching up with Volusenus. Dreading having to deal with the surly Pilus Prior, Porcinus was nevertheless curious about something.

"Any idea why we came to a stop and just stood there in a perfect spot for an ambush?" he asked him as they made their way forward.

Volusenus gave a humorless laugh.

"You didn't see? Our Primus Pilus had us marching up this fucking ravine without any flank security."

Porcinus stared, not sure he had heard Volusenus correctly, but he was assured this was the case by the sidelong glance the other Pilus Prior gave him.

"That's...disturbing," was the only thing Porcinus could think to say, prompting another laugh from Volusenus, although this time, there seemed to be some humor in it.

Reaching the command group, now Porcinus saw the reason for the halt; they had reached a point where another ravine intersected the one they were currently standing in, and he tried to recall from the large model whether or not it was known where this eastward ravine led. He assumed that Tiberius was going to split his forces even more.

Tiberius confirmed Porcinus' guess by telling Volusenus and Porcinus, "I'm going to continue in this direction with the First, but I want the Second and the Fourth searching this ravine that branches off to the east. The scouts say that it should eventually curve back to the north. You can decide between yourselves how to arrange your men."

"I want the Second to lead the way," Barbatus interrupted, prompting even more astonished gasps from everyone within hearing.

Which, unfortunately, Porcinus noted dismally, were the Tribunes and the men of the First Century. He had long since learned how damaging it could be to not just morale, but discipline when rankers were witness to shows of discord between their superiors. Consequently, something caught his eye, and he turned in time to catch the knowing smirks exchanged between two men standing side by side, who were men he didn't recognize. Instantly understanding that these two men had to be some of the Praetorians brought by Barbatus, Porcinus scanned the ranks of the rest of the Century. In the limited time he had, he saw at least three more faces that were unknown to him, and Porcinus wondered if Barbatus had salted all of his spies just in his Century, or if they were spread out. He reminded himself to look into that further, then his attention was returned to the moment by Tiberius' response to Barbatus.

"As you wish," Tiberius said coldly, but once more glared down at the Primus Pilus from his horse.

Then he wheeled the horse about and moved back just behind the vanguard. Meanwhile, Volusenus and Porcinus returned to their Centuries, where Porcinus waited for the Second to begin its movement up this defile to the east. If anything, Porcinus could see that this was even narrower a passage than the one they had taken into this part of the search area. Volusenus had perceived much the same thing, and reduced his own front to just two men wider than they would have been if they were marching on a road, in column, although their spacing was for battle instead of the march. If men were alert and tense before, now they were getting nervous, it quickly becoming apparent that the slopes on their right side steepened to the point where it wouldn't have taken much effort to drop the abundant rocks littering the hill down onto their collective heads. Compounding the difficulty even further, Volusenus quickly determined that the slope to the right was simply too steep for a section to travel it, at least with any hope of them keeping pace with the men down below, sending word back to Porcinus.

"I don't like this at all." Ovidius had made his way from the opposite rear side of the formation to confer with Porcinus, but all Porcinus did was nod in agreement, keeping his eyes to the right. "At least we have flanking patrols on the other side," Ovidius continued, "but all it would take is a handful of those bastards to kick some rocks loose and we'd be fucked."

"I know that," Porcinus finally answered, his tone terse, "and the mud doesn't help. But we still need to keep our eyes open to the left. In fact," only then did he drop his gaze, looking at Ovidius. "I want you to send word back to the others that I still want everyone to send out a flank guard, but they're all going to be on the left. At least," he amended, "until this levels out a bit. Then we can put them back on the right as well."

Ovidius saluted, then spun and began trotting back to where the Second Century and Urso were marching, who in turn sent his own Optio to do the same thing, before returning to his place. Behind him, Porcinus heard not only his Optio, but the others shouting the number of the section that would be flanking to the left. Meanwhile, Volusenus pressed forward, and with every pace taken, the net thrown by Tiberius was tightening, shrinking the possible hiding spots down. At least, that was what Tiberius, and to be fair to the Legate, all of the Centurions thought.

What Tiberius or Porcinus had no way of knowing was that this formation of rock was part of a system of ridges that extended to the west. In fact, young Titus Porcinianus Pullus could have been a great help at this moment because, while he wouldn't have realized it, he would at least have seen how similar the terrain was to that lone ridge he had used to escape the Latobici. It was true that in the twenty-odd miles between that lone ridge and this area the ground was, while not flat, of a gentler grade than these two points, and appeared to be gently rolling. The fact that the underlying rock was of the same composition nobody knew, not even those native tribes who had inhabited the area for living memory. What they did know was if they started from the lone ridge to the west and rode east, it was relatively flat until they reached this part of the country, whereupon the terrain was almost identical to that of the lone ridge. And that feature that had allowed Titus to escape, in the form of the numerous caves riddling these hills, now revealed the secret of why the rebels were so hard to find. Porcinus' first sign was in the blast of a *cornu* up from where Volusenus was followed, although the note was cut dramatically short, almost instantly by the surprised shouts and sudden commands of the Centurions of the Second, just up ahead. What Porcinus would never know was whether or not there had been some prearranged signal, or the other Varciani had heard the shortened note of the *cornu* and used it as their own signal. What he did recognize was that, almost simultaneously, he heard the flanking patrols to his left shout their warnings; to Porcinus it sounded like just his Century and the Second were under attack at the moment, while out of the corner of his vision, he caught a blur of motion coming from the opposite direction and, before he could react, a large rock came bouncing off the slope to hit with a tremendous spray of pebbles and mud just in front of him. From a nervous silence to a riot of sound and motion, Porcinus was suddenly assailed by threats from both sides.

"*Testudo!*"

Even as he bellowed the word over and over, he understood he was making a bad choice, but the only other one was worse. Forming a *testudo* would protect the men for the most part from the rocks that were beginning to cascade down the steep slope to the right, yet it robbed men of mobility and the ability to see what was coming their way from the other direction. The only thing that could have made it worse was if the rebels fielded even a small number of mounted troops, but Porcinus discounted that as a possibility, not aware that there, in fact, were several caves large enough to handle up to a dozen mounted men. His command was obeyed instantly, as the men on the most vulnerable side turned outward to bring their shields to bear, while their comrades who had been to their left, but were now behind them, provided what was at least as important, overhead protection. The men moved quickly; even so, Porcinus heard a dull, sodden thudding noise, accompanied by a dull snap that he had heard before. As quickly as his mind registered the sound of the impact, there was a shrill, sharp scream of pain, and he glanced to his right just in time to see one of his men about halfway down his Century go to the ground, leaving a momentarily gaping hole in the *testudo*. Rocks were now bounding down from the right all along the column, but Porcinus knew that whatever real attack would come from the left, because it was the only practicable slope. Bitterly, he had to salute the rebel chief, who clearly knew what he was about. His men had just formed up into a compact *testudo*, and Porcinus could see that Urso had done the same thing. Porcinus had quickly moved to the left side of the formation, since he was without a shield, yet it took a huge effort of will for him to turn his back to the cascading stones to pay attention to where he knew the real threat would come from. His eyes scanned the slope, trying to see through the thick foliage, for any sign of his section of men, looking for movement of some sort that would give him a hint where they were. Just as he caught sight of one of them who had just leaped over a fallen tree to land lower down on the slope nearer to Porcinus, his eye was drawn by even more movement directly up the hill from his man.

He caught a glimpse of motion that his mind at first couldn't grasp, and he was only vaguely aware that he spoke aloud, saying, "Can that be…?"

"Cavalry!"

The shout came from up the slope; Porcinus saw that it was his man who had jumped the log, and only now could he see who it was as he turned to shout a warning. His name was Placus, one of Porcinus' most experienced men, but before Porcinus could even blink, he watched a slow-motion horror of a large black horse, its rider raising the long cavalry sword, burst into view from just behind Placus, the horse already beginning its leap over the fallen tree. Placus' hands were still cupped around his mouth when the horse slammed into him, yet Porcinus tore his eyes away, as close to panic as he had ever been, knowing that he was just a few heartbeats from disaster.

"Porcupine! Porcupine! Porcupine!"

Even as he shouted it, he was sure it was too late, although he couldn't spare a glance as he spun back around just in time for the black horse to come bounding down the slope, having run down Placus, whose body Porcinus caught a flashing glimpse of, still tumbling down the slope with that limpness that comes from either being dead or unconscious. Now the horse was close enough that Porcinus could see the flecks of foam on its muzzle, and immediately above it the ferocious smile of its rider as he aimed at a hated Centurion of Rome. Without thinking, or hesitation, Porcinus made a diving leap, except instead of his direction being backward, towards his men, he went the opposite way, his goal being to drop just underneath the hooves of the black as it flew overhead, its rider aiming his beast at the spot where Porcinus had been an eyeblink before. As Porcinus tucked his head down, preparing to roll when he hit the ground, he understood he had to get to his feet instantly or he would be trampled by the other horses he had seen behind the black and, for a brief instant, he thought he had gotten away cleanly. Then his foot slipped in the mud, so that one of its rearmost hooves caught him a glancing blow on the shoulder, sending a lightning bolt of pain through his upper body. More importantly, it knocked his body out of its tightly tucked position, and he hit the ground with tremendous impact at an awkward angle. Stars exploded behind his eyes as his helmet slammed into the rocky ground with terrific force, knocking him unconscious. And saving his life.

Porcinus' next conscious memory was opening his eyes to see nothing but what seemed to be a green veil, and it took him a moment to recognize that what he initially thought of as a veil actually was the screen of green leaves of a bush. Accompanying the sight were the sounds of fighting going on just a dozen paces away, and it was this that caused Porcinus to start rising from where he was lying in the mud, hidden from sight by the large shrub that he had clearly fallen, or been thrown, into. Fortunately, he caught himself, stifling the urge to try struggling to his feet and, while it was initially to allow his head and, most importantly, his vision to clear, a moment later, he realized that if he were just to appear in the midst of this fight, in all likelihood, he would be cut down. For Porcinus, it was some of the worst moments of his life as he lay there, helplessly listening to the sounds of his men, his boys, in what was clearly a desperate fight. Even in the short time it took before the leaves just above his face finally came into enough focus that he could tell the individual leaves apart instead of the single green mass it had been before, he heard the sound of one of his men crying out in his tongue, a strangled cry for his mother that Porcinus had heard too many times before. Despite this, he didn't rise, instead rolling over slightly to peer through the bushes. Perhaps a dozen paces away was what appeared to be the back line of the rebel infantry, pressing in around a single line of enemy cavalrymen who were slashing down at what he could see was essentially an intact formation. Although this was encouraging, just as troubling was the number of men he could see in a similar position to his, prone in the mud. Fortunately, most of them were moving or, in another sign of veterans, had pulled their shields over their bodies while curling up in as tight a ball as possible. He heard Ovidius shouting orders to his Century, and he was slightly relieved to see that a fair number of men had managed to thrust their javelins out in between the space of their shields. Also, he saw that there weren't as many horsemen as he had feared; from his vantage point, he saw no more than a half-dozen, although they were still pushing hard against the thin wall of shields of his Century. That was all the time Porcinus could spend to the larger situation before getting back into the action, but he was mindful of not drawing unwanted attention. Carefully, he pulled his feet underneath him, while watching the rebels to his immediate front. He had determined that he hadn't been out long, yet it was long enough that any warriors who were going to participate in the battle were already down in the ravine. Nevertheless, he still checked over his shoulder just before he burst forth from the shrub that had concealed him. He understood that his initial advantage of surprise, compounded by attacking from behind, would only serve him for a matter of a few heartbeats, so he had to maximize his impact. Seeing a somewhat larger gap between a pair of cavalrymen, he realized that one of them was the warrior on the black, and sensing that this was at the very least the leader of this bunch of warriors, he aimed for him, his plan to cut down the two infantrymen who stood in that gap between the black and the horseman to his right, mounted on a large roan and armed with a spear instead of sword. The two infantrymen were pushing up against his men, while the Legionaries directly behind the first line had at least been able to drop their shields in their normal position now that whoever had been rolling the rocks down would undoubtedly hit their own men if they continued. It was a good tactic but it had run its course; now the rebels had to take advantage of it and press home the attack. Drawing himself up, Porcinus dropped into a crouch, the Gallic-forged sword that had once been in his father's in his own hand, drawn back and ready to strike. He gathered himself, taking the time to draw in a deep breath.

"Now or never, Gaius," he muttered.

Then, without any more hesitation, he took his first stride back into the action, yet he had only gone a step when his foot slipped in the mud again. Despite this, he didn't stop, instead mentally adjusting for the reduced traction, as the detached part of his mind recognized that the rain, in fact, had been to the Romans' advantage, because not only had the enemy cavalry been forced to chop the stride of their mounts and thereby reduce speed to compensate, when they had slammed into his men, the men in the front ranks actually slid backwards, but kept their feet, rather than being knocked flat on their backs. None of that mattered in the moment, however, as he closed the distance, his eyes fixed on the back of the warrior to the right, next to the roan horse. When he came within a half-dozen paces, he was close enough to look past the man's shoulders, so that he saw the Legionary facing the warrior glance past his adversary and see his Centurion approaching, a look of grim determination fixed on Porcinus' face. The Legionary was relatively new to the Cohort, having been part of the last replacement draft, but he still thought quickly by making a sudden lunging thrust that, under normal circumstances would have put him in grave danger. But the warrior, seeing only that his enemy was overcommitting himself, made his own attack, sure that he had a kill to his credit. Porcinus' blade struck low and hard into the man's back, yet even before the Varciani had fallen, Porcinus yanked the blade free, bringing it across his body to strike the second man on foot, who was beginning to turn, just sensing this unexpected threat. The point of Porcinus' sword punched into the man, right under the breastbone, causing the warrior's breath to burst out of his lungs with a whooshing sound that was audible to Porcinus even above the other sounds of fighting. The Roman was blasted with a smell of wine, and a foul odor that Porcinus knew was caused by rotting teeth, yet he didn't pause, wrenching the blade free and ripping it sideways as he was trained, no longer noticing the sudden appearance of intestines that came bulging out of his enemy's body. By this time, the warrior on the black had turned at the disturbance he had spotted out of the corner of his eye, but while it was understandable, it was a fatal mistake. Even as he brought his own longer sword to bear on Porcinus, who was forced to step to his left to avoid the offal and falling body of his second victim, he opened himself up to the Legionary across from him, one of the men who had managed to bring a javelin to bear. It was just at the edge of his reach, but it was enough, the triangular point of the javelin tearing an awful, gashing wound in the mounted man's face. Understandably, any intention he had held of dealing with Porcinus was no longer a priority, and he dropped his sword with an awful scream of pain that was cut short when Porcinus gave a hard, upward thrust just below the warrior's ribcage. Before the man could topple from the saddle, Porcinus used his free hand to grab the black's bridle, yanking its head around while using the flat of his bloody sword to swat the horse on the rump. As with all creatures, the horse leapt forward, following its head, which was pointed down the ravine, its now-dead rider falling limply from the saddle. And with that, Porcinus entered back into the relative safety of his men, the two across from him moving their shields aside just enough to let him back into the security of the formation.

Ovidius, who had been in Porcinus' spot, just inside the *testudo*, grinned at the sight of his mud-spattered Centurion, shouting, "Good to see you're alive!"

"Good to be alive," Porcinus said wearily, then turned his attention to the fight.

As Porcinus took in the situation, he saw that it was composed of equal parts good and bad. It wasn't just his Century under attack; because of his height, he was able to see that Urso's Century was similarly engaged, and seemed to have suffered the same amount of casualties. Although he couldn't see past Urso and his men, Porcinus had to assume that the rest of the Cohort was under attack as well, or they would have already come to the aid of his and Urso's Century. Both Centuries he could see were being pressed from all sides, with the gap that had been between them as they marched now filled with Varciani warriors, roughly divided equally in facing the opposite direction, one half pressing what was the front of Urso's Century and the other half attacking what had been the rear of the First Century. There wasn't enough room in the flat area of the ravine floor for any of the Centuries to form a true *orbis* with a large cleared area in the middle, although that was essentially the formation his men were in, if only because they were now being pressed from all sides. What this meant was that there was no place to which to drag the wounded, or where they could crawl under their own power if they were able. Instead, men were lying where they had fallen, or at most had been dragged just a couple of paces behind the front line. This was an additional hazard for the men still fighting, as they were forced to keep one eye on the enemy they were facing and their footing at the same time. The gap between Porcinus' Cohort and Volusenus' was also teeming with Varciani, but there were even more because Porcinus had kept the normal spacing of at least a hundred paces between Cohorts. From his quick estimate, he thought there were at least two hundred rebel warriors, and the concentration of cavalry was the thickest in that space as well, since there was more room for the horsemen to maneuver. He was slightly relieved to see that there weren't as many mounted troops as he had initially feared, but there were still enough to cause problems. Fortunately, they had managed to weather the first assault, and he was grimly pleased that most of the men on that side of the fight had managed to thrust their javelins out far enough to keep the horses at bay. And, in fact, the lack of space was now working against the Varciani cavalry because the riders didn't have the area they needed to build their momentum back up to slam into his lines. Instead, the cavalrymen were being pressed hard by their own infantry as the rebels, understanding that they had achieved surprise and had the hated Romans on the defensive, were eagerly pushing the horses up against the bristling points of the javelins. Not surprisingly, the horses weren't willing to have these hardened iron tips poking into their flesh, and most of them were balking. Nevertheless, they were still dangerous and in some ways even more so, because as Porcinus watched, first one, then another reared up, lashing out with their hooves at the threatening Legionaries. Before he could shout out the command, he saw one of his men struck flush in the face by one of the hardened hooves that were deadly weapons on their own.

"The next time those bastards do that, step forward and gut the *cunni* with your javelins," Porcinus roared, wincing at the stab of pain the effort caused in his head.

Fortunately, his men heard the command and, an instant later, when a horse the color of cream with a rider clad in mail of a quality that marked him as a Varciani noble, rose up in response to the hard shove to its hindquarters that forced it onto the point of the javelin of the Legionary in front of it, the man responded as Porcinus had commanded. Taking a short step forward, which put him at risk to a blow from the mounted men on either side, the Legionary braved the danger to launch a hard thrust up into the tender belly of the horse. Unleashing a scream that was almost human, the horse instinctively twisted away while still on its rear legs, which wrenched the javelin from the Legionary's hand. Luckily for the man, Porcinus saw that it was one of his most veteran men, a Spaniard like himself named Artorius, the struggles of the cream-colored gelding distracted the cavalrymen on either side long enough for the Roman to leap back into the safety of the formation. Seeing that this part of his lines were intact, the Pilus Prior turned his attention back to the larger situation. Cursing as he slipped because the already muddy ground was churned up by the scrabbling of the Legionaries as the Varciani pushed in from all sides, Porcinus forced himself between the ranks, struggling to make his way back to what had been the rear of his Century. That was where he found Ovidius, who was in the process of using his neckerchief to bind up what Porcinus could see was a gaping leg wound of one of the newest men from the last replacement draft, who was staring down wide-eyed at the sight of his own blood. Porcinus knew the look, understood that the boy; Porcinus wasn't sure, but thought his name was Strabo, was on the verge of panic, and despite understanding that he couldn't spare the time, felt compelled to do something. Squatting down, he grabbed Strabo by the shoulder, squeezing it hard enough to drag his attention away from Ovidius working, the Optio's hands already slick with blood as he expertly tied the bandage off.

"It hurts like Dis, doesn't it?" Porcinus' tone was conversational, at least as much as it was possible to be under the circumstances, as if he and Strabo were sitting in a tavern, having a cup of wine.

Strabo jerked in surprise, unaware of the Centurion's presence until just then, looking up at Porcinus.

Swallowing hard, at first Strabo just nodded, then seemed to realize that this wasn't a sufficient response to his Centurion's question, replying hoarsely, "Yes, sir. It does. Will I...will I be all right?"

Porcinus had seen enough before Ovidius bound the wound to know that while it was a deep and ugly wound, and the blood was copiously flowing, it wasn't the bright red that spurted in arcs with every beat of a man's heart, allowing him to say with an assurance that didn't sound false to his ears, "Absolutely! You'll be sore for a bit, no doubt. But think of the bright side; you'll be on easy duty for at least a month. And women love a warrior with scars."

He gave the boy a grin and a man-to-man wink, and was pleased to see that his words seemed to have the effect he was hoping, Strabo giving him a weak smile back. That was all the time Porcinus could give to one man; he had a whole Cohort to worry about. Patting Ovidius, he leaned close to his Optio's ear.

"We're going to have to close this gap between us and Urso. Get the men of the second line on this side ready to follow me."

Ovidius' response was to stare at his Centurion, a clear question on his face, and without having to say anything, Porcinus understood.

"We need to worry about ourselves first," Porcinus said, as quietly as he could and still be heard over the din of the fighting going on all around them. "Until we link up with Urso, then we do the same with the rest of the Cohort; there's nothing we can do for Volusenus. They're going to have to take care of themselves until we can get organized and I get a better idea of what's going on."

Ovidius considered for only a moment, then gave an abrupt nod.

"Yes, sir. I understand, and I will obey."

Without waiting, the Optio turned and shoved his way towards what had been the rear of the formation until he reached the men of the second row, who were busy bracing their comrades of the now-front line. As Ovidius did this, Porcinus followed behind, but then moved off to the right side, stopping only to pick up a shield that had been set on its edge, somewhat out of the way in the middle of the formation. The man it belonged to was lying face-up, but covered with mud, the sign that he had fallen face first and his comrades had turned him over to check on him. But as his friends had seen and Porcinus saw now, he needed no help, the wound to his throat still seeping blood, trickling down into the mud. Because of the filth caking his face, Porcinus didn't immediately recognize the man; he would learn his identity soon enough. Provided, of course, that he survived the day as well. With that cheerful thought, he hefted the shield and moved to the far side of the second line. Right now, his sword was needed more than his leadership, and he prepared himself for what had to be done.

Somewhat surprisingly, Porcinus and the men of the second line were able to leap from behind the first line and after striking down a dozen or more Varciani, easily scattered the remaining warriors facing them. Then, they fell onto the few Varciani who had either not heard or ignored their comrades' shouts of warning and were still engaged with Urso's men at what was the front of the Second's column, the Romans killing another handful while scattering the remaining warriors. These last men scrambled to the relative safety of the throng of warriors who were still pressing Urso's Century from the direction of both slopes, as Ovidius, left in command of the First, bellowed the orders for the bulk of the Century to sidestep into the now-vacated gap. If the Varciani in that part of the fight were better led, Porcinus thought, as he pushed his way past the men of the Second looking for Urso, they could have made his men fight for this gap all over again, flowing back into the vacated space the same way water does when a finger is pulled out of it. Porcinus and the eight men with him had made it with only one man wounded, fortunately minor, yet there was a span of time, however brief, when that area was still empty of everything but bodies and the detritus of battle, as the First fought its way, one step to the side at a time, to link up with the Second. Fortunately, the Varciani seemed resigned to the idea that the two Centuries would combine. In the span of a hundred heartbeats, the First Century managed to close the gap so that at least two Centuries of the Fourth Cohort were together. In their wake, they left only those

Legionaries who were already dead, or who their comrades had seen were beyond hope; the rest were dragged, most of them howling with pain, along with their comrades who were still in the fight. There was no doubt they would be grateful, although that would come later. At the moment, however, more than one of them cursed the man who had grabbed their harness to drag them through the mud, along with their benefactor's mother and ancestors. Meanwhile, Porcinus found his Cohort's second in command at the far end of the Century, where just like Porcinus had done, Urso had picked up a shield and was adding the weight of his own sword to the fight. Unlike Porcinus, Urso had been wounded, but had either not noticed or hadn't taken the time to bind up what Porcinus could see was a deep puncture wound in his left forearm. He must have overextended himself when he was following up with his shield, Porcinus thought, stopping just behind the Centurion, knowing from experience to wait for a moment when Urso wouldn't be put in danger by being distracted. Urso's use of the shield didn't seem compromised by the wound, but Porcinus also knew that as time passed, that would change, especially if he didn't bind the wound. Although it wasn't bleeding heavily – for some reason, deep wounds like that often didn't – the toll was still cumulative. Launching a vicious underhand thrust that, despite his vision being obscured by Urso's body, Porcinus could tell had landed a probably mortal blow just from the shrill shriek that followed so closely behind it as to appear to be simultaneous, only after Urso recovered his position did Porcinus reach out and tap his second on the hip. This was something more commonly done by the man immediately behind the Centurion, usually the *signifer* of the Century, and as expected, Urso didn't turn his head, but leaned back so he could hear.

"It's Porcinus. Call a relief so we can talk."

Despite himself, Urso glanced over his shoulder in surprise at the sound of his Pilus Prior's voice, but gave a quick nod. The man immediately next to Porcinus who was directly behind Urso, heard the exchange and tapped his Centurion on his shoulder, letting him know he was ready. Making a sudden thrust with his shield, the boss punched into the body of the Varciani who had stepped into the place of the man Urso had just dispatched, and was thrown back a step. It was a maneuver that had been perfected by the Legions of Rome, and there was no fighting force in the world who did it better. Even before the warrior had finished staggering backward, Urso took a step to the side, while his relief made a step forward, at almost exactly the same time, so that even if the man across from the Romans was ready, there would have been no opportunity to exploit a gap that lasted for less than a heartbeat. The exchange accomplished, only then did Urso give any sign that he was aware of the wound, grimacing as he lowered the shield, letting it drop on the ground.

As he was doing so, Porcinus had taken off his neckerchief and before Urso could react, was already wrapping it around the Centurion's forearm, saying, "Tell me when it's tight enough."

Porcinus pulled the ends of the neckerchief until Urso gave a grunt that Porcinus took to be the answer, then quickly tied them off.

Once he was done, Porcinus indicated the area just on the other side of the first line of Legionaries, who were being pressed by what appeared to be two Varciani for every Roman, while just behind those warriors was a fairly solid mass of barbarians, waving their own weapons and shouting encouragement to the men currently engaged. One slight relief was that there was no cavalry, and again, thanks to his height, Porcinus could look across the space to the Third Century, and see that there were no horsemen there either.

"We need to drive these bastards out of this space and link up with the Third," Porcinus repeated to Urso.

Urso's reaction was slightly different, but nonetheless one that Porcinus noted, as the Centurion stiffened, his face turning hard, and Porcinus realized that he took it as a rebuke.

"That's what I was about to order, Centurion." Urso' tone was as rigid as the position of *intente* he was holding, which was one of those incongruous sights that often would cause Porcinus to burst out laughing at the oddest times.

Like now, he thought, yet he managed to refrain and, in fact, he decided not to respond in a manner that, while it would reinforce their respective roles, Porcinus knew would just further strain a relationship that was already fraught with tension.

"You're right, Urso," Porcinus said, although now he had to fight the urge to laugh even more strongly as he saw Urso's jaw drop in clear astonishment. "I know you were already aware of the need, so I apologize. It's just a habit." This time, he did smile. "And I'm a little distracted."

Now it was Urso who laughed, but he still rendered a salute.

"I understand, Centurion." Turning back to face the front, he said briskly, "Now, let's get these *cunni* sorted out so we can go save Munacius' bacon!"

He shouted this last, prompting a cheer from his men, reminding Porcinus that, his problems with Urso aside, the man was a great leader.

It was in this manner that, over the next sixth part of a watch, the Fourth Cohort closed the gaps between their Centuries to form one solid wall of wood, iron, and flesh. It would have taken longer, but Corvinus, seeing the situation and reading it in exactly the same way as his Pilus Prior, had already fought his way to Verrens and the Sixth Century. Porcinus did have to suppress the urge to quibble with Corvinus about his decision to head away from the bulk of the Cohort, but he quickly realized that it didn't really make a difference; either way he went, the rest of the Cohort would have had to move in that direction. But while Porcinus had done what was necessary to protect his Cohort, he had also moved farther away from the Second and Volusenus. Porcinus estimated that the men of his Cohort were facing perhaps a thousand warriors, pressing in from all sides. Only to what had been the right, where the slope was the steepest, was there not a press of Varciani at least four men deep. The only blessing, at least for the most part, was that there weren't archers, slingers, or javelineers flinging missiles down on their head. However, as Porcinus quickly learned, this was only partially true. Once the entire Cohort coalesced, Porcinus pushed his way all the way to the Sixth Century, not only to find Verrens, but to assess the situation at what was essentially the other end of the fight in order to see what his options were, if any. As he stopped briefly with each Century and made a quick check, his mind had begun working on forming a plan, one that would allow him to detach at least the Sixth, to clamber up the lesser of the two slopes, then move back up the draw until they were roughly above the expanse of ground that was between his Cohort and the Second. As formidable as a Roman Cohort was, two were even more so, although from what

Porcinus had seen, Volusenus was more hard-pressed than he was himself. However, that nascent plan was dashed almost immediately after he found Verrens. It was not only what he said, but the appearance of the Hastatus Posterior and the men of his Century who, unlike the other Centuries, hadn't abandoned the *testudo*. When Porcinus closed on Verrens, spotting the transverse crest, he had to crouch beneath the shelter of the shields, and there was a spattering of the hollow sound that Porcinus knew were arrows striking shields. His Hastatus Posterior was in the same posture as his men, holding a shield aloft with arms that Porcinus could clearly see trembling, telling him that the Centurion and his men had been under missile fire for some time. Further proof was provided by the half-dozen arrows protruding from the shield he had picked up from a man who no longer needed it.

"The cocksuckers have us pinned pretty well," was Verrens' comment when he was alerted of Porcinus' approach by the call of his men.

"So I see," Porcinus said before asking for the overall situation.

"Tiburinus is dead," Verrens said. That had been the Optio of the Century. "He took an arrow in the eye." Verrens gave a laugh that held no humor. "That's how we found out they had archers."

Porcinus uttered a soft curse, then made a silent prayer for the Optio, who Porcinus believed had shown a great deal of potential. Pushing that out of his mind, Porcinus began telling Verrens what he had in mind, but before he got very far, he was cut off.

"Follow me," was all Verrens said.

So, crouching and holding his own shield up, Porcinus followed Verrens to the farthest end of the formation. Before he had gone a half-dozen paces, the shield he was carrying was suddenly almost jerked from his hand, as what sounded very much like a mallet striking a block of wood assailed Porcinus' left ear so loud that it made it ring. He managed to maintain his hold, but when he glanced up at the shield, he saw the barbed head of an arrow poking through, with perhaps two inches of shaft showing, towards the lower left corner of the shield. The amount of shaft visible told Porcinus that these missiles were being fired at close range, although he wasn't willing to take the risk of peeking from behind his only protection to locate where the threat was coming from. That, Porcinus thought, as he stayed tight on

Verrens' hip, was probably how Tiburinus had died, trying to find where the bastards were, taking an arrow through the eye for his trouble. By this point, Verrens reached what had been the last rank of the last Century of the column, but had now become in essence a front line. Porcinus saw that, unlike the rest of the formation, there was only a thin screen of perhaps fifty Varciani warriors who were staying just out of the range of the javelins.

This sight puzzled Porcinus, who asked Verrens, "Why aren't they pressing us on this side too?"

"They don't have to," Verrens replied bitterly, then pointed to a spot beyond where the warriors were gathered. "See that? The bastards had this planned, no doubt about it." His tone turned to one of grudging respect. "And they did a good job of it."

Even as Verrens spoke, Porcinus was looking and he realized with a sinking heart that his Hastatus Posterior was accurate in his assessment. Not more than fifty paces behind the warriors, who even then were shouting taunts and challenges in a combination of their own tongue and camp Latin, was a pile of muddy rubble, partially blocking the ravine.

"Pluto's cock," Porcinus swore softly.

"That sums it up," Verrens agreed.

Just then, another arrow came thudding down into Verrens' shield, and both men heard a cracking sound they knew signaled that the shield was failing. Within another two or perhaps three strikes, the shield would be useless. The missile fire itself wasn't the heaviest that Porcinus had experienced, although it was just enough to keep the men of the Sixth Century holding their shields up. The only blessing was that the men on the outer edges of the formation, where they were closest to the enemy, were safe from the danger of being struck by an arrow because of the proximity to their own comrades. Porcinus also guessed that the barbarian archers were saving their arrows for the moment they hoped was coming, when the Romans made an attempt to clear the ravine.

While it was similar in conception to what the Daesitiates had attempted a year before, that time with trees instead of rocks, Porcinus could see that the Varciani were only partially successful. Probably because of the mud, he thought, yet despite the fact that the floor of the ravine wasn't completely blocked, from his examination, such as it was, it informed him that men would have to use two hands just to climb over the pile of large rocks, debris, and mud. And of course, that would spell the death of a great number of any Century he tried to send over the pile, no matter which one it was. He immediately understood Verrens was correct, that there was no way to detach a Century, and this was when he realized what he must do. As he had learned from his father, even when a decision is forced on you, hesitation only makes matters worse.

"We need to send word to Tiberius," Porcinus decided. "This has the smell of something a lot bigger than we thought."

Without waiting for an answer, he turned to make his way back forward, knowing who the best man for the job he needed done was, and not liking it a bit.

Publius Paperius was one of the most popular men, not just in his Century, the Fifth, but in the entire Cohort. He was irrepressibly cheerful, always willing to help one of his comrades, and never shirked his duties, no matter how onerous. He was also dangerously close to being an imbecile, yet he was so likable that even in the normally harsh, mocking world of the Legions, rather than make him the butt of the kind of cruel jokes men liked to play on simpler comrades, they were extremely protective of him. But Paperius had a talent that Porcinus needed, and he needed it desperately now; he was able to disappear. Although it wasn't quite literally true, Paperius' ability to move stealthily, without detection, had made him a legend, not just in the Cohort, but in the entire 8th Legion. This was the Gregarius that Porcinus sought out, even as he knew that Corvinus would argue about it, and it was hard to blame him. His father had warned him on many occasions, as Porcinus climbed through the ranks, of the peril of becoming attached to rankers, but it was a lesson that Porcinus had been forced to learn the hard way some time before. Unfortunately, it was a lesson Corvinus still had to learn, yet Porcinus hoped that this wouldn't be the occasion when his subordinate and friend learned the harsh reality, that every man was expendable, particularly when it came to the welfare of the entire Cohort. Despite the fact that Porcinus didn't need to, he still sought out Corvinus first, finding his friend conferring with his Optio, Sulpicius. Seeing Porcinus approach, Corvinus sketched a quick salute while sending Sulpicius on his way with a quiet word. As the two men talked, it would have been hard to imagine that, no more than twenty paces in any direction, there were men still fighting and dying. One small blessing was that the battle had reached its ebb, when the initial energy created by the fear, rage, and pent-up hostility of the combatants had first come exploding out of each of them, meaning that men were now more judicious in their attacks, while the defenders wasted no more energy than they were forced to. Often it was the case where, at this point in the fight, men did little more than pant like dogs in the hottest part of a summer day and curse the enemy across from them. Although it was less frenetic, Porcinus also knew that this was the most dangerous part of the battle. All it would take was a lapse by one of his men, and whether it was caused by inattentiveness or fatigue made no difference, one careless man could very quickly trigger a complete collapse.

"I need Paperius," Porcinus told Corvinus. "I need a runner to go to Tiberius."

Porcinus had half-hoped that Corvinus would simply agree, but he wasn't surprised when his friend stiffened.

"Why Paperius?" Corvinus asked, but this was neither the time nor the place to indulge his friend.

"You know very well why," Porcinus snapped. "He's the only one who we can count on slipping past these bastards."

"But they've got archers," Corvinus argued, pointing in the direction of the Sixth Century. "He'll look like a porcupine if you try and send him back that way!"

"I'm not sending him back up the ravine," Porcinus replied with a patience he didn't feel. "He's going to have to climb the slope and get past these *cunni* first."

"No," Corvinus replied immediately, the absolute worst thing he could have said under the circumstances.

"That wasn't a request, Hastatus Prior," Porcinus didn't raise his voice above what he needed to in order to be heard over the fighting. "That's an order."

Corvinus refused to be cowed, although he snapped, "Yes, sir. I understand, and will obey." Turning on his heel, he muttered, "And whatever happens to him is on your head."

Porcinus chose to ignore the comment, but he recognized that he had allowed Corvinus to become too close a friend, to the point where he forgot, even if it was temporary, that Porcinus was his superior. That, he reflected as he saw Paperius, a grin on his face despite the desperate circumstance and, making his way towards Porcinus, was something he would have to correct sooner rather than later. Especially with Barbatus in command. Paperius reached them, and there was nothing sloppy or forced in his salute.

Corvinus told Paperius, "The Pilus Prior needs you, Paperius. Go with him."

Porcinus again ignored the tone Corvinus used for these words, choosing to clap Paperius on the shoulder, saying only, "Come with me, Paperius. You're going to save the Cohort."

The sudden attack by the Sixth Century, as Porcinus had hoped, caught the Varciani by surprise. With no blast of the *cornu* to alert them, the only signal given was a shout by Porcinus, as he and Verrens, along with a handpicked group of twenty men pulled from the Fifth and the Sixth, went rushing forward. They headed directly for the knot of warriors standing in front of the landfall, and as he had hoped, caught them completely by surprise. Best of all, the assault happened so quickly that the archers higher up on the slope only had a handful of heartbeats to move their aim from the mass of Romans down in the ravine to this new threat that detached itself from the main body. Fortunately for Porcinus and the others, there was time to launch no more than a dozen arrows before the Romans were hopelessly entangled with their own comrades, and only one of those struck a fleshy target. That man was lucky and unlucky at the same time; the wound wasn't fatal, but it would cause him a great deal of embarrassment, provided he survived, as he went hobbling back to the larger group of Romans, the shaft of an arrow protruding from his left buttock. He was welcomed back to the safety of the *testudo* with laughs, although they were the kind of laughs tinged with hysteria that sometimes happened in combat. Meanwhile, Porcinus and Verrens had already struck down a number of barbarians who had tried to stand their ground. Porcinus, by virtue of his longer legs, was the first to go smashing into the Varciani, except this time he was careful to account for the slippery footing. Nevertheless, he still felt his left foot sliding as he delivered his first, underhand thrust, with the shield hard against his shoulder, thereby robbing him of some of the power. It was still enough to seriously wound the barbarian warrior and put him out of the fight and, at this point, Porcinus was less concerned with killing as many of the enemy as he could, as he was in achieving enough of a surprise that it alarmed the Varciani in the area and drew their attention in his direction. It did exactly that, drawing some of the men who were in the rear ranks of the warriors, pressing in on the flanks along each slope to this part of the fight. Porcinus had no intention of staying separated from the main group, yet he and his group of men stayed away from the rest of the Cohort long enough to inflict a good number of casualties and to achieve his main purpose. From the perspective of the rebels, it seemed as if this had been an attempt at least to examine the pile of rock and mud more closely, if not to try and scale it. In reality, it was neither; although Porcinus never looked directly to where Paperius was using the distraction to scramble up the slope before slipping into the heavy underbrush, he had seen the man signal when he reached the far side of the landfall, then turn and begin his run to Tiberius and the First. Only then did Porcinus give the command, and as quickly as they had struck, all but two of the men Porcinus had started with began a fighting withdrawal, formed into a rough circle. One of the two was the unfortunate with the wound in his nether regions, but they were also leaving a man behind, dead. The only satisfaction that his comrades could take was the fact that there were well more than twenty Varciani bodies scattered around the Roman corpse. Some of them showed signs of life, dragging themselves off to get help, or to die alone in the mud, like an animal. In the span of perhaps two hundred heartbeats, Porcinus, Verrens, and the rest were reunited with the rest of the Cohort.

"Now, we just need to hold on until Tiberius and the First show up," Porcinus said to Verrens.

"We will," Verrens assured him.

"I know you will," Porcinus replied, even as he was already moving back in the direction of his own Century.

Because of the clouds, it was impossible for Porcinus to estimate with any accuracy, but he guessed that perhaps a third of a watch had passed since the attack had begun. Making his way back to his Century, he stopped to get a report on casualties from each Centurion, and the news was disheartening. At least ten men were out of action in every Century; the Fourth was the worst off, with fifteen down, although there didn't seem to be any real threat of collapse anywhere along his lines. But while his Legionaries were holding firm, he could see they were getting fatigued. More troubling was that from what he could tell, even with as many Varciani as they had slain or wounded, there seemed to be as many warriors pushing against his men as when the attack first started. Porcinus could only assume that these men had been hiding in the hills as well, and had continued streaming down from wherever they were concealed. Well, he thought grimly, Tiberius wanted to find these bastards; now we have. He wondered briefly if Volusenus had been able to send a runner earlier than he had, but he doubted it. Besides that, from what he recalled of the map, the draw they were following to the east went deeper into the mountains before it turned back to the north, making it highly unlikely a messenger would reach the other Cohorts. The Third, the Fifth, the and Sixth were deployed about two miles to the east, while the Seventh, the Eighth, and the Ninth were about that distance, even farther east, and both of them were under the same orders to push to the north. If possible, once they penetrated into this rough country, they were to follow similar draws and ravines towards the west if they found them, in an attempt to drive the enemy into the center, where they would be surrounded. The fact that it was, at the very least, Porcinus' and Volusenus' Cohorts that were surrounded wasn't lost on Porcinus, but he refused to think about it at the moment, since it didn't help with the situation they were currently in. His fear wasn't as much that the Varciani would defeat his men as his boys would finally just wear out. By the time he returned to his Century, Ovidius had already put the Century through five rotations, which he reported to Porcinus. The most rotations that Porcinus could ever remember going through was close to twenty, but he had been a Gregarius in Parthia, and it was one thing when you were a ranker and all you had to do was to shut off your mind and remember your training. When you were responsible for almost five hundred other souls, it was another matter entirely, and it was just one more worry for the Quartus Pilus Prior as he wondered how many more his boys had in them.

Publius Paperius had no idea why he was so good at moving undetected through any kind of terrain, but it was a great source of pride to him. While he didn't spend much time thinking about it, he supposed it came from his early days, when it was just him, his sister, and mother. His father had either died or run off; over the years, Paperius heard so many different versions about the fate of the elder Paperius that he had long since given up ever knowing the truth. But that had meant that Paperius was the sole support for his family at the age of eight, and he was very proud of the fact that he had managed to do so. How he did it was another story, and was one he preferred not to think about. Still, he imagined that learning to move about the narrow streets and alleys of the Subura, sneaking into the *insulae* to steal whatever he could lay his hands on, had at least given him this skill that was so valuable now. Despite the danger of detection, Paperius moved swiftly, using every fallen log, clump of bushes, or mass of deadfall to give him cover from detection. He would dart from one form of cover to the other, while his eyes and, most importantly, his ears did their work. Only twice was he forced to go to ground, once when a small group of Varciani warriors came trotting across the slope, coming from the west, and Paperius assumed that these men were hurrying to join their comrades. The second time was when a pair of mounted barbarians, who Paperius decided had to be scouts assigned to look for the very kind of thing that he was doing, had paused for a moment just a matter of twenty paces up the slope from where he was squatting in the middle of what to the scouts looked like an impenetrable tangle of brambles and dead wood. Even with the danger, Paperius couldn't stop himself from grinning as he thought what their reaction would be if they were informed that the very thing they were looking for was happening right under their noses, almost literally. Having long since learned the danger of actually trying to watch the pair, knowing that animals of every type could sense when there were eyes on them, instead Paperius listened and was rewarded by the sounds of a man relieving himself, while the other man continued with a running commentary that had first alerted Paperius to their approach. The commentary never stopped, and as soon as the other man was finished with his business, the pair continued moving down the slope at an angle in the general direction of where the Fourth and Second Cohorts were fighting for their collective lives. Once he deemed it safe, Paperius resumed his journey, but only after checking his belt to make sure that the tablet Porcinus had handed him was still snug and secure. It was true Paperius wasn't very bright; however, he was smart enough to know that his friends were in desperate trouble, and they were all counting on him, so he resumed his quick pace. The easiest thing for him to do would have been to head west, parallel and above the ravine where his Cohort and the Second had branched off, until he came to the intersection with the main one where presumably Tiberius was still heading north. However, he somehow understood that while it would ensure that he wouldn't get lost, it would also take a great deal more time than he was willing to spare, so he moved at an angle, heading roughly northwest. His one fear in doing so was that he might come upon the other ravine at a point ahead of Tiberius and his men, which would require him to either wait for them to come to him, or force him to head south, back in their direction. As it turned out, he didn't have to worry; he had just finished picking his way around a mass of fallen trees and a bunch of boulders that looked to him as if some giant had just tossed a handful of sticks and pebbles on the ground, when he saw where the trees of the forest suddenly dropped away, and beyond the farthest edge was an open area. Despite the fact that the sun wasn't shining because of the heavy cloud cover, it was nonetheless brighter, telling Paperius that he, in all likelihood, had run into the ravine that Tiberius and the First were following. In a matter of just a moment, he discovered he was right, and to his delight, he saw the churned mass of muddy ground that looked like a black ribbon, heading to the north, the telltale sign of a large body of men. Clapping his hands in delight, Paperius was genuinely happy, sure that he would get his message to someone higher ranking and smarter than he was, and they would come to help his friends. Sliding down the slope, he quickly determined that this ravine was quite a bit wider than the one his Cohort was in, so instead of having to struggle over ground that had been chopped and churned by the feet of the First Cohort and the hooves of all the cavalry and officers, he ran closer to the slope he had just descended and was able to make good progress. He hadn't gone more than a stadia when, coming out of a gradual bend in the ravine as the watercourse that had formed it turned west, he saw that his vision had been blocked. Not more than three hundred paces ahead were the six riders that composed the rearguard of Tiberius' force. He opened his mouth to shout, then realized with some chagrin that he was too far away, so he broke into a full run, only slowing down when he was certain he could be heard. Immediately after he began shouting, the riders wheeled their mounts, and with no discernible hesitation, kicked their horses to come galloping towards Paperius. It was only then that Paperius realized that he had forgotten the daily watchword. Fortunately, none of the cavalrymen thought he was a Varciani disguised as a Legionary, wearing a dead man's uniform. After a brief conversation, the ranking man held his hand down and pulled Paperius up behind him, then turned and began at the fast trot to take his cargo to the officers. Paperius normally didn't like horses; this time, he didn't mind the ride and, in fact, he quite enjoyed it when they caught up with the boys of the First Cohort, starting with the Sixth Century, most of the men knowing him at least by sight, and he waved at them as he passed. He had done it; he had delivered the message, and Publius Paperius couldn't have been happier than at that moment.

"Do you think we should try to close the gap between us and Volusenus?"

Porcinus wasn't sure who was the most surprised; himself for asking the question or Urso for being the man he asked. It was due to the fact that, during this fight at least, Porcinus had put away his antipathy and suspicion of his Pilus Posterior, acknowledging to himself that he was, in fact, an extremely experienced Centurion. And at this moment, Porcinus needed Urso because he wasn't sure what to do. It was as if there were two separate battles going on, except now they were separated by more than three hundred paces. This was the result of two events; the first being that both Cohorts did essentially the same thing in closing the gaps between them to form one larger unit. Unfortunately, what Porcinus could now see was that he and Volusenus had gone in opposite directions in collapsing their Cohorts. Although Porcinus had taken the First to link up to the Second, and then the Third, it appeared very much as if Volusenus had, in essence, ordered his Centurions to come to him, meaning that now the two Cohorts and their respective problems were compounded by the extra distance between them. Once he recovered from his clear surprise, Urso considered the question with what looked to Porcinus like a great deal of care. Before he answered, he stood on a shield, looking to the east in the direction of the Second Cohort, once again oblivious to the fact that there were men trying to kill each other twenty paces in two directions, and that he was making himself a tempting target. However, for the reasons Porcinus assumed was to keep his men pinned down and not going for help, none of the archers that were just two hundred paces away, down by the Sixth Cohort, had made their way to this part of the fight. At least, he thought, not yet, although there was also the hope that was growing stronger that the Varciani archers were either conserving or, better yet, had run out of arrows. Urso used Porcinus' shoulder to steady himself as he stretched up on his toes, still staring across the little more than a quarter mile of ground between the two Cohorts.

Finally, he hopped down to the ground and shook his head, saying, "If anything, he should come to us. We're the ones closest to Tiberius and the First."

Porcinus made no attempt to hide his relief.

"That's what I thought as well," he replied to Urso. "In fact, I've been expecting him to do that very thing. But I can't see the sense in us fighting our way to him, just to have Tiberius either come to us, or order us to come to him."

"Not much chance of that," Urso commented. "We're stuck in this ravine like a cork in a bottle." He shook his head again, with a frown on his face. "No, I think we either have to stay put. Or," he paused before he looked Porcinus directly in the eye, "we fight our way out of here and go to Tiberius on our own."

"And leave the Second?" Porcinus asked, although, being completely truthful with himself, he had thought of this. "No," he said, "we're not going to do that."

"With all due respect, Pilus Prior," Urso said as quietly as he could get away with, "if we stay here, we're just going to get worn down. I'm surprised there hasn't been a breakthrough somewhere along our lines yet."

This, Porcinus knew, was nothing more than the truth; a bitter one, to be sure, but it was only slightly more unpleasant because it was uttered by Urso.

"I know," he finally replied wearily.

Porcinus took off his helmet and was going to mop his brow with his neckerchief before he remembered that it was tied around his counterpart's forearm. Sighing, the best he could do was to lean down to use a corner of his tunic to absorb the sweat, before he squeezed the moisture out of the liner and put the helmet back on. As he was doing so, Urso had been watching the men of his Century, and he lifted the bone whistle attached to the lanyard around his neck to give a long, sharp blast, his signal for the men of the front two lines to switch places.

"How many is that for you?" Porcinus asked.

Urso didn't need more than that, answering flatly, "Nine."

Amid the noise, the chaos, the shouts, curses, and cries of men who were fighting, killing, and dying, Porcinus tried to shut it all out and think. As he saw it, there was no right answer to be had; if he gave the order to link up with the Second, it would be the men of his Century who would bear the brunt of the fighting as they cut and hacked their way through the mass of warriors between the Fourth and the Second, and as Urso had pointed out, it would put both Cohorts farther east in the event Tiberius came to their aid. If he chose to stand fast, Urso's answer told him that he had perhaps a third of a watch, at most, before his men would simply be too exhausted to hold off these Varciani. He had determined some time before that not only were those slain enemy warriors being replaced by new arrivals in the form of small bands of combatants answering what was either a summons or the sounds of battle, Tiberius' scouts had woefully underestimated the numbers of the Varciani.

"Unless all seven thousand are here," Porcinus muttered under his breath.

Urso's head turned, his flat, black eyes searching his Pilus Prior's face, but when Porcinus looked up, he turned his attention back to his men. Porcinus knew he needed to get back to his own Century; as much as he trusted Ovidius, his boys needed him. He had lost count of how many times he had traveled back and forth from the far end where Verrens and his Century had at least been able to drop their shields now that the rain of arrows had almost completely stopped. He tried to calculate how long Paperius had been gone; certainly less than a third of a watch, not that the knowledge helped any. There were too many things he didn't know for him to have anything more than a wild guess about when he and his men would hear the welcome sound of the *cornu*, telling him that Tiberius was on the way. Shaking his head, he left Urso without saying anything more, intent on joining his Century.

As it turned out, Publius Paperius didn't ever see Tiberius. The Legate, along with the detachment of cavalry and the Tribunes, had pushed ahead of the vanguard to scout what looked to be a likely spot for an enemy ambush. Consequently, it was to Barbatus that the cavalry trooper took Paperius, where the men of the First Cohort had come to a halt, letting the Legionary slide off the horse before turning and trotting back to his spot in the rearguard. Barbatus eyed the Gregarius with suspicion, and if the truth were known, Paperius was a bit nervous himself, yet his voice was firm as he rendered his salute.

Once it was returned, Paperius said, "I was sent here by Pilus Prior Porcinus, sir. The Fourth and the Second are in, well, they're in a bit of a fight."

Barbatus had stepped to the side, while the men of the Cohort stood, waiting for the return of the Legate, and the Primus Pilus' expression was one that was hard for a man like Paperius to decipher.

"A bit of a fight?" Barbatus repeated, his lip curling up. "I find that hard to believe. We haven't seen anything more than some tracks."

"That might be because all those bastards are over there trying to kill us," Paperius replied helpfully, then remembered, "sir."

Then, Paperius remembered the tablet, quickly withdrawing and handing it to Barbatus. Paperius was puzzled by this new Primus Pilus' behavior, who acted as if the tablet had been dipped in *cac* before being handed to him. Because Paperius had made it a practice to avoid contact with Centurions of a certain rank; he could count the number of times he had been this close to any Primus Pilus on one hand and have fingers left over, he just ascribed Barbatus' attitude to one of the many odd habits of superior officers. Consequently, like good rankers everywhere, he quickly adopted the position of *intente*, and started staring at a spot above Barbatus' head. Meanwhile, Barbatus eyed Paperius up and down, his frown deepening as he opened the tablet and began reading. Paperius wasn't sure, but he thought he heard his Primus Pilus suddenly take in a breath, the way one does when surprised by something, which Paperius supposed was understandable. Barbatus read the message not once, but twice, then snapped the tablet shut, his expression again unreadable.

"Wait here," he ordered Paperius, who gave the only acceptable answer, keeping his eyes above the transverse crest of the Primus Pilus.

Spinning on his heel, Barbatus walked quickly over to the First Century, but while Paperius didn't move his head, like any veteran, he had developed the ability to observe actions at the edge of his vision. And he was puzzled why a Primus Pilus of a Legion would pull a Gregarius out of the ranks of the First Cohort and take him on the far side of the formation from Paperius so Paperius' view of the pair was now blocked. His mind wasn't his best asset, so he had reached no firm conclusion when Barbatus and the other man came striding from where they had been conferring to come back to stand before Paperius, who was still at *intente*.

"This is Gregarius Philo," Barbatus said curtly. "He'll go back with you to ascertain exactly what the situation is, and determine if matters are as your Pilus Prior says they are, or if he's being a bit...dramatic."

Only then did Paperius drop his gaze to look directly in Barbatus' eyes, his astonishment and alarm overriding the discipline instilled in him. When his eyes met Barbatus', the Primus Pilus' face flushed, confusing Paperius even more; the thought that flashed through the

Gregarius' mind was, why does he look guilty, like he's done something wrong? Perhaps if Publius Paperius had been smarter, he would at the very least have been on his guard and suspicious enough to be alert to what was about to happen to him, but between his shortcomings and the obedience drilled into him from his first day as a *tiro*, his fate was sealed.

Still confused, all he could manage was a salute and a weak, "I understand, Primus Pilus, and I will obey."

For a long moment, Barbatus said nothing, just stared into Paperius' eyes, making the Gregarius feel as if the Primus Pilus were trying to probe his thoughts.

Finally, he gave another curt nod, and said only, "Very well. Now, go with Philo. You need to guide him back to your Cohort so he can see for himself. Then he'll report back to me and we'll decide then."

With that, Barbatus turned away and walked back to the front of the Cohort, sending a clear sign of dismissal.

"Come on, then," the Gregarius introduced as Philo said.

Without waiting to see if he was obeyed, Philo began moving at a quick trot back down the column, in the direction of the Sixth Century and the way back to the Fourth.

Sighing, Paperius turned to follow, calling out, "Wait! You don't know the way."

Retracing their steps, nothing was said between the men for some time, but Paperius kept glancing over his shoulder at the man following him.

Finally, Philo had enough and, in between gasping breaths, snarled, "What the fuck are you looking at?"

Paperius wasn't prepared for this kind of hostility, so he hurried to explain.

"Nothing! I mean…it's just that I've never seen you before."

Philo's expression didn't change, although his tone softened fractionally as he explained, "That's because I'm new. To the Cohort, that is," he added quickly, but he kept his eyes ahead of him, refusing to look Paperius in the eyes. "But I've been around. I'm no *tiro*," he gave a breathless laugh that was humorless. What Paperius didn't hear was Philo's muttered, "Believe me, I've been around."

Satisfied for the moment, Paperius returned his attention to the path; he was retracing his steps, something he normally wouldn't have done, but time was even more pressing now that the Primus Pilus had insisted that this Philo come along. However, Publius Paperius was naturally a friendly sort, so it wasn't long before he resumed his questions. They had just stopped for a quick breather, Philo following Paperius' example of dropping down at the base of a tree that was surrounded by small shrubbery.

"So what Legion did you come from?" he asked Philo.

Again, Philo didn't look at Paperius, choosing instead to stare off to the east in the direction they were headed.

For a moment, Paperius thought Philo hadn't heard the question, then the other man answered, "No Legion. I'm from the Praetorians."

Even Paperius could hear the pride in the man's voice as he said this; Paperius' reaction was decidedly different. He turned his head to examine the man more fully, a sense of caution suddenly flooding through him. What he saw didn't comfort him. Philo, still resolutely looking in the other direction, was obviously a tough man, with a nose that had clearly been broken more than once, and a heavy jaw that looked as if it always needed to be shaved. Instinctively, Paperius glanced down to look at Philo's hands, and the sight of the scarred and misshapen knuckles confirmed what he was beginning to believe. Philo reminded him of the kind of tough man that the leaders of the *collegia* gangs who controlled the back alleys and shady streets of Rome used as muscle. There was no doubt these men were hard men, and it was true when Paperius joined the Legions, they served as his example of what a tough man looked and acted like. But his years under the standard had taught him the truth, and in his ten years with the 8th, he had seen more than one of these supposedly tough men show up full of loud talk and boasts of all the battles they had already won, only to break down in the middle of a fight against men who weren't just scared bakers and tanners, but full-fledged warriors.

"So what's it like in the Praetorians?" Paperius tried to make it sound as casual as he could, and he was thankful that Philo didn't seem to hear the catch in his voice. "Is it good duty?"

Philo gave a grunting laugh, understanding what Paperius meant by "good duty."

"Well, there's none of this marching about and bending your fucking back like a slave to dig a ditch," he allowed. "There's women and wine, and plenty of both." Philo thought a moment, then finished, "So, yes. I suppose it is good duty."

"This must be a big change," Paperius laughed, but Philo didn't share in his amusement.

"You have no idea," he replied.

Then he stood, and looked down at Paperius.

"Shouldn't we be going?"

Paperius gave a start, feeling guilty that this man had to remind him. In answer, he gave a quick nod, then resumed leading the way. Philo followed behind, staring at the man's back, feeling regretful about what he was going to do. That wouldn't stop him, but it was a shame nonetheless; this Paperius seemed to be a really good sort.

The pair heard the sounds of the fighting when Paperius estimated they were still almost a half-mile away.

Turning to Philo, he said in a tone that the Praetorian hadn't heard from him before in the short time they had known each other, "Now we slow down. And we keep our eyes open. It won't do anyone any good if we get caught by a patrol this close."

Philo gave a simple nod in answer, and Paperius turned back to scan the wooded slope. He didn't see Philo reach down and quietly draw his *pugio* partway out of the scabbard, as if checking to make sure it would slide out easily. Moving in a crouch, Philo followed Paperius as the Gregarius essentially repeated the performance that had enabled him to complete the first part of his task. Only once were they forced to dive for cover, when Paperius hissed a warning as what he could tell was the same pair of mounted warriors he had hidden from the first time, mainly because he recognized the voice of the man who had been talking earlier, passed by. Again, despite the circumstances, Paperius had to stifle a grin as the pair crossed in front of the two Romans, this time much closer than the first time, as he thought that it sounded very much like the Varciani had never stopped talking. Poor bastard, he thought, feeling sympathy for the other warrior who had to endure whatever this man was chattering about. Allowing them to pass, only when they disappeared through the trees did Paperius stand, beckoning to Philo as he began moving down the slope. The sounds of battle were clear now, to the point where the pair could hear the individual shouts of men, both in their own tongue and in the language of the barbarians, yet they were still unable to see anything. Finally, after another hundred paces, Paperius caught a glimpse through the trees, and was relieved to see that he had maneuvered the pair past the rubble blocking the ravine; he had no desire to scramble over that. Motioning to Philo, Paperius began creeping even more slowly, until he reached a point perhaps fifty paces up the slope from the bottom of the ravine, and directly across from what he recognized was the Sixth Century. They were close enough now that he could distinguish faces, and he saw Verrens, engaged at that moment with a Varciani warrior armed with a spear, his own blade flashing in quick but brutal movements.

"Now what?" Philo's voice startled Paperius, who had become absorbed watching the Centurion waging his own private battle.

Paperius considered for a moment, then pointed to a spot.

"See there? Right where those bodies are?"

Philo followed Paperius' finger, and he did indeed see what Paperius was indicating. Because of one of those quirks of battle, where either one or two Legionaries had been particularly deadly, or more likely because the Varciani had dragged these fallen men out of the way, then the flow of the fighting had seen a slight shift in position that coalesced around the pile, there was a gap in the warriors pressing against the Sixth Century. It wasn't much, a space perhaps ten paces wide, and the footing would be tricky in the extreme as they clambered over the bodies to make the safety of the formation, yet although Philo was much less experienced in this kind of fighting, he saw that Paperius had picked the best spot.

"Yes," Philo said softly, giving a nod. "I see."

Paperius gave him a grin, then slapped him on the shoulder as he rose from his crouch.

"Follow me," he said.

He had no chance, as one of the hands Paperius had examined earlier brutally clamped over his mouth. There was a searing, but thankfully very brief, pain in his neck, followed quickly by...nothing. Dropping the body back behind the bush that they had used as cover,

Philo gave a brief glance down at his hands, and began wiping his hands before stopping, realizing it would help his story.

"I'm sorry," he said quietly to the corpse of Paperius, his face turned up to the sky, wearing that surprised look like so many of Philo's victims had, the wide gash in his throat looking like a gruesome second mouth, still leaking blood.

The fact was that Philo was sorry; in the short time that he knew the man, he had liked Paperius. But orders were orders, so there wasn't any use dwelling on the injustice of it all. Squaring his shoulders, he took a deep breath, and made himself ready.

"Man coming in!"

Verrens, having just dispatched the Varciani with the spear that the now-dead Paperius had been watching him fight, whirled around, looking to his left towards the end of his Century. At first, he didn't see anything, then his eye was caught by a darting movement at the very base of the slope, just a few paces behind the last line of enemy warriors. Whoever it was moved so fast that it was impossible for Verrens to catch more than a glimpse, but it was enough to see that it was a Legionary. Then the man was lost from view, blocked by the mob of barbarian warriors, and Verrens saw some of the Varciani near their rear suddenly turn about. This was immediately followed by a roar that reverberated above the rest of the noise of the fighting, as those warriors shouted in alarm, presumably from the actions of Verrens' men to chop a path for the incoming Legionary. Verrens began pushing his way to the rear of the formation; before he had taken more than two steps, he heard answering shouts, these in his own language that told him that at the very least his men were aware and doing something to protect this incoming messenger. He had been informed by Porcinus that the Pilus Prior sent Paperius for help, and that was who he expected to see, yet when he reached the small knot of men who were surrounding a figure seated on the ground, he was in for a surprise. As his men parted, Verrens stared down at the panting man, confused for a moment; he didn't recognize this man, was sure he had never seen him before, and his initial thought was that this was a Varciani dressed in a dead Legionary's uniform.

However, before he could say anything, one of his men said, "He knew the watchword, sir. Besides, I recognize him. He's one of the new men in the First Cohort."

While this assuaged Verrens' concern about the chances of the man being a spy, it also puzzled him; why would Tiberius, or Barbatus for that matter, send a new man? And more importantly, where was Paperius? By this point, the new arrival had climbed to his feet, and while the salute he rendered was proper, there was something in the man's manner Verrens didn't care for. Verrens shook that off; this wasn't the time or place to worry about the man's deportment.

"You bring a message from Tiberius?" Verrens demanded.

Philo hesitated, but it was so brief that Verrens didn't notice.

"Yes, sir," Philo replied.

"Good. Follow me," Verrens said curtly, then turned about. Calling over his shoulder, he said, "Stay close to me. We've got a ways to go to get to the Pilus Prior."

As it turned out, they didn't have to go as far as Verrens assumed. Porcinus had started on another of his checks on the status of the other Centuries, and resultantly was with Munacius and the Third when Verrens called his name. He had to shout it three times before Porcinus heard, the tall Roman finally turning to watch Verrens and Philo approach. Movement was even more difficult, between the bodies of the wounded who had crawled to the middle of the formation, the pile of cracked and ruined shields, broken swords, and bent javelins, items of each scattered about. Finally, after weaving their way through, Verrens and Philo stood in front of Porcinus.

"Gregarius Philo, reporting to…."

"We can skip the formalities, Philo," Porcinus cut him off, examining the man wearily, while Philo silently did the same out of the corner of his vision now that he had the time, much as Paperius had with Barbatus.

What Philo saw was a tall, rangy, blood-spattered Centurion, although from what Philo could see, none of the blood was his own.

"What's your report? Is Tiberius on his way?"

Philo hesitated, but again, it was only a brief one. Except Porcinus *did* notice, and Philo saw the other man's eyes narrow.

"Actually, er, no, sir," Philo replied. "In fact, I come from Primus Pilus Barbatus. He commands that you disengage and come to our aid immediately. We're also under attack, and the Legate has either been isolated and is under attack himself, or has been killed. The Primus Pilus says that the only way he can break out is with the help of your Cohort."

Porcinus suddenly staggered, as if taking a physical blow, but Verrens was no less affected, so he couldn't help steady his Pilus Prior.

"What?" he gasped. "Repeat your orders!" he snapped.

Philo repeated what Barbatus had instructed him to say, and he was prepared when Porcinus held his hand out.

"Let me see the written orders," he demanded.

Philo regretfully shook his head, telling Porcinus another lie he had been instructed to give to the Pilus Prior by Barbatus, "I'm sorry, sir, but the Primus Pilus is out of tablets. That's why he sent me personally. We've served together a long time, and he knows I can be trusted."

The revelation that Philo was from the Praetorian Guard would have meant more to Porcinus, and might have alerted him, but his mental state was already shaken.

"Where's Paperius?" Verrens was the one who asked the question.

"He's dead," Philo said. "Just before we got here, we were surprised by a mounted patrol. He held them off and allowed me to make it the rest of the way."

That made Porcinus look sharply at Philo; more than the news that Philo was a Praetorian, this jarred him. He knew Paperius well, meaning that he had a hard time believing that the most reliable messenger would allow himself to be surprised. Philo saw the look, and he felt a trickle of sweat colder than the rest that covered his body run down his back.

Thinking quickly, he hurried on, "Actually, sir, it was probably my fault. I was following him, and they came up from behind and probably saw me." He managed to look regretful, which was only partially feigned as he finished, "I'm sorry, sir. He seemed like a good man."

"He was, but why would he do that? Why would he have sacrificed himself to save a man he didn't know when he knew how important this was? Didn't he hear the message as well? He could have given it to me."

Porcinus was still suspicious, but Philo merely gave a shrug. Porcinus recognized the gesture, the universal sign of a ranker who has run out of answers. Consequently, he dropped what was ultimately an unimportant line of questioning. Or, at least, so he believed at the time.

"How are we supposed to do that?"

It was not only a sensible question, Porcinus knew; the fact that it came from Urso was even more comforting, albeit in a very odd way. Porcinus had called a meeting of the Pili Priores, and they were now all huddled in a crouching knot in the midst of the Third Century, recognizing that the sight of all six transverse crests in one place was liable to cause a sudden surge in the fury of the Varciani attack. If they managed to penetrate and strike down even two or three Centurions, the Cohort would be in even more trouble than they already were. As the rankers around them held the Varciani at bay, Porcinus considered Urso's question, glancing around at the other faces, hoping that they might have some idea. Unfortunately, they all had essentially the same expression on their faces.

This forced Porcinus' hand, but all he could do was shake his head and say, "I really don't know." He paused, then continued with a grimace, "Other than fight our way step by step."

"But what about that pile of *cac* blocking the way? Granted, it's not across the whole ravine, but we'd have to squeeze down to maybe three men across. Not only would that take forever, if they still have arrows that they've been saving, a lot of men are going to get picked off," Verrens pointed out.

Considering his Century had already borne the brunt of the missiles, Porcinus found it hard to blame him for being so concerned; besides, what he was saying was true. When Porcinus led the sortie out to give Paperius time to slip away, he had been able to examine the rubble pile and, in his opinion, Verrens was being optimistic. There was space for perhaps two men side by side to pass the pile while still keeping their shields up to protect them from any arrows.

However, his gut instinct told him that the Varciani had exhausted their supply of missiles, and he asked Verrens, "When's the last time they've loosed any at you?"

"It's been a while," Verrens said grudgingly, then insisted, "but that could be because they're waiting for us to do what we're talking about doing!"

That, Porcinus knew, he couldn't argue.

"What about the wounded?" Corvinus asked, and this was yet another consideration.

Even as Porcinus said the words, he hated himself for them, knowing that his Centurions would like it even less, "Anyone who can't keep up gets left behind."

As he expected, this created a chorus of objections. Even as they protested, above the other noises came a sharp scream of pain.

"Glaxus is down!"

Munacius swore bitterly, risking standing to look in the direction of Glaxus' spot in the formation.

"Pluto's cock, it's his leg. He can barely walk."

Munacius turned to look accusingly at Porcinus.

"He's one of my best! We can't leave him behind."

Porcinus sighed, rubbing his face for what he was sure was the hundredth time.

"Gaius, we can't leave anyone behind," Corvinus said softly.

Despite the fact that, no matter what their relationship was during off-duty hours, Corvinus had no business addressing him by his praenomen, Porcinus also knew Corvinus was right. Even if his Cohort survived this day, it would be gutted and shattered, the survivors racked with the guilt that came from leaving comrades behind who still had a breath of life in them. That was when it came to him, with utter clarity, and it shocked him so much that he stood upright.

"That's what he wants," Porcinus gasped. "That *cunnus* is trying to destroy this Cohort!"

"Who?" Urso was clearly confused. "Tiberius? Nonsense! Why would he want to do that?"

"Not Tiberius." Porcinus shook his head as the sick certainty threatened to make his stomach lurch and eject whatever was in it. "Barbatus."

In that moment, he realized that he hadn't told the others the full contents of Philo's message, that, according to Barbatus, Tiberius was either in mortal danger or already dead. Initially he hadn't wanted to pass news that he knew would, if not cause a panic among the rankers, at the very least increase their worry to the point it put them one step closer to it. He knew from experience that, especially in this case where men were just four or five paces away, the rankers on relief holding onto the leathers of the man in front of them would be listening intently to everything the Centurions said. Anything to have a hint of what their future held, particularly when it was possibly so short. Despite this, Porcinus went ahead and told them the rest of the story that Philo had relayed, about Tiberius and the possibility that he was dead. He saw Corvinus shoot a glance over to Verrens, who he knew was the man to bring Philo to Porcinus. In turn, Verrens looked to Porcinus, and the Pilus Prior gave a curt nod. Although he had initially told Verrens not to divulge what Philo had said, he now realized that not only did his Centurions have the right to know, he also was certain of one thing, that this was a ruse on the part of Barbatus. Verrens confirmed what Porcinus said, and there were bitter curses all around.

"But I'm sure that Barbatus is lying. At least," he amended, "the part about Tiberius. They may be under attack, but I don't believe that he's missing, or dead, for that matter."

"But why would he lie?" Pacuvius asked. Before Porcinus could answer, someone else provided the answer.

"Because of Porcinus here," Urso said, yet so softly he was forced to repeat it when Munacius said he couldn't hear.

Porcinus stared hard at Urso, his mind spinning with the import of his Pilus Posterior's words, before looking directly at Corvinus, who refused to meet his gaze. Neither Munacius nor Pacuvius seemed to have any understanding of what was happening, while Verrens looked only slightly less puzzled. Has Corvinus betrayed me? he thought bitterly. Why would he tell the man I trust the least about what happened with Barbatus? That, he realized in the moment, was a jug that was broken and couldn't be mended, so he forced himself to put that consideration away. He began to open his mouth, but he was stopped, again by Urso.

"Our Primus Pilus is from the Praetorian Guard," Urso explained. "And where is the Praetorian Guard located?"

"In Rome." Munacius supplied the answer, a slow look of dawning on his face.

"Exactly," Urso confirmed. "And it appears that our Pilus Prior has aroused the ire of someone very powerful."

"But why Porcinus?" Pacuvius asked, still puzzled.

Urso turned and gave Pacuvius a long, level look, and whatever he silently communicated was enough.

"Ah." Pacuvius nodded, then turned to Porcinus. "This is somehow about your unc...I mean, your father, isn't it?"

Now it was Porcinus' turn to sigh, wondering how much he should divulge, then quickly decided he owed these men the truth. A partial truth at least.

"Yes," he answered at last, eliciting a groan from one of the others; he didn't know which.

"Wait," Verrens interjected. "So you're saying that this *cunnus* is willing to drop us in the *cac* just because Augustus or someone close to him is still angry with Prefect Pullus?" He shook his head. "Sorry, but there has to be more to it than that."

"Does it really matter right now?" This came from Corvinus, who turned to look at Porcinus for the first time since Urso's revelation. "All that matters at the moment is what we need to do, not why it's happening."

There was no more argument after that, each Centurion tacitly accepting this as fact. Once more, they all turned to Porcinus, who was furiously thinking, only half-listening to the back and forth.

Finally, he said, "The way I see it, either way we go, we're fucked. I don't like the idea of leaving the Second any more than you do. But," he took a deep breath, and continued with a grimace, hating the bitter taste of the words, "if Barbatus is telling the truth, losing the First Cohort and the Legate at the same time is a shame we'll never be able to live with. At least, I won't. Anyone disagree?"

He was prepared for some objection, and even more ready to override their protest, yet he was somewhat relieved to see that the other five Centurions seemed to accept this.

"Fine," he said at last. "We're going to fight our way to the First. Now," he asked with a bitter chuckle, "anyone have any idea how we're going to do it and still have more than a Century left?"

He had meant it as a rhetorical question, but Corvinus spoke up.

"I do," he said calmly. "I don't know if it will work, but I do have an idea."

As plans went, it was simple, yet as the men of the Fourth Cohort discovered, it was effective. It required Verrens and his Century to detach itself from the other five Centuries, whereupon they sidestepped back to the west, until they reached the base of the muddy rubble. Their initial role was to act as bait, and for perhaps the first time that day, the gods rewarded the men of the Fourth Cohort in the form of a complete absence of missile fire. Just as Porcinus had hoped, the Varciani had run out of arrows. Once it became obvious that the Varciani weren't simply withholding their arrow fire, the Sixth shifted its formation to form a solid line of men, only three deep instead of the more standard eight or ten, but this was done in order to provide other men for what was needed. Verrens formed them up so the line curved slightly, to prevent any Varciani from getting behind the men who would be guarding their comrades of the working party. The rest of Verrens' Century worked frantically, hampered by the lack of tools, to widen the gap in the rubble pile to a point where a full Century could march through it. Not surprisingly, the Varciani weren't willing to let this effort go unmolested, and one of the warriors, probably a noble, in that area of the fight, rallied a force of perhaps fifty men to throw themselves at the Romans who were defending their comrades. This was when the second piece of Corvinus' plan went into effect, as the men of his Fifth Century, now at what was the end of the Fourth's battle line, suddenly launched first one, then another volley of javelins at the barbarians, who were, at that moment, running into the now-vacated space where the Sixth had been, leaving behind dozens of bodies, mostly Varciani, but a distressingly large number of Romans as well. The javelins were scrounged from all the other Centuries, passed down through the compact formation, and as they so often did, proved devastatingly effective. This was particularly true because Corvinus waited until the last possible moment to give the command, so that a large number of Varciani had their backs turned to his men as they prepared to fall on Verrens' Century. They had done so secure in the knowledge that their own comrades would wrap around the end of Corvinus' Century now that it was the last one in the Cohort and protect their rear. But while they did keep Corvinus and his men from falling on them from behind with swords, they were completely unprepared for the volley of the heavy, weighted missiles arcing through the air to slice down into them with a terrific impact. Enough javelins had been gathered for four volleys from Corvinus, yet he quickly saw that any more than two would be wasted, as the Varciani charge at Verrens' men was shattered almost before it got started. The survivors of that group were forced back into the main body of the Varciani, retreating to the relative safety provided by their comrades, who were still pressing the sides of the Roman formation. They did so grudgingly, shaking their weapons and shouting curses at the men of Corvinus' Century, who jeered and hurled their own insults. By this point in the battle, the action was desultory, most men on both sides having expended most of their energy staying alive. There was a ripple of motion up and down the entire length of both sides of the Fourth's battle lines, as a Varciani would summon the energy to launch an attack against the Roman across from him, while the men around him only half-heartedly moved with him in support.

Porcinus, back in his spot with the First Century, wasn't sure if the sounds of the fighting had actually subsided, or he had just become so accustomed to them he barely noticed, although he suspected it was a little of both. At that moment, however, his attention was riveted on the sight of the Second Cohort, and he realized with a peculiar mix of emotions that whoever was commanding this Varciani attack had seemed to realize that his only hope of destroying at least one Cohort was to concentrate his forces on one of them. From what Porcinus could see, that was the Second, although the Varciani commander wasn't leaving the Fourth completely unmolested. To Porcinus, it appeared that he was leaving just enough men surrounding the Fourth to keep them occupied, but not enough to exploit a breakthrough. While this made the coming ordeal facing the Fourth easier, Porcinus couldn't suppress the feeling of guilt at the idea of leaving Volusenus and his men to their collective fate. His hope was that he and his men could extract themselves, go to the aid of the First, then either return to rescue the Second, or what seemed more likely, that mounted couriers would be sent galloping to the east to order the other Cohorts to come to the rescue of the Second. For all Porcinus knew, Barbatus had already done that very thing, yet somehow, he doubted it. If he were being brutally honest with himself, he didn't believe for a moment that Tiberius was either missing or dead, or that the First was in as much trouble as this Philo said. It wasn't lost on Porcinus that he had never seen Philo before, telling him that he was one of Barbatus' Praetorians. He was also worried about Paperius; something about Philo's story just didn't add up to him, but he also had more important matters to worry about. Turning away from the Second Cohort, he actually closed his eyes for a moment, trying to banish what he hoped wouldn't be the last image of the Second from being burned into his mind. Their normally ordered ranks had become hopelessly muddled, and while he wasn't sure, it had looked to Porcinus like the Varciani had managed to penetrate the Second's formation to a point where it appeared that there were only perhaps three or four men keeping the two forces of warriors from meeting and cutting the Cohort in half. If that happened, Porcinus knew that the Second would be doomed, as it could then be chopped up piecemeal. Regardless of this looming possibility, it wasn't his most immediate problem, and when he opened his eyes, he was ready to command his Cohort.

Painstakingly, one step to the side at a time, the five Centuries of the Fourth Cohort moved slowly to link up with Verrens and his men, who were still arrayed in their defensive formation, now augmented by the men who had essentially pulled and dragged the largest rocks from the rubble pile blocking the way. The latter Legionaries were easy to spot because they were uniformly filthy, and they had taken spots at the rear of the formation. As difficult as moving in this manner was, it was made even more so because a large number of otherwise healthy men had become noncombatants as they helped those wounded comrades who couldn't move under their own power. These unfortunates were crammed into the center of the formation, each Century taking care of its own wounded, except for the Third, who had more casualties than the other Centuries and not enough men still standing to both fight and help their wounded. Their plight was such that men from the Second had to be sent to help with their wounded comrades. In practical terms, what this meant was that in the Second and Third Centuries, there was only the man on the outside of the formation, with one comrade behind him, also sidestepping while holding the harness of the man in front. It was a cumbersome, slow method of movement, but there was no avoiding it, at least until such time that Porcinus deemed it to be safe to resume a more normal mode of march.

"One...two...one...two..."

Like some huge, multi-legged beast, the compact formation that had become the Fourth Cohort slowly made its way back to the west. They reached the men of the Sixth Century who, instead of folding themselves back into the formation in their normal spot, adjusted their position so that they could screen the rest of the Cohort more effectively. This had been prearranged; the Sixth would maintain its position until the entire Cohort had made it through the choke point, then they would fall into a spot in front of the First. It was unusual, but it was the best that the combined minds of the Centurions could come up with. When the Fourth began their maneuver, there was a flurry of renewed assaults up and down the now-moving line, as the Varciani threw themselves at the Legionaries, who kept their shields up in the first position, elbows locked in the hollow just above their hipbones. Inevitably, some of those attacks were successful, as a man became momentarily distracted by being forced to step over the body of friend or foe who had already been struck down, or in one or two cases, sweat suddenly blinded a man. There would be a blur of motion from among the milling warriors as one of them spotted an opening, followed by a sharp cry and curses from the Romans around the unfortunate man. If the victim was lucky, he was able to take a staggering step out of the front line in order for his relief to take his spot, then join the mass of wounded in the middle of the formation. That was what usually happened; unfortunately, some men lost their balance, falling amid the shuffling feet of their comrades. This was the most dangerous moment, if the man next to him wasn't alert and stepped over his fallen comrade or, more commonly, got his own feet tangled up as he tried to make a quick check on a comrade who was almost always a friend. This only happened twice, once on one side of the formation with the Second Century, and once on the other with the Fourth. Then, for several agonizing moments, the entire Cohort was forced to stop as the men in that area fought desperately to blunt the savage incursions of Varciani who had spotted their chance to break the Roman formation. Both attacks were turned back, and the progress resumed, as the Centurions called out the same, monotonous rhythm. Nevertheless, as tired as the men of the Fourth were, their superior training, conditioning, and, most importantly, discipline began showing now, as the Varciani attempt to stop their progress became more desperate. The Fifth, then Fourth, Third, and Second Centuries managed to make it through the choke point without having to alter their formation. In the beginning of this maneuver, some Varciani attempted to continue their pressure by scrambling up the muddy pile of rocks and debris to get on the other side, when the final wrinkle of what Corvinus had proposed made itself known. Being the first through the gap, the Fifth hurried and got into a position across the width of the ravine floor, basically paralleling the rubble pile, but within javelin range. The moment the first of the more intrepid Varciani appeared at the top of the pile, a dozen missiles went hurtling toward them, wiping them from the pile as if they had never been there. It only took two more such volleys to convince even the most ardent warrior that only death waited for them on the other side, leaving them to shout their frustration as Porcinus' Cohort made its way to what would be the safety on the other side of the rubble. Finally, Porcinus' Century passed through the gap, while Verrens and his men changed their orientation so that they were essentially backing through the gap. To provide cover, Corvinus ordered those men still with javelins to clamber partway up the pile, just high enough that they could hurl their remaining missiles down on any Varciani who appeared to be putting too much pressure on Verrens' men.

Even with all the pressing problems and worries of the moment, Gaius Porcinus had never been prouder of his Cohort than he was in this retreat from what had turned out to be a well-planned and well-executed ambush. The teamwork and precision, forged by what the men grumbled were endless and pointless watches of practice were bearing fruit right then, and it would mark a turning point for the men of the Fourth that survived to see another winter. No longer would they complain so vociferously when they were summoned from the warmth of their huts during the cold winter months to practice maneuvers of this sort, all of them remembering this day.

Finally, Verrens and his Century were on the same side of the pile as the rest of the Cohort, but Corvinus still kept his men standing on their precarious perch, each of them holding at least two javelins, waiting to see what the Varciani had in mind. Fortunately, they seemed content to stay just out of javelin range, hurling only taunts and challenges at the retreating Romans, pointing to the line of Roman corpses being left behind. Fairly quickly, one of the Varciani got the idea to escalate the verbal harassment, running over to the nearest dead Roman. As Verrens' men, still walking backward, looking over their shields, could only watch in impotent fury, the warrior's arm raised, a battle-axe in his hand, hovering above his head for an instant before slashing down. Then the warrior bent over, and because the Legionary's chin strap had been securely tied, was able to pick up the dead man's head by the horsetail plume of the helmet, holding it up and displaying it to the enraged Legionaries. There was a sudden roar of sound as Romans howled in impotent fury, while the Varciani matched them with their triumphant shouts, as the warrior holding his grisly trophy danced and capered about, waving the still-dripping head above his own, completely heedless of the bits of gore dripping down onto him.

"Shut your mouths," Verrens roared, before finally lashing out with his *vitus* at two or three of the most vocal of his men when they became so enraged they stopped their movement with their comrades. "There's nothing we can do about it now. The faster we get back to the First, the sooner we can come back and take our revenge on these *cunni!*"

After that, there was nothing more to be said, and Porcinus waited to call a halt until they were almost three hundred paces to the west of the rubble. As he trotted down the side of the formation, his ears were assailed by the sounds of panting, cursing men; even worse were the moans of so many wounded. He thought briefly about taking the time for a full butcher's bill, then dismissed it, for a number of reasons. What he did do was order the Centuries back into their normal spots, with the exception that men from both the Second and the Fourth were detailed to assist with the Third's casualties, using shields as makeshift stretchers for men who couldn't walk. Once matters were to his satisfaction, he told Nigidius, who was wounded in at least two places he could see, to sound the notes to resume the march. Immediately, the battered Fourth Cohort retraced its steps back to the west, leaving a piece of itself behind, along with the Second Cohort.

Chapter 7

The Fourth moved as quickly as possible, given the circumstances, but even so, it was a third of a watch before there was a shouted warning from the section of men Porcinus had sent ahead. The advance guard was halted just before a slight dogleg in the wider northward passage, which Porcinus estimated was at least three times as wide as the ravine he and his men had been traversing, making it almost a small valley. Certainly wide enough for a full Cohort to spread out, he mused, which deepened his suspicions about the supposed peril that the First was in. Ordering a halt to the main column, Porcinus called Ovidius up to his spot.

"Wait here; if it's some sort of trap, you know what to do."

Ovidius saluted, assuring Porcinus that he did, and the Pilus Prior trotted forward, where his scouts were standing, staring farther up the ravine. Not until he was within twenty paces of them could he see that they were watching as an even half-dozen riders approached, yet while he couldn't make out their features, he saw they were Roman. Despite his suspicion, he felt himself relax, reaching his advance guard a moment before the cavalrymen came trotting up. Porcinus instantly recognized one of the men as Silva's troopers; if he remembered correctly, he had been one of the men who had escorted his son back to Siscia.

"*Salve*, Centurion," the same man called out, confirming Porcinus' guess. "What brings you up here? We weren't expecting to see you and the Second."

"It's not the Second. It's just us," Porcinus replied, eyeing all the troopers with a growing unease.

None of them looked as if they had been in a fight, or harried in some way, and he felt a lead ball start to form in his stomach.

Nevertheless, he kept his voice as neutral as he could as he asked, "What say you? Everything all right up here?"

The trooper – Porcinus thought his name was Albinus, which would fit because his hair was the color of the sun when it was masked by clouds – gave a snort of disgust.

"Bah," he replied. "This has been a total waste of a day so far. We haven't seen anything but a lot of tracks. Although," he added in what was clearly an afterthought, "most of them seemed to be headed in your direction. Did you see anything?"

Porcinus had to bite down hard on the retort that came to his lips, knowing that none of this was Albinus' fault, if that really was his name. Instead of giving a verbal answer, Porcinus simply spun around on his heel and beckoned the riders to follow him. He walked until they passed the slight bend, enabling them to see the column of the Fourth Cohort, and they didn't have to get close to see what Porcinus intended. He heard more than one man gasp behind him, and he turned to face them, his face cold.

"Pluto's cock, what happened? Sir?" one of the other men with Albinus blurted out, his agitation such that he had to remember to append the correct courtesy to the end of his question.

"What does it look like?" Porcinus snapped.

He instantly regretted at least his tone, so in a quiet voice, he briefly explained the events that had occurred, finishing with, "Then we got a runner telling us we needed to leave the Second and come to help the First because they were under attack and that Tiberius had either been cut off or was dead."

Porcinus would long remember the expressions of shock from every one of the troopers, but it was Albinus who answered. "I don't know who told you that, Centurion. But we haven't had as much as a sling bullet come our way. It's true that Tiberius and the mounted advance guard have ridden ahead at least twice that I know of when they thought there might be some sort of mischief waiting for us. But," he shook his head emphatically, "we haven't been in any kind of fight, let alone one where we'd need help."

Porcinus had opened his mouth to tell Albinus that this desperate news had come from the man who was the second in command of this part of the army, then thought better of it.

Instead, he said simply, "There's only one way to find out. How far ahead are they?"

"No more than a half-mile," Albinus answered instantly. "If you want, I'll give you my horse, Centurion."

Porcinus was tempted, but decided against it. Whatever was going to happen, he wanted the support of his boys, no matter whether it was only in spirit, so he shook his head.

"No, thank you. We'll just march at the double quick and catch up."

Albinus nodded, then turned his horse to head back, but Porcinus stopped him.

"I'd like you to drop back and make sure there are none of those bastards on our trail," he told Albinus.

This made sense; Albinus saluted and beckoned his men to follow. While it was true that this was a standard method, that wasn't why Porcinus didn't want to give Barbatus any prior warning. In fact, he was so anxious to see the Primus Pilus' face when he brought the Fourth, he trotted to march with the advance guard, wanting to be the first to meet him.

As it turned out, before he had the chance to confront Barbatus, he was met by a clearly agitated Tiberius, who came galloping back toward the end of the marching column of the First when he was alerted to the presence of approaching troops. His normal scowl was in place, but Porcinus could see that there was also a considerable amount of agitation and, worse for a commander, confusion.

"Pilus Prior...Porcinus?" He stared hard down at the tall Roman, taking in the condition of the Centurion's armor, which was covered in blood, and with that look men who had just been in battle seemed to have in the immediate aftermath. "What are you doing here? Where's the Second?" He sat taller in his saddle to peer past Porcinus, looking at the ranks of the Fourth, then trying to see beyond them.

Porcinus opened his mouth to give an immediate answer, then hesitated.

Instead of giving the kind of report that might be expected at that moment, he asked, "Sir, were you ever in danger?"

Tiberius quite naturally looked startled at the question, his eyebrows suddenly plunging downward and coming so close together they were almost touching.

"What? What do you mean 'in danger'? I would assume we're all in danger every moment we spend here in this gods-forsaken stretch of country. Would you mind not speaking in riddles, Centurion?"

"I received a message that you had disappeared and that the First was being hard-pressed and needed help. I was ordered to come to your aid immediately."

Now Tiberius looked hopelessly confused, and although it gave Porcinus a spark of vindication that his guess was correct, it was outweighed by the feeling of dread that came rushing up from his gut, as he understood that a man like Barbatus wouldn't do something like this without at least covering his tracks.

"'Come to my aid'? What for? We haven't seen anything more than some churned-up mud." His gaze moved from Porcinus' face down to his uniform, then he looked past the Centurion to the leading ranks of the Fourth Cohort, who had been brought to a halt by Ovidius a short distance away. There was clearly no mistaking the signs that the Fourth Cohort had been in battle, and it prompted Tiberius to say, "But you've clearly been in a fight, and from the looks of it, a bad one." Porcinus didn't know Tiberius that well, but he could recognize the dawning of realization on the face of the young Legate. "Where's the Second?" he asked Porcinus softly.

It took all of Porcinus' discipline to keep his tone level and not give in to the fear and desperation of the moment as he went on to explain in as few words as possible the events of the preceding time since they had separated.

"How long ago was this?" was Tiberius' first question.

Unfortunately, with the clouds still hanging so heavy, it was hard for Porcinus to give an estimate with any accuracy, but he finally ventured, "Since the attack started? A watch. No more than that, but probably a full watch."

"And you...left the Second behind?" Porcinus didn't have to know Tiberius well to hear the quiet menace in the man's tone, reminding the Centurion that, even with his youth, he was an extremely powerful man.

"Because I was ordered to." Porcinus struggled to keep his tone matter-of-fact.

"By whom?" Tiberius demanded. "I certainly didn't order it." And when Porcinus uttered the name of the Primus Pilus, he couldn't be sure, but he thought he saw Tiberius' lip curl in a sort of disdain, as if he was smelling something unpleasant. In response, Tiberius simply said, "Well, let's go talk to the Primus Pilus."

Without waiting for a reply, he wheeled his horse about and began trotting back to the head of the column, forcing Porcinus to break into a run to keep up.

"I did what?" Barbatus gasped, his mouth opening in astonishment. "I did no such thing!"

Despite being prepared for it, Porcinus felt his own jaw drop as he stared at his Primus Pilus. The expression on the other man's face was one of pure shock, reminding Porcinus where the other man had spent most of his time, in a place where duplicity and double-dealing had to be as common as the whores of the Subura.

Regardless, Porcinus couldn't stop himself from blurting, "That's a lie! You sent your man Philo to tell me that you were under attack, that the situation was desperate, and you ordered me to march immediately to the aid of the First! You said that Tiberius was either dead or had been cut off!"

Only later would Porcinus admit that the flush that came to Barbatus' face was a nice touch, but in the moment, he had to fight to retain control as his Primus Pilus snapped, "I don't know what you're talking about! I never said anything of the sort!" Turning to Tiberius, Barbatus said coolly, "There's a simple way to clear this up, sir." When he turned to Porcinus, Tiberius also looked to the Pilus Prior, so he missed the gleam of malicious triumph in the coiffed Primus Pilus' eye as he finished, "Why don't you go get Philo? He can clear this up, I'm sure."

Despite the fact that Porcinus was sure he knew what Philo would say, he nevertheless summoned the man from the ranks, where he had been marching with the First Century. As the Gregarius approached, Porcinus watched him carefully, yet there was no sign from the man that he could point to as something suspicious. Philo presented himself to the three men, with Tiberius still astride his horse, and as much as it pained Porcinus, there was nothing in the man's manner to arouse doubt in the man's story, other than the normal apprehension that any ranker had when standing in front of the most senior commanders in the army.

Before anyone else could speak, Tiberius took advantage of his status, looking down at the Legionary, a severe look on his face as he demanded, "What was the message you were given by Primus Pilus Barbatus?"

As much as Porcinus hated to admit it, the look on Philo's face, as he looked first to Barbatus, then over to Porcinus, before turning his gaze back to the mounted Legate, was a perfect example of the kind of confusion and apprehension that one would expect from a perfectly innocent man.

"Sir?" Philo asked, his tone cautious. "I'm not sure what you mean."

"I can't make it any plainer," Tiberius snapped, his face flushing. "Repeat back to me the message that was relayed to you by Primus Pilus Barbatus that you were to give to Pilus Prior Porcinus."

Philo stiffened even more than he had been, as he recited in a clipped voice, "I was told by Primus Pilus Barbatus to relay to Pilus Prior Porcinus that since there had been no contact with the enemy on the part of the First Cohort that he was to make every effort to link up with the Second."

"That's a lie!" Porcinus gasped, unable to stop himself from the outburst, despite half-expecting it.

"Why would he lie?" Barbatus interjected before Philo could make his own response. "That's ridiculous!"

"Yes, Pilus Prior." Tiberius made no attempt to hide his skepticism. "Why would this man lie about a message that important?"

"I...I don't know why," Porcinus stammered. He was unwilling to expose the entire history of his dealings with the Praetorian Primus Pilus, so instead, he just repeated stubbornly, "But it's a lie. He told me a completely different story."

"And what was that?"

Porcinus was unsettled by the fact the question came not from Tiberius, who could have been reasonably expected to ask that question, but from Barbatus, but it also put him on his guard.

"That you were under attack, and that you were in danger of being overwhelmed. And," Porcinus added, "that you," he turned then to Tiberius, "had either been isolated and couldn't get back to the Cohort, or that you were already dead. We were ordered to come to your aid immediately."

Barbatus' laughter was harsh, and it was mocking.

"What?" He shook his head. "That's preposterous! I said no such thing; why would I? We haven't seen more than a few tracks of the enemy!" He turned now, sneering at Porcinus, his contemptuous tone as lacerating as his words, especially because they were so patently false. "I think you lost your nerve, you abandoned the Second Cohort because they were in trouble, and you came scurrying back here with some concocted story that the message I sent you was what you say it is!" He turned to Tiberius, while indicating Philo. "Why would this man lie? He's a Gregarius. He has no reason to do anything other than repeat exactly what I told him to!"

"Where did he come from? I mean, what Legion was he in before this?" Porcinus asked the questions quietly, but he was pleased to see Barbatus' face flush and, more importantly, Tiberius look sharply between the Primus Pilus and Philo, who was staring off into space, acting as if he wasn't listening to a word.

"What does that matter?" Barbatus demanded, yet Porcinus felt a flicker of hope because of the look of discomfort that flashed across the Primus Pilus' features.

"It doesn't." It was Tiberius who spoke up and, for an instant, Porcinus thought that hope was dashed, but then Tiberius finished, "So why don't you answer the question?"

He gave Barbatus a cold smile. Barbatus' composure faltered, and his eyes shot over to Philo, who seemed to be made of the same marble as the statues in the forum of every Roman city.

Then, he surprised Porcinus by saying, "I'm somewhat ashamed to say that I don't know, sir. If you remember, this man was part of the replacements that arrived the same time as I did. And I haven't had the time to go through every man's record." He turned to Philo and snapped, "What Legion are you from, Gregarius?"

"9th Legion, Primus Pilus," Philo responded crisply, with no hesitation. "First Century, Second Cohort."

Porcinus was suddenly thrown so off-balance that he actually took a staggering step backward, which Tiberius noticed.

"Why are you reacting like this is a surprise, Pilus Prior?"

Tiberius' gaze pierced him and, with a great effort, Porcinus replied, "Because that's not what I was told."

"And what was it you were told?"

"That Philo is from the Praetorian Guard."

Tiberius jerked in his saddle, and he shot a look at Philo, who Porcinus had to admit was continuing to stand stolidly at *intente*, his expression still the blank stare.

Before Tiberius could say anything, Barbatus responded with a sneer, "Do you believe everything you hear, Pilus Prior? It's true that a handful of men came with me, but I can assure you that not only did I have nothing to do with their assignment, Philo isn't one of them."

Suddenly, Tiberius let out a hiss of frustration, making a chopping motion with his hand.

"Enough. We don't have time to go into this now." He turned back to Porcinus. "Do you think the Second can hold until we get there?"

"Only if we move at the double quick," Porcinus answered.

"We'll sort this business out later," Tiberius said, then ordered, "Porcinus, you need to reverse your course and lead us back to the Second. When we get close, you're going to let the First take the lead, and they'll be the ones to sort those bastards out."

He had begun to turn away, but Porcinus didn't move, prompting Tiberius to wheel his horse about to glare at the Pilus Prior.

"Well?"

"It's just that if we wait until we're in the ravine where we were at, that one isn't wide enough for two Cohorts to change places."

Despite his irritation, Tiberius recognized that Porcinus was right, and he relented.

"Very well. When we reach the junction of the two, that's when you'll let the First take the lead. Now, start moving!"

Tiberius didn't see the looks exchanged between Barbatus and Porcinus, but if he had, he might have been curious about the malicious smile the Primus Pilus was giving one of his Centurions.

The First and Fourth Cohorts did arrive to save the Second, driving the Varciani away, but inflicting few more casualties than had already been caused by the Second and Fourth in the original fight. However, the Second Cohort had been savaged, with more than half its numbers dead or wounded. As might be expected, the First Century was particularly hard hit, and while Volusenus lived, he had lost an eye to a spear thrust. Somehow, he had not only survived, but had continued fighting, and was able to meet Tiberius still on his feet, despite a blood-soaked makeshift bandage tied around his head that obscured his damaged eye. Porcinus wasn't that surprised when he was told about Volusenus; despite his unpleasant demeanor and surly attitude, he had a well-deserved reputation for being one of the toughest men of the Legion, and this only added luster to it. Tiberius sent Silva's troopers out in force, but the Varciani host simply melted away, although they left a large portion of their warriors dead or wounded on the field. Those wounded were only in that state for the amount of time that it took for Tiberius' Legionaries to dispatch them with a thrust or a slash of their own blades. Couriers arrived from the two other groups of Cohorts; only one of them, the Seventh, Eighth, and Ninth Cohorts, under the nominal command of one of the Tribunes, but led by Aulus Amulius, the Septimus Pilus Prior, had made any contact with the Varciani, repulsing what was described as a probing attack by a band of perhaps five hundred warriors. The other Cohorts, just like the First under Tiberius, had only seen signs of activity, in the form of tracks, leading in the general direction of the ravine where the Second and the Fourth were ambushed. It took another full watch for the wounded to be treated and stabilized to the point they could be transported, and the Roman dead gathered up. Wagons were sent for, yet with the ravine too narrow for them to turn around, the survivors had been required to carry their fallen comrades back west down the ravine, to the intersection of the north/south ravine, where the wagons waited. It was a somber procession back to the camp, one that Porcinus would never forget as he shambled alongside his Cohort, his mind still reeling from the scene earlier. Yet when Corvinus came trotting up from his spot, he was rebuffed by his friend and Pilus Prior, unusual in itself. However, Porcinus needed time to think about all that had transpired. He had been informed by a mounted messenger sent by Tiberius that he was confined to his quarters upon their return to camp, while the commander investigated the allegations made by Barbatus, and Porcinus' response. Not surprisingly, his mind was fully occupied by how he was going to defend himself, yet by the time they arrived back at the main camp, he had been unable to come up with any kind of answer.

Later that evening, when Corvinus once more tried to talk to Porcinus, this time he relented, but their time together was quickly interrupted.

"Pilus Posterior Canidius is here," Lysander announced as Porcinus and Corvinus sat in Porcinus' private quarters, both of them moodily occupied in sipping unwatered wine.

Although Porcinus wasn't in the mood to deal with Urso, he also understood that he couldn't turn him away, so he indicated to Lysander to allow him entry. Porcinus wasn't sure what to expect from his second in command, but Urso's mien was such that it was impossible for Porcinus to reconcile his suspicion of the man with what he was seeing. More out of an automatic reflex, Porcinus offered him some wine, as Lysander brought another stool, so there were three men sitting, staring morosely into their cups.

Finally, Urso broke the silence, looking at Porcinus in the eye. "I want you to know that what Barbatus is trying to do is unjust, and it needs to be stopped."

Porcinus wasn't sure how to respond, so he looked at Urso over his cup; Corvinus wasn't so circumspect.

"That's certainly true," he agreed with Urso, but his tone was cool as he continued. "Although if he has his way, you'll get what we all know you wanted. You'll be Pilus Prior."

Urso' features darkened even more than normal, yet he didn't reply immediately, and Porcinus saw his free hand clench into a fist. He tensed, preparing himself to leap from his own chair to stop Urso from striking Corvinus, who didn't look the least bit worried. Then Urso did something completely unexpected, suddenly exhaling by giving a harsh chuckle.

"I suppose I deserved that," he said and, for a moment, Porcinus wasn't sure he had heard correctly; Corvinus looked as shocked as he felt as Urso went on, either ignoring or oblivious to their reactions.

"But while I have ambitions of my own, I don't want to get promoted like this."

Although there was a part of Porcinus that desperately wanted to believe Urso, he was still wary. However, what Urso said next, while not dispelling his suspicions altogether, made such sense that he felt himself relenting a bit in his distrust.

"Besides," Urso pointed out, "if he does this to you and gets away with it, it's going to destroy this Legion, mark my words. Every one of us is going to be looking over our shoulders, wondering who will be next to run afoul of him."

Out of the corner of his eye, Porcinus could see that Corvinus was no less impressed with Urso's words than he was.

"That's true," Porcinus granted, then heaved a sigh. "But I don't know what I can do about it."

Before he got any further, Lysander interrupted again to tell Porcinus that other visitors had arrived.

"Let them in," Porcinus grumbled. "We might as well have a festival. It'll probably be my last one as Pilus Prior."

"Not if we have anything to do with it," Urso said, just beating Corvinus, who was about to say the same thing.

Before Porcinus could respond, the other Centurions of the Fourth Cohort entered, along with Ovidius, who did his best to appear inconspicuous since he was the man who had summoned the rest of them, except for Urso.

"We're here to tell you that we're behind you." Munacius took the lead, acting as the representative of the group, while the others added their agreement.

Porcinus reacted to this with a mixture of embarrassment and gratitude, mumbling his thanks. Urso, acting in his role as the Pilus Posterior, took command.

"We need to come up with a plan," he said. "First, we need to prove that this Philo *cunnus* came from the Praetorians. That alone may be enough, if we can show him we have proof."

"I agree that's a good start, but I don't think that will be enough," Corvinus put in.

Urso looked irritated, but it was Sabinus who asked the obvious question. "Why not? What else do we need to do?"

Corvinus put his cup down, then looked around the tent at the others. "Because this isn't just about our Pilus Prior. Barbatus isn't here just for Porcinus."

"What does that mean?" Munacius demanded.

Corvinus didn't answer; instead, he looked to Porcinus, giving him a long, level look, eliciting a sigh from his superior. Porcinus understood Corvinus' silent message perfectly, and although he was reluctant to divulge the details, he realized that he needed these men to be his allies. Consequently, he gave the others a recounting of his meeting with Barbatus, leaving nothing out. When he was through, there was a silence for several moments.

"I'm still not sure why that means that exposing the fact that the Gregarius isn't from the 9th Legion like he claimed won't solve the problem." Sabinus was the one who said it, but Porcinus could see that he wasn't alone in his confusion.

"He's here to keep an eye on Tiberius." Urso was the one who supplied the answer. "He was sent by Augustus to make sure that he's loyal and doesn't have…ambitions."

"Ambitions like what?" This came from Verrens. "Augustus is still a relatively young man. It's true he was sickly, but that was in the past. Besides, Tiberius isn't Augustus' blood."

"Which is why he bears watching," Corvinus pointed out patiently. "Because as we all know, a man with an army can create a lot of mischief." He turned to Porcinus and pointed to his superior. "Porcinus' father is an example of that with the Primus affair. I know none of us have forgotten that."

None of them had; every man in the room had been in the 8th Legion when Marcus Primus took them on campaign. It was a tumultuous time, and if they were being honest, the most disturbing aspect of the entire campaign was how unprofitable it had been. In fact, when Marcus Primus was relieved of command and taken to Rome for trial, Titus Pullus had been put in command of the army as it returned back to Siscia. With a hugely unhappy army deprived of what had become an accustomed bonus in the form of money derived from loot and the sale of slaves taken during the campaign, Pullus was forced to come up with an accommodation. Few people knew that Pullus considered it the most shameful and underhanded thing he had done in his forty-two year career; Gaius Porcinus was one of those who did, and he well remembered the self-imposed anguish his father had suffered. Although in the army archives the attack of the town of Naissus had been a completely justifiable act, taking place after the ambush of the lead element of the army as it passed nearby, by a group of warriors from the tribe that the town belonged to, what Porcinus knew was that it wouldn't have mattered. Pullus had already made the decision to attack Naissus and let his men strip it clean; the fact that the army was attacked in retaliation for the first assault on the town five years before under the command of Marcus Crassus' grandson was just a happy accident. Therefore, just the mention of what had been a turbulent campaign that ultimately saw the execution of Marcus Primus, and the tribunal of Titus Pullus, was still a powerful memory to these men.

"That's what Augustus is worried about," Corvinus continued. "But I think there's even more to it than just that."

Porcinus was puzzled and saw that he wasn't the only one, prompting him to ask, "What else do you think is going on?"

"I think Barbatus has his own ambitions," Corvinus said evenly. "I think that he's viewing this as an opportunity to not only destroy your career, but to put Tiberius in an awkward spot, where he's in a position where he owes Barbatus a debt."

"How do you think he plans on doing that?"

Urso no longer sounded doubtful, accepting Corvinus' reasoning, and Porcinus couldn't help the thought flashing through his mind that this was the type of thing that Urso might have done. You're being unfair, Gaius, he admonished himself as he listened to Corvinus explain.

"We got a bloody nose today, there's no doubt about that," Corvinus said. "And I think that Barbatus is going to do what he can to at least insinuate to Tiberius that Augustus will be very interested in knowing the causes of what happened." He took a sip before he continued, "And I think that Barbatus will do his utmost to convince Tiberius that he can either do Tiberius a great amount of good, or a great deal of harm, simply by the way he reports the results of today's action to Augustus."

One of the men gave a low whistle, although that wasn't the only reaction.

"That's a very, very dangerous game to play," was Urso's comment.

"Yes it is," Corvinus agreed. "But remember, Barbatus is a Praetorian. He's been posted in Rome for the gods know how long. He knows how to play politics. The fact that he's survived and is trusted by Augustus to be his spy speaks for itself."

That, Porcinus had to acknowledge, was an undeniable truth.

"So you think that he's going to use me as the reason for what happened today?" Porcinus asked, trying to ignore the hard lump in his throat.

Corvinus looked regretful, but he was frank in his reply. "I think that's a strong possibility. In fact, I think that what he's going to do is present this as a way for Tiberius to escape censure by Augustus."

"And if I were Tiberius, I'd jump at this chance to make sure my name isn't spattered with the *cac*," Porcinus concluded, unable to hide his misery.

"That may be true," Urso spoke up. "But he may also not like the idea of being in a position where he feels Barbatus has something to hold over his head like Damocles' sword."

To Porcinus, that seemed an awfully slim possibility to hang his hopes on, but he did at least appreciate the gesture from Urso.

"The best thing for everyone would be if he'd never shown up," Sabinus said, reddening slightly as he became aware that every eye had turned on him.

"Well, thank you for that observation." Verrens' tone was dry, yet there was no real censure in it. "Except it's a bit late for that."

"Then that leaves one other thing," Corvinus muttered, although only Urso heard him.

Porcinus' second in command didn't make any comment; there was no need to draw attention to what the Hastatus Prior had said, because it would put Porcinus in a position that, if he were to go by regulations, would require him to report his best friend. Instead, Urso just stared thoughtfully at the other man as the conversation finally dwindled down to a long silence. The only thing that was clear was that there wasn't much that could be done until Porcinus was informed of how much danger he was in.

Porcinus would never be able to decide if it was a good or bad thing that he didn't have to wait long, although given the outcome, he tended to think it was the former, not the latter.

"I've decided that there will be no further action taken in regards to what happened yesterday," Tiberius informed Porcinus, who had been summoned shortly after dawn to the *praetorium*.

His first hint that something unusual was taking place was when he was ushered into the private office of the Legate, and the only others present besides Tiberius and him were two clerks, and the burly former gladiator that Porcinus knew was Tiberius' bodyguard.

Porcinus, standing at *intente*, had a sudden horrifying feeling that he was going to faint dead away in front of his commanding officer, yet he managed to maintain not only his feet, but his composure.

"Yes, sir." He finally found his voice, but was unsure how to respond. "Er, thank you, sir."

Tiberius didn't reply, verbally anyway. Instead, he gave a perfunctory nod. Tiberius was sitting behind his desk, and he stared up at the Centurion, who was standing at *intente*, unsure if the audience was over. In fact, Tiberius was almost in as much of a quandary as Porcinus was, although his face still had the same scowl that was more or less his permanent expression, giving nothing of his inner turmoil away. Finally, Tiberius seemed to come to a decision of some sort, because he picked up a scroll, opened it, and began looking at it.

"That will be all," he said curtly. "You're dismissed."

Still a mass of confusion, Porcinus fell back on the familiar security of military protocol, saluting and facing about. He had gone about halfway to the heavy leather flap that served as the entrance to Tiberius' office when the young Legate spoke.

"I know why Barbatus is here," he said, just loudly enough for Porcinus to hear him. "And I know what he's trying to do, not just with you, but with me."

Porcinus wasn't sure how to react, although he stopped and turned around, resuming his position of *intente*, his helmet under his left arm.

"Sir?" he asked cautiously. "I'm not sure I understand."

In the time it took for Porcinus to walk to his current point, Tiberius had chosen to stand, and he was leaning forward, both fists on his desk as he looked at Porcinus intently.

"I think you do," Tiberius replied evenly, but without any visible sign of rancor or impatience at this display of the Stupid Legionary act that all rankers used when in uncertain situations with a superior.

Porcinus met Tiberius' gaze, and he swallowed the lump down in his throat, deciding at that moment to match his Legate's honesty with his own.

"Yes, sir, I do," Porcinus finally said.

He couldn't be sure, but there seemed to be a subtle change in the younger man's demeanor, as if Porcinus had passed some sort of test.

"So," Tiberius said softly. "It would seem that you and I have fallen afoul of the Princeps for some reason. I know why in my case, but I'm curious about you. What could you have done, out here in the wilds of Pannonia to merit his attention?"

Porcinus opened his mouth; it was a moment before the words came, as his mind raced through every possible answer he could give. He was more trusting in nature than his adoptive father was, yet he had witnessed so much of what had befallen Titus Pullus that he understood in reality the choice he was facing was really not one at all. It was the choice between drawing the immediate ire of Tiberius by refusing to enter into what could be viewed as some sort of conspiracy against the Princeps, a virtual certainty if Barbatus were to get wind of this meeting and chose to paint it in the most sinister light possible. And that, Porcinus knew, was exactly what Barbatus would do. In all likelihood, Tiberius would take Porcinus' refusal to reveal what he knew to be the cause of his situation with Augustus as a personal insult, a repudiation of the confidence that Tiberius had just shown to him. On the other hand, if he was honest with Tiberius, he stood to become viewed as even more of a potential problem for the Princeps. Porcinus wasn't sure how much of what Barbatus had said about his supposed mission of "keeping an eye" on Porcinus was direct orders from Augustus and how much was just a matter of Barbatus viewing the situation as a means to an end to compromise his real target, Tiberius. After the discussion of the night before,

Porcinus felt more confident that, although Augustus was certainly aware of him and, in all likelihood, had mentioned Porcinus to Barbatus, it had only been in passing. Barbatus' main mission and target was Tiberius, but Barbatus had chosen to use Porcinus and Augustus' suspicion of him as the lever on Tiberius. However, as cautiously sure as he was that this was the truth of the situation he was facing, Porcinus also recognized that he would probably never know the exact circumstances. Then, seemingly unbidden, a memory suddenly flooded Porcinus, an ostensibly disconnected bit of random recollection of an event from the past, and he would always take that moment as the evidence that his father was still helping him.

"It has to do with my father," Porcinus began.

By the time Porcinus left the *praetorium*, while in some ways his mind was clearer than it had been for some time, it was also beset by a whole new set of worries and uncertainty. He had ended up spending a third of a watch with Tiberius, as both men revealed to the other what they knew of their individual circumstances in an attempt to put the pieces of what Porcinus was realizing was a huge puzzle into place. Yet, more sobering than the enormity of what was confronting the two men was the danger, and from what Porcinus could tell, solving this problem appeared likely to be as hazardous as not and allowing events to unfold without any attempt to steer them. He did feel slightly better in one regard; his assumption about his importance to Augustus seemed to be correct. After comparing their respective bits of information, it seemed clear to Porcinus that Barbatus' hostility and interest in Porcinus was peripheral and mostly of his own making. While Tiberius was clearly under scrutiny by the Princeps, he also was close to Augustus, and he swore to Porcinus that if the Princeps had truly been as interested in Porcinus' aspirations to emulate his father as Barbatus had claimed, Tiberius would have been told when he took command.

"He's using you, and your...situation to get to me," was how Tiberius had put it, and Porcinus accepted this as truth.

That didn't make it any less unsettling, or any less dangerous, but it at least reinforced to Porcinus something his father had tried to impress upon him more times than Porcinus could count over the years.

"Men like us," Pullus would say, "are pieces in a game to the upper classes. Some of us are more valuable than others, but never forget, Gaius, that in the end, we're not men to them. We're not human beings with families, and hopes and dreams of our own. We're merely pieces on a board to be used. And sacrificed to win the game," he had finished ominously.

Nothing in Porcinus' experience had given him reason to doubt Pullus; if anything, this crisis demonstrated how true it was.

The immediate threat to Porcinus was ended; Tiberius had given his assurance that not only would Tiberius not endorse Barbatus' official accusation against Porcinus that he had disobeyed orders and abandoned the Second Cohort, but in turn, he was putting the Primus Pilus under close watch.

"If he tries to get a message out to Augustus, or anyone, for that matter, I'll know about it," Tiberius assured Porcinus just before he finally left the Legate. "I have men I trust watching him every moment of the day. Nothing will happen that I don't know about."

However, Porcinus was under no illusions that his problems were solved. Tiberius had confirmed one fear of the Pilus Prior's, that there was also no way for the Legate to replace Barbatus as the Primus Pilus. In fact, Porcinus worried that in some ways his predicament was still at least as precarious, if not worse. Tiberius could protect Porcinus from this particular threat, but he understood that Barbatus would be, in all likelihood, more determined than ever to punish Porcinus, especially since he couldn't lash out at Tiberius. No, matters were far from settled, Porcinus understood, walking out of the *praetorium*. Porcinus didn't head back to his tent. As was traditional, the army wasn't moving this day after the battle while the Second Cohort was reorganized and the missing leadership spots were filled, either permanently in the case of the Hastatus Posterior, who was killed, or temporarily, like Volusenus who, from his hospital bed, had assured anyone and everyone that he would be back in action. This was actually where Porcinus was headed now, and it was with only slightly less dread than he felt facing Tiberius that he entered the hospital tent to talk to Volusenus. He was easy to find; not only were wounded

Centurions kept in a segregated area, Porcinus only had to follow in the opposite direction of the fleeing *medicus*, who had blood streaming from a wound in his scalp. A few paces away from Volusenus' cot lay the shattered remains of a cup, with a puddle around the shards of clay that Porcinus assumed had contained some potion concocted by the camp physician.

"If you try to make me drink that piss again, I'll flay you, you cocksucking son of a whore," Volusenus roared, raising up partway from his cot, half his face obscured by the bandage over his eye.

Attracted by the movement, the Secundus Pilus Prior turned to examine Porcinus with his good eye, flopping back on the cot as he muttered, "What do you want?"

Porcinus had braced himself for some sort of outburst; at the very least, he expected some recrimination and accusation from Volusenus. But now that he was facing the man, he desperately wished he were anywhere else.

"I just wanted to come check on you," he forced himself to sound casual.

"Came to see your handiwork?" Volusenus shot back bitterly.

Despite expecting something like this, Porcinus felt the rush of blood to his face.

"Volusenus." He knelt next to the other man's cot, although he was careful to stay just out of reach. "I swear to you by Mars and Bellona, we would never have left if we hadn't been told to by Barbatus! But he sent one of his..." Porcinus' mouth twisted into a bitter grimace, "...lackeys to pull us away. He told us that the First was under threat!" He shook his head emphatically. "We would never have left otherwise! We were working out how to link up with you when the message arrived."

Porcinus stopped, forcing himself to meet Volusenus' gaze, who stared hard with his one eye. The silence stretched out for what seemed like a watch, then there was a sudden relaxation in the posture of Volusenus, accompanied by a gust of air from his lungs that blasted Porcinus, and he recognized the smell, a mixture of wine and herbs favored by the *medici* for wounded men. It made Porcinus wonder what had been in the cup Volusenus had thrown since he had obviously ingested at least one dose.

"I know that," Volusenus muttered, shocking Porcinus. Oblivious to the other man's reaction, Volusenus said, "I know exactly what happened, and I know why it happened." Only then did he turn to face Porcinus, his lone eye blazing with a fierce intensity. "You're not the only one who has friends in places who tell him things! And I know exactly what our Primus Pilus is made of and why he's here! You," he gave a wave in Porcinus' direction, as if dismissing a slave, "are just a tool."

Porcinus was torn; on one hand, he was relieved that Volusenus didn't blame him and knew the true cause of what had happened to him and his Cohort, yet on the other, he didn't care for the way Volusenus seemed to be grimly amused. Regardless, the latter was a minor consideration to the larger relief he felt. Just when he felt the surprises were over, Volusenus proved him wrong.

Seemingly out of nowhere, Volusenus blurted, "Besides, you're not a bad sort. Mind you, you're a trifle…" He paused for a moment, and Porcinus finished for him.

"Soft," he said with a smile. "I'm a bit soft for your taste."

Volusenus gave Porcinus what he was beginning to realize was the man's version of a smile, which looked as much like a grimace as anything else.

"Exactly," Volusenus grunted. Then, "But I see how those misbegotten bastards in your Cohort respond to you, and how your Centurions seem to think your *cac* doesn't stink." Porcinus laughed, which seemed to please Volusenus, who hastened to add, "Now, your boys aren't the equal of mine, mind you. But, they're not bad."

While Porcinus might have been disposed to argue this last point, he knew this wasn't the time, especially when he saw the cold, harsh mask of his counterpart slip and reveal the true man as the memory of those men he had lost, his beloved boys, overwhelmed him with grief. A solitary tear rolled down from his remaining eye, and that lone symbol of anguish threatened Porcinus' own composure as he felt the tears coming to his two good eyes. He was still kneeling near the cot, but moved closer so that he could put a gentle hand on Volusenus' arm. The other man had closed his good eye as he grieved, and the touch of Porcinus' hand caused him to jerk in surprise, yet when he looked at the other Pilus Prior, he saw in Porcinus' eyes a man who understood the sorrow and loss he was experiencing, so he didn't pull away. They stayed that way for some time, neither man saying anything.

Finally, Volusenus told Porcinus in a hoarse whisper, "That *cunnus* needs to pay for what he did to my boys."

"He will," Porcinus promised, despite having no idea how that was going to happen.

After his visit to Volusenus, he returned to his tent, where he was met by the Centurions. He briefly recounted the exchange between him and the Legate, relaying Tiberius' assurance that nothing would come of Barbatus' attempt to damage Porcinus. He didn't feel the need to relate the fact that he was being protected out of Tiberius' own interests, thinking that it was obvious. It was Urso who touched on the thing that still worried him.

"Barbatus isn't going to be happy, at all," Urso commented. "But he can't do anything to Tiberius. At least," he amended, "not overtly. But you?" He pointed at Porcinus, then finished, "And that means us. So while I'll say that you managed to dodge the sword thrust this time, there's going to be more coming."

"Well, at least you know Tiberius is aware of what's going on," Corvinus pointed out. "And I'm willing to bet that even now, he's sent messages back to Rome to his own spies in the Praetorian Guard to find out dirt on Barbatus and those *cunni* he brought with him."

That prompted an interruption, from an unlikely source. Lysander had been serving the assembled men refreshments, and he cleared his throat in a signal that Porcinus had learned meant he had something to say. Normally, Porcinus would have been irritated at the slave's impertinence, except that not only was this not a normal day, much had changed as far as his opinion of the Thracian. This adjustment had started when Porcinus discovered that Lysander's frequent absences during those interminable days when he was in Siscia, waiting for his family, was due to the fact that Lysander was on the wall of the camp, looking for their arrival himself. Consequently, he now waved the others to silence, looking at Lysander, who appeared embarrassed with all eyes on him.

"I apologize, Centurion," he mumbled as he held the tray, now empty of cups. "It's just that when I turned in the morning report to the *praetorium,* I ran into Crito." This was the name of Lysander's counterpart in the First Cohort. Hearing the slave's name wrought an instant change in the atmosphere of Porcinus' office, and Lysander hurried on. "And he told me that there's been a desertion in the First Cohort."

Porcinus sat back, a sick feeling in his stomach, knowing the name without asking.

"Philo."

It was Corvinus who supplied the name, and Lysander nodded, his face showing regret at being the bearer of this news.

"Deserter?" Urso scoffed. "He's no more a deserter than I am. Barbatus has just salted him away somewhere, and is saving both himself and this bastard from Tiberius' own men sniffing out and proving that he's not from the 9th Legion."

Porcinus considered Urso's words and nodded slowly, accepting this as the most likely explanation.

"Not that there's anything we can do about it," Urso finished his thought, and Porcinus knew that this was true as well.

"Still, you have Tiberius as an ally," Corvinus insisted. "You're not going to be like your father when he was hung out to dry and had to win his fight all on his own."

Porcinus opened his mouth, then thought better of it; this wasn't the time or the place to correct Corvinus.

"That's true," he said, instead of telling Corvinus the reality, that if Tiberius was an ally, it was only because it was convenient for him to be one.

That reality was an entirely different matter from the case with the men in this tent, he realized as his eyes traveled the room. He was beginning to accept the idea that Urso could be depended on in this fight, and perhaps completely, while with the others he had no doubts that he could trust them with his life. On the other hand, Tiberius would help him as long as it was in his interests to do so, and the best that Porcinus could do was hope that remained the case.

"We go back out tomorrow." Porcinus deliberately changed the subject, understanding that nothing more could be accomplished by further talk. "So make sure the men are ready to go. What's our strength?"

One by one, each Centurion rattled off the numbers from their respective wax tablets, upon which the figures were compiled. Porcinus knew the number of dead men; that was always the first and most bitter number he had to hear. In fact, that was what this day would be about for the rankers, sending their comrades on their way, releasing their souls by fire, cleansing their immortal essence by burning away the flesh that kept it trapped here on the earth. Then each survivor's close comrade, the man responsible for holding the other's will, would open it and, to the extent possible, fulfill the bequests in it. Not that many men had to actually read their deceased friend's will; as Porcinus well knew, this was a very common topic around the fires every night, as men bickered back and forth about their plans for their property, and who should get what. He couldn't count the number of times he had heard one man threaten another with amending his will in order to cut the other man out from some prized possession. Shaking his head, he banished those thoughts, forcing himself to concentrate on the numbers being recited. After the dead were the number of wounded, divided into a number of sub-categories; wounded, expected to die; wounded, expected to live but be crippled and therefore be cashiered out; wounded and expected to return to the standard, but were currently in the hospital. Finally, there were those men who were wounded but had been cleared by the *medici* to return to duty, and were also further sub-divided by what level of duties they could perform. Once every man was finished, Porcinus did his own figures, writing the numbers laboriously down in his tablet, then sat back, slightly stunned.

"We're only going to be at half-strength when we march tomorrow," he said hoarsely.

Although each Centurion knew the specific numbers in their own Century, and were generally aware of the losses in the others, none of them had heard the numbers once they were combined in regard to the entire Cohort. Hearing it put so baldly took them all by surprise, and it was a very glum group that sat there for several moments.

Realizing that it was up to him to lift the spirits of his subordinates, Porcinus pointed out with an optimism that was only partially feigned,

"But we have a really high number of men who can't march tomorrow but will be back under the standard. By this time next month, we'll be at about eighty percent strength."

As he had hoped, that seemed to cheer the others some, even if it was tempered by the knowledge that they were going to possibly face the Varciani once more with severely depleted ranks. Dismissing the Centurions, Porcinus sat at his desk, lost in thought.

Mention of the ordeal his father had gone through, and how the common perception was that he had managed to defeat the designs of "them" back in Rome, which was how other men of his class always referred to this episode to Porcinus, occupied his thoughts for the rest of the time he sat in his office, before he got up and went about the business of making sure his men were ready for the next day. What Porcinus understood was that those men who talked to him of such matters only referred to "them" because of their fear of pointing to one man, and one man alone. Because that was the open secret about what became the last notable chapter of the remarkable career of Titus Pullus, that Augustus had been the unseen mover behind the tribunal of the Camp Prefect. However, Gaius Porcinus was one of the few people who knew that this was only partially true; it was certainly the case that Augustus had a hand in arranging a Tribunal, but from everything that Diocles, Pullus, and his friend Scribonius could gather during that time, the true architect had been another patrician. This man had seen a dual threat in Pullus; his son Claudius had been a participant in a scheme carried out by the Primus Pilus of the 13th Legion to squeeze the men of his Legion, and although it was true that Pullus had become aware of the younger Claudius' participation, he never had any intention of exposing the young nobleman's secret, not once they had made amends after Pullus saved Claudius' life. Understandably, this event had a huge impact on Claudius, and while Pullus would never count a man of Claudius' class a friend, they had forged a relationship based on mutual respect nonetheless. However, the man's father not only considered Pullus' knowledge of Claudius' activities with the 13th a threat, what Porcinus had always believed was the elder Claudius' real objection lay in what Pullus represented. Styling himself as an "old Roman," what it meant was that he took a very dim view of any man of Pullus' status elevating himself from the Head Count into the Equestrian class. Diocles' belief was that Augustus hadn't been the driving force behind Pullus' tribunal. Instead, the Princeps had merely been the facilitator, either doing or returning a favor to a man who was not only a member of his own class, but known to be close friends with the Princeps. The fact that, according to those who only knew the bare bones of all that had gone on, Pullus had managed to somehow outwit and defeat the combined forces of Roman nobility, all on his own, had just added the final luster to the sheen of his legend. And while Porcinus was as proud as any man of his adoptive father, even more so, he also had learned that it was a burden. Like earlier that day, when Corvinus had unwittingly brought up the episode. Porcinus had almost blurted out what, as far as he knew, only he, Diocles, and probably Scribonius were familiar with, that Pullus hadn't thwarted Augustus' plans by his own wit and courage. Naturally, Porcinus hadn't been in Rome with Pullus when he stood trial, yet when Pullus returned to Siscia not only free but exonerated, the Camp Prefect was a changed man. Porcinus thought his then-uncle would have been elated, but while he was happy the ordeal was over, he seemed to be in a thoughtful, pensive mood, one that lasted for several weeks. And although Titus Pullus never divulged it, Porcinus had learned from Diocles about an event that occurred on the night that Pullus had been found not guilty by the tribunal that, to Porcinus, at least partially explained his father's attitude. Not surprisingly, the Greek and Pullus had been in a celebratory mood, and from Diocles' accounting, they were on their third or fourth cup of unwatered wine when there was a knock on the door. Diocles had described to Porcinus everything that happened.

"The man who showed up looked like a slave," Diocles had explained to Porcinus one night in Siscia. "And he brought a message. He looked scared half to death. Although," Diocles had given a chuckle at the memory, "I suppose that's understandable. Titus yanked the door open and had his sword in his hand. Anyway," Diocles continued, "the man carried a scroll that he handed to Titus. But before he did, he made your father promise that he would never divulge the contents of the message, or the identity of who sent it." Diocles laughed again, although this had a bitter edge to it. "Oh, he did not like that and, for a moment, I thought he'd refuse. You see, he was just so worn down by all that he'd been through, all the secrets, and the intrigue, and the double-dealing. He just wanted to come back here and be allowed to do his job without worrying about politics." That Porcinus had known, and understood, very well. "But I think he also realized that he didn't really have a choice. So, he agreed." Diocles tapped the side of his nose with his finger, winking at Porcinus as he pressed on, "But your father wasn't dumb, not by any stretch. He wasn't as smart as Scribonius, although I haven't met many men who are. So when he took the scroll, he made a great show of having to turn it to the light. To get it to the proper angle, you know, so that he could read it. I remember he even made a joke about his old eyes and his short arms. Anyway, he had positioned himself so that I could see the scroll from where I was sitting, and he was close enough that I could read it. Most of it, at least," Diocles corrected himself. "Enough to know who it was from, anyway. And what he had done, more or less."

This conversation in Siscia that Porcinus was recalling now in his tent had actually been fairly recently; in fact, it had been one night, late, shortly after Diocles had arrived with his news about the death of his father.

When Porcinus saw that Diocles was waiting to be asked, he sighed at the theatrics but gave in, asking the Greek.

"It was from Marcus Agrippa," Diocles said quietly, clearly savoring the look of shock on Porcinus' face. "He wanted to let Titus know that he had been the man who made sure the prosecutor was so inept, and that we had the best possible defender in Lucius Calpurnius Piso. He also told Titus that Augustus was very angry at being thwarted, and while Agrippa could protect himself, he warned Titus that he needed to leave Rome immediately. You see," Diocles had sat back, looking off into the distance, "Agrippa is a soldier at heart. And he knew that an injustice was being done. But, because of his position, he couldn't openly come out on Titus' side. So," the Greek said with a shrug, "he did what he could."

Sitting alone in his own office in camp, Porcinus recalled those words and wished that he could count on Tiberius to be his Marcus Agrippa, but nothing he had heard or seen gave him any confidence that Porcinus was anything other an ally of convenience, and would be discarded, or even worse, expended should the need arise. With that thought haunting him, Porcinus rose to go rouse the men and get them ready.

When the army marched out the next day, it was almost as a whole Legion; Tiberius wasn't willing to divide his forces again, not after what happened the previous time. The Second Cohort, or what was left of it, remained, this time along with the Ninth, much to the dismay of Maxentius, their Pilus Prior. Every man in the 8th Legion was thirsting for revenge; despite all the rivalry between Cohorts, the relationship between men from different Cohorts in a Legion could be likened to that of siblings who fight each other all the time. At least until an outside threat shows up, and then to hurt one of them is to hurt all of them, meaning that it was an angry army at Tiberius' back, ready to bring death to the remaining Varciani.

Silva and his troopers had been hard at work, scouring the surrounded area, and Tiberius had sent couriers to each camp, ordering them to change their tactics. When the First and Fourth had returned to the site of the ambush, Tiberius ordered a count of the enemy dead. Porcinus and all of the men of the Second and Fourth Cohorts had taken grim satisfaction when they heard that there were almost four thousand Varciani dead left behind. Although there had been signs that small bands of Varciani, no more than twenty or thirty men at a time, were slipping past the patrols sent out by Tiberius to join the main body, Silva's scouts' best estimate was that the slain left to rot accounted for a bit more than half the total strength of the remaining Varciani. Early on in this endeavor, Tiberius had hoped that by surrounding this area and placing camps at the most commonly used routes into the interior of this hilly country, that he could starve out the Varciani. He was quickly disabused of this notion by men like the Primus Pilus of the 13th, Traianus, who was a veteran of Pannonia and knew that these hills hid a variety and abundance of game, especially for skilled hunters like the Varciani. The Legate had even briefly considered employing the drastic tactic of using the prevailing winds and starting fires in the hope that it would drive the Varciani to a location in this area that favored Tiberius and his men. He was talked out of that very quickly, it being pointed out to him that conflagrations of that size were impossible to control. There was really only one way to end this, and that prospective end was announced by the tramping sound of hobnailed soles marching out of the camp one more time. Between the casualties and the fact that campaigns where the goal was suppressing a rebellion were soundly hated by all ranks, the men were in a surly mood as they left, completely foregoing the normal ritual of calling to the guard Cohorts about being left behind. Neither was there the normal chatter as the men passed the time spent on a march by resuming conversations where they had been left off the night before around the fire or, in some cases, picking a story back up that was only told while on the march.

The 8th was as grim and silent as Porcinus had ever seen it, and it gave him a sense of quiet satisfaction knowing what that meant for the Varciani. Unlike Pullus, Porcinus didn't immediately hate the men he was facing, but once whoever the adversary was had shed the blood of even one of his men, it became a different story. And, with each death and each wounded man, that initial feeling of mild dislike turned into something else, growing and hardening into what he was feeling now, a silent fury waiting to be unleashed. He had often wondered why the gods hadn't seen fit to pass on the gift of battle madness to him that was such a defining characteristic of Titus Pullus. Most of the time, however, he was thankful that they had passed him over. Not this time; as they marched north on the now-familiar trail, Porcinus offered up a prayer that was slightly different from the normal one he offered whenever he and his men went into battle, and that was that if there was a fight today, that the gods bestow on Porcinus the gift that would enable him to exact vengeance on these Varciani who had so savaged his Cohort. He was praying when Silva, who had just seen to the rearguard element of his cavalry, came trotting up the column. Seeing Porcinus, he veered over to him.

"*Salve*, Porcinus," Silva called out.

Porcinus almost tripped over his feet, so caught by surprise was he, and when he turned to look up at Silva, the mounted man burst into laughter.

"You look like I'm Cerberus about to catch you and chew your balls off," the Decurion said.

Porcinus was about to make a retort, then bit it off, knowing Silva meant no harm by it, and he understood that Silva wasn't the type just to stop and chat, meaning there was something on the man's mind.

"Sorry," he said instead. "I was thinking about something else."

"That's all right," Silva replied genially. "You gave me something to smile about." His expression changed, a look that Porcinus would describe as apprehensive if he didn't know Silva better. "Gods know there hasn't been much to smile about the last few days."

"That's true," Porcinus granted, but he was unwilling to spend time on what would be an unpleasant topic, prompting him to ask, "What can I do for you, Decurion?"

Silva started, as if he was reminded of something, and he replied, "Ah, yes. Sorry. I did want to tell you something. But," he said as he glanced over Porcinus' shoulder, where his men were marching alongside in formation, each of them trying to appear as if they weren't listening intently to every word. "I think it's better if you come this way."

Without waiting for an answer, Silva laid the reins over his horse's neck, a coal black stallion that he had ridden for almost his entire time here in Pannonia, moving just out of earshot of the column. Porcinus was intrigued and irritated in equal parts, not relishing the idea of having to go trotting off, then come scampering back, not to mention walk alongside Silva's horse. Normally, Porcinus would expect a man to dismount and walk alongside whoever he was giving a message to, but Porcinus knew Silva well, and knew that he was more or less molded to the saddle, disdaining the idea of walking a step when he could ride, so he didn't take it as a personal insult. Reaching Silva's side, he gave the Decurion an inquiring glance.

"I wanted to talk to you about something that one of my boys found," Silva began and, despite the distance away from the column, he took care to keep his voice low. "At first, we didn't know who the man we found belonged to. But when we brought him into camp, someone identified him as belonging to you." Porcinus' face clearly reflected the confusion he was feeling, compelling Silva to explain further. "It's about your man. Paperius, is it?"

Porcinus' chest tightened, but he nodded and said, "Yes, Paperius is one of mine. Or was," Porcinus corrected himself. "What's this about?"

"Well, like I said, one of my boys was scouting the area around the battle, trying to pick up some sort of signs that would tell us where we could find these bastards. That was when he found your man, off by himself."

"I know," Porcinus sighed. "He and Philo were ambushed on their way back from the First the other day. It's a shame he died because he could have cleared up exactly what Barbatus did or didn't say."

Porcinus wasn't looking at Silva when he said this, so Porcinus only became aware that he had uttered something Silva considered important when there was a long silence. Finally, he glanced up at Silva to see him staring down at Porcinus intently.

"Tell me exactly what you know about your man being killed," Silva said, and Porcinus relayed the story he had been told by Philo.

When he was finished, Silva shook his head slowly.

"That's not very likely," he began. "First, my man only found him by accident. When he was riding by a bunch of thick underbrush surrounding a tree, his horse suddenly shied. He thinks his horse smelled your man Paperius' body, and I think he's right. It was when he was getting the horse back under him that he saw his legs sticking out from under the brush. When he described it to me, I also agree with him that he wasn't likely to have fallen into that bush after being killed. It's probable that whoever killed him dragged him there to hide him."

Although his heart wasn't in it, Porcinus felt compelled to point out, "That could have been the work of the Varciani."

"Why would they do that?" Silva made no attempt to hide his skepticism. "They have no reason to try and hide a body of one of ours. In fact, they're more likely to make a spectacle of it than hide it."

Although it wasn't Silva's intent, Porcinus' mind immediately recalled the sight of the Varciani dancing about, holding the grisly trophy of a Roman head aloft. Silva had made his point and Porcinus said as much.

Nodding to Silva to continue, he listened as the Decurion said, "But not only did the location of where the body was found look strange, the nature of the wound that killed him is even more...troubling." Now he made sure to make eye contact with Porcinus as he finished quietly, "His throat was cut from ear to ear. The way that only someone who's up close to you can do it."

Porcinus felt a sudden sickness in the pit of his stomach, and it was only through willpower that he didn't actually expel its contents. Part of this feeling came from the recognition that he had suspected this to be the case, that Philo had murdered Paperius. Nevertheless, having it confirmed was still a shock. Suddenly, Porcinus was struck by a thought.

"When did this happen? I mean, when did your man bring Paperius in?"

Silva looked away guiltily and replied, "Yesterday. I would have told you sooner, but we didn't know at first, and when we did find out who it was, I already had orders to go out on patrol."

Porcinus motioned with a wave, assuring Silva that there was no need to apologize. An idea had begun forming in his mind, but he needed to be sure.

"Were you there when your man came in?"

"No," Silva said, seemingly dashing Porcinus' hopes, but continued, "at least not when he first entered the camp. But he knew I was in the *praetorium*, and he came to get me and show me the body. He had slung it behind the saddle. At least," Silva grimaced, "as much as he could. The poor bastard was stiff as a board, so you can imagine it was difficult." Seeing Porcinus' expression and recognizing that this wasn't just any man they were talking about, but one from Porcinus' own Cohort, he hurried on, "I didn't recognize him, so we asked some of the men walking around to come take a look at him. That was how he was identified. A Gregarius who said he was from the First Cohort said he recognized him."

"Did any of them..." Porcinus began, but cut his question off as the import of what Silva had just offered sunk in. "Wait, you said a Gregarius from the First Cohort?"

Silva nodded.

"Yes, and from the way he acted, I guessed they might have been friends. He looks the way a man does when it's someone he knows by more than just sight."

Porcinus' heart started beating harder, and he asked quickly, "What did he look like?"

Silva shrugged, then seeing Porcinus' intent look, tried to think.

"Actually, if I had to describe him, I'd say he looked like one of those bully boys that you see running around Rome. His nose had clearly been broken, more times than just once, if you know what I'm saying. And he had one of those complexions where he always looks like he needs a shave."

The description Silva had just provided perfectly matched a man who Porcinus had only seen briefly, but had cause to remember. Philo had been the man who correctly identified Paperius, there was no doubt in Porcinus' mind.

It wasn't until the first break that Porcinus had the opportunity to call all of his Centurions aside and let them know what Silva had told him. He was most worried about Corvinus, whose Century Paperius had belonged to, and it was clear that his friend was enraged by what he heard.

"That cocksucking son of a whore," he spat to emphasize his anger. "That's why he ran. Barbatus probably didn't have anything to do with it. He knew that we would be able to add everything up and know that Paperius was murdered by one of our own, not by these barbarian *cunni*."

Porcinus glanced around and saw that every other man accepted Corvinus' reasoning.

Then Urso added, "This may actually turn out to be a good thing."

Every man looked at him in surprise, but he was unruffled at the attention.

"How so?" Porcinus finally asked.

"Because if Barbatus isn't the one who sent him running, that means it's pretty likely Barbatus isn't going to like the idea of him being on the loose somewhere. What if he's caught and we somehow get wind of it before Barbatus does?" Urso shook his head. "No, he'd be feeling a lot safer than he is right now if he actually knew where

Philo was. As it stands right now, there is just as much chance of Philo getting caught and us learning about it, and he's no fool. You can count on the fact that he knows we've figured out that Paperius was murdered."

Corvinus had been listening to all of this, but he couldn't contain his outburst.

"You sound like you hope they catch this bastard and bring him back alive!" he exclaimed, clearly angry. "I know he wasn't in your Century, but Pluto's cock, man, he was one of the Fourth! Why aren't you angrier than this?"

Urso actually did seem very calm and dispassionate, but his response was simple.

"I don't get mad at the sword because the man who wielded it stuck it in me." Urso shrugged. "Philo was just following orders. Just like we have in the past."

"Not to kill our own men," Corvinus blazed back.

"True," Urso granted. "Oh, don't mistake me. I want to see him punished, but I don't feel like he deserves to have done to him what you want to do. In fact," he said, "I think he feels badly about it."

"Badly about it?" Corvinus gasped, but Porcinus had the same thought pass through his mind that Urso now voiced.

"Why else would he be the man who stepped forward to identify Paperius?" the Pilus Posterior pointed out. "If he didn't feel anything about it, he wouldn't have lifted a finger to help them find out. In fact, he made his own life more dangerous by helping speed up the process of trying to determine who Paperius was and where he belonged."

Corvinus didn't immediately respond, yet while he was still fuming, Porcinus could see that Urso's argument hadn't been completely in vain.

"Well, I still plan on gutting the bastard if I find him," he finally said.

Then the break was over, and the men returned to their Centuries. Little by little, pieces were coming together that at least gave Porcinus a better idea of what he was facing, and this was what occupied his thoughts as the march continued.

It was shortly before the midday break that there was a flurry of motion at the front of the column, followed shortly by the blast of the *cornu* signaling the senior Centurions to come to meet with Tiberius. Porcinus made sure that he was at the back of the seven men as they came from their respective spots to gather in front of where Tiberius had dismounted. Even with his attempt, the crowd was too small for him to escape the notice of Barbatus, and Porcinus could feel the man's poisonous stare, but he ignored it and concentrated on what Tiberius had to say.

"Silva's men have come across fresh tracks, just two miles from here." Tiberius made no attempt to hide his excitement. "And his scouts say that it looks to be a mixed force of about three thousand men. In all likelihood, that's the main body. It looks like they're trying to escape to the west and squeeze in between us and the 15th." He pounded a fist into his palm as he finished. "But we're going to run them down. Prepare the men for a hard, fast march until we catch up and crush them. The estimate is that they're no more than a third of a watch ahead of us. That's all."

He turned away, but then Barbatus once more cleared his throat.

"Excuse me…sir," he began as Tiberius spun on his heel to glare at the Primus Pilus. "But if I might suggest…"

He got no farther, as Tiberius held up a hand and made a chopping motion in a clear command to stop.

"No, you may not suggest anything," Tiberius said, his tone and expression matching in coldness. "You've been given your orders. Now, let's not waste any more time."

"But, sir," Barbatus protested, "I wanted to…"

"Do not say another word."

The words weren't yelled, yet, at least to Porcinus, that made them even more menacing. Tiberius stared at Barbatus, but unlike the last time, Barbatus was either unable or unwilling to stand up to the scrutiny of those eyes. In front of the other Centurions, the carefully coiffed Primus Pilus seemed to wilt in front of them.

"Yes, sir," he finally managed in a small voice.

However, if he expected that to be the end of it, he was quickly shown this wasn't the case. Barbatus and the others began to turn to head back to their respective Cohorts, but again, Tiberius held up a hand.

"I believe I gave an order, Primus Pilus," he said in the same quiet voice.

Now Barbatus looked confused, and his eyes began to shift from one face to the next. He found no friendliness anywhere as the other Centurions gazed at him with expressions that ranged from indifference to outright hostility. Despite knowing that he should be cautious, Porcinus was one of the latter, returning the malevolent look Barbatus had given him in kind.

"Sir? I'm not sure what you mean."

"You don't? That's interesting. You seem to know everything else." Tiberius now made no attempt to stop a sneer from taking over his face. "But since we don't have time to educate you in how the Legions, the real Legions, do things, I'll remind you. When a superior gives an order, the standard response is…what?"

Only then did Barbatus seem to understand what Tiberius was demanding, and it was his turn not to hide his feelings as his face twisted into a bitter grimace.

"Yes, sir. I understand…and I will obey."

Only then were all the men dismissed, and immediately, the air was filled with the sounds of Centurions warning their men that they were about to earn their pay for once.

Piecing it together later, the Centurions came to the conclusion that this attempt on the part of the Varciani to escape from what had been their stronghold was born out of desperation. Either the game was becoming scarce, or more likely, the men of the Varciani army themselves had begun agitating to take some sort of action. Whatever the cause, it put the Varciani in the perfect position to be brought to battle, and on ground that favored the Roman way of fighting. Tiberius and the 8th followed the churned ground made by thousands of feet to the west, and it wasn't long before the men at the front of the column spotted the telltale sign that they were closing the gap, in the form of a low, hovering cloud of dust that was on the horizon just ahead, looking like a dirty smudge. They were following the course of one of the larger streams that ended in the Savus to the south, but then they turned away from that to scale a low pass leading to the more open country beyond. For the first time, there was a buzz of conversation in the ranks, although it was in the form of short, terse statements or questions, snatched between the rapid breathing caused by the pace. They weren't trotting, yet, although Porcinus was sure the order would be coming at any moment. When the Varciani hit the slope of the pass they intended to use, there was a natural slowing of their pace, allowing the lead elements of Tiberius' force to come within a half-mile of the straggling end of what was little more than a mob, at least to a Roman eye. There were no ordered ranks, no neat division between clans or between types of fighting men; spear warriors were jostling with archers and other skirmish troops, all of whom were being shoved aside by the larger bodies of the horses, ridden by Varciani nobles and their retainers. Even from the distance they currently were, the Legionaries in the vanguard could see that the Varciani were close to panic in their haste, scrambling up the narrow track that led over the shoulder between two steep hills. Just on the other side, after they descended the slope, was the widest expanse of what passed for open ground. Perhaps two miles farther west of that was a solid line of green, representing a forest that screened the view of the country immediately beyond, but off in the distance, perhaps ten miles away, was another series of hills and ridges similar in composition in size to the area the Varciani were fleeing. This was clearly their goal, but as every man in Tiberius' part of the army knew, the 15th Legion was somewhere on the other side of this forest, waiting to fall on the remnants of the rebel army. Despite the fact that, to a Roman eye especially, the sight before them of the Varciani was little more than a disorganized mess, as Porcinus and every veteran of Pannonia knew, there was a hidden advantage that the barbarian tribes exhibited at certain moments, particularly in those just before battle. Perhaps their best weapon was the rapidity with which they could engage their enemy, as there was no need for excessive maneuvering or movements to bring warriors to bear. In fact, it was more about who was the swiftest among them in throwing themselves at their enemy, rather than having to issue and listen for a series of commands that brought the right troops into position. What this meant was that Porcinus and his counterparts weren't necessarily fooled at this sign of impending panic, knowing how quickly that could change. Hitting the slope, Porcinus felt the burning in his thighs start, but being a Centurion meant that one could never show they were under the same kind of strain as the rankers, that they were just as tired as the men puffing alongside. And it was at moments like this when Porcinus felt his age, thinking that he was just a couple years short of forty; not as old as most Pili Priores, yet still old enough to feel this pace more acutely than most of his boys. When he was laboring in this manner, he found it useful to think of other things, and he supposed it was natural that he would reflect on how many different faces there were around him. He tried to calculate how many men were missing from among the ranks compared to his first day as Pilus Prior. Just in the little more than three years since he first took command, he estimated that at least a third of his Century, and perhaps a quarter of the entire Cohort were different. Almost immediately, he regretted that train of thought, since the next natural step was to wonder if that meant that in another six years, none of the originals from his Century would be there. Following that was the worst thought; what if he weren't there? What would his family do if he fell? Like every Centurion, and indeed every man with a family, he was acutely aware of the possibility, but he usually managed to put that aside, stuffed and locked away in some deeply buried box in his mind. Unfortunately, sometimes that thought managed to trick the rest of his mind into unlocking the box, and it would come roaring out, almost paralyzing him with the fear it brought. Ironically enough, the only time it was never lurking there, creeping around the corners of his consciousness, reminding him of its presence and instead was safely secure, was in battle. And Porcinus had learned that, for him at least, once he had been made Optio, and then Centurion, nothing helped goad that snarling beast of fear back into its box better than actually thinking about the upcoming fight. He had often wondered about why this was so, and had come to the conclusion that since his mind was so occupied with all the myriad details that came with the job, there was no room for the beast. Not lost on him was that this was based in his love for his boys, and his desire that they see another day, and the best thing he could do to ensure that was to be as prepared as possible. Porcinus didn't know the word for it, but it was this symbiotic relationship, where he as

Centurion, and his men as his other half, fed the other's desire to live, and as they all knew, the best way to survive was to win. Just as his Cohort crested the pass, Porcinus felt the moment of nerves pass, and despite the fact that he felt as if he were breathing pure fire, and his legs were screaming for relief, he felt a smile form on his lips as he realized there was nowhere he would rather be than right here, at this moment.

"All right, boys." Despite his best effort, he knew he was panting some, although he noted with quiet satisfaction that none of the men were even able to talk. "There they are, just waiting for us to cut them down!"

The fact that the cheer was ragged was the best part for him as he began the descent down the slope, following the rest of the army in front of him, as eager for vengeance as any man there.

There was no pause to rest for Tiberius' men, and it was this moment where the superior conditioning of the Legions saw the gap close down to a matter of a few hundred paces from the swirling knot of men that had been designated as the rearguard. The Romans were close enough to see that it was composed of a high number of missile troops, some cavalry, probably consisting of the lower ranking members of each nobleman's mounted contingent, and perhaps two to three hundred infantry. It was the archers that Tiberius worried about, although it wasn't enough of one for him to call a halt. He was young, but this campaign season had seen him grow with experience as a commander, and he knew that some casualties would be inevitable. Even so, the shields of his men would protect the vast majority of them, allowing them to close on the rearguard. What concerned him were two things; the enemy cavalry, which could prevent his men from forming *testudo*, and the length of the delay to his main body as they brushed the rearguard aside. If the enemy rearguard were led by a determined and capable man, they could prove effective enough to hold Tiberius' men for the amount of time it would take to allow the rest of the Varciani to make it into the heavy forest, now a mile ahead of them. Although this wasn't a huge problem in the grand design of his plan, since Quirinus and the 15th were waiting on the other side of that forest, he was determined that it would be the 8th who would exact vengeance. The fact that it was more than glory for its own sake was something he didn't make any attempt to communicate to the Centurions, particularly to that *cunnus* Barbatus, but the more elemental reason and truth was that, in his own way, he loved these men as much as the Centurions did. Perhaps even more so, because this was the first time that Tiberius Claudius Nero felt like he belonged somewhere. For almost as long as he could remember, Tiberius had felt like an outsider, and although he wasn't one to dwell on such things, he supposed it started from the day his mother Livia Drusilla had married the man then known as Gaius Octavianus Caesar. It was true that Tiberius had lacked for nothing, and his stepfather hadn't been excessively harsh, at least for a Roman father. Nevertheless, Octavian had made it abundantly clear that neither Tiberius nor Drusus were his natural sons. And yet, Tiberius also knew that Augustus was much, much fonder of his younger brother Drusus. Despite this, for reasons that Tiberius himself didn't really understand, he felt no malice towards his younger sibling because of his obvious favor with the man who was the sole power in Rome. It was probably because Drusus was so...likeable himself that it was impossible for Tiberius to hate him. The fact that Drusus so obviously adored his older brother had something to do with it, and in a life where he experienced very little of the kind of love among family members that was supposed to be there, it was no surprise that Tiberius returned that kind of affection with his own. He had resigned himself that, in all probability, it would be Drusus who would take the reins from Augustus, and if he were being honest, he was actually relieved that this was the case. Still, this command, his first real command, one where he was clearly in charge, without some older, more experienced crony of Augustus looking over his shoulder, was one he would never forget. And it was this bond he felt with the men marching at his back that drove him to be determined to let them exact their vengeance. Despite the excitement and apprehension of the moment, his internal musings had let his mind touch on the festering boil that was Barbatus. Again, he had known that Augustus didn't view him with the same affection as he did Drusus, but having one of the Princeps' creatures sent to spy on him, to find something with which he could exert some form of pressure on him that would ensure Tiberius would dance to the Princeps' tune, no matter what it was; that was almost too much for him to bear. He longed to send a message, subtle and one that only Augustus would understand that, while he was loyal to the Princeps, he was still his own man and didn't take such things as having eyes on him at all times lightly, nor would he tolerate it. Consequently, it was with some grim satisfaction that he allowed himself to savor what, hopefully, was in store for Barbatus. As pleasant a thought as that was, his attention needed to be elsewhere, and the sight of something out of the ordinary served to yank his thoughts back to the moment. Without any warning, he pulled his horse to a stop to stare ahead, but it wasn't at the rearguard of the Varciani, or even the main body, which had separated itself by this point as they hurried on toward the relative safety of the forest. Instead, he was looking beyond at the forest itself, or just above it, and he swore bitterly, not caring who heard.

"What idiot did that?"

"I don't know, but things just got more interesting," Porcinus commented, his eyes not leaving the sight, the same one that had caused Tiberius' reaction.

Ovidius was the one who called his attention to it, and he was now standing next to him as both men stared ahead. When Ovidius pointed it out, Porcinus initially thought it was dust, probably churned up by the men of the 15th, who he knew were waiting on the far side of the forest, but very quickly he saw that it was not only different in color, it was quickly spreading across the entire front.

"I thought he had decided against doing that," Ovidius said.

"He did, but either someone didn't get the message, or they decided to do it anyway," was Porcinus' guess. "But there's nothing we can do about it now." Shrugging, he slapped Ovidius on the shoulder, sending the signal that his Optio needed to return to his spot as he finished, "Like I said, it just makes things more interesting."

"And hot. And smoky," Ovidius grumbled as he turned to return to his spot.

Porcinus laughed at his Optio's grousing, calling after him, "Do you really want things to be easy all the time?"

"Yes!"

This was uttered not just by Ovidius, but by all the men within earshot who were avidly listening to their superiors talking, causing

Porcinus to give them a glare, while they cheerfully grinned back at their Centurion marching alongside.

"Nosy bastards," he muttered in a voice loud enough to be heard, knowing that they would get a laugh, which they did.

It was yet another lesson learned from Titus Pullus, that men needed a laugh from time to time, especially right before they were about to throw themselves into the terrorizing chaos of battle. Despite making light of it, Porcinus eyed the rapidly growing line of smoke, rising higher and spreading out by the heartbeat with some trepidation, increased by the feeling of the fresh breeze in his face, which was sending the flames in their general direction. From his perspective, this was almost equal parts good and bad; the fire now effectively cut off the escape route of the Varciani, but the barbarians would still reach the edge of the forest on this side before the fire did. As he saw it, the best thing that could happen was that the Varciani commander, seeing this new threat, would call a halt and turn to fight, yet Porcinus felt sure that he would still lead his men into the forest. It would mean they would have a fire at their back, and heading their way, but it also meant that they would no longer be in the open, and could fight on terrain where the Legions weren't as effective. Before any of that could happen, however, the *cornu* sounded, calling the Pili Priores to meet with Tiberius. Trotting up from his spot, Porcinus hurried a bit to catch up with Fronto, whose Cohort was actually marching behind the First this day, since the Second was back in camp.

"Ready for this?" the Tertius Pilus Prior asked his counterpart.

"Very," Porcinus replied grimly, prompting a grunted laugh from Fronto.

"That makes one of us," he said, getting a laugh in return from Porcinus.

Then they were there, where Tiberius and Barbatus were already waiting, the Primus Pilus glaring at the two Centurions as if they had arrived late, despite the fact they were the first Pili Priores to arrive. The look caused Porcinus to reflect that he hadn't come to hate a man in such a short period of time in his entire life, and shooting a glance at Fronto, he was heartened to see the disgust plainly written on the other man's face. Tiberius, on the other hand, favored both men with his version of a smile, looking down from his horse, once more choosing to stay mounted. In another moment, the other five Centurions were gathered, and Tiberius wasted no time.

"We're going in a double line of Cohorts, on a three-Century front," he told the Centurions.

So far, this was standard, and it meant there would be four Cohorts, and Porcinus immediately looked over to the spot where he was sure his men would line up, third Cohort from the right, with the Third to their right and the Fifth to the left. But Tiberius had other plans.

"I want the First on the right." This was standard and caused no comment, but the surprise was coming, "But I want the Fourth next to the First." Turning to Fronto, Tiberius said, "Fronto, I want your Cohort to anchor the other end, with the Fifth to your right."

This was slightly unusual, but Porcinus realized that the fact they were marching without Volusenus' Cohort was also unusual, and he saw that Fronto didn't appear to be overly upset. The only man who looked put out was Barbatus, and Porcinus saw the man open his mouth to object, except the look Tiberius gave him was apparently enough that he quickly shut it. It was with equal parts amusement and relief that Porcinus saw someone else who hated Barbatus as much as he did, and he supposed that he and the Legate, at least in the moment, had more in common than one would suppose just from looking at them.

"I want the First there." Tiberius pointed to the base of a small rise to the north of their position that would put the First just to the right of the outermost edge of the rough line formed by the Varciani rearguard that, even then, was shaking out into their own version of a formation. Continuing, Tiberius said, "I'm putting half of Silva's *ala* on the top of that rise." He twisted in the saddle to look in the opposite direction, back where the Third would be. Pointing, he addressed Fronto. "The other half is going to be just next to that stream. You'll use them as your left marker." With his dispositions made, Tiberius snapped, "Well, hurry up! The faster we get formed up, the faster we can get those bastards. I want the men put in position at the double time."

As the Centurions hurried away, Fronto muttered to Porcinus, "Notice he didn't mention that huge fucking fire headed our way?"

In fact, Porcinus had, but the best he could come up with was, "I guess he realizes there's nothing we can do about it. That's probably why he wants us to double time to get in place."

"But we're going to have to pause to catch our breath," Fronto argued.

Although it was a valid complaint, Porcinus wasn't so sure, and he said, "Maybe not. You've seen the boys. They're wound as tight as a ballista rope. They just want to get stuck in with these bastards. And so do I," he finished.

Fronto didn't appear convinced, but they had reached the Third, and the pair paused just long enough for a quick clasp of arms.

"Mars and Fortuna," Fronto said, in an abbreviated form of the blessing that the Centurions of the 8th had used to wish each other luck since long before Porcinus had been in the Centurionate.

"Mars and Fortuna," Porcinus repeated, then turned and resumed his jog back to the Fourth.

"All right, you misbegotten sons of whores," he roared. "It's time to earn our pay and avenge our brothers!"

The answering roar told Porcinus that his men were more than ready.

Moving into their respective positions as quickly as Porcinus could ever remember seeing, the 8th quickly brushed the rearguard out of the way, and with a minimum of casualties. The archers were particularly ineffective, mainly because, from what Porcinus saw, only a handful launched more than two or three arrows before turning to flee, following the main body into the forest. There was a slight pause when the small cavalry force with the rearguard suddenly came galloping forward with the clear goal of catching the Romans off balance. However, the men of the Roman front line all quickly thrust their javelins out in front of them, the bristling points convincing the Varciani cavalry they would be foolish to try and penetrate that line. Shearing away, they galloped parallel to the Roman front, and some horses and riders were actually taken down by quicker thinking men, who hurled one of their two javelins as they thundered by. Then the troopers belonging to Silva stationed on the small rise came down at the gallop, quickly dispatching those Varciani nobles whose courage overruled their brains. Meanwhile, the front line barely paused in their relentless advance, as the Centurions of both lines bawled out orders to keep the alignment as close to parade-ground perfect as it was possible to do over rough, broken ground. Within three hundred heartbeats after the last of the rearguard either fled, or in one case consisting of a small knot of rebel infantry who made a foolish stand and were cut down, the Romans in the front line were within javelin range of the edge of the forest. Only then was a halt called, both Centurions and Optios working quickly as they straightened lines with a shove here and a push there. Just inside the forest, Porcinus could see the mass of Varciani, who had begun their own pre-battle ritual, meaning that the noise level rose rapidly, as individual warriors came darting out from the safety of the trees to shout their challenges and taunts while shaking their weapons at the Romans. It was a familiar sight to the veterans, and it had no effect on any man in the Roman ranks, most of whom stood there, shields grounded in front of them, the only signs of nerves either a drumming of fingers on the shield, or excessive yawning. While there was a noise coming from the ranks as the Legionaries talked quietly to each other, it was a low buzz compared to the roar from the Varciani. Although it was difficult for Porcinus, in his spot slightly ahead of his Century, to hear what was said, he caught enough to know that the men were beginning to get concerned about the smoke that was finally beginning to drift from the forest, and what was causing it.

Realizing he needed to say something, Porcinus turned about and bellowed loudly, "Look, boys! Hades has already gotten the fires going for when we drive those bastards into them! You're going to get to watch them burn!"

There was a roar of approval, and very quickly, men on either side of his Century who hadn't heard relayed his words, causing a rolling reaction that could be followed both directions down the line. For the moment at least, the fire became an ally, the flames another weapon, waiting for the 8th to drive these rebels right into them. The cheering was interrupted by the sound of the *cornu* assigned to Tiberius, coming from behind the center of the Roman lines.

"Prepare javelins!"

Porcinus and all the other Centurions of the first line bellowed the order. And, as before, he didn't have to turn around, hearing the rustling, creaking sound of men drawing their arms back. Personally, Porcinus thought this was a waste of javelins, since the trees would block most of the missiles, but he supposed every man or shield taken down now was one less they would have to face in just a few dozen heartbeats. The *cornu* blast that followed served as the command to release, the air filling with streaking missiles, and even with the extra protection of the trees, Porcinus clearly heard the low moan coming from the forest as those men who were the most exposed tried to track the progress of the javelins on their earthward arc. The sound of the weighted shafts slamming into targets, both wooden and flesh, was oddly muffled compared to other times, which Porcinus assumed was because of the trees, but he had no time to wonder why.

"Prepare javelins!"

The rustling sound again, except this time, the command given was verbal, making the second volley more ragged, as each Centurion chose to wait varying lengths of time before thundering, "Release!"

With this second volley, even as the missiles were in the air, Tiberius' *cornu* sounded again, with the three-note blast that unleashed the full fury of the Legions of Rome, only beginning their charge on the third note.

"Come on, boys! Don't let those bastards next to us get there first!" Porcinus roared, holding his blade above his head, then bringing it down in a chopping motion, even as he began the dash towards the waiting enemy.

The second volley had just landed, giving the Varciani less than a dozen heartbeats before they had to prepare to receive the smashing impact of the Legionaries of the leading Cohorts, all of the men on the front line holding their shields hard against their left shoulder to put the weight of their bodies behind the first impact. This would be the only time they would use this tactic, but as always, it was devastatingly effective, and the immense, deafening crash of the impact as usual drowned out all other noise. Porcinus, not yet having a shield, had to be more judicious in his attack, although it was only marginally so, as he counted on his size and the sheer ferocity of his assault to make up for his lack of the other offensive weapon. As always, he chose either the largest warrior, or the one who had the appearance of being a leader or high-ranking noble. In this case, it was the former, a burly man who seemed to be as wide as he was tall, heavily muscled and adorned with several arm rings on each limb. This Varciani was armed with a heavy spear and a round wooden shield; in addition, he also had a mail coat that hung down to his knees, along with a helmet adorned with the antlers of a stag. As he approached at a run, Porcinus drew his sword back so the point was close to his ear, which was his favored method of starting a first attack. The Varciani, eyes narrowed into slits as he focused on this tall Roman, concentrated on the point of the blade, which was exactly what Porcinus had hoped for, starting what looked like a downward thrust when he was still two paces away. If the Varciani had had the time, he would have given a grim smile at the sight of this supposed veteran warrior, which he knew all Centurions were supposed to be, committing too early in this first crucial attack, so that even if the point struck him, it would be at the farthest end of the Roman's reach. Still, he had no desire to be stuck at all and his shield arm rose, responding as of its own mind, the result of his own endless practice, preparing to block a thrust that would never come. Even as Porcinus took his next step, his sword arm was changing direction, moving the sword from a high thrust aimed at the Varciani's chest, to one that came from beneath the lower edge of the man's shield, slightly from the left. As it had done to literally thousands of men over its life, the point of what had been Titus Pullus' Gallic sword punched through the mail of the Varciani, plunging deep into the warrior's vitals just under the ribcage. In one smooth motion, Porcinus twisted, not his arm but his entire body, holding the sword rigid by keeping his upper arm tight against his chest. The result was as inevitable as it was devastating, the keen blade ripping across the abdomen, cutting through the muscles and metal links of mail with an ease that belied the enormous strength it took perform such a movement. The Varciani's eyes bulged as his mouth opened and let out a blood-curdling shriek of pain, but Porcinus was already moving past the now-dead man before the Varciani even dropped to his knees. If Porcinus had the time or inclination, he would have acknowledged with some chagrin that this move, taught to him by his father, was one that Titus Pullus could perform without the need to brace himself, and, in fact, could disembowel a man with his arm fully extended. But there was no shame in what Porcinus had to do; he had never seen anyone else who could do it as Pullus had. Moving quickly, Porcinus crossed the two paces so that he was now tight up against the rest of his Century's formation. Seeing an opportunity presented by a gap between two Varciani, he chose the Varciani that was engaged by the Legionary to his left, dispatching the man with a quick thrust to the back. There was a howl of outrage from the nearest Varciani, who leapt forward, bringing his long sword down in a smashing blow, trying to catch Porcinus before he could turn to face the new threat. It would have succeeded, but the Gregarius who Porcinus had helped returned the favor, taking a single step forward to the right, raising his shield to stop the blade, which struck the boss in a shower of sparks before bouncing off at an awkward angle. Again, Porcinus' blade snaked out, this time coming in high as he noticed the warrior carrying his shield a bit lower than normal, the point catching the man in the throat, a spray of bright red arterial blood erupting from the gaping wound.

"Thanks," Porcinus gasped, while never taking his eyes off the Varciani across from him.

"Welcome," the Legionary grunted. "Just remember that when it's my turn to clean the latrines."

Porcinus laughed, and although it was forced, it was not only for the benefit of his men, but he knew that such behavior served to rattle their enemies, the idea that there were men who could laugh at such moments as this adding to the mystique and intimidation of the Legions. His front line had already pushed more than a dozen paces inside the forest, and Porcinus' eyes had adjusted to the dimmer lighting. Following immediately behind the laugh, however, came a string of curses as Porcinus swore at the sight before him. He wasn't sure why he was surprised, but he realized he had been irrationally hoping that somehow this forest would be different from the others in this area, that there would be less underbrush, and worse, the ground wouldn't be littered with the trunks and large branches of fallen trees. This was the worst type of terrain for men of the Legions to fight on, yet he also understood that the only way to deal with this effectively was to break down into smaller groups that were more nimble and didn't require as much open space. Fortunately, his men possessed plenty of experience in this kind of fighting, although they loathed it as much as Porcinus did.

"Break down by sections!" He bellowed the order several times, risking quick glances to make sure the section leaders, all ten of them, had heard and acknowledged the order. Once he saw them signal with a nod or a wave that they had heard, he finished, "Wait for my command!"

Then he turned his attention back to the front, waving his *vitus* and pointing it forward in a signal to press onward, closing back up to the Varciani, who had shuffled backward. Over the heads and behind the enemy, Porcinus saw what was taking the form of a gray wall of smoke, billowing upward and, more importantly, coming in their direction.

"Get your neckerchiefs out and ready," he suddenly ordered. "We're about to be in that smoke, so those men who can, douse them with your canteens! And if I smell wine on any of you bastards, I'll stripe you, I swear on the black stone I will!"

The was a combination of muted laughs and curses, and Porcinus grimaced, knowing that more than one of his men had violated the regulations about only water being in the canteens of men going into battle. However, that was a worry for later. Like the men of the front line, he couldn't take the risk of wetting his neckerchief, so it would be extremely unpleasant for some time to come. Then they were again within a couple paces of the Varciani, yet before he could give any more orders, a trio of warriors darted from their lines, screaming their defiance as they aimed at Porcinus. This wasn't the time for reckless bravery, so instead of moving to meet them, the Centurion took a step back and to his left, bringing him hard up against his Century. In one smooth motion that betrayed the experience and training of the Legions, the man on the outside of the second rank took a step forward at an oblique angle to the right, placing himself to Porcinus' right, instantly creating a solid line of Romans, now ready to meet the onrushing barbarians man for man. Two of them never faltered, but the third man, the one in the middle, either more timid or perhaps wiser, suddenly chopped his steps, as if changing his mind about the attack. This left Porcinus unengaged, meaning that it was short work for him to end the Varciani attacking the Gregarius to his right, the man from the second rank. Before he could turn his attention to the second man, he was already down, while the third man scrambled back to his own lines, accompanied by the jeers and taunts of the Romans who saw it happen. Still, the Varciani were backpedaling, then over the shouting and sounds of the fighting taking place to the right and to the left, there were screams from the rear of the Varciani formation. They were shrill with the kind of panic that told Porcinus in clear terms what had happened; the fire had just caught up with the rear ranks of the Varciani. The move backward was over.

Not more than a handful of moments later, the entire area of battle was enveloped in smoke, reducing the visibility in any direction to less than thirty paces. Compounding the difficulty was the smoke itself, which soon had men's eyes streaming, the sounds of coughing, gagging, and cursing now competing with the normal din of fighting. One unfortunate consequence of the fire was that, whether by choice or circumstance, it stiffened the resolve of the Varciani, as most of them understandably chose the relatively quick death offered by a blade rather than the lingering, horrific pain that came from fire. Very quickly, the ordered ranks of the Romans broke down as well, although this was by design, pursuing groups of rebels who took advantage of the clumps of underbrush, deadfalls of logs, and hidden gullies, using them as makeshift defensive barricades. It was a nightmare world of quick glimpses of darting warriors, moving from a clump of brush to leap behind a fallen tree, using it as a breastwork, while the Legionaries stood on the other side, thrusting over and down at their enemies, cursing in frustration.

Porcinus was everywhere, moving from one section of his Century to another, adding his sword where it was needed, or giving directions about the best way to dislodge a stubborn handful of warriors. There were no more lines, ordered or otherwise, and once the smoke had settled like a choking blanket, there was no discernible direction. Porcinus worried that the poor visibility would allow a fair number of the Varciani to slip past his men, but he knew that, in all likelihood, Tiberius had kept the second line Cohorts positioned at the edge of the forest, waiting for just such a development. Regardless of Tiberius' plans, this was something beyond his control and he gave it no more than a passing thought. What was of more immediate concern was the change in the ground as they penetrated deeper into the forest; the terrain was becoming more undulating, with creases and folds in the ground showing up with more frequency. If the wood was a difficult place to clear under the best of circumstances, between the smoke and these new obstacles, it was now a nightmare. Even as this was occupying his thoughts, he took a step forward and immediately discovered that the ground wasn't where he thought it would be. For a sickening moment, he felt himself pitching forward, and he had more of an impression than actual view of a steeply sloping gully, the bottom of which was filled with a tangle of dead branches and logs. Windmilling his arms, he managed to recover his balance, then shouted a warning over his shoulder at the section of men following just behind. Directly across from him on the other side of the gully, which was perhaps twenty-five paces wide, he caught a glimpse of movement, yet before he could react, a Varciani spear came hissing through the smoke, missing him by a hand's breadth. He ducked, then chided himself for doing so much too late for it do any good, whether it was an understandable reflex or not. Stepping back a pace, he crouched to present a smaller target as he strained his eyes, trying to see where the gully returned to the ground level either to his right or left, so that he could move his men around it. Finally thinking he saw the spot, he called to the section with him, and began skirting the gully. Even as he navigated around it, Porcinus was trying to get his bearings, realizing with a sinking feeling that he had lost track of where he and his men were in relation to anything familiar. The temperature had risen several degrees, but he could no longer tell in which direction the fire was, nor did he know where the edge of the forest where he and his men had entered should be any longer. It was nothing but shadows and smoke, and the only thing he was sure of was the direction those Varciani on the opposite side of the gully had headed.

"Follow me," he called, then plunged after them.

He only became aware that he was alone when he turned back around a dozen heartbeats later and nobody was there. Cursing softly, he opened his mouth wider to call out for his men then, realizing it would just as likely attract unwanted attention, shut it. There were already men shouting all around him, but it was impossible to pinpoint their location with any precision, and although many were shouting in clear Latin, just as many were either in the Varciani tongue, or worse, unintelligible. If he followed his ears to one of those men, he could walk right into a bunch of Varciani. Consequently, he began moving slowly, pausing every few paces to wipe his eyes in an attempt to clear his vision, except the smoke had gotten so thick that it was impossible to keep them from tearing up almost immediately. Then he saw a dark shape lying off to his left, and he approached cautiously, sword at the ready. It wasn't until he got within a half-dozen paces that he saw that it was a Roman and, with a curse, he hurried to the man's body. It was with equal parts relief and guilt when he saw that it wasn't one of his men, but one from the First Cohort; if he remembered, the Third Century, although he couldn't recall the man's name. The one bright spot was that he now had a shield, and as he hefted it, he said a brief prayer for the dead man. Turning his mind to the immediate problem, he tried to determine the meaning of his discovery. Had he wandered so far from his own Cohort that he was now in the First Cohort's area? Just then, he heard a shout, and recognized the voice as belonging to Frontinus, somewhere off to his right. That told him, in all likelihood, he was in between the Second and Third Century of the First Cohort, meaning that somehow, his own men were back to his left. However, now if he moved directly left, he would run into that gully he had bypassed, so with a quiet curse, he turned about to reverse his course. Before he moved three paces, there was another shout, directly from behind him.

"There they are, boys! Gut those bastards!"

It was Urso! He was sure of it, back in the direction he had just been headed, so he reversed course once more, still carefully moving, but doing so more swiftly than he had before. That meant he once more almost took a tumbling fall, except this time, he managed to stop himself, and he paused again to wipe his eyes, peering through the smoke. Before him was another gully; unlike the first one, this one ran across his front, perpendicular to the first one he had almost fallen into, meaning that, most likely, this one intersected it somewhere to his left. He began searching for a way across, either by a place that wasn't as steep as what was in front of him, or for where this one ended, which he assumed would be off to his right, back in the direction of the First Cohort. That was the direction he moved now, intent on getting across so that he could at least rejoin his Pilus Posterior; maybe then, he could sort this mess out. Twice, he saw fleeting shapes, yet each time, they were fleeing in the same direction he was headed, and he couldn't tell whether they were friend or foe, so he didn't call out. He thought about using his bone whistle; he had heard several blasts in all directions, then decided against it since he was alone. Again, he paused for a moment, wiping his eyes one more time with the neckerchief, hoping that he would find a way across quickly so he could get back in the fight with his men.

The blow, when it came, was completely unexpected. In fact, it was more of a shove, and before he could react, Porcinus felt himself sprawling to his left, into the empty space above the gully. The impact as his left side hit the ground drove the wind from his lungs in an explosive whoosh, the only blessing being that the ground was soft enough that it didn't break his shoulder. Unfortunately, that was where the good news ended, as he felt himself tumbling end over end, the sight before him a rapidly whirling landscape where sky and ground switched places faster than his brain could account for the change. Then everything before that in the form of the impact from hitting the ground perhaps a half-dozen times seemed to be the whisper of a child compared to the shouts of a thousand men as his right leg met a log near the bottom of the gully. Slamming into the wood with horrific force, the two bones of his lower right leg just above his greave snapped as if they were twigs themselves, and he was only vaguely aware that the horrible scream of pain came from his own lips. Then he was still, lying on his back, much as he had been just a couple of days before, looking up at a tangled mass of vegetation, both living and dead. Somehow, he didn't know how, he didn't lose consciousness, although a part of him was praying that he would do so, anything to put him out of the most intense pain he had ever experienced. After a moment, when he realized he wouldn't be passing out, at least right away, he tried to catch as much of his breath as he could in the choking smoke, which seemed to be thicker here than up on the forest floor. Then, with a dread that he would never be able to describe, he tried to lever himself upright into a sitting position. It was only with the help of a thick branch attached to the larger log that he assumed had broken his leg that he managed, pulling himself up to a point where he could look at his leg. He immediately wished he hadn't, as without any warning, the sight of his leg, grotesquely twisted so that it formed a right angle, with the sole of his right foot pressed against his left calf, caused him to vomit. It happened so quickly that he couldn't even turn his head, and the feeling of the warm bile splattering over his lap and upper legs only meant that he couldn't stop until he was retching and nothing more was coming up. Each spasm of his stomach sent bolts of exquisite pain shooting through his lower right leg, and it wasn't just the smoke that was causing the tears to stream from his eyes. Spent, he fell back down onto his back, staring up at the smoky sky, moaning with the pain, and for the first time in his life, he understood other men who had begged for their comrades to kill them. That was when he became aware of another sound, and with every fiber of his being, he forced himself to lie still, listening. It took just a moment for him to determine that it was the sound of someone, or something, large, coming down the slope of the gully from the side on which he had been. He opened his mouth to shout, realizing that he was almost completely hidden here at the bottom of the gully, covered over with the branches and leaves of the deadfall. Then, the part of his mind still aware of his overall situation clamped down on his mouth, firmly shutting it. Carefully, he began moving his head, looking all around him for his sword, but when he found it, he couldn't stop himself from a small groan of frustration. It had landed low on the opposite side of the gully, just up the slope, the point partially buried in the dirt underneath the leaves. It had obviously been flung from his hand with a great deal of force for it to have landed where it had, with the point embedded in the earth. Even if moving at all wasn't an agony that he was sure would cause him finally to pass out, for him to retrieve it he would have to lift himself up from his hiding spot. Instead, he reached down and was only slightly comforted by the feel of the handle of his *pugio*, still secure in its sheath, although he recoiled as his hands touched the sticky slime from his vomit coating the handle. The *pugio* would only be useful if he could somehow lure the Varciani close enough, and he decided that appearing to be dead was his best bet. If it was a Roman, it wouldn't matter. Focusing all of his rapidly waning resolve and concentration, he slowed his breathing down to the point that he hoped from a distance at least, he would appear not to be breathing at all. Shutting his eyes so they were barely slit, he waited as the sounds of moving leaves and trickling dirt signaled the location of whoever it was coming down the gully. Finally, Porcinus heard a soft thud, in the direction of his feet, telling him that whoever it was had jumped the last distance down into the bottom of the gully. Then he heard a deeper rustling, followed by a dragging sound that Porcinus assumed was the man searching for him. This confirmed he was well hidden, and he began to hope that perhaps whoever it was, at least if it was the enemy, would give up and go scrambling back up the gully. If he did that, then Porcinus could at least risk a peek through the branches of his spot to see if it was friend or foe. As it turned out, there was no need for this; there was a vibration under Porcinus' body that presaged the sudden removal of one of the branches above him. Just that movement caused Porcinus to want to scream out, but he clenched his teeth together tightly, praying to every god he could think of that whoever it was couldn't see him. Then, he made out movement through the thicket of his eyelashes, and he let out a burst of pent-up breath as he fully opened his eyes.

"Thank the gods," he groaned. "I thought it was those Varciani bastards."

Porcinus' relief was justified; even through the combined obscurity of eyes almost shut and the heavy smoke, there was no mistaking the silhouette of the transverse crest of the Roman Centurion. However, that relief was also misplaced; in fact, he was in the most danger of his life.

Porcinus' first hint that all was not right, that he hadn't been rescued, was in the silence that greeted Porcinus' own words. He had been trying to struggle to a position where he would be easier to retrieve from the tangle of vegetation, but the lack of response stopped him. It seemed that time suddenly came to a complete standstill, as Porcinus raised his eyes to look up at the Centurion, still standing no more than five paces from him, hands on hips and with a smile on his face. But it was a smile that held nothing but a promise of pure malice.

"Barbatus," Porcinus breathed the name, and even above the throbbing agony, he felt a stab of such fear that, for a brief instant, the pain in his leg was forgotten.

"Pilus Prior Porcinus." Barbatus drew each word out, almost lovingly, as if he was savoring each one like a sweet grape. "The gods are indeed kind. They've answered one of our prayers."

"What...what do you mean?" Porcinus asked, trying to shove the panic down to force his mind to ignore the pain and think clearly.

"I think you know what I mean," Barbatus replied evenly, then took a step toward Porcinus.

That was when Porcinus knew he had one chance, and one only, so that even understanding the agony it would cause him, he used his powerful arms to lever himself upright before grabbing two handfuls of the slope to begin pulling himself up, towards his sword, the Gallic blade that was so tantalizingly close. Barbatus didn't react immediately; instead, he just stood there, watching with interest as Porcinus, emitting a whining groan that was almost feral in its intensity, pulled himself up towards the sword. However, just as Porcinus got to a point where he was sure the sword was within reach and he extended his right arm, Barbatus, without any real hurry, took a couple steps closer. Then, raising one foot, he brought one hobnailed boot down, hard, on Porcinus' ruined leg. The shriek that emanated from Porcinus was so loud and so shrill that it not only caused Barbatus to wince from the noise, he cast a quick, slightly nervous glance up to the top of the gully, looking quickly to both sides before he drew his sword. Porcinus was now soaked in sweat, panting and almost out of his mind with the pain, but he still had the presence of mind to draw his own *pugio*, the sight of which only caused Barbatus to laugh.

"You brought a dagger to a sword fight, Porcinus," he sneered. Then, taking another step forward, he drew his sword arm back. "I'm going to enjoy this, you *cunnus*. You thought you were so much better than me, so much smarter than me! I've killed a lot of men, but I'm really going to enjoy sending the heir of the great Titus Pullus to Hades where he belongs! Oh," his lips pulled back in a sneering smile, "and when I get back to Siscia, your brat is going to have an accident. Then your whore of a wife. Then the rest of your children. That will teach you who the better man is!"

"You cocksucker." Porcinus' voice was part snarl, part shriek. "I swear by all the gods that I'll piss on you, even if it's from the afterlife. Why don't you come closer and we'll see who the better man is, you...*minion!*"

"Shut your mouth." Barbatus' voice was no less savage than Porcinus', and even through the fog of pain and the fear, Porcinus saw that he had hit a nerve.

"Why? What are you going to do? Kill me?" Porcinus spat back. "Then you're probably going to roll me over and fuck me, aren't you? Oh wait," Porcinus didn't know how, but he found a way at least to make the approximation of a laugh, although it was more of a wheezing cough. "I forgot. You don't like to give; you like to receive. Is that what Augustus does for you? Is it? He gives you the fucking you like? How big is your asshole, Barbatus? How much of his seed have you taken up your ass? In your mouth? When you fart, does it sound like a sigh?"

"SHUT YOUR MOUTH!" Barbatus screamed this, but Porcinus only had eyes for the man's sword and saw that the point of the blade was wavering, so overcome with rage was the Primus Pilus.

"At least tell me why." Porcinus hoped he sufficiently tamped down any pleading quality in his question. From his viewpoint, the only way to win at least a few more heartbeats of life was to play on the man's vanity and pride. The memory of those grooming implements in the Primus Pilus' quarters came to his mind now, and Porcinus was gambling that Barbatus was a man with a highly inflated sense of himself and his place in their world. "Did Augustus tell you to do this? Were those his orders?"

Of all the guesses and leaps of intuition that Gaius Porcinus made in his life, this was the shrewdest, because it stopped Barbatus who, if anything, looked amused.

Staring down at the prone Centurion, he finally gave a shrug, then answered, "Not that it matters now. You won't be telling anyone. No, the Princeps didn't tell me to kill you. Oh," he hurried to add, "he knows about you. Don't think he doesn't. But he clipped your wings and frankly, you don't matter. No," he shook his head as his mouth twisted into an expression that gave Porcinus the full impact of the depth of Barbatus' hatred, "this is my idea. Your uncle thought he was so much better than men just like him! Well, he wasn't the only man who had plans! Who had dreams! But he had to rub the patricians' faces in the *cac* and let them know he was the great Titus Pullus! And because of him, none of us in the ranks can count on reaping the rewards we deserve! So what better way to avenge myself on your *cunnus* of an uncle by stamping out his line?"

Finished, Barbatus took another step and Porcinus knew it was over, that, at most, he had won a few more heartbeats of life, yet, in those last moments, his thoughts were only for his family, and he was filled with the hopeless dread that comes when a man realizes that everything he holds dear will be destroyed. Except Barbatus didn't strike. Instead, he did something quite strange. He gave a little coughing sound, and with a slowness completely out of character for what he had been about to do, he made a slight half-turn, as if he wanted to make one last check over his shoulder. Then, he turned back around, and Porcinus would never forget the look on the man's face, a puzzled expression that was marred by the stream of blood bubbling from his mouth. Barbatus took a staggering step forward before collapsing to his knees, his eyes wide but unseeing, then toppled forward on his face to land with a heavy thud just inches from Porcinus' feet. Porcinus stared down at the prone body of the Primus Pilus uncomprehendingly, his mind barely registering the puckered hole oozing blood in his back. Only then did he lift his head, with an almost comical slowness, to see a man, this one dressed identically to both Porcinus and Barbatus, now lying dead in the gully, as Porcinus should have been. Porcinus felt his mouth working, but it took several tries before anything came out, a croaking combination of recognition and question.

"Urso?"

Porcinus' Pilus Posterior didn't answer immediately. Instead, he moved quickly to where Porcinus was lying, shoving the branches out of the way to kneel by his side. His face was grim as he looked at the mangled leg of his Pilus Prior, while Porcinus studied the other man for a clue as to how bad it really was. He had looked once, although he couldn't bring himself to do so again, thinking that seeing it would only increase the agony he was already feeling.

"Porcinus, I'm going to have to lift you up, and I won't lie, it's going to hurt like Dis," Urso said.

Porcinus barely heard the other man, still studying the darker features of his second in command, before he whispered a hoarse, "Thank you."

Urso just shrugged, seeming to be embarrassed by Porcinus' gratitude.

"You're welcome, but there's no real need to thank me. I'd expect you to haul me out of here instead of burning to death."

"That's not what I was talking about," Porcinus answered quietly. "I'm talking about saving me from Barbatus."

Porcinus would never forget Urso's reply, not only for what he said, but for what happened immediately afterward.

"There's no need for that either," Urso replied conversationally as he reached down to put a hand under Porcinus' armpits. "That debt was paid by the man I work for."

Then, before Porcinus could respond, or even make sense of what he had just heard, Urso lifted Porcinus up with a grunt. Sparks of a thousand colors exploded in Porcinus' head as the pain simply became too overwhelming, and that was the last thing he remembered for some time. From what he pieced together later, the next full watch of his life was passed with him slipping in and out of consciousness; he had faint memories of hearing Urso's harsh breath as he labored up the slope of the gully, then the shouts of other Romans before he slipped away again. His next memory was of intense heat, and he was lying on the ground, except there was something hard underneath him as he vaguely realized that he had been placed on a shield. He was only strong enough to turn his head, seeing the dirty legs and *caligae* of Legionaries, but it was what was beyond them that was the most vivid memory. It looked like a wall of flame, and it helped him to distinguish the meaning of the line of men, frantically chopping and tearing brush out in an attempt to slow the fire by creating a firebreak. Clearly, he and the others escaped the flames, because the next time he opened his eyes, he was staring up at a clear but smoky sky, while the shouts and calls that were so familiar to him of a Legion forming up sounded all around him. He remained conscious long enough to feel himself lifted up and a pair of hands, once again under his arms, dragging him backward onto a flat, hard surface.

"Sorry, Centurion," a voice with a tinge of Greek spoke, "but this is going to be bumpy getting back to camp. I'm afraid it's going to be pretty painful."

Whoever told him that was right; he stayed awake until shortly after the wagon started moving. Then it hit a hole, sending a shuddering jolt through the floor of the wagon and up into Porcinus' body. Once more, he heard a shout of pain, just before all went dark again.

It was dark in the tent when Porcinus woke up next, although that was always the case in the hospital tent. The first sensation that was strong enough to cut through the pain was an almost overwhelming thirst, and he turned his head, looking for a *medicus*.

Seeing nobody near, he opened his mouth to call, except all that came out was a croak that he didn't recognize himself.

"Water."

When nobody came, he braced himself, knowing that the effort would cause him agony.

"Water!"

"Coming, Centurion! I'm coming!"

Then there was someone there, the *medicus* who Porcinus recognized as the one whose head Volusenus had bounced the cup off, and there was still a bandage in place, covering the wound. What was most important was that he brought a ladle and, lifting Porcinus' head, he put it to the stricken man's lips. He drank greedily, sure that he had never tasted water so sweet.

"More," he commanded once he had finished the ladle.

"I'm sorry, Centurion, but that's all you get. The physician still has to set your leg, and if you have too much in your stomach, you'll regret it."

Porcinus opened his mouth to argue then, realizing the wisdom in the *medicus'* words, just nodded his head weakly in acceptance. The *medicus* hurried off, presumably to inform the physician that Porcinus had awakened. Soon enough, an older man, bald and wearing a leather apron that Porcinus saw was stained with blood, came into view, and Porcinus recognized that it was Philandros, the physician who had worked on Titus.

"Well now, Centurion," he said with a geniality that Porcinus had heard before, knowing it to be the false heartiness that men like him saved for the gravely injured. "Let's see what we can do about this leg, shall we?"

Porcinus didn't answer verbally, instead just giving a grim nod. Philandros, who Porcinus knew was the most senior among the staff, pulled the thin cover that had been lain over Porcinus' lower body, and even that slight disturbance caused him to wince. His eyes never left Philandros, something that he would regret later, because he saw the man's expression change instantly as soon as he looked down at the ruined appendage. Heaving a sigh, he suddenly seemed to be looking everywhere but in Porcinus' eyes.

"I regret to say that the damage to your leg is more...severe than I was led to believe," he said at last.

Porcinus waited for more, but when Philandros said nothing else, it prompted him to demand, "Well? What does that mean?"

"It means," the physician said softly, "that you are unlikely to survive what it would take for me to set the leg straight, and that even if I did, and you did live, the chance of it mending straight is...poor."

Porcinus didn't reply for long moments, his fatigued mind struggling to make sense of what Philandros was telling him.

Finally, he opened his mouth; it took him three tries before anything came out, and he protested, "But I'm strong and in good health! I survived breaking it. I'm not going to die when you set it!"

"No, you may not," the physician agreed, sending Porcinus' hopes rising, if just for a moment. "In fact, I think you probably would, particularly since you don't seem to have any other wounds, just some bumps and bruises. How did this happen, by the way? We don't often see injuries like this after a battle."

"I was...I fell," Porcinus mumbled, changing his mind in mid-sentence about telling the truth.

In fact, this was the first time he had thought about the circumstances that led him to his current condition, and his next was the memory of Barbatus lying at his feet, with Urso standing, holding a bloody sword. Unaware of Porcinus' musings, Philandros gave him a surprised look.

"That's strange," he said, staring at Porcinus for the first time, with an expression that the Centurion couldn't readily decipher. Then, he shrugged and finished, "But I've seen stranger things happen on a battlefield. Just your bad luck."

"Yes, just my bad luck," Porcinus agreed through gritted teeth. "So, set my leg."

The physician gave him a long, searching look, before asking, "Centurion, are you sure? Because even if you survive, I can tell you that the chances of it healing straight again are not good. It will have to be in a splint for several weeks, and the broken ends of your bones have poked through the skin in two places. Frankly, I've seldom seen breaks this bad, and I've never seen one worse. At least, where the patient lived."

Porcinus felt a flare of temper, and he grabbed the physician, using the considerable strength of his right hand, made even more powerful by the conditioning exercises prescribed for all who used the Vinician grip. He was rewarded by a yelp of pain from the physician; under normal circumstances, Porcinus would have relented because he normally didn't like exerting his strength to hurt men who weren't enemies, but this wasn't a normal moment.

"Listen to me," he hissed. "Set. My. Fucking. Leg. Now." Only then did he relent with his grip, dropping his head back on the bolster, his hair and face soaked with sweat. "You let me worry about the rest of it."

"Very well, Centurion," Philandros relented, rubbing his forearm and glaring at the prone Roman. "Have it your way. But don't say I didn't warn you." Motioning to the nearest *medicus*, the physician ordered him to come assist, pointing to a stoppered bottle, which the *medicus* picked up. Pouring a spoonful, he indicated to Porcinus to open his mouth, which he did. When he swallowed the bitter concoction, he made a face that seemed to amuse the physician. "Poppy syrup. Tastes horrible from what I've been told. But you'll be thanking me later. Not," he rubbed his arm again, "that you deserve it. But I suppose this will be enough punishment as it is, even with the syrup."

As he spoke, the *medicus* tapped Porcinus on the jaw softly, in a signal for the Centurion to open his mouth. Porcinus did, the *medicus* shoving a round dowel wrapped with several layers of leather into his mouth and, as Porcinus clamped down on it, he could feel the grooves and indentations made by only the gods knew how many other teeth. That was when the fear hit him, a fresh spate of sweat bursting out all over his body as he prepared himself for his trial. Philandros, seeing that all was ready, did…nothing. In fact, he seemed more interested in continuing what had been a one-sided conversation, as it was, even before Porcinus clamped down on the gag.

"I have seen at least two cases where the men in question were able to walk, but it was with a decided limp," he continued on, in a tone that suggested he was talking with a colleague over a cup of wine, and not to a patient. "And one of them was actually able to return to the standard, although, if I'm being honest, he was a Gregarius near the end of his enlistment and not a Centurion. So he was consigned to guard duty for the most part. Still, he was able to retire and receive his full pension. I do think it's very wise of Augustus to amend the regulations so that men who fall just a year or two short of their retirement don't leave with nothing to show for it, don't you?"

Porcinus had no idea whether he was expected to answer; there was no way he could have responded in any fashion because just as the physician finished what he was saying, he suddenly reached down, grabbed Porcinus' heel and gave a hard pull. Whereupon Porcinus' world instantly went black.

Porcinus opened his eyes, although it took a moment for them to focus on the roof of the hospital tent. It was even darker than when he had come to the first time, telling him that it was now nighttime. Turning his head, just that slight movement made his head pound; he had heard this was a side effect of ingesting poppy syrup, yet he was oddly thankful because it gave him something else to concentrate on other than the throbbing agony in his leg. His movement had another effect, as he heard a grunt from a few feet away.

"So you're awake. It's about time."

Porcinus recognized the voice as belonging to Volusenus, and he remembered that the Secundus Pilus Prior had now been there for two days, since the first attack. Had it really only been two days? he wondered. So much had happened in that time, it was hard for him to imagine that such a short interval had passed. There was a shuffling sound, then suddenly the face of Volusenus loomed above him, still with the bandage wrapped around half his face and covering his ruined eye. The good one stared down at Porcinus, and there was something in the other man's expression that Porcinus had never seen before. His mind was still dulled from the syrup, forcing him to struggle a bit to try and identify the look, but he quickly regretted it, recognizing the pity in the man's face. Perhaps if it was coming from someone other than Volusenus, it wouldn't have been such a shock to his system.

"That bad?" he whispered.

There was a fleeting look of surprise, then Volusenus' face flushed a little as his good eye suddenly looked away, embarrassed at the display. He opened his mouth, seemingly about to deny this, but then his mouth set in a grim frown, and he nodded his head.

"I'm sorry," Volusenus said awkwardly, clearly unaccustomed to apologizing for anything. Yet, the truth was that he not only respected Gaius Porcinus, but in his own way, he liked the younger man a great deal, despite their prior differences. "But yes, it's pretty bad."

"I thought so," Porcinus sighed, then without thinking, he held out a hand and asked, "Will you help me up? I want to look for myself."

Volusenus looked startled, and he hesitated, asking, "Are you sure? I'm telling you, lad, it's pretty ugly."

It was a sign of Porcinus' combination of discomfort and astonishment that Volusenus had uttered what for him could be called a term of endearment that he didn't take offense at being called "lad." Nevertheless, he was insistent and finally, Volusenus complied with a sigh, taking his hand and letting Porcinus pull against it. And Porcinus immediately regretted doing so, both because the sudden movement caused his stomach to lurch, threatening to send whatever was left in it back up, and for the sight of his leg. Philandros had pulled it straight, at least as straight as it was possible for him to do, aligning the bones so that the ends no longer poked through the skin. The two places where they had done so were clearly visible in the form of two large red spots on the linen bandage that was tightly wrapped around his lower right leg. Outside the bandage were two flat boards, one on either side, which were also wrapped with linen in two spots, one just below his knee and the other above his ankle. That was distressing enough; it was the sight of his foot that caused Porcinus to let out an audible gasp. It was horribly swollen, a dark purple in color, and although he was no physician, he understood this was a bad sign.

Girding himself, he turned to Volusenus. "Touch my foot."

The other Centurion recoiled, and gave a disbelieving laugh, shaking his head in refusal.

"I'm not going to tickle your foot for you!"

"Please," Porcinus implored him. "I need to see if I can feel it."

Volusenus mouthed a curse, but relented, and walked to the end of Porcinus' cot.

"Close your eyes," Volusenus commanded.

Porcinus did so, and without thinking, started holding his breath.

"Feel that?"

At first, Porcinus held the wild hope that Volusenus was tricking him, and he opened one eye. When he saw the other Pilus Prior firmly grasping his big toe, he felt his heart rise in his throat, along with a healthy dose of bile. He felt nothing, nothing at all; no pressure, no sensation whatsoever.

"Maybe it's temporary," he muttered.

"It probably is," Volusenus agreed, and although he didn't sound sincere, Porcinus chose to ignore that and took his words at face value.

"I imagine by tomorrow I'll get feeling back in my foot," he said with the desperate hopefulness of the man who knows that he's lying to himself, if not everyone else.

Volusenus decided to change the subject.

"Did you hear about our Primus Pilus?"

Of all the things Volusenus could have said, in terms of jerking Porcinus' attention away from his current plight, he couldn't have found a better topic.

"No." Porcinus tried to keep his voice level. "I've been…occupied."

Volusenus gave that snort that Porcinus had determined was his version of a laugh.

"I suppose so," Volusenus agreed. "Well, he's gone missing."

"Missing?" Porcinus echoed. "How? When?"

"What do you remember about the fight?" Volusenus asked. "Because I don't want to waste my breath going over things you already know."

Porcinus considered, then replied, "I remember going into the forest, and as soon as we did, we broke down by sections because of the ground. It was really chopped up. Then there was the fire." Porcinus thought of something. "By the way, what about that fire? Who started it? I thought Tiberius had decided against it."

"He did," Volusenus agreed, "but apparently, the courier sent to Quirinus got intercepted because not only did he not get the message, the courier hasn't been heard from since."

That made sense to Porcinus and he fell silent, waiting for Volusenus to continue.

Seeing that Porcinus was listening, Volusenus went on. "So as I was saying, Barbatus hasn't been seen since just before the Legion pulled out of the forest because of the fire. It's about burned out now, so Tiberius has sent men in to search for survivors. Not," he finished grimly, "that there's likely to be."

"What about the Varciani?" Porcinus asked. "Did they manage to slip away?"

"No." Volusenus made no attempt to hide his satisfaction. "We slaughtered those *cunni* almost to the last man. Only a handful were captured, and they were wounded or high-ranking nobles that Tiberius ordered be kept alive. Our boys didn't spare anyone else."

Porcinus shared his counterpart's satisfaction, even if his mind was still focused on the news about Barbatus.

"Are there any ideas about what happened to Barbatus?" he asked cautiously. "Did anyone…see anything?"

Evidently, there was something in Porcinus' tone that caused Volusenus to look at him sharply, his lone eye boring into Porcinus' pair, searching for something.

"Not that I've heard," Volusenus said at last. Then, "Why? What do you know?"

Porcinus' heart, which was already beating at an elevated pace, suddenly started behaving like a runaway horse, and he was sure that Volusenus could see the movement of his tunic, which he watched, with a dull horror, leaping rhythmically out of the corner of his eye.

He tried to ignore the sight as he concentrated his gaze on Volusenus and protested, "Nothing!" Thinking quickly, he added, "Besides, how could I? I fell down that fucking gully pretty early on, and I passed out. The next thing I remember is Urso standing there."

Volusenus grunted, seemingly satisfied with Porcinus' answer, although he was moved to ask, "About that. How in Hades did you manage to do that? Trip over your own feet? I've never known you to be so clumsy."

"There's a first time for everything, I suppose," Porcinus said lightly, then gave the other man a shrug. "I don't really remember much. One moment I was trying to get to one of my sections after we got separated, the next I was tumbling down into the gully."

"Just bad luck then," Volusenus concluded, but Porcinus thought he heard as much question as statement, which he chose to ignore.

"Bad luck," Porcinus agreed.

There was an awkward silence, then finally, Volusenus broke it, saying, "Well. Right, then. I suppose you need your rest." He turned to go, but then seemed to think of something. Turning back around, he said quietly, "I'm going to make a sacrifice that your leg mends good as new, Gaius."

Before Porcinus could respond, he hurried away, not returning to his own cot, but exiting the tent, leaving an astonished fellow Pilus Prior staring at his retreating back.

Porcinus spent a fitful night, dropping off to sleep, then being jerked awake when he made the slightest movement in his slumber, the pain shooting up his leg making him gasp. Finally, Philandros ordered one of the *medici* working the night shift to spoon another mouthful of poppy syrup into Porcinus, and although he was grateful, in some ways, it made matters worse, because he almost immediately dropped into a deeper sleep. Consequently, whenever he made that kind of move that all people do when they sleep, the shock of pain seemed even more severe than before. It was also a difficult place to sleep because of the activity that always took place in the aftermath of a battle, although this one had seen relatively light casualties. However, the nature of the injuries of those who had been unlucky, Porcinus included, were different from most fights. There were two men in particular who served to make Porcinus feel, if not fortunate, then at least not as cursed as he could have been. They were two Gregarii, from different Cohorts, who had been trapped by the flames set by Quirinus' men, both of them suffering horrible burns. One of them had been knocked into a line of burning underbrush, and his lower legs had suffered horrific burns, looking to Porcinus like charred meat. He had only gotten a glimpse of the man, moaning with a pain that Porcinus couldn't even imagine as the unfortunate Gregarius was carried through the Centurion's area on the way to Charon's Boat. The small blessing was that Philandros, knowing the man couldn't be saved, ordered that he be drugged insensible so that his suffering was eased during his passage to the afterlife. But it was the other man who Porcinus was thankful that he didn't even see; he concluded he must have been asleep when this man was carried past his cot, and he shuddered just to think about him. He had heard the whispered conversation of two *medici* discussing the case.

"His face is burned off," one told the other, and there was no mistaking the shudder in the man's voice. "He's got no nose, no lips, no ears. Nothing's left."

"How is he even alive?" the other *medicus* had asked, and despite his revulsion, it was a question Porcinus had asked himself.

"Who knows?" the first man said; Porcinus couldn't see him shrug. "Sometimes, the *animus* in a man is just too strong for its own good. Truly, it would be a blessing for all of us if he just…let go."

Despite accepting the truth in what the *medicus* was saying, Porcinus felt a surge of anger at the man's words. What would this…orderly, this non-combatant know of such things? What it took to stay alive on a battlefield? He thought about calling the man over, but he was too tired, and too addled in his mind to do more than silently curse the man, so he let it pass. As it would turn out, while both Gregarii did die, it was the man whose legs were burned who succumbed first, while the other man stubbornly clung to life well into the next day. The night passed, the *bucina* sounding the changes in the watches of the night, telling Porcinus what time it was, and it was shortly after the call that signaled the start of a new day for the Legions that he had his first visitors. It was Corvinus and Ovidius, both men still dressed in their full uniforms and covered with the grime and soot from what was clearly an exhausting battle and aftermath. They had at least washed their faces, although their eyes were still red-rimmed from the smoke, and Porcinus could see that both of them were near the end of their tethers, weaving with fatigue.

"Sorry it took us so long," Ovidius began, but Porcinus waved him off.

"I have a feeling you've been busy," he joked weakly.

The truth was that he wasn't in the mood for visitors; the enormity of what had happened to him was beginning to settle in, and he was finding it difficult to keep his mind from going to a bleak place. And yet, neither did he feel like dismissing these two men that he considered friends, knowing that the company would probably do him more good than harm.

"You could say that," Corvinus agreed wearily, signaling to a *medicus*. "Bring two stools, now!"

A moment later, the pair was settled next to Porcinus, and he noticed that their eyes clearly had trouble staying away from the sight of his leg.

"Pretty ugly, isn't it?" he asked lightly.

Ovidius was the first to reply, clearly relieved that Porcinus had brought it up.

"It's not good," he agreed, then hastened to add, "but I've seen worse."

"Really? Care to tell me when? Because I'd love to know." Porcinus made sure by his tone that he meant this as a joke, but Ovidius' face flushed anyway.

Then, he realized his superior was teasing him, and he gave a short laugh.

"All right," he retorted. "I've never seen anything this bad before! There, feel better?"

"At least you're being honest," Porcinus said equably. Then, seeing the pair's discomfort, he hastened to ask, "So, how are the boys?"

"They're fine," Ovidius assured him. "We only had one wounded, that stupid bastard Figulus. But I'm half-convinced he stabbed himself, he's so fucking clumsy."

Without thinking, Porcinus laughed, sending a stab of pain up his leg that immediately wrenched a gasp from him. Ovidius jumped up, his face showing the alarm he felt, and the sight was so comical to Porcinus that, despite himself, he felt another laugh coming. Which of course was immediately followed by another gasp of pain.

"Pluto's cock." Ovidius was almost beside himself by this point, awkwardly patting Porcinus' shoulder. "I didn't mean to make you laugh!"

"Yes you did, you bastard," Porcinus wheezed, the tears streaming from his eyes as he alternated between what was now a guffaw of laughter, punctuated by increasingly sharp gasps of pain.

The effect on the other two was that, despite their best efforts, they joined in with Porcinus until the trio were laughing hysterically, and all three of them were streaming tears. Finally, Philandros was forced to come over, his expression severe.

"This is a hospital, not a mime show!" he hissed. "And you're Centurions, not rankers! I expect better behavior from men like you!"

The trio did their best to look chastised, hanging their heads like schoolboys caught whispering in class, a posture that lasted as long as it took for Philandros to give them a last, stern look before going back to his duties. He wasn't gone more than a few heartbeats before the snickering resumed, albeit in a quieter tone. However, the mirth was sufficiently dampened that it allowed more normal conversation to resume.

"So, did you hear about Barbatus?" Corvinus was the man who asked Porcinus, echoing Volusenus, but only after assuring his superior that his Century had emerged unscathed from the battle, and that as far as he knew, the other Centuries only had a couple minor wounds.

"Yes, Volusenus mentioned something about it," Porcinus said carefully.

The Secundus Pilus Prior, evidently deciding he was sufficiently recovered, had checked himself out of the hospital shortly before Ovidius and Corvinus came to visit, but there were two other Centurions that had been wounded seriously enough to be in this part of the hospital tent, so Porcinus made sure his voice was pitched low.

"What did he tell you?" Corvinus pressed.

"Only that he was missing."

"Well," Corvinus replied, "they found him." His expression changed to one of grim satisfaction. "And the *cunnus* is dead."

"Really?" Porcinus tried to affect surprise, but he was sure that his friends weren't fooled, although if they saw through him, they gave no sign.

"Yes," Corvinus assured him. "He's dead, all right. But I won't deny it's a bit strange."

"Oh? What's strange about it?" Porcinus' throat almost closed around the words.

"Well, the fire passed over the gully that he was found in, although the entire area above him was burned to a crisp. So he wasn't even singed."

"So what killed him?" Porcinus asked Corvinus, once more sure that the beating of his heart would be visible to his friend.

"One of the Varciani must have gotten behind him, because he was stabbed in the back." Corvinus, if he knew any differently, was remarkably composed and sounded completely sincere in his own belief. He gave a harsh laugh. "So I guess his Praetorians either weren't that fond of him, or they weren't all he thought they were, because it's very strange for a Primus Pilus to be isolated that way."

"True," Porcinus agreed, then gave what he hoped was a casual shrug, "but maybe he got separated. Like I did. It was impossible to see because of all the fucking smoke."

"You're right about that." Corvinus nodded. Then, he seemed to think of something. "But Urso said he found you in a gully too. I know the ground was really broken up and it was a nightmare, but what are the odds that two first-grade Centurions would end up like that?"

"I'd guess pretty low," Porcinus said, desperately wishing that Ovidius would speak up or that Corvinus would change the topic.

"Well, at least we're rid of that bastard," Corvinus concluded, and much to Porcinus' relief, did change the subject. "I heard we're going to be here for another day, then we head back to Siscia."

"When we get back, you'll at least be able to be at home," Ovidius said, and while he meant it as a way to cheer Porcinus up, it, in fact, had the opposite effect.

"I suppose," was all Porcinus would say, but the truth was he had thought of this earlier, and didn't relish the idea.

He knew that his children would want to help, yet he understood that, in all likelihood, they would only cause Iras to become cross as she fussed over him. More than anything, though, was that he didn't want his family to see him so helpless; although he had been wounded before, it had happened before he had a family, or was on campaign and had mended before returning at the end of the season. This would be a new experience for all of them, and one he wasn't looking forward to in the slightest. Porcinus made a great show of yawning, then blinking his eyes several times, but was forced to repeat this twice more before the two men took the hint.

"We'll let you get some rest," Corvinus finally said, standing up.

"Let me know what happens about Barbatus," Porcinus said without thinking.

"What do you mean?" Corvinus, who had been about to leave, turned about, looking down at Porcinus sharply. "What more is there to know? He's dead."

"I meant if Tiberius makes any decision about a new Primus Pilus," Porcinus said hastily.

"Ah. Don't worry, I will," Corvinus assured him, seemingly accepting Porcinus' words.

Still, long after the pair left, Porcinus lay there, deep in thought.

As Corvinus had predicted, the army broke camp the next day. By that time, Porcinus' condition was worsening, and the only evidence he needed was the sight of his foot. Rather than slowly returning to a normal color, it remained a deep purple, almost the hue of a plum, and he still had no feeling in it, nor could he do more than barely wiggle his big toe. Philandros was doing his best to minimize the severity of Porcinus' plight, but the Centurion could tell the physician wasn't optimistic. Outside the hospital tent, there was the normal noise, composed of shouted orders, braying mules, and the constant chattering as men talked while they worked, striking their tents before filling in the ditches. Being transferred to a wagon was just the beginning of what was an ordeal for every wounded man, and one that Porcinus never had to endure before. The other times he was wounded, either the camp had stayed in place long enough for him to be discharged, or he had only been required to stay overnight. Consequently, he gained a new appreciation for the horrible pain and discomfort that was part of being wounded with an army on the move. Because of his rank, he and the other Centurions at least had their own wagon, which only made the misery marginally less; bouncing and jolting in the back of a wagon over the kind of rough ground they had to cover was uncomfortable whether it was with ten men or four. Philandros did what he could to make his charges more comfortable, offering them each a spoonful of poppy syrup, but when Porcinus learned he was only doing this for the Centurions, he refused his dose, a decision he would later regret, but didn't reverse. Instead, he occupied himself by trying to think of anything and everything other than the creeping rot that he knew was claiming his leg. Although it was true that when his bandage was changed, his leg, while not as purple as his foot and not displaying the livid red streaks that every experienced Legionary knew to fear, was still horribly swollen, looking very much like the skin would burst, and the area around the places the bones had poked through were an angry red and leaking pus. Even if he hadn't seen that, Philandros' expression was eloquent in itself, so Porcinus forced himself to think of other things. Naturally, his family was on his mind, yet most of the time, he dwelled on what had happened in those last moments before Barbatus was killed. He had resigned himself to never knowing exactly why Barbatus had tried to kill him; he didn't accept Barbatus' claim that he was going to kill Porcinus because of some grudge he held against his father, but that was actually less important to him than why Urso had saved him. There were two reasons for his concern; the first and most obvious was that even if he was convinced he knew the purpose of Barbatus' attack, the man was dead. Consequently, what was even more important and urgent to him was not only why Urso had chosen to save him, but under whose authority or protection he had taken action. When Porcinus had first regained consciousness, he had almost convinced himself that he imagined Urso's statement, but in the intervening watches between then and now in the wagon, he forced himself to acknowledge that what he tried to pass off as vision or dream was very, very real. That left a simple but, for Porcinus and his future, extremely crucial question; who was Urso's master? There turned out to be one blessing concerning his refusal to take the poppy syrup, in that his mind was clear and he was able to concentrate, even through the pain. As the wagon bounced along and he rocked in the slung hammock the wagons carrying the wounded used to transport their cargo, he ran through the possibilities. The most obvious candidate was Tiberius, and Porcinus tried to calculate whether this was a good or a bad thing as far as he was concerned. It was true that they shared a common enemy, or at least they had, in Barbatus, but Porcinus forced himself to acknowledge that there was another man who, if not an enemy, certainly wasn't an ally, and that was Augustus. And while Barbatus had posed the more immediate threat, Porcinus was under no illusions about who was the most dangerous. Regardless, Porcinus mused, he still didn't think that Augustus truly cared about Gaius Porcinus, as long as Gaius Porcinus didn't get any lofty ambitions. But what if somehow Augustus learned of the truth behind the death of Barbatus, his handpicked Primus Pilus, and if the dead man was to be believed, in fact, his agent? Even worse, what if Augustus discovered that Urso did indeed work for Tiberius? Would the fact that Urso was the second in command of his Cohort mean Porcinus would be considered guilty by association? And, in fact, wasn't he guilty by association? No matter why he had done it, Urso had saved Porcinus' life, and that was a debt that must be paid, or Porcinus would never be able to live with the shame of it. If that meant that he was implicated by Augustus, and considered a threat to the Princeps, then that was what the gods had willed. Unlike his father, who had severed all ties with the gods after Miriam died, Porcinus did pray and make sacrifices, although it wasn't something he did with any real regularity. No, he decided, about halfway back to Siscia on the second day of the miserable march, even if it meant being considered an accomplice, he would never betray Urso for saving his life. He also realized that he would have to face Urso at some point in time, and he dreaded the idea, yet he knew it was not only inevitable, but necessary.

The march back to Siscia took three days, and by the time the army marched back through the gates, Gaius Porcinus was delirious with fever, and if anything, his leg had become even more swollen. It was at dawn of the second day when Philandros ordered the dressing changed that Porcinus saw the red streaks he had been dreading. By the midday halt, Porcinus' fever was so high that he had made the final break with reality, and was living in a world where shadows were solid, and men who had been dead for some time were sitting next to him in the wagon. And the wagon wasn't the wagon; it was alternately his own apartment back in Siscia, or the farmhouse in which he'd grown up. He wasn't particularly surprised to see Titus Pullus show up, staring down at him with a mock frown that Porcinus knew he used to hide when he was worried.

"What stupid thing did you go and do now?" he asked Porcinus.

When Porcinus, at least in his own mind, explained what had happened, Pullus had been anything but sympathetic.

"How many times have I told you that you can't trust anyone associated with men like Augustus?" the Camp Prefect, looking exactly the same as the last time Porcinus had seen him in the flesh, had pressed. "You never turn your back on any of them!"

"But I was in the middle of a battle," Porcinus protested. "How was I supposed to know that the bastard would sneak up on me and push me?"

"You should have known," Pullus insisted, and there was a part of Porcinus' mind that, understanding that no matter how real the conversation might seem, it was taking place in his mind. Nevertheless, he fervently wished his father had somewhere else to be.

"Does it really matter?" Porcinus asked, and only then did his imaginary visitor relent.

"I suppose not." Pullus, or his ghost, pointed to Porcinus' leg. "You know you're going to lose that leg, don't you?"

In Porcinus' fevered mind, he glared at his adoptive father, and shouted at him, "That's not true! Philandros will come up with something! I'm not losing my fucking leg!"

"Gaius," Pullus' shade said, and this time he did sound sympathetic, "you know that's not the truth. You saw it when they changed the dressing. You have the red streaks, and you know what that means. Besides, how many times have they had to change your dressing? Every time the army stops? Because the places where the bones poked through have become corrupt." Pullus' shade shook his head. "No, I'm sorry, Gaius. But when you get to Siscia, you need to listen to what Philandros tells you."

"Noooooooooooo," Porcinus moaned, and if he had been lucid, he would have been aware that he wasn't just saying the word in his mind; in the wagon, his voice was raised to a shout, and his head was thrashing back and forth, flinging sweat in every direction. His condition had deteriorated to the point where Philandros had ordered a *medicus* ride in the wagon, yet no amount of sponging could keep up with the torrent of fluid oozing from every inch of Porcinus' skin. The only blessing, at least for Porcinus, was that he accepted the ladles of water that the *medicus* put to his lips, although a fair amount of the liquid spilled and splashed when the wagon would suddenly bounce over a bump or drop into a hole. Better yet was that Porcinus managed to keep the water down, although it was a never-ending cycle as his body raged with fever, and he fought a battle in his mind, not just with his father, but with himself.

"Stop it," Pullus' shade snapped, standing to his full height over Porcinus, as he had done on multiple occasions in real life. "Stop indulging in self-pity; you know I can't stand that! This is what The Fates have ordained for you, and I'll be the first to admit that it's a bad one. But it's not as bad as it could be! Do I have to remind you about Didius?"

The mention of this name, in fact, did have meaning for Porcinus, although he had never personally met the man. However, he had certainly heard of Spurius Didius, one of his father's original tentmates, back when the 10th Legion was formed in Hispania. Moreover, he had heard about Didius and the role he played in Pullus' life from two of the other members of the tent section of the First Century, Second Cohort, led by Gaius Crastinus. Scribonius, Porcinus' first Centurion and Pullus' best friend, had relayed many tales of the battles that Pullus waged within their Century with the one man who had convinced himself that he was, if not a better man, at least the equal of Titus Pullus. And while it was true that when it came to strength, Didius was a match for Pullus, in every other way, he was sadly lacking in the qualities that make a man a great Legionary and a great leader. It was in the first civil war, after Pharsalus, when the 10th was back in Hispania, where Divus Julius had crushed the last remnants of rebellion by the sons of Pompeius Magnus, and Didius suffered a wound that, like Porcinus', became corrupt. He had lost his leg almost all the way up to the hip, and it had happened just a few weeks before the enlistment of the 10th was completed. Back then, under the regulations, it meant that Didius was eligible for nothing in the way of the retirement bonus that had been promised to the men. No land, no money, nothing; at least, if the regulations were followed. Nevertheless, even if the regulations had been followed, it still shouldn't have been a catastrophe; Didius, like Scribonius, Vellusius, and Pullus, were veterans of the Gallic campaign, and each of them had received a portion of the proceeds from the sale of slaves taken by Divus Julius. A very small portion, it was true, but when a million souls had been sold into slavery, even a tiny part of the proceeds was a staggering sum. Yet, Didius was broke, although as Porcinus had been told by many men, he wasn't unusual. A disturbingly high proportion of the Legionaries who by rights should have been wealthy had pissed their money away on wine, women, and gambling, usually in some combination of all three vices. In Didius' case, he was an inveterate gambler, and while in his early days had actually been fabulously successful, by the time he was wounded, more than a decade of looking over his shoulder, always waiting to be caught cheating, had taken its toll. Pullus had become Primus Pilus by this point, making his relationship with Didius naturally more distant, so he was unaware that Didius had not only gone straight, but had turned out to be a much better cheater than an honest gambler. Without his leg, and with the prospect of no retirement bonus, Spurius Didius' prospects were bleak, and it was the mention of the man's name that forced Porcinus to realize something.

"Yes, I remember Didius," he said, even weary in his dream. "And I understand what you're saying. But…it's my leg," he finished quietly.

"I know, boy," Pullus' shade replied, his tone gentle this time. "But if you fight Philandros on this, by the time he does what's inevitable, it may be too late. And as much as I miss you, I'm not ready for you to join me yet." Once he regained his senses, Gaius Porcinus would always believe that the hand that reached down to grasp his shoulder was as real as he himself was, and didn't belong to a shade. "You know what needs to be done."

And Porcinus did. Now the only question was whether his internal decision would be uttered to the external world, which could only happen if he regained his senses.

Whether it was by coincidence, or from some other force, Gaius Porcinus' fever broke almost at the exact moment the army arrived in Siscia. He had a difficult time opening his eyes, as they seemed to be gummed shut, and he finally was forced to use his fingers to pull his eyelids apart. The movement alerted the *medicus*, who at that moment was peering out the back flap of the wagon, watching as the wagon they were in rolled through the gates.

"Centurion! You're awake!" The *medicus* practically leaped over to Porcinus' side, beaming down at the prone Roman as if he had something to do with this change in condition.

"I guess I am." To Porcinus, his voice sounded like a rusty hinge, and his throat was so dry that he could barely get the words out. "Where are we?"

"We're just arriving in Siscia," the *medicus* told him.

Porcinus frowned. "How long have I been...out?"

"For a bit more than a day," the other man replied. "You became delirious shortly after noon yesterday."

"What time is it now?" Porcinus asked, and the *medicus* leaned over to glance out through the flaps of the wagon.

"About a watch before dark," he told Porcinus.

Even as he spoke, the wagon came to a halt, and Porcinus heard the shouted commands that told him they had arrived at their destination. The *medicus* got up, and was about to leap out of the wagon, but Porcinus stopped him.

"Go get Philandros and tell him I need to see him," Porcinus told the *medicus*.

"He'll be seeing you fairly shortly, Centurion," the other man replied. "Right now, we have to begin unloading the wounded."

"That wasn't a request," Porcinus said shortly, fixing the man with a cold stare. "I need to see him. Now."

"Very well, Centurion," the *medicus* answered stiffly. "As you command."

Without waiting for a reply, he pushed through the flaps of the wagon.

"Fucking right 'as you command,'" a new voice interrupted. "These little bastards have some nerve!"

Porcinus craned his neck, but although he couldn't see the face of the man who was slung above him, he recognized the voice as belonging to the Secundus Hastatus Prior, commander of Volusenus' Fifth Century who had taken a serious wound to his thigh that, while it was healing cleanly, would leave him with a limp. But at least he'll have his leg, Porcinus couldn't stop the bitter thought from flashing through his mind, and was only half-hearted in chastising himself. Fortunately, he didn't have long to dwell on the injustice; the wagon flap was pulled aside, and Porcinus saw Philandros peer in, although he didn't bother climbing up into the wagon.

"Yes, Pilus Prior?" Philandros made no attempt to hide his impatience, but Porcinus was beyond caring.

"How soon can you do it?" he asked the physician quietly.

For a moment, Philandros didn't seem to understand. Then the meaning dawned on him and he stared hard at the Roman, who gazed back calmly, his face still flushed from the fever.

"Why, as soon as you're ready," Philandros finally answered. His expression was grave, but he assured Porcinus, "You're doing the right thing, Centurion."

"I know." Porcinus couldn't hide the bitterness. "That doesn't make it any fucking easier."

"I understand," Philandros replied.

Porcinus opened his mouth to utter a retort, then realized there was nothing to be gained from speaking harshly to Philandros. Despite his own pain and anxiety for what was about to come, he also understood that the physician had seen more than his share of suffering. Porcinus knew Philandros was a kind man by nature, and most of the time, he took no pleasure in his job; in fact, from Porcinus' viewpoint, it was hard to understand why anyone would practice his profession.

"I can be ready in less than a third of a watch," Philandros said.

"Not that soon," Porcinus hurriedly replied. "There's something I need to do first."

Philandros opened his mouth, but shrugged instead.

"Very well. A full watch then?" he asked.

Porcinus nodded grimly.

"That will be enough time."

In order to have some privacy for what he had planned, Porcinus ended up bribing the *medicus* who had been caring for him to leave him in the wagon until last, and make sure the wagon remained parked next to the hospital until Porcinus was done. To make this happen he also had to promise the wagon driver a bribe, who he asked to go find Quintus Pacuvius, the son of the Centurion who had accompanied his father. The youth had survived his first campaign, short as it was, and he would never look at the profession of his father in the same way again. In fact, although the elder Pacuvius had yet to be told, the son had decided that there were other occupations that he would rather pursue than being a man of the Legions, something that the father would have no argument with whatsoever.

"I need you to go find Titus," Porcinus had told him. "Just Titus, not his brother or sister. You understand?" Then he gave the youth a weak grin and finished, "And by the gods, not his mother."

Young Pacuvius needed no extra incentive to avoid Iras; he had not only witnessed her wrath, he had been the recipient of it on more than one occasion when he and his best friend Titus had gotten involved in one misdeed or another. Assuring Porcinus that he would be back shortly, with Titus, he slipped out of the wagon. For the first time, Porcinus was completely alone, his only companion the sounds of the army settling in to their permanent quarters. The 8th, in particular, had been badly bloodied, and while Porcinus wasn't sure whether Tiberius had plans to go back out in pursuit of the Latobici and the Colapiani, the tribe who lived to the south of the Latobici and west of Siscia, he assumed that Tiberius would do so. There was still at least a month left in the season, and he had learned during his time in Pannonia that it didn't do well to let these rebellions fester over the winter months if it could be avoided. However, he was reasonably sure that the 8th wouldn't be part of Tiberius' army even if he did continue the campaign. But that, he forced himself to remember, was no longer his concern, because in a matter of a watch, his career would be over.

Quintus Pacuvius arrived with Titus, and although Porcinus had prepared himself for this meeting with his son as much as he could, his composure almost crumbled when he saw that the boy needed help from his friend to climb into the wagon, favoring his left arm as he did so.

"Father?" Porcinus could clearly hear the strain in his son's voice, yet he had remembered to address his father more formally, even if it was only in front of Quintus. "Quintus said you've been hurt and that you wanted to see me! What is it?"

"I just didn't want you to be the only wounded man in the family," Porcinus joked, but Titus' expression didn't change, his eyes wide and not leaving his father's splinted leg.

"What happened?" Titus gasped, reaching out to touch Porcinus' foot before pulling his hand back.

"You can touch it; it won't hurt," Porcinus assured him. "But I need to talk to you about something." Turning to Quintus, he asked, "Quintus, would you please wait outside the wagon? There's something I need to talk about with Titus." Quintus had been expecting this command, even if it was in the form of a question, but then, Porcinus added, "In fact, go find your father. I'm sure he needs your help unloading his mule."

Quintus' face fell, prompting a small smile from Porcinus, who had known that if he hadn't sent him away, the youth's ear would be pressed against the side of the wagon. What he had to share with Titus nobody else needed to hear.

Once the other boy was gone, Titus pointed to the wooden bench. "Sit down. I need to tell you something." Titus did as he was told, his face tight with tension, but before Porcinus began on the subject he had summoned Titus to discuss, he asked, "How's your arm?"

In reply, Titus moved his left arm in a circular motion, but although he tried, he couldn't stifle the wince.

"That's what I thought." Porcinus shook his head. "Why isn't your arm still in a sling?"

"I don't need it," Titus protested, but Porcinus was unmoved.

"From the looks of it, that's not exactly true," was all Porcinus said, however. "So I want you to put it back in a sling for at least another week."

His son opened his mouth to argue, then the combination of the look on his father's face, and the fact that, for the first time in his life, Titus saw his father helpless, caused him simply to agree.

"Now," Porcinus began. "I want to prepare you for something that's about to happen. But before I do, I'm going to tell you that I expect you to act like a man, Titus. Do you understand me?"

"Yes," Titus answered, although he was still sullen about the command to return his arm to the sling, his tone prompting his father to speak in a manner that Titus had never heard before, at least when he was the focus of his father's anger.

"Pluto's cock," Porcinus snarled, his face, still gleaming with sweat, hardening into an expression that Titus had rarely seen before and never aimed at him. "I don't have time for this! It's time for you to grow up, boy! Your mother, and I," Porcinus conceded, "have spoiled you. But that ends today! It has to, because…" Now it was Porcinus' turn for emotion almost to overwhelm him, but he forced himself to continue, although in a softer tone. "…I need you, Titus. More importantly, your mother is going to need you, as will your brother and sisters."

Now all rebellion and unhappiness had fled Titus' face, to be replaced by a fear that he had never experienced before, even when the Latobici had chased him.

"Why?" he asked Porcinus, searching his father's face. "What's going to happen? Tata?"

It was the last word that did it, Porcinus realized with some chagrin as his son suddenly began shimmering in front of him.

"Because," Porcinus was doing his utmost to keep his tone matter-of-fact, as if this was just a routine matter of business that had to be dealt with, "I'm having my leg amputated in a little while."

For the rest of his days, Porcinus would often think of that moment as he watched his son change into a man in front of his eyes. Titus' first reaction was a widening of the eyes, and Porcinus saw the sudden sheen in them that signaled his own tears were forming. Yet, somehow, they didn't fall. As he watched Titus absorb what he'd just been told, there was a detached part of Porcinus that observed and tracked the emotions that went rippling through the boy. First, there was the understandable response of a child, as along with the tears, Porcinus saw his son's lower lip jut out, a sure sign throughout Titus' life that he was refusing to accept whatever decision or parental edict with which he was presented. Then, something happened. Suddenly, Titus sat up straighter, and while his lower lip was still jutting out, it was joined by his jaw in a look that, frankly, Porcinus had never seen before, transforming not only his son's face, but his entire body. In that moment, Gaius Porcinus realized that his son didn't look like him, at least in the way he was presenting himself; he looked how Porcinus imagined a young Titus Pullus had, as an almost palpable aura of hardened resolve emanated from the boy's body.

"What do you need me to do?" Titus asked quietly.

Porcinus suddenly exhaled, only then aware that he had been holding his breath.

"You're going to have to be strong for your mother," he told Titus. "And that means you can't argue about whatever it is she tells you to do. Also, you're going to have to explain to your brother and sister what this means."

"What does it mean, Tata?" Titus sounded remarkably composed, although Porcinus could hear how clipped his words were, a telling sign of his son's struggle to keep his poise.

And Titus wasn't the only one struggling, especially as Porcinus was forced to voice what had been preying on his mind ever since he came to his decision.

"It means my time under the standard is done, my son," he said quietly. "I'm going to be retired and my days in the Legion will come to an end." Seeing the anguish in his son's face, he sought to reassure him, "But, Titus, it's not all bad. Remember, your Avus has left us in a very, very good….position."

"Not if Augustus finds out," Titus burst out, the bitterness causing his face to twist in a mask of sorrow and rage.

Despite the fact that his son's outburst wasn't that loud, Porcinus still put up a cautioning hand and replied sternly, "And that's the last you're going to say anything like that! Do you hear me? I know Diocles already talked to you about this, Titus. He told me the night before I left on campaign. But now, it's even more important than ever that you never, ever say anything that can be considered as disloyal to the Princeps."

Suddenly, Titus eyed his father keenly, so that despite the fact it was his ten-year-old son, Porcinus felt acutely uncomfortable under the scrutiny.

"I know, Tata. Diocles explained why, but what's different now? What happened?"

For a brief moment, Porcinus considered telling his son everything, his rationale being that, since he was saddling Titus with the responsibilities of an adult before his natural time came, as a man, he deserved to know the entire scope of the hazards that might lie in wait.

Yet, he couldn't bring himself to burden his son in that way, so instead, he merely replied, "Nothing's different. I just need you to understand and take to heart how important it is."

"I do, and I will," Titus promised.

For a moment, the pair sat there, suddenly awkward as neither of them quite knew what to do. Finally, Porcinus spoke.

"Now that you're taking over duties as the man of the family, I do have one request."

"What, Tata?" Titus asked, eager to repay his father for what he knew was not only an enormous responsibility, but was a compliment of the same stature. "What can I do?"

"Come give your Tata one last hug and kiss like a little boy," Porcinus said huskily, holding his hands out from his hammock.

And Titus did, without protest.

When Titus left, it was with the task of going to the Fourth Cohort area and finding Urso.

"I need to talk to him about the Cohort," Porcinus had explained to Titus, which was true enough.

Porcinus wasn't sure how long it was before he heard the footsteps outside his wagon. He was too uncomfortable to doze off, but he fell into some sort of daze as he waited, because the sound of voices caused him to jerk, sending a bolt of pain through his leg. Later, he would be thankful, since it served to yank him out of wherever he had been, and forced him to concentrate. The flap of the wagon was pulled aside, and Urso's face appeared, his expression impossible to read.

Over his shoulder, Porcinus could see Titus, and he called to his son, "Go on home now, Titus. You know what you need to do."

Titus nodded and quickly disappeared, but Porcinus still waited a moment before motioning his second in command into the wagon.

As Urso climbed in, Porcinus commented, "This is my last official act as Pilus Prior."

Although he had meant it as a joke, he also understood the truth in the statement, and he could see that Urso did as well. Still, for whatever reason, there was no hint of triumph in the expression of the Pilus Posterior as he unconsciously mimicked Titus, settling in the same spot on the bench of the wagon. If anything, Porcinus noted with some confusion, he looked...sad? Why would that be? he wondered. He has to know that he's going to be the Pilus Prior, especially if he does work for Tiberius.

"Pilus Prior," Urso said, "I just want you to know something. It's no secret I wanted your post, and as hard as it is for me to admit, in the beginning, I thought it was because you weren't qualified for the job." Urso's eyes bored into Porcinus', and the suspicious part of his brain thought that if Urso was making a point to be sincere even if he wasn't, he was doing a good job of it. "But I was about as wrong about you as a man can be, and no matter what you have to say, I wanted you to know that. Your leadership of the Cohort has been exemplary."

Everything that Porcinus had carefully rehearsed in his mind fled as he felt his jaw dropping in astonishment, and if he were honest, with more than a little shame.

"I...I thank you for that, Urso. And, since we're baring our souls," he was heartened to see the Pilus Posterior chuckle, "I have to say that I've been suspicious of your motives."

"I know," Urso replied, his tone matter-of-fact. "And, in the beginning, you should have been, frankly. But I've watched how you lead this Cohort, and I can't deny that it's not been without a bit of surprise that I've seen how your...style of leading is effective. Mind you, it's not mine," he emphasized, "but if anything, you've taught me that there's more than one way to lead a Cohort."

"Well, now it's yours to lead, and I can't think of a better man to lead it," Porcinus replied, and, like Urso, he was more than a little surprised as he realized that he was being honest.

For moment, neither man spoke, with Porcinus staring at the ceiling and Urso examining the floor. Finally, Porcinus cleared his throat.

"Yes. Well," he began, trying to remember the words he had rehearsed in his mind. "That's only part of the reason I called you here."

"Oh?" Urso suddenly looked cautious. "And what would be the rest of the reason?"

"Who do you work for?" Porcinus asked bluntly. "Because you said that my debt was paid by the man you work for. Not," he felt compelled to add, "that I agree. About the debt. You saved my life, and no matter why you did it, I owe you."

Urso stared at him, his face revealing nothing, then said, "Does it matter, really? Who I work for?"

"It does to me," Porcinus replied fervently. "Because I need to know who I need to worry about."

Urso didn't reply immediately, but then he inclined his head in tacit acceptance of Porcinus' argument.

"I work for Tiberius," he said evenly, confirming Porcinus' first guess. "And I meant what I said. You owe me nothing." Seeing Porcinus' skepticism, Urso assured him, "I swear on Jupiter's black stone, Porcinus. Even if I wasn't working for him, I would have saved you."

"Why?" Porcinus was surprised that the question came out, but once it was, he didn't do anything to modify it. "Why did you save me?" he demanded.

"Because Barbatus didn't deserve to be Primus Pilus," Urso replied immediately, "and what he was doing was wrong."

"Since when does right and wrong have anything to do with things nowadays?" Porcinus couldn't stop his bitter outburst. "All that matters is what side you're on!"

"That's true, but only to an extent," Urso said, seemingly unperturbed by Porcinus' words. "I'd like to think that I would have stopped Barbatus even if I thought he was in the right, or that you weren't a worthy Pilus Prior. Things," he finished soberly, "aren't always as simple as they seem."

Porcinus couldn't argue that truth, at least of the last part of Urso's statement, but he couldn't resist answering bitterly, "I wish they were! Life would be so much easier!"

"Yes, it would," Urso agreed evenly. "But that isn't the world that you and I live in." Seemingly moved by some internal urge, he leaned forward to pin Porcinus with his eyes. "Don't you think I know that you and I are just pieces in some game that the upper classes play?"

Of all the things that he could have said, Urso couldn't have picked a better statement, echoing as it did Porcinus' own father's words.

Either oblivious or ignoring Porcinus' eyeing of him, Urso continued, "So if we're going to be used, why not make sure you pick the right horse to back in this absurd game?"

"And you're backing Tiberius," Porcinus said slowly.

Although Urso didn't make any reply, neither did he deny it.

"You really think he's going to come out on top? Compared to all the others?" Porcinus asked, more curious than anything.

Urso shrugged.

"He's as good a one as any," was how he put it. "Ideally, I think Drusus is probably the smartest choice. But there's just something about Drusus." He shrugged again. "I can't explain it, but my gut tells me that when it's all settled, and Augustus does shuffle off into the afterlife, it will be Tiberius who's left."

Although Porcinus didn't have a feeling one way or another, he supposed that Urso's reasoning was sound, and while he didn't want to admit it, and like Urso, there was something about Drusus that had caused him to hesitate when viewing the patrician as the likely heir to what Romans were only just now coming to understand was the throne of all that was Rome and what it stood for, the shining light in an otherwise dark world.

Porcinus regarded Urso, and he finally accepted not only his counterpart's argument, but his lot as decreed by The Fates.

"I suppose so," he said slowly. "And nothing I've seen about him gives me the shivers. But," he finally moved to the subject that worried him above all, "if Barbatus was being honest, and he was sent by

Augustus, and he had doubts about Tiberius, where does that leave us?"

"That," Urso conceded, "is a good question. And one that I can't answer with any certainty. Other than to say that Tiberius has his own allies, and they're very powerful."

"Who?" Porcinus asked, but when Urso balked, he persisted, "Look, as far as I'm concerned, you and I are in the same *trireme*. Whether we're chained together like galley slaves, or we're there of our own free will, does it really matter? This is where we are."

Urso started to continue arguing, but quickly recognized that there was really nothing he could summon to refute what Porcinus had said.

"Livia Drusilla," he finally said, and was rewarded by the sight of Porcinus' own mouth dropping open.

Porcinus had been expecting a name, but of all those that he had prepared himself to hear, the name of Augustus' wife was the last. And yet, the moment Urso uttered it, he realized that it made sense. Augustus' wife, by all accounts, was a formidable woman even without her association with the Princeps. And she was Tiberius' mother, so her support of both him and Drusus was understandable. He let out a low whistle.

"Well, if you're going to have a backer, you could do worse," he mused.

Urso nodded, clearly relieved that Porcinus accepted what he had said without pressing for more.

"That's what I thought," he agreed. "But I also think that Tiberius is a good man, and he'll do what's best for Rome."

"Of course," Porcinus said blandly.

The truth was that he didn't care about how fit Tiberius was to run Rome, and he suspected that it wasn't high on Urso's list either. Regardless of this truth, there were some conventions that had to be served, even in the privacy of a wagon.

"Well," Porcinus said awkwardly, "I still thank you for what you did. No matter why, you saved my life."

"Don't forget that I helped the Legion," Urso pointed out, "because that *cunnus* had no business running a Century, let alone a Legion."

Even if he had been so disposed, this was something that Porcinus couldn't argue.

"Whatever the case," Porcinus said, "you're going to be the Pilus Prior. And," his throat threatened to close over the words, but they had to be uttered, "you're the best man for the job. Take care of our boys."

Urso inclined his head in acknowledgment, not just of what Porcinus was saying, but all that it meant.

"I will try," he told Porcinus, and the other man would have been greatly surprised to know that Urso was being completely sincere, "to do as good a job as you've done with the Cohort. You've done a magnificent job, and I just hope that I can follow in your footsteps."

Then the two men, long-time rivals and adversaries who only wanted the same thing, clasped arms in the Roman manner, Urso rising from the bench.

"May the gods watch over you, and I'll sacrifice to make it so," were Urso's parting words, and Porcinus was too affected to respond, just nodding in reply.

As Urso turned to exit the wagon, Porcinus gave his last order as Secundus Pilus Prior.

"Go find Philandros. Tell him I'm ready."

Epilogue

It had been an extremely eventful and busy six months, Titus realized one morning, shortly after he had taken Ocelus out for his morning ride. The horse, still knowing the territory better than his rider, had headed west on the Via Domitia, out of Arelate. The fact that this was his old home, and his rider's new one, was the least of the changes that both Titus and Ocelus had experienced. The day that Titus' father had undergone the amputation of his right leg was one that Titus would never forget, since it had marked a turning point, not only in his own life, but in the direction of the Porcinus family. Titus was just happy that his father was able to walk, after a fashion at least, even if it was with the help of a crutch. Only now, six months and a couple weeks after that day, did Titus' father seem to be coming out from under the cloud of despondency and bitterness. The trip from Siscia to Arelate hadn't been as dangerous as the first time, because the flames of rebellion had been so thoroughly stamped out that not even the normal banditry on the roads was a worry, meaning that the party of travelers, which included Gallus, who was now a permanent part of the Porcinus household, didn't have to be on constant guard. Not that it hadn't been arduous; any kind of trip of the length between Siscia and Arelate would be wearing. It was even more so for Porcinus, who was still coming to grips with the new reality that faced him. His leg was amputated just below the knee, and for more than a week, he refused to see anyone, including his family. It was the most trying time of young Titus' life, but his father had endowed him with a huge responsibility, so he stood firm against his mother, who tried on more than one occasion to charge past Titus. However, he had appointed himself as guard over Porcinus, and Iras had seen another side to her son which, when put together with what she had seen both in Arelate and with the Latobici, had signaled to her that the son she knew was gone forever. Ten years old or not, young Titus was steadfast in his responsibilities, to the point that Ocelus had gone for almost a week without his customary exercise. The paperwork that was required to be filled out was expedited, thanks to Tiberius, who, as expected, had promoted Urso. However, what hadn't been expected was that Urso had been named Primus Pilus of the 8th Legion to replace the departed but unlamented Barbatus. Even more surprising was the fact that his promotion was ratified, ostensibly by the nameless, faceless bureaucracy of the army. Despite this appearance, everyone in the Legions knew it meant that Augustus had endorsed it. The only one who didn't appear to be shocked was Porcinus himself, but he made no comment on the event that had the entire army buzzing, although his lack of surprise was due more to indifference.

Titus didn't like dwelling on the past, but despite this, as he rode Ocelus outside of Arelate, he couldn't fight the urge to think back to those dark times when his father had insisted on shutting himself away from everyone, with Titus his only link to the larger world, and the one who kept everyone else at bay. This had tested his relationship with his mother more than any other event, yet even as he understood that his guardianship of his father's privacy came at a heavy price, he was also proud of himself. Never before had he so consistently stood his ground against his mother; the sword was one thing, but this crisis had lasted for many, many days. Regardless of the strife it caused between the two, until his father was ready, there was no fiercer guardian than young Titus, who barred all visitors to the room that Porcinus had appropriated as his own in their apartment. It wasn't easy; Porcinus had been surly and hard to deal with, even for Titus, who was the only person with whom the former Pilus Prior had any real interaction. Somehow, Titus had persevered, absorbing his father's anger and abuse, but in a completely unexpected way, the relationship between the two solidified into a bond that would last them for the rest of their respective lives. For Porcinus, the prospect of life using a crutch was such that it was extremely difficult for him to accept this new reality. Unsurprisingly, he lashed out, and most of the time it was young Titus who had to bear the brunt of the anger and misery from his father. There had been no real scrutiny on what happened; the official story that he had made a misstep and fallen down the steep slope of a gully was accepted without much question. The same was true for the official story of what happened to Barbatus, but while Titus had no reason to disbelieve both, he could tell, just from the reaction of his father whenever it came up, that there was much more to the story, no matter what Porcinus said about it. That, he had mused as he let Ocelus take him where the big gray horse wanted, was understandable. Titus Porcinianus Pullus had become a man, in more ways than one, just as his father had hoped, so it was with the mind of an adult that he recognized that his father carried secrets that would only be revealed when it was appropriate, if they ever were. Titus was still too young to appreciate the irony that the severing of his leg gave Gaius Porcinus a certain level of freedom, yet what he did know was that, not more than three weeks after the amputation of his leg, Porcinus had decreed that his family would be moving to Arelate. Ironically, Iras had been the major obstacle, not wanting to uproot her life and that of her family, no matter that her family, in the form of Valeria and Sextus, had agitated for the move. The fact that it was young Titus who, behind the scenes, was pushing his siblings to put pressure on his mother was something he was sure Iras didn't need to hear. What he knew was that moving to Arelate would remove his father from the pain of seeing the Fourth Cohort being led by another man, and that was enough, at least as far as Titus was concerned. Everything else was secondary to that reality, and it was with a vigor and sense of command that the other members of the family Porcinus obeyed the new, young, and temporary *paterfamilias*. For his part, Titus had never felt such a weight on his young shoulders, understanding that this would be the way his life would be for as long as he was alive. That was enough to make him angry, but he found what he needed within himself to quell the flaring of resentment he felt at the injustice of the entire situation. His entire being had ended up focusing on this wrong, but heeding his father's warning, he hadn't spoken a word of his true feelings. Instead, he used it as fuel for what he thought of as his quest to right what had been done to his family. Although he never uttered a word about it, Titus Porcinianus Pullus understood that he was on a mission of vengeance. All that remained was the fulfillment.

Finally, Titus realized that it was time to turn around and head back for Arelate, although Ocelus was clearly eager to keep going.

"No, boy," he admonished his horse, who kept trying to jerk the reins from Titus' hands.

It was a game that Ocelus had played with his Avus, Titus knew, and while it was somewhat irritating, it gave him an odd sense of security, a sign of stability in his world that had seen so much upheaval. Finally, Ocelus accepted that they were indeed headed home, and Titus settled back into his reverie, focusing on what he was sure had been the turning point for his father, and seemed to be the reason for his return to the land of the living. Although Diocles had continued his tutoring of Titus, and the boy had begun to get a glimmering that perhaps there was something to be learned from books, it was still surprising to him that it appeared to be a book that was responsible for his father's recovery. Actually, he thought, it wasn't really a book. It was more like a lot of books, just judging from the number of scrolls contained in a box that Titus had seen in his Avus' study. During his visit, Titus had only expressed an idle curiosity, since the box was clearly not part of the library contained in the cubbyholes lining two walls of the study.

However, when he opened the box and started to pick up one, Diocles had spoken to him, using a tone he rarely heard from the Greek.

"Don't touch those," he had snapped.

Titus was more startled than afraid, but he had jumped away from the box, the lid slamming shut with a bang that made both of them flinch. That had seemed to snap Diocles out of his irritation, because he gave an embarrassed laugh.

"Sorry about that, Titus," he muttered apologetically. "It's just that those are very…valuable."

This was something that Titus still had problems fathoming, that there could be anything worthwhile in a bunch of scrolls, but his curiosity was now fully aroused.

"Why?" he asked, with more than a little suspicion. "What's in them?"

Diocles didn't answer right away, but when he did, if anything, it confused Titus even more.

"That," Diocles finally said quietly, "is your legacy."

Whatever was in the scrolls, however, had elicited a change in Titus' father that the boy would never have dreamed possible. Although his mental state had improved somewhat by the time they arrived in Arelate, Porcinus was still withdrawn and prone to bouts of sullen melancholy that was hard to endure, even for his family. Then, one day, Diocles asked to speak to Porcinus privately after the evening meal. Their conversation took place in the study, which, to that point, Titus knew Porcinus had avoided entering. But after that night, it was almost impossible to get him out of it, and every time Titus came to check on his father, he found him poring over what Titus was sure was a scroll from the box, since it was sitting next to Porcinus' chair. Porcinus began staying up late, and while it was gradual, his family began noticing a change coming over the *paterfamilias*, and even on one occasion, he had laughed at the dinner table when Valeria hit Sextus over the head with her spoon when she caught him trying to filch an extra candied fig from her plate. Yet, when Titus finally worked up the nerve to enter his Avus' study while his father was reading, to ask Porcinus what was contained in what he had begun to think of as some sort of magic scroll, his father's answer had been anything but satisfactory.

"You'll find out soon enough," Porcinus said, rolling up the scroll he had been reading when he saw Titus leaning forward, trying to catch a glimpse of what was on it. "In fact," Porcinus held the scroll up and pointed at Titus with it, "you'll inherit these. But not until you're a man."

"Ta...Father," Titus corrected himself, making sure not to whine. "I'm as big as a man. And I've killed in battle," he pointed out, although he said it quietly, not in a boastful manner at all, just a simple statement of fact.

For a moment, Porcinus seemed to waver, regarding his son with an appraising expression.

Then, he shook his head and replied, "Not yet, Titus." As much as Titus tried to hide it, his father saw the disappointment in his son's face, which prompted him to add, "I'll make you a deal. When you put on the *toga virilis*, I'll let you start reading these. But," he hurried on, "I'm going to keep them in my possession, at least until I die. Only then will you have them."

Titus would remember this conversation, and it was with some chagrin he recalled that, in the moment, he hadn't cared about this last condition, not seeing how having physical possession of these scrolls would be meaningful. Over the years, he would have cause to regret that.

"Get up."

The command, rousing Titus from sleep, had come a little less than two months after they had moved to Arelate, and the boy opened his eyes to see his father standing there, his now customary crutch under one shoulder. However, it was the expression on Porcinus' face that brought him fully awake. There was no hint of warmth, no smile or any other sign that would give Titus a hint about what was to come. Rubbing the sleep from his eyes, he hurried to obey his father, hurriedly throwing on his tunic. His father watched, face impassive, then when Titus was dressed, turned about.

"Follow me," he said curtly, the now-accustomed sound of his crutch thumping across the floor as he left the room without looking back over his shoulder.

Titus followed his father, and was surprised when they didn't stop in the room where the meals were prepared; Titus was hungry, but he saw his father didn't seem interested in either his own hunger or that of his son. Porcinus continued moving, throwing open the door that led to the courtyard, and Titus saw that it was only then beginning to dawn, the eastern sky above the enclosing wall rimmed with pink. Following his father, Titus was completely confused, but he had to hurry to match his father's pace, since he had become adept at moving quickly, even with a crutch. It was only when Porcinus stopped that Titus understood; actually, it was where his father was standing that gave Titus a hint about what the coming day held for him. Porcinus, who still hadn't spoken since his initial command, had clearly prepared for this beforehand, because there were a pair of *rudii* thrust point-first into the dirt, just a few paces away from the set of stakes that Titus Pullus had placed in the courtyard when he had first moved into the villa.

"Show me your forms," Porcinus commanded, pointing first to a *rudis,* then to a stake.

Titus only hesitated a moment before walking over and picking up the *rudis*, holding it in the way that Vulso had required. Before he could take more than a step towards the stake, his father spoke again.

"Wrong," Porcinus said, his tone flat, his face still showing no hint of warmth. "You've seen the way I hold...held," Porcinus corrected himself, and now there was no mistaking the bitterness in his voice, "my sword. Hold it like that."

Titus did as he was told, but the grip felt awkward, made even more so by the fact that the handle of the *rudis* was normally sized, and although the boy was large in every aspect, his hands were still on the small side of a full-grown man's at this point. Porcinus saw this and grunted.

"We're going to have shave down the handle a bit so it matches your real sword," he muttered, yet when Titus reverted to the conventional grip, his father shook his head. "No, today I just want to see how bad you are on your forms, so it doesn't matter if your hand is a little sore. Besides, I'll show you some exercises I want you to do to make your hand stronger. Now," he indicated the stake again, "show me."

And Titus did as his father commanded, dropping his body into the required position as he scowled at the wooden stake, which had apparently been his Avus' favorite, since it was the one that showed the most scars from countless strikes and thrusts. He performed the series of movements that he had watched hundreds, if not thousands, of men do when they were training for the Legions, including his father, who continued to stand there, observing impassively, the boy's own muscles quickly recalling the training with Vulso. Only when Titus had performed one complete set of the movements did his father make any comment, and it was a day the boy would long remember.

"I've seen worse," Porcinus said, and for the first time, Titus saw just a glimmer of a smile on his father's face. "Granted, you've got some bad habits to unlearn that they taught you at that *ludus*, but nothing that can't be undone. No," Porcinus concluded, "all in all, not a bad beginning."

So began Titus' tutelage in the art of being a Legionary, trained by a man who had been taught by Titus Pullus, the next link in a chain of iron men who marched in the Legions and for Rome. Gaius

Porcinus had rediscovered his purpose, even if his command was shrunk to a complement of one, and Titus Porcinianus Pullus began training for the Legions at an even younger age than his Avus, which Porcinus was quick to point out. And both of them, father and son, were united in their desire to find a way to right the injustice done to their family, the beginning of that quest prompted by a set of scrolls.